EVERYMAN'S LIBRARY

EVERYMAN,
I WILL GO WITH THEE,
AND BE THY GUIDE,
IN THY MOST NEED
TO GO BY THY SIDE

THOMAS MANN

Collected Stories

Translated from the German by
H. T. Lowe-Porter

with an Introduction by
Daniel Johnson

EVERYMAN'S LIBRARY

196

This book is one of 250 volumes in Everyman's Library
which have been distributed to 4500 state schools
throughout the United Kingdom.
The project has been supported by a grant of £4 million
from the Millennium Commission.

Collected shorter fiction of Thomas Mann first included in
Everyman's Library, 2001
This translation first published by Secker & Warburg in 1961 as
Stories of a Lifetime

Selections from the shorter fiction of Thomas Mann previously
published in Everyman's Library in 1940 and 1991

Typography by Peter B. Willberg

ISBN 1-85715-196-8

A CIP catalogue record for this book is available from the
British Library

Published by Everyman Publishers plc,
Gloucester Mansions, 140A Shaftesbury Avenue,
London WC2H 8HD

Distributed by Random House (UK) Ltd.,
20 Vauxhall Bridge Road, London SW1V 2SA

THOMAS MANN

CONTENTS

INTRODUCTION

If Goethe was Germany's greatest man of letters, Thomas Mann made himself her greatest literary composer. As a disciple of Schopenhauer and Nietzsche, this son of the *fin de siècle* agreed with Walter Pater that all art constantly aspires towards the condition of music. There is something odd about this. Mann was a writer who made a virtue of prolixity, who never used one subordinate clause when half a dozen would do. The heavenly lengths of his mellifluous periods achieved a certain notoriety even in a land of sermonizing pastors and pedants; sometimes only irony rescues his sentences from sententiousness. Yet it is as absurd to accuse Mann of using too many words as it was of Joseph II to tell Mozart that he used too many notes. There was method in Mann's wordiness: it was a means to an end beyond words. The endless melody of Wagner was to find its counterpart in Mann's musical prose.

Deployed on a grand scale in the novels, that prose could achieve effects of symphonic complexity or operatic opulence. But his linguistic instrumentation is no less masterly in miniature. In his shorter prose pieces he demonstrated that he could be a virtuoso of economy and brevity, too. The stories are, indeed, Mann's chamber music.

The present volume is a miscellany, ranging from novellas, substantial enough to have been published separately, to the briefest of impressionistic sketches, besides Mann's meditation on his dog and his only stage play. The bulk of it, however, is made up of the short stories proper, which mostly date from his early years and frequently display an experimental character. The two volumes of stories which Mann published in 1898 (*Little Herr Friedemann*) and 1903 (*Tristan*) were essentially parerga and paralipomena, ideas related to but omitted from his first two major works, the novel *Buddenbrooks* and the novella 'Tonio Kröger'.

Mann's first published work, and the first item in that first collection, was 'Little Herr Friedemann'. He was twenty and eking out a precarious existence in Rome on his small private income when it was accepted by Oskar Bie, the editor of the *Neue Deutsche Rundschau*, then as now the leading German literary journal. He later paid tribute to his 'discoverer', seeing the hand of destiny in the fact that Bie, a prominent music critic, had brought to light 'a writer whose work was from the first marked by a deep inward affinity to [music] and a tendency to apply its technique in his own field'. Slight though it is, 'Little Herr Friedemann' is already a mature work, anticipating *Buddenbrooks* with its mordant wit and world-weary melancholia. Its unsparing treatment of the psychological effects of physical disability may strike a modern reader as crude; but the subject was then topical because the Kaiser, Wilhelm II, had been born with a withered arm and there was much speculation about its consequences for his volatile character. Little Herr Friedemann, the hunchback, is a man of delicate aesthetic sensibilities, whose renunciation of sexual love is compensated for by books and music, especially Wagner. Confronted by the flirtatious and, as it transpires, sadistic wife of the district commandant, however, his carefully cultivated defences collapse: 'That was all lies and my imagination.' Mann's characteristically dialectical mode of fiction – a ceaseless dialogue between art and life, between *vita activa* and *vita contemplativa*, between morbid love and eroticized death – is already established.

The other stories in Mann's first slim volume are variations on the same themes. 'Disillusionment' was actually the first to be written, in 1896. Though a mere *jeu d'esprit*, it is notable for its delicate irony and its Venetian setting. Many of the early stories oscillate, as the young Mann himself did, between Germany and Italy, the two temperamental poles which he associated with his austere, Teutonic father and his sensual, Latin mother. Mann identified Venice, the crossroads of north and south, east and west, with the flowering of German romanticism – its melancholy magnificence had inspired everyone from Goethe to Wagner, who had even chosen to die there – so the theme of disillusionment already anticipates the leitmotif of his own oeuvre: the stripping of the altar of a culture which had degenerated into an ideology. By this time the twenty-one-year-old Mann had already immersed himself in the presiding philosophical genius of his youth. Arthur Schopenhauer saw the empirical world as a cruel illusion, the shimmering, deceptive mask of the immanent will. Venice is a metaphor for this metaphor, and one to which Mann would do justice in the greatest novella of his maturity, 'Death in Venice'.

'The Dilettante', written in the first person, is more obviously autobiographical. Until his vocation as a writer became clear with the success of *Buddenbrooks*, Mann constantly castigated himself for his dilettantism, evidently suffering from a sense of inferiority by comparison with his elder brother Heinrich, who radiated a cosmopolitan worldliness, sexual and literary precocity. The German title of this sketch, 'Der Bajazzo', really means a clown or buffoon, and the narcissistic narrator professes to be filled with disgust whenever he contemplates himself. Yet Mann, in writing this *reductio ad absurdum* of his own existence, was also purging himself of such self-abnegation, or rather turning it to good use. Suicide, too, is a mere pose, and one which the narrator will never carry through. The thematic complex adumbrated here will recur throughout Mann's oeuvre, from 'Tonio Kröger' to *Felix Krull.*

'Tobias Mindernickel' is a caricature of Schopenhauer, who famously preferred the companionship of his poodle to that of men. He feels such pity (*Mitleid*, 'suffering with') for his dog Esau that he kills his fellow creature to spare it the pain of existence – thereby plunging himself back into solitary misery. But this grotesque, a parody of the misanthropy and depression to which all the Manns were prey, has sinister undertones, hints even of an unhealthy interest in children. It is characteristic of Mann that even his hero, Schopenhauer, should be lampooned and the potential destructiveness of his pessimism ruthlessly exposed.

'Little Lizzy' is another expression of the young author's ferocious sexual pessimism. The portly Jacoby is too ludicrous a cuckold to inspire sympathy, and his end is encompassed by a musical means normally reserved for grand opera. Yet the artificiality of this artifice does not detract from its impact. In 'Tristan', in *The Magic Mountain* and above all in *Doctor Faustus*, Mann returns to the idea of music, and the song in particular, as a harbinger of death: not so much a *Liebestod* as a *Liedertod.* 'Luischen', to give the tale its German title, shares with 'Little Herr Friedemann' a gently satirical eye for the detail of bourgeois life which betrays Mann's new preoccupation, the evocation of his native Lübeck on a scale incomparably grander than anything he had hitherto attempted: *Buddenbrooks.*

By the time the *Little Herr Friedemann* volume appeared in May 1898, Mann had already written much of the novel. The stories sold only 413 copies, but his Jewish publisher from Hamburg, Samuel Fischer, had faith in the young writer. Though scarcely a commercial success, these strange tales revealed a promise which raised Mann's status among his fellow literati and artists, for whom he had hitherto been merely Heinrich's little brother. At the age of twenty-three, he had arrived.

Work on the great novel explains a gap of a few years before the next two stories. Mann was already in the midst of that prodigious epic when he dashed off a ghost story, 'The Wardrobe', while 'The Way to the Churchyard' was written while he was recuperating from that 'arduous task'. The teeming vivacity of *Buddenbrooks*, however, is absent from these two tales; slight as they are, they look forward to the new symbolist aesthetic of *Jugendstil* rather than back to the naturalism of Flaubert and Zola. Van der Qualen, the sickly traveller of 'The Wardrobe', is a forerunner of Gustave von Aschenbach, the protagonist of 'Death in Venice', while in 'The Way to the Churchyard' the confrontation between Praisegod (Gottlob) Piepsam and the blond, blue-eyed cyclist whom Mann dubs 'Life' is a grotesque prelude to the dialectic between art and life in 'Tonio Kröger'. The eponymous wardrobe – a gateway to another world which anticipates that of C. S. Lewis by half a century – was, in reality, part of his landlady's furniture in an apartment on the Marktstrasse in the Schwabing district of Munich which he rented in 1898.

Buddenbrooks appeared in two cheap volumes at the turn of the century. Originally conceived as a novella, it recounts the decline and fall of a dynasty of Hanseatic patricians modelled on the Mann family. It is surely the most accomplished first novel ever written by an unknown youth in his early twenties. It made a fortune for its publisher, Samuel Fischer, and eventually won the Nobel Prize for its author. Its all-too-recognizable portraits from the life landed Mann in hot water with some of his acquaintances in Lübeck, but such indignation was an inevitable hazard of his *modus operandi*. Blurring the boundaries between fact and fiction became habitual to Mann and helps to explain why a writer who craved respectability was dogged by controversy throughout his life.

By the time he wrote *Buddenbrooks*, Mann had already fled from the mercantile world of the Baltic ports to the fleshpots of Italy, before eventually settling down in Munich, where he would remain for the next three decades, until the Nazis drove him into exile. The Bavarian capital was a unique milieu for Germany, a combination of bohemia and Ruritania – both sustained by the wealth of a rising class of capitalists. The theme of old money meeting new money, so central to the French and English nineteenth-century novel, had loomed less large in German literature, with a few exceptions such as the Prussian novels of Theodor Fontane. Only with Mann's generation, however, did the German novel take full account of the social transformation wrought by industrialization and unification. The new discipline of sociology was busily creating a vocabulary in which to describe this permanent revolution. Ferdinand Tönnies discerned a shift from *Gemeinschaft* (community) to *Gesellschaft* (society), Max Weber derived the spirit of capitalism from the worldly asceticism of the Protestant work ethic, while Georg Simmel's *Philosophy of Money* depicted the attenuated, formalized relationships characteristic of a cosmopolitan, urban society such as Berlin.

Though in 'The Blood of the Walsungs' he cruelly satirized the pretensions to high culture of the Berlin bourgeoisie, and the Jewish bourgeoisie in particular, Mann was not at home in the Prussian capital, nor did his style suit the 'asphalt literature' that it spawned. He preferred the less hectic, more Mediterranean atmosphere of Munich, with occasional forays to Italy itself.

'Gladius Dei', one of the best early stories, begins with a

celebrated cameo of the Bavarian capital. Mann contrasts this 'radiant' and prosperous metropolis of art, a latter-day Renaissance Florence, with the gloomy iconoclasm of Hieronymus, a Savonarola-like ascetic who is so scandalized by a lascivious Madonna in the window that he harangues the (evidently Jewish) art-dealer and finds himself thrown out. 'At the Prophet's' mercilessly sends up the aesthetes who based themselves in the Munich suburb of Schwabing at the turn of the century. Mann doubtless had in mind the circle around the poet Stefan George, who styled themselves 'secret Germany' and prophesied a new Reich. Two members of the group, the philosopher and graphologist Ludwig Klages and the literary historian Ernst Bertram, were at various times friendly with Mann. George himself and most of his circle, however, despised Mann as a bourgeois, an establishment writer in the naturalist tradition, and he responded in kind. Yet his light-hearted squibs are more than polemics in the culture wars of the day; they hint at a more sinister undertone of fanaticism, which Mann was to take more seriously in later works such as *The Magic Mountain* and 'Mario and the Magician'.

Mann was by now aware of his own growing status, as one of the leading young writers in the German-speaking world. In 'A Weary Hour', he draws a charming vignette of Friedrich Schiller, one of his literary heroes, whose *Don Carlos* symbolizes the romantic idealism of youth for Tonio Kröger. A century ago Schiller was a far more popular writer than his friend Goethe, and Mann did not need to mention his name for every reader to identify him. What they may not have spotted so easily was that this is also a self-portrait. To assume the mantle of one of the icons of Weimar classicism would have seemed blasphemous to an educated German of the 1900s, so Mann needed to disguise himself. He would do so repeatedly throughout his career, identifying with Goethe in *Lotte in Weimar*, for example, or with Nietzsche in *Doctor Faustus*. All his essays on writers, composers and thinkers are in part autobiographical; and 'A Weary Hour' anticipates a veritable orgy of introspection, the colossal *Reflections of an Unpolitical Man* to which he devoted most of the First World War. Here we glimpse the great man's inner turmoil; but the world beyond sees only the indomitable will to overcome every obstacle, physical or psychological.

For Mann's was an acutely self-conscious conscience, and the hero as man of letters was a role that suited him in life, precisely because he could reveal his own vulnerability in his work. When, during the Second World War, he was acknowledged everywhere except in his homeland as the living embodiment of the good German, of a Germany uncontaminated by Nazism, it seemed to him only natural that he should judge his countrymen, just as he had sat in permanent judgment over himself. Disciple of the arch-atheists Schopenhauer and Nietzsche as he was, Mann had internalized the Protestant sense of duty, and the austere ethics of another Balt, Immanuel Kant, had been absorbed as a kind of literary imperative: write as if every word were to be read everywhere, by everybody, for all eternity. In short, once he had written *Buddenbrooks*, Thomas Mann took himself very seriously indeed.

Yet the decade that followed his emergence as the leading novelist of the younger generation yielded only a meagre harvest. His only novel of the period, *Royal Highness*, was entertaining enough, with many thinly veiled allusions to the Kaiser and his court; but it was not a novel of ideas, while as satire it lacked the bite of his brother Heinrich's ruthless dissections of the German bourgeoisie. The truth is that, after a mildly adventurous bohemian period, Mann had settled down to become an ornament of that middle class, both by virtue of his own success, but even more by marrying Katja Pringsheim, the highly educated daughter of a Jewish professor. Mann's most popular and substantial work of this period was the novella 'Tonio Kröger', which always retained a special place in his affections – possibly because the eponymous hero is a portrait of the author as a young aesthete. The narrative, such as it is, was, indeed, so closely based on his own experience as to be virtually an autobiographical fragment. It is very much of its period, the period of *Jugendstil* arts and crafts. And yet its indubitable charm derives from the refraction of the harsh, bright, monotonous light of experience into a magical spectrum of sensibilities, illuminating the twilight zone where life confronts literature.

A mellow melancholy pervades the divine comedy of Tonio's tale. Once again it is set in the bleak Baltic landscape. His adolescent adoration, first of Hans Hansen and later of Inge Holm, goes unrequited: the two blond beasts are as unconscious of his torments as they are indifferent to his intellectual adventures. The scenic technique suggests the then recently invented cinema: it consists of episodes, tableaux and flashbacks rather than a continuous narrative. Like Goethe's Faust, two souls dwell in Tonio's breast: the artist and the bourgeois. The only woman who understands him, the bohemian artist Lisabeta Ivanovna (based on Mann's friend Ida Boy-Ed), cannot save him. When Tonio returns to his homeland, by now an established writer, he is treated as an alien being and nearly arrested. Finally he recognizes the lost loves of his youth, Hans and Inge, and he realizes that his destiny is to love, chronicle and yet be a stranger to both worlds, the bourgeois and the bohemian. The novella is deliberately inconclusive: the struggle will go on, the antitheses of Tonio's personality are irreconcilable, but he now sees his inability to abandon 'the ordinary, the living and the human' is not a defect but a strength.

In 1911, Thomas Mann took a holiday in Venice with his wife, Katja, and his brother, Heinrich. En route they had a series of uncanny encounters: an old man with a painted face, a sinister gondolier, and finally a beautiful Polish boy, Tadzio, at the Hôtel des Bains on the Lido. They attempted to escape to Bolzano, but returned after Heinrich's luggage was temporarily lost. Thomas was glad to return to the thirteen-year-old youth, who had captivated him, but another harbinger of doom paid them a visit, this time a hideous crooner. After Tadzio's family had left, rumours of a cholera outbreak reached their ears. A travel agent at Thomas Cook advised the Manns to leave, which they promptly did. Soon after returning to Munich, Thomas Mann began work on a novella, which took a year to complete. Almost every detail of the Venetian expedition was exploited in this story.

A decade separated 'Tonio Kröger' from 'Death in Venice',

which was first serialized in *Der Neue Rundschau* in 1912 and appeared in book form the following year. If the earlier novella was the author's favourite, its successor was immediately recognized as his masterpiece, not only in Germany but abroad. Alone among Mann's works, 'Death in Venice' has attained the status of a modern myth. Why its only character, Gustave von Aschenbach, should so quickly have acquired this legendary aureole is not immediately obvious. *Buddenbrooks* remains not only the most popular of his books, but of all German novels. For most Europeans, *The Magic Mountain* has always been seen as the twentieth century's richest novel of ideas. Mann himself devoted more effort to his vast *Joseph* tetralogy than to anything else, and it remains the most ambitious historical novel of all time. *Doctor Faustus* was the extraordinary monument of his old age, at once a celebration and an indictment of the secret Germany, the romantic culture that all but perished between 1933 and 1945. More than any of these sprawling epics – a larger number, certainly, than any other German novelist has bequeathed – this taut, concise, stylized novella, published just before World War I, has entered the inventory of Western literary consciousness. Prophetic of the impending political crisis in its symbol-laden account of the corporeal and moral disintegration of Aschenbach, yet deliberately ironical in its linguistic formality, the story has become the model of all subsequent attempts to address Western civilization's self-immolation, of which modernist literature is itself one of the symptoms. As in 'Tonio Kröger', but to a more intensely self-conscious degree, the hero of 'Death in Venice' is an artist to his fingertips, a spiritual sovereign of his time. He is, in short, an archetype of modern heroism, the intellectual who succumbs to the instinctual.

Aschenbach's capitulation before his ineluctable Dionysian destiny – and, with him, that of the high culture of old Europe – was not left on a harmlessly abstract plane. 'Death in Venice' is also the first serious, undisguised study of homoerotic love in the modern novel. It has a good claim to be the final breakthrough in ending the Judeo-Christian taboo on homosexuality as a literary theme, which had persisted in the West since the conversion of Europe from Greco-Latin paganism. There were, of course, precedents: in the ambiguous sonnets of Michelangelo or Shakespeare, in Marlowe's tortured Edward II, in the androgynous aesthetics of Winckelmann or the lyrical allegories of Rimbaud, in the dark insinuations of Stevenson's Jekyll and Hyde or Wilde's Dorian Gray. E. M. Forster's posthumously published homosexual novel *Maurice* is exactly contemporary with 'Death in Venice'. There is even a clear precedent in Mann's own fiction. 'The Fight Between Jappe and Do Escobar', published in 1911, hardly bothers to conceal its fascination with adolescent male sexuality. All the youths involved in this unofficial boxing match seem foppish or exhibitionist; while the referee turns out to be Herr Knaak, the effeminate, theatrical dancing-master who made a public exhibition of the young Tonio Kröger's clumsiness, here taking another bow – the only such reappearance in Mann's entire oeuvre. Knaak is, of course, a comic figure, in no way comparable to Aschenbach; but he is the first clearly identifiable homosexual in Mann's fiction.

'Death in Venice' transcends the pseudo-medical concept of homosexuality, the mainly German theory of which dates only from 1869. It is not a thinly disguised tract on behalf of what would now be called gay liberation, like Gide's *Corydon* or some of the novels of Klaus Mann, Thomas's eldest son. There is none of the innocence with which earlier writers might have endowed their unmentionable yearnings, and a few still did even after 1900; Housman's Shropshire lad is one case in point. Though Aschenbach's (and Mann's) choice as a hero of the most famous bisexual in German history, Frederick the Great, was not accidental, it would have seemed innocent to most of his patriotic readers. But the self-lacerating guilt feelings of a Wittgenstein or the hostility of a D. H. Lawrence (who hated 'Death in Venice') were more typical responses of the day. Since Aschenbach set eyes on Tadzio, a dimension of human experience which had hitherto been unaware of itself finally emerged into the glare of the Venetian sun. Homosexuality became a respectable, and eventually even a fashionable, subject for explicit treatment by novelists. Mann's true forerunner in this endeavour was the philosopher he most revered, Schopenhauer, whose extraordinary essay on the metaphysics of sexual love remarks upon the re-emergence of adolescent homosexual desires in late middle age. Except in his diaries, however, Mann was unable publicly to acknowledge his own homoerotic tendencies, even later in life when several of his children (Erika, Klaus and Golo) openly came out. Like Aschenbach, he was repelled by his own compulsions.

Aschenbach's fate may be seen as a coda to the Wilhelminian epoch, in which the cult of masculinity and the sublimation of femininity had broken down at certain points to reveal a subculture or anticulture in which homosexuality took on socially acceptable forms. Homosexuality was not an accidental aspect of the story: it was the essential metaphor for the author's underlying preoccupation with mortality. Aschenbach's sterile love, divorced fom procreation, subversive of the natural order and scornful of the social one, is here depicted as a steadily encroaching contagion, which overcomes the lover's moral antibodies to the point at which erotic surrender passes effortlessly into oceanic infinity. Nor should one forget that, only a generation after Mann brought homosexuality into the German public arena, homosexuals were incarcerated in concentration camps.

'Death in Venice' does not begin with so much as a suggestion of its central theme, but rather with a political allusion which fixes the story precisely in time: 1911, the year of Agadir. The threatening aspect of that year, to which the German original refers in the very first sentence, was the 'gunboat diplomacy' practised by the Imperial German government in pursuit of its colonial ambitions in Morocco. Agadir was a near-miss for Europe, and for a few perceptive individuals it triggered far-reaching reflections on the fragility of their comfortable world. The pre-war period suddenly realized that it was pre-war. In Berlin and Vienna, expressionist art and poetry took on a warlike, catastrophic aspect. In Munich, less conscious of the proximity of political and military power, the paintings of the Blaue Reiter school, like the other products of bohemian Schwabing, were untinged with impending doom, and now seem all the more poignant for that.

But Munich, where Aschenbach's story begins, was also the place where the confrontation at Agadir spawned its most gigantic offspring. A lonely and unemployed teacher of mathematics, Oswald Spengler, began writing a prodigious philosophy of history, the first volume of which would appear seven years and a world war later, in 1918. Thomas Mann was one of the first and most avid readers of *The Decline of the West*, and he adapted its cyclical morphology of culture for his own purposes.

'Death in Venice', Mann wrote many years later, is 'a crystallization in the true sense of the word; it is a structure, and an image, shedding light from so many facets, by its nature of such inexhaustible allusiveness, that it might well dazzle the eyes of its creator himself as it took shape'. Readers who wish to know more about its myriad sources, and about its sexual and political background, may wish to consult my introduction to the earlier Everyman volume, *Death in Venice and Other Stories* (London, 1991), which goes into much greater detail, and on which I have drawn for the present preface.

The best-known inspiration for Aschenbach is Gustav Mahler, whom Mann knew and revered. In Visconti's film of 'Death in Venice', Dirk Bogarde resembles the composer so closely that many have supposed that Aschenbach was closely based on Mahler. In fact, Mann used only Mahler's aquiline features, his age and his early death of heart disease in May 1911. In a letter, however, Mann testified to having sought to attain a vicarious 'consciousness of greatness' in his character, such as he had sensed in Mahler's presence.

Of Mann's contemporaries, Stefan George was perhaps the nearest approximation to Aschenbach. George elevated his infatuation with the young poet Maximin, who died in adolescence, into a neo-pagan cult; like Aschenbach, he saw the object of his adoration as a revelation from another world. George's austere, formalist conception of art also had much in common with Aschenbach's, though Mann laughed at his hieratic, sacerdotal pretensions. Closer to Mann's artistic ideal was an earlier romantic poet, August von Platen, whose homosexuality led to his disgrace and exile, after he was satirized by his rival Heinrich Heine. Resident in Venice for much of his life, Platen earned Mann's admiration for his classical severity and modern sensibility. His most celebrated poem, 'Tristan', already anticipates Aschenbach. 'He who has seen Beauty with his eyes/Is already prey to Death.'

As in so many of Mann's works, the presence of Nietzsche is palpable. A frequent visitor to Venice whose gondolier's song was set by Mahler in his Third Symphony, Nietzsche notoriously fell in love with the teenage Lou Andreas-Salomé, before a sudden breakdown cost him his sanity. Mann's fascination with the psychological effects of physical illness – whether tertiary syphilis, tuberculosis, cancer or, as here, cholera – was evidently stimulated by the case of Nietzsche; but the novella is full of homages to the philosopher, most notably in the classical allusions, which develop the Apollonian and Dionysian dialectic of *The Birth of Tragedy*.

For Mann, as for most other Germans of his day, Goethe was the pattern of all genius. But it was one of the most disturbing episodes of the great man's life that here provided Mann with a model. His 'terrible, beautiful, grotesque and deeply stirring' love for the young Ulrike von Levetzow (he was seventy-two, she only seventeen) was originally intended to provide the biographical framework for 'Death in Venice'. There are many connections between Mann's story and Goethe's great memorial to Ulrike, the 'Marienbad Elegy', which ends with a bitter rebuke to the gods: 'They separate us, and drive me to destruction.' But Mann transposed the idea of an ageing man of letters at the mercy of his passion for an adolescent from the elegiac plane of an impossible but still permissible love to that of mortification, by the simple device of changing the sex of the beloved.

Perhaps the most indispensable of Aschenbach's godparents was Wagner, the only one whose death actually occurred in Venice. Mann was writing an article on Wagner as the story germinated on holiday at the Lido, in which he argued that Wagner's manipulation of ecstasy must give way to 'a new classicism', the very creed he attributed to Aschenbach. Later in his career, Mann liked to suggest that the formal, over-elaborate style of this novella was a kind of parody of Aschenbach's style. But at the time Mann actually held the views he attributes to Aschenbach. Indeed, one may see the story as part of Mann's lifelong struggle to free himself from the tyranny of Wagnerian influence — a struggle which would one day become the pretext for his exile. Though Aschenbach's character and convictions are deliberately intended to be the antithesis of Wagner's, the debts are still ubiquitous – not least in the final scene, a caricature of Isolde's *Liebestod*.

The success of 'Death in Venice' left Mann with mixed feelings: 'A nation in which such a novella can be not merely accepted, but to some extent acclaimed, is perhaps in need of a war.' Germany did not have long to wait. For Mann, however, the success of this work unblocked a well-spring of creativity: two of his finest novels, *Felix Krull* and *The Magic Mountain*, were both begun on the eve of war. The war itself caused him to abandon fiction almost entirely, in favour of the political, aesthetic and personal polemics of *Reflections of an Unpolitical Man*. This apologia for German exceptionalism, and for his own nationalism against his brother Heinrich's cosmopolitanism, appeared just as defeat loomed, plunging the country into revolution and Mann into despair.

'A Man and his Dog', written during the last summer of the war, is as idyllic as 'Death in Venice' had been elegiac. For once, Mann is at ease, off duty, laid back. He takes innocent pleasure in the companionship of Bashan, his German pointer, delights in the landscape and reflects on nature. Here Mann the bourgeois leaves Mann the artist in the shade. The shaggy-dog story was an immediate success, and has remained popular ever since. It is, by some distance, the worst thing that Mann ever wrote. This pot-boiler does not really belong in a collection of short fiction, but it is included here as a curiosity.

'Disorder and Early Sorrow' dates from 1925 and is expressly associated with the great inflation of 1923. Like 'A Man and his Dog', this is a *symphonia domestica*, a thinly disguised autobiographical sketch of the Mann family at home rather than a story. Here, too, the prose is ingratiating and conversational, bourgeois rather than noble, present rather than past tense. But 'Disorder and Early Sorrow' has more to say than the vacuous canine idyll. Though the references to the hyper-inflation are casual and understated, they are resonant. No less telling are the portraits of Klaus and Erika, his two eldest children, as Bert and Ingrid; their camp theatricality hints at the social and sexual liberation of post-war German culture. Though the charm of the story is undeniable, it is steeped in irony, and there are hints of more ominous preoccupations. Professor Cornelius, the historian, is devoted to the past, a past which is 'immortalized; that is to say, it is dead; and death is the root of all godliness and all abiding significance'. He is also devoted to his little girl, Ellie, and this devotion, too, 'has something to do with death'. The professor fears the present and the future; his predilection for the innocence of his youngest daughter is a kind of refuge. And yet, as the denouement demonstrates, all children grow up, there is no escape from the contemporary world, symbolized by the teenagers' party, with its modern dances and jazz. The impotent rage of Ellie when she is sent to bed by her father, who is furiously jealous of the five-year-old's hopeless infatuation with a grown-up youth, is a sign that she too wants to belong to the present, not to the patriarchal past. Max Hergesell (the name means 'master-apprentice'), the elegant engineering student who is the object of her infantile passion, will inherit the earth. Cornelius has ambivalent feelings towards this younger generation, but he has no inkling of its susceptibility to the forces unleashed by defeat, revolution, inflation and depression. Indeed, the story barely hints at the bitterness of the ruined middle classes, the pervasive disillusionment with democracy, the fear of communism and the embrace of anti-Semitism. The author had recently courted the hostility of his former allies in the nationalist camp by embracing the Weimar Republic; he compounded this betrayal of the Right by providing the intellectual justification in his great novel, *The Magic Mountain*. Hence in this incomparably slighter work, Mann did not set out to write a political parable, rather a fleeting glimpse of the *Zeitgeist*. At that level, 'Disorder and Early Sorrow' succeeds brilliantly; it is, perhaps, the most characteristic of all his stories.

A political parable, on the other hand, is precisely what 'Mario and the Magician' (1929) set out to be. Like the other stories of the Weimar period, this one is openly autobiographical; once again, it records an Italian journey. Though Mussolini's name is never mentioned, his presence haunts the narrative, though the manifestations of authoritarianism are suggestive rather than shocking. The narrator's youngest child is not allowed to bathe naked on the beach; the hotel is unfriendly; an ostentatious patriotism is ubiquitous. Even the most obvious metaphor for Mussolini, the magician himself, seems at first more grotesque than sinister. The title is ironical: der Zauberer, 'the magician', was Mann's own family nickname, and Cipolla is in any case not a magician at all, but a hypnotist.

And yet this story is one of the most effective parables about fascism ever written. The slow build-up to the performance heightens our expectations, so that – like the narrator, who keeps reminding us of his reluctance, of how he ought never to have found himself in such vulgar company – one finds oneself drawn in by, yet impatient of, Cipolla's freakish showmanship. Once he starts to work on his audience, which by now includes us, there is no escape. Whoever we are, naive or sentimental, ignorant or educated, Cipolla holds us spellbound by an eloquence that humiliates even as it captivates. Like the Duce, the Cavaliere has the trick of dominating his listeners even though they know what is happening to them: 'Even against your will.' His is, indeed, a triumph of the will.

Schopenhauer, whose extensive writings about 'animal magnetism' would have been familiar to Mann, saw hypnosis as a window onto the inner reality of the world. In the world of appearances, Cipolla is a huckstering hunchback, a pitiable specimen, less demon than gargoyle. In the world of the will, however, he is master of all he surveys. In his laughing Cavaliere, Mann shows us the power of the demonic over the human.

'Mario and the Magician' is, after 'Death in Venice', Mann's finest and most famous work of shorter fiction. Though separated by nearly two decades, the two stories have much in common. Both are set in an Italian resort; in both the author generates a tense, ominous air of expectancy; both end with the death of the principal character. Cipolla is a kind of distillation of several figures in Mann's fiction, Settembrini and Naphta in *The Magic Mountain* being the most obvious examples. But the relationship between Cipolla and Mario is a kind of caricature of that between Aschenbach and Tadzio. The hideous hypnotist masquerades as the young waiter's girlfriend, they kiss, and then the spell is broken. As Rilke wrote, man cannot bear very much reality, and Mario cannot bear it at all. His resort to violence is a suicidal act of desperation. Mann seems to be saying that sometimes the only answer to the tyrant is tyrannicide.

In 1913, the year that 'Death in Venice' appeared, a young Austrian artist came to Munich. He lived above a tailor's shop called Popp at Schleissheimerstrasse 34. Since his paintings did not sell well, he spent much of his time reading in public libraries. He did not like books which represented German culture as decadent, unmanly heroes, sexual ambivalence. But he was interested in death. He volunteered as soon as the war began. He was decorated, wounded, decorated again. He was not considered officer material, but achieved the rank of corporal, serving as a messenger between the trenches – one of the most dangerous of all military tasks. Finally he was gassed and invalided out, just as the war ended. During the war he wrote: 'I think about Munich so often, and each of us has only one wish, that the final settlement with that gang will soon come, that we'll be able to go at them, no matter what the cost, and that those of us who have the good fortune to see our homeland again will find it purer and more purified of foreignism, so that by the sacrifices and sufferings which so many hundreds of us are undergoing daily, by the torrent of blood which is pouring out here day after day against an international world of enemies, not only Germany's enemies outside will be shattered, but also our inner internationalism.' The artist-soldier returned to Munich to become a politician. This messenger of death was Adolf Hitler.

Cavaliere Cipolla, the metaphysical mountebank, is hardly a depiction of Hitler, who – despite his attempted putsch in 1923 – was not yet considered a serious threat in 1929. Mussolini is more obviously Mann's model, and the rise of fascism plays the same role in 'Mario and the Magician' that cholera plays in 'Death in Venice'. And yet the Italian backdrop to these great works should not deceive us: their frame of reference was as profoundly German as their intended readership. 'Death in Venice' foreshadows the disintegration of German culture, just as Hermann Broch's *The Death of Virgil* looks back upon it in retrospect. 'Mario and the Magician' foreshadows the submission of German society to Hitler, just as Günter Grass's *The Tin Drum* deconstructs it after the event. The didactic purpose is in both cases implicit, but it is all the more powerful for being understated. Unlike Bertolt Brecht, for example, Mann never tried to portray a fictional Hitler. Nor did he – like Ernst Jünger, say, or Hermann Broch, or his own son Klaus – attempt a more explicit Hitlerian allegory. When he came to write *Doctor Faustus*, some fifteen years after 'Mario and the Magician', the demonic forces that destroy Germany and her culture are sublimated into the life of a composer.

Thomas Mann, the self-styled unpolitical German, became the most political of all Hitler's intellectual opponents; so much so, indeed, that after the defeat and conquest of Germany he was seriously considered (by the Allies and the exiles, never by the Germans) as a candidate for the presidency of a new republic. Yet this musician of literature could never bring himself to write a straightforwardly political novel. 'Mario and the Magician' is the nearest he ever came to one.

The last story, 'The Black Swan', is a suitable coda. A middle-aged woman falls in love with a young American officer; she believes herself to have miraculously conceived; but the pregnancy is a phantom one, a tumour which rapidly kills her. Here, within a brief compass, are many of the themes which by now we have come to expect: the intimate connections between love and death, between sexuality and disease, between illusion and reality. As usual, there is a homoerotic and autobiographical subtext. There is also political symbolism, for this is a tale of the occupation. Germany, the menopausal matriarch, has fallen for her invader, imagining that America will restore her creativity. Instead, the New World proves fatal to the Old.

Three of Mann's stories belong in the canon of world literature: 'Tonio Kröger', 'Death in Venice' and 'Mario and the Magician'. Among his German-speaking contemporaries, only Kafka contributed more. Remember, too, that Kafka saw the story as his principal vehicle, whereas Mann gradually abandoned shorter fiction in favour of novels, several executed on the grandest possible scale. Mann's stories are uneven in quality, but there is much to learn from and to enjoy in almost all of them. A century after the earliest of them appeared, it is high time that these works were rediscovered by the English-speaking world.

Daniel Johnson

Daniel Johnson, formerly Literary Editor of the *Times*, is now an Associate Editor of the *Daily Telegraph*. He is currently writing an intellectual history of Germany.

SELECT BIBLIOGRAPHY

WORKS BY THOMAS MANN

There are two good German editions of Mann: the East German Aufbau Verlag edition in twelve volumes (Berlin, 1956), long out of print; and the more complete Stockholmer Ausgabe, published by S. Fischer Verlag, in twenty volumes (Frankfurt am Main, 1965). For dates of first publication, see the chronology.

Most English editions of Mann date from his lifetime, when the author made Mrs Helen Lowe-Porter the exclusively copyrighted translator of almost all his works. Only in the last thirty years have newer translations of Mann's earlier works begun to appear as they enter the public domain. Most English editions have been published by Secker & Warburg. The works listed below, with dates of first publication in English, are still in print. An English translation of Mann's treatise *Reflections of an Unpolitical Man* (1918) is also now available. Penguin Modern Classics publish paperback editions.

The Buddenbrooks, 1924.
Royal Highness, 1916.
Death in Venice, Tristan, Tonio Kröger, 1928.
A Man and his Dog, 1923.
The Magic Mountain, 1927.
Disorder and Early Sorrow, 1929.
Mario and the Magician, 1930.
A Sketch of my Life, 1930.
Joseph and his Brothers, 1934–44.
Lotte in Weimar, 1940.
Essays of Three Decades, 1947.
Doctor Faustus, 1948.
The Holy Sinner, 1951.
Confessions of Felix Krull, 1955.
Last Essays, 1959.
Stories of a Lifetime, Vols I and II, 1961.
Letters to Paul Amann, 1961.
The Letters of Thomas Mann, Vols I and II, 1970.

Thomas Mann Diaries, 1918–1939, edited by Hermann Kesten, translated by Richard and Clara Winston (André Deutsch, 1983). Fragmentary but still eloquent testament of Mann's inner life.

Thomas Mann: Pro and Contra Wagner, translated by Allan Blunden, introduction by Erich Heller (Faber & Faber, 1985). Documents the lifelong obsession of an imperfect Wagnerite.

GENERAL BIBLIOGRAPHY

BLACKBOURN, DAVID, and EVANS, RICHARD J., eds, *The German Bourgeoisie,* Routledge, 1991. Historical essays on Mann's milieu.

BRUFORD, W. H., *The German Tradition of Self-Cultivation. 'Bildung' from Humboldt to Thomas Mann*, Cambridge University Press, 1975. Chapters on *The Magic Mountain* and 'The Conversion of an Unpolitical Man' by a great scholar.

CARNEGY, PATRICK, *Faust as Musician: A Study of Thomas Mann's Novel 'Doctor Faustus'*, Chatto & Windus, 1973. Subtle investigation of Mann and music by a leading opera critic and producer.

DE MENDELSSOHN, PETER, *Der Zauberer. Das Leben des deutschen Schriftstellers Thomas Mann*, Frankfurt, 1975. The standard German biography.

GRAY, R. D., *The German Tradition in Literature 1871–1945*, Cambridge University Press, 1965. A highly critical account of Mann's contemporaries and their ideas.

HAMILTON, NIGEL, *The Brothers Mann*, Secker & Warburg, and Yale University Press, New Haven, Conn., 1978. A biographical study of Thomas Mann and his elder brother Heinrich, an eminent novelist in his own right.

HAYMAN, RONALD, *Thomas Mann: A Biography*, Bloomsbury, 1995. Reliable life and times by the author of biographies of Kafka, Brecht, Nietzsche and Proust.

HEILBUT, ANTHONY, *Thomas Mann: Eros and Literature*, Macmillan, 1995. Revisionist biography, emphasizing links between Mann's homosexuality and his works.

HELLER, ERICH, *The Ironic German. A Study of Thomas Mann*, Secker & Warburg, 1956. This remains far and away the best book on Mann. Heller's best-known book, *The Disinherited Mind*, Bowes and Bowes, 1975, gives the intellectual background to Mann. His German collection, *Die Wiederkehr der Unschuld und andere Essays*, Suhrkamp, Frankfurt am Main, 1977, contains three essays on Mann. One of them is 'Thomas Mann in Venice', published in *The Poet's Self and the Poem*, Athlone Press, 1976. Heller, who died in 1991, also wrote an introduction to the earlier Everyman volume of *Thomas Mann: Stories and Episodes*, Dent, 1960.

HOLLINGDALE R. J., *Thomas Mann. A Critical Study*, Rupert Hart-Davies, 1971. The author, a Nietzsche scholar and translator, is especially worth reading on Mann's debts to the philosopher.

JOHNSON, DANIEL, introduction to Thomas Mann's *Death in Venice and Other Stories*, Everyman's Library, 1991. Background to Mann's most celebrated story.

LAWRENCE, D. H., 'German Books: Thomas Mann' (1913), in: *A Selection from Phoenix*, Peregrine, 1971. Among the first English reviews of *Death in Venice.* Lawrence rampant: 'Thomas Mann is old – and we are young.'

MANN, GOLO, *Reminiscences and Reflections: Growing Up in Germany*, Faber & Faber, 1990. Chilling, unsparing account of Thomas Mann as a father by his historian son.

PASCAL, ROY, *From Naturalism to Expressionism. German Literature and Society 1880–1918*, Weidenfeld, 1973. Fine on background to the young Mann.

PRATER, DONALD, *Thomas Mann: A Life*, Oxford University Press, 1995. The best of the recent crop of biographies, placing Mann in his literary, social and political context.

REED, T. J., *Thomas Mann: The Uses of Tradition*, Oxford University Press, 1974. Careful scholarship by the author of a critical edition of *Death in Venice.*

REICH-RANICKI, MARCEL, *Thomas Mann and His Family*, Fontana Press, 1989. Provocative essays on Thomas, Heinrich, Klaus, Katja, Erika and Golo Mann by Germany's most influential literary critic, based in part on personal acquaintance.

SONTHEIMER, KURT, *Thomas Mann und die Deutschen*, Fischer, Frankfurt am Main, 1965. A lively German apologia for Mann the political contortionist.

STERN, J. P., *Hitler. The Führer and the People*, Fontana, 1975; *A Study of Nietzsche*, Cambridge University Press, 1979. Opposite poles of Mann's cosmos.

TAYLOR, RONALD, *Literature and Society in Germany, 1918–1945*, Harvester, 1980. Reliable work on the period of Mann's triumph and exile.

WYSLING, HANS (ed.), *Letters of Heinrich and Thomas Mann, 1900–1949*, University of California Press, 1998. Riveting chronicle of fraternal rivalry.

CHRONOLOGY

DATE	AUTHOR'S LIFE	LITERARY CONTEXT
1871	Birth of Heinrich Mann	
1872		Nietzsche: *The Birth of Tragedy*.
1873		Tolstoy: *Anna Karenina* (to 1877).
1874		Wagner's *Ring* finished.
1875	Birth, 6 June, of Thomas Mann in Lübeck as second son of Consul Thomas Mann and his Brazilian wife, Julia da Silva Bruhns.	
1876		
1880		Zola: *Nana*.
1883		
1889		
1890		
1891	Death of Mann's father.	Wilde: *The Picture of Dorian Gray*. Rimbaud dies.
1894	Mann leaves school and joins his mother in Munich.	Heinrich Mann's first novel, *In a Family*.
1896		Fontane: *Poggenpuhls*.
1898	Mann's first stories, *Little Herr Friedemann*, are published by S. Fischer.	
1899	Mann reads Schopenhauer and Platen. In the autumn he returns to Lübeck and visits Denmark.	Proust abandons society, later to write *A la recherche du temps perdu*.
1900		
1901	*Buddenbrooks* appears.	
1903	*Tristan* (second volume of stories), 'Tonio Kröger'.	
1905	Mann marries Katja Pringsheim, who is Jewish. Daughter, Erika, born. *Fiorenza* appears. 'The Blood of the Walsungs' is withdrawn.	
1906	Son, Klaus, is born.	Musil: *Young Törless*. Galsworthy: *A Man of Property* (*Forsyte Saga*).
1907		
1909	*Royal Highness* appears. Son, Golo, born. *The Confessions of Felix Krull, Confidence Man* begun, set aside in 1911 and resumed in 1951.	

HISTORICAL EVENTS

Germany unified by Bismarck.

Wagner founds Bayreuth Festival.

Wagner dies.
Birth of Hitler.
Fall of Bismarck. Wilhelm II's personal rule begins.

German Navy Law begins the arms race.

Bülow becomes Imperial Chancellor.

First Morocco crisis.

Homosexual scandal shakes Imperial court.

DATE	AUTHOR'S LIFE	LITERARY CONTEXT
1910	Suicide of Mann's sister Carla. Daughter, Monika, born. Mann meets Mahler at Pringsheims, hears Eighth Symphony.	E. M. Forster: *Howards End.*
1911	May: Manns visit Venice. July: begins 'Death in Venice'. Work continues for a year.	Heinrich Mann's manifesto, *Spirit and Deed.*
1912	Katja stays four months at sanatorium in Davos. Mann wrongly diagnosed as tubercular while visiting her in May–June. September: 'Death in Venice' serialized.	Heinrich Mann begins his most famous book, *Man of Straw.*
1913	*The Magic Mountain* begun, set aside 1916, resumed 1919. Mann resigns from Munich Board of Censors over Frank Wedekind.	Lawrence: *Sons and Lovers.*
1914	November: 'Thoughts in Wartime' appears. Mann declares his support for German war aims.	January: *Man of Straw* starts serialization; July: interrupted.
1915	'Frederick and the Grand Coalition', a pro-war tract, appears. Break with Heinrich.	H. Mann's *Zola*, an anti-war tract, appears.
1917	Mann influenced by Hans Pfitzner's opera *Palestrina.*	
1918	Daughter, Elisabeth, born. September: *Reflections of an Unpolitical Man* appears.	Spengler: *The Decline of the West.*
1919	'A Man and his Dog' appears. Mann's life spared by Ernst Toller, Soviet leader. Son, Michael, born.	Musil begins *The Man without Qualities* (1930).
1920		Janowitz and Mayer film, *The Cabinet of Dr Caligari.*
1921	'Goethe and Tolstoy'. 'The Blood of the Walsungs' printed privately.	
1922	Mann brothers reconciled. Thomas supports Weimar Republic.	James Joyce: *Ulysses.*
1923	Mother dies. Befriends Gerhart Hauptmann in Bolzano.	Rilke: *Duino Elegies*, *Sonnets to Orpheus.*
1924	*The Magic Mountain.*	E. M. Forster: *A Passage to India.*
1925		André Gide: *Corydon.*

CHRONOLOGY

HISTORICAL EVENTS

Tolstoy dies.

Mahler dies. Agadir crisis.

Social Democrats are the largest German party.

August: World War I begins.

Russian Revolution.

June: Germans near Paris. November: Germany defeated. Revolution.

Weimar Republic. March: Munich Soviet republic suppressed.

Rise of fascism in Italy.

Walter Rathenau assassinated.

Munich putsch by Nazis. Hyper-inflation.

Hindenburg becomes German President.

DATE	AUTHOR'S LIFE	LITERARY CONTEXT
1926	'Disorder and Early Sorrow'. Klaus engaged to Pamela Wedekind. Erika engaged to Gustaf Gründgens. Mann begins *Joseph* tetralogy.	
1927	Sister Julia's suicide.	Proust: *A la recherche du temps perdu.*
1929	Mann receives Nobel Prize (200,000 Marks) for *Buddenbrooks.*	Döblin: *Berlin Alexanderplatz.*
1930	'Mario and the Magician', 'A Sketch of My Life', 'Appeal to Reason'.	Film, *The Blue Angel*, based on a novel by Heinrich. Musil: *The Man without Qualities.*
1931	'The Rebirth of Decency'.	
1932	'Goethe as Representative of the Bourgeois Age' (lecture).	Heinrich Mann: *The Acceptance of Internationalism.*
1933	'The Tales of Jacob'. 'Sufferings and Greatness of Richard Wagner' (lecture). March: Mann warned not to return from Switzerland. Exile begins but Mann's books continue to appear in Germany.	Strauss and Pfitzner are among forty-five to sign protest against Mann's lecture on Wagner.
1934	*The Young Joseph.* Klaus Mann edits *Die Sammlung.*	
1935	Mann's publisher, Bermann-Fischer, moves to Vienna.	Canetti: *Auto da Fé.*
1936	*Joseph in Egypt.* 'Freud and the Future'. Loses German citizenship; becomes Czech citizen.	Klaus Mann: *Mephisto.*
1938	Lectures in America, decides to stay in Princeton.	Freud: *Moses and Monotheism.*
1939	*Lotte in Weimar.* 9 September: Manns leave Europe.	Isherwood: *Goodbye to Berlin.*
1940	'The Transposed Heads'. October: Mann gives the first of forty-five broadcasts for BBC. Heinrich Mann escapes from Vichy via Lisbon.	Jünger: *On the Marble Cliffs.*
1941	Roosevelt fêtes Mann as leader of German exiles. Manns move to California.	
1943	*Joseph the Provider.* Mann begins *Doctor Faustus.*	Hesse: *The Glass Bead Game.* Brecht: *Galileo.*

CHRONOLOGY

HISTORICAL EVENTS

World economic crisis.

Nazis win 18 per cent of vote. Brüning uses Hindenburg's emergency powers.

In Germany 4.6 million unemployed.
April: Nazis gain 37 per cent. November: 33 per cent. Brüning succeeded by Papen, Schleicher.
January: Hitler becomes Chancellor. February: Reichstag fire. March: Nazis gain 44 per cent. Hitler creates Third Reich; concentration camps set up for dissidents.

Hitler orders Röhm and other rivals shot.

Nuremberg laws. Germany re-arms.

Rhineland is remilitarized. Spanish Civil War.

March: *Anschluss*. September: Munich crisis.

World War II begins, 1 September.

Fall of France.

USSR invaded. Hitler's Final Solution. Pearl Harbor: US at war.

Germans retreat in Russia, Africa, Italy.

DATE	AUTHOR'S LIFE	LITERARY CONTEXT
1944	'The Tables of the Law'. Becomes American citizen.	
1945	December: Mann gives radio broadcast on why he will not return to Germany. Storm of criticism.	Broch: *The Death of Virgil.*
1946	Mann has operation for lung cancer, recovers.	Golo Mann: *Life of Gentz.*
1947	*Doctor Faustus* appears, is attacked by Schoenberg. Mann returns to Europe, is attacked by Döblin and others.	Camus: *The Plague.*
1948	Klaus attempts suicide. 'The Genesis of a Novel'.	Eliot: *Notes Towards the Definition of Culture.*
1949	'Nietzsche in the Light of our Experience'. Klaus Mann kills himself. Mann returns to Germany; lectures in East and West.	
1950	Heinrich Mann dies. Mann working on *Felix Krull.* He attacks McCarthyism.	
1951	'The Holy Sinner'.	
1952	Moves to Switzerland.	
1953	'The Black Swan'.	Beckett: *Waiting for Godot.*
1954	*The Confessions of Felix Krull, Confidence Man.*	
1955	12 August: Mann dies of arteriosclerosis, aged eighty. He is buried in Kilchberg.	Nabokov: *Lolita.*

CHRONOLOGY

HISTORICAL EVENTS

Germany besieged.

April: Hitler's suicide. May: Germany surrenders. August: atom bombs on Japan.

Iron curtain speech by Churchill.

Gruppe 47 founded by young German writers.

Erhard launches the Deutschemark.

Germany is divided: Adenauer is Chancellor of West, Ulbricht rules East.

Korean War. West German production outstrips pre-war Reich.

Death of Stalin.

Death of Albert Einstein.

THOMAS MANN

THE COLLECTED STORIES

LITTLE HERR FRIEDEMANN

IT WAS the nurse's fault. When they first suspected, Frau Consul Friedemann had spoken to her very gravely about the need of controlling her weakness. But what good did that do? Or the glass of red wine which she got daily besides the beer which was needed for the milk? For they suddenly discovered that she even sank so low as to drink the methylated spirit which was kept for the spirit lamp. Before they could send her away and get someone to take her place, the mischief was done. One day the mother and sisters came home to find that little Johannes, then about a month old, had fallen from the couch and lay on the floor, uttering an appallingly faint little cry, while the nurse stood beside him quite stupefied.

The doctor came and with firm, gentle hands tested the little creature's contracted and twitching limbs. He made a very serious face. The three girls stood sobbing in a corner and the Frau Consul in the anguish of her heart prayed aloud.

The poor mother, just before the child's birth, had already suffered a crushing blow: her husband, the Dutch Consul, had been snatched away from her by sudden and violent illness, and now she was too broken to cherish any hope that little Johannes would be spared to her. But by the second day the doctor had given her hand an encouraging squeeze and told her that all immediate danger was over. There was no longer any sign that the brain was affected. The facial expression was altered, it had lost the fixed and staring look... Of course, they must see how things went on – and hope for the best, hope for the best.

The grey gabled house in which Johannes Friedemann grew up stood by the north gate of the little old commercial city. The front door led into a large flag-paved entry, out of which a stair with a white wooden balustrade led up into the second storey. The faded wall-paper in the living-room had a landscape pattern, and straight-backed chairs and sofas in dark-red plush stood round the heavy mahogany table.

Often in his childhood Johannes sat here at the window, which always had a fine showing of flowers, on a small footstool at his mother's feet, listening to some fairy-tale she told him, gazing at her smooth grey head, her mild and gentle face, and breathing in the faint scent she exhaled. She showed him the picture of his father, a kindly man with grey side-whiskers – he was now in heaven, she said, and awaiting them there.

Behind the house was a small garden where in summer they spent much of their time, despite the smell of burnt sugar which came over from the refinery close by. There was a gnarled old walnut tree in whose shade little Johannes would sit, on a low wooden stool, cracking walnuts, while Frau Friedemann and her three daughters, now grown women, took refuge from the sun under a grey canvas tent. The mother's gaze often strayed from her embroidery to look with sad and loving eyes at her child.

He was not beautiful, little Johannes, as he crouched on his stool industriously cracking his nuts. In fact, he was a strange sight, with his pigeon breast, humped back, and disproportionately long arms. But his hands and feet were delicately formed, he had soft red-brown eyes like a doe's, a sensitive mouth, and fine, light-brown hair. His head, had it not sat so deep between his shoulders, might almost have been called pretty.

When he was seven he went to school, where time passed swiftly and uniformly. He walked every day, with the strut deformed people often have, past the quaint gabled houses and shops to the old schoolhouse with the vaulted arcades. When he had done his preparation he would read in his books with the lovely title-page illustrations in colour, or else work in the garden, while his sisters kept house for their invalid mother. They went out too, for they belonged to the best society of the town; but unfortunately they had not married, for they had not much money nor any looks to recommend them.

Johannes too was now and then invited out by his schoolmates, but it is not likely that he enjoyed it. He could not take part in their games, and they were always embarrassed in his company, so there was no feeling of good fellowship.

There came a time when he began to hear certain matters talked about, in the courtyard at school. He listened wide-eyed and large-eared, quite silent, to his companions' raving over this or that little girl. Such things, though they entirely engrossed the attention of these others, were not, he felt, for him; they belonged in the same category as the ball games and gymnastics. At times he felt a little sad. But at length he had become quite used to standing on one side and not taking part.

But after all it came about – when he was sixteen – that he felt suddenly drawn to a girl of his own age. She was the sister of a classmate of his, a blond, hilarious hoyden, and he met her when calling at her brother's house. He felt strangely embarrassed in her neighbourhood; she too was embarrassed and treated him with such artificial cordiality that it made him sad.

One summer afternoon as he was walking by himself on the wall outside the town, he heard a whispering behind a jasmine bush and peeped cautiously through the branches. There she sat on a bench beside a long-legged, red-haired youth of his acquaintance. They had their arms about each other and he was imprinting on her lips a kiss, which she returned amid giggles. Johannes looked, turned round, and went softly away.

His head was sunk deeper than ever between his shoulders, his hands trembled, and a sharp pain shot upwards from his chest to his throat. But he choked it down, straightening himself as well as he could. "Good," said he to himself. "That is over. Never again will I let myself in for any of it.

To the others it brings joy and happiness, for me it can only mean sadness and pain. I am done with it. For me that is all over. Never again."

The resolution did him good. He had renounced, renounced for ever. He went home, took up a book, or else played on his violin, which despite his deformed chest he had learned to do.

At seventeen Johannes left school to go into business, like everybody else he knew. He was apprenticed to the big lumber firm of Herr Schlievogt down on the river-bank. They were kind and considerate, he on his side was responsive and friendly, time passed with peaceful regularity. But in his twenty-first year his mother died, after a lingering illness.

This was a sore blow for Johannes Friedemann, and the pain of it endured. He cherished this grief, he gave himself up to it as one gives oneself to a great joy, he fed it with a thousand childhood memories; it was the first important event in his life and he made the most of it.

Is not life in and for itself a good, regardless of whether we may call its content "happiness"? Johannes Friedemann felt that it was so, and he loved life. He, who had renounced the greatest joy it can bring us, taught himself with infinite, incredible care to take pleasure in what it had still to offer. A walk in the springtime in the parks surrounding the town; the fragrance of a flower; the song of a bird – might not one feel grateful for such things as these?

And that we need to be taught how to enjoy, yes, that our education is always and only equal to our capacity for enjoyment – he knew that too, and he trained himself. Music he loved, and attended all the concerts that were given in the town. He came to play the violin not so badly himself, no matter what a figure of fun he made when he did it; and took delight in every beautiful soft tone he succeeded in producing. Also, by much reading he came in time to possess a literary taste the like of which did not exist in the place. He kept up with the new books, even the foreign ones; he knew how to savour the seductive rhythm of a lyric or the ultimate flavour of a subtly told tale – yes, one might almost call him a connoisseur.

He learned to understand that to everything belongs its own enjoyment and that it is absurd to distinguish between an experience which is "happy" and one which is not. With a right good will he accepted each emotion as it came, each mood, whether sad or gay. Even he cherished the unfulfilled desires, the longings. He loved them for their own sakes and told himself that with fulfilment the best of them would be past. The vague, sweet, painful yearning and hope of quiet spring evenings – are they not richer in joy than all the fruition the summer can bring? Yes, he was a connoisseur, our little Herr Friedemann.

But of course they did not know that, the people whom he met on the street, who bowed to him with the kindly, compassionate air he knew so well. They could not know that this unhappy cripple, strutting comically along in his light overcoat and shiny top hat – strange to say, he was a little vain – they could not know how tenderly he loved the mild flow of his life, charged with no great emotions, it is true, but full of a quiet and tranquil happiness which was his own creation.

But Herr Friedemann's great preference, his real passion, was for the theatre. He possessed a dramatic sense which was unusually strong; at a telling theatrical effect or the catastrophe of a tragedy his whole small frame would shake with emotion. He had his regular seat in the first row of boxes at the opera-house; was an assiduous frequenter and often took his sisters with him. Since their mother's death they kept house for their brother in the old home which they all owned together.

It was a pity they were unmarried still; but with the decline of hope had come resignation – Friederike, the eldest, was seventeen years further on than Herr Friedemann. She and her sister Henriette were over-tall and thin, whereas Pfiffi, the youngest, was too short and stout. She had a funny way, too, of shaking herself as she talked, and water came in the corners of her mouth.

Little Herr Friedemann did not trouble himself overmuch about his three sisters. But they stuck together loyally and were always of one mind. Whenever an engagement was announced in their circle they with one voice said how very gratifying that was.

Their brother continued to live with them even after he became independent, as he did by leaving Herr Schlievogt's firm and going into business for himself, in an agency of sorts, which was no great tax on his time. His offices were in a couple of rooms on the ground floor of the house so that at mealtimes he had but the pair of stairs to mount – for he suffered now and then from asthma.

His thirtieth birthday fell on a fine warm June day, and after dinner he sat out in the grey canvas tent, with a new head-rest embroidered by Henriette. He had a good cigar in his mouth and a good book in his hand. But sometimes he would put the latter down to listen to the sparrows chirping blithely in the old nut tree and look at the clean gravel path leading up to the house between lawns bright with summer flowers.

Little Herr Friedemann wore no beard, and his face had scarcely changed at all, save that the features were slightly sharper. He wore his fine light-brown hair parted on one side.

Once, as he let the book fall on his knee and looked up into the sunny blue sky, he said to himself: "Well, so that is thirty years. Perhaps there may be ten or even twenty more, God knows. They will mount up without a sound or a stir and pass by like those that are gone; and I look forward to them with peace in my heart."

Now, it happened in July of the same year that a new appointment to the office of District Commandant had set the whole town talking. The stout and jolly gentleman who had for many years occupied the post had been very popular in social circles and they saw him go with great regret. It was in compliance with goodness knows what regulations that Herr von Rinnlingen and no other was sent hither from the capital.

In any case the exchange was not such a bad one. The new Commandant was married but childless. He rented a spacious villa in the southern suburbs of the city and seemed to intend to set up an establishment. There was a report that he was very rich – which received confirmation in the fact that he brought with him four servants, five riding and carriage horses, a landau and a light hunting-cart.

Soon after their arrival the husband and wife left cards on all the best society, and their names were on every tongue. But it was not Herr von Rinnlingen, it was his wife who was the centre of interest. All the men were dazed, for the moment too dazed to pass judgment; but their wives were quite prompt and definite in the view that Gerda von Rinnlingen was not their sort.

"Of course, she comes from the metropolis, her ways would naturally be different," Frau Hagenström, the lawyer's wife, said, in conversation with Henriette Friedemann. "She smokes, and she rides. That is of course. But it is her manners – they are not only free, they are positively brusque, or even worse. You see, no one could call her ugly, one might even say she is pretty; but she has not a trace of feminine charm in her looks or gestures or her laugh – they completely lack everything that makes a man fall in love with a woman. She is not a flirt – and goodness knows I would be the last to disparage her for that. But it is strange to see so young a woman – she is only twenty-four – so entirely wanting in natural charm. I am not expressing myself very well, my dear, but I know what I mean. All the men are simply bewildered. In a few weeks, you will see, they will be disgusted."

"Well," Fräulein Friedemann said, "she certainly has everything she wants."

"Yes," cried Frau Hagenström, "look at her husband! And how does she treat him? You ought to see it – you will see it! I would be the first to approve of a married woman behaving with a certain reserve towards the other sex. But how does she behave to her own husband? She has a way of fixing him with an ice-cold stare and saying 'My dear friend!' with a pitying expression that drives me mad. For when you look at him – upright, correct, gallant, a brilliant officer and a splendidly preserved man of forty! They have been married four years, my dear."

Herr Friedemann was first vouchsafed a glimpse of Frau von Rinnlingen in the main street of the town, among all the rows of shops, at mid-day, when he was coming from the Bourse, where he had done a little bidding.

He was strolling along beside Herr Stephens, looking tiny and important, as usual. Herr Stephens was in the wholesale trade, a huge stocky man with round side-whiskers and bushy eyebrows. Both of them wore top hats; their overcoats were unbuttoned on account of the heat. They tapped their canes along the pavement and talked of the political situation; but half-way down the street Stephens suddenly said:

"Deuce take it if there isn't the Rinnlingen driving along."

"Good," answered Herr Friedemann in his high, rather sharp voice, looking expectantly ahead. "Because I have never yet set eyes on her. And here we have the yellow cart we hear so much about."

It was in fact the hunting-cart which Frau von Rinnlingen was herself driving today with a pair of thoroughbreds; a groom sat behind her, with folded arms. She wore a loose beige coat and skirt and a small round straw hat with a brown leather band, beneath which her well-waved red-blond hair, a good, thick crop, was drawn into a knot at the nape of her neck. Her face was oval, with a dead-white skin and faint bluish shadows lurking under the close-set eyes. Her nose was short but well-shaped, with a becoming little saddle of freckles; whether her mouth was as good or not could not be told, for she kept it in continual motion, sucking the lower and biting the upper lip.

Herr Stephens, as the cart came abreast of them, greeted her with a great show of deference; little Herr Friedemann lifted his hat too and looked at her with wide-eyed attention. She lowered her whip, nodded slightly, and drove slowly past, looking at the houses and shop-windows.

After a few paces Herr Stephens said:

"She has been taking a drive and was on her way home."

Little Herr Friedemann made no answer, but stared before him at the pavement. Presently he started, looked at his companion, and asked: "What did you say?"

And Herr Stephens repeated his acute remark.

Three days after that Johannes Friedemann came home at mid-day from his usual walk. Dinner was at half past twelve, and he would spend the interval in his office at the right of the entrance door. But the maid came across the entry and told him that there were visitors.

"In my office?" he asked.

"No, upstairs with the mistresses."

"Who are they?"

"Herr and Frau Colonel von Rinnlingen."

"Ah," said Johannes Friedemann. "Then I will – "

And he mounted the stairs. He crossed the lobby and laid his hand on the knob of the high white door leading into the "landscape room". And then he drew back, turned round, and slowly returned as he had come. And spoke to himself, for there was no one else there, and said: "No, better not."

He went into his office, sat down at his desk, and took up the paper. But after a little he dropped it again and sat looking to one side out of the window. Thus he sat until the maid came to say that luncheon was ready; then he went up into the dining-room where his sisters were already waiting, and sat down in his chair, in which there were three music-books.

As she ladled the soup Henriette said:

"Johannes, do you know who were here?"

"Well?" he asked.

"The new Commandant and his wife."

"Indeed? That was friendly of them."

"Yes," said Pfiffi, a little water coming in the corners of her mouth. "I found them both very agreeable."

"And we must lose no time in returning the call," said Friederike. "I suggest that we go next Sunday, the day after tomorrow."

"Sunday," Henriette and Pfiffi said.

"You will go with us, Johannes?" asked Friederike.

"Of course he will," said Pfiffi, and gave herself a little shake. Herr Friedemann had not heard her at all; he was eating his soup, with a hushed and troubled air. It was as though he were listening to some strange noise he heard.

Next evening *Lohengrin* was being given at the opera, and everybody in society was present. The small auditorium was crowded, humming with voices and smelling of gas and perfumery. And every eye-glass in the stalls was directed towards box thirteen, next to the stage; for this was the first appearance of Herr and Frau von Rinnlingen and one could give them a good looking-over.

When little Herr Friedemann, in flawless dress clothes and glistening white pigeon-breasted shirt-front, entered his box, which was number thirteen, he started back at the door, making a gesture with his hand towards his brow. His nostrils dilated feverishly. Then he took his seat, which was next to Frau von Rinnlingen's.

She contemplated him for a little while, with her under lip stuck out; then she turned to exchange a few words with her husband, a tall, broad-shouldered gentleman with a brown, good-natured face and turned-up moustaches.

When the overture began and Frau von Rinnlingen leaned over the balustrade Herr Friedemann gave her a quick, searching side glance. She wore a light-coloured evening frock, the only one in the theatre which was slightly low in the neck. Her sleeves were full and her white gloves came up to her elbows. Her figure was statelier than it had looked under the loose coat; her full bosom slowly rose and fell and the knot of red-blond hair hung low and heavy at the nape of her neck.

Herr Friedemann was pale, much paler than usual, and little beads of perspiration stood on his brow beneath the smoothly parted brown hair. He could see Frau von Rinnlingen's left arm, which lay upon the balustrade. She had taken off her glove and the rounded, dead-white arm and ringless hand, both of them shot with pale blue veins, were directly under his eye – he could not help seeing them.

The fiddles sang, the trombones crashed, Telramund was slain, general jubilation reigned in the orchestra, and little Herr Friedemann sat there motionless and pallid, his head drawn in between his shoulders, his forefinger to his lips and one hand thrust into the opening of his waistcoat.

As the curtain fell, Frau von Rinnlingen got up to leave the box with her husband. Johannes Friedemann saw her without looking, wiped his handkerchief across his brow, then rose suddenly and went as far as the door into the foyer, where he turned, came back to his chair, and sat down in the same posture as before.

When the bell rang and his neighbours re-entered the box he felt Frau von Rinnlingen's eyes upon him, so that finally against his will he raised his head. As their eyes met, hers did not swerve aside; she continued to gaze without embarrassment until he himself, deeply humiliated, was forced to look away. He turned a shade paler and felt a strange, sweet pang of anger and scorn. The music began again.

Towards the end of the act Frau von Rinnlingen chanced to drop her fan; it fell at Herr Friedemann's feet. They both stooped at the same time, but she reached it first and gave a little mocking smile as she said: "Thank you."

Their heads were quite close together and just for a second he got the warm scent of her breast. His face was drawn, his whole body twitched, and his heart thumped so horribly that he lost his breath. He sat without moving for half a minute, then he pushed back his chair, got up quietly, and went out.

He crossed the lobby, pursued by the music; got his top hat from the cloak-room, his light overcoat and his stick, went down the stairs and out of doors.

It was a warm, still evening. In the gas-lit street the gabled houses towered towards a sky where stars were softly beaming. The pavement echoed the steps of a few passers-by. Someone spoke to him, but he heard and saw nothing; his head was bowed and his deformed chest shook with the violence of his breathing. Now and then he murmured to himself:

"My God, my God!"

He was gazing horror-struck within himself, beholding the havoc which had been wrought with his tenderly cherished, scrupulously managed feelings. Suddenly he was quite overpowered by the strength of his tortured longing. Giddy and drunken he leaned against a lamp-post and his quivering lips uttered the one word: "Gerda!"

The stillness was complete. Far and wide not a soul was to be seen. Little Herr Friedemann pulled himself together and went on, up the street in which the opera-house stood and which ran steeply down to the river, then along the main street northwards to his home.

How she had looked at him! She had forced him, actually, to cast down his eyes! She had humiliated him with her glance. But was she not a woman and he a man? And those strange brown eyes of hers – had they not positively glittered with unholy joy?

Again he felt the same surge of sensual, impotent hatred mount up in him; then he relived the moment when her head had touched his, when he had breathed in the fragrance of her body – and for the second time he halted, bent his deformed torso backwards, drew in the air through clenched teeth, and murmured helplessly, desperately, uncontrollably:

"My God, my God!"

Then went on again, slowly, mechanically, through the heavy evening air, through the empty echoing streets until he stood before his own house. He paused a minute in the entry, breathing the cool, dank inside air; then he went into his office.

He sat down at his desk by the open window and stared straight ahead of him at a large yellow rose which somebody had set there in a glass of water. He took it up and smelt it with his eyes closed, then put it down with a gesture of weary sadness. No, no. That was all over. What was even that fragrance to him now? What any of all those things that up to now had been the well-springs of his joy?

He turned away and gazed into the quiet street. At intervals steps passed and the sound died away. The stars stood still and glittered. He felt so weak, so utterly tired to death. His head was quite vacant, and suddenly his despair began to melt into a gentle, pervading melancholy. A few lines of a poem flickered through his head, he heard the *Lohengrin* music in his ears, he saw Frau von Rinnlingen's face and her round white arm on the red velvet – then he fell into a heavy fever-burdened sleep.

Often he was near waking, but feared to do so and managed to sink back into forgetfulness again. But when it had grown quite light, he opened his eyes and looked round him with a wide and painful gaze. He remembered everything, it was as though the anguish had never been intermitted by sleep.

His head was heavy and his eyes burned. But when he had washed up and bathed his head with cologne he felt better and sat down in his place by the still open window. It was early, perhaps only five o'clock. Now and then a baker's boy passed; otherwise there was no one to be seen. In the opposite house the blinds were down. But birds were twittering and the sky was luminously blue. A wonderfully beautiful Sunday morning.

A feeling of comfort and confidence came over little Herr Friedemann. Why had he been distressing himself? Was not everything just as it had been? The attack of yesterday had been a bad one. Granted. But it should be the last. It was not too late, he could still escape destruction. He must avoid every occasion of a fresh seizure, he felt sure he could do this. He felt the strength to conquer and suppress his weakness.

It struck half past seven and Friederike came in with the coffee, setting it on the round table in front of the leather sofa against the rear wall.

"Good morning, Johannes," said she; "here is your breakfast."

"Thanks," said little Herr Friedemann. And then: "Dear Friederike, I am sorry, but you will have to pay your call without me, I do not feel well enough to go. I have slept badly and have a headache – in short, I must ask you –"

"What a pity!" answered Friederike. "You must go another time. But you do look ill. Shall I lend you my menthol pencil?"

"Thanks," said Herr Friedemann. "It will pass." And Friederike went out.

Standing at the table he slowly drank his coffee and ate a croissant. He felt satisfied with himself and proud of his firmness. When he had finished he sat down again by the open window, with a cigar. The food had done him good and he felt happy and hopeful. He took a book and sat reading and smoking and blinking into the sunlight.

Morning had fully come, wagons rattled past, there were many voices and the sound of the bells on passing trams. With and among it all was woven the twittering and chirping; there was a radiant blue sky, a soft mild air.

At ten o'clock he heard his sisters cross the entry; the front door creaked, and he idly noticed that they passed his window. An hour went by. He felt more and more happy.

A sort of hubris mounted in him. What a heavenly air – and how the birds were singing! He felt like taking a little walk. Then suddenly, without any transition, yet accompanied by a terror namelessly sweet came the thought: "Suppose I were to go to her!" And suppressing, as though by actual muscular effort, every warning voice within him, he added with blissful resolution: "I will go to her!"

He changed into his Sunday clothes, took his top hat and his stick, and hurried with quickened breath through the town and into the southern suburbs. Without looking at a soul he kept raising and dropping his head with each eager step, completely rapt in his exalted state until he arrived at the avenue of chestnut trees and the red brick villa with the name of Commandant von Rinnlingen on the gate-post.

But here he was seized by a tremor, his heart throbbed and pounded in his breast. He went across the vestibule and rang at the inside door. The die was cast, there was no retreating now. "Come what come may," thought he, and felt the stillness of death within him.

The door suddenly opened and the maid came towards him across the vestibule; she took his card and hurried away up the red-carpeted stair. Herr Friedemann gazed fixedly at the bright colour until she came back and said that her mistress would like him to come up.

He put down his stick beside the door leading into the salon and stole a look at himself in the glass. His face was pale, the eyes red, his hair was sticking to his brow, the hand that held his top hat kept on shaking.

The maid opened the door and he went in. He found himself in a rather large, half-darkened room, with drawn curtains. At his right was a piano, and about the round table in the centre stood several arm-chairs covered in brown silk. The sofa stood along the left-hand wall, with a landscape painting in a heavy gilt frame hanging above it. The wall-paper too was dark in tone. There was an alcove filled with potted palms.

A minute passed, then Frau von Rinnlingen opened the portières on the right and approached him noiselessly over the thick brown carpet. She wore a simply cut frock of red and black plaid. A ray of light, with motes dancing in it, streamed from the alcove and fell upon her heavy red hair so that it shone like gold. She kept her strange eyes fixed upon him with a searching gaze and as usual stuck out her under lip.

"Good morning, Frau Commandant," began little Herr Friedemann, and looked up at her, for he came only as high as her chest. "I wished to pay you my respects too. When my sisters did so I was unfortunately out...I regretted sincerely..."

He had no idea at all what else he should say; and there she stood and gazed ruthlessly at him as though she would force him to go on. The blood rushed to his head. "She sees through me," he thought, "she will torture and despise me. Her eyes keep flickering...."

But at last she said, in a very high, clear voice:

"It is kind of you to have come. I have also been sorry not to see you before. Will you please sit down?"

She took her seat close beside him, leaned back, and put her arm along the arm of the chair. He sat bent over, holding his hat between his knees. She went on:

"Did you know that your sisters were here a quarter of an hour ago? They told me you were ill."

"Yes," he answered, "I did not feel well enough to go out, I thought I should not be able to. That is why I am late."

"You do not look very well even now," said she tranquilly, not shifting her gaze. "You are pale and your eyes are inflamed. You are not very strong, perhaps?"

"Oh," said Herr Friedemann, stammering, "I've not much to complain of, as a rule."

"I am ailing a good deal too," she went on, still not turning her eyes from him, "but nobody notices it. I am nervous, and sometimes I have the strangest feelings."

She paused, lowered her chin to her breast, and looked up expectantly at him. He made no reply, simply sat with his dreamy gaze directed upon her. How strangely she spoke, and how her clear and thrilling voice affected him! His heart beat more quietly and he felt as though he were in a dream. She began again:

"I am not wrong in thinking that you left the opera last night before it was over?"

"Yes, madam."

"I was sorry to see that. You listened like a music-lover – though the performance was only tolerable. You are fond of music, I am sure. Do you play the piano?"

"I play the violin, a little," said Herr Friedemann. "That is, really not very much – "

"You play the violin?" she asked, and looked past him consideringly. "But we might play together," she suddenly said. "I can accompany a little. It would be a pleasure to find somebody here – would you come?"

"I am quite at your service – with pleasure," said he, stiffly. He was still as though in a dream. A pause ensued. Then suddenly her expression changed. He saw it alter for one of cruel, though hardly perceptible mockery, and again she fixed him with that same searching, uncannily flickering gaze. His face burned, he knew not where to turn; drawing his head down between his shoulders he stared confusedly at the carpet, while there shot through him once more that strangely sweet and torturing sense of impotent rage.

He made a desperate effort and raised his eyes. She was looking over his head at the door. With the utmost difficulty he fetched out a few words:

"And you are so far not too dissatisfied with your stay in our city?"

"Oh, no," said Frau Rinnlingen indifferently. "No, certainly not; why should I not be satisfied? To be sure, I feel a little hampered, as though everybody's eyes were upon me, but – oh, before I forget it," she went on quickly, "we are entertaining a few people next week, a small, informal company. A little music, perhaps, and conversation. . . . There is a charming garden at the back, it runs down to the river. You and your sisters will be receiving an invitation in due course, but perhaps I may ask you now to give us the pleasure of your company?"

Herr Friedemann was just expressing his gratitude for the invitation when the door-knob was seized energetically from without and the Commandant entered. They both rose and Frau von Rinnlingen introduced the two men to each other. Her husband bowed to them both with equal courtesy. His bronze face glistened with the heat.

He drew off his gloves, addressing Herr Friedemann in a

powerful, rather sharp-edged voice. The latter looked up at him with large vacant eyes and had the feeling that he would presently be clapped benevolently on the shoulder. Heels together, inclining from the waist, the Commandant turned to his wife and asked, in a much gentler tone:

"Have you asked Herr Friedemann if he will give us the pleasure of his company at our little party, my love? If you are willing I should like to fix the date for next week and I hope that the weather will remain fine so that we can enjoy ourselves in the garden."

"Just as you say," answered Frau von Rinnlingen, and gazed past him.

Two minutes later Herr Friedemann got up to go. At the door he turned and bowed to her once more, meeting her expressionless gaze still fixed upon him.

He went away, but he did not go back to the town; unconsciously he struck into a path that led away from the avenue towards the old ruined fort by the river, among well-kept lawns and shady avenues with benches.

He walked quickly and absently, with bent head. He felt intolerably hot, as though aware of flames leaping and sinking within him, and his head throbbed with fatigue.

It was as though her gaze still rested on him – not vacantly as it had at the end, but with that flickering cruelty which went with the strange still way she spoke. Did it give her pleasure to put him beside himself, to see him helpless? Looking through and through him like that, could she not feel a little pity?

He had gone along the river-bank under the moss-grown wall; he sat down on a bench within a half-circle of blossoming jasmine. The sweet, heavy scent was all about him, the sun brooded upon the dimpling water.

He was weary, he was worn out; and yet within him all was tumult and anguish. Were it not better to take one last look and then to go down into that quiet water; after a brief struggle to be free and safe at peace? Ah, peace, peace – that was what he wanted! Not peace in an empty and soundless void, but a gentle, sunlit peace, full of good, of tranquil thoughts.

All his tender love of life thrilled through him in that moment, all his profound yearning for his vanished "happiness". But then he looked about him into the silent, endlessly indifferent peace of nature, saw how the river went its own way in the sun, how the grasses quivered and the flowers stood up where they blossomed, only to fade and be blown away; saw how all that was bent submissively to the will of life; and there came over him all at once that sense of acquaintance and understanding with the inevitable which can make those who know it superior to the blows of fate.

He remembered the afternoon of his thirtieth birthday and the peaceful happiness with which he, untroubled by fears or hopes, had looked forward to what was left of his life. He had seen no light and no shadow there, only a mild twilight radiance gently declining into the dark. With what a calm and superior smile had he contemplated the years still to come – how long ago was that?

Then this woman had come, she had to come, it was his fate that she should, for she herself was his fate and she alone. He had known it from the first moment. She had come – and though he had tried his best to defend his peace, her coming had roused in him all those forces which from his youth up he had sought to suppress, feeling, as he did, that they spelled torture and destruction. They had seized upon him with frightful, irresistible power and flung him to the earth.

They were his destruction, well he knew it. But why struggle, then, and why torture himself? Let everything take its course. He would go his appointed way, closing his eyes before the yawning void, bowing to his fate, bowing to the overwhelming, anguishingly sweet, irresistible power.

The water glittered, the jasmine gave out its strong, pungent scent, the birds chattered in the tree-tops that gave glimpses among them of a heavy, velvety-blue sky. Little hump-backed Herr Friedemann sat long upon his bench; he sat bent over, holding his head in his hands.

Everybody agreed that the Rinnlingens entertained very well. Some thirty guests sat in the spacious dining-room, at the long, prettily decorated table, and the butler and two hired waiters were already handing round the ices. Dishes clattered, glasses rang, there was a warm aroma of food and perfumes. Here were comfortable merchants with their wives and daughters; most of the officers of the garrison; a few professional men, lawyers and the popular old family doctor – in short, all the best society.

A nephew of the Commandant, on a visit, a student of mathematics, sat deeply in conversation with Fräulein Hagenström, whose place was directly opposite Herr Friedemann's, at the lower end of the table. Johannes Friedemann sat there on a rich velvet cushion, beside the unbeautiful wife of the Colonial Director and not far off Frau von Rinnlingen, who had been escorted to table by Consul Stephens. It was astonishing, the change which had taken place in little Herr Friedemann in these few days. Perhaps the incandescent lighting in the room was partly to blame; but his cheeks looked sunken, he made a more crippled impression even than usual, and his inflamed eyes, with their dark rings, glowed with an inexpressibly tragic light. He drank a great deal of wine and now and then addressed a remark to his neighbour.

Frau von Rinnlingen had not so far spoken to him at all; but now she leaned over and called out:

"I have been expecting you in vain these days, you and your fiddle."

He looked vacantly at her for a while before he replied. She wore a light-coloured frock with a low neck that left the white throat bare; a Maréchal Niel rose in full bloom was fastened in her shining hair. Her cheeks were a little flushed, but the same bluish shadows lurked in the corners of her eyes.

Herr Friedemann looked at his plate and forced himself to make some sort of reply; after which the school superintendent's wife asked him if he did not love Beethoven and he had to answer that too. But at this point the Commandant, sitting at the head of the table, caught his wife's eye, tapped on his glass and said:

"Ladies and gentlemen, I suggest that we drink our coffee in the next room. It must be fairly decent out in the garden too, and whoever wants a little fresh air, I am for him."

Lieutenant von Deidesheim made a tactful little joke to cover the ensuing pause, and the table rose in the midst of laughter. Herr Friedemann and his partner were among the last to quit the room; he escorted her through the "old German" smoking-room to the dim and pleasant living-room, where he took his leave.

He was dressed with great care: his evening clothes were irreproachable, his shirt was dazzlingly white, his slender, well-shaped feet were encased in patent-leather pumps, which now and then betrayed the fact that he wore red silk stockings.

He looked out into the corridor and saw a good many people descending the steps into the garden. But he took up a position at the door of the smoking-room, with his cigar and coffee, where he could see into the living-room.

Some of the men stood talking in this room, and at the right of the door a little knot had formed round a small table, the centre of which was the mathematics student, who was eagerly talking. He had made the assertion that one could draw through a given point more than one parallel to a straight line; Frau Hagenström had cried that this was impossible, and he had gone on to prove it so conclusively that his hearers were constrained to behave as though they understood.

At the rear of the room, on the sofa beside the red-shaded lamp, Gerda von Rinnlingen sat in conversation with young Fräulein Stephens. She leaned back among the yellow silk cushions with one knee slung over the other, slowly smoking a cigarette, breathing out the smoke through her nose and sticking out her lower lip. Fräulein Stephens sat stiff as a graven image beside her, answering her questions with an assiduous smile.

Nobody was looking at little Herr Friedemann, so nobody saw that his large eyes were constantly directed upon Frau von Rinnlingen. He sat rather droopingly and looked at her. There was no passion in his gaze nor scarcely any pain. But there was something dull and heavy there, a dead weight of impotent, involuntary adoration.

Some ten minutes went by. Then as though she had been secretly watching him the whole time, Frau von Rinnlingen approached and paused in front of him. He got up as he heard her say:

"Would you care to go into the garden with me, Herr Friedemann?"

He answered:

"With pleasure, madam."

"You have never seen our garden?" she asked him as they went down the steps. "It is fairly large. I hope that there are not too many people in it; I should like to get a breath of fresh air. I got a headache during supper; perhaps the red wine was too strong for me. Let us go this way." They passed through a glass door, the vestibule, and a cool little courtyard, whence they gained the open air by descending a couple more steps.

The scent of all the flower-beds rose into the wonderful, warm, starry night. The garden lay in full moonlight and the guests were strolling up and down the white gravel paths, smoking and talking as they went. A group had gathered round the old fountain, where the much-loved old doctor was making them laugh by sailing paper boats.

With a little nod Frau von Rinnlingen passed them by, and pointed ahead of her, where the fragrant and well-cared-for garden blended into the darker park.

"Shall we go down this middle path?" asked she. At the beginning of it stood two low, squat obelisks.

In the vista at the end of the chestnut alley they could see the river shining green and bright in the moonlight. All about them was darkness and coolness. Here and there side paths branched off, all of them probably curving down to the river. For a long time there was not a sound.

"Down by the water," she said, "there is a pretty spot where I often sit. We could stop and talk a little. See the stars glittering here and there through the trees."

He did not answer, gazing, as they approached it, at the river's shimmering green surface. You could see the other bank and the park along the city wall. They left the alley and came out on the grassy slope down to the river, and she said:

"Here is our place, a little to the right, and there is no one there."

The bench stood facing the water, some six paces away, with its back to the trees. It was warmer here in the open. Crickets chirped among the grass, which at the river's edge gave way to sparse reeds. The moonlit water gave off a soft light.

For a while they both looked in silence. Then he heard her voice; it thrilled him to recognize the same low, gentle, pensive tone of a week ago, which now as then moved him so strangely:

"How long have you had your infirmity, Herr Friedemann? Were you born so?"

He swallowed before he replied, for his throat felt as though he were choking. Then he said, politely and gently:

"No, *gnädige Frau*. It comes from their having let me fall, when I was an infant."

"And how old are you now?" she asked again.

"Thirty years old."

"Thirty years old," she repeated. "And these thirty years were not happy ones?"

Little Herr Friedemann shook his head, his lips quivered.

"No," he said, "that was all lies and my imagination."

"Then you have thought that you were happy?" she asked.

"I have tried to be," he replied, and she responded:

"That was brave of you."

A minute passed. The crickets chirped and behind them the boughs rustled lightly.

"I understand a good deal about unhappiness," she told him. "These summer nights by the water are the best thing for it."

He made no direct answer, but gestured feebly across the water, at the opposite bank, lying peaceful in the darkness.

"I was sitting over there not long ago," he said.

"When you came from me?" she asked. He only nodded.

Then suddenly he started up from his seat, trembling all over; he sobbed and gave vent to a sound, a wail which yet seemed like a release from strain, and sank slowly to the ground before her. He had touched her hand with his as it lay beside him on the bench, and clung to it now, seizing the other as he knelt before her, this little cripple, trembling and shuddering; he buried his face in her lap and stammered between his gasps in a voice which was scarcely human:

"You know, you understand . . . let me . . . I can no longer . . . my God, oh, my God!"

She did not repulse him, neither did she bend her face towards him. She sat erect, leaning a little away, and her close-set eyes, wherein the liquid shimmer of the water seemed to be mirrored, stared beyond him into space.

Then she gave him an abrupt push and uttered a short, scornful laugh. She tore her hands from his burning fingers, clutched his arm, and flung him sidewise upon the ground. Then she sprang up and vanished down the wooded avenue.

He lay there with his face in the grass, stunned, unmanned, shudders coursing swiftly through his frame. He pulled himself together, got up somehow, took two steps, and fell again, close to the water. What were his sensations at this moment? Perhaps he was feeling that same luxury of hate which he had felt before when she had humiliated him with her glance, degenerated now, when he lay before her on the ground and she had treated him like a dog, into an insane rage which must at all costs find expression even against himself – a disgust, perhaps of himself, which filled him with a thirst to destroy himself, to tear himself to pieces, to blot himself utterly out.

On his belly he dragged his body a little further, lifted its upper part, and let it fall into the water. He did not raise his head nor move his legs, which still lay on the bank.

The crickets stopped chirping a moment at the noise of the little splash. Then they went on as before, the boughs lightly rustled, and down the long alley came the faint sound of laughter.

DISILLUSIONMENT

I CONFESS that I was completely bewildered by the conversation which I had with this extraordinary man. I am afraid that I am even yet hardly in a state to report it in such a way that it will affect others as it did me. Very likely the effect was largely due to the candour and friendliness with which an entire stranger laid himself open to me.

It was some two months ago, on an autumnal afternoon, that I first noticed my stranger on the Piazza di San Marco. Only a few people were abroad; but on the wide square the standards flapped in the light sea-breeze in front of that sumptuous marvel of colour and line which stood out with luminous enchantment against a tender pale-blue sky. Directly before the centre portal a young girl stood strewing corn for a host of pigeons at her feet, while more and more swooped down in clouds from all sides. An incomparably blithe and festive sight.

I met him on the square and I have him in perfect clarity before my eye as I write. He was rather under middle height and a little stooped, walking briskly and holding his cane in his hands behind his back. He wore a stiff black hat, a light summer overcoat, and dark striped trousers. For some reason I mistook him for an Englishman. He might have been thirty years old, he might have been fifty. His face was smooth-shaven, with a thickish nose and tired grey eyes; round his mouth played constantly an inexplicable and somewhat simple smile. But from time to time he would look searchingly about him, then stare upon the ground, mutter a few words to himself, give his head a shake and fall to smiling again. In this fashion he marched perseveringly up and down the square.

After that first time I noticed him daily; for he seemed to have no other business than to pace up and down, thirty, forty, or fifty times, in good weather and bad, always alone and always with that extraordinary bearing of his.

On the evening which I mean to describe there had been a concert by a military band. I was sitting at one of the little tables which spread out into the piazza from Florian's café; and when after the concert the concourse of people had begun to disperse, my unknown, with his accustomed absent smile, sat down in a seat left vacant near me.

The evening drew on, the scene grew quieter and quieter, soon all the tables were empty. Hardly any strollers were left, the majestic square was wrapped in peace, the sky above it thick with stars; a great half-moon hung above the splendid spectacular façade of San Marco.

I had been reading my paper, with my back to my neighbour, and was about to surrender the field to him when I was obliged instead to turn in his direction. For whereas I had not heard a single sound, he now suddenly began to speak.

"You are in Venice for the first time, sir?" he asked, in bad French. When I essayed to answer in English he went on in good German, speaking in a low, husky voice and coughing often to clear it.

"You are seeing all this for the first time? Does it come up to your expectations? Surpasses them, eh? You did not picture it as finer than the reality? You mean it? You would not say so in order to seem happy and enviable? Ah!" He leaned back and looked at me, blinking rapidly with a quite inexplicable expression.

The ensuing pause lasted for some time. I did not know how to go on with this singular conversation and once more was about to depart when he hastily leaned towards me.

"Do you know, my dear sir, what disillusionment is?" he asked in low, urgent tones, both hands leaning on his stick. "Not a miscarriage in small, unimportant matters, but the great and general disappointment which everything, all of life, has in store? No, of course, you do not know. But from my youth up I have carried it about with me; it has made me lonely, unhappy, and a bit queer, I do not deny that.

"You could not, of course, understand what I mean, all at once. But you might; I beg of you to listen to me for a few minutes. For if it can be told at all it can be told without many words.

"I may begin by saying that I grew up in a clergyman's family, in quite a small town. There reigned in our home a punctilious cleanliness and the pathetic optimism of the scholarly atmosphere. We breathed a strange atmosphere, compact of pulpit rhetoric, of large words for good and evil, beautiful and base, which I bitterly hate, since perhaps they are to blame for all my sufferings.

"For me life consisted utterly of those large words; for I knew no more of it than the infinite, insubstantial emotions which they called up in me. From man I expected divine virtue or hair-raising wickedness; from life either ravishing loveliness or else consummate horror; and I was full of avidity for all that and of a profound, tormented yearning for a larger reality, for experience of no matter what kind, let it be glorious and intoxicating bliss or unspeakable, undreamed-of anguish.

"I remember, sir, with painful clearness the first disappointment of my life; and I would beg you to observe that it had not at all to do with the miscarriage of some cherished hope, but with an unfortunate occurrence. There was a fire at night in my parents' house, when I was hardly more than a child. It had spread insidiously until the whole small storey was in flames up to my chamber door, and the stairs would soon have been on fire as well. I discovered it first, and I remember that I went rushing through the house shouting over and over: 'Fire, fire!' I know exactly what I said and what feeling underlay the words, though at the time it could scarcely have come to the surface of my consciousness. 'So this,' I thought, 'is a fire. This is what it is like to have the house on fire. Is this all there is to it?'

"Goodness knows it was serious enough. The whole house burned down, the family was only saved with difficulty, and

I got some burns. And it would be wrong to say that my fancy could have painted anything much worse than the actual burning of my parents' house. Yet some vague, formless idea of an event even more frightful must have existed somewhere within me, by comparison with which the reality seemed flat. This fire was the first great event in my life. It left me defrauded of my hope of fearfulness.

"Do not fear lest I go on to recount my disappointments to you in detail. Enough to tell you that I zealously fed my magnificent expectations of life with the matter of a thousand books and the works of all the poets. Ah, how I have learned to hate them, those poets who chalked up their large words on all the walls of life – because they had no power to write them on the sky with pencils dipped in Vesuvius! I came to think of every large word as a lie or a mockery.

"Ecstatic poets have said that speech is poor: 'Ah, how poor are words,' so they sing. But no, sir. Speech, it seems to me, is rich, is extravagantly rich compared with the poverty and limitations of life. Pain has its limits: physical pain in unconsciousness and mental in torpor; it is not different with joy. Our human need for communication has found itself a way to create sounds which lie beyond these limits.

"Is the fault mine? Is it down my spine alone that certain words can run so as to awaken in me intuitions of sensations which do not exist?

"I went out into that supposedly so wonderful life, craving just one, one single experience which should correspond to my great expectations. God help me, I have never had it. I have roved the globe over, seen all the best-praised sights, all the works of art upon which have been lavished the most extravagant words. I have stood in front of these and said to myself: 'It is beautiful. And yet – is that all? Is it no more beautiful than that?'

"I have no sense of actualities. Perhaps that is the trouble. Once, somewhere in the world, I stood by a deep, narrow gorge in the mountains. Bare rock went up perpendicular on either side, and far below the water roared past. I looked down and thought to myself: 'What if I were to fall?' But I knew myself well enough to answer: 'If that were to happen you would say to yourself as you fell: "Now you are falling, you are actually falling. Well, and what of it?"'

"You may believe me that I do not speak without experience of life. Years ago I fell in love with a girl, a charming, gentle creature, whom it would have been my joy to protect and cherish. But she loved me not, which was not surprising, and she married another. What other experience can be so painful as this? What tortures are greater than the dry agonies of baffled lust? Many a night I lay wide-eyed and wakeful; yet my greatest torture resided in the thought: 'So this is the greatest pain we can suffer. Well, and what then – is this all?'

"Shall I go on to tell you of my happiness? For I have had my happiness as well and it too has been a disappointment. No, I need not go on; for no heaping up of bald examples can make clearer to you that it is life in general, life in its dull, uninteresting, average course which has disappointed me – disappointed, disappointed!

"What is man? asks young Werther – man, the glorious half-god? Do not his powers fail him just where he needs them most? Whether he soars upwards in joy or sinks down in anguish, is he not always brought back to bald, cold consciousness precisely at the point where he seeks to lose himself in the fullness of the infinite?

"Often I have thought of the day when I gazed for the first time at the sea. The sea is vast, the sea is wide, my eyes roved far and wide and longed to be free. But there was the horizon. Why a horizon, when I wanted the infinite from life?

"It may be narrower, my horizon, than that of other men. I have said that I lack a sense of actualities – perhaps it is that I have too much. Perhaps I am too soon full, perhaps I am too soon done with things. Am I acquainted in too adulterated a form with both joy and pain?

"I do not believe it; and least of all do I believe in those whose views of life are based on the great words of the poets –

it is all lies and poltroonery. And you may have observed, my dear sir, that there are human beings so vain and so greedy of the admiration and envy of others that they pretend to have experienced the heights of happiness but never the depths of pain?

"It is dark and you have almost ceased to listen to me; so I can the more easily confess that I too have tried to be like these men and make myself appear happy in my own and others' eyes. But it is some years since that the bubble of this vanity was pricked. Now I am alone, unhappy, and a little queer, I do not deny it.

"It is my favourite occupation to gaze at the starry heavens at night – that being the best way to turn my eyes away from earth and from life. And perhaps it may be pardoned in me that I still cling to my distant hopes? That I dream of a freer life, where the actuality of my fondest anticipations is revealed to be without any torturing residue of disillusionment? Of a life where there are no more horizons?

"So I dream and wait for death. Ah, how well I know it already, death, that last disappointment! At my last moment I shall be saying to myself: 'So this is the great experience – well, and what of it? What is it after all?'

"But it has grown cold here on the piazza, sir – that I can still feel – ha ha! I have the honour to bid you a very good night."

THE DILETTANTE

IT CAN all be summed up, beginning, middle, and end – yes, and fitting valediction too, perhaps – in the one word: "disgust". The disgust which I now feel for everything and for life as a whole; the disgust that chokes me, that shatters me, that hounds me out and pulls me down, and that one day may give me strength to break the whole fantastic and ridiculous situation across my knee and finish with it once and for all. I may go on for another month or so, perhaps for six months or a year; eat and drink and fill my days somehow or other. Outwardly my life may proceed as peacefully, regularly, and mechanically as it has been doing all this winter, in frightful contrast to the process of dry rot and dissolution going on within. It would seem that the more placid, detached, and solitary a man's outer life, the more strenuous and violent his inner experiences are bound to be. It comes to the same thing: if you take care not to be a man of action, if you seek peace in solitude, you will find that life's vicissitudes fall upon you from within and it is upon that stage you must prove yourself a hero or a fool.

I have bought this new note-book in order to set down my story in it – but to what end, after all? Perhaps just to fill in the time? Out of interest in the psychological, and to soothe myself with the conviction that it all had to be? There is such consolation in the inevitable! Or perhaps in order to give myself a temporary illusion of superiority and therewith a certain indifference to fate? For even indifference, as I know full well, might be a sort of happiness.

It lies so far behind me, the little old city with its narrow, irregular, gabled streets, its Gothic churches and fountains, its busy, solid, simple citizens, and the big patrician house, hoary with age, where I grew up!

It stood in the centre of the town and had lasted out four generations of well-to-do, respected business men and their families. The motto over the front door was "*Ora et labora*". You entered through a large flagged court, with a wooden gallery, painted white, running round it up above; and mounted the stairs to a good-sized lobby and a dark little columned hall, whence you had access, through one of the tall white-enamelled doors, to the drawing-room, where my mother sat playing the piano.

The room was dull, for thick dark-red curtains half-shrouded the windows. The white figures of gods and goddesses on the wall hangings stood out plastically from their blue background and seemed as though listening to the deep, heavy first notes of a Chopin nocturne which was her favourite piece. She always played it very slowly, as though to enjoy to the full each melancholy cadence. The piano was old and its resonance had suffered; but by using the soft pedal you could give the notes a veiled, dull silvery sound and so produce quite extraordinary effects.

I would sit on the massive, straight-backed mahogany sofa listening, and watching my mother as she played. She was small and fragile and wore as a rule a soft, pale-grey gown. Her narrow face was not beautiful, it was more like that of a quiet, gentle, dreamy child, beneath the parted, slightly waved indefinitely blond hair. Sitting at the piano, her head a little on one side, she looked like one of those touching little angels who sit in old pictures at the Madonna's feet and play on their guitars.

When I was little she often used to tell me, in her low, deprecatory voice, such fairy-tales as nobody else knew; or she would simply put her hands on my head as it lay in her lap and sit there motionless, not saying a word. Those, I think, were the happiest, peacefullest days of my life. – Her hair did not grey, she became no older; only her figure grew more fragile with the years and her face thinner, stiller, and more dreaming.

But my father was a tall, broad-shouldered gentleman, in fine black broadcloth trousers and coat, with a white waistcoat on which his gold eye-glasses dangled. He wore grey mutton-chop whiskers, with a firm round chin coming out between them, smooth-shaven like his upper lip. Between his brows stood permanently two horizontal folds. He was a powerful man, of great influence in public affairs. I have seen men leave his presence, some with quickened breath and sparkling eyes, others quite broken and in despair. For it sometimes happened that I, and I suppose my mother and my two elder sisters as well, were witnesses at such scenes – either because our father wanted to rouse my ambitions and stimulate me to get on in the world, or else, as I have since suspected, because he needed an audience. He had a way of leaning back in his chair, with one hand thrust into the opening of his waistcoat, and looking after the favoured or the disappointed man, which even as a child led me vaguely to such a conclusion.

I sat in my corner looking at my father and mother, and it was as though I would choose between them: whether I would spend my life in deeds of power or in dreamy musing. And always in the end my eyes would rest upon my mother's quiet face.

Not that I could have been at all like her outwardly, for my occupations were for the most part quite lively and bustling. One of them I still remember, which I vastly preferred to any sort of game with my schoolmates. Even now, at thirty, I still recall it with a heightened sense of pleasure.

I owned a large and well-equipped puppet theatre, and I would shut myself in alone with it to perform the most wonderful musical dramas. My room was in the second storey and had two dark and grisly-bearded ancestral portraits hanging on the wall. I would draw the curtains and set a lamp near the theatre, for it heightened the atmosphere to have artificial light. I, as conductor, took my place directly in front of the stage, my left hand resting upon a large round pasteboard box which was the sole visible orchestral instrument.

The performers would now enter; I had drawn them myself with pen and ink, cut them out, and fitted them into little wooden blocks so that they could stand up. There were the most beautiful ladies, and gentlemen in overcoats and top hats.

"Good evening, ladies and gentlemen," I would say. "Everybody all right? I got here betimes, for there was still some work to do. But it is quite time for you to go to your dressing-rooms."

They went behind the stage and soon came back transfigured, in the gayest and most beautiful costumes, to look through the peep-hole which I had cut in the curtain and see if there was a good house. The house was in fact not so bad; and I rang the bell to let myself know that the performance was about to begin, lifted my baton, and paused to enjoy the sudden stillness which my gesture evoked. Another motion called up the dull warning rumble of the drums with which the overture began – this I performed with my left hand on the top of the box. Then came in the horns, clarinets, and flutes; these I reproduced with my own voice in most inimitable fashion, and so it went on until upon a powerful crescendo the curtain rose and the play began, in a setting of gloomy forest or glittering palace hall.

I would mentally sketch out the drama beforehand and then improvise the details as I went along. The shrilling of the clarinets, the beating of the drums accompanied singing of great passion and sweetness; I chanted splendid bombastic verse with more rhyme than reason; in fact it seldom had any connected meaning, but rolled magnificently on, as I drummed with my left hand, performed both song and accompaniment with my own voice, and directed with my right hand both music and acting down to the minutest detail. The applause at the end of each act was so enthusiastic that there were repeated curtain calls, and even the conductor had sometimes to rise from his seat and bow low in pride and gratitude.

Truly, when after such a strenuous performance I put my toy theatre away, all the blood in my body seemed to have risen to my head and I was blissfully exhausted as is a great artist at the triumphant close of a production to which he has given all that is in him. Up to my thirteenth or fourteenth year this was my favourite occupation.

I recall so very little of my childhood and boyhood in the great house, where my father conducted his business on the ground floor, my mother sat dreaming in her easy-chair, and my sisters, who were two and three years older than I, bustled about in kitchen and laundry.

I am clear that I was an unusually brisk and lively lad. I was well born, I was an adept in the art of imitating my schoolmasters, I knew a thousand little play-acting tricks and had a quite superior use of language – so that it was not hard for me to be popular and respected among my mates. But lessons were a different matter; I was too busy taking in the attitudes and gestures of my teachers to have attention left over for what they were saying, while at home my head was too full of my verses, my theatre, and all sorts of airy trifles to be in a state to do any serious work.

"You ought to be ashamed," my father would say, the furrows in his brow getting deeper as he spoke, when I brought him my report into the drawing-room after dinner and he perused it with one hand stuck in his waistcoat. "It does not make very good reading for me and that's a fact. Will you kindly tell me what you expect will become of you? You will never get anywhere in life like this."

Which was depressing; but it did not prevent me from reading aloud to my parents and sisters after the evening meal a poem which I had written during the afternoon. My father laughed so that his pince-nez bounced about all over his waistcoat. "What sort of fool's tricks are those?" he cried again and again. But my mother drew me to her and stroked my hair. "It is not bad at all, my dear," she said. "I find there are some quite pretty lines in it."

Later on, when I was at an older stage, I taught myself a way of playing the piano. Being attracted by the black keys, I began with the F-sharp major chords, explored modulations over into other scales, and by assiduous practice arrived at a certain skill in various harmonies without time or tune, but imparting all possible expressiveness to my mystical billows of sound.

My mother said that my attack displayed a taste for piano, and she got a teacher for me. The lessons went on for six months, but I had not sufficient manual dexterity or sense of rhythm to succeed.

Well, the years passed, and despite my troubles at school I found life very jolly. In the circle of my relatives and friends I was high-spirited and popular, being amiable out of sheer pleasure in playing the amiable part; though at the same time I began instinctively to look down on all these people, finding them arid and unimaginative.

One afternoon, when I was some eighteen years old and about to enter the highest class at school, I overheard a little conversation between my parents. They were sitting together at the round table in the sitting-room and did not see me dawdling by the window in the adjacent dining-room, staring at the pale sky above the gabled roofs. I heard my own name and slipped across to the half-open white-enamelled folding doors.

My father was leaning back in his chair with his legs crossed and the financial newspaper in one hand while with the other he slowly stroked his chin between the mutton-chops. My mother sat on the sofa with her placid face bent over her embroidery. The lamp was on the table between.

My father said: "It is my view that we ought to take him out of school and apprentice him to some good well-known firm."

"Oh!" answered my mother looking up in dismay. "Such a gifted child!"

My father was silent for a moment, meticulously brushing a speck from his coat. Then he lifted his shoulders and put out his hands, palms up. Said he:

"If you think, my love, that it takes no brains to be a business man you are much mistaken. And besides, I realize to my regret that the lad is accomplishing absolutely nothing at school. His gifts to which you refer are of the dilettante variety – though let me hasten to add that I by no means underestimate the value of that sort of thing. He can be very charming when he likes; he knows how to flatter and amuse his company, and he needs to please and be successful. Many a man has before now made a fortune with this equipment. Possessing it, and in view of his indifference to other fields of endeavour, he is not unadapted to a business career in the larger sense."

My father leaned back in some self-satisfaction, took a cigarette out of his case, and slowly lighted it.

"You are quite right," said my mother, looking about the room with a saddened face. "Only I have often thought and to some extent hoped that we might make an artist of him. I suppose it is true that no importance can be attached to his musical talent, which has remained undeveloped; but have you noticed that since he went to that art exhibition he has been doing a little drawing? It does not seem at all bad to me."

My father blew out smoke from his cigarette, sat erect, and said curtly:

"That is all stuff and nonsense. Anyhow, we can easily ask him."

I asked myself. What indeed did I really want? The prospect of any sort of change was most welcome to me. So in the end I put on a solemn face and said that I was quite ready to leave school and become a business man. I was apprenticed to the wholesale lumber business of Herr Schlievogt, down on the river-bank.

The change was only superficial, of course. I had but the most moderate interest in the lumber business; I sat in my revolving chair under the gas burner in the dark, narrow counting-room, as remote and indifferent as on the bench at school. This time I had fewer cares – that was the great difference.

Herr Schlievogt was a stout man with a red face and stiff grey nautical beard; he troubled himself very little about me, being mostly in the mills, at some distance from the counting-house and yards. The clerks treated me with respect. I had social relations with but one of them, a talented and self-satisfied young man of good family whom I had known when I was at school. His name was Schilling. He made as much fun of everything in the world as I did, but he displayed a lively interest in the lumber business and every day gave utterance to his firm resolve that he would some day and somehow become a rich man.

As for me, I mechanically performed my necessary tasks and for the rest spent my time sauntering among the workmen in the yards, between the stacks of lumber, looking at the river beyond the high wooden lattice, where now and then a freight train rolled past, and thinking about some theatre or concert I had lately attended or some book which I had read.

For I read a great deal, read everything I could lay my hands on, and my capacity for impressions was great. I had an emotional grasp of each character created by an author; in each one I thought to see myself, and identified myself wholly with the atmosphere of a book – until it was the turn of a new one to have its effect upon me. I would sit in my room – with a book on my knee instead of the toy theatre to occupy me – and look up at my two ancestral portraits while I savoured the style of the book in which I was then absorbed, my brain filled with an unproductive chaos of half-thoughts and fanciful imaginings.

My sisters had married in quick succession. When I was not at the office I would often go down to the drawing-room, where my mother sat, now almost always alone. She was a little ailing, her face had grown even more childlike and placid, and when she played Chopin to me or I showed her a new sequence of harmonies which I had discovered, she would ask me whether I was content and happy in my calling. – And there was no doubt that I was happy.

I was not much more than twenty, my choice of a career was still provisional, and the idea was not foreign to me that I need not always spend my life with Herr Schlievogt or with some bigger lumber-dealer. I knew that one day I could free myself, leave my gabled birthplace, and live somewhere more in accordance with my tastes: read good and well-written novels, attend the theatre, make a little music. Was I not happy? Did I not eat excellently well, go dressed in the best? And as in my schooldays I realized that there were poor and badly dressed boys who behaved with subservience to me and my life, so now I was stimulated by the consciousness that I belonged to the upper classes, the rich and enviable ones, born to look down with benevolent contempt upon the unlucky and dissatisfied. Why should I not be happy? Let things take their course. And there was a certain charm in the society of these relations and friends. It gave me a blithe feeling of superiority to smile at their limitations and yet to gratify my desire to please by behaving towards them with the extreme of affability. I basked in the sunshine of their somewhat puzzled approbation – puzzled because while they approved, they vaguely discerned elements of contradiction and extravagance.

A change began to take place in my father. Each day when he came to table at four o'clock the furrows on his brow seemed to have got deeper. He no longer thrust his hand imposingly between his waistcoat buttons, his bearing was depressed and self-conscious. One day he said to me:

"You are old enough now to share with me the cares which are undermining my health. And it is even my duty to acquaint you with them, to prevent you from cherishing false expectations. You know that I made considerable sacrifices to give your sisters their marriage portions. And of late the firm has lost a deal of money as well. I am an old man, and a discouraged one; I do not feel that things will change much for the better. I must ask you to realize that you will be flung upon your own resources."

These things he said some two months before his death.

One day he was found sitting in his arm-chair in the office, waxen-faced, paralysed, and unable to articulate. A week later the whole town attended his funeral.

My mother sat by the table in the drawing-room, fragile and silent, with her eyes mostly closed. My sisters and I hovered about her; she would nod and smile, but still be motionless and silent, her hands in her lap and her strange, wide, melancholy gaze directed at one of the white deities on the wall. Gentlemen in frock-coats would come in to tell her about the progress of the liquidation; she would nod and smile and shut her eyes again.

She played Chopin no more. When she passed her pale, delicate hand over her smoothly parted hair it would tremble with fatigue and weakness. Scarcely six months after my father's death she laid herself down and died, without a murmur, without one struggle for life.

So it was all over now – and what was there to hold me to the place? For good or ill, the business of the firm had been liquidated; I turned out to have fallen heir to some hundred thousand marks, enough to make me independent. I had no duties and on some ground or other had been declared unfit for service.

There was no longer any bond between me and those among whom I had grown up. Their point of view was too one-sided for me to share it, and on their side they regarded me with more and more puzzled eyes. Granted that they knew me for what I was, a perfectly useless human being – as such, indeed, did I know myself. But I was cynical and fatalistic enough to look on the bright side of what my father had called my dilettante talents, self-satisfied enough to want to enjoy life in my own way.

I drew my little competence out of the bank and almost without any formal farewell left my native town to pursue my travels.

I remember as though they were a beautiful, far-away dream those next three years, in which I surrendered myself greedily to a thousand new, rich, and varied sensations. How long ago was it that I spent a New Year's Day amid snow and ice among the monks at the top of the Simplon Pass? How long since I was sauntering across Piazza Erbe in Verona? Since I entered the Piazza di San Pietro from the Borgo San Spirito, trod for the first time beneath the colonnades, and let my gaze stray abashed into the distances of that mammoth square? Since I looked down from Corso Vittorio Emmanuele on the city of Naples, white in the brilliant light, and saw far off across the bay the charming silhouette of Capri, veiled in deep-blue haze? All that was some six years ago, hardly more.

I lived very carefully within my means, in simple lodgings or in modest pensions. But what with travelling and the difficulty of giving up all at once the good bourgeois comforts I was used to, my expenses were after all not small. I had set apart for my travels the sum of fifteen thousand marks out of my capital – but I overstepped this limit.

For the rest I fared very well among the people with whom I came into contact: disinterested and often very attractive characters, to whom of course I could not be the object of respect that I had been in my former surroundings, but from whom, on the other hand, I need not fear disapproving or questioning looks.

My social gifts sometimes made me genuinely popular – I recall for instance a scene in Pensione Minelli at Palermo, where there was a circle of French people of all ages. One evening I improvised for them "a music drama by Richard Wagner" with a lavishness of tragic gesture, recitative, and rolling harmonies, finishing amid enormous applause. An old gentleman hurried up to me; he had scarcely a hair on his head, his sparse white mutton-chops straggled down across his grey tweed jacket. He seized my hands, tears in his eyes, and cried:

"But it is amazing! Amazing, my dear sir! I swear to you that not for thirty years have I been so pricelessly entertained. Permit me to thank you from the bottom of my heart. But you must, you certainly must become an actor or a musician!"

Truly, on such an occasion I felt something of the arrogance of a great painter who draws a caricature on the table-cloth to amuse his friends. – But after dinner I sat down alone in the salon and spent a sad and solitary hour trying sustained chords on the piano in an effort to express the mood evoked in me by the sight of Palermo.

Leaving Sicily, I had just touched the African coast, then gone on into Spain. In the country near Madrid, on a gloomy, rainy winter afternoon, I felt the first time the desire – and the necessity – for a return to Germany. For aside from the fact that I began to crave a settled and regular life, I saw without any prolonged calculation that however carefully I lived I should have spent twenty thousand marks before my return.

I did not hesitate many days before setting out on the long journey through France, which was protracted to nearly six months by lengthy sojourns in this place and that. I recall with painful distinctness the summer evening of my arrival at the capital city in the centre of Germany which even before setting out on my travels I had selected as my home. Hither I had now come: a little wiser, equipped with a little experience and knowledge, and full of childish joy at the prospect of here setting up my rest and establishing – carefree, independent, and in enjoyment of my modest means – a life of quiet and contemplation.

The spot was not badly chosen. It is a city of some size, yet not so bustling as a metropolis, nor marred by a too obtrusive business life. It has some fine old squares and its atmosphere is not lacking in either elegance or vivacity. Its suburbs are charming; best of all I liked the well-laid-out promenade leading up to the Lerchenberg, a long ridge against which most of the town is built. From this point there is an extended view over houses, churches, and the river winding gently away into the distance. From some positions, and especially when the band is playing on a summer afternoon and carriages and pedestrians are moving to and fro, it recalls the Pincio. – But I will return to this promenade later on.

It would be hard to overestimate the peculiar pleasure I drew from the arrangement of the bedroom and sitting-room I had taken in a busy quarter in the centre of the city. Most of our family effects had passed into the possession of my sisters, but enough was left for my needs: adequate and even handsome furniture, my books, and my two ancestral portraits, even the old grand piano, which my mother had willed to me.

When everything had been placed and the photographs which I had acquired on my travels were hung on the walls or arranged on the heavy mahogany writing-desk and the bow-front chest of drawers, and when ensconced in my new fastness I sat down in an arm-chair by the window to survey by turns my abode within and the busy street life outside, my comfort and pleasure were no small thing. And yet – I shall never forget the moment – besides my satisfaction and confidence something else stirred in me, a faint sense of anxiety and unrest, a faint consciousness of being on the defensive, of rousing myself against some power that threatened my peace: the slightly depressing thought that I had now for the first time left behind the temporary and provisional and exchanged it for the definite and fixed.

I will not deny that these and like sensations repeated themselves from time to time. But must they not come, now and then, those afternoon hours in which one sits and looks out into the growing twilight, perhaps into a slowly falling rain, and becomes prey to gloomy foreboding? True, my future was secure. I had entrusted the round sum of eighty thousand marks to the bank, the interest came to about six hundred marks the quarter – my God, but the times are bad! – so that I could live decently, buy books, and now and then visit the theatre or enjoy some lighter kind of diversion.

My days in fact conformed very well to the ideal which I had always had in view. I got up at about ten, breakfasted, and spent the rest of the morning at the piano or reading some book or magazine. Then I strolled up the street to my little restaurant, ate my dinner, and took a long walk, through the city streets, to a gallery, the suburbs, or the Lerchenberg. I came back and resumed the same occupations: read, played the piano, amused myself with drawings of a sort, or wrote a letter, slowly and carefully. Perhaps I attended the theatre or a concert after my evening meal; if not, I sat in a café and read the papers until bedtime. That was a good day, with a solid and gratifying content, when I had discovered a motif on the piano which seemed to me new and pleasing, or when I had carried away from a painting in the gallery or from the book I had read some fine and abiding impression.

I must say too that my programme was seriously conceived with the view of giving my days as much ideal content as possible. I ate modestly, had as a rule only one suit at a time; in short, I limited my material demands in order to be able to get a good seat at the opera or concert, to buy the latest books or visit this or that art exhibition.

But the days went by, they turned into weeks and months – of boredom? Yes, I confess it. One has not always a book at hand which will absorb one for hours on end. I might sit all the morning at the piano and have no success with my improvisations. I would be seated at the window smoking cigarettes and feel stealing over me a distaste of all the world, myself included. I would be possessed by fear, spring up and go out of doors, there to shrug my shoulders and watch with a superior smile the business men and labourers on the street, who lacked the spiritual and material gifts which would fit them for the enjoyment of leisure.

But is a man of seven-and-twenty able seriously to believe – no matter how likely it is – that his days are now fixed and unchangeable up to the end? A span of blue sky, the twitter of a bird, some half-vanished dream of the night before – everything has power to suffuse his heart with undefined hopes and fill it with the solemn expectation of some great and nameless joy. – I dawdled from one day to the next – aimless, dreamy, occupied with this or that little thing to look forward to, even if it were only the date of a forthcoming publication, with the lively conviction that I was certainly very happy even though now and again weary of my solitude.

They were not precisely infrequent, those hours in which I was painfully conscious of my lack of contact with my kind. That I had none needs no explanation. I was not in touch with society – neither the first circles nor the second. To introduce myself as a *fêtard* among the gilded youth, I lacked means for that, God knew – and on the other hand, bohemia? But I was well brought up, I wear clean linen and a whole suit, and it does not amuse me to carry on anarchistic conversations with shabby young people at tables sticky with absinthe. In short, there was no one sphere to which I could naturally gravitate, and the chance connections I made from time to time were few, slight, and superficial – though this was largely my own fault, for I held back, I know, being insecure myself and unpleasantly aware that I could not make clear even to a drunken painter exactly who and what I was.

Besides, of course, I had given up society; I had broken with it when I took the liberty of going my own way regardless of its claims upon me. So if in order to be happy I needed "people", then I had to ask myself whether I should not have been by now busy and useful making money as a business man in a large way and becoming the object of respect and envy.

But meanwhile? The fact remained that my philosophic isolation disturbed me far too much. It refused to fit in with my conception of happiness, with the consciousness or conviction that I was happy – and from this conviction I was utterly unable to part. That I was not happy, that I was in fact unhappy – certainly that was unthinkable. And there the matter rested, until the next time came, when I found myself sitting alone, withdrawn and remote, alarmingly morose – and, in short, in an intolerable state.

But are happy people morose? I thought of my home life in the limited circle where I had moved in the pleasing consciousness of my own talents and parts, sociable, charming, my eyes bright with fun and mockery and good feeling of a rather condescending sort; viewed as a little odd and yet quite generally liked. Then I had been happy, despite Herr Schlievogt and the lumber business, whereas now – ?

But some vastly interesting book would appear, a new French novel, which I would spend the money to buy and, sitting in my comfortable arm-chair, would enjoy at my leisure. Three hundred unexplored pages of charming blague and literary art! Certainly life was going as I would have it. Was I asking myself whether I was happy? Such a question is sheer rubbish, nothing else.

So ends another day, undeniably a full one, thank God! Evening is here, the curtains are drawn, the lamp burns on the writing-table, it is nearly midnight. I might go to bed, but I remain sprawled in my arm-chair with idle hands, gazing up at the ceiling in order to concentrate on the vague gnawing and boring of an indefinite ache which I know not how to dispel.

I have spent the past hours immersed in a great work of art: one of those tremendous and ruthless works of genius which rack and deafen, enrapture and shatter the reader with their decadent and dilettante splendours. My nerves still quiver, my imagination is rampant, my mind seethes with strange fancies, with moods mingled of yearning, religious fervour, triumph, and a mystical peace. And with all that the compulsion, which for ever urges them upwards and outwards, to display them, to share them, to "make something of them".

Suppose I were an artist in very truth, capable of giving utterance to my feelings in music, in verse, in sculpture – or best of all, to be honest, in all of them at once? It is true that I can do a little of everything. For instance, I can sit at my piano in my quiet little room and express the fullness of my feelings, to my heart's content – ought that not to be enough? Of course, if I needed "people" in order to be happy, then I could understand. But supposing that I set store by success, by recognition, praise, fame, envy, love? My God, when I recall that scene at Palermo I have to admit to myself that something like that at this moment would be a great encouragement to me now!

If I am honest with myself I cannot help admitting the sophistical and ridiculous distinction between the two kinds of happiness, inward and outward. Outward happiness – of what does it consist? There are men, the favourites of the gods, it would seem, whose happiness is genius and their genius happiness; children of light, who move easily through life with the reflection and image of the sun in their eyes; easy, charming, amiable, while all the world surrounds them with praise, admiration, envy, and love – for even envy is powerless to hate them. And they mingle in the world like children, capricious, arrogant, spoiled, friendly as the sunshine, as certain of their genius and their joy as though it were impossible things should be otherwise.

As for me, weak though I may be, I confess that I should like to be like them. Rightly or wrongly I am possessed with the feeling that I once belonged among them – but what matter? For when I am honest with myself I know that the real point is what one thinks of oneself, to what one gives oneself, to what one feels strong enough to give oneself!

Perhaps the truth is that I resigned my claim to this "outward happiness" when I withdrew myself from the demands of society and arranged my life to do without people. But of my inward satisfaction there is no doubt at all – it cannot, it must not be doubted; for I repeat, with emphasis of desperation, that happy I must and will be, for I conceive too profoundly of happiness as a virtue, as genius, refinement, charm; and of unhappiness as something ugly, mole-like, contemptible – in a word, absurd – to be able to be unhappy and still preserve my self-respect.

I could not permit myself to be unhappy, could not stand the sight of myself in such a role. I should have to hide in the dark like a bat or an owl and gaze with envy at the children of light. I should have to hate them with a hatred which would be nothing but a festered love – and I should have to despise myself!

Hide in the dark! Ah, there comes to my mind all that I have been thinking and feeling these many months about my philosophic isolation – and my fit takes me again, my familiar, my too-much-feared fear! I am conscious of anger against some force which threatens me.

Certainly I found consolations, ameliorations, oblivion for the time and for another time and yet another. But my fear always returned, returned a thousand times in the course of the months and the years.

There are autumn days that are like a miracle. Summer is past, the trees are yellow and brown, all day the wind whistles round the corners, and turbid water fills all the gutters. You have come to terms with the time of year; you have come home, so to speak, to sit by the stove and let the winter go over your head. Then one morning you wake to see with unbelieving eyes a narrow strip of luminous blue shine through your bedroom curtains. You spring astonished out of bed and open the window, a tremulous wave of sunshine streams towards you, while through all the street noises you hear the blithe twitter of a bird. It is as though the fresh light atmosphere of an early October day were to breathe the ineffably sweet and spicy air which belongs to the promiseful winds of May. It is spring – obviously, despite the calendar, a day in spring. You fling on your clothes to hurry through the streets and into the country, out under the open sky.

Now, such an unhoped-for blessing of a day there was, some four months ago – we are now in the month of February. And on that day I saw a lovely sight. I had got up before nine, in a bright and joyful mood, possessed by vague hopes of change, of unexpected and happy events. I took the road to the Lerchenberg, mounting the right side of the hill and following along the ridge on the main road, close to the low stone parapet, in order to keep in sight all the way – it takes perhaps half an hour – the view over the slightly terraced city on the slope below, the river winding and glittering in the sun, and the green hilly landscape dim in the distance.

Hardly anyone was up here. The benches were empty, here and there among the trees a white statue looked out; a faded leaf straggled down. Watching the bright panorama as

I walked, I went on undisturbed until I had reached the end of the ridge, where my road slanted down among old chestnut trees. Then I heard the ringing of horses' hoofs and the rolling of a wagon coming on at a lively trot. It would pass me at about the middle of the descent, so I moved to one side and stood still.

It was a small, light, two-wheeled cart drawn by two large, briskly snorting, glossy light bays. A young lady of nineteen or twenty years held the reins, seated beside a dignified elderly gentleman with bushy white eyebrows and moustaches brushed up *à la russe*. A servant in plain black and silver livery adorned the seat behind.

The pace of the horses had been slowed down at the top of the descent, which seemed to have made one of them nervous; it swung out sidewise from the shaft, tucked down its head, and braced its forelegs, trembling. The old gentleman leaned over to help his companion, drawing in one rein with his elegantly gloved hand. The driving seemed to have been turned over to her only temporarily and half as a game; at least she seemed to do it with a childish air of mingled importance and inexperience. She made a vexed little motion of the head as she tried to quiet the shying and stumbling animal.

She was slender and brunette. Her hair was gathered to a firm knot in the back of her neck, but lay loose and soft on brow and temples so that I could see the single bright brown strands; atop it perched a round dark straw hat trimmed with a ribbon bow. For the rest she wore a short dark-blue jacket and a simple skirt of light-grey cloth. The brunette skin of her finely formed oval face looked freshened and rosy in the morning air; the most attractive features in it were the long, narrow eyes, whose scarcely visible iris was a shining black, above which arched brows so even that they looked as though they were drawn with a pen. The nose was perhaps a little long and the mouth might have been smaller, though the lips were clear-cut and fine. It was charming to see the gleaming white well-spaced teeth of her upper jaw, which, in her efforts to control the struggling horse, she pressed hard upon her lower lip, lifting her chin, which was almost as round as a child's.

It would not be true to say that this face possessed any striking or exceptional beauty. What it had was youth, the charm of gaiety and freshness, polished, as it were, refined and heightened by ease, well-being, and luxurious living-conditions. Certainly those bright narrow eyes, now looking in displeasure at the refractory horse, would assume next minute their accustomed expression of happy security. The sleeves of her jacket, which were wide at the shoulders, came close round the slender wrists and she had an enchantingly dainty and elegant way of holding the reins in her slim ungloved white hands.

I stood by the edge of the path unnoted as the cart drove past, and walked slowly on when the horses quickened their pace again and took it out of sight. I felt pleasure and admiration, but at the same time a strange and poignant pain – was it envy, love, self-contempt? I did not dare to think.

The image in my mind as I write is that of a beggar, a poor wretch standing at a jeweller's window and staring at a costly jewel within. The man will not even feel any conscious desire to possess the stone, the bare idea would make him laugh at his own absurdity.

It came about quite by chance that I saw this same young lady again, only a week later, at the opera, during a performance of Gounod's *Faust*. Hardly had I entered the brightly lighted auditorium to betake myself to my seat in the stalls when I became aware of her seated at the old gentleman's side in a proscenium box on the other side of the stage. To my surprise I felt a little startled and confused, and in consequence perhaps averted my eyes, letting them rove over the other tiers and boxes. It was only when the overture had begun that I summoned resolution to look at the pair more closely.

The old gentleman wore a buttoned-up frock-coat and a black tie. He leaned back in his seat with dignified calm, one of his brown-gloved hands resting on the ledge in front of him while the other slowly stroked his beard or the close-cropped grey hair. The young girl – undoubtedly his daughter – leaned forward with lively interest, clasping her fan with both hands and resting them on the velvet upholstery of the ledge. Now and then with a quick gesture she tossed back the bright, soft brown hair from her brow and temples.

She wore a light-coloured silk blouse with a bunch of violets in her girdle. In the bright light her narrow eyes seemed to sparkle even more than before; and the position of the lips and mouth which I had noticed proved to be habitual with her; for she constantly set her even, shining, well-spaced white teeth on her under lip and drew the chin upwards a little. This innocent little face, quite devoid of coquetry, the detached and merrily roving glance, the delicate white throat, confined only by a ribbon the colour of her blouse, the gesture with which she called the old gentleman's attention to something in the stalls, on the stage, or in a box – all this gave the impression of an unspeakably refined and charming child, though it had nothing touching about it and did not arouse any of those emotions of pity which we sometimes feel for children. It was childlike in an elevated, tempered, and superior way that rested upon a security born of physical well-being and good breeding. Her evident high spirits did not have their source in pride, but in an inward and unconscious poise.

Gounod's music, spirited and sentimental by turns, seemed not a bad accompaniment to this young lady's appearance. I listened without looking at the stage, lost in a mild and pensive mood which without the music might have been more painful than it was. But after the first act there disappeared from his place in the stalls a gentleman of between twenty-five and thirty years who presently with a very easy bow appeared in the box on which my eye was fastened. The old man put out his hand at once, the young lady gave him hers with a gay nod, and he carried it respectfully to his lips as they invited him to sit down.

I was quite ready to admit that this gentleman's shirt-front was the most incomparable I had ever had the pleasure of beholding. It was fully exposed, for the waistcoat was the narrowest of black strips; his dress coat was not fastened save by a single button which came below his middle, and it was cut out from the shoulders in a sweeping curve. A stand-up collar with turned-over points met the shirt-front beneath a wide black tie, and his studs were two large square black buttons, standing out on the admirably starched, dazzlingly white expanse of shirt, which however did not lack flexibility, for it had a pleasing little concavity in the neighbourhood of the waist and swelled out again just as pleasingly and glossily below.

Of course, this shirt-front was what took the eye; but there was a head atop, entirely round and covered with close-cropped very blond hair and boasting such adornments as a pair of eye-glasses without rims or cord, a rather weedy, waving blond moustache, and a host of little duelling scars running up to the temple on one cheek. For the rest the gentleman was faultlessly built and moved with assurance.

In the course of the evening – for he remained in the box – I noted two attitudes characteristic of him. If the conversation languished he sat leaning jauntily back with one leg cocked over the other and his opera-glasses on his knee, bent his head and stuck out his whole mouth as far as it would go, to plunge into absorbed contemplation of his moustache, quite hypnotized, it would seem, and turning the while his head slowly to and fro. On the other hand, taken up in a conversation with the young lady, he would, to be sure, respectfully alter the position of his legs; then leaning even further back and seizing his chair with both hands, he would elevate his chin as high as possible and smile down upon his young neighbour with his mouth wide open, assuming an amiable and slightly superior air. What wonderfully happy self-confidence such a young man must rejoice in!

In all seriousness, I do not undervalue the possession. Upon none of his motions, however airily audacious, did the faintest self-consciousness ensue – he was buoyed up by his own self-respect. And why not? It was plain that he had made his way –

not necessarily by pushing – and was on the straight road to a plain and profitable goal. He dwelt in the shade of good understanding with all the world and in the sunshine of general approbation. And so he sat there chatting with a young girl for whose pure and priceless charms he probably had an eye – and if he had he need feel no hesitation in asking for her hand. Certainly I have no desire to utter one contemptuous word in the direction of this young gentleman.

But as for me? I sat far off in the darkness below, sulkily observing that priceless and unobtainable young creature as she laughed and prattled happily with this unworthy male. Shut out, unregarded, disqualified, unknown, *hors ligne – déclassé*, pariah, a pitiable object even to myself!

I stopped on till the end and came on the three in the cloak-room, where they lingered a little getting their furs, chatting with this or that acquaintance, here a lady, there an officer. When they left, the young gentleman accompanied the young lady and her father, and I followed at a little remove through the vestibule.

It was not raining, there were a few stars in the sky, they did not take a cab. Talking easily, the three passed on ahead and I followed, timid, oppressed, tortured by my poignant, mocking, miserable feelings. – They had not far to go; not more than one turning and they stopped in front of a stately house with a plain façade, and father and daughter disappeared after a cordial leave-taking from their companion, who walked off with a brisk tread.

On the heavy, carved house-door was a plate with the name: Justizrat Rainer.

I am determined to see these notes to a finish, though my inward resistance is so great that I am tempted every minute to spring up and escape. I have dug and burrowed into this mess until I am perfectly exhausted. I am sick to death of it all.

Not quite three months since, I read in the paper that a charity bazaar was to be held in the Rathaus under the auspices of the best society in the city. I read the announcement attentively and made up my mind to go. "She will be there," I thought; "perhaps she will have a stall, and nothing can prevent my speaking to her. After all I am a man of good birth and breeding, and if I like this Fräulein Rainer I am just as well qualified as the man with the shirt-front to address her and exchange a few light words."

It was a windy, rainy afternoon when I betook myself to the Rathaus, before whose doors was a press of carriages and people. I made my way into the building, paid the entrance fee, left my hat and coat, and with some difficulty gained the broad and crowded staircase up to the first floor and so into the hall. I was greeted by a waft of heavy scent – wine, food, perfume, and pine needles – and a confused hurly-burly of laughter, talk, cries, and ringing gongs.

The immensely high and large space was gaily adorned with flags and garlands; along the walls and down the middle were the stalls, both open and closed, fantastically arrayed gentlemen acting as barkers in front of the latter and shouting at the top of their lungs. Ladies, likewise in costume, were everywhere selling flowers, embroideries, tobacco, and various refreshments. On the stage at the upper end, decorated with potted plants, a noisy band was in action, while a compact procession of people moved slowly forward in the narrow lanes between the rows of stalls.

A little confused by the noise of the music, the barkers, and the grab-bags, I joined the procession, and in no time at all, scarcely four paces from the entrance, I found her whom I sought. She was selling wine and lemonade and wore the bright-coloured skirt, the square white head-dress and short stays of the Albanian peasant costume, her tender arms bare to the elbow. She was looking rather flushed, leaning back against her serving-table, playing with her gaudy fan and talking with a group of gentlemen round the stall. Among them I saw at the first glance a well-known face – my gentleman of the shirt-front stood beside her at the table with four fingers of each hand thrust in the side pockets of his jacket.

I pushed my way over, meaning to approach her when she

was less surrounded. This was a test: we should see whether I still had in me some remnant of the blithe self-assurance and conscious ability of yore, or whether my present moroseness and pessimism were only too well justified. What was it ailed me? Why did the sight of this girl – I confess it – make my cheeks burn with the same old mingled feelings of envy, yearning, chagrin, and bitter exasperation? A little straight forwardness, in the devil's name, a little gaiety and self-confidence, as befits a talented and happy man! With nervous eagerness I summoned the apt word, the light Italian phrase with which I meant to address her.

It took some time for me to make the circuit of the hall in that slowly moving stream of people; and when once more I stood in front of her booth all the gentlemen save one had gone. He of the shirt-front still leaned against her table, discoursing blithely with the fair vendeuse. I would take the liberty of interrupting their conversation. And turning quickly, I edged myself out of the stream and stood before her stall.

What happened? Ah, nothing at all, or hardly anything. The conversation broke off, the young man stepped aside and, holding his rimless, ribbonless pince-nez with all five fingers, stared at me through them and it, while the young lady swept me with a calm and questioning gaze – from my suit down to my boots. My suit was by no means new and my boots were muddy, as I was well aware. I was hot too, and very likely my hair was ruffled. I was not cool, I was not unconcerned, I was not equal to the occasion. Here was I, a stranger, not one of the elect, intruding and making myself absurd; hatred and helpless hapless misery prevented me from looking at her at all, and in desperation I carried through my stout resolve by saying gruffly, with a scowl and in a hoarse voice:

"I'd like a glass of wine."

What matter whether she really did, as I thought, cast a quick mocking glance at her companion? We stood all three in silence as she gave me the wine; without raising my eyes, red and distraught with pain and fury, a wretched and ridiculous figure, I stood between the two, drank a few sips, laid the money on the table, and rushed out of the hall.

Since that moment it is all up with me; it added but little to my bitter cup when a few days later I read in the paper that Herr Justizrat Rainer had the honour to announce his daughter Anna's engagement to Herr Dr Alfred Witznagel.

Since that moment it is all up with me. My last remaining shreds of happiness and self-confidence have been blown to the winds, I can do no more. Yes, I am unhappy; I freely admit it, I seem a lamentable and absurd figure even to myself. And that I cannot bear. I shall make an end of it. Today, or tomorrow, or some time, I will shoot myself.

My first impulse, my first instinct, was a shrewd one: I would make copy of the situation, I would contribute my pathetic sickness to swell the literature of unhappy love. But that was all folly. One does not die of an unhappy love-affair. One revels in it. It is not such a bad pose. But what is destroying me is that hope has been destroyed with the destruction of all pleasure in myself.

Was I – if I might ask the question – was I in love with this girl? Possibly. . . . But how – and why? Such love, if it existed, was a monstrosity born of a vanity which had long since become irritable and morbid, rasped into torment at sight of an unattainable prize. Love was the mere pretext, escape, and hope of salvation for my feelings of envy, hatred, and self-contempt.

Yes, it was all superficial. And had not my father once called me a dilettante?

No, I had not been justified, I less than most people, in keeping aloof and ignoring society – I, who am too vain to support her indifference or contempt, who cannot do without her and her applause. But here was not a matter of justification, rather one of necessity; and was it just my impractical dilettantism that made me useless for society? Ah, well, it was precisely my dilettantism that was killing me!

Indifference, I know, would be a sort of happiness. But

I cannot be indifferent to myself, I am not in a position to look at myself with other eyes than those of "people" – and all innocent as I am, I am being destroyed by my bad conscience. But is a bad conscience ever anything but a festering vanity?

There is only one kind of unhappiness: to suffer the loss of pleasure in oneself. No longer to be pleasant to oneself – that is the worst that can happen; and I have known it for such a long time! All else is the play of life, it enriches life; any other kind of suffering can leave one perfectly satisfied with oneself, one can get on quite well with it. It is the conflict in oneself, the suffering with a bad conscience, the struggle with one's vanity – it is these make you a pitiable and disgusting spectacle.

An old acquaintance of mine turned up, a man named Schilling, in whose company I had once served society by working in Herr Schlievogt's lumber-yard. He was in the city on business and came to see me: a cynical individual with his hands in his trouser pockets, black-rimmed pince-nez, and a convincingly tolerant shoulder-shrug. He arrived one evening and said: "I am stopping for a few days." We went to a wine-house.

He met me as though I were still the happy and self-satisfied individual he had known; and in the belief that he was merely confirming my own conviction he said:

"My God, young fellow, but you have done yourself well here! Independent, eh? And you are right too, deuce take me if you aren't! Man lives but once as they say, and that's all there is to it. You are the cleverer of us two, I must say. But you were always a bit of a genius." And went on just as of yore, wholeheartedly recognizing my claims to superiority and being agreeable without suspecting for a moment that I on my side was afraid of his opinion.

I struggled desperately to retain his high opinion of me, to appear happy and self-satisfied. All in vain. I had not the backbone, the courage, or the countenance; I was languid and ill at ease, I betrayed my insecurity – and with astonishing quickness he grasped the situation. He had been perfectly ready to grant my superiority – but it was frightful to see how he saw through me, was first astonished, then impatient, then cooled off and betrayed his contempt and disgust with every word he spoke. He left me early and next day I received a curt note saying that after all he found he was obliged to go away.

It is a fact that everybody is much too preoccupied with himself to form a serious opinion about another person. The world displays a readiness, born of indolence, to pay a man whatever degree of respect he himself demands. Be as you will, live as you like – but be bold about it, display a good conscience and nobody will be moral enough to condemn you. But once suffer yourself to become split, forfeit your own self-esteem, betray that you despise yourself, and your view will be blindly accepted by all and sundry. As for me, I am a lost soul.

I cease to write, fling the pen from me – full of disgust, full of disgust! I will make an end of it – alas, that is an attitude too heroic for a dilettante. In the end I shall go on living, eating, sleeping; I shall gradually get used to the idea that I am dull, that I cut a wretched and ridiculous figure.

Good God, who would have thought, who could have thought, that such is the doom which overtakes the man born a dilettante!

TOBIAS MINDERNICKEL

ONE OF the streets running steeply up from the docks to the middle town was named Grey's Road. At about the middle of it, on the right, stood Number 47, a narrow, dingy-looking building no different from its neighbours. On the ground floor was a chandler's shop where you could buy overshoes and castor oil. Crossing the entry along a courtyard full of cats and mounting the mean and shabby, musty-smelling stair, you arrived at the upper storeys. In the first, on the left, lived a cabinet-maker; on the right a midwife. In the second, on the left a cobbler, on the right a lady who began to sing loudly whenever she heard steps on the stair. In the third on the left, nobody; but on the right a man named Mindernickel – and Tobias to boot. There was a story about this man; I tell it, because it is both puzzling and sinister, to an extraordinary degree.

Mindernickel's exterior was odd, striking, and provoking to laughter. When he took a walk, his meagre form moving up the street supported by a cane, he would be dressed in black from head to heels. He wore a shabby old-fashioned top hat with a curved brim, a frock-coat shining with age, and equally shabby trousers, fringed round the bottoms and so short that you could see the elastic sides to his boots. True, these garments were all most carefully brushed. His scrawny neck seemed longer because it rose out of a low turn-down collar. His hair had gone grey and he wore it brushed down smooth on the temples. His wide hat-brim shaded a smooth-shaven sallow face with sunken cheeks, red-rimmed eyes which were usually directed at the floor, and two deep, fretful furrows running from the nose to the drooping corners of the mouth.

Mindernickel seldom left his house – and this for a very good reason. For whenever he appeared in the street a mob of children would collect and sally behind him, laughing, mocking, singing – "Ho, ho, Tobias!" they would cry, tugging at his coat-tails, while people came to their doors to laugh. He made no defence; glancing timidly round, with shoulders drawn up and head stuck out, he continued on his way, like a man hurrying through a driving rain without an umbrella. Even while they were laughing in his face he would bow politely and humbly to people as he passed. Further on, when the children had stopped behind and he was not known, and scarcely noted, his manner did not change. He still hurried on, still stooped, as though a thousand mocking eyes were on him. If it chanced that he lifted his timid, irresolute gaze from the ground, you would see that, strangely enough, he was not able to fix it steadily upon anyone or anything. It may sound strange, but there seemed to be missing in him the natural superiority with which the normal, perceptive individual looks out upon the phenomenal world. He seemed to measure himself against each phenomenon, and find himself wanting; his gaze shifted and fell, it grovelled before men and things.

What was the matter with this man, who was always alone and unhappy even beyond the common lot? His clothing belonged to the middle class; a certain slow gesture he had, of his hand across his chin, betrayed that he was not of the common people among whom he lived. How had fate been playing with him? God only knows. His face looked as though life had hit him between the eyes, with a scornful laugh. On the other hand, perhaps it was a question of no cruel blow but simply that he was not up to it. The painful shrinking and humility expressed in his whole figure did indeed suggest that nature had denied him the measure of strength, equilibrium, and backbone which a man requires if he is to live with his head erect.

When he had taken a turn up into the town and come back to Grey's Road, where the children welcomed him with lusty bawlings, he went into the house and up the stuffy stair into his own bare room. It had but one piece of furniture worthy the name, a solid Empire chest of drawers with brass handles, a thing of dignity and beauty. The view from the window was hopelessly cut off by the heavy side wall of the next house; a flower-pot full of earth stood on the ledge, but there was nothing growing in it. Tobias Mindernickel went up to it sometimes and smelled at the earth. Next to this room was a dark little bedchamber. Tobias on coming in would lay hat and stick on the table, sit down on the dusty green-covered sofa, prop his chin with his hand, and stare at the floor with his eyebrows raised. He seemed to have nothing else to do.

As for Tobias Mindernickel's character, it is hard to judge of that. Some favourable light seems to be cast by the following episode. One day this strange man left his house and was pounced upon by a troop of children who followed him with laughter and jeers. One of them, a lad of ten years, tripped over another child's foot and fell so heavily to the pavement that blood burst from his nose and ran from his forehead. He lay there and wept. Tobias turned at once, went up to the lad, and began to console him in a mild and quavering voice. "You poor child," said he, "have you hurt yourself? You are bleeding – look how the blood is running down from his forehead. Yes, yes, you do look miserable, you weep because it hurts you so. I pity you. Of course, you did it yourself, but I will tie my handkerchief round your head. There, there! Now pull yourself together and get up." And actually with the words he bound his own handkerchief round the bruise and helped the lad to his feet. Then he went away. But he looked a different man. He held himself erect and stepped out firmly, drawing longer breaths under his narrow coat. His eyes looked larger and brighter, he looked squarely at people and things, while an expression of joy so strong as to be almost painful tightened the corners of his mouth.

After this for a while there was less tendency to jeer at him among the denizens of Grey's Road. But they forgot his astonishing behaviour with the lapse of time, and once more the cruel cries resounded from dozens of lusty throats behind the bent and infirm man: "Ho, ho, Tobias!"

One sunny morning at eleven o'clock Mindernickel left the house and betook himself through the town to the Lerchenberg, a long ridge which constitutes the afternoon walk of good society. Today the spring weather was so fine that even in the forenoon there were some carriages as well as pedestrians moving about. On the main road, under a tree, stood a man with a young hound on a leash, exhibiting it for sale. It was a muscular little animal about four months old, with black ears and black rings round its eyes.

Tobias at a distance of ten paces noticed this; he stood still, rubbed his chin with his hand, and considered the man, and the hound alertly wagging its tail. He went forward, circling three times round the tree, with the crook of his stick pressed against his lips. Then he stepped up to the man, and keeping his eye fixed on the dog, he said in a low, hurried tone: "What are you asking for the dog?"

"Ten marks," answered the man.

Tobias kept still a moment, then he said with some hesitation: "Ten marks?"

"Yes," said the man.

Tobias drew a black leather purse from his pocket, took out a note for five marks, one three-mark and one two-mark piece, and quickly handed them to the man. Then he seized the leash, and two or three people who had been watching the bargain laughed to see him as he gave a quick, frightened look about him and, with his shoulders stooped, dragged away the whimpering and protesting beast. It struggled the whole of the way, bracing its forefeet and looking up pathetically in its new master's face. But Tobias pulled, in silence, with energy and succeeded in getting through the town.

An outcry arose among the urchins of Grey's Road when Tobias appeared with the dog. He lifted it in his arms, while they danced round, pulling at his coat and jeering; carried it up the stair and bore it into his own room, where he set it on the floor, still whimpering. Stooping over and patting it with kindly condescension he told it:

"There, there, little man, you need not be afraid of me; that is quite unnecessary."

He took a plate of cooked meat and potatoes out of a drawer and tossed the dog a part of it, whereat it ceased to whine and ate the food with loud relish, wagging its tail.

"And I will call you Esau," said Tobias. "Do you understand? That will be easy for you to remember." Pointing to the floor in front of him he said, in a tone of command:

"Esau!"

And the dog, probably in the hope of getting more to eat, did come up to him. Tobias clapped him gently on the flank and said:

"That's right, good doggy, good doggy!"

He stepped back a few paces, pointed to the floor again, and commanded:

"Esau!"

And the dog sprang to him quite blithely, wagging its tail, and licked its master's boots.

Tobias repeated the performance with unflagging zest, some twelve or fourteen times. Then the dog got tired, it wanted to rest and digest its meal. It lay down, in the sagacious and charming attitude of a hunting dog, with both long, slender forelegs stretched before it, close together.

"Once more," said Tobias. "Esau!"

But Esau turned his head aside and stopped where he was.

"Esau!" Tobias's voice was raised, his tone more dictatorial still. "You've got to come, even if you are tired."

But Esau laid his head on his paws and came not at all.

"Listen to me," said Tobias, and his voice was now low and threatening; "you'd best obey or you will find out what I do when I am angry."

But the dog hardly moved his tail.

Then Mindernickel was seized by a mad and extravagant fit of anger. He clutched his black stick, lifted up Esau by the nape of the neck, and in a frenzy of rage he beat the yelping animal, repeating over and over in a horrible, hissing voice:

"What, you do not obey me? You dare to disobey me?"

At last he flung the stick from him, set down the crying animal, and with his hands upon his back began to pace the room, his breast heaving, and flinging upon Esau an occasional proud and angry look. When this had gone on for some time, he stopped in front of the dog as it lay on its back, moving its fore-paws imploringly. He crossed his arms on his chest and spoke with a frightful hardness and coldness of look and tone – like Napoleon, when he stood before a company that had lost its standard in battle:

"May I ask you what you think of your conduct?"

And the dog, delighted at this condescension, crawled closer, nestled against its master's leg, and looked up at him bright-eyed.

For a while Tobias gazed at the humble creature with silent contempt. Then as the touching warmth of Esau's body communicated itself to his leg he lifted Esau up.

"Well, I will have pity on you," he said. But when the good beast essayed to lick his face his voice suddenly broke with melancholy emotion. He pressed the dog passionately to his breast, his eyes filling with tears, unable to go on. Chokingly he said:

"You see, you are my only . . . my only . . ." He put Esau to bed, with great care, on the sofa, supported his own chin with his hand, and gazed at him with mild eyes, speechlessly.

Tobias Mindernickel left his room now even less often than before; he had no wish to show himself with Esau in public. He gave his whole time to the dog, from morning to night; feeding him, washing his eyes, teaching him commands, scolding him, and talking to him as though he were human. Esau, alas, did not always behave to his master's satisfaction. When he lay beside Tobias on the sofa, dull with lack of air and exercise, and gazed at him with soft, melancholy eyes,

Tobias was pleased. He sat content and quiet, tenderly stroking Esau's back as he said:

"Poor fellow, how sadly you look at me! Yes, yes, life is sad, that you will learn before you are much older."

But sometimes Esau was wild, beside himself with the urge to exercise his hunting instincts; he would dash about the room, worry a slipper, leap on the chairs, or roll over and over with sheer excess of spirits. Then Tobias followed his motions from afar with a helpless, disapproving, wandering air and a hateful, peevish smile. At last he would brusquely call Esau to him and say:

"That's enough now, stop dashing about like that – there is no reason for such high spirits."

Once it even happened that Esau got out of the room and bounced down the stairs to the street, where he at once began to chase a cat, to eat dung in the road, and jump up at the children frantic with joy. But when the distressed Tobias appeared with his wry face, half the street roared with laughter to see him, and it was painful to behold the dog bounding away in the other direction from his master. That day Tobias in his anger beat him for a long time.

One day, when he had had the dog for some weeks, Tobias took a loaf of bread out of the chest of drawers and began stooping over to cut off little pieces with his big bone-handled knife and let them drop on the floor for Esau to eat. The dog was frantic with hunger and playfulness: it jumped up at the bread, and the long-handled knife in the clumsy hands of Tobias ran into its right shoulder-blade. It fell bleeding to the ground.

In great alarm Tobias flung bread and knife aside and bent over the injured animal. Then the expression of his face changed, actually a gleam of relief and happiness passed over it. With the greatest care he lifted the wounded animal to the sofa – and then with what inexhaustible care and devotion he began to tend the invalid. He did not stir all day from its side, he took it to sleep on his own bed, he washed and bandaged, stroked and caressed and consoled it with unwearying solicitude.

"Does it hurt so much?" he asked. "Yes, you are suffering a good deal, my poor friend. But we must be quiet, we must try to bear it." And the look on his face was one of gentle and melancholy happiness.

But as Esau got better and the wound healed, so the spirits of Tobias sank again. He paid no more attention to the wound, confining his sympathy to words and caresses. But it had gone on well, Esau's constitution was sound; he began to move about once more. One day after he had finished off a whole plate of milk and white bread he seemed quite right again; jumped down from the sofa to rush about the room, barking joyously, with all his former lack of restraint. He tugged at the bed-covers, chased a potato round the room, and rolled over and over in his excitement.

Tobias stood by the flower-pot in the window. His arms stuck out long and lean from the ragged sleeves and he mechanically twisted the hair that hung down from his temples. His figure stood out black and uncanny against the grey wall of the next building. His face was pale and drawn with suffering and he followed Esau's pranks unmoving, with a sidelong, jealous, wicked look. But suddenly he pulled himself together, approached the dog, and made it stop jumping about; he took it slowly in his arms.

"Now, poor creature," he began, in a lachrymose tone – but Esau was not minded to be pitied, his spirits were too high. He gave a brisk snap at the hand which would have stroked him; he escaped from the arms to the floor, where he jumped mockingly aside and ran off, with a joyous bark.

That which now happened was so shocking, so inconceivable, that I simply cannot tell it in any detail. Tobias Mindernickel stood leaning a little forward, his arms hanging down; his lips were compressed, the balls of his eyes vibrated uncannily in their sockets. Suddenly with a sort of frantic leap, he seized the animal, a large bright object gleamed in his hand – and then he flung Esau to the ground with a cut which ran from the right shoulder deep into the chest. The dog made no sound, he simply fell on his side, bleeding and quivering.

The next minute he was on the sofa with Tobias kneeling before him, pressing a cloth on the wound and stammering:

"My poor brute, my poor dog! How sad everything is! How sad it is for both of us! You suffer – yes, yes, I know. You lie there so pathetic – but I am with you, I will console you – here is my best handkerchief – "

But Esau lay there and rattled in his throat. His clouded, questioning eyes were directed upon his master, with a look of complaining, innocence, and incomprehension – and then he stretched out his legs a little and died.

But Tobias stood there motionless, as he was. He had laid his face against Esau's body and he wept bitter tears.

LITTLE LIZZY

THERE ARE marriages which the imagination, even the most practised literary one, cannot conceive. You must just accept them, as you do in the theatre when you see the ancient and doddering married to the beautiful and gay, as the given premisses on which the farce is mechanically built up.

Yes, the wife of Jacoby the lawyer was lovely and young, a woman of unusual charm. Some years – shall we say thirty years? – ago, she had been christened with the names of Anna, Margarete, Rosa, Amalie; but the name she went by was always Amra, composed of the initials of her four real ones; it suited to perfection her somewhat exotic personality. Her soft, heavy hair, which she wore parted on one side and brushed straight back above her ears from the narrow temples, had only the darkness of the glossy chestnut; but her skin displayed the dull, dark sallowness of the south and clothed a form which southern suns must have ripened. Her slow, voluptuous indolent presence suggested the harem; each sensuous, lazy movement of her body strengthened the impression that with her the head was entirely subordinate to the heart. She needed only to have looked at you once, with her artless brown eyes, lifting her brows in the pathetically narrow forehead, horizontally, in a quaint way she had, for you to be certain of that. But she herself was not so simple as not to know it too. Quite simply, she avoided exposing herself, she spoke seldom and little – and what is there to say against a woman who is both beautiful and silent? Yes, the word "simple" is probably the last which should be applied to her. Her glance was artless; but also it had a kind of luxurious cunning – you could see that she was not dull, also that she might be a mischief-maker. In profile her nose was rather too thick; but her full, large mouth was utterly lovely, if also lacking in any expression save sensuality.

This disturbing phenomenon was the wife of Jacoby the lawyer, a man of forty. Whoever looked at him was bound to be amazed at the fact. He was stout, Jacoby the lawyer; but stout is not the word, he was a perfect colossus of a man! His legs, in their columnar clumsiness and the slate-grey trousers he always wore, reminded one of an elephant's. His round, fat-upholstered back was that of a bear, and over the vast round of his belly his funny little grey jacket was held by a single button strained so tight that when it was unbuttoned the jacket came wide open with a pop. Scarcely anything which could be called a neck united this huge torso with the little head atop. The head had narrow watery eyes, a squabby nose, and a wee mouth between cheeks drooping with fullness. The upper lip and the round head were covered with harsh, scanty, light-coloured bristles that showed the naked skin, as on an overfed dog. There was no doubt that Jacoby's fatness was not of a healthy kind. His gigantic body, tall as well as stout, was not muscular, but flabby. The blood would sometimes rush to his puffy face, then ebb away leaving it of a yellowish pallor; the mouth would be drawn and sour.

Jacoby's practice was a limited one; but he was well-to-do, partly from his wife's side; and the childless pair lived in a comfortable apartment in the Kaiserstrasse and entertained a good deal. This must have been Frau Amra's taste, for it is unthinkable that the lawyer could have cared for it; he participated with an enthusiasm of a peculiarly painful kind. This fat man's character was the oddest in the world. No human being could have been politer, more accommodating, more complaisant than he. But you unconsciously knew that this over-obligingness was somehow forced, that its true source was an inward insecurity and cowardice – the impression it gave was not very pleasant. A man who despises himself is a very ugly sight; worse still when vanity combines with his cowardice to make him wish to please. This was the case,

I should say, with Jacoby: his obsequiousness was almost crawling, it went beyond the bounds of personal decency. He was quite capable of saying to a lady as he escorted her to table: "My dear lady, I am a disgusting creature, but will you do me the honour?" No humour would be mingled with the remark; it was simply cloying, bitter, self-tortured – in a word, disgusting, as he said.

The following once actually happened: the lawyer was taking a walk, and a clumsy porter with a hand-cart ran over his foot. Too late the man stopped his cart and turned round – whereupon Jacoby, quite pale and dazed, his cheeks shaking up and down, took off his hat and stuttered: "I b-beg your pardon." A thing like that is infuriating. But this extraordinary colossus seemed perpetually to suffer from a plague of conscience. When he took a walk with his wife on the Lerchenberg, the Corso of the little city, he would roll his eyes round at Amra, walking with her wonderful elastic gait at his side, and bow so anxiously, diligently, and zealously in all directions that he seemed to be begging pardon of all the lieutenants they met for being in unworthy possession of such a beautiful wife. His mouth had a pathetically ingratiating expression, as though he wanted to disarm their scorn.

I have already hinted that the reason why Amra married Jacoby is unfathomable. As for him, he was in love with her, ardently, as people of his physical make-up seldom are, and with such anxious humility as fitted the rest of his character. Sometimes, late in the evening, he would enter their large sleeping-chamber with its high windows and flowered hangings – softly, so softly that there was no sound, only the slow shaking of floor and furniture. He would come up to Amra's massive bed, where she already lay, kneel down, and with infinite caution take her hand. She would lift her brows in a level line, in the quaint way she had, and look at her husband, abject before her in the dim light, with a look of malice and sensuality combined. With his puffy, trembling hands he would softly stroke back the sleeve and press his tragic fat face into the soft brown flesh of her wrist, where little blue veins stood out. And he would speak to her, in a shaking, half-smothered voice, as a sensible man in everyday life never speaks:

"Amra, my dear Amra! I am not disturbing you? You were not asleep yet? Dear God! I have been thinking all day how beautiful you are and how much I love you. I beg you to listen, for it is so very hard to express what I feel: I love you so much that sometimes my heart contracts and I do not know where to turn. I love you beyond my strength. You do not understand that, I know; but you believe it, and you must say, just one single time, that you are a little grateful to me. For, you see, such a love as mine to you is precious, it has its value in this life of ours. And that you will never betray or deceive me, even if you cannot love me, just out of gratitude for this love. I have come to you to beg you, as seriously, as fervently as I can . . ." here the lawyer's speech would be dissolved in sobs, in low, bitter weeping, as he knelt. Amra would feel moved; she would stroke her husband's bristles and say over and over, in the soothing, contemptuous singsong one uses to a dog who comes to lick one's feet: "Yes, yes, good doggy, good doggy!"

And this behaviour of Amra's was certainly not that of a moral woman. For to relieve my mind of the truth which I have so far withheld, she did already deceive her husband; she betrayed him for the embraces of a gentleman named Alfred Läutner, a gifted young musician, who at twenty-seven had made himself a small reputation with amusing little compositions. He was a slim young chap with a provocative face, a flowing blond mane, and a sunny smile in his eyes, of which he was quite aware. He belonged to the present-day race of small artists, who do not demand the utmost of themselves, whose first requirement is to be jolly and happy, who employ their pleasing little talents to heighten their personal charms. It pleases them to play in society the role of the naïve genius. Consciously childlike, entirely unmoral and unscrupulous, merry and self-satisfied as they are, and healthy enough to enjoy even their disorders, they are agreeable even in their vanity, so long as that has not been wounded. But woe to these wretched little poseurs when serious misfortune befalls them, with which there is no coquetting, and when they can no longer be pleasant in their own eyes. They will not know how to be wretched decently and in order, they do not know how to attack the problem of suffering. They will be destroyed. All that is a story in itself. But Herr Alfred Läutner wrote pretty things, mostly waltzes and mazurkas. They would have been rather too gay and popular to be considered music as I understand it, if each of them had not contained a passage of some originality, a modulation, a harmonic phrasing, some sort of bold effect that betrayed wit and invention, which was evidently the point of the whole and which made it interesting to genuine musicians. Often these two single measures would have a strange plaintive, melancholy tone which would come out abruptly in the midst of a piece of dance-music and as suddenly be gone.

Amra Jacoby was on fire with guilty passion for this young man, and as for him he had not enough moral fibre to resist her seductions. They met here, they met there, and for some years an immoral relation had subsisted between them, known to the whole town, who laughed at it behind the lawyer's back. But what did he think? Amra was not sensitive enough to betray herself on account of a guilty conscience, so we must take it as certain that, however heavy the lawyer's heart, he could cherish no definite suspicions.

Spring had come, rejoicing all hearts; and Amra conceived the most charming idea.

"Christian," said she – Jacoby's name was Christian – "let us give a party, a beer party to celebrate the new beer – of course quite simply, but let's have a lot of people."

"Certainly," said the lawyer, "but could we not have it a little later?"

To which Amra made no reply, having passed on to the consideration of details.

"It will be so large that we cannot have it here, we must hire a place, some sort of outdoor restaurant where there is plenty of room and fresh air. You see that, of course. The place I am thinking of is Wendelin's big hall at the foot of the Lerchenberg. The hall is independent of the restaurant and brewery, connected by a passage only. We can decorate it for the occasion and set up long tables, drink our bock, and dance – we must have music and even perhaps some sort of entertainment. There is a little stage, as I happen to know, that makes it very suitable. It will be a very original party and no end of fun."

The lawyer's face had gone a pale yellow as she spoke, and the corners of his mouth went down. He said:

"My dear Amra! How delightful it will be! I can leave it all to you, you are so clever. Make any arrangements you like."

And Amra made her arrangements. She took counsel of various ladies and gentlemen, she went in person to hire the hall, she even formed a committee of people who were invited or who volunteered to co-operate in the entertainment. These were exclusively men, except for the wife of Herr Hildebrandt, an actor at the Hoftheater, who was herself a singer. Then there was Herr Hildebrandt, an Assessor Witznagel, a young painter, Alfred Läutner the musician, and some students brought in by Herr Witznagel, who were to do Negro dances.

A week after Amra had made her plan, this committee met in Amra's drawing-room in the Kaiserstrasse – a small, crowded, over-heated room, with a heavy carpet, a sofa with quantities of cushions, a fan palm, English leather chairs, and a splay-legged mahogany table with a velvet cover, upon which rested several large illustrated morocco-bound volumes. There was a fireplace too, with a small fire still burning, and on the marble chimney-top were plates of dainty sandwiches, glasses, and two decanters of sherry. Amra reclined in one corner of the sofa under the fan palm, with her legs crossed. She had the beauty of a warm summer night. A thin blouse of light-coloured silk covered her bosom, but her skirt was of heavy dark stuff embroidered with large flowers. Sometimes she put up one hand to brush back the chestnut hair from her narrow forehead. Frau Hildebrandt sat beside her on the sofa; she had red hair and wore riding clothes. Opposite the two all the gentlemen formed a semicircle – among them Jacoby himself, in the lowest chair he could find. He looked unutterably wretched, kept drawing a long breath and swallowing as though struggling against increasing nausea. Herr Alfred Läutner was in tennis clothes – he would not take a chair, but leaned decoratively against the chimney-piece, saying merrily that he could not sit still so long.

Herr Hildebrandt talked sonorously about English songs. He was a most respectable gentleman, in a black suit, with a Roman head and an assured manner – in short a proper actor for a court theatre, cultured, knowledgeable, and with enlightened tastes. He liked to hold forth in condemnation of Ibsen, Zola, and Tolstoi, all of whom had the same objectionable aims. But today he was benignly interested in the small affair under discussion.

"Do you know that priceless song 'That's Maria!'?" he asked. "Perhaps it is a little racy – but very effective. And then" so-and-so – he suggested other songs, upon which they came to an agreement and Frau Hildebrandt said that she would sing them. The young painter, who had sloping shoulders and a very blond beard, was to give a burlesque conjuring turn. Herr Hildebrandt offered to impersonate various famous characters. In short, everything was developing nicely, the programme was apparently arranged, when Assessor Witznagel, who had command of fluent gesture and a good many duelling scars, suddenly took the word.

"All very well, ladies and gentlemen, it looks like being most amusing. But if I may say so, it still lacks something; it wants some kind of high spot, a climax as it were, something a bit startling, perhaps, to round the thing off. I leave it to you, I have nothing particular in mind, I only think..."

"That is true enough!" Alfred Läutner's tenor voice came from the chimney-piece where he leaned. "Witznagel is right. We need a climax. Let us put our heads together!" He settled his red belt and looked engagingly about him.

"Well, if we do not consider the famous characters as the high spot," said Herr Hildebrandt. Everybody agreed with the Assessor. Something piquant was wanted for the principal number. Even Jacoby nodded, and murmured: "Yes, yes, something jolly and striking. . . ." They all reflected.

At the end of a minute's pause, which was broken only by stifled exclamations, an extraordinary thing happened. Amra was sitting reclined among the cushions, gnawing as busily as a mouse at the pointed nail of her little finger. She had a very odd look on her face: a vacant, almost an irresponsible smile, which betrayed a sensuality both tormented and cruel. Her eyes, very bright and wide, turned slowly to the chimney-piece, where for a second they met the musician's. Then suddenly she jerked her whole body to one side as she sat, in the direction of her husband. With both hands in her lap she stared into his face with an avid and clinging gaze, her own growing visibly paler, and said in her rich, slow voice:

"Christian, suppose you come on at the end as a *chanteuse*, in a red satin baby frock, and do a dance."

The effect of these few words was tremendous. The young painter essayed to laugh good-humouredly; Herr Hildebrandt, stony-faced, brushed a crumb from his sleeve; his wife coloured up, a rare thing for her; the students coughed and used their handkerchiefs loudly; and Herr Assessor Witznagel simply left the field and got himself a sandwich. The lawyer sat huddled on his little chair, yellow in the face, with a terrified smile. He looked all round the circle, and stammered:

"But, my God . . . I – I – I am not up to – not that I – I beg pardon, but . . ."

Alfred Läutner had lost his insouciant expression; he even seemed to have reddened a little, and he thrust out his neck to peer searchingly into Amra's face. He looked puzzled and upset.

But she, Amra, holding the same persuasive pose, went on with the same impressiveness:

"And you must sing, too, Christian, a song which Herr Läutner shall compose, and he can accompany you on the piano. We could not have a better or more effective climax."

There was a pause, an oppressive pause. Then this extraordinary thing happened, that Herr Läutner, as it were seized upon and carried away by his excitement, took a step forward and his voice fairly trembled with enthusiasm as he said:

"Herr Jacoby, that is a priceless idea, and I am more than ready to compose something. You must have a dance and song, anything else is unthinkable as a wind-up to our affair. You will see, it will be the best thing I have ever written or ever shall write. In a red satin baby frock. Oh, your wife is an artist, only an artist could have hit upon the idea! Do say yes, I beg of you. I will do my part, you will see, it will be an achievement."

Here the circle broke up and the meeting became lively. Out of politeness, or out of malice, the company began to storm the lawyer with entreaties – Frau Hildebrandt went so far as to say, quite loudly, in her Brünnhilde voice:

"Herr Jacoby, after all, you are such a jolly and entertaining man!"

But the lawyer had pulled himself together and spoke, a little yellow, but with a strong effort at resolution:

"But listen to me, ladies and gentlemen – what can I say to you? It isn't my line, believe me. I have no comic gift, and besides . . . in short, no, it is quite impossible, alas!"

He stuck obstinately to his refusal, and Amra no longer insisted, but sat still with her absent look. Herr Läutner was silent too, staring in deep abstraction at a pattern in the rug. Herr Hildebrandt changed the subject, and presently the committee meeting broke up without coming to a final decision about the "climax".

On the evening of the same day Amra had gone to bed and was lying there with her eyes wide open; her husband came lumbering into the bedroom, drew a chair up beside the bed, dropped into it, and said, in a low, hesitating voice:

"Listen, Amra; to be quite frank, I am feeling very disturbed. I refused them today – I did not mean to be offensive – goodness knows I did not mean that. Or do you seriously feel that – I beg you to tell me."

Amra was silent for a moment, while her brows rose slowly. Then she shrugged her shoulders and said:

"I do not know, my dear friend, how to answer you. You behaved in a way I should not have expected from you. You were unfriendly, you refused to support our enterprise in a way which they flatteringly considered to be indispensable to it. To put it mildly, you disappointed everybody and upset the whole company with your rude lack of compliance. Whereas it was your duty as host –"

The lawyer hung his head and sighed heavily. He said:

"Believe me, Amra, I had no intention to be disobliging. I do not like to offend anybody; if I have behaved badly I am ready to make amends. It is only a joke, after all, an innocent little dressing-up – why not? I will not upset the whole affair, I am ready to..."

The following afternoon Amra went out again to "make preparations". She drove to Number 78 Holzstrasse and went up to the second storey, where she had an appointment. And when she lay relaxed by the expression of her love she pressed her lover's head passionately to her breast and whispered:

"Write it for four hands. We will accompany him together while he sings and dances. I will see to the costume myself."

And an extraordinary shiver, a suppressed and spasmodic burst of laughter went through the limbs of both.

For anyone who wants to give a large party out of doors Herr Wendelin's place on the slope of the Lerchenberg is to be recommended. You enter it from the pretty suburban street through a tall trellised gateway and pass into the parklike garden, in the centre of which stands a large hall, connected only by a narrow passage with restaurant, kitchen, and brewery. It is a large, brightly painted wooden hall, in an amusing mixture of Chinese and Renaissance styles. It has folding doors which stand open in good weather to admit the woodland air, and it will hold a great many people.

On this evening as the carriages rolled up they were greeted from afar by the gleam of coloured lights. The whole gateway, the trees, and the hall itself were set thick with lanterns, while the interior made an entrancing sight. Heavy garlands were draped across the ceiling and studded with paper lanterns. Hosts of electric lights hung among the decorations of the walls, which consisted of pine boughs, flags, and artificial flowers; the whole hall was brilliantly lighted. The stage had foliage plants grouped on either side, and a red curtain with a painted design of a presiding genius hovering in the air. A long row of decorated tables ran almost the whole length of the hall. And at these tables the guests of Attorney Jacoby were doing themselves well on cold roast veal and bock beer. There were certainly more than a hundred and fifty people: officers, lawyers, business men, artists, upper officials, with their wives and daughters. They were quite simply dressed, in black coats and light spring toilettes, for this was a jolly, informal occasion. The gentlemen carried their mugs in person to the big casks against one of the walls; the spacious, festive, brightly lighted room was filled with a heavy sweetish atmosphere of evergreen boughs, flowers, beer, food, and human beings; and there was a clatter and buzz of laughter and talk – the loud, simple talk and the high, good-natured, unrestrained, carefree laughter of the sort of people there assembled.

The attorney sat shapeless and helpless at one end of the table, near the stage. He drank little and now and then addressed a laboured remark to his neighbour, Frau Regierungsrat Havermann. He breathed offensively, the corners of his mouth hung down, he stared fixedly with his bulging watery eyes into the lively scene, with a sort of melancholy remoteness, as though there resided in all this noisy merriment something inexpressibly painful and perplexing.

Large fruit tarts were now being handed round for the company to cut from; they drank sweet wine with these, and the time for the speeches arrived. Herr Hildebrandt celebrated the new brew in a speech almost entirely composed of classical quotations, even Greek. Herr Witznagel, with florid gestures and ingenious turns of phrase, toasted the ladies, taking a handful of flowers from the nearest vase and comparing each flower to some feminine charm. Amra Jacoby, who sat opposite him in a pale-yellow silk frock, he called "a lovelier sister of the Maréchal Niel".

Then she nodded meaningfully to her husband, brushing back her hair from her forehead; whereupon the fat man arose and almost ruined the whole atmosphere by stammering a few words with painful effort, smiling a repulsive smile. Some half-hearted bravos rewarded him, then there was an oppressive pause, after which jollity resumed its sway. All smoking, all a little elevated by drink, they rose from table and with their own hands and a great deal of noise removed the tables from the hall to make way for the dancing.

It was after eleven and high spirits reigned supreme. Some of the guests streamed out into the brightly lighted garden to get the fresh air; others stood about the hall in groups, smoking, chatting, drawing beer from the kegs, and drinking it standing. Then a loud trumpet call sounded from the stage, summoning everybody to the entertainment. The band arrived and took its place before the curtains; rows of chairs were put in place and red programmes distributed on them; the gentlemen ranged themselves along the walls. There was an expectant hush.

The band played a noisy overture, and the curtains parted to reveal a row of Negroes horrifying to behold in their barbaric costumes and their blood-red lips, gnashing their teeth and emitting savage yells.

Certainly the entertainment was the crowning success of Amra's party. As it went on, the applause grew more and more enthusiastic. Frau Hildebrandt came on in a powdered wig, pounded with a shepherdess's crook on the floor and sang – in too large a voice – "That's Maria!" A conjuror in a dress coat covered with orders performed the most amazing feats; Herr Hildebrandt impersonated Goethe, Bismarck, and Napoleon in an amazingly lifelike manner; and a newspaper editor, Dr Wiesensprung, improvised a humorous lecture which had as its theme bock beer and its social significance. And now the suspense reached its height, for it was time for the last, the mysterious number which appeared on the programme framed in a laurel wreath and was entitled: "*Little Lizzy*. Song and Dance. Music by Alfred Läutner."

A movement swept through the hall, and people's eyes met as the band sat down at their instruments and Alfred Läutner came from the doorway where he had been lounging with a cigarette between his pouting lips to take his place beside Amra Jacoby at the piano, which stood in the centre of the stage in front of the curtains. Herr Läutner's face was flushed and he turned over his manuscript score nervously; Amra for her part was rather pale. She leaned one arm on the back of her chair and looked loweringly at the audience. The bell rang, the pianists played a few bars of an insignificant accompaniment, the curtains parted, little Lizzy appeared.

The whole audience stiffened with amazement as that tragic and bedizened bulk shambled with a sort of bear-dance into view. It was Jacoby. A wide, shapeless garment of crimson satin, without folds, fell to his feet; it was cut out above to make a repulsive display of the fat neck, stippled with white powder. The sleeves consisted merely of a shoulder puff, but the flabby arms were covered by long lemon-coloured gloves; on the head perched a high blond wig with a swaying green feather. And under the wig was a face, a puffy, pasty, unhappy, and desperately mirthful face, with cheeks that shook pathetically up and down and little red-rimmed eyes that strained in anguish towards the floor and saw nothing else at all. The fat man hoisted himself with effort from one leg to the other, while with his hands he either held up his skirts or else weakly raised his index fingers – these two gestures he had and knew no others. In a choked and gasping voice he sang; to the accompaniment of the piano.

The lamentable figure exhaled more than ever a cold breath of anguish. It killed every light-hearted enjoyment and lay like an oppressive weight upon the assembled audience. Horror was in the depths of all these spellbound eyes, gazing at this pair at the piano and at that husband there. The monstrous, unspeakable scandal lasted five long minutes.

Then came a moment which none of those present will forget as long as they live. Let us picture to ourselves what happened in that frightful and frightfully involved little instant of time.

You know of course the absurd little jingle called "Lizzy". And you remember the lines:

> I can polka until I am dizzy,
> I can waltz with the best and beyond,
> I'm the popular pet, little Lizzy,
> Who makes all the menfolks so fond –

which form the trivial and unlovely refrain to three longish stanzas. Alfred Läutner had composed a new setting to the verses I have quoted, and it was, as he had said it would be, his masterpiece. He had, that is, brought to its highest pitch his little artifice of introducing into a fairly vulgar and humorous piece of hackwork a sudden phrase of genuine creative art. The melody, in C-sharp major, had been in the first bars rather pretty and perfectly banal. At the beginning of the refrain the rhythm became livelier and dissonances occurred, which by means of the constant accentuation of a B-natural made one expect a transition into F-sharp major. These dissonances went on developing until the word "beyond"; and after the "I'm the" a culmination into F-sharp major should have followed. Instead of which the most surprising thing happened. That is, through a harsh turn, by means of an inspiration which was almost a stroke of genius, the key changed to F-major, and this little interlude which followed, with the use of both pedals on the long-drawn-out first syllable of the word "Lizzy", was indescribably, almost gruesomely effective. It was a complete surprise, an abrupt assault on the nerves, it shivered down the back, it was a miracle, a revelation, it was like a curtain suddenly torn away to reveal something nude.

And on the F-major chord Attorney Jacoby stopped dancing. He stood still, he stood as though rooted to the stage with his two forefingers lifted, one a little lower than the other. The word "Lizzy" stuck in his throat, he was dumb; almost at the same time the accompaniment broke sharp off, and the incredible, absurd, and ghastly figure stood there frozen, with his head thrust forward like a steer's, staring with inflamed eyes straight before him. He stared into the brightly lighted, decorated, crowded hall, in which, like an exhalation from all these people, the scandal hung and thickened into visibility. He stared at all these upturned faces, foreshortened and distorted by the lighting, into these hundreds of pairs of eyes all directed with the same knowing expression upon himself and the two at the piano. In a frightful stillness, unbroken by the smallest sound, his gaze travelled slowly and uneasily from the pair to the audience, from the audience to the pair, while his eyes widened more and more. Then knowledge seemed to flash across his face, like a sudden rush of blood, making it red as the frock he wore, only to give way to a waxen yellow pallor – and the fat man collapsed, making the platform creak beneath his weight.

For another moment the stillness reigned. Then there came shrieks, hubbub ensued, a few gentlemen took heart to spring upon the platform, among them a young doctor – and the curtains were drawn together.

Amra Jacoby and Alfred Läutner still sat at the piano. They had turned a little away from each other, and he, with his head bent, seemed to be listening to the echo of his F-major chord, while she, with her birdlike brain, had not yet grasped the situation, but gazed round her with vacant face.

The young doctor came back presently. He was a little Jewish gentleman with a serious face and a small pointed beard. Some people surrounded him at the door with questions – to which he replied with a shrug of the shoulders and the words:

"All over."

THE WARDROBE

IT WAS cloudy, cool, and half-dark when the Berlin–Rome express drew in at a middle-sized station on its way. Albrecht van der Qualen, solitary traveller in a first-class compartment with lace covers over the plush upholstery, roused himself and sat up. He felt a flat taste in his mouth, and in his body the none-too-agreeable sensations produced when the train comes to a stop after a long journey and we are aware of the cessation of rhythmic motion and conscious of calls and signals from without. It is like coming to oneself out of drunkenness or lethargy. Our nerves, suddenly deprived of the supporting rhythm, feel bewildered and forlorn. And this the more if we have just roused out of the heavy sleep one falls into in a train.

Albrecht van der Qualen stretched a little, moved to the window, and let down the pane. He looked along the train. Men were busy at the mail van, unloading and loading parcels. The engine gave out a series of sounds, it snorted and rumbled a bit, standing still, but only as a horse stands still, lifting its hoof, twitching its ears, and awaiting impatiently the signal to go on. A tall, stout woman in a long raincoat, with a face expressive of nothing but worry, was dragging a hundred-pound suitcase along the train, propelling it before her with pushes from one knee. She was saying nothing, but looking heated and distressed. Her upper lip stuck out, with little beads of sweat upon it – altogether she was a pathetic figure. "You poor dear thing," van der Qualen thought. "If I could help you, soothe you, take you in – only for the sake of that upper lip. But each for himself, so things are arranged in life; and I stand here at this moment perfectly carefree, looking at you as I might at a beetle that has fallen on its back."

It was half-dark in the station shed. Dawn or twilight – he did not know. He had slept, who could say whether for two, five, or twelve hours? He had sometimes slept for twenty-four, or even more, unbrokenly, an extraordinarily profound sleep. He wore a half-length dark-brown winter overcoat with a velvet collar. From his features it was hard to judge his age: one might actually hesitate between twenty-five and the end of the thirties. He had a yellowish skin, but his eyes were black like live coals and had deep shadows round them. These eyes boded nothing good. Several doctors, speaking frankly as man to man, had not given him many more months. – His dark hair was smoothly parted on one side.

In Berlin – although Berlin had not been the beginning of his journey – he had climbed into the train just as it was moving off – incidentally with his red leather hand-bag. He had gone to sleep and now at waking felt himself so completely absolved from time that a sense of refreshment streamed through him. He rejoiced in the knowledge that at the end of the thin gold chain he wore round his neck there was only a little medallion in his waistcoat pocket. He did not like to be aware of the hour or of the day of the week, and moreover he had no truck with the calendars. Some time ago he had lost the habit of knowing the day of the month or even the month of the year. Everything must be in the air – so he put it in his mind, and the phrase was comprehensive though rather vague. He was seldom or never disturbed in this programme, as he took pains to keep all upsetting knowledge at a distance from him. After all, was it not enough for him to know more or less what season it was? "It is more or less autumn," he thought, gazing out into the damp and gloomy train shed. "More I do not know. Do I even know where I am?"

His satisfaction at this thought amounted to a thrill of pleasure. No, he did not know where he was! Was he still in Germany? Beyond a doubt. In North Germany? That remained to be seen. While his eyes were still heavy with sleep the window of his compartment had glided past an illuminated sign; it probably had the name of the station on it, but not the picture of a single letter had been transmitted to his brain. In still dazed condition he had heard the conductor call the name two or three times, but not a syllable had he grasped. But out there in a twilight of which he knew not so much as whether it was morning or evening lay a strange place, an unknown town. – Albrecht van der Qualen took his felt hat out of the rack, seized his red leather hand-bag, the strap of which secured a red and white silk and wool plaid into which was rolled an umbrella with a silver crook – and although his ticket was labelled Florence, he left the compartment and the train, walked along the shed, deposited his luggage at the cloak-room, lighted a cigar, thrust his hands – he carried neither stick nor umbrella – into his overcoat pockets, and left the station.

Outside in the damp, gloomy, and nearly empty square five or six hackney coachmen were snapping their whips, and a man with braided cap and long cloak in which he huddled shivering inquired politely: "*Hotel zum braven Mann?*" Van der Qualen thanked him politely and held on his way. The people whom he met had their coat-collars turned up; he put his up too, nestled his chin into the velvet, smoked, and went his way, not slowly and not too fast.

He passed along a low wall and an old gate with two massive towers; he crossed a bridge with statues on the railings and saw the water rolling slow and turbid below. A long wooden boat, ancient and crumbling, came by, sculled by a man with a long pole in the stern. Van der Qualen stood for a while leaning over the rail of the bridge. "Here," he said to himself, "is a river; here is *the* river. It is nice to think that I call it that because I do not know its name." – Then he went on.

He walked straight on for a little, on the pavement of a street which was neither very narrow nor very broad; then he turned off to the left. It was evening. The electric arc-lights came on, flickered, glowed, sputtered, and then illuminated the gloom. The shops were closing. "So we may say that it is in every respect autumn," thought van der Qualen, proceeding along the wet black pavement. He wore no galoshes, but his boots were very thick-soled, durable, and firm, and withal not lacking in elegance.

He held to the left. Men moved past him, they hurried on their business or coming from it. "And I move with them," he thought, "and am as alone and as strange as probably no man has ever been before. I have no business and no goal. I have not even a stick to lean upon. More remote, freer, more detached, no one can be, I owe nothing to anybody, nobody owes anything to me. God has never held out His hand over me, He knows me not at all. Honest unhappiness without charity is a good thing; a man can say to himself: I owe God nothing."

He soon came to the edge of the town. Probably he had slanted across it at about the middle. He found himself on a broad suburban street with trees and villas, turned to his right, passed three or four cross-streets almost like village lanes, lighted only by lanterns, and came to a stop in a somewhat wider one before a wooden door next to a commonplace house painted a dingy yellow, which had nevertheless the striking feature of very convex and quite opaque plate-glass windows. But on the door was a sign: "In this house on the third floor there are rooms to let." "Ah!" he remarked; tossed away the end of his cigar, passed through the door along a boarding which formed the dividing line between two properties, and then turned left through the door of the house itself. A shabby grey runner ran across the entry. He covered it in two steps and began to mount the simple wooden stair.

The doors to the several apartments were very modest too; they had white glass panes with woven wire over them and on some of them were name-plates. The landings were lighted by oil lamps. On the third storey, the top one, for the attic came next, were entrances right and left, simple brown doors without name-plates. Van der Qualen pulled the brass bell in the middle. It rang, but there was no sign from within. He knocked left. No answer. He knocked right. He heard light steps within, very long, like strides, and the door opened.

A woman stood there, a lady, tall, lean, and old. She wore a cap with a large pale-lilac bow and an old-fashioned, faded black gown. She had a sunken birdlike face and on her brow there was an eruption, a sort of fungus growth. It was rather repulsive.

"Good evening," said van der Qualen. "The rooms?"

The old lady nodded; she nodded and smiled slowly, without a word, understandingly, and with her beautiful long white hand made a slow, languid, and elegant gesture towards the next, the left-hand door. Then she retired and appeared again with a key. "Look," he thought, standing behind her as she unlocked the door; "you are like some kind of banshee, a figure out of Hoffmann, madam." She took the oil lamp from its hook and ushered him in.

It was a small, low-ceiled room with a brown floor. Its walls were covered with straw-coloured matting. There was a window at the back in the right-hand wall, shrouded in long, thin white muslin folds. A white door also on the right led into the next room. This room was pathetically bare, with staring white walls, against which three straw chairs, painted pink, stood out like strawberries from whipped cream. A wardrobe, a washing-stand with a mirror. . . . The bed, a mammoth mahogany piece, stood free in the middle of the room.

"Have you any objections?" asked the old woman, and passed her lovely long, white hand lightly over the fungus growth on her forehead. – It was as though she had said that by accident because she could not think for the moment of a more ordinary phrase. For she added at once: " – so to speak?"

"No, I have no objections," said van der Qualen. "The rooms are rather cleverly furnished. I will take them. I'd like to have somebody fetch my luggage from the station, here is the ticket. You will be kind enough to make up the bed and give me some water. I'll take the house key now, and the key to the apartment. . . . I'd like a couple of towels. I'll wash up and go into the city for supper and come back later."

He drew a nickel case out of his pocket, took out some soap, and began to wash his face and hands, looking as he did so through the convex window-panes far down over the muddy, gas-lit suburban streets, over the arc-lights and the villas. – As he dried his hands he went over to the wardrobe. It was a square one, varnished brown, rather shaky, with a simple curved top. It stood in the centre of the right-hand wall exactly in the niche of a second white door, which of course led into the rooms to which the main and middle door on the landing gave access. "Here is something in the world that is well arranged," thought van der Qualen. "This wardrobe fits into the door niche as though it were made for it." He opened the wardrobe door. It was entirely empty, with several rows of hooks in the ceiling; but it proved to have no back, being closed behind by a piece of rough, common grey burlap, fastened by nails or tacks at the four corners.

Van der Qualen closed the wardrobe door, took his hat, turned up the collar of his coat once more, put out the candle, and set forth. As he went through the front room he thought to hear mingled with the sound of his own steps a sort of ringing in the other room: a soft, clear, metallic sound – but perhaps he was mistaken. As though a gold ring were to fall into a silver basin, he thought, as he locked the outer door. He went down the steps and out of the gate and took the way to the town.

In a busy street he entered a lighted restaurant and sat down at one of the front tables, turning his back to all the world. He ate a *soupe aux fines herbes* with croûtons, a steak with a poached egg, a compote and wine, a small piece of green gorgonzola and half a pear. While he paid and put on his coat he took a few puffs from a Russian cigarette, then lighted a cigar and went out. He strolled for a while, found his homeward route into the suburb, and went leisurely back.

The house with the plate-glass windows lay quite dark and silent when van der Qualen opened the house-door and mounted the dim stair. He lighted himself with matches as he went, and opened the left-hand brown door in the third storey. He laid hat and overcoat on the divan, lighted the lamp on the big writing-table, and found there his hand-bag as well as the plaid and umbrella. He unrolled the plaid and got a bottle of cognac, then a little glass and took a sip now and then as he sat in the arm-chair finishing his cigar. "How fortunate, after all," thought he, "that there is cognac in the world!" Then he went into the bedroom, where he lighted the candle on the night-table, put out the light in the other room, and began to undress. Piece by piece he put down his good, unobtrusive grey suit on the red chair beside the bed; but then as he loosened his braces he remembered his hat and overcoat, which still lay on the couch. He fetched them into the bedroom and opened the wardrobe.... He took a step backwards and reached behind him to clutch one of the large dark-red mahogany balls which ornamented the bedposts. The room, with its four white walls, from which the three pink chairs stood out like strawberries from whipped cream, lay in the unstable light of the candle. But the wardrobe over there was open and it was not empty. Somebody was standing in it, a creature so lovely that Albrecht van der Qualen's heart stood still a moment and then in long, deep, quiet throbs resumed its beating. She was quite nude and one of her slender arms reached up to crook a forefinger round one of the hooks in the ceiling of the wardrobe. Long waves of brown hair rested on the childlike shoulders – they breathed that charm to which the only answer is a sob. The candlelight was mirrored in her narrow black eyes. Her mouth was a little large, but it had an expression as sweet as the lips of sleep when after long days of pain they kiss our brow. Her ankles nestled and her slender limbs clung to one another.

Albrecht van der Qualen rubbed one hand over his eyes and stared... and he saw that down in the right corner the sacking was loosened from the back of the wardrobe. "What –" said he... "won't you come in – or how should I put it – out? Have a little glass of cognac? Half a glass?" But he expected no answer to this and he got none. Her narrow, shining eyes, so very black that they seemed bottomless and inexpressive – they were directed upon him, but aimlessly and somewhat blurred, as though they did not see him.

"Shall I tell you a story?" she said suddenly in a low, husky voice.

"Tell me a story," he answered. He had sunk down in a sitting posture on the edge of the bed, his overcoat lay across his knees with his folded hands resting upon it. His mouth stood a little open, his eyes half-closed. But the blood pulsated warm and mildly through his body and there was a gentle singing in his ears. She had let herself down in the cupboard and embraced a drawn-up knee with her slender arms, while the other leg stretched out before her. Her little breasts were pressed together by her upper arm, and the light gleamed on the skin of her flexed knee. She talked . . . talked in a soft voice, while the candle-flame performed its noiseless dance.

Two walked on the heath and her head lay on his shoulder. There was a perfume from all growing things, but the evening mist already rose from the ground. So it began. And often it was in verse, rhyming in that incomparably sweet and flowing way that comes to us now and again in the half-slumber of fever. But it ended badly; a sad ending: the two holding each other indissolubly embraced and, while their lips rest on each other, one stabbing the other above the waist with a broad knife – and not without good cause. So it ended. And then she stood up with an infinitely sweet and modest gesture, lifted the grey sacking at the right-hand corner – and was no more there.

From now on he found her every evening in the wardrobe and listened to her stories – how many evenings? How many days, weeks, or months did he remain in this house and in this city? It would profit nobody to know. Who would care for a miserable statistic? And we are aware that Albrecht van der Qualen had been told by several physicians that he had but a few months to live. She told him stories. They were sad stories, without relief; but they rested like a sweet burden upon the heart and made it beat longer and more blissfully. Often he forgot himself. – His blood swelled up in him, he stretched out his hands to her, and she did not resist him. But then for several evenings he did not find her in the wardrobe, and when she came back she did not tell him anything for several evenings and then by degrees resumed, until he again forgot himself.

How long it lasted – who knows? Who even knows whether Albrecht van der Qualen actually awoke on that grey afternoon and went into the unknown city; whether he did not remain asleep in his first-class carriage and let the Berlin–Rome express bear him swiftly over the mountains? Would any of us care to take the responsibility of giving a definite answer? It is all uncertain. "Everything must be in the air. . . ."

THE WAY TO THE CHURCHYARD

THE WAY to the churchyard ran along beside the highroad, ran beside it all the way to the end; that is to say, to the churchyard. On the other side of it were houses, new suburban houses, some of them still unfinished; after the houses came fields. The highroad was flanked by trees, gnarled beeches of considerable age, and half of it was paved and half not. But the way to the churchyard had a sprinkling of gravel, which made it seem like a pleasant foot-path. Between highroad and path ran a narrow dry ditch, filled with grass and wild flowers.

It was spring, it was nearly summer. The world was smiling, God's blue sky was filled with nothing but small, round, dense little morsels of cloud, tufted all over with funny little dabs of snowy white. The birds were twittering in the beeches, and a soft wind blew across the fields.

A wagon from the next village was going along the highroad towards the town, half on the paved, half on the unpaved part of the road. The driver's legs were hanging down both sides of the shaft, he was whistling out of tune. At the end of the wagon, with its back to the driver, sat a little yellow dog. It had a pointed muzzle and it gazed with an unspeakably solemn and collected air back over the way by which it had come. It was a most admirable little dog, good as gold, a pleasure to contemplate. But no, it does not belong to the matter in hand, we must pass it by. – A troop of soldiers came along, from the barracks close at hand; they marched in their own dust and sang. Another wagon passed, coming from the town and going to the next village. The driver was asleep and there was no dog; hence this wagon is devoid of interest. Two journeymen followed after it, one of them a giant, the other a hunchback. They walked barefoot, because they were carrying their boots on their backs; they shouted a good-natured greeting to the sleeping driver and went their way. Yes, this was but a moderate traffic, which pursued its ends without complications or incidents.

On the path to the churchyard walked a single figure, going slowly, with bent head, and leaning on a black stick. This man was named Piepsam, Praisegod Piepsam and no other name. I mention it expressly because of his ensuing most singular behaviour.

He wore black, for he was on his way to visit the graves of his loved ones. He had on a furry top hat with a wide brim, a frock-coat shiny with age, trousers both too tight and too short, and black kid gloves with all the shine rubbed off. His neck, a long, shrivelled neck with a huge Adam's apple, rose out of a frayed turn-over collar – yes, this turn-over collar was already rough at the corners. Sometimes the man raised his head to see how far away the churchyard still was; and then you got a glimpse of a strange face, a face, unquestionably, which you would not easily forget.

It was smooth-shaven and pallid. But a knobbly nose stuck out between the sunken cheeks, and this nose glowed with immoderate and unnatural redness and swarmed with little pimples, unhealthy excrescences which gave it an uneven and fantastic outline. The deep glow of the nose stood out against the dead paleness of the face; there was something artificial and improbable about it, as though he had put it on, like a carnival nose, and was wearing it as a sort of funereal joke. But it was no joke. – His mouth was big, with drooping corners, and he held it tightly compressed. His eyebrows were black, strewn with little white hairs, and when he glanced up from the ground he lifted them till they disappeared under the brim of his hat and you got a good view of the pathetically inflamed and red-rimmed eyes. In short, this was a face bound in the end to evoke one's pity.

Praisegod Piepsam's appearance was not enlivening, it fitted ill into the lovely afternoon; even for a man who was visiting the graves of his dear departed he looked much too depressed. His inner man, however, could one have seen within him, amply explained and justified the outward state. Yes, he was a bit depressed, a bit unhappy, a little hardly treated – is it so hard for happy people like yourselves to enter into his feelings? But the fact was, things were not going just a little badly with him, they were bad in a very high degree.

In the first place, he drank. We shall come on to that later. And he was a widower, bereft and forsaken of all the world, there was not a soul on earth to love him. His wife, born Lebzelt, had been taken from him six months before, when she had presented him with a child. It was the third child, and it was born dead. The others were dead too, one of diphtheria, the other of nothing in particular, save general insufficiency. And as though that were not enough, he had lost his job, been deprived with contumely of his position and his daily bread – naturally on account of his vice, which was stronger than Piepsam.

Once he had been able to resist it, to some extent, though yielding to it by bouts. But when his wife and child were snatched from him, when he had no work and no position, nothing to support him, when he stood alone on this earth, then his weakness took more and more the upper hand. He had been a clerk in the office of a benefit society, a sort of superior copyist who got ninety marks a month. But he had been drunken and negligent and after repeated warnings had finally been discharged.

Certainly this did not improve Piepsam's morale. Indeed he declined more and more to his fall. Wretchedness, in fact, is destructive to our human dignity and self-respect – it does us no harm to get a little understanding of these matters. For there is much that is strange about them, not to say thrilling. It does the man no good to keep on protesting that he is not guilty, for in most cases he despises himself for his own unhappiness. And self-contempt and bad conduct stand in the most frightful mutual relation: they feed each other, they play into each other's hands, in a way shocking to behold. Thus was it with Piepsam. He drank because he had no self-respect, and he had no self-respect because the continual breakdown of his good intentions ate it away. At home in his wardrobe he kept a bottle with a poisonous-coloured liquor in it, the name of which I will refrain from mentioning. Before this wardrobe Praisegod Piepsam had before now gone literally on his knees, and in his wrestlings had bitten his tongue – and still in the end capitulated. I do not like even to mention such things – but after all they are very instructive.

Now he was taking his way to the churchyard, striking his black stick before him as he went. The gentle breeze played about his nose too, but he felt it not. A lost and most miserable human being, he stared straight ahead of him with lifted brows. – Suddenly he heard a noise behind him and listened; it was a little rustling sound coming on swiftly from the distance. He turned round and stopped. – A bicycle was approaching at full tilt, its pneumatic tyres crunching the gravel; it slowed down because Piepsam stood directly in the way.

A young man perched on the saddle, a youth, a blithe and carefree cyclist. He made no claims to belong to the great and mighty of this earth – oh, dear me, not at all! He rode a cheapish machine, of no matter what make, worth perhaps two hundred marks, at a guess. On it he rode abroad, he came out from the city and the sun glittered on his pedals as he rode straight into God's great out-of-doors – hurrah, hurrah! He wore a coloured shirt with a grey jacket, gaiters, and the sauciest cap in the world, a perfect joke of a cap, brown checks and a button on top. Underneath it a thick sheaf of blond hair stuck out on his forehead. His eyes were blue lightnings. He came on, like life itself, ringing his bell. But Piepsam did not budge a hair's breadth out of the way. He stood there and looked at Life – unbudgeably.

Life flung him an angry glance and went past – whereupon Piepsam too began to move forwards. When Life got abreast of him he said slowly, with dour emphasis:

"Number nine thousand seven hundred and seven." He clipped his lips together and looked unflinchingly at the ground, feeling Life's angry eye upon him.

Life had turned round, grasping the saddle behind it with one hand and slowly pedalling.

"What did you say?" asked Life.

"Number nine thousand seven hundred and seven," Piepsam reiterated. "Oh, nothing. I am going to report you."

"You are going to report me?" asked Life; turned round still further and rode still slower, so that it had to keep its balance by straightening the handle-bars.

"Certainly," said Piepsam, some five or six paces away.

"Why?" asked Life, getting off. It stood there in an expectant attitude.

"You know very well yourself."

"No, I do not know."

"You must know."

"No, I do not know," said Life, "and besides, it interests me very little, I must say." It turned to its bicycle as though to mount. Life certainly had a tongue in its head.

"I am going to report you for riding here on the path to the churchyard instead of out on the highroad," said Piepsam.

"But, my dear sir," said Life with a short impatient laugh, turning round again, "look at the marks of bicycles all the way along. Everybody uses this path."

"It makes no difference to me," replied Piepsam. "I am going to report you all the same."

"Just as you please," said Life, and mounted its machine. It really mounted at one go, with a single push of the foot, secured its seat in the saddle, and bent to the task of getting up as much speed as its temperament required.

"Well, if you go on riding here on the foot-path I will certainly report you," said Piepsam again, his voice rising and trembling. But Life paid no attention at all; it went on gathering speed.

If you could have seen Praisegod Piepsam's face at that moment, it would have shocked you deeply. He compressed his lips so tightly that his cheeks and even his red-hot nose were drawn out of shape. His eyebrows were lifted as high as they would go and he stared after the departing bicycle with a maniac expression. Suddenly he gave a forward rush and covered running the small space between him and Life. He laid hold on the little leather pocket behind the saddle and held fast with both hands. He clung to it with lips drawn out of human semblance, and tugged wild-eyed and speechless, with all his strength, at the moving and wobbling machine. It seemed from the appearances in doubt whether he was seeking with malice aforethought to stop it or whether he had been struck with the idea of mounting behind Life and riding with glittering pedals into God's great out-of-doors, hurrah, hurrah! No bicycle could stand the weight; it stopped, it leaned over, it fell.

But now Life became violent. It had come to a stop with one leg on the ground; it stretched out its right arm and gave Herr Piepsam such a push in the chest that he staggered several steps backwards. Then it said, its voice swelling to a threat:

"You are probably drunk, fellow! But if you continue to try to stop me, my fine lad, I'll just chop you into little bits – do you understand? I'll tear you limb from limb. Kindly get that through your head." Then Life turned its back on Herr Piepsam, pulled its cap furiously down on its brow, and once more mounted its bicycle. Yes, Life certainly had a tongue in its head. And it mounted as neatly as before, in one go, settled into the saddle, and had the machine at once under control. Piepsam saw its back retreating faster and faster.

He stood there gasping, staring after Life. And Life did not fall over, no mishap occurred, no tyre burst, no stone lay in the way. It moved off on its rubber wheels. Then Piepsam began to shriek and rail; his voice was no longer melancholy at all, you might call it a roar.

"You are not to go on!" he shouted. "You shall not go on. You are to ride out on the road and not here on the way to the churchyard – do you hear? Get off, get off at once! I will report you, I will enter an action against you. Oh, Lord, oh, God, if you were to fall off, if you would only fall off, you rascally windbag, I would stamp on you, I would stamp on your face with my boots, you damned villain, you –"

Never was seen such a sight. A man raving mad on the way to the churchyard, a man with his face swollen with roaring, a man dancing with rage, capering, flinging his arms about, quite out of control. The bicycle was out of sight by this time, but still Piepsam stood where he was and raved.

"Stop him, stop him! Ride on the path to the churchyard, will he? You blackguard! You outrageous puppy, you! You damned monkey, I'd like to skin you alive, you with the blue eyes, you silly cur, you windbag, you blockhead, you ignorant ninny! You get off! Get off this very minute! Won't anybody pitch him off in the dirt? Riding, eh? On the way to the churchyard! Pull him down, damned puppy.... Oh, if I had hold of you, eh? What wouldn't I do? Devil scratch your eyes out, you ignorant, ignorant, ignorant fool!"

Piepsam went on from this to expressions which cannot be set down. Foaming at the mouth, he uttered the most shameless objurgations, while his voice cracked in his throat and his writhings grew more fantastic. A few children with a fox-terrier and a basket crossed over from the road; they climbed the ditch, surrounded the shrieking man and peered into his distorted face. Some labourers at work on the new houses, just about to take their mid-day rest, saw that something was going on and joined the group – there were both men and women among them. But Piepsam went on, his frenzy grew worse and worse. Blind with rage he shook his fist at all four quarters of the heavens, whirled round on himself, bounded and bent his knees and bobbed up again in the extremity of his effort to shriek even louder. He did not stop for breath and where all his words came from was the greatest wonder. His face was frightfully puffed out, his top hat sat on the back of his neck, and his shirt hung out of his waistcoat. By now he had passed on from the particular to the general and was making remarks which had nothing at all to do with the situation: references to his own vicious mode of life, and religious allusions which certainly sounded strange in such a voice, mingled as they were with his dissolute curses.

"Come on, come on, all of you!" he bellowed. "Not only you and you and you but all the rest of you, with your blue-lightning eyes and your little caps with buttons. I will shriek the truth in your ears and it will fill you with everlasting horror.... So you are grinning, so you are shrugging your shoulders? I drink... well, yes, of course I drink. I am even a drunkard, if you want to know. What does that signify? It is not yet the last day of all. The day will come, you good-for-nothing vermin, when God shall weigh us all in the balance... ah, the Son of Man shall come in the clouds, you filth, and His justice is not of this world. He will hurl you into outer darkness, all you light-headed breed, and there shall be wailing and..."

He was now surrounded by a crowd of some size. People were laughing at him, some were frowning. More hod-carriers and labourers, men and women, came over from the unfinished buildings. A driver got down from his wagon and jumped the ditch, whip in hand. One man shook Piepsam by the arm, but nothing came of it. A troop of soldiers marched by, turning to look at the scene and laughing. The fox-terrier could no longer contain itself; it braced its fore-feet and howled into Piepsam's face with its tail between its legs.

Then Praisegod Piepsam screamed once more with all his strength: "Get off, get off at once, you ignorant fool!" He described with one arm a wide half-circle – and collapsed. He lay there, his voice abruptly silenced, a black heap surrounded by the curious throng. His wide-brimmed hat blew off, bounced once, and then lay on the ground.

Two masons bent over the motionless Piepsam and considered his case in the moderate and reasonable tone that working-people have. One of them then got on his legs and went off at a run. The other made experiments with the unconscious man. He sprinkled him with water from a tub, he poured out brandy in the hollow of his hand and rubbed

Piepsam's temples with it. None of these efforts was crowned with success.

Some little time passed. Then the sound of wheels was heard and a wagon came along the road. It was an ambulance with a great red cross on each side, drawn by two charming little horses. Two men in neat uniforms got down from the box; one went to the back of the wagon, opened it, and drew out a stretcher; the other ran over to the path, pushed away the yokels standing round Piepsam, and with the help of one of them got Herr Piepsam out of the crowd and into the road. He was laid out on the stretcher and shoved into the wagon as one shoves a loaf of bread into the oven. The door clicked shut and the two men climbed back on to the box. All that went off very efficiently, with but few and practised motions, as though in a theatre. And then they drove Praisegod Piepsam away.

THE HUNGRY

THERE CAME the moment when Detlef was struck by the sense of his own superfluity; as though by chance he let himself be borne away by the bustling throng and disappeared from the sight of his two companions without taking leave.

He gave himself to the current which bore him the whole length of the splendid auditorium; not until he knew that he was far away from Lily and the little painter did he resist the tide and stop in his tracks. He was by then near the stage, leaning against the heavily gilt projecting front of a proscenium box, between a bearded baroque caryatid with neck bent to his burden and his female counterpart whose swelling bosoms were thrust out into the hall. He put on as well as he could the air of a complacent observer, lifting his glasses now and then to his eyes – but in the brilliant circle which they swept he avoided one single point.

The fête was at its height. At the back of these swelling boxes eating and drinking were going on at laden tables, gentlemen in black and coloured dress suits, with mammoth chrysanthemums in their buttonholes, bent over the powdered shoulders of fantastically garbed and extravagantly coiffed ladies, talking and pointing down upon the motley and the bustle in the hall below as it formed eddies and currents, got choked and streamed on again, in quick and colourful play.

There were women in flowing robes, with barge-shaped hats fastened in outlandish curves beneath their chins, leaning on tall staves, holding long-handled lorgnons to their eyes. The puffed sleeves of the men came almost to the brims of their grey top hats. Loud jests mounted to the upper tiers, healths were wafted thitherwards in brimming glasses of champagne and beer. People pushed their way up closer to the stage and stood craning their necks to see the screaming turn then being performed. When the curtains rustled together, everybody pushed away again amid laughter and applause. The orchestra blared. The crowd wreathed and sauntered in and out and to and fro. The golden-yellow light, far brighter than day, gave brilliance to every eye; every breast heaved with quickened breath, idly yet avidly drinking in the intoxication of an atmosphere reeking with odours of food and drink, flowers and scent, dust and over-heated human flesh.

The orchestra stopped. People stood where they were, arm in arm, looking up at the stage, where a new turn was beginning with a din of sound. Four or five actors in peasant costume were parodying with clarinets and stringed instruments the chromatic wrestlings of the *Tristan* music. Detlef closed his eyes a moment, the lids burned. His senses were so keen that even this wanton distortion of the music could not fail to bring home to him poignantly that yearning for unity which it supremely expresses. It evoked in him overwhelmingly the suffocating melancholy of the lonely man who has lost himself in love and longing for some light and common child of life.

Lily. His soul, in imploring tenderness, shaped the name; his gaze, do what he would, turned towards her distant form. Yes, they were still there, they stood on the spot where he had left them and as the crowd thinned he would catch glimpses of her figure, leaning against the wall in her milk-white, silver-trimmed gown; her head slightly on one side, she talked with the little artist and looked into his eyes with lingering, mischievous gaze. And his eyes were just as blue, just as wide apart and unclouded as her own.

Ah, that prattle of theirs, flowing so blithely from an inexhaustible fount of simple, artless, unassuming gaiety – how could he share in it, he, a slow and serious man whose life was compact of knowledge and dreams, of paralysing insight and the inexorable urge to create! So he had left them, stolen away in a spasm of defiance and despair, in which there mingles a queer sort of magnanimity; stolen away and left these two children of life to themselves. But even at this distance came the strangling jealousy in his throat with the knowledge that they had smiled with relief at being freed of his oppressive presence.

Why had he come, why had he come here again? To move, with his tormented soul, among these carefree throngs, knowing himself to be with but not of them? Ah, well he knew! Why then this craving for contact with them? "We lonely ones," so he had written once in a quiet hour of self-communing, "we isolated dreamers, disinherited of life, who spend our introspective days remote in an artificial, icy air and spread abroad a cold breath as from strange regions so soon as we come among living human beings and they see our brows marked with the sign of knowledge and of fear; we poor ghosts of life, who are met with an embarrassed glance and left to ourselves as soon as possible, that our hollow and knowledgeable eye may not blight all joy... we all cherish a hidden and unappeased yearning for the harmless, simple, and real in life; for a little friendly, devoted, familiar human happiness. That 'life' from which we are shut out – we do not envisage it as wild beauty and cruel splendour, it is not as the extraordinary that we crave it, we extraordinary ones. The kingdom of our longing love is the realm of the pleasant, the normal, and the respectable, it is life in all its tempting, banal everydayness that we want...."

He looked over at them again as they stood there talking. The whole hall rang with shouts of laughter and the whining of the clarinets, as the passionate, cloying music was being distorted into shrieking sentimentality. "That is you," he thought. "You are warm, mad, sweet and lovely life, that which stands in eternal opposition to the spirit. Think not that it despises you. Think not it feels one single motion of contempt. Ah, no, we abase ourselves, we denizens of the profound, mute with our monstrous weight of knowledge, we stand afar and in our eyes there burns an avid longing to be like you.

"Do we feel pride stirring? Would we deny that we are lonely? Does our self-respect make us boast that the motions of the spirit bring to love a loftier union with life, at all times and in all places? Ah, but with whom, with what? Always only with our like, with the suffering and the yearning and the poor – never with you, you blue-eyed ones who have no need of spirit!"

Now the curtains had fallen again, dancing began afresh. The band crashed and lilted. Couples turned and glided, wove in and out upon the polished floor. And Lily danced with the little painter. How pricelessly her dainty head rose out of the stiff chalice of her silver-embroidered collar! They moved in a constricted space, with effortless, elastic turnings and pacings. His face was turned towards hers, they continued to talk and smile as they moved in obedience to the sweet and trivial measures from the band.

Suddenly the lonely man felt his spirit reach out to grasp and form as with hands. "After all, you are mine," he thought, "and I am above you. Can I not see through your simple souls with a smile? Do I not observe and perpetuate, half in love and half in mockery, each naïve motion that you make? The sight of your artless activities arouses in me the forces of the Word, the power of irony. It makes my heart beat with desire and the lustful knowledge that I can reshape you as I will and by my art expose your foolish joys for the world to gape at." But then all his defiance collapsed again quite suddenly, leaving only dull longing in its wake. Ah, to be not an artist but a man, if only once, if only on a night like this! If only once to escape the inexorable doom which rang in his ears: "You may not live, you must create; you may not love, you must know." Ah, just once to live, to love and to give thanks, to feel and know that feeling is all! Just once to share your life, ye living ones, just once to drink in magic draughts the bliss of the commonplace!

He shuddered and turned away. As he looked at all these

charming, over-heated faces it seemed to him that they peered into his and then turned away in disgust. He was overpowered by a desire to void the field, to seek out stillness and darkness – yes, he would go away, withdraw without a word, as he had withdrawn from Lily's side; go home and lay his burning, throbbing head upon a cool pillow. He strode to the exit.

Would she see him go? He was so used to this sensation, this going away, this silent, proud, despairing withdrawal from a room, a garden, from any place where society was gathered, with the secret hope of causing even one pang in the light heart of her for whom he longed! He paused, looked across at her again; he implored her in his thoughts. Should he stay, stick it out, should he remain near her, though separated by the length of the hall, remain and await some unhoped-for bliss? No, it would all be in vain. There would be no approach, no understanding, no hope. – "Go out into the darkness, put your head in your hands and weep, if you can – if in your world of rigid desolation, of ice, of spirit, and of art there are tears left to shed." – He left the hall.

He felt a burning, gnawing pain in his breast and at the same time a wild and senseless expectation. She *must* see him, must understand, must come, must follow him, even if only out of pity; must come half-way and say to him: Stay here, be glad, I love you. He moved very slowly, although well he knew, was certain to the point of absurdity, that she would not come at all, that little laughing, dancing, chattering Lily!

It was two o'clock. The corridors were empty and behind the long tables in the cloak-room the attendants nodded sleepily. No one but himself thought of going home. He wrapped himself in his cloak, took his hat and stick, and left the theatre.

Long rows of carriages stood on the square; lamps illumined the white mist of the winter night. The horses stood blanketed, with hanging heads; groups of well-bundled coachmen stamped the hard snow to warm their feet. Detlef beckoned to one, and as the man uncovered his horse he waited in the vestibule and let the cool dry air play about his throbbing temples.

The flat after-taste of the champagne made him want a smoke. Mechanically he drew out a cigarette and lighted it. But at the moment when the match went out he saw something strange. He did not at first understand it and stood there puzzled and aghast, with hanging arms. He could not get over it, could not put it out of his mind.

Out of the dark, as his vision recovered from the blindness caused by the flame from the match, there came a red-bearded, hollow-cheeked, lawless face, with horribly inflamed, red-rimmed eyes that stared with sardonic despair and a certain greedy curiosity into his own. The owner of this anguished face stood only two or three paces off, leaning against one of the lamp-posts which flanked the entrance of the theatre, with fists thrust deep into his trouser pockets and the collar of his tattered jacket turned up. His gaze travelled over Detlef's whole figure, from the opera-glass round the neck, down over the fur coat to the patent-leather shoes, then back again to search the other's face with that avid stare. Once the man gave a short, contemptuous snort; then his body relaxed, he shuddered, his flabby cheeks seemed to grow even hollower, while the eyelids quivered and closed and the mouth drooped at the corners with an expression both tragic and malign.

Detlef stood transfixed. He struggled to understand. He had a sudden insight as to how he must look as he stood there; his air of prosperity and well-being as he left the gay gathering, beckoned to the coachman, took the cigarette from his silver box. Involuntarily he lifted his hand in the act to strike his brow. He took a step towards the man, he drew breath to speak, to explain – but what he did was to mount silently into the waiting carriage, almost forgetting, in his distraction, to give the coachman his address. He was confounded by the inadequacy of any explanation he might make.

My God, what an error, what a crass misunderstanding! This starving, outcast man had looked at him with the bitter craving, the violent scorn that spring from envy and longing. Had he not put himself there to be looked at, this hungry man? Had not his shivering body, his tragic and malignant face, been deliberately calculated to make an impression, to give him, Detlef – as an arrogantly happy human being – one moment of misgiving, of sympathy, of distress – But you mistake, my friend – that was not the effect they had. "You thought to show me a horrifying warning out of a strange and frightful world, to arouse my remorse. But we are *brothers*.

"Have you a weight here, my friend, a burning weight on your breast? How well I know it! And why did you come? Why did you not hug your misery in the shadow instead of taking your stand under the lighted windows behind which are music and laughter? Do not I too know the morbid yearning that drove thee hither, to feed this thy wretchedness, which may just as well be called love as hate?

"Nothing is strange to me of all the sorrow that moves thee – and thou thoughtest to shame me! What is mind but the play of hatred? What art, but yearning in act to create? We are both at home in the land of the betrayed, the hungering, the lamenting, the denying; and common to us both are those hours full of betraying self-contempt, when we lose ourselves in a shameful love of life and of mad happiness.

"Wrong, all wrong!" – And as this pity wholly filled him he felt kindled somewhere deep within an intuition at once painful and sweet. "Is it only he who errs? Where is the end of error? Is not all longing on earth an error, this of mine first of all, which craves the simple and the instinctive, dumb life itself, ignorant of the enlightenment which comes through mind and art, the release through the Word? Ah, we are all brothers, we creatures of the restlessly suffering will, yet we do not recognize ourselves as such. Another love is needed, another love."

And when at home he sat among his books and pictures, and the busts ranged along the wall looked down upon him, he felt moved to utter those gentle words:

"Little children, love one another."

TRISTAN

EINFRIED, THE sanatorium. A long, white, rectilinear building with a side wing, set in a spacious garden pleasingly equipped with grottoes, bowers, and little bark pavilions. Behind its slate roofs the mountains tower heavenwards, evergreen, massy, cleft with wooded ravines.

Now as then Dr Leander directs the establishment. He wears a two-pronged black beard as curly and wiry as horsehair stuffing; his spectacle-lenses are thick, and glitter; he has the look of a man whom science has cooled and hardened and filled with silent, forbearing pessimism. And with this beard, these lenses, this look, and in his short, reserved, preoccupied way, he holds his patients in his spell: holds those sufferers who, too weak to be laws unto themselves, put themselves into his hands that his severity may be a shield unto them.

As for Fräulein von Osterloh, hers it is to preside with unwearying zeal over the housekeeping. Ah, what activity! How she plies, now here, now there, now upstairs, now down, from one end of the building to the other! She is queen in kitchen and storerooms, she mounts the shelves of the linen-presses, she marshals the domestic staff; she ordains the bill of fare, to the end that the table shall be economical, hygienic, attractive, appetizing, and all these in the highest degree; she keeps house diligently, furiously; and her exceeding capacity conceals a constant reproach to the world of men, to no one of whom has it yet occurred to lead her to the altar. But ever on her cheeks there glows, in two round, carmine spots, the unquenchable hope of one day becoming Frau Dr Leander.

Ozone, and stirless, stirless air! Einfried, whatever Dr. Leander's rivals and detractors may choose to say about it, can be most warmly recommended for lung patients. And not only these, but patients of all sorts, gentlemen, ladies, even children, come to stop here. Dr Leander's skill is challenged in many different fields. Sufferers from gastric disorders come, like Frau Magistrate Spatz – she has ear trouble into the bargain – people with defective hearts, paralytics, rheumatics, nervous sufferers of all kinds and degrees. A diabetic general here consumes his daily bread amid continual grumblings. There are several gentlemen with gaunt, fleshless faces who fling their legs about in that uncontrollable way that bodes no good. There is an elderly lady, a Frau Pastor Höhlenrauch, who has brought fourteen children into the world and is now incapable of a single thought, yet has not thereby attained to any peace of mind, but must go roving spectre-like all day long up and down through the house, on the arm of her private attendant, as she has been doing this year past.

Sometimes a death takes place among the "severe cases", those who lie in their chambers, never appearing at meals or in the reception-rooms. When this happens no one knows of it, not even the person sleeping next door. In the silence of the night the waxen guest is put away and life at Einfried goes tranquilly on, with its massage, its electric treatment, douches, baths; with its exercises, its steaming and inhaling, in rooms especially equipped with all the triumphs of modern therapeutic.

Yes, a deal happens hereabouts – the institution is in a flourishing way. When new guests arrive, at the entrance to the side wing, the porter sounds the great gong; when there are departures, Dr Leander, together with Fräulein von Osterloh, conducts the traveller in due form to the waiting carriage. All sorts and kinds of people have received hospitality at Einfried. Even an author is here stealing time from God Almighty – a queer sort of man, with a name like some kind of mineral or precious stone.

Lastly there is, besides Dr Leander, another physician, who

takes care of the slight cases and the hopeless ones. But he bears the name of Müller and is not worth mentioning.

At the beginning of January a business man named Klöterjahn – of the firm of A. C. Klöterjahn & Co. – brought his wife to Einfried. The porter rang the gong, and Fräulein von Osterloh received the guests from a distance in the drawing-room on the ground floor, which, like nearly all the fine old mansion, was furnished in wonderfully pure Empire style. Dr Leander appeared straightaway. He made his best bow, and a preliminary conversation ensued, for the better information of both sides.

Beyond the windows lay the wintry garden, the flower-beds covered with straw, the grottoes snowed under, the little temples forlorn. Two porters were dragging in the guests' trunks from the carriage drawn up before the wrought-iron gate – for there was no drive up to the house.

"Be careful, Gabriele, *doucement, doucement*, my angel, keep your mouth closed," Herr Klöterjahn had said as he led his wife through the garden; and nobody could look at her without tender-heartedly echoing the caution – though, to be sure, Herr Klöterjahn might quite as well have uttered it all in his own language.

The coachman who had driven the pair from the station to the sanatorium was an uncouth man, and insensitive; yet he sat with his tongue between his teeth as the husband lifted down his wife. The very horses, steaming in the frosty air, seemed to follow the procedure with their eyeballs rolled back in their heads out of sheer concern for so much tenderness and fragile charm.

The young wife's trouble was her trachea; it was expressly so set down in the letter Herr Klöterjahn had sent from the shores of the Baltic to announce their impending arrival to the director of Einfried – the trachea, and not the lungs, thank God! But it is a question whether, if it had been the lungs, the new patient could have looked any more pure and ethereal, any remoter from the concerns of this world, than she did now as she leaned back pale and weary in her chaste white-enamelled arm-chair, beside her robust husband, and listened to the conversation.

Her beautiful white hands, bare save for the simple wedding-ring, rested in her lap, among the folds of a dark, heavy cloth skirt; she wore a close-fitting waist of silver-grey with a stiff collar – it had an all-over pattern of arabesques in high-pile velvet. But these warm, heavy materials only served to bring out the unspeakable delicacy, sweetness, and languor of the little head, to make it look more than ever touching, exquisite, and unearthly. Her light-brown hair was drawn smoothly back and gathered in a knot low in her neck, but near the right temple a single lock fell loose and curling, not far from the place where an odd little vein branched across one well-marked eyebrow, pale-blue and sickly amid all that pure, well-nigh transparent spotlessness. That little blue vein above the eye dominated quite painfully the whole fine oval of the face. When she spoke, it stood out still more; yes even when she smiled – and lent her expression a touch of strain, if not actually of distress, that stirred vague fear in the beholder. And yet she spoke, and she smiled: spoke frankly and pleasantly in her rather husky voice, with a smile in her eyes – though they again were sometimes a little diffident and showed a tendency to avoid a direct gaze. And the corners of her eyes, both sides the base of the slender little nose, were deeply shadowed. She smiled with her mouth too, her beautiful wide mouth, whose lips were so pale and yet seemed to flash – perhaps because their contours were so exceedingly pure and well-cut. Sometimes she cleared her throat, then carried her handkerchief to her mouth and afterwards looked at it.

"Don't clear your throat like that, Gabriele," said Herr Klöterjahn. "You know, darling, Dr Hinzpeter expressly forbade it, and what we have to do is to exercise self-control, my angel. As I said, it is the trachea," he repeated. "Honestly, when it began, I thought it was the lungs, and it gave me a scare, I do assure you. But it isn't the lungs – we don't mean to let ourselves in for that, do we, Gabriele, my love, eh? Ha ha!"

"Surely not," said Dr Leander, and glittered at her with his eye-glasses.

Whereupon Herr Klöterjahn ordered coffee, coffee and rolls; and the speaking way he had of sounding the *c* far back in his throat and exploding the *b* in "butter" must have made any soul alive hungry to hear it.

His order was filled; and rooms were assigned to him and his wife, and they took possession with their things.

And Dr Leander took over the case himself, without calling in Dr Müller.

The population of Einfried took unusual interest in the fair new patient; Herr Klöterjahn, used as he was to see homage paid her, received it all with great satisfaction. The diabetic general, when he first saw her, stopped grumbling a minute; the gentlemen with the fleshless faces smiled and did their best to keep their legs in order; as for Frau Magistrate Spatz, she made her her oldest friend on the spot. Yes, she made an impression, this woman who bore Herr Klöterjahn's name! A writer who had been sojourning a few weeks in Einfried, a queer sort, he was, with a name like some precious stone or other, positively coloured up when she passed him in the corridor, stopped stock-still and stood there as though rooted to the ground, long after she had disappeared.

Before two days were out, the whole little population knew her history. She came originally from Bremen, as one could tell by certain pleasant small twists in her pronunciation; and it had been in Bremen that, two years gone by, she had bestowed her hand upon Herr Klöterjahn, a successful business man, and become his life-partner. She had followed him to his native town on the Baltic coast, where she had presented him, some ten months before the time of which we write, and under circumstances of the greatest difficulty and danger, with a child, a particularly well-formed and vigorous son and heir. But since that terrible hour she had never fully recovered her strength – granting, that is, that she had ever had any. She had not been long up, still extremely weak, with extremely impoverished vitality, when one day after coughing she brought up a little blood – oh, not much, an insignificant quantity in fact; but it would have been much better to be none at all; and the suspicious thing was that the same trifling but disquieting incident recurred after another short while. Well, of course, there were things to be done, and Dr Hinzpeter, the family physician, did them. Complete rest was ordered, little pieces of ice swallowed; morphine administered to check the cough, and other medicines to regulate the heart action. But recovery failed to set in; and while the child, Anton Klöterjahn, junior, a magnificent specimen of a baby, seized on his place in life and held it with prodigious energy and ruthlessness, a low, unobservable fever seemed to waste the young mother daily. It was, as we have heard, an affection of the trachea – a word that in Dr Hinzpeter's mouth sounded so soothing, so consoling, so reassuring, that it raised their spirits to a surprising degree. But even though it was not the lungs, the doctor presently found that a milder climate and a stay in a sanatorium were imperative if the cure was to be hastened. The reputation enjoyed by Einfried and its director had done the rest.

Such was the state of affairs; Herr Klöterjahn himself related it to all and sundry. He talked with a slovenly pronunciation, in a loud, good-humoured voice, like a man whose digestion is in as capital order as his pocket-book; shovelling out the words pell-mell, in the broad accents of the northern coast-dweller; hurtling some of them forth so that each sound was a little explosion, at which he laughed as at a successful joke.

He was of medium height, broad, stout, and short-legged; his face full and red, with watery blue eyes shaded by very fair lashes; with wide nostrils and humid lips. He wore English side-whiskers and English clothes, and it enchanted him to discover at Einfried an entire English family, father, mother, and three pretty children with their nurse, who were stopping here for the simple and sufficient reason that they knew not where else to go. With this family he partook of a good

English breakfast every morning. He set great store by good eating and drinking and proved to be a connoisseur both of food and wines, entertaining the other guests with the most exciting accounts of dinners given in his circle of acquaintance back home, with full descriptions of the choicer and rarer dishes; in the telling his eyes would narrow benignly, and his pronunciation take on certain palatal and nasal sounds, accompanied by smacking noises at the back of his throat. That he was not fundamentally averse to earthly joys of another sort was evinced upon an evening when a guest of the cure, an author by calling, saw him in the corridor trifling in not quite permissible fashion with a chambermaid – a humorous little passage at which the author in question made a laughably disgusted face.

As for Herr Klöterjahn's wife, it was plain to see that she was devotedly attached to her husband. She followed his words and movements with a smile: not the rare arrogant toleration the ailing sometimes bestow upon the well and sound, but the sympathetic participation of a well-disposed invalid in the manifestations of people who rejoice in the blessing of abounding health.

Herr Klöterjahn did not stop long in Einfried. He had brought his wife hither, but when a week had gone by and he knew she was in good hands and well looked after, he did not linger. Duties equally weighty – his flourishing child, his no less flourishing business – took him away; they compelled him to go, leaving her rejoicing in the best of care.

Spinell was the name of that author who had been stopping some weeks in Einfried – Detlev Spinell was his name, and his looks were quite out of the common. Imagine a dark man at the beginning of the thirties, impressively tall, with hair already distinctly grey at the temples, and a round, white, slightly bloated face, without a vestige of beard. Not that it was shaven – that you could have told; it was soft, smooth, boyish, with at most a downy hair here and there. And the effect was singular. His bright, doe-like brown eyes had a gentle expression, the nose was thick and rather too fleshy.

Also, Herr Spinell had an upper lip like an ancient Roman's, swelling and full of pores; large, carious teeth, and feet of uncommon size. One of the gentlemen with the rebellious legs, a cynic and ribald wit, had christened him "the dissipated baby"; but the epithet was malicious, and not very apt. Herr Spinell dressed well, in a long black coat and a waistcoat with coloured spots.

He was unsocial and sought no man's company. Only once in a while he might be overtaken by an affable, blithe, expansive mood; and this always happened when he was carried away by an aesthetic fit at the sight of beauty, the harmony of two colours, a vase nobly formed, or the range of mountains lighted by the setting sun. "How beautiful!" he would say, with his head on one side, his shoulders raised, his hands spread out, his lips and nostrils curled and distended. "My God! look, how beautiful!" And in such moments of ardour he was quite capable of flinging his arms blindly round the neck of anybody, high or low, male or female, that happened to be near.

On his table, for anybody to see who entered his room, there always lay the book he had written. It was a novel of medium length, with a perfectly bewildering drawing on the jacket, printed on a sort of filter-paper. Each letter of the type looked like a Gothic cathedral. Fräulein von Osterloh had read it once, in a spare quarter-hour, and found it "very cultured" – which was her circumlocution for inhumanly boresome. Its scenes were laid in fashionable salons, in luxurious boudoirs full of choice *objets d'art*, old furniture, gobelins, rare porcelains, priceless stuffs, and art treasures of all sorts and kinds. On the description of these things was expended the most loving care; as you read you constantly saw Herr Spinell, with distended nostrils, saying: "How beautiful! My God! look, how beautiful!" After all, it was strange he had not written more than this one book; he so obviously adored writing. He spent the greater part of the day doing it, in his room, and sent an extraordinary number of letters to the post, two or three nearly every day – and that made it more striking, even almost funny, that he very seldom received one in return.

Herr Spinell sat opposite Herr Klöterjahn's wife. At the first meal of which the new guests partook, he came rather late into the dining-room, on the ground floor of the side wing, bade good-day to the company generally in a soft voice, and betook himself to his own place, whereupon Dr Leander perfunctorily presented him to the new-comers. He bowed, and self-consciously began to eat, using his knife and fork rather affectedly with the large, finely shaped white hands that came out from his very narrow coat-sleeves. After a little he grew more at ease and looked tranquilly first at Herr Klöterjahn and then at his wife, by turns. And in the course of the meal Herr Klöterjahn addressed to him sundry queries touching the general situation and climate of Einfried; his wife, in her charming way, added a word or two, and Herr Spinell gave courteous answers. His voice was mild, and really agreeable; but he had a halting way of speaking that almost amounted to an impediment – as though his teeth got in the way of his tongue.

After luncheon, when they had gone into the salon, Dr Leander came up to the new arrivals to wish them *Mahlzeit*, and Herr Klöterjahn's wife took occasion to ask about their *vis-à-vis*.

"What was the gentleman's name?" she asked. "I did not quite catch it. Spinelli?"

"Spinell, not Spinelli, madame. No, he is not an Italian; he only comes from Lemberg, I believe."

"And what was it you said? He is an author, or something of the sort?" asked Herr Klöterjahn. He had his hands in the pockets of his very easy-fitting English trousers, cocked his head towards the doctor, and opened his mouth, as some people do, to listen the better.

"Yes . . . I really don't know," answered Dr Leander. "He writes. . . . I believe he has written a book, some sort of novel. I really don't know what."

By which Dr Leander conveyed that he had no great

opinion of the author and declined all responsibility on the score of him.

"But I find that most interesting," said Herr Klöterjahn's wife. Never before had she met an author face to face.

"Oh, yes," said Dr Leander obligingly. "I understand he has a certain amount of reputation," which closed the conversation.

But a little later, when the new guests had retired and Dr Leander himself was about to go, Herr Spinell detained him in talk to put a few questions for his own part.

"What was their name?" he asked. "I did not understand a syllable, of course."

"Klöterjahn," answered Dr Leander, turning away.

"What's that?" asked Herr Spinell.

"*Klöterjahn* is their name," said Dr Leander, and went his way. He set no great store by the author.

Have we got as far on as where Herr Klöterjahn went home? Yes, he was back on the shore of the Baltic once more, with his business and his babe, that ruthless and vigorous little being who had cost his mother great suffering and a slight weakness of the trachea; while she herself, the young wife, remained in Einfried and became the intimate friend of Frau Spatz. Which did not prevent Herr Klöterjahn's wife from being on friendly terms with the rest of the guests – for instance with Herr Spinell who, to the astonishment of everybody, for he had up to now held communion with not a single soul, displayed from the very first an extraordinary devotion and courtesy, and with whom she enjoyed talking whenever she had any time left over from the stern service of the cure.

He approached her with immense circumspection and reverence, and never spoke save with his voice so carefully subdued that Frau Spatz, with her bad hearing, seldom or never caught anything he said. He tiptoed on his great feet up to the arm-chair in which Herr Klöterjahn's wife leaned, fragilely smiling; stopped two paces off, with his body bent forward and one leg poised behind him, and talked in his halting way, as though he had an impediment in his speech; with ardour, yet prepared to retire at any moment and vanish at the first sign of fatigue or satiety. But he did not tire her; she begged him to sit down with her and the Rätin; she asked him questions and listened with curious smiles, for he had a way of talking sometimes that was so odd and amusing, different from anything she had ever heard before.

"Why are you in Einfried, really?" she asked. "What cure are you taking, Herr Spinell?"

"Cure? Oh, I'm having myself electrified a bit. Nothing worth mentioning. I will tell you the real reason why I am here, madame. It is a feeling for style."

"Ah?" said Herr Klöterjahn's wife; supported her chin on her hand and turned to him with exaggerated eagerness, as one does to a child who wants to tell a story.

"Yes, madame. Einfried is perfect Empire. It was once a castle, a summer residence, I am told. This side wing is a later addition, but the main building is old and genuine. There are times when I cannot endure Empire, and then times when I simply must have it in order to attain any sense of well-being. Obviously, people feel one way among furniture that is soft and comfortable and voluptuous, and quite another among the straight lines of these tables, chairs, and draperies. This brightness and hardness, this cold, austere simplicity and reserved strength, madame – it has upon me the ultimate effect of an inward purification and rebirth. Beyond a doubt, it is morally elevating."

"Yes, that is remarkable," she said. "And when I try I can understand what you mean."

Whereto he responded that it was not worth her taking any sort of trouble, and they laughed together. Frau Spatz laughed too and found it remarkable in her turn, though she did not say she understood it.

The reception-room was spacious and beautiful. The high, white folding doors that led to the billiard-room were wide open, and the gentlemen with the rebellious legs were disporting themselves within, others as well. On the opposite side of the room a glass door gave on the broad veranda and the garden. Near the door stood a piano. At a green-covered folding table the diabetic general was playing whist with some other gentlemen. Ladies sat reading or embroidering. The rooms were heated by an iron stove, but the chimney-piece, in the purest style, had coals pasted over with red paper to simulate a fire, and chairs were drawn up invitingly.

"You are an early riser, Herr Spinell," said Herr Klöterjahn's wife. "Two or three times already I have chanced to see you leaving the house at half past seven in the morning."

"An early riser? Ah, with a difference, madame, with a vast difference. The truth is, I rise early because I am such a late sleeper."

"You really must explain yourself, Herr Spinell." Frau Spatz too said she demanded an explanation.

"Well, if one is an early riser, one does not need to get up so early. Or so it seems to me. The conscience, madame, is a bad business. I, and other people like me, work hard all our lives to swindle our consciences into feeling pleased and satisfied. We are feckless creatures, and aside from a few good hours we go around weighted down, sick and sore with the knowledge of our own futility. We hate the useful; we know it is vulgar and unlovely, and we defend this position, as a man defends something that is absolutely necessary to his existence. Yet all the while conscience is gnawing at us, to such an extent that we are simply one wound. Added to that, our whole inner life, our view of the world, our way of working, is of a kind – its effect is frightfully unhealthy, undermining, irritating, and this only aggravates the situation. Well, then, there are certain little counter-irritants, without which we would most certainly not hold out. A kind of decorum, a hygienic regimen, for instance, becomes a necessity for some of us. To get up early, to get up ghastly early, take a cold bath, and go out walking in a snowstorm – that may give us a sense of self-satisfaction that lasts as much as an hour. If I were to act out my true character, I should be lying in bed late into the afternoon. My getting up early is all hypocrisy, believe me."

"Why do you say that, Herr Spinell? On the contrary, I call it self-abnegation." Frau Spatz, too, called it self-abnegation.

"Hypocrisy or self-abnegation – call it what you like, madame. I have such a hideously downright nature –"

"Yes, that's it. Surely you torment yourself far too much."

"Yes, madame, I torment myself a great deal."

The fine weather continued. Rigid and spotless white the region lay, the mountains, house and garden, in a windless air that was blinding clear and cast bluish shadows; and above it arched the spotless pale-blue sky, where myriads of bright particles of glittering crystals seemed to dance. Herr Klöterjahn's wife felt tolerably well these days: free of fever, with scarce any cough, and able to eat without too great distaste. Many days she sat taking her cure for hours on end in the sunny cold on the terrace. She sat in the snow, bundled in wraps and furs, and hopefully breathed in the pure icy air to do her trachea good. Sometimes she saw Herr Spinell, dressed like herself, and in fur boots that made his feet a fantastic size, taking an airing in the garden. He walked with tentative tread through the snow, holding his arms in a certain careful pose that was stiff yet not without grace; coming up to the terrace he would bow very respectfully and mount the first step or so to exchange a few words with her.

"Today on my morning walk I saw a beautiful woman – good Lord! how beautiful she was!" he said; laid his head on one side and spread out his hands.

"Really, Herr Spinell. Do describe her to me."

"That I cannot do. Or, rather, it would not be a fair picture. I only saw the lady as I glanced at her in passing, I did not actually see her at all. But that fleeting glimpse was enough to rouse my fancy and make me carry away a picture so beautiful that – good Lord! how beautiful it is!"

She laughed. "Is that the way you always look at beautiful women, Herr Spinell? Just a fleeting glance?"

"Yes, madame; it is a better way than if I were avid of actuality, stared them plump in the face, and carried away with me only a consciousness of the blemishes they in fact possess."

"'Avid of actuality' – what a strange phrase, a regular literary phrase, Herr Spinell; no one but an author could have said that. It impresses me very much, I must say. There is a lot in it that I dimly understand; there is something free about it, and independent, that even seems to be looking down on reality though it is so very respectable – is respectability itself, as you might say. And it makes me comprehend, too, that there is something else besides the tangible, something more subtle –"

"I know only one face," he said suddenly, with a strange lift in his voice, carrying his closed hands to his shoulders as he spoke and showing his carious teeth in an almost hysterical smile, "I know only one face of such lofty nobility that the mere thought of enhancing it through my imagination would be blasphemous; at which I could wish to look, on which I could wish to dwell, not minutes and not hours, but my whole life long; losing myself utterly therein, forgotten to every earthly thought. . . ."

"Yes, indeed, Herr Spinell. And yet don't you find Fräulein von Osterloh has rather prominent ears?"

He replied only by a profound bow; then, standing erect, let his eyes rest with a look of embarrassment and pain on the strange little vein that branched pale-blue and sickly across her pure translucent brow.

An odd sort, a very odd sort. Herr Klöterjahn's wife thought about him sometimes; for she had much leisure for thought. Whether it was that the change of air began to lose its effect or some positively detrimental influence was at work, she began to go backward, the condition of her trachea left much to be desired, she had fever not infrequently, felt tired and exhausted, and could not eat. Dr Leander most emphatically recommended rest, quiet, caution, care. So she sat, when indeed she was not forced to lie, quite motionless, in the society of Frau Spatz, holding some sort of sewing which she did not sew, and following one or another train of thought.

Yes, he gave her food for thought, this very odd Herr Spinell; and the strange thing was she thought not so much about him as about herself, for he had managed to rouse in her a quite novel interest in her own personality. One day he had said, in the course of conversation:

"No, they are positively the most enigmatic facts in nature – women, I mean. That is a truism, and yet one never ceases to marvel at it afresh. Take some wonderful creature, a sylph, an airy wraith, a fairy dream of a thing, and what does she do? Goes and gives herself to a brawny Hercules at a country fair, or maybe to a butcher's apprentice. Walks about on his arm, even leans her head on his shoulder and looks round with an impish smile as if to say: 'Look on this, if you like, and break your heads over it.' And we break them."

With this speech Herr Klöterjahn's wife had occupied her leisure again and again.

Another day, to the wonderment of Frau Spatz, the following conversation took place:

"May I ask, madame – though you may very likely think me prying – what your name really is?"

"Why, Herr Spinell, you know my name is Klöterjahn!"

"H'm. Yes, I know that – or, rather, I deny it. I mean your own name, your maiden name, of course. You will in justice, madame, admit that anybody who calls you Klöterjahn ought to be thrashed."

She laughed so hard that the little blue vein stood out alarmingly on her brow and gave the pale sweet face a strained expression most disquieting to see.

"Oh, no! Not at all, Herr Spinell! Thrashed, indeed! Is the name Klöterjahn so horrible to you?"

"Yes, madame. I hate the name from the bottom of my heart. I hated it the first time I heard it. It is the abandonment of ugliness; it is grotesque to make you comply with the custom so far as to fasten your husband's name upon you; is barbarous and vile."

"Well, and how about Eckhof? Is that any better? Eckhof is my father's name."

"Ah, you see! Eckhof is quite another thing. There was a great actor named Eckhof. Eckhof will do nicely. You spoke of your father – Then is your mother – ?"

"Yes, my mother died when I was little."

"Ah! Tell me a little more of yourself, pray. But not if it tires you. When it tires you, stop, and I will go on talking about Paris, as I did the other day. But you could speak very softly, or even whisper – that would be more beautiful still. You were born in Bremen?" He breathed, rather than uttered, the question with an expression so awed, so heavy with import, as to suggest that Bremen was a city like no other on earth, full of hidden beauties and nameless adventures, and ennobling in some mysterious way those born within its walls.

"Yes, imagine," said she involuntarily. "I was born in Bremen."

"I was there once," he thoughtfully remarked.

"Goodness me, you have been there, too? Why, Herr Spinell, it seems to me you must have been everywhere there is between Spitzbergen and Tunis!"

"Yes, I was there once," he repeated. "A few hours, one evening. I recall a narrow old street, with a strange, warped-looking moon above the gabled roofs. Then I was in a cellar that smelled of wine and mould. It is a poignant memory."

"Really? Where could that have been, I wonder? Yes, in just such a grey old gabled house I was born, one of the old merchant houses, with echoing wooden floor and white-painted gallery."

"Then your father is a business man?" he asked hesitatingly.

"Yes, but he is also, and in the first place, an artist."

"Ah! In what way?"

"He plays the violin. But just saying that does not mean much. It is *how* he plays, Herr Spinell – it is that that matters! Sometimes I cannot listen to some of the notes without the tears coming into my eyes and making them burn. Nothing else in the world makes me feel like that. You won't believe it – "

"But I do. Oh, very much I believe it! Tell me, madame, your family is old, is it not? Your family has been living for generations in the old gabled house – living and working and closing their eyes on time?"

"Yes. Tell me why you ask."

"Because it not infrequently happens that a race with sober, practical bourgeois traditions will towards the end of its days flare up in some form of art."

"Is that a fact?"

"Yes."

"It is true, my father is surely more of an artist than some that call themselves so and get the glory of it. I only play the piano a little. They have forbidden me now, but at home, in the old days, I still played. Father and I played together. Yes, I have precious memories of all those years; and especially of the garden, our garden, back of the house. It was dreadfully wild and overgrown, and shut in by crumbling mossy walls. But it was just that gave it such charm. In the middle was a fountain with a wide border of sword-lilies. In summer I spent long hours there with my friends. We all sat round the fountain on little camp-stools – "

"How beautiful!" said Herr Spinell, and flung up his shoulders. "You sat there and sang?"

"No, we mostly crocheted."

"But still – "

"Yes, we crocheted and chattered, my six friends and I – "

"How beautiful! Good Lord! think of it, *how beautiful*!" cried Herr Spinell again, his face quite distorted with emotion.

"Now, what is it you find so particularly beautiful about that, Herr Spinell?"

"Oh, there being six of them besides you, and your being not one of the six, but a queen among them . . . set apart from your six friends. A little crown showed in your hair – quite a modest, unostentatious little crown, still it was there – "

"Nonsense, there was nothing of the sort."

"Yes, there was; it shone unseen. But if I had been there,

standing among the shrubbery, one of those times, I should have seen it."

"God knows what you would have seen. But you were not there. Instead of that, it was my husband who came out of the shrubbery one day, with my father. I was afraid they had been listening to our prattle – "

"So it was there, then, madame, that you first met your husband?"

"Yes, there it was I saw him first," she said, in quite a glad, strong voice; she smiled, and as she did so the little blue vein came out and gave her face a constrained and anxious expression. "He was calling on my father on business, you see. Next day he came to dinner, and three days later he proposed for my hand."

"Really? It all happened as fast as that?"

"Yes. Or, rather, it went a little slower after that. For my father was not very much inclined to it, you see, and consented on condition that we wait a long time first. He would rather I had stopped with him, and he had doubts in other ways too. But – "

"But?"

"But I had set my heart on it," she said, smiling; and once more the little vein dominated her whole face with its look of constraint and anxiety.

"Ah, so you set your heart on it."

"Yes, and I displayed great strength of purpose, as you see – "

"As I see. Yes."

"So that my father had to give way in the end."

"And so you forsook him and his fiddle and the old house with the overgrown garden, and the fountain and your six friends, and clave unto Herr Klöterjahn – "

"'And clave unto' – you have such a strange way of saying things, Herr Spinell. Positively biblical. Yes, I forsook all that; nature has arranged things that way."

"Yes, I suppose that is it."

"And it was a question of my happiness – "

"Of course. And happiness came to you?"

"It came, Herr Spinell, in the moment when they brought little Anton to me, our little Anton, and he screamed so lustily with his strong little lungs – he is very, very strong and healthy, you know –"

"This is not the first time, madame, that I have heard you speak of your little Anton's good health and great strength. He must be quite uncommonly healthy?"

"That he is. And looks so absurdly like my husband!"

"Ah! . . . So that was the way of it. And now you are no longer called by the name of Eckhof, but a different one, and you have your healthy little Anton, and are troubled with your trachea."

"Yes. And you are a perfectly enigmatic man, Herr Spinell, I do assure you."

"Yes. God knows you certainly are!" said Frau Spatz, who was present on this occasion.

And that conversation, too, gave Herr Klöterjahn's wife food for reflection. Idle as it was, it contained much to nourish those secret thoughts of hers about herself. Was this the baleful influence which was at work? Her weakness increased and fever often supervened, a quiet glow in which she rested with a feeling of mild elevation, to which she yielded in a pensive mood that was a little affected, self-satisfied, even rather self-righteous. When she had not to keep her bed, Herr Spinell would approach her with immense caution, tiptoeing on his great feet; he would pause two paces off, with his body inclined and one leg behind him, and speak in a voice that was hushed with awe, as though he would lift her higher and higher on the tide of his devotion until she rested on billowy cushions of cloud where no shrill sound nor any earthly touch might reach her. And when he did this she would think of the way Herr Klöterjahn said: "Take care, my angel, keep your mouth closed, Gabriele," a way that made her feel as though he had struck her roughly though well-meaningly on the shoulder. Then as fast as she could she would put the memory away and rest in her weakness and elevation of spirit upon the clouds which Herr Spinell spread out for her.

One day she abruptly returned to the talk they had had about her early life. "Is it really true, Herr Spinell," she asked, "that you would have seen the little gold crown?"

Two weeks had passed since that conversation, yet he knew at once what she meant, and his voice shook as he assured her that he would have seen the little crown as she sat among her friends by the fountain – would have caught its fugitive gleam among her locks.

A few days later one of the guests chanced to make a polite inquiry after the health of little Anton. Herr Klöterjahn's wife gave a quick glance at Herr Spinell, who was standing near, and answered in a perfunctory voice:

"Thanks, how should he be? He and my husband are quite well, of course."

There came a day at the end of February, colder, purer, more brilliant than any that had come before it, and high spirits held sway at Einfried. The "heart cases" consulted in groups, flushed of cheek, the diabetic general carolled like a boy out of school, and the gentlemen of the rebellious legs cast aside all restraint. And the reason for all these things was that a sleighing party was in prospect, an excursion in sledges into the mountains, with cracking whips and sleigh-bells jingling. Dr Leander had arranged this diversion for his patients.

The serious cases, of course, had to stop at home. Poor things! The other guests arranged to keep it from them; it did them good to practise this much sympathy and consideration. But a few of those remained at home who might very well have gone. Fräulein von Osterloh was of course excused, she had too much on her mind to permit her even to think of going. She was needed at home, and at home she remained. But the disappointment was general when Herr Klöterjahn's wife announced her intention of stopping away. Dr Leander exhorted her to come and get the benefit of the fresh air – but in vain. She said she was not up to it, she had a headache, she felt too weak – they had to resign themselves. The cynical gentleman took occasion to say:

"You will see, the dissipated baby will stop at home too."

And he proved to be right, for Herr Spinell gave out that he intended to "work" that afternoon – he was prone thus to characterize his dubious activities. Anyhow, not a soul regretted his absence; nor did they take more to heart the news that Frau Magistrate Spatz had decided to keep her young friend company at home – sleighing made her feel sea-sick.

Luncheon on the great day was eaten as early as twelve o'clock, and immediately thereafter the sledges drew up in front of Einfried. The guests came through the garden in little groups, warmly wrapped, excited, full of eager anticipation. Herr Klöterjahn's wife stood with Frau Spatz at the glass door which gave on the terrace, while Herr Spinell watched the setting-forth from above, at the window of his room. They saw the little struggles that took place for the best seats, amid joking and laughter; and Fräulein von Osterloh, with a fur boa round her neck, running from one sleigh to the other and shoving baskets of provisions under the seats; they saw Dr Leander, with his fur cap pulled low on his brow, marshalling the whole scene with his spectacle-lenses glittering, to make sure everything was ready. At last he took his own seat and gave the signal to drive off. The horses started up, a few of the ladies shrieked and collapsed, the bells jingled, the short-shafted whips cracked and their long lashes trailed across the snow; Fräulein von Osterloh stood at the gate waving her handkerchief until the train rounded a curve and disappeared; slowly the merry tinkling died away. Then she turned and hastened back through the garden in pursuit of her duties; the two ladies left the glass door, and almost at the same time Herr Spinell abandoned his post of observation above.

Quiet reigned at Einfried. The party would not return before evening. The serious cases lay in their rooms and suffered. Herr Klöterjahn's wife took a short turn with her friend, then they went to their respective chambers. Herr Spinell kept to his, occupied in his own way. Towards four o'clock the ladies were served with half a litre of milk apiece, and Herr Spinell with a light tea. Soon after, Herr Klöterjahn's wife tapped on the wall between her room and Frau Spatz's and called:

"Shan't we go down to the salon, Frau Spatz? I have nothing to do up here."

"In just a minute, my dear," answered she. "I'll just put on my shoes – if you will wait a minute. I have been lying down."

The salon, naturally, was empty. The ladies took seats by the fireplace. The Frau Magistrate embroidered flowers on a strip of canvas; Herr Klöterjahn's wife took a few stitches too, but soon let her work fall in her lap and, leaning on the arm of her chair, fell to dreaming. At length she made some remark, hardly worth the trouble of opening her lips for; the Frau Magistrate asked what she said, and she had to make the effort of saying it all over again, which quite wore her out. But just then steps were heard outside, the door opened, and Herr Spinell came in.

"Shall I be disturbing you?" he asked mildly from the threshold, addressing Herr Klöterjahn's wife and her alone; bending over her, as it were, from a distance, in the tender, hovering way he had.

The young wife answered:

"Why should you? The room is free to everybody – and besides, why would it be disturbing us? On the contrary, I am convinced that I am boring Frau Spatz."

He had no ready answer, merely smiled and showed his carious teeth, then went hesitatingly up to the glass door, the ladies watching him, and stood with his back to them looking out. Presently he half turned round, still gazing into the garden, and said:

"The sun has gone in. The sky clouded over without our seeing it. The dark is coming on already."

"Yes, it is all overcast," replied Herr Klöterjahn's wife. "It looks as though our sleighing party would have some snow after all. Yesterday at this hour it was still broad daylight, now it is already getting dark."

"Well," he said, "after all these brilliant weeks a little dullness is good for the eyes. The sun shines with the same penetrating clearness upon the lovely and the commonplace, and I for one am positively grateful to it for finally going under a cloud."

"Don't you like the sun, Herr Spinell?"

"Well, I am no painter . . . when there is no sun one becomes more profound. . . . It is a thick layer of greyish-white cloud. Perhaps it means thawing weather for tomorrow. But, madame, let me advise you not to sit there at the back of the room looking at your embroidery."

"Don't be alarmed; I am not looking at it. But what else is there to do?"

He had sat down on the piano-stool, resting one arm on the lid of the instrument.

"Music," he said. "If we could only have a little music here. The English children sing darky songs, and that is all."

"And yesterday afternoon Fräulein von Osterloh rendered 'Cloister Bells' at top speed," remarked Herr Klöterjahn's wife.

"But you play, madame!" said he, in an imploring tone. He stood up. "Once you used to play every day with your father."

"Yes, Herr Spinell, in those old days I did. In the time of the fountain, you know."

"Play to us, today," he begged. "Just a few notes – this once. If you knew how I long for some music –"

"But our family physician, as well as Dr Leander, expressly forbade it, Herr Spinell."

"But they aren't here – either of them. We are free agents. Just a few bars –"

"No, Herr Spinell, it would be no use. Goodness knows what marvels you expect of me – and I have forgotten everything I knew. Truly. I know scarcely anything by heart."

"Well, then, play that scarcely anything. But there are notes here too. On top of the piano. No, that is nothing. But here is some Chopin."

"Chopin?"

"Yes, the Nocturnes. All we have to do is to light the candles –"

"Pray don't ask me to play, Herr Spinell. I must not. Suppose it were to be bad for me –"

He was silent; standing there in the light of the two candles, with his great feet, in his long black tail-coat, with his beardless face and greying hair. His hands hung down at his sides.

"Then, madame, I will ask no more," he said at length, in a low voice. "If you are afraid it will do you harm, then we shall leave the beauty dead and dumb that might have come alive beneath your fingers. You were not always so sensible; at least not when it was the opposite question from what it is today, and you had to decide to take leave of beauty. Then you did not care about your bodily welfare; you showed a firm and unhesitating resolution when you left the fountain and laid aside the little gold crown. Listen," he said, after a pause, and his voice dropped still lower; "if you sit down and play as you used to play when your father stood behind you and brought tears to your eyes with the tones of his violin – who knows but the little gold crown might glimmer once more in you hair. . . ."

"Really," said she, with a smile. Her voice happened to break on the word, it sounded husky and barely audible. She cleared her throat and went on:

"Are those really Chopin's Nocturnes you have there?"

"Yes, here they are open at the place; everything is ready."

"Well, then, in God's name, I will play one," said she. "But only one – do you hear? In any case, one will do you, I am sure."

With which she got up, laid aside her work, and went to the piano. She seated herself on the music-stool, on a few bound volumes, arranged the lights, and turned over the notes. Herr Spinell had drawn up a chair and sat beside her, like a music-master.

She played the Nocturne in E major, opus 9, number 2. If her playing had really lost very much then she must originally have been a consummate artist. The piano was mediocre, but after the first few notes she learned to control it. She displayed a nervous feeling for modulations of timbre and a joy in mobility of rhythm that amounted to the fantastic. Her attack was at once firm and soft. Under her hands the very last drop of sweetness was wrung from the melody; the embellishments seemed to cling with slow grace about her limbs.

She wore the same frock as on the day of her arrival, the dark, heavy bodice with the velvet arabesques in high relief, that gave her head and hands such an unearthly fragile look. Her face did not change as she played, but her lips seemed to become more clear-cut, the shadows deepened at the corners of her eyes. When she finished she laid her hands in her lap and went on looking at the notes. Herr Spinell sat motionless.

She played another Nocturne, and then a third. Then she stood up, but only to look on the top of the piano for more music.

It occurred to Herr Spinell to look at the black-bound volumes on the piano-stool. All at once he uttered an incoherent exclamation, his large white hands clutching at one of the books.

"Impossible! No, it cannot be," he said. "But yes, it is. Guess what this is – what was lying here! Guess what I have in my hands."

"What?" she asked.

Mutely he showed her the title-page. He was quite pale; he let the book sink and looked at her, his lips trembling.

"Really? How did that get here? Give it me," was all she said; set the notes on the piano and after a moment's silence began to play.

He sat beside her, bent forward, his hands between his knees, his head bowed. She played the beginning with exaggerated and tormenting slowness, with painfully long pauses between the single figures. The *Sehnsuchtsmotiv*, roving lost and forlorn like a voice in the night, lifted its trembling question. Then silence, a waiting. And lo, an answer: the same timorous, lonely note, only clearer, muted *sforzando*, like mounting passion, the love-motif came in; reared and soared and yearned ecstatically upward to its consummation, sank back, was resolved; the cellos taking up the melody to carry it on with their deep, heavy notes of rapture and despair.

Not unsuccessfully did the player seek to suggest the orchestral effects upon the poor instrument at her command. The violin runs of the great climax rang out with brilliant precision. She played with a fastidious reverence, lingering on each figure, bringing out each detail, with the self-forgotten concentration of the priest who lifts the Host above his head. Here two forces, two beings, strove towards each other, in transports of joy and pain; here they embraced and became one in delirious yearning after eternity and the absolute.... The prelude flamed up and died away. She stopped at the point where the curtains part, and sat speechless, staring at the keys.

But the boredom of Frau Spatz had by now reached that pitch where it distorts the countenance of man, makes the eyes protrude from the head, and lends the features a corpse-like and terrifying aspect. More than that, this music acted on the nerves that controlled her digestion, producing in her dyspeptic organism such *malaise* that she was really afraid she would have an attack.

"I shall have to go up to my room," she said weakly. "Goodbye; I will come back soon."

She went out. Twilight was far advanced. Outside the snow fell thick and soundlessly upon the terrace. The two tapers cast a flickering, circumscribed light.

"The Second Act," he whispered, and she turned the pages and began.

What was it dying away in the distance – the ring of a horn? The rustle of leaves? The rippling of a brook? Silence and night crept up over grove and house; the power of longing had full sway, no prayers or warnings could avail against it. The holy mystery was consummated. The light was quenched; with a strange clouding of the timbre the death-motif sank down: white-veiled desire, by passion driven, fluttered towards love as through the dark it groped to meet her.

Ah, boundless, unquenchable exultation of union in the eternal beyond! Freed from torturing error, escaped from fettering space and time, the Thou and the I, the Thine and the Mine at one forever in a sublimity of bliss! The day might part them with deluding show; but when night fell, then by the power of the potion they would see clear. To him who has looked upon the night of death and known its secret sweets, to him day never can be aught but vain, nor can he know a longing save for night, eternal, real, in which he is made one with love.

O night of love, sink downwards and enfold them, grant them the oblivion they crave, release them from this world of partings and betrayals. Lo, the last light is quenched. Fancy and thought alike are lost, merged in the mystic shade that spread its wings of healing above their madness and despair. "Now, when deceitful daylight pales, when my raptured eye grows dim, then all that from which the light of day would shut my sight, seeking to blind me with false show, to the stanchless torments of my longing soul – then, ah, then, O wonder of fulfilment, even then I am the world!" Followed Brangäna's dark notes of warning, and then those soaring violins so higher than all reason.

"I cannot understand it all, Herr Spinell. Much of it I only divine. What does it mean, this 'even then I am the world'?"

He explained, in a few low-toned words.

"Yes, yes. It means that. How is it you can understand it all so well, yet cannot play it?"

Strangely enough, he was not proof against this simple question. He coloured, twisted his hands together, shrank into his chair.

"The two things seldom happen together," he wrung from his lips at last. "No, I cannot play. But go on."

And on they went, into the intoxicated music of the love-mystery. Did love ever die? Tristan's love? The love of thy Isolde, and of mine? Ah, no, death cannot touch that which can never die – and what of him could die, save what distracts and tortures love and severs united lovers? Love joined the two in sweet conjunction, death was powerless to sever such a bond, save only when death was given to one with the very life of the other. Their voices rose in mystic unison, rapt in the wordless hope of that death-in-love, of endless oneness in the wonder-kingdom of the night. Sweet night! Eternal night of love! And all-encompassing land of rapture! Once envisaged or divined, what eye could bear to open again on desolate dawn? Forfend such fears, most gentle death! Release these lovers quite from need of waking. Oh tumultuous storm of rhythms! Oh, glad chromatic upward surge of metaphysical perception! How find, how bind this bliss so far remote from parting's torturing pangs? Ah, gentle glow of longing, soothing and kind, ah, yielding sweet-sublime, ah, raptured sinking into the twilight of eternity! Thou Isolde, Tristan I, yet no more Tristan, no more Isolde. . . .

All at once something startling happened. The musician broke off and peered into the darkness with her hand above her eyes. Herr Spinell turned round quickly in his chair. The corridor door had opened, a sinister form appeared, leant on the arm of a second form. It was a guest of Einfried, one of those who, like themselves, had been in no state to undertake the sleigh-ride, but had passed this twilight hour in one of her pathetic, instinctive rounds of the house. It was that patient who had borne fourteen children and was no longer capable of a single thought; it was Frau Pastor Höhlenrauch, on the arm of her nurse. She did not look up; with groping step she paced the dim background of the room and vanished by the opposite door, rigid and still, like a lost and wandering soul. Stillness reigned once more.

"That was Frau Pastor Höhlenrauch," he said.

"Yes, that was poor Frau Höhlenrauch," she answered. Then she turned over some leaves and played the finale, played Isolde's song of love and death.

How colourless and clear were her lips, how deep the shadows lay beneath her eyes! The little pale-blue vein in her transparent brow showed fearfully plain and prominent. Beneath her flying fingers the music mounted to its unbelievable climax and was resolved in that ruthless, sudden *pianissimo* which is like having the ground glide from beneath one's feet, yet like a sinking too into the very deeps of desire. Followed the immeasurable plenitude of that vast redemption and fulfilment; it was repeated, swelled into a deafening, unquenchable tumult of immense appeasement that wove and welled and seemed about to die away, only to swell again and weave the *Sehnsuchtsmotiv* into its harmony; at length to breathe an outward breath and die, faint on the air, and soar away. Profound stillness.

They both listened, their heads on one side.

"Those are bells," she said.

"It is the sleighs," he said. "I will go now."

He rose and walked across the room. At the door he halted, then turned and shifted uneasily from one foot to the other. And then, some fifteen or twenty paces from her, it came to pass that he fell upon his knees, both knees, without a sound. His long black coat spread out on the floor. He held his hands clasped over his mouth, and his shoulders heaved.

She sat there with hands in her lap, leaning forward, turned away from the piano, and looked at him. Her face wore a distressed, uncertain smile, while her eyes searched the dimness at the back of the room, searched so painfully, so dreamily, she seemed hardly able to focus her gaze.

The jingling of sleigh-bells came nearer and nearer, there was the crack of whips, a babel of voices.

The sleighing party had taken place on the twenty-sixth of February, and was talked of for long afterwards. The next day, February twenty-seventh, a day of thaw, that set everything to melting and dripping, splashing and running, Herr Klöterjahn's wife was in capital health and spirits. On the twenty-eighth she brought up a little blood – not much, still it was blood, and accompanied by far greater loss of strength than ever before. She went to bed.

Dr Leander examined her, stony-faced. He prescribed according to the dictates of science – morphia, little pieces of ice, absolute quiet. Next day, on account of pressure of work, he turned her case over to Dr Müller, who took it on in humility and meekness of spirit and according to the letter of his contract – a quiet, pallid, insignificant little man, whose unadvertised activities were consecrated to the care of the slight cases and the hopeless ones.

Dr Müller presently expressed the view that the separation between Frau Klöterjahn and her spouse had lasted overlong. It would be well if Herr Klöterjahn, in case his flourishing business permitted, were to make another visit to Einfried. One might write him – or even wire. And surely it would benefit the young mother's health and spirits if he were to bring young Anton with him – quite aside from the pleasure it would give the physicians to behold with their own eyes this so healthy little Anton.

And Herr Klöterjahn came. He got Dr Müller's little wire and arrived from the Baltic coast. He got out of the carriage, ordered coffee and rolls, and looked considerably aggrieved.

"My dear sir," he asked, "what is the matter? Why have I been summoned?"

"Because it is desirable that you should be near your wife," Dr Müller replied.

"Desirable! Desirable! But is it *necessary*? It is a question of expense with me – times are poor and railway journeys cost money. Was it imperative I should take this whole day's journey? If it were the lungs that are attacked, I should say nothing. But as it is only the trachea, thank God – "

"Herr Klöterjahn," said Dr Müller mildly, "in the first place the trachea is an important organ. . . ." He ought not to have said "in the first place", because he did not go on to the second.

But there also arrived at Einfried, in Herr Klöterjahn's company, a full-figured personage arrayed all in red and gold and plaid, and she it was who carried on her arm Anton Klöterjahn, junior, that healthy little Anton. Yes, there he was, and nobody could deny that he was healthy even to excess. Pink and white and plump and fragrant, in fresh and immaculate attire, he rested heavily upon the bare red arm of his bebraided body-servant, consumed huge quantities of milk and chopped beef, shouted and screamed, and in every way surrendered himself to his instincts.

Our author from the window of his chamber had seen him arrive. With a peculiar gaze, both veiled and piercing, he fixed young Anton with his eye as he was carried from the carriage into the house. He stood there a long time with the same expression on his face.

Herr Spinell was sitting in his room "at work".

His room was like all the others at Einfried – old-fashioned, simple, and distinguished. The massive chest of drawers was mounted with brass lions' heads; the tall mirror on the wall was not a single surface, but made up of many little panes set in lead. There was no carpet on the polished blue paved floor, the stiff legs of the furniture prolonged themselves on it in clear-cut shadows. A spacious writing-table stood at the window, across whose panes the author had drawn the folds of a yellow curtain, in all probability that he might feel more retired.

In the yellow twilight he bent over the table and wrote – wrote one of those numerous letters which he sent weekly to the post and to which, quaintly enough, he seldom or never received an answer. A large, thick quire of paper lay before him, in whose upper left-hand corner was a curious involved drawing of a landscape and the name Detlev Spinell in the very latest thing in lettering. He was covering the page with a small, painfully neat, and punctiliously traced script.

"Sir:" he wrote, "I address the following lines to you because I cannot help it; because what I have to say so fills and shakes and tortures me, the words come in such a rush, that I should choke if I did not take this means to relieve myself."

If the truth were told, this about the rush of words was quite simply wide of the fact. And God knows what sort of vanity it was made Herr Spinell put it down. For his words did not come in a rush; they came with such pathetic slowness, considering the man was a writer by trade, you would have drawn the conclusion, watching him, that a writer is one to whom writing comes harder than to anybody else.

He held between two finger-tips one of those curious downy hairs he had on his cheek, and twirled it round and round, whole quarter-hours at a time, gazing into space and not coming forwards by a single line; then wrote a few words, daintily, and stuck again. Yet so much was true: that what had managed to get written sounded fluent and vigorous, though the matter was odd enough, even almost equivocal, and at times impossible to follow.

"I feel," the letter went on, "an imperative necessity to make you see what I see; to show you through my eyes, illuminated by the same power of language that clothes them for me, all the things which have stood before my inner eye for weeks, like an indelible vision. It is my habit to yield to the impulse which urges me to put my own experiences into flamingly right and unforgettable words and to give them to the world. And therefore hear me.

"I will do no more than relate what has been and what is: I will merely tell a story, a brief, unspeakably touching story, without comment, blame, or passing of judgment; simply in my own words. It is the story of Gabriele Eckhof, of the woman whom you, sir, call your wife – and mark you this: it is your story, it happened to you, yet it will be I who will for the first time lift it for you to the level of an experience.

"Do you remember the garden, the old, overgrown garden behind the grey patrician house? The moss was green in the crannies of its weather-beaten wall, and behind the wall dreams and neglect held sway. Do you remember the fountain in the centre? The pale mauve lilies leaned over its crumbling rim, the little stream prattled softly as it fell upon the riven paving. The summer day was drawing to its close.

"Seven maidens sat circlewise round the fountain; but the seventh, or rather the first and only one, was not like the others, for the sinking sun seemed to be weaving a queenly coronal among her locks. Her eyes were like troubled dreams, and yet her pure lips wore a smile.

"They were singing. They lifted their little faces to the leaping streamlet and watched its charming curve droop earthward – their music hovered round it as it leaped and danced. Perhaps their slim hands were folded in their laps the while they sang.

"Can you, sir, recall the scene? Or did you ever see it? No, you saw it not. Your eyes were not formed to see it nor your ears to catch the chaste music of their song. You saw it not, or else you would have forbidden your lungs to breathe, your heart to beat. You must have turned aside and gone back to your own life, taking with you what you had seen to preserve it in the depth of your soul to the end of your earthly life, a sacred and inviolable relic. But what did you do?

"That scene, sir, was an end and culmination. Why did you come to spoil it, to give it a sequel, to turn it into the channels of ugly and commonplace life? It was a peaceful apotheosis and a moving, bathed in a sunset beauty of decadence, decay and death. An ancient stock, too exhausted and refined for life and action, stood there at the end of its days; its latest manifestations were those of art: violin notes, full of that melancholy understanding which is ripeness for death.... Did you look into her eyes – those eyes where tears so often stood, lured by the dying sweetness of the violin? Her six friends may have had souls that belonged to life; but hers, the queen's and sister's, death and beauty had claimed for their own.

"You saw it, that deathly beauty; saw, and coveted. The sight of that touching purity moved you with no awe or trepidation. And it was not enough for you to see, you must possess, you must use, you must desecrate.... It was the refinement of a choice you made – you are a gourmand, sir, a plebeian gourmand, a peasant with taste.

"Once more let me say that I have no wish to offend you. What I have just said is not an affront; it is a statement, a simple, psychological statement of your simple personality – a personality which for literary purposes is entirely uninteresting. I make the statement solely because I feel an impulse to clarify for you your own thoughts and actions; because it is my inevitable task on this earth to call things by their right names, to make them speak, to illuminate the unconscious. The world is full of what I call the unconscious type, and I cannot endure it; I cannot endure all these unconscious types! I cannot bear all this dull, uncomprehending, unperceiving living and behaving, this world of maddening naïveté about me! It tortures me until I am driven irresistibly to set it all in relief, in the round, to explain, express, and make self-conscious everything in the world – so far as my powers will reach – quite unhampered by the result, whether it be for good or evil, whether it brings consolation and healing or piles grief on grief.

"You, sir, as I said, are a plebeian gourmand, a peasant with taste. You stand upon an extremely low evolutionary level; your own constitution is coarse-fibred. But wealth and a sedentary habit of life have brought about in you a corruption of the nervous system, as sudden as it is unhistoric; and this corruption has been accompanied by a lascivious refinement in your choice of gratifications. It is altogether possible that the muscles of your gullet began to contract, as at the sight of some particularly rare dish, when you conceived the idea of making Gabriele Eckhof your own.

"In short, you lead her idle will astray, you beguile her out of that moss-grown garden into the ugliness of life, you give her your own vulgar name and make of her a married woman, a housewife, a mother. You take that deathly beauty – spent, aloof, flowering in lofty unconcern of the uses of this world – and debase it to the service of common things, you sacrifice it to that stupid, contemptible, clumsy graven image we call 'nature' – and not the faintest suspicion of the vileness of your conduct visits your peasant soul.

"Again. What is the result? This being, whose eyes are like troubled dreams, she bears you a child; and so doing she endows the new life, a gross continuation of its author's own, with all the blood, all the physical energy she possesses

– and she dies. She dies, sir! And if she does not go hence with your vulgarity upon her head; if at the very last she has lifted herself out of the depths of degradation, and passes in an ecstasy, with the deathly kiss of beauty on her brow – well, it is I, sir, who have seen to that! You, meanwhile, were probably spending your time with chambermaids in dark corners.

"But your son, Gabriele Eckhof's son, is alive; he is living and flourishing. Perhaps he will continue in the way of his father, become a well-fed, trading, tax-paying citizen; a capable, philistine pillar of society; in any case, a tone-deaf, normally functioning individual, responsible, sturdy, and stupid, troubled by not a doubt.

"Kindly permit me to tell you, sir, that I hate you. I hate you and your child, as I hate the life of which you are the representative: cheap, ridiculous, but yet triumphant life, the everlasting antipodes and deadly enemy of beauty. I cannot say I despise you – for I am honest. You are stronger than I. I have no armour for the struggle between us, I have only the Word, avenging weapon of the weak. Today I have availed myself of this weapon. This letter is nothing but an act of revenge – you see how honourable I am – and if any word of mine is sharp and bright and beautiful enough to strike home, to make you feel the presence of a power you do not know, to shake even a minute your robust equilibrium, I shall rejoice indeed. – DETLEV SPINELL."

And Herr Spinell put this screed into an envelope, applied a stamp and a many-flourished address, and committed it to the post.

Herr Klöterjahn knocked on Herr Spinell's door. He carried a sheet of paper in his hand covered with neat script, and he looked like a man bent on energetic action. The post office had done its duty, the letter had taken its appointed way: it had travelled from Einfried to Einfried and reached the hand for which it was meant. It was now four o'clock in the afternoon.

Herr Klöterjahn's entry found Herr Spinell sitting on the sofa reading his own novel with the appalling cover-design. He rose and gave his caller a surprised and inquiring look, though at the same time he distinctly flushed.

"Good afternoon," said Herr Klöterjahn. "Pardon the interruption. But may I ask if you wrote this?" He held up in his left hand the sheet inscribed with fine clear characters and struck it with the back of his right and made it crackle. Then he stuffed that hand into the pocket of his easy-fitting trousers, put his head on one side, and opened his mouth, in a way some people have, to listen.

Herr Spinell, curiously enough, smiled; he smiled engagingly, with a rather confused, apologetic air. He put his hand to his head as though trying to recollect himself, and said:

"Ah! – yes, quite right, I took the liberty – "

The fact was, he had given in to his natural man today and slept nearly up to mid-day, with the result that he was suffering from a bad conscience and a heavy head, was nervous and incapable of putting up a fight. And the spring air made him limp and good-for-nothing. So much we must say in extenuation of the utterly silly figure he cut in the interview which followed.

"Ah? Indeed! Very good!" said Herr Klöterjahn. He dug his chin into his chest, elevated his brows, stretched his arms, and indulged in various other antics by way of getting down to business after his introductory question. But unfortunately he so much enjoyed the figure he cut that he rather overshot the mark and the rest of the scene hardly lived up to this preliminary pantomime. However, Herr Spinell went rather pale.

"Very good!" repeated Herr Klöterjahn. "Then permit me to give you an answer in person; it strikes me as idiotic to write pages of letter to a person when you can speak to him any hour of the day."

"Well, idiotic . . ." Herr Spinell said, with his apologetic smile. He sounded almost meek.

"Idiotic!" repeated Herr Klöterjahn, nodding violently in

token of the soundness of his position. "And I should not demean myself to answer this scrawl; to tell the truth, I should have thrown it away at once if I had not found in it the explanation of certain changes – however, that is no affair of yours, and has nothing to do with the thing anyhow. I am a man of action, I have other things to do than to think about your unspeakable visions."

"I wrote '*indelible vision*'," said Herr Spinell, drawing himself up. This was the only moment at which he displayed a little self-respect.

"Indelible, unspeakable," responded Herr Klöterjahn, referring to the text. "You write a villainous hand, sir; you would not get a position in my office, let me tell you. It looks clear enough at first, but when you come to study it, it is full of shakes and quavers. But that is your affair, it's no business of mine. What I have come to say to you is that you are a tomfool – which you probably know already. Furthermore, you are a cowardly sneak; I don't suppose I have to give the evidence for that either. My wife wrote me once that when you meet a woman you don't look her square in the face, but just give her a side squint, so as to carry away a good impression, because you are afraid of the reality. I should probably have heard more of the same sort of stories about you, only unfortunately she stopped mentioning you. But this is the kind of thing you are: you talk so much about 'beauty'; you are all chicken-livered hypocrisy and cant – which is probably at the bottom of your impudent allusion to out-of-the-way corners too. That ought to crush me, of course, but it just makes me laugh – it doesn't do a thing but make me laugh! Understand? Have I clarified your thoughts and actions for you, you pitiable object, you? Though of course it is not my invariable calling –"

"'*Inevitable*' was the word I used," Herr Spinell said; but he did not insist on the point. He stood there, crestfallen, like a big, unhappy, chidden, grey-haired schoolboy.

"Invariable or inevitable, whichever you like – anyhow you are a contemptible cur, and that I tell you. You see me every day at table, you bow and smirk and say good-morning – and one fine day you send me a scrawl full of idiotic abuse. Yes, you've a lot of courage – on paper! And it's not only this ridiculous letter – you have been intriguing behind my back. I can see that now. Though you need not flatter yourself it did any good. If you imagine you put any ideas into my wife's head you never were more mistaken in your life. And if you think she behaved any different when we came from what she always does, then you just put the cap on to your own foolishness. She did not kiss the little chap, that's true, but it was only a precaution, because they have the idea now that the trouble is with her lungs, and in such cases you can't tell whether – though that still remains to be proved, no matter what you say with your 'She dies, sir,' you silly ass!"

Here Herr Klöterjahn paused for breath. He was in a furious passion; he kept stabbing the air with his right forefinger and crumpling the sheet of paper in his other hand. His face, between the blond English mutton-chops, was frightfully red and his dark brow was rent with swollen veins like lightnings of scorn.

"You hate me," he went on, "and you would despise me if I were not stronger than you. Yes, you're right there! I've got my heart in the right place, by God, and you've got yours mostly in the seat of your trousers. I would most certainly hack you into bits if it weren't against the law, you and your gabble about the 'Word', you skulking fool! But I have no intention of putting up with your insults; and when I show this part about the vulgar name to my lawyer at home, you will very likely get a little surprise. My name, sir, is a first-rate name, and I have made it so by my own efforts. You know better than I do whether anybody would ever lend you a penny piece on yours, you lazy lout! The law defends people against the kind you are! You are a common danger, you are enough to drive a body crazy! But you're left this time, my master! I don't let individuals like you get the best of me so fast! I've got my heart in the right place – "

Herr Klöterjahn's excitement had really reached a pitch. He

shrieked, he bellowed, over and over again, that his heart was in the right place.

"'They were singing.' Exactly. Well, they weren't. They were knitting. And if I heard what they said, it was about a recipe for potato pancakes; and when I show my father-in-law that about the old decayed family you'll probably have a libel suit on your hands. 'Did you see the picture?' Yes, of course I saw it; only I don't see why that should make me hold my breath and run away. I don't leer at women out of the corner of my eye; I look at them square, and if I like their looks I go for them. I have my heart in the right place –"

Somebody knocked. Knocked eight or ten times, quite fast, one after the other – a sudden, alarming little commotion that made Herr Klöterjahn pause; and an unsteady voice that kept tripping over itself in its haste and distress said:

"Herr Klöterjahn, Herr Klöterjahn – oh, is Herr Klöterjahn there?"

"Stop outside," said Herr Klöterjahn, in a growl.... "What's the matter? I'm busy talking."

"Oh, Herr Klöterjahn," said the quaking, breaking voice, "you must come! The doctors are there too – oh, it is all so dreadfully sad –"

He took one step to the door and tore it open. Frau Magistrate Spatz was standing there. She had her handkerchief before her mouth, and great egg-shaped tears rolled into it, two by two.

"Herr Klöterjahn," she got out. "It is so frightfully sad.... She has brought up so much blood, such a horrible lot of blood.... She was sitting up quite quietly in bed and humming a little snatch of music... and there it came... my God, such a quantity you never saw...."

"Is she dead?" yelled Herr Klöterjahn. As he spoke he clutched the Rätin by the arm and pulled her to and fro on the sill. "Not quite? Not dead; she can see me, can't she? Brought up a little blood again, from the lung, eh? Yes, I give in, it may be from the lung. Gabriele!" he suddenly cried out, and his eyes filled with tears; you could see what a burst of good, warm, honest human feeling came over him. "Yes, I'm coming," he said, and dragged the Rätin after him as he went with long strides down the corridor. You could still hear his voice, from quite a distance, sounding fainter and fainter: "Not quite, eh? From the lung?"

Herr Spinell stood still on the spot where he had stood during the whole of Herr Klöterjahn's rudely interrupted call and looked out the open door. At length he took a couple of steps and listened down the corridor. But all was quiet, so he closed the door and came back into the room.

He looked at himself awhile in the glass, then he went up to the writing-table, took a little flask and a glass out of a drawer, and drank a cognac – for which nobody can blame him. Then he stretched himself out on the sofa and closed his eyes.

The upper half of the window was down. Outside in the garden birds were twittering; those dainty, saucy little notes held all the spring, finely and penetratingly expressed. Herr Spinell spoke once: "*Invariable calling*," he said, and moved his head and drew in the air through his teeth as though his nerves pained him violently.

Impossible to recover any poise or tranquillity. Crude experiences like this were too much – he was not made for them. By a sequence of emotions, the analysis of which would lead us too far afield, Herr Spinell arrived at the decision that it would be well for him to have a little out-of-doors exercise. He took his hat and went downstairs.

As he left the house and issued into the mild, fragrant air, he turned his head and lifted his eyes, slowly, scanning the house until he reached one of the windows, a curtained window, on which his gaze rested awhile, fixed and sombre. Then he laid his hands on his back and moved away across the gravel path. He moved in deep thought.

The beds were still straw-covered, the trees and bushes bare; but the snow was gone, the path was only damp in spots. The large garden with its grottoes, bowers and little pavilions lay in the splendid colourful afternoon light, strong shadow and rich, golden sun, and the dark network of branches stood out sharp and articulate against the bright sky.

It was about that hour of the afternoon when the sun takes shape, and from being a formless volume of light turns to a visibly sinking disk, whose milder, more saturated glow the eye can tolerate. Herr Spinell did not see the sun, the direction the path took hid it from his view. He walked with bent head and hummed a strain of music, a short phrase, a figure that mounted wailingly and complainingly upward – the *Sehnsuchtsmotiv*.... But suddenly, with a start, a quick, jerky intake of breath, he stopped, as though rooted to the path, and gazed straight ahead of him, with brows fiercely gathered, staring eyes, and an expression of horrified repulsion.

The path had curved just here, he was facing the setting sun. It stood large and slantwise in the sky, crossed by two narrow strips of gold-rimmed cloud; it set the tree-tops aglow and poured its red-gold radiance across the garden. And there, erect in the path, in the midst of the glory, with the sun's mighty aureola above her head, there confronted him an exuberant figure, all arrayed in red and gold and plaid. She had one hand on her swelling hip, with the other she moved to and fro the graceful little perambulator. And in this perambulator sat the child – sat Anton Klöterjahn, junior, Gabriele Eckhof's fat son.

There he sat among his cushions, in a woolly white jacket and large white hat, plump-cheeked, well cared for, and magnificent; and his blithe unerring gaze encountered Herr Spinell's. The novelist pulled himself together. Was he not a man, had he not the power to pass this unexpected, sun-kindled apparition there in the path and continue on his walk? But Anton Klöterjahn began to laugh and shout – most horrible to see. He squealed, he crowed with inconceivable delight – it was positively uncanny to hear him.

God knows what had taken him; perhaps the sight of Herr Spinell's long, black figure set him off; perhaps an attack of sheer animal spirits gave rise to his wild outburst of merriment. He had a bone teething-ring in one hand and a tin rattle in the other; and these two objects he flung aloft with shoutings, shook them to and fro, and clashed them together in the air, as though purposely to frighten Herr Spinell. His eyes were almost shut, his mouth gaped open till all the rosy gums were displayed; and as he shouted he rolled his head about in excess of mirth.

Herr Spinel turned round and went thence. Pursued by the youthful Klöterjahn's joyous screams, he went away across the gravel, walking stiffly, yet not without grace; his gait was the hesitating gait of one who would disguise the fact that, inwardly, he is running away.

GLADIUS DEI

MUNICH WAS radiant. Above the gay squares and white columned temples, the classicistic monuments and the baroque churches, the leaping fountains, the palaces and parks of the Residence there stretched a sky of luminous blue silk. Well-arranged leafy vistas laced with sun and shade lay basking in the sunshine of a beautiful day in early June.

There was a twittering of birds and a blithe holiday spirit in all the little streets. And in the squares and past the rows of villas there swelled, rolled, and hummed the leisurely, entertaining traffic of that easy-going, charming town. Travellers of all nationalities drove about in the slow little droshkies, looking right and left in aimless curiosity at the house-fronts; they mounted and descended museum stairs. Many windows stood open and music was heard from within: practising on piano, cello, or violin – earnest and well-meant amateur efforts; while from the Odeon came the sound of serious work on several grand pianos.

Young people, the kind that can whistle the Nothung motif, who fill the pit of the Schauspielhaus every evening, wandered in and out of the University and Library with literary magazines in their coat pockets. A court carriage stood before the Academy, the home of the plastic arts, which spreads its white wings between the Türkenstrasse and the Siegestor. And colourful groups of models, picturesque old men, women and children in Albanian costume, stood or lounged at the top of the balustrade.

Indolent, unhurried sauntering was the mode in all the long streets of the northern quarter. There life is lived for pleasanter ends than the driving greed of gain. Young artists with little round hats on the backs of their heads, flowing cravats and no canes – carefree bachelors who paid for their lodgings with colour-sketches – were strolling up and down to let the clear blue morning play upon their mood, also to look at the little girls, the pretty, rather plump type, with the brunette bandeaux, the too large feet, and the unobjectionable morals. Every fifth house had studio windows blinking in the sun. Sometimes a fine piece of architecture stood out from a middle-class row, the work of some imaginative young architect; a wide front with shallow bays and decorations in a bizarre style very expressive and full of invention. Or the door to some monotonous façade would be framed in a bold improvisation of flowing lines and sunny colours, with bacchantes, naiads, and rosy-skinned nudes.

It was always a joy to linger before the windows of the cabinet-makers and the shops for modern articles *de luxe*. What a sense for luxurious nothings and amusing, significant line was displayed in the shape of everything! Little shops that sold picture-frames, sculptures, and antiques there were in endless number; in their windows you might see those busts of Florentine women of the Renaissance, so full of noble poise and poignant charm. And the owners of the smallest and meanest of these shops spoke of Mino da Fiesole and Donatello as though he had received the rights of reproduction from them personally.

But on the Odeonsplatz, in view of the mighty loggia with the spacious mosaic pavement before it, diagonally opposite to the Regent's palace, people were crowding round the large windows and glass show-cases of the big art-shop owned by M. Blüthenzweig. What a glorious display! There were reproductions of the masterpieces of all the galleries in the world, in costly decorated and tinted frames, the good taste of which was precious in its very simplicity. There were copies of modern paintings, works of a joyously sensuous fantasy, in which the antiques seemed born again in humorous and realistic guise; bronze nudes and fragile ornamental glassware; tall, thin earthenware vases with an iridescent glaze produced by a bath in metal steam; *éditions de luxe* which were triumphs of modern binding and presswork, containing the works of the most modish poets, set out with every possible advantage of sumptuous elegance. Cheek by jowl with these, the portraits of artists, musicians, philosophers, actors, writers, displayed to gratify the public taste for personalities. – In the first window, next the book-shop, a large picture stood on an easel, with a crowd of people in front of it, a fine sepia photograph in a wide old-gold frame, a very striking reproduction of the sensation at this year's great international exhibition, to which public attention is always invited by means of effective and artistic posters stuck up everywhere on hoardings among concert programmes and clever advertisements of toilet preparations.

If you looked into the windows of the book-shop your eye met such titles as *Interior Decoration Since the Renaissance*, *The Renaissance in Modern Decorative Art*, *The Book as Work of Art*, *The Decorative Arts, Hunger for Art*, and many more. And you would remember that these thought-provoking pamphlets were sold and read by the thousand and that discussions on these subjects were the preoccupation of all the salons.

You might be lucky enough to meet in person one of the famous fair ones whom less fortunate folk know only through the medium of art; one of those rich and beautiful women whose Titian-blond colouring Nature's most sweet and cunning hand did *not* lay on, but whose diamond parures and beguiling charms had received immortality from the hand of some portrait-painter of genius and whose love-affairs were the talk of the town. These were the queens of the artist balls at carnival-time. They were a little painted, a little made up, full of haughty caprices, worthy of adoration, avid of praise. You might see a carriage rolling up the Ludwigstrasse, with such a great painter and his mistress inside. People would be pointing out the sight, standing still to gaze after the pair. Some of them would curtsy. A little more and the very policemen would stand at attention.

Art flourished, art swayed the destinies of the town, art

stretched above it her rose-bound sceptre and smiled. On every hand obsequious interest was displayed in her prosperity, on every hand she was served with industry and devotion. There was a downright cult of line, decoration, form, significance, beauty. Munich was radiant.

A youth was coming down the Schellingstrasse. With the bells of cyclists ringing about him he strode across the wooden pavement towards the broad façade of the Ludwigskirche. Looking at him it was as though a shadow passed across the sky, or cast over the spirit some memory of melancholy hours. Did he not love the sun which bathed the lovely city in its festal light? Why did he walk wrapped in his own thoughts, his eyes directed on the ground?

No one in that tolerant and variety-loving town would have taken offence at his wearing no hat; but why need the hood of his ample black cloak have been drawn over his head, shadowing his low, prominent, and peaked forehead, covering his ears and framing his haggard cheeks? What pangs of conscience, what scruples and self-tortures had so availed to hollow out these cheeks? It is frightful, on such a sunny day, to see care sitting in the hollows of the human face. His dark brows thickened at the narrow base of his hooked and prominent nose. His lips were unpleasantly full, his eyes brown and close-lying. When he lifted them, diagonal folds appeared on the peaked brow. His gaze expressed knowledge, limitation, and suffering. Seen in profile his face was strikingly like an old painting preserved at Florence in a narrow cloister cell whence once a frightful and shattering protest issued against life and her triumphs.

Hieronymus walked along the Schellingstrasse with a slow, firm stride, holding his wide cloak together with both hands from inside. Two little girls, two of those pretty, plump little creatures with the bandeaux, the big feet, and the unobjectionable morals, strolled towards him arm in arm, on pleasure bent. They poked each other and laughed, they bent double with laughter, they even broke into a run and ran away still laughing, at his hood and his face. But he paid them no heed. With bent head, looking neither to the right nor to the left, he crossed the Ludwigstrasse and mounted the church steps.

The great wings of the middle portal stood wide open. From somewhere within the consecrated twilight, cool, dank, incense-laden, there came a pale red glow. An old woman with inflamed eyes rose from a prayer-stool and slipped on crutches through the columns. Otherwise the church was empty.

Hieronymus sprinkled brow and breast at the stoup, bent the knee before the high altar, and then paused in the centre nave. Here in the church his stature seemed to have grown. He stood upright and immovable; his head was flung up and his great hooked nose jutted domineeringly above the thick lips. His eyes no longer sought the ground, but looked straight and boldly into the distance, at the crucifix on the high altar. Thus he stood awhile, then retreating he bent the knee again and left the church.

He strode up the Ludwigstrasse, slowly, firmly, with bent head, in the centre of the wide unpaved road, towards the mighty loggia with its statues. But arrived at the Odeonsplatz, he looked up, so that the folds came out on his peaked forehead, and checked his step, his attention being called to the crowd at the windows of the big art-shop of M. Blüthenzweig.

People moved from window to window, pointing out to each other the treasures displayed and exchanging views as they looked over one another's shoulders. Hieronymus mingled among them and did as they did, taking in all these things with his eyes, one by one.

He saw the reproductions of masterpieces from all the galleries in the world, the priceless frames so precious in their simplicity, the Renaissance sculpture, the bronze nudes, the exquisitely bound volumes, the iridescent vases, the portraits of artists, musicians, philosophers, actors, writers; he looked at everything and turned a moment of his scrutiny upon each object. Holding his mantle closely together with both hands from inside, he moved his hood-covered head in short turns from one thing to the next, gazing at each awhile with a dull, inimical, and remotely surprised air, lifting the dark brows which grew so thick at the base of the nose. At length he stood in front of the last window, which contained the startling picture. For a while he looked over the shoulders of people before him and then in his turn reached a position directly in front of the window.

The large red-brown photograph in the choice old-gold frame stood on an easel in the centre. It was a Madonna, but an utterly unconventional one, a work of entirely modern feeling. The figure of the Holy Mother was revealed as enchantingly feminine and beautiful. Her great smouldering eyes were rimmed with darkness, and her delicate and strangely smiling lips were half-parted. Her slender fingers held in a somewhat nervous grasp the hips of the Child, a nude boy of pronounced, almost primitive leanness. He was playing with her breast and glancing aside at the beholder with a wise look in his eyes.

Two other youths stood near Hieronymus, talking about the picture. They were two young men with books under their arms, which they had fetched from the Library or were taking thither. Humanistically educated people, that is, equipped with science and with art.

"The little chap is in luck, devil take me!" said one.

"He seems to be trying to make one envious," replied the other. "A bewildering female!"

"A female to drive a man crazy! Gives you funny ideas about the Immaculate Conception."

"No, she doesn't look exactly immaculate. Have you seen the original?"

"Of course; I was quite bowled over. She makes an even more aphrodisiac impression in colour. Especially the eyes."

"The likeness is pretty plain."

"How so?"

"Don't you know the model? Of course he used his little dress-maker. It is almost a portrait, only with a lot more emphasis on the corruptible. The girl is more innocent."

"I hope so. Life would be altogether too much of a strain if there were many like this *mater amata.*"

"The Pinakothek has bought it."

"Really? Well, well! They knew what they were about, anyhow. The treatment of the flesh and the flow of the linen garment are really first-class."

"Yes, an incredibly gifted chap."

"Do you know him?"

"A little. He will have a career, that is certain. He has been invited twice by the Prince Regent."

This last was said as they were taking leave of each other.

"Shall I see you this evening at the theatre?" asked the first. "The Dramatic Club is giving Machiavelli's *Mandragola.*"

"Oh, bravo! That will be great, of course, I had meant to go to the Variété, but I shall probably choose our stout Niccolo after all. Good-bye."

They parted, going off to right and left. New people took their places and looked at the famous picture. But Hieronymus stood where he was, motionless, with his head thrust out; his hands clutched convulsively at the mantle as they held it together from inside. His brows were no longer lifted with that cool and unpleasantly surprised expression; they were drawn and darkened; his cheeks, half-shrouded in the black hood, seemed more sunken than ever and his thick lips had gone pale. Slowly his head dropped lower and lower, so that finally his eyes stared upwards at the work of art, while the nostrils of his great nose dilated.

Thus he remained for perhaps a quarter of an hour. The crowd about him melted away, but he did not stir from the spot. At last he turned slowly on the balls of his feet and went thence.

But the picture of the Madonna went with him. Always and ever, whether in his hard and narrow little room or kneeling in the cool church, it stood before his outraged soul, with its smouldering, dark-rimmed eyes, its riddlingly smiling lips – stark and beautiful. And no prayer availed to exorcize it.

But the third night it happened that a command and summons from on high came to Hieronymus, to intercede and lift his voice against the frivolity, blasphemy, and arrogance of beauty. In vain like Moses he protested that he had not the gift of tongues. God's will remained unshaken; in a loud voice He demanded that the faint-hearted Hieronymus go forth to sacrifice amid the jeers of the foe.

And since God would have it so, he set forth one morning and wended his way to the great art-shop of M. Blüthenzweig. He wore his hood over his head and held his mantle together in front from inside with both hands as he went.

The air had grown heavy, the sky was livid and thunder threatened. Once more crowds were besieging the show-cases at the art-shop and especially the window where the photograph of the Madonna stood. Hieronymus cast one brief glance thither; then he pushed up the latch of the glass door hung with placards and art magazines. "As God wills," said he, and entered the shop.

A young girl was somewhere at a desk writing in a big book. She was a pretty brunette thing with bandeaux of hair and big feet. She came up to him and asked pleasantly what he would like.

"Thank you," said Hieronymus in a low voice and looked her earnestly in the face, with diagonal wrinkles in his peaked brow. "I would speak not to you but to the owner of this shop, Herr Blüthenzweig."

She hesitated a little, turned away, and took up her work once more. He stood there in the middle of the shop.

Instead of the single specimens in the show-windows there were here a riot and a heaping-up of luxury, a fullness of colour, line, form, style, invention, good taste, and beauty. Hieronymus looked slowly round him, drawing his mantle close with both hands.

There were several people in the shop besides him. At one of the broad tables running across the room sat a man in a yellow suit, with a black goat's beard, looking at a portfolio of French drawings, over which he now and then emitted a bleating laugh. He was being waited on by an undernourished and vegetarian young man, who kept on dragging up fresh portfolios. Diagonally opposite the bleating man sat an elegant old dame, examining art embroideries with a pattern of fabulous flowers in pale tones standing together on tall perpendicular stalks. An attendant hovered about her too. A leisurely Englishman in a travelling-cap, with his pipe in his mouth, sat at another table. Cold and smooth-shaven, of indefinite age, in his good English clothes, he sat examining bronzes brought to him by M. Blüthenzweig in person. He was holding up by the head the dainty figure of a nude young girl, immature and delicately articulated, her hands crossed in coquettish innocence upon her breast. He studied her thoroughly, turning her slowly about. M. Blüthenzweig, a man with a short, heavy brown beard and bright brown eyes of exactly the same colour, moved in a semicircle round him, rubbing his hands, praising the statuette with all the terms his vocabulary possessed.

"A hundred and fifty marks, sir," he said in English. "Munich art – very charming, in fact. Simply full of charm, you know. Grace itself. Really extremely pretty, good, admirable, in fact." Then he thought of some more and went on: "Highly attractive, fascinating." Then he began again from the beginning.

His nose lay a little flat on his upper lip, so that he breathed constantly with a slight sniff into his moustache. Sometimes he did this as he approached a customer, stooping over as though he were smelling at him. When Hieronymus entered, M. Blüthenzweig had examined him cursorily in this way, then devoted himself again to his Englishman.

The elegant old dame made her selection and left the shop. A man entered. M. Blüthenzweig sniffed briefly at him as though to scent out his capacity to buy and left him to the young book-keeper. The man purchased a faience bust of young Piero de' Medici, son of Lorenzo, and went out again. The Englishman began to depart. He had acquired the statuette of the young girl and left amid bowings from

M. Blüthenzweig. Then the art-dealer turned to Hieronymus and came forward.

"You wanted something?" he said, without any particular courtesy.

Hieronymus held his cloak together with both hands and looked the other in the face almost without winking an eyelash. He parted his big lips slowly and said:

"I have come to you on account of the picture in the window there, the big photograph, the Madonna." His voice was thick and without modulation.

"Yes, quite right," said M. Blüthenzweig briskly and began rubbing his hands. "Seventy marks in the frame. It is unfadable – a first-class reproduction. Highly attractive and full of charm."

Hieronymus was silent. He nodded his head in the hood and shrank a little into himself as the dealer spoke. Then he drew himself up again and said:

"I would remark to you first of all that I am not in the position to purchase anything, nor have I the desire. I am sorry to have to disappoint your expectations. I regret if it upsets you. But in the first place I am poor and in the second I do not love the things you sell. No, I cannot buy anything."

"No? Well, then?" asked M. Blüthenzweig, sniffing a good deal. "Then may I ask – "

"I suppose," Hieronymus went on, "that being what you are you look down on me because I am not in a position to buy."

"Oh – er – not at all," said M. Blüthenzweig. "Not at all. Only – "

"And yet I beg you to hear me and give some consideration to my words."

"Consideration to your words. H'm – may I ask – "

"You may ask," said Hieronymus, "and I will answer you. I have come to beg you to remove that picture, the big photograph, the Madonna, out of your window and never display it again."

M. Blüthenzweig looked awhile dumbly into Hieronymus's face – as though he expected him to be abashed at the words he had just uttered. But as this did not happen he gave a violent sniff and spoke himself:

"Will you be so good as to tell me whether you are here in any official capacity which authorizes you to dictate to me, or what does bring you here?"

"Oh, no," replied Hieronymus, "I have neither office nor dignity from the state. I have no power on my side, sir. What brings me hither is my conscience alone."

M. Blüthenzweig, searching for words, snorted violently into his moustache. At length he said:

"Your conscience... well, you will kindly understand that I take not the faintest interest in your conscience." With which he turned round and moved quickly to his desk at the back of the shop, where he began to write. Both attendants laughed heartily. The pretty Fräulein giggled over her account-book. As for the yellow gentleman with the goat's beard, he was evidently a foreigner, for he gave no sign of comprehension but went on studying the French drawings and emitting from time to time his bleating laugh.

"Just get rid of the man for me," said M. Blüthenzweig shortly over his shoulder to his assistant. He went on writing. The poorly paid young vegetarian approached Hieronymus, smothering his laughter, and the other salesman came up too.

"May we be of service to you in any other way?" the first asked mildly. Hieronymus fixed him with his glazed and suffering eyes.

"No," he said, "you cannot. I beg you to take the Madonna picture out of the window, at once and for ever."

"But – why?"

"It is the Holy Mother of God," said Hieronymus in a subdued voice.

"Quite. But you have heard that Herr Blüthenzweig is not inclined to accede to your request."

"We must bear in mind that it is the Holy Mother of God," said Hieronymous again and his head trembled on his neck.

"So we must. But should we not be allowed to exhibit any Madonnas – or paint any?"

"It is not that," said Hieronymus, almost whispering. He drew himself up and shook his head energetically several times. His peaked brow under the hood was entirely furrowed with long, deep cross-folds. "You know very well that it is vice itself that is painted there – naked sensuality. I was standing near two simple young people and overheard with my own ears that it led them astray upon the doctrine of the Immaculate Conception."

"Oh, permit me – that is not the point," said the young salesman, smiling. In his leisure hours he was writing a brochure on the modern movement in art and was well qualified to conduct a cultured conversation. "The picture is a work of art," he went on, "and one must measure it by the appropriate standards as such. It has been very highly praised on all hands. The state has purchased it."

"I know that the state has purchased it," said Hieronymus. "I also know that the artist has twice dined with the Prince Regent. It is common talk – and God knows how people interpret the fact that a man can become famous by such work as this. What does such a fact bear witness to? To the blindness of the world, a blindness inconceivable, if not indeed shamelessly hypocritical. This picture has its origin in sensual lust and is enjoyed in the same – is that true or not? Answer me! And you too answer me, Herr Blüthenzweig!"

A pause ensued. Hieronymus seemed in all seriousness to demand an answer to his question, looking by turns at the staring attendants and the round back M. Blüthenzweig turned upon him, with his own piercing and anguishing brown eyes. Silence reigned. Only the yellow man with the goat's beard, bending over the French drawings, broke it with his bleating laugh.

"It is true," Hieronymus went on in a hoarse voice that shook with his profound indignation. "You do not dare deny it. How then can honour be done to its creator, as though he had endowed mankind with a new ideal possession? How can one stand before it and surrender unthinkingly to the base enjoyment which it purveys, persuading oneself in all seriousness that one is yielding to a noble and elevated sentiment, highly creditable to the human race? Is this reckless ignorance or abandoned hypocrisy? My understanding falters, it is completely at a loss when confronted by the absurd fact that a man can achieve renown on this earth by the stupid and shameless exploitation of the animal instincts. Beauty? What is beauty? What forces are they which use beauty as their tool today – and upon what does it work? No one can fail to know this, Herr Blüthenzweig. But who, understanding it clearly, can fail to feel disgust and pain? It is criminal to play upon the ignorance of the immature, the lewd, the brazen, and the unscrupulous by elevating beauty into an idol to be worshipped, to give it even more power over those who know not affliction and have no knowledge of redemption. You are unknown to me, and you look at me with black looks – yet answer me! Knowledge, I tell you, is the profoundest torture in the world; but it is the purgatory without whose purifying pangs no soul can reach salvation. It is not infantile, blasphemous shallowness that can save us, Herr Blüthenzweig; only knowledge can avail, knowledge in which the passions of our loathsome flesh die away and are quenched."

Silence. – The yellow man with the goat's beard gave a sudden little bleat.

"I think you really must go now," said the underpaid assistant mildly.

But Hieronymus made no move to do so. Drawn up in his hooded cape, he stood with blazing eyes in the centre of the shop and his thick lips poured out condemnation in a voice that was harsh and rusty and clanking.

"Art, you cry; enjoyment, beauty! Enfold the world in beauty and endow all things with the noble grace of style! – Profligate, away! Do you think to wash over with lurid colours the misery of the world? Do you think with the sounds of feasting and music to drown out the voice of the tortured earth? Shameless one, you err! God lets not Himself be mocked, and your impudent deification of the glistering surface of things is an abomination in His eyes. You tell me that I blaspheme art. I say to you that you lie. I do not blaspheme art. Art is no conscienceless delusion, lending itself to reinforce the allurements of the fleshly. Art is the holy torch which turns its light upon all the frightful depths, all the shameful and woeful abysses of life; art is the godly fire laid to the world that, being redeemed by pity, it may flame up and dissolve altogether with its shames and torments. – Take it out, Herr Blüthenzweig, take away the work of that famous painter out of your window – you would do well to burn it with a hot fire and strew its ashes to the four winds – yes, to all the four winds – "

His harsh voice broke off. He had taken a violent backwards step, snatched one arm from his black wrappings, and stretched it passionately forth, gesturing towards the window with a hand that shook as though palsied. And in this commanding attitude he paused. His great hooked nose seemed to jut more than ever, his dark brows were gathered so thick and high that folds crowded upon the peaked forehead shaded by the hood; a hectic flush mantled his hollow cheeks.

But at this point M. Blüthenzweig turned round. Perhaps he was outraged by the idea of burning his seventy-mark reproduction; perhaps Hieronymus's speech had completely exhausted his patience. In any case he was a picture of stern and righteous anger. He pointed with his pen to the door of the shop, gave several short, excited snorts into his moustache, struggled for words, and uttered with the maximum of energy those which he found:

"My fine fellow, if you don't get out at once I will have my packer help you – do you understand?"

"Oh, you cannot intimidate me, you cannot drive me away, you cannot silence my voice!" cried Hieronymus as he clutched his cloak over his chest with his fists and shook his head doughtily. "I know that I am single-handed and powerless, but yet I will not cease until you hear me, Herr Blüthenzweig! Take the picture out of your window and burn it even today! Ah, burn not it alone! Burn all these statues and busts, the sight of which plunges the beholder into sin! Burn these vases and ornaments, these shameless revivals of paganism, these elegantly bound volumes of erotic verse! Burn everything in your shop, Herr Blüthenzweig, for it is a filthiness in God's sight. Burn it, burn it!" he shrieked, beside himself, describing a wild, all-embracing circle with his arm. "The harvest is ripe for the reaper, the measure of the age's shamelessness is full – but I say unto you – "

"Krauthuber!" Herr Blüthenzweig raised his voice and shouted towards a door at the back of the shop. "Come in here at once!"

And in answer to the summons there appeared upon the scene a massive overpowering presence, a vast and awe-inspiring, swollen human bulk, whose limbs merged into each other like links of sausage – a gigantic son of the people, malt-nourished and immoderate, who weighed in, with puffings, bursting with energy, from the packing-room. His appearance in the upper reaches of his form was notable for a fringe of walrus beard; a hide apron fouled with paste covered his body from the waist down, and his yellow shirt-sleeves were rolled back from his heroic arms.

"Will you open the door for this gentleman, Krauthuber?" said M. Blüthenzweig; "and if he should not find the way to it, just help him into the street."

"Huh," said the man, looking from his enraged employer to Hieronymus and back with his little elephant eyes. It was a heavy monosyllable, suggesting reserve force restrained with difficulty. The floor shook with his tread as he went to the door and opened it.

Hieronymus had grown very pale. "Burn – " he shouted once more. He was about to go on when he felt himself turned round by an irresistible power, by a physical preponderance to which no resistance was even thinkable. Slowly and inexorably he was propelled towards the door.

"I am weak," he managed to ejaculate. "My flesh cannot

bear the force . . . it cannot hold its ground, no . . . but what does that prove? Burn –"

He stopped. He found himself outside the art-shop. M. Blüthenzweig's giant packer had let him go with one final shove, which set him down on the stone threshold of the shop, supporting himself with one hand. Behind him the door closed with a rattle of glass.

He picked himself up. He stood erect, breathing heavily, and pulled his cloak together with one fist over his breast, letting the other hang down inside. His hollow cheeks had a grey pallor; the nostrils of his great hooked nose opened and closed; his ugly lips were written in an expression of hatred and despair and his red-rimmed eyes wandered over the beautiful square like those of a man in a frenzy.

He did not see that people were looking at him with amusement and curiosity. For what he beheld upon the mosaic pavement before the great loggia were all the vanities of this world: the masked costumes of the artist balls, the decorations, vases and art objects, the nude statues, the female busts, the picturesque rebirths of the pagan age, the portraits of famous beauties by the hands of masters, the elegantly bound erotic verse, the art brochures – all these he saw heaped in a pyramid and going up in crackling flames amid loud exultations from the people enthralled by his own frightful words. A yellow background of cloud had drawn up over the Theatinerstrasse, and from it issued wild rumblings; but what he saw was a burning fiery sword, towering in sulphurous light above the joyous city.

"*Gladius Dei super terram . . .*" his thick lips whispered; and drawing himself still higher in his hooded cloak while the hand hanging down inside it twitched convulsively, he murmured, quaking: "*cito et velociter!*"

TONIO KRÖGER

THE WINTER sun, poor ghost of itself, hung milky and wan behind layers of cloud above the huddled roofs of the town. In the gabled streets it was wet and windy and there came in gusts a sort of soft hail, not ice, not snow.

School was out. The hosts of the released streamed over the paved court and out at the wrought-iron gate, where they broke up and hastened off right and left. Elder pupils held their books in a strap high on the left shoulder and rowed, right arm against the wind, towards dinner. Small people trotted gaily off, splashing the slush with their feet, the tools of learning rattling amain in their walrus-skin satchels. But one and all pulled off their caps and cast down their eyes in awe before the Olympian hat and ambrosial beard of a master moving homewards with measured stride. . . .

"Ah, there you are at last, Hans," said Tonio Kröger. He had been waiting a long time in the street and went up with a smile to the friend he saw coming out of the gate in talk with other boys and about to go off with them. . . . "What?" said Hans, and looked at Tonio. "Right-oh! We'll take a little walk, then."

Tonio said nothing and his eyes were clouded. Did Hans forget, had he only just remembered that they were to take a walk together today? And he himself had looked forward to it with almost incessant joy.

"Well, good-bye, fellows," said Hans Hansen to his comrades. "I'm taking a walk with Kröger." And the two turned to their left, while the others sauntered off in the opposite direction.

Hans and Tonio had time to take a walk after school

because in neither of their families was dinner served before four o'clock. Their fathers were prominent business men, who held public office and were of consequence in the town. Hans's people had owned for some generations the big wood-yards down by the river, where powerful machine-saws hissed and spat and cut up timber; while Tonio was the son of Consul Kröger, whose grain-sacks with the firm name in great black letters you might see any day driven through the streets; his large, old ancestral home was the finest house in all the town. The two friends had to keep taking off their hats to their many acquaintances; some folk did not even wait for the fourteen-year-old lads to speak first, as by rights they should.

Both of them carried their satchels across their shoulders and both were well and warmly dressed: Hans in a short sailor jacket, with the wide blue collar of his sailor suit turned out over shoulders and back, and Tonio in a belted grey overcoat. Hans wore a Danish sailor cap with black ribbons, beneath which streamed a shock of straw-coloured hair. He was uncommonly handsome and well built, broad in the shoulders and narrow in the hips, with keen, far-apart, steel-blue eyes; while beneath Tonio's round fur cap was a brunette face with the finely chiselled features of the south; the dark eyes, with delicate shadows and too heavy lids, looked dreamily and a little timorously on the world. Tonio's walk was idle and uneven, whereas the other's slim legs in their black stockings moved with an elastic, rhythmic tread.

Tonio did not speak. He suffered. His rather oblique brows were drawn together in a frown, his lips were rounded to whistle, he gazed into space with his head on one side. Posture and manner were habitual.

Suddenly Hans shoved his arm into Tonio's, with a sideways look – he knew very well what the trouble was. And Tonio, though he was silent for the next few steps, felt his heart soften.

"I hadn't forgotten, you see, Tonio," Hans said, gazing at the pavement, "I only thought it wouldn't come off today because it was so wet and windy. But I don't mind that at all, and it's jolly of you to have waited. I thought you had gone home, and I was cross. . . ."

Everything in Tonio leaped and jumped for joy at the words.

"All right; let's go over the wall," he said with a quaver in his voice. "Over the Millwall and the Holstenwall, and I'll go as far as your house with you, Hans. Then I'll have to walk back alone, but that doesn't matter; next time you can go round my way."

At bottom he was not really convinced by what Hans said; he quite knew the other attached less importance to this walk than he did himself. Yet he saw Hans was sorry for his remissness and willing to be put in a position to ask pardon, a pardon that Tonio was far indeed from withholding.

The truth was, Tonio loved Hans Hansen, and had already suffered much on his account. He who loves the more is the inferior and must suffer; in this hard and simple fact his fourteen-year-old soul had already been instructed by life; and he was so organized that he received such experiences consciously, wrote them down as it were inwardly, and even, in a certain way, took pleasure in them, though without ever letting them mould his conduct, indeed, or drawing any practical advantage from them. Being what he was, he found this knowledge far more important and far more interesting than the sort they made him learn in school; yes, during his lesson hours in the vaulted Gothic classrooms he was mainly occupied in feeling his way about among these intuitions of his and penetrating them. The process gave him the same kind of satisfaction as that he felt when he moved about in his room with his violin – for he played the violin – and made the tones, brought out as softly as ever he knew how, mingle with the splashing of the fountain that leaped and danced down there in the garden beneath the branches of the old walnut tree.

The fountain, the old walnut tree, his fiddle, and away in the distance the North Sea, within sound of whose summer murmurings he spent his holidays – these were the things he loved, within these he enfolded his spirit, among these things his inner life took its course. And they were all things whose names were effective in verse and occurred pretty frequently in the lines Tonio Kröger sometimes wrote.

The fact that he had a note-book full of such things, written by himself, leaked out through his own carelessness and injured him no little with the masters as well as among his fellows. On the one hand, Consul Kröger's son found their attitude both cheap and silly, and despised his schoolmates and his masters as well, and in his turn (with extraordinary penetration) saw through and disliked their personal weaknesses and bad breeding. But then, on the other hand, he himself felt his verse-making extravagant and out of place and to a certain extent agreed with those who considered it an unpleasing occupation. But that did not enable him to leave off.

As he wasted his time at home, was slow and absent-minded at school, and always had bad marks from the masters, he was in the habit of bringing home pitifully poor reports, which troubled and angered his father, a tall, fastidiously dressed man, with thoughtful blue eyes, and always a wild flower in his buttonhole. But for his mother, she cared nothing about the reports – Tonio's beautiful black-haired mother, whose name was Consuelo, and who was so absolutely different from the other ladies in the town, because father had brought her long ago from some place far down on the map.

Tonio loved his dark, fiery mother, who played the piano and mandolin so wonderfully, and he was glad his doubtful standing among men did not distress her. Though at the same time he found his father's annoyance a more dignified and respectable attitude and despite his scoldings understood him very well, whereas his mother's blithe indifference always seemed just a little wanton. His thoughts at times would run something like this: "It is true enough that I am what I am and will not and cannot alter: heedless, self-willed, with my mind on things nobody else thinks of. And so it is right they should scold and punish me and not smother things all up with kisses and music. After all, we are not gypsies living in a green wagon; we're respectable people, the family of Consul Kröger." And not seldom he would think: "Why is it I am different, why do I fight everything, why am I at odds with the masters and like a stranger among the other boys? The good scholars, and the solid majority – they don't find the masters funny, they don't write verses, their thoughts are all about things that people do think about and can talk about out loud. How regular and comfortable they must feel, knowing that everybody knows just where they stand! It must be nice! But what is the matter with me, and what will be the end of it all?"

These thoughts about himself and his relation to life played an important part in Tonio's love for Hans Hansen. He loved him in the first place because he was handsome; but in the next because he was in every respect his own opposite and foil. Hans Hansen was a capital scholar, and a jolly chap to boot, who was head at drill, rode and swam to perfection, and lived in the sunshine of popularity. The masters were almost tender with him, they called him Hans and were partial to him in every way; the other pupils curried favour with him; even grown people stopped him on the street, twitched the shock of hair beneath his Danish sailor cap, and said: "Ah, here you are, Hans Hansen, with your pretty blond hair! Still head of the school? Remember me to your father and mother, that's a fine lad!"

Such was Hans Hansen; and ever since Tonio Kröger had known him, from the very minute he set eyes on him, he had burned inwardly with a heavy, envious longing. "Who else has blue eyes like yours, or lives in such friendliness and harmony with all the world? You are always spending your time with some right and proper occupation. When you have done your prep you take your riding-lesson, or make things with a fret-saw; even in the holidays, at the seashore, you row and sail and swim all the time, while I wander off somewhere and lie down in the sand and stare at the strange and mysterious changes that whisk over the face of the sea. And all that is why your eyes are so clear. To be like you . . ."

He made no attempt to be like Hans Hansen, and perhaps hardly even seriously wanted to. What he did ardently, painfully want was that, just as he was, Hans Hansen should love him; and he wooed Hans Hansen in his own way, deeply, lingeringly, devotedly, with a melancholy that gnawed and burned more terribly than all the sudden passion one might have expected from his exotic looks.

And he wooed not in vain. Hans respected Tonio's superior power of putting certain difficult matters into words; moreover, he felt the lively presence of an uncommonly strong and tender feeling for himself; he was grateful for it, and his response gave Tonio much happiness – though also many pangs of jealousy and disillusion over his futile efforts to establish a communion of spirit between them. For the queer thing was that Tonio, who after all envied Hans Hansen for being what he was, still kept on trying to draw him over to his own side; though of course he could succeed in this at most only at moments and superficially. . . .

"I have just been reading something so wonderful and splendid . . ." he said. They were walking and eating together out of a bag of fruit toffees they had bought at Iverson's sweetshop in Mill Street for ten pfennigs. "You must read it, Hans, it is Schiller's *Don Carlos* . . . I'll lend it you if you like. . . ."

"Oh, no," said Hans Hansen, "you needn't, Tonio, that's not anything for me. I'll stick to my horse books. There are wonderful cuts in them, let me tell you. I'll show them to you when you come to see me. They are instantaneous photography – the horse in motion; you can see him trot and canter and jump, in all positions, that you never can get to see in life, because they happen so fast. . . ."

"In all positions?" asked Tonio politely. "Yes, that must be great. But about *Don Carlos* – it is beyond anything you could possibly dream of. There are places in it that are so lovely they make you jump . . . as though it were an explosion –"

"An explosion?" asked Hans Hansen. "What sort of an explosion?"

"For instance, the place where the king has been crying because the marquis betrayed him... but the marquis did it only out of love for the prince, you see, he sacrifices himself for his sake. And the word comes out of the cabinet into the antechamber that the king has been weeping. 'Weeping? The king been weeping?' All the courtiers are fearfully upset, it goes through and through you, for the king has always been so frightfully stiff and stern. But it is so easy to understand why he cried, and I feel sorrier for him than for the prince and the marquis put together. He is always so alone, nobody loves him, and then he thinks he has found one man, and then *he* betrays him...."

Hans Hansen looked sideways into Tonio's face, and something in it must have won him to the subject, for suddenly he shoved his arm once more into Tonio's and said:

"How had he betrayed him, Tonio?"

Tonio went on.

"Well," he said, "you see all the letters for Brabant and Flanders – "

"There comes Irwin Immerthal," said Hans.

Tonio stopped talking. If only the earth would open and swallow Immerthal up! "Why does he have to come disturbing us? If he only doesn't go with us all the way and talk about the riding-lessons!" For Irwin Immerthal had riding-lessons too. He was the son of the bank president and lived close by, outside the city wall. He had already been home and left his bag, and now he walked towards them through the avenue. His legs were crooked and his eyes like slits.

"'lo, Immerthal," said Hans. "I'm taking a little walk with Kröger...."

"I have to go into town on an errand," said Immerthal. "But I'll walk a little way with you. Are those fruit toffees you've got? Thanks, I'll have a couple. Tomorrow we have our next lesson, Hans." He meant the riding-lesson.

"What larks!" said Hans. "I'm going to get the leather gaiters for a present, because I was top lately in our papers."

"You don't take riding-lessons, I suppose, Kröger?" asked

Immerthal, and his eyes were only two gleaming cracks.

"No . . ." answered Tonio, uncertainly.

"You ought to ask your father," Hans Hansen remarked, "so you could have lessons too, Kröger."

"Yes . . ." said Tonio. He spoke hastily and without interest; his throat had suddenly contracted, because Hans had called him by his last name. Hans seemed conscious of it too, for he said by way of explanation: "I call you Kröger because your first name is so crazy. Don't mind my saying so, I can't do with it all. Tonio – why, what sort of name is that? Though of course I know it's not your fault in the least."

"No, they probably called you that because it sounds so foreign and sort of something special," said Immerthal, obviously with intent to say just the right thing.

Tonio's mouth twitched. He pulled himself together and said:

"Yes, it's a silly name – Lord knows I'd rather be called Heinrich or Wilhelm. It's all because I'm named after my mother's brother Antonio. She comes from down there, you know. . . ."

There he stopped and let the others have their say about horses and saddles. Hans had taken Immerthal's arm; he talked with a fluency that *Don Carlos* could never have roused in him. . . . Tonio felt a mounting desire to weep pricking his nose from time to time; he had hard work to control the trembling of his lips.

Hans could not stand his name – what was to be done? He himself was called Hans, and Immerthal was called Irwin; two good, sound, familiar names, offensive to nobody. And Tonio was foreign and queer. Yes, there was always something queer about him, whether he would or no, and he was alone, the regular and usual would none of him; although after all he was no gypsy in a green wagon, but the son of Consul Kröger, a member of the Kröger family. But why did Hans call him Tonio as long as they were alone and then feel ashamed as soon as anybody else was by? Just now he had won him over, they had been close together, he was sure. "How had he betrayed him, Tonio?" Hans asked, and took his arm. But he had breathed easier directly Immerthal came up, he had dropped him like a shot, even gratuitously taunted him with his outlandish name. How it hurt to have to see through all this!... Hans Hansen did like him a little, when they were alone, that he knew. But let a third person come, he was ashamed, and offered up his friend. And again he was alone. He thought of King Philip. The king had wept....

"Goodness, I have to go," said Irwin Immerthal. "Good-bye, and thanks for the toffee." He jumped upon a bench that stood by the way, ran along it with his crooked legs, jumped down, and trotted off.

"I like Immerthal," said Hans, with emphasis. He had a spoilt and arbitrary way of announcing his likes and dislikes, as though graciously pleased to confer them like an order on this person and that.... He went on talking about the riding-lessons where he had left off. Anyhow, it was not very much farther to his house; the walk over the walls was not a long one. They held their caps and bent their heads before the strong, damp wind that rattled and groaned in the leafless trees. And Hans Hansen went on talking, Tonio throwing in a forced yes or no from time to time. Hans talked eagerly, had taken his arm again; but the contact gave Tonio no pleasure. The nearness was only apparent, not real; it meant nothing....

They struck away from the walls close to the station, where they saw a train puff busily past, idly counted the coaches, and waved to the man who was perched on top of the last one bundled in a leather coat. They stopped in front of the Hansen villa on the Lindenplatz, and Hans went into detail about what fun it was to stand on the bottom rail of the garden gate and let it swing on its creaking hinges. After that they said good-bye.

"I must go in now," said Hans. "Good-bye, Tonio. Next time I'll take you home, see if I don't."

"Good-bye, Hans," said Tonio. "It was a nice walk."

They put out their hands, all wet and rusty from the garden gate. But as Hans looked into Tonio's eyes, he bethought himself, a look of remorse came over his charming face.

"And I'll read *Don Carlos* pretty soon, too," he said quickly. "That bit about the king in his cabinet must be nuts." Then he took his bag under his arm and ran off through the front garden. Before he disappeared he turned and nodded once more.

And Tonio went off as though on wings. The wind was at his back; but it was not the wind alone that bore him along so lightly.

Hans would read *Don Carlos*, and then they would have something to talk about, and neither Irwin Immerthal nor another could join in. How well they understood each other! Perhaps – who knew? – some day he might even get Hans to write poetry! . . . No, no, that he did not ask. Hans must not become like Tonio, he must stop just as he was, so strong and bright, everybody loved him as he was, and Tonio most of all. But it would do him no harm to read *Don Carlos*. . . . Tonio passed under the squat old city gate, along by the harbour, and up the steep, wet, windy, gabled street to his parents' house. His heart beat richly: longing was awake in it, and a gentle envy; a faint contempt, and no little innocent bliss.

Ingeborg Holm, blonde little Inge, the daughter of Dr Holm, who lived on Market Square opposite the tall old Gothic fountain with its manifold spires – she it was Tonio Kröger loved when he was sixteen years old.

Strange how things come about! He had seen her a thousand times; then one evening he saw her again; saw her in a certain light, talking with a friend in a certain saucy way, laughing and tossing her head; saw her lift her arm and smooth her back hair with her schoolgirl hand, that was by no means particularly fine or slender, in such a way that the thin sleeve slipped down from her elbow; heard her speak a word or two, a quite indifferent phrase, but with a certain intonation, with a warm ring in her voice; and his heart throbbed with ecstasy, far stronger than that he had once felt when he looked at Hans Hansen long ago, when he was still a little, stupid boy.

That evening he carried away her picture in his eye: the thick blond plait, the longish, laughing blue eyes, the saddle of pale freckles across the nose. He could not go to sleep for hearing that ring in her voice; he tried in a whisper to imitate the tone in which she had uttered the commonplace phrase, and felt a shiver run through and through him. He knew by experience that this was love. And he was accurately aware that love would surely bring him much pain, affliction, and sadness, that it would certainly destroy his peace, filling his heart to overflowing with melodies which would be no good to him because he would never have the time or tranquillity to give them permanent form. Yet he received this love with joy, surrendered himself to it, and cherished it with all the strength of his being; for he knew that love made one vital and rich, and he longed to be vital and rich, far more than he did to work tranquilly on anything to give it permanent form.

Tonio Kröger fell in love with merry Ingeborg Holm in Frau Consul Hustede's drawing-room on the evening when it was emptied of furniture for the weekly dancing-class. It was a private class, attended only by members of the first families; it met by turns in the various parental houses to receive instruction from Knaak, the dancing-master, who came from Hamburg expressly for the purpose.

François Knaak was his name, and what a man he was! "*J'ai l'honneur de me vous représenter,*" he would say, "*mon nom est Knaak.* . . . This is not said during the bowing, but after you have finished and are standing up straight again. In a low voice, but distinctly. Of course one does not need to introduce oneself in French every day in the week, but if you can do it correctly and faultlessly in French you are not likely to make a mistake when you do it in German." How marvellously the silky black frock-coat fitted his chubby hips! His trouser-legs fell down in soft folds upon his patent-leather pumps with their wide satin bows, and his brown eyes glanced about him with languid pleasure in their own beauty.

All this excess of self-confidence and good form was positively overpowering. He went trippingly – and nobody tripped like him, so elastically, so weavingly, rockingly, royally – up to the mistress of the house, made a bow, waited for a hand to be put forth. This vouchsafed, he gave murmurous voice to his gratitude, stepped buoyantly back, turned on his left foot, swiftly drawing the right one backwards on its toe-tip, and moved away, with his hips shaking.

When you took leave of a company you must go backwards out at the door; when you fetched a chair, you were not to shove it along the floor or clutch it by one leg; but gently, by the back, and set it down without a sound. When you stood, you were not to fold your hands on your tummy or seek with your tongue the corners of your mouth. If you did, Herr Knaak had a way of showing you how it looked that filled you with disgust for that particular gesture all the rest of your life.

This was deportment. As for dancing, Herr Knaak was, if possible, even more of a master at that. The salon was emptied of furniture and lighted by a gas-chandelier in the middle of the ceiling and candles on the mantel-shelf. The floor was strewn with talc, and the pupils stood about in a dumb semicircle. But in the next room, behind the portières, mothers and aunts sat on plush-upholstered chairs and watched Herr Knaak through their lorgnettes, as in little springs and hops, curtsying slightly, the hem of his frock-coat held up on each side by two fingers, he demonstrated the single steps of the mazurka. When he wanted to dazzle his audience completely he would suddenly and unexpectedly spring from the ground, whirling his two legs about each other with bewildering swiftness in the air, as it were trilling with them, and then, with a subdued bump, which nevertheless shook everything within him to its depths, returned to earth.

"What an unmentionable monkey!" thought Tonio Kröger to himself. But he saw the absorbed smile on jolly little Inge's face as she followed Herr Knaak's movements; and that, though not that alone, roused in him something like admiration of all this wonderfully controlled corporeality. How tranquil, how imperturbable was Herr Knaak's gaze! His eyes did not plumb the depth of things to the place where life becomes complex and melancholy; they knew nothing save that they were beautiful brown eyes. But that was just why his bearing was so proud. To be able to walk like that, one must be stupid; then one was loved, then one was lovable. He could so well understand how it was that Inge, blonde, sweet little Inge, looked at Herr Knaak as she did. But would never a girl look at him like that?

Oh, yes, there would, and did. For instance, Magdalena Vermehren, Attorney Vermehren's daughter, with the gentle mouth and the great, dark, brilliant eyes, so serious and adoring. She often fell down in the dance; but when it was "ladies' choice" she came up to him; she knew he wrote verses and twice she had asked him to show them to her. She often sat at a distance, with drooping head, and gazed at him. He did not care. It was Inge he loved, blonde, jolly Inge, who most assuredly despised him for his poetic effusions . . . he looked at her, looked at her narrow blue eyes full of fun and mockery, and felt an envious longing; to be shut away from her like this, to be for ever strange – he felt it in his breast, like a heavy, burning weight.

"First couple *en avant*," said Herr Knaak; and no words can tell how marvellously he pronounced the nasal. They were to practise the quadrille, and to Tonio Kröger's profound alarm he found himself in the same set with Inge Holm. He avoided her where he could, yet somehow was for ever near her; kept his eyes away from her person and yet found his gaze ever on her. There she came, tripping up hand-in-hand with red-headed Ferdinand Matthiessen; she flung back her braid, drew a deep breath, and took her place opposite Tonio. Herr Heinzelmann, at the piano, laid bony hands upon the keys, Herr Knaak waved his arm, the quadrille began.

She moved to and fro before his eyes, forwards and back, pacing and swinging; he seemed to catch a fragrance from her hair or the folds of her thin white frock, and his eyes grew sadder and sadder. "I love you, dear, sweet Inge," he said to himself, and put into his words all the pain he felt to see her so intent upon the dance with not a thought of him. Some lines of an exquisite poem by Storm came into his mind: "I would sleep, but thou must dance." It seemed against all sense, and most depressing, that he must be dancing when he was in love. . . .

"First couple *en avant*," said Herr Knaak; it was the next figure. "*Compliment! Moulinet des dames! Tour de main!*" and he swallowed the silent *e* in the "*DE*", with quite indescribable ease and grace.

"Second couple *en avant*!" This was Tonio Kröger and his partner. "*Compliment!*" And Tonio Kröger bowed. "*Moulinet des dames!*" And Tonio Kröger, with bent head and gloomy brows, laid his hand on those of the four ladies, on Ingeborg Holm's hand, and danced the *moulinet*.

Roundabout rose a tittering and laughing. Herr Knaak took a ballet pose conventionally expressive of horror. "Oh, dear! Oh, dear!" he cried. "Stop! Stop! Kröger among the ladies! *En arrière*, Fräulein Kröger, step back, *fi donc!* Everybody else understood it but you. Shoo! Get out! Get away!" He drew out his yellow silk handkerchief and flapped Tonio Kröger back to his place.

Everyone laughed, the girls and the boys and the ladies beyond the portières; Herr Knaak had made something too utterly funny out of the little episode, it was as amusing as a play. But Herr Heinzelmann at the piano sat and waited, with a dry, businesslike air, for a sign to go on; he was hardened against Herr Knaak's effects.

Then the quadrille went on. And the intermission followed. The parlourmaid came clinking in with a tray of wine-jelly glasses, the cook followed in her wake with a load of plum-cake. But Tonio Kröger stole away. He stole out into the corridor and stood there, his hands behind his back, in front of a window with the blind down. He never thought that one could not see through the blind and that it was absurd to stand there as though one were looking out.

For he was looking within, into himself, the theatre of so much pain and longing. Why, why was he here? Why was he not sitting by the window in his own room, reading Storm's *Immensee* and lifting his eyes to the twilight garden outside, where the old walnut tree moaned? That was the place for him! Others might dance, others bend their fresh and lively minds upon the pleasure in hand! . . . But no, no, after all, his place was here, where he could feel near Inge, even although he stood lonely and aloof, seeking to distinguish the warm notes of her voice amid the buzzing, clattering, and laughter within. Oh, lovely Inge, blonde Inge of the narrow, laughing blue eyes! So lovely and laughing as you are one can only be if one does not read *Immensee* and never tries to write things like it. And that was just the tragedy!

Ah, she *must* come! She *must* notice where he had gone, must feel how he suffered! She must slip out to him, even pity must bring her, to lay her hand on his shoulder and say: "Do come back to us, ah, don't be sad – I love you, Tonio." He listened behind him and waited in frantic suspense. But not in the least. Such things did not happen on this earth.

Had she laughed at him too like all the others? Yes, she had, however gladly he would have denied it for both their sakes. And yet it was only because he had been so taken up with her that he had danced the *moulinet des dames*. Suppose he had – what did that matter? Had not a magazine accepted a poem of his a little while ago – even though the magazine had failed before his poem could be printed? The day was coming when he would be famous, when they would print everything he wrote; and *then* he would see if that made any impression on Inge Holm! No, it would make no impression at all; that was just it. Magdalena Vermehren, who was always falling down in the dances, yes, she would be impressed. But never Ingeborg Holm, never blue-eyed, laughing Inge. So what was the good of it?

Tonio Kröger's heart contracted painfully at the thought. To feel stirring within you the wonderful and melancholy play of strange forces and to be aware that those others you yearn for are blithely inaccessible to all that moves you – what a pain is this! And yet! He stood there aloof and alone, staring hopelessly at a drawn blind and making, in his distraction, as though he could look out. But yet he was happy. For he lived. His heart was full; hotly and sadly it beat for thee, Ingeborg Holm, and his soul embraced thy blonde, simple, pert, commonplace little personality in blissful self-abnegation.

Often after that he stood thus, with burning cheeks, in lonely corners, whither the sound of the music, the tinkling of glasses and fragrance of flowers came but faintly, and tried to distinguish the ringing tones of thy voice amid the distant happy din; stood suffering for thee – and still was happy! Often it angered him to think that he might talk with Magdalena Vermehren, who always fell down in the dance. She understood him, she laughed or was serious in the right places; while Inge the fair, let him sit never so near her, seemed remote and estranged, his speech not being her speech. And still – he was happy. For happiness, he told himself, is not in being loved – which is a satisfaction of the vanity and mingled with disgust. Happiness is in loving, and perhaps in snatching fugitive little approaches to the beloved object. And he took inward note of this thought, wrote it down in his mind; followed out all its implications and felt it to the depths of his soul.

"Faithfulness," thought Tonio Kröger. "Yes, I will be faithful, I will love thee, Ingeborg, as long as I live!" He said this in the honesty of his intentions. And yet a still small voice whispered misgivings in his ear: after all, he had forgotten Hans Hansen utterly, even though he saw him every day! And the hateful, the pitiable fact was that this still, small, rather spiteful voice was right: time passed and the day came when Tonio Kröger was no longer so unconditionally ready as once he had been to die for the lively Inge, because he felt in himself desires and powers to accomplish in his own way a host of wonderful things in this world.

And he circled with watchful eye the sacrificial altar, where flickered the pure, chaste flame of his love; knelt before it and tended and cherished it in every way, because he so wanted to be faithful. And in a little while, unobservably, without sensation or stir, it went out after all.

But Tonio Kröger still stood before the cold altar, full of regret and dismay at the fact that faithfulness was impossible upon this earth. Then he shrugged his shoulders and went his way.

He went the way that go he must, a little idly, a little irregularly, whistling to himself, gazing into space with his head on one side; and if he went wrong it was because for some people there is no such thing as a right way. Asked what in the world he meant to become, he gave various answers, for he was used to say (and had even already written it) that he bore within himself the possibility of a thousand ways of life, together with the private conviction that they were all sheer impossibilities.

Even before he left the narrow streets of his native city, the threads that bound him to it had gently loosened. The old Kröger family gradually declined, and some people quite rightly considered Tonio Kröger's own existence and way of life as one of the signs of decay. His father's mother, the head of the family, had died, and not long after his own father followed, the tall, thoughtful, carefully dressed gentleman with the field-flower in his buttonhole. The great Kröger house, with all its stately tradition, came up for sale, and the firm was dissolved. Tonio's mother, his beautiful, fiery mother, who played the piano and mandolin so wonderfully and to whom nothing mattered at all, she married again after a year's time; married a musician, moreover, a virtuoso with an Italian name, and went away with him into remote blue distances. Tonio Kröger found this a little irregular, but who was he to call her to order, who wrote poetry himself and could not even give an answer when asked what he meant to do in life?

And so he left his native town and its tortuous, gabled streets with the damp wind whistling through them; left the fountain in the garden and the ancient walnut tree, familiar friends of his youth; left the sea too, that he loved so much, and felt no pain to go. For he was grown up and sensible and had come to realize how things stood with him; he looked down on the lowly and vulgar life he had led so long in these surroundings.

He surrendered utterly to the power that to him seemed the highest on earth, to whose service he felt called, which promised him elevation and honours: the power of intellect, the power of the Word, that lords it with a smile over the unconscious and inarticulate. To this power he surrendered with all the passion of youth, and it rewarded him with all it had to give, taking from him inexorably, in return, all that it is wont to take.

It sharpened his eyes and made him see through the large words which puff out the bosoms of mankind; it opened for him men's souls and his own, made him clairvoyant, showed him the inwardness of the world and the ultimate behind men's words and deeds. And all that he saw could be put in two words: the comedy and the tragedy of life.

And then, with knowledge, its torment and its arrogance, came solitude; because he could not endure the blithe and innocent with their darkened understanding, while they in turn were troubled by the sign on his brow. But his love of the word kept growing sweeter and sweeter, and his love of form; for he used to say (and had already said it in writing) that knowledge of the soul would unfailingly make us melancholy if the pleasure of expression did not keep us alert and of good cheer.

He lived in large cities and in the south, promising himself a luxuriant ripening of his art by southern suns; perhaps it was the blood of his mother's race that drew him thither. But, his heart being dead and loveless, he fell into adventures of the flesh, descended into the depths of lust and searing sin, and suffered unspeakably thereby. It might have been his father in him, that tall, thoughtful, fastidiously dressed man with the wild flower in his buttonhole, that made him suffer so down there in the south; now and again he would feel a faint, yearning memory of a certain joy that was of the soul; once it had been his own, but now, in all his joys, he could not find it again.

Then he would be seized with disgust and hatred of the senses; pant after purity and seemly peace, while still he breathed the air of art, the tepid, sweet air of permanent spring, heavy with fragrance where it breeds and brews and burgeons in the mysterious bliss of creation. So for all result he was flung to and fro for ever between two crass extremes: between icy intellect and scorching sense, and what with his pangs of conscience led an exhausting life, rare, extraordinary, excessive, which at bottom he, Tonio Kröger, despised. "What a labyrinth!" he sometimes thought. "How could I possibly have got into all these fantastic adventures? As though I had a wagonful of travelling gypsies for my ancestors!"

But as his health suffered from these excesses, so his artistry was sharpened; it grew fastidious, precious, *raffiné*, morbidly sensitive in questions of tact and taste, rasped by the banal. His first appearance in print elicited much pleasure; there was joy among the elect, for it was a good and workmanlike performance, full of humour and acquaintance with pain. In no long time his name – the same by which his masters had reproached him, the same he had signed to his earliest verses on the walnut tree and the fountain and the sea, those syllables compact of the north and the south, that good middle-class name with the exotic twist to it – became a synonym for excellence; for the painful thoroughness of the experiences he had gone through, combined with a tenacious ambition and a persistent industry, joined battle with the irritable fastidiousness of his taste and under grinding torments issued in work of a quality quite uncommon.

He worked, not like a man who works that he may live; but as one who is bent on doing nothing but work; having no regard for himself as a human being but only as a creator; moving about grey and unobtrusive among his fellows like an actor without his make-up, who counts for nothing as soon as he stops representing something else. He worked withdrawn out of sight and sound of the small fry, for whom he felt nothing but contempt, because to them a talent was a social asset like another; who, whether they were poor or not, went about ostentatiously shabby or else flaunted startling cravats, all the time taking jolly good care to amuse themselves, to be artistic and charming without the smallest notion of the fact that good work only comes out under pressure of a bad life; that he who lives does not work; that one must die to life in order to be utterly a creator.

"Shall I disturb you?" asked Tonio Kröger on the threshold of the atelier. He held his hat in his hand and bowed with some ceremony, although Lisabeta Ivanovna was a good friend of his, to whom he told all his troubles.

"Mercy on you, Tonio Kröger! Don't be so formal," answered she, with her lilting intonation. "Everybody knows you were taught good manners in your nursery." She transferred her brush to her left hand, that held the palette, reached him her right, and looked him in the face, smiling and shaking her head.

"Yes, but you are working," he said. "Let's see. Oh, you've been getting on," and he looked at the colour-sketches leaning against chairs at both sides of the easel and from them to the large canvas covered with a square linen mesh, where the first patches of colour were beginning to appear among the confused and schematic lines of the charcoal sketch.

This was in Munich, in a back building in Schellingstrasse, several storeys up. Beyond the wide window facing the north were blue sky, sunshine, birds twittering; the young sweet breath of spring streaming through an open pane mingled with the smells of paint and fixative. The afternoon light, bright golden, flooded the spacious emptiness of the atelier; it made no secret of the bad flooring or the rough table under the window, covered with little bottles, tubes, and brushes; it illumined the unframed studies on the unpapered walls, the torn silk screen that shut off a charmingly furnished little living-corner near the door; it shone upon the inchoate work on the easel, upon the artist and the poet there before it.

She was about the same age as himself – slightly past thirty. She sat there on a low stool, in her dark-blue apron, and leant her chin in her hand. Her brown hair, compactly dressed, already a little grey at the sides, was parted in the middle and waved over the temples, framing a sensitive, sympathetic, dark-skinned face, which was Slavic in its facial structure, with flat nose, strongly accentuated cheek-bones, and little bright black eyes. She sat there measuring her work with her head on one side and her eyes screwed up; her features were drawn with a look of misgiving, almost of vexation.

He stood beside her, his right hand on his hip, with the other furiously twirling his brown moustache. His dress, reserved in cut and a soothing shade of grey, was punctilious and dignified to the last degree. He was whistling softly to himself, in the way he had, and his slanting brows were gathered in a frown. The dark-brown hair was parted with severe correctness, but the laboured forehead beneath showed a nervous twitching, and the chiselled southern features were sharpened as though they had been gone over again with a graver's tool. And yet the mouth – how gently curved it was, the chin how softly formed! . . . After a little he drew his hand across his brow and eyes and turned away.

"I ought not to have come," he said.

"And why not, Tonio Kröger?"

"I've just got up from my desk, Lisabeta, and inside my head it looks just the way it does on this canvas. A scaffolding, a faint first draft smeared with corrections and a few splotches of colour; yes, and I come up here and see the same thing. And the same conflict and contradiction in the air," he went on, sniffing, "that has been torturing me at home. It's extraordinary. If you are possessed by an idea, you find it expressed everywhere, you even *smell* it. Fixative and the breath of spring; art and – what? Don't say nature, Lisabeta, 'nature' isn't exhausting. Ah, no, I ought to have gone for a walk, though it's doubtful if it would have made me feel better. Five minutes ago, not far from here, I met a man I know, Adalbert, the novelist. 'God damn the spring!' says he in the aggressive way he has. 'It is and always has been the most ghastly time of the year. Can you get hold of a single sensible idea, Kröger? Can you sit still and work out even the smallest effect, when your blood tickles till it's positively indecent and you are teased by a whole host of irrelevant sensations that when you look at them turn out to be unworkable trash? For my part, I am going to a café. A café is neutral territory, the change of the seasons doesn't affect it; it represents, so to speak, the detached and elevated sphere of the literary man, in which one is only capable of refined ideas.' And he went into the café . . . and perhaps I ought to have gone with him."

Lisabeta was highly entertained.

"I like that, Tonio Kröger. That part about the indecent tickling is good. And he is right too, in a way, for spring is really not very conducive to work. But now listen. Spring or no spring, I will just finish this little place – work out this little effect, as your friend Adalbert would say. Then we'll go into the 'salon' and have tea, and you can talk yourself out, for I can perfectly well see you are too full for utterance. Will you just compose yourself somewhere – on that chest, for instance, if you are not afraid for your aristocratic garments – "

"Oh, leave my clothes alone, Lisabeta Ivanovna! Do you want me to go about in a ragged velveteen jacket or a red waistcoat? Every artist is as bohemian as the deuce, inside! Let him at least wear proper clothes and behave outwardly like a respectable being. No, I am not too full for utterance," he said as he watched her mixing her paints. "I've told you, it is only that I have a problem and a conflict, that sticks in my mind and disturbs me at my work. . . . Yes, what was it we were just saying? We were talking about Adalbert, the novelist, that stout and forthright man. 'Spring is the most ghastly time of the year,' says he, and goes into a café. A man has to know what he needs, eh? Well, you see he's not the only one; the spring makes me nervous, too; I get dazed with the triflingness and sacredness of the memories and feelings it evokes; only that I don't succeed in looking down on it; for the truth is it makes me ashamed; I quail before its sheer naturalness and triumphant youth. And I don't know whether I should envy Adalbert or despise him for his ignorance....

"Yes, it is true; spring is a bad time for work; and why? Because we are feeling too much. Nobody but a beginner imagines that he who creates must feel. Every real and genuine artist smiles at such naïve blunders as that. A melancholy enough smile, perhaps, but still a smile. For what an artist talks about is never the main point; it is the raw material, in and for itself indifferent, out of which, with bland and serene mastery, he creates the work of art. If you care too much about what you have to say, if your heart is too much in it, you can be pretty sure of making a mess. You get pathetic, you wax sentimental; something dull and doddering, without roots or outlines, with no sense of humour – something tiresome and banal grows under your hand, and you get nothing out of it but apathy in your audience and disappointment and misery in yourself. For so it is, Lisabeta; feeling, warm, heartfelt feeling, is always banal and futile; only the irritations and icy ecstasies of the artist's corrupted nervous system are artistic. The artist must be unhuman, extra-human; he must stand in a queer aloof relationship to our humanity; only so is he in a position, I ought to say only so would he be tempted, to represent it, to present it, to portray it to good effect. The very gift of style, of form and expression, is nothing else than this cool and fastidious attitude towards humanity; you might say there has to be this impoverishment and devastation as a preliminary condition. For sound natural feeling, say what you like, has no taste. It is all up with the artist as soon as he becomes a man and begins to feel. Adalbert knows that; that's why he betook himself to the café, the neutral territory – God help him!"

"Yes, God help him, Batuschka," said Lisabeta, as she washed her hands in a tin basin. "You don't need to follow his example."

"No, Lisabeta, I am not going to; and the only reason is that I am now and again in a position to feel a little ashamed of the springtime of my art. You see sometimes I get letters from strangers, full of praise and thanks and admiration from people whose feelings I have touched. I read them and feel touched myself at these warm if ungainly emotions I have called up; a sort of pity steals over me at this naïve enthusiasm; and I positively blush at the thought of how these good people would freeze up if they were to get a look behind the scenes. What they, in their innocence, cannot comprehend is that a properly constituted, healthy, decent man never writes, acts, or composes – all of which does not hinder me from using his admiration for my genius to goad myself on; nor from taking it in deadly earnest and aping the airs of a great man. Oh, don't talk to me, Lisabeta. I tell you I am sick to death of depicting humanity without having any part or lot in it. . . . Is an artist a male, anyhow? Ask the females! It seems to me we artists are all of us something like those unsexed papal singers . . . we sing like angels; but –"

"Shame on you, Tonio Kröger. But come to tea. The water is just on the boil, and here are some *papyros*. You were talking about singing soprano, do go on. But really you ought to be ashamed of yourself. If I did not know your passionate devotion to your calling and how proud you are of it –"

"Don't talk about 'calling', Lisabeta Ivanovna. Literature is not a calling, it is a curse, believe me! When does one begin to feel the curse? Early, horribly early. At a time when one ought by rights still to be living in peace and harmony with God and the world. It begins by your feeling yourself set apart, in a curious sort of opposition to the nice, regular people; there is a gulf of ironic sensibility, of knowledge, scepticism, disagreement, between you and the others; it grows deeper and deeper, you realize that you are alone; and from then on any *rapprochement* is simply hopeless! What a fate! That is, if you still have enough heart, enough warmth of affections, to feel how frightful it is! . . . Your self-consciousness is kindled, because you among thousands feel the sign on your brow and know that everyone else sees it. I once knew an actor, a man of genius, who had to struggle with a morbid self-consciousness and instability. When he had no role to play, nothing to represent, this man, consummate artist but impoverished human being, was overcome by an exaggerated consciousness of his ego. A genuine artist – not one who has taken up art as a profession like another, but artist foreordained and damned – you can pick out, without boasting very sharp perceptions, out of a group of men. The sense of being set apart and not belonging, of being known and observed, something both regal and incongruous shows in his face. You might see something of the same sort on the features of a prince walking through a crowd in ordinary clothes. But no civilian clothes are any good here, Lisabeta. You can disguise yourself, you can dress up like an attaché or a lieutenant of the guard on leave; you hardly need to give a glance or speak a word before everyone knows you are not a human being, but something else: something queer, different, inimical.

"But what is it, to be an artist? Nothing shows up the general human dislike of thinking, and man's innate craving to be comfortable, better than his attitude to this question. When these worthy people are affected by a work of art, they say humbly that that sort of thing is a 'gift'. And because in their innocence they assume that beautiful and uplifting results must have beautiful and uplifting causes, they never dream that the 'gift' in question is a very dubious affair and rests upon extremely sinister foundations. Everybody knows that artists are 'sensitive' and easily wounded; just as everybody knows that ordinary people, with a normal bump of self-confidence, are not. Now you see, Lisabeta, I cherish at the bottom of my soul all the scorn and suspicion of the artist gentry – translated into terms of the intellectual – that my upright old forebears there on the Baltic would have felt for any juggler or mountebank that entered their houses. Listen to this. I know a banker, grey-haired business man, who has a gift for writing stories. He employs this gift in his idle hours, and some of his stories are of the first rank. But despite – I say despite – this excellent gift his withers are by no means unwrung: on the contrary, he has had to serve a prison sentence, on anything but trifling grounds. Yes, it was actually first *in prison* that he became conscious of his gift, and his experiences as a convict are the main theme in all his works. One might be rash enough to conclude that a man has to be at home in some kind of jail in order to become a poet. But can you escape the suspicion that the source and essence of his being an artist had less to do with his life in prison than they had with the reasons that *brought him there*? A banker who writes – that is a rarity, isn't it? But a banker who isn't a criminal, who is irreproachably respectable, and yet writes – he doesn't exist. Yes, you are laughing, and yet I am more than half serious. No problem, none in the world, is more tormenting than this of the artist and his human aspect. Take the most miraculous case of all, take the most typical and therefore the most powerful of artists, take such a morbid and profoundly equivocal work as *Tristan and Isolde*, and look at the effect it has on a healthy young man of thoroughly normal feelings. Exaltation, encouragement, warm, downright enthusiasm, perhaps incitement to 'artistic' creation of his own. Poor young dilettante! In us artists it looks fundamentally different from what he wots of, with his 'warm heart' and 'honest enthusiasm'. I've seen women and youths go mad over artists . . . and I *knew* about them . . . ! The origin, the accompanying phenomena, and the conditions of the artist life – good Lord, what I haven't observed about them, over and over!"

"Observed, Tonio Kröger? If I may ask, only 'observed'?"

He was silent, knitting his oblique brown brows and whistling softly to himself.

"Let me have your cup, Tonio. The tea is weak. And take another cigarette. Now, you perfectly know that you are looking at things as they do not necessarily have to be looked at. . . ."

"That is Horatio's answer, dear Lisabeta. ''Twere to consider too curiously, to consider so.'"

"I mean, Tonio Kröger, that one can consider them just exactly as well from another side. I am only a silly painting female, and if I can contradict you at all, if I can defend your own profession a little against you, it is not by saying anything new, but simply by reminding you of some things you very well know yourself: of the purifying and healing influence of letters, the subduing of the passions by knowledge and eloquence; literature as the guide to understanding, forgiveness, and love, the redeeming power of the word, literary art as the noblest manifestation of the human mind, the poet as the most highly developed of human beings, the poet as saint. Is it to consider things not curiously enough, to consider them so?"

"You may talk like that, Lisabeta Ivanovna, you have a perfect right. And with reference to Russian literature, and the works of your poets, one can really worship them; they really come close to being that elevated literature you are talking about. But I am not ignoring your objections, they are part of the things I have in my mind today. . . . Look at me, Lisabeta. I don't look any too cheerful, do I? A little old and tired and pinched, eh? Well, now to come back to the 'knowledge'. Can't you imagine a man, born orthodox, mild-mannered, well-meaning, a bit sentimental, just simply over-stimulated by his psychological clairvoyance, and going to the dogs? Not to let the sadness of the world unman you; to read, mark, learn, and put to account even the most torturing things and to be of perpetual good cheer, in the sublime consciousness of moral superiority over the horrible invention of existence – yes, thank you! But despite all the joys of expression once in a while the thing gets on your nerves. '*Tout comprendre c'est tout pardonner.*' I don't know about that. There is something I call being sick of knowledge, Lisabeta: when it is enough for you to see through a thing in order to be sick to death of it, and not in the least in a forgiving mood. Such was the case of Hamlet the Dane, that typical literary man. He knew what it meant to be called to knowledge without being born to it. To see things clear, if even through your tears, to recognize, notice, observe – and have to put it all down with a smile, at the very moment when hands are clinging, and lips meeting, and the human gaze is blinded with feeling – it is infamous, Lisabeta, it is indecent, outrageous – but what good does it do to be outraged?

"Then another and no less charming side of the thing, of course, is your ennui, your indifferent and ironic attitude towards truth. It is a fact that there is no society in the world so dumb and hopeless as a circle of literary people who are hounded to death as it is. All knowledge is old and tedious to them. Utter some truth that it gave you considerable youthful joy to conquer and possess – and they will all chortle at you for your naïveté. Oh, yes, Lisabeta, literature is a wearing job. In human society, I do assure you, a reserved and sceptical man can be taken for stupid, whereas he is really only arrogant and perhaps lacks courage. So much for 'knowledge'. Now for the 'Word'. It isn't so much a matter of the 'redeeming power' as it is of putting your emotions on ice and serving them up chilled! Honestly, don't you think there's a good deal of cool cheek in the prompt and superficial way a writer can get rid of his feelings by turning them into literature? If your heart is too full, if you are overpowered with the emotions of some sweet or exalted moment – nothing simpler! Go to the literary man, he will put it all straight for you *instanter*. He will analyse and formulate your affair, label it and express it and discuss it and polish it off and make you indifferent to it for time and eternity – and not charge you a farthing. You will go home quite relieved, cooled off, enlightened; and wonder what it was all about and why you were so mightily moved. And will you seriously enter the lists in behalf of this vain and frigid charlatan? What is uttered, so runs this *credo*, is finished and done with. If the whole world could be expressed, it would be saved, finished and done.... Well and good. But I am not a nihilist –"

"You are not a –" said Lisabeta.... She was lifting a teaspoonful of tea to her mouth and paused in the act to stare at him.

"Come, come, Lisabeta, what's the matter? I say I am not a nihilist, with respect, that is, to lively feeling. You see, the literary man does not understand that life may go on living, unashamed, even after it has been expressed and therewith finished. No matter how much it has been redeemed by becoming literature, it keeps right on sinning – for all action is sin in the mind's eye –

"I'm nearly done, Lisabeta. Please listen. I love life – this is an admission. I present it to you, you may have it. I have never made it to anyone else. People say – people have even written and printed – that I hate life, or fear or despise or abominate it. I liked to hear this, it has always flattered me; but that does not make it true. I love life. You smile; and I know why, Lisabeta. But I implore you not to take what I am saying for literature. Don't think of Cæsar Borgia or any drunken philosophy that has him for a standard-bearer. He is nothing to me, your Cæsar Borgia. I have no opinion of him, and I shall never comprehend how one can honour the extraordinary and daemonic as an ideal. No, life as the eternal antinomy of mind and art does not represent itself to us as a vision of savage greatness and ruthless beauty; we who are set apart and different do not conceive it as, like us, unusual; it is the normal, respectable, and admirable that is the kingdom of our longing: life, in all its seductive banality! That man is very far from being an artist, my dear, whose last and deepest enthusiasm is the *raffiné*, the eccentric and satanic; who does not know a longing for the innocent, the simple, and the living, for a little friendship, devotion, familiar human happiness – the gnawing, surreptitious hankering, Lisabeta, for the bliss of the commonplace. . . .

"A genuine human friend. Believe me, I should be proud and happy to possess a friend among men. But up to now all the friends I have had have been daemons, kobolds, impious monsters, and spectres dumb with excess of knowledge – that is to say, literary men.

"I may be standing upon some platform, in some hall in front of people who have come to listen to me. And I find myself looking round among my hearers, I catch myself secretly peering about the auditorium, and all the while I am thinking who it is that has come here to listen to me, whose grateful applause is in my ears, with whom my art is making me one. . . . I do not find what I seek, Lisabeta, I find the herd. The same old community, the same old gathering of early Christians, so to speak: people with fine souls in uncouth bodies, people who are always falling down in the dance, if you know what I mean; the kind to whom poetry serves as a sort of mild revenge on life. Always and only the poor and suffering, never any of the others, the blue-eyed ones, Lisabeta – they do not need mind. . . .

"And, after all, would it not be a lamentable lack of logic to want it otherwise? It is against all sense to love life and yet bend all the powers you have to draw it over to your own side, to the side of finesse and melancholy and the whole sickly aristocracy of letters. The kingdom of art increases and that of health and innocence declines on this earth. What there is left of it ought to be carefully preserved; one ought not to tempt people to read poetry who would much rather read books about the instantaneous photography of horses.

"For, after all, what more pitiable sight is there than life led astray by art? We artists have a consummate contempt for the dilettante, the man who is leading a living life and yet thinks he can be an artist too if he gets the chance. I am speaking from personal experience, I do assure you. Suppose I am in a company in a good house, with eating and drinking going on, and plenty of conversation and good feeling; I am glad and grateful to be able to lose myself among good regular people for a while. Then all of a sudden – I am thinking of something that actually happened – an officer gets up, a lieutenant, a stout, good-looking chap, whom I could never have believed guilty of any conduct unbecoming his uniform, and actually in good set terms asks the company's permission to read some verses of his own composition. Everybody looks disconcerted, they laugh and tell him to go on, and he takes them at their word and reads from a sheet of paper he has up to now been hiding in his coat-tail pocket – something about love and music, as deeply felt as it is inept. But I ask you: a lieutenant! A man of the world! He surely did not need to. . . . Well, the inevitable result is long faces, silence, a little artificial applause, everybody thoroughly uncomfortable. The first sensation I am conscious of is guilt – I feel partly responsible for the disturbance this rash youth has brought upon the company; and no wonder, for I, as a member of the same guild, am a target for some of the unfriendly glances. But next minute I realize something else: this man for whom just now I felt the greatest respect has suddenly sunk in my eyes. I feel a benevolent pity. Along with some other brave and good-natured gentlemen I go up and speak to him. 'Congratulations, Herr Lieutenant,' I say, 'that is a very pretty talent you have. It was charming.' And I am within an ace of clapping him on the shoulder. But is that the way one is supposed to feel towards a lieutenant – benevolent? . . . It was his own fault. There he stood, suffering embarrassment for the mistake of thinking that one may pluck a single leaf from the laurel tree of art without paying for it with his life. No, there I go with my colleague, the convict banker – but don't you find, Lisabeta, that I have quite a Hamlet-like flow of oratory today?"

"Are you done, Tonio Kröger?"

"No. But there won't be any more."

"And quite enough too. Are you expecting a reply?"

"Have you one ready?"

"I should say. I have listened to you faithfully, Tonio, from beginning to end, and I will give you the answer to everything you have said this afternoon and the solution of the problem that has been upsetting you. Now: the solution is that you, as you sit there, are, quite simply, a bourgeois."

"Am I?" he asked a little crestfallen.

"Yes; that hits you hard, it must. So I will soften the judgment just a little. You are a bourgeois on the wrong path, a bourgeois *manqué*."

Silence. Then he got up resolutely and took his hat and stick.

"Thank you, Lisabeta Ivanovna; now I can go home in peace. I am expressed."

* * *

Towards autumn Tonio Kröger said to Lisabeta Ivanovna:

"Well, Lisabeta, I think I'll be off. I need a change of air. I must get away, out into the open."

"Well, well, well, little Father! Does it please your Highness to go down to Italy again?"

"Oh, get along with your Italy, Lisabeta. I'm fed up with Italy, I spew it out of my mouth. It's a long time since I imagined I could belong down there. Art, eh? Blue-velvet sky, ardent wine, the sweets of sensuality. In short, I don't want it – I decline with thanks. The whole *bellezza* business makes me nervous. All those frightfully animated people down there with their black animal-like eyes; I don't like them either. These Romance peoples have no soul in their eyes. No, I'm going to take a trip to Denmark."

"To Denmark?"

"Yes. I'm quite sanguine of the results. I happen never to have been there, though I lived all my youth so close to it. Still I have always known and loved the country. I suppose I must have this northern tendency from my father, for my mother was really more for the *bellezza*, in so far, that is, as she cared very much one way or the other. But just take the books that are written up there, that clean, meaty, whimsical Scandinavian literature, Lisabeta, there's nothing like it, I love it. Or take the Scandinavian meals, those incomparable meals, which can only be digested in strong sea air (I don't know whether I can digest them in any sort of air); I know them from my home too, because we ate that way up there. Take even the names, the given names that people rejoice in up north; we have a good many of them in my part of the country too: Ingeborg, for instance, isn't it the purest poetry – like a harp tone? And then the sea – up there it's the Baltic! . . . In a word, I am going, Lisabeta. I want to see the Baltic again and read the books and hear the names on their native heath; I want to stand on the terrace at Kronberg, where the ghost appeared to Hamlet, bringing despair and death to that poor, noble-souled youth. . . ."

"How are you going, Tonio, if I may ask? What route are you taking?"

"The usual one," he said, shrugging his shoulders, and blushed perceptibly. "Yes, I shall touch my – my point of departure, Lisabeta, after thirteen years, and that may turn out rather funny."

She smiled.

"That is what I wanted to hear, Tonio Kröger. Well, be off, then, in God's name. Be sure to write to me, do you hear? I shall expect a letter full of your experiences in – Denmark."

And Tonio Kröger travelled north. He travelled in comfort (for he was wont to say that anyone who suffered inwardly more than other people had a right to a little outward ease); and he did not stay until the towers of the little town he had left rose up in the grey air. Among them he made a short and singular stay.

The dreary afternoon was merging into evening when the train pulled into the narrow, reeking shed, so marvellously familiar. The volumes of thick smoke rolled up to the dirty glass roof and wreathed to and fro there in long tatters, just as they had, long ago, on the day when Tonio Kröger, with nothing but derision in his heart, had left his native town. – He arranged to have his luggage sent to his hotel and walked out of the station.

There were the cabs, those enormously high, enormously wide black cabs drawn by two horses, standing in a rank. He did not take one, he only looked at them, as he looked at everything: the narrow gables, and the pointed towers peering above the roofs close at hand; the plump, fair, easy-going populace, with their broad yet rapid speech. And a nervous laugh mounted in him, mysteriously akin to a sob. He walked on, slowly, with the damp wind constantly in his face, across the bridge, with the mythological statues on the railings, and some distance along the harbour.

Good Lord, how tiny and close it all seemed! The comical little gabled streets were climbing up just as of yore from the port to the town! And on the ruffled waters the smoke-stacks and masts of the ships dipped gently in the wind and twilight. Should he go up that next street, leading, he knew, to a certain house? No, tomorrow. He was too sleepy. His head was heavy from the journey, and slow, vague trains of thought passed through his mind.

Sometimes in the past thirteen years, when he was suffering from indigestion, he had dreamed of being back home in the echoing old house in the steep, narrow street. His father had been there too, and reproached him bitterly for his dissolute manner of life, and this, each time, he had found quite as it should be. And now the present refused to distinguish itself in any way from one of those tantalizing dream-fabrications in which the dreamer asks himself if this be delusion or reality and is driven to decide for the latter, only to wake up after all in the end. . . . He paced through the half-empty streets with his head inclined against the wind, moving as though in his sleep in the direction of the hotel, the first hotel in the town, where he meant to sleep. A bow-legged man, with a pole at the end of which burned a tiny fire, walked before him with a rolling, seafaring gait and lighted the gas-lamps.

What was at the bottom of this? What was it burning darkly beneath the ashes of his fatigue, refusing to burst out into a clear blaze? Hush, hush, only no talk. Only don't make words! He would have liked to go on so, for a long time, in the wind, through the dusky, dreamily familiar streets – but everything was so little and close together here. You reached your goal at once.

In the upper town there were arc-lamps, just lighted. There was the hotel with the two black lions in front of it; he had been afraid of them as a child. And there they were, still looking at each other as though they were about to sneeze; only they seemed to have grown much smaller. Tonio Kröger passed between them into the hotel.

As he came on foot, he was received with no great ceremony. There was a porter, and a lordly gentleman dressed in black, to do the honours; the latter, shoving back his cuffs with his little fingers, measured him from the crown of his head to the soles of his boots, obviously with intent to place him, to assign him to his proper category socially and hierarchically speaking and then mete out the suitable degree of courtesy. He seemed not to come to any clear decision and compromised on a moderate display of politeness. A mild-mannered waiter with yellow-white side-whiskers, in a dress suit shiny with age, and rosettes on his soundless shoes, led him up two flights into a clean old room furnished in patriarchal style. Its windows gave on a twilit view of courts and gables, very mediaeval and picturesque, with the fantastic bulk of the old church close by. Tonio Kröger stood a while before this window; then he sat down on the wide sofa, crossed his arms, drew down his brows, and whistled to himself.

Lights were brought and his luggage came up. The mild-mannered waiter laid the hotel register on the table, and Tonio Kröger, his head on one side, scrawled something on it that might be taken for a name, a station, and a place of origin. Then he ordered supper and went on gazing into space from his sofa-corner. When it stood before him he let it wait long untouched, then took a few bites and walked up and down an hour in his room, stopping from time to time and closing his eyes. Then he very slowly undressed and went to bed. He slept long and had curiously confused and ardent dreams.

It was broad day when he woke. Hastily he recalled where he was and got up to draw the curtains; the pale-blue sky, already with a hint of autumn, was streaked with frayed and tattered cloud; still, above his native city the sun was shining.

He spent more care than usual upon his toilette, washed and shaved and made himself fresh and immaculate as though about to call upon some smart family where a well-dressed and flawless appearance was *de rigueur*; and while occupied in this wise he listened to the anxious beating of his heart.

How bright it was outside! He would have liked better a twilight air like yesterday's, instead of passing through the streets in the broad sunlight, under everybody's eye. Would he meet people he knew, be stopped and questioned and have to submit to be asked how he had spent the last thirteen years? No, thank goodness, he was known to nobody here; even if anybody remembered him, it was unlikely he would be recognized – for certainly he had changed in the meantime! He surveyed himself in the glass and felt a sudden sense of security behind his mask, behind his work-worn face, that was older than his years. . . . He sent for breakfast, and after that he went out; he passed under the disdainful eyes of the porter and the gentleman in black, through the vestibule and between the two lions, and so into the street.

Where was he going? He scarcely knew. It was the same as yesterday. Hardly was he in the midst of this long-familiar scene, this stately conglomeration of gables, turrets, arcades, and fountains, hardly did he feel once more the wind in his face, that strong current wafting a faint and pungent aroma from far-off dreams, than the same mistiness laid itself like a veil about his senses. . . . The muscles of his face relaxed, and he looked at men and things with a look grown suddenly calm. Perhaps right there, on that street corner, he might wake up after all. . . .

Where was he going? It seemed to him the direction he took had a connection with his sad and strangely rueful dreams of the night. . . . He went to Market Square, under the vaulted arches of the Rathaus, where the butchers were weighing out their wares red-handed, where the tall old Gothic fountain stood with its manifold spires. He paused in front of a house, a plain narrow building, like many another, with a fretted baroque gable; stood there lost in contemplation. He read the plate on the door, his eyes rested a little while on each of the windows. Then slowly he turned away.

Where did he go? Towards home. But he took a roundabout way outside the walls – for he had plenty of time. He went over the Millwall and over the Holstenwall, clutching his hat, for the wind was rushing and moaning through the trees. He left the wall near the station, where he saw a train puffing busily past, idly counted the coaches, and looked after the man who sat perched upon the last. In the Lindenplatz he stopped at one of the pretty villas, peered long into the garden and up at the windows, lastly conceived the idea of swinging the gate to and fro upon its hinges till it creaked. Then he looked awhile at his moist, rust-stained hand and went on, went through the squat old gate, along the harbour, and up the steep, windy street to his parents' house.

It stood aloof from its neighbours, its gable towering above them; grey and sombre, as it had stood these three hundred years; and Tonio Kröger read the pious, half-illegible motto above the entrance. Then he drew a long breath and went in.

His heart gave a throb of fear, lest his father might come out of one of the doors on the ground floor, in his office coat, with the pen behind his ear, and take him to task for his excesses. He would have found the reproach quite in order; but he got past unchidden. The inner door was ajar, which appeared to him reprehensible though at the same time he felt as one does in certain broken dreams, where obstacles melt away of themselves, and one presses onward in marvellous favour with fortune. The wide entry, paved with great square flags, echoed to his tread. Opposite the silent kitchen was the curious projecting structure, of rough boards, but cleanly varnished, that had been the servants' quarters. It was quite high up and could only be reached by a sort of ladder from the entry. But the great cupboards and carven presses were gone. The son of the house climbed the majestic staircase, with his hand on the white-enamelled, fret-work balustrade. At each step he lifted his hand, and put it down again with the next as though testing whether he could call back his ancient familiarity with the stout old railing.... But at the landing of the entresol he stopped. For on the entrance door was a white plate; and on it in black letters he read: "Public Library".

"Public Library?" thought Tonio Kröger. What were either literature or the public doing here? He knocked... heard a "Come in," and obeying it with gloomy suspense gazed upon a scene of most unhappy alteration.

The storey was three rooms deep, and all the doors stood open. The walls were covered nearly all the way up with long rows of books in uniform bindings, standing in dark-coloured bookcases. In each room a poor creature of a man sat writing behind a sort of counter. The farthest two just turned their heads, but the nearest got up in haste and, leaning with both hands on the table, stuck out his head, pursed his lips, lifted his brows, and looked at the visitor with eagerly blinking eyes.

"I beg pardon," said Tonio Kröger without turning his eyes from the book-shelves. "I am a stranger here, seeing the sights. So this is your Public Library? May I examine your collection a little?"

"Certainly, with pleasure," said the official, blinking still more violently. "It is open to everybody.... Pray look about you. Should you care for a catalogue?"

"No, thanks," answered Tonio Kröger, "I shall soon find my way about." And he began to move slowly along the walls, with the appearance of studying the rows of books. After a while he took down a volume, opened it, and posted himself at the window.

This was the breakfast-room. They had eaten here in the morning instead of in the big dining-room upstairs, with its white statues of gods and goddesses standing out against the blue walls.... Beyond there had been a bedroom, where his father's mother had died – only after a long struggle, old as she was, for she had been of a pleasure-loving nature and clung to life. And his father too had drawn his last breath in the same room: that tall, correct, slightly melancholy and pensive gentleman with the wild flower in his buttonhole.... Tonio had sat at the foot of his death-bed, quite given over to unutterable feelings of love and grief. His mother had knelt at the bedside, his lovely, fiery mother, dissolved in hot tears; and after that she had withdrawn with her artist into the far blue south.... And beyond still, the small third room, likewise full of books and presided over by a shabby man – that had been for years on end his own. Thither he had come after school and a walk – like today's; against that wall his table had stood with the drawer where he had kept his first clumsy, heartfelt attempts at verse. . . . The walnut tree . . . a pang went through him. He gave a sidewise glance out at the window. The garden lay desolate, but there stood the old walnut tree where it used to stand, groaning and creaking heavily in the wind. And Tonio Kröger let his gaze fall upon the book he had in his hands, an excellent piece of work, and very familiar. He followed the black lines of print, the paragraphs, the flow of words that flowed with so much art, mounting in the ardour of creation to a certain climax and effect and then as artfully breaking off. . . .

"Yes, that was well done," he said; put back the book and turned away. Then he saw that the functionary still stood bolt-upright, blinking with a mingled expression of zeal and misgiving.

"A capital collection, I see," said Tonio Kröger. "I have already quite a good idea of it. Much obliged to you. Good-bye." He went out; but it was a poor exit, and he felt sure the official would stand there perturbed and blinking for several minutes.

He felt no desire for further researches. He had been home. Strangers were living upstairs in the large rooms behind the pillared hall; the top of the stairs was shut off by a glass door which used not to be there, and on the door was a plate. He went away, down the steps, across the echoing corridor, and left his parental home. He sought a restaurant, sat down in a corner, and brooded over a heavy, greasy meal. Then he returned to his hotel.

"I am leaving," he said to the fine gentleman in black. "This afternoon." And he asked for his bill, and for a carriage to take him down to the harbour where he should take the boat for Copenhagen. Then he went up to his room and sat there stiff and still, with his cheek on his hand, looking down on the table before him with absent eyes. Later he paid his bill and packed his things. At the appointed hour the carriage was announced and Tonio Kröger went down in travel array.

At the foot of the stairs the gentleman in black was waiting.

"Beg pardon," he said, shoving back his cuffs with his little fingers.... "Beg pardon, but we must detain you just a moment. Herr Seehaase, the proprietor, would like to exchange two words with you. A matter of form.... He is back there.... If you will have the goodness to step this way.... It is *only* Herr Seehaase, the proprietor."

And he ushered Tonio Kröger into the background of the vestibule.... There, in fact, stood Herr Seehaase. Tonio Kröger recognized him from old time. He was small, fat, and bow-legged. His shaven side-whisker was white, but he wore the same old low-cut dress coat and little velvet cap embroidered in green. He was not alone. Beside him, at a little high desk fastened into the wall, stood a policeman in a helmet, his gloved right hand resting on a document in coloured inks; he turned towards Tonio Kröger with his honest, soldierly face as though he expected Tonio to sink into the earth at his glance.

Tonio Kröger looked at the two and confined himself to waiting.

"You came from Munich?" the policeman asked at length in a heavy, good-natured voice.

Tonio Kröger said he had.

"You are going to Copenhagen?"

"Yes, I am on the way to a Danish seashore resort."

"Seashore resort? Well, you must produce your papers," said the policeman. He uttered the last word with great satisfaction.

"Papers...?" He had no papers. He drew out his pocket-book and looked into it; but aside from notes there was nothing there but some proof-sheets of a story which he had taken along to finish reading. He hated relations with officials and had never got himself a passport....

"I am sorry," he said, "but I don't travel with papers."

"Ah!" said the policeman. "And what might be your name?"

Tonio replied.

"Is that a fact?" asked the policeman, suddenly erect, and expanding his nostrils as wide as he could....

"Yes, that is a fact," answered Tonio Kröger.

"And what are you, anyhow?"

Tonio Kröger gulped and gave the name of his trade in a firm voice. Herr Seehaase lifted his head and looked him curiously in the face.

"H'm," said the policeman. "And you give out that you are not identical with an individdle named" – he said "individdle" and then, referring to his document in coloured inks, spelled out an involved, fantastic name which mingled all the sounds of all the races – Tonio Kröger forgot it next minute – "of unknown parentage and unspecified means," he went on, "wanted by the Munich police for various shady transactions, and probably in flight towards Denmark?"

"Yes, I give out all that, and more," said Tonio Kröger, wriggling his shoulders. The gesture made a certain impression.

"What? Oh, yes, of course," said the policeman. "You say you can't show any papers –"

Herr Seehaase threw himself into the breach.

"It is only a formality," he said pacifically, "nothing else. You must bear in mind the official is only doing his duty. If you could only identify yourself somehow – some document..."

They were all silent. Should he make an end of the business, by revealing to Herr Seehaase that he was no swindler without specified means, no gypsy in a green wagon, but the son of the late Consul Kröger, a member of the Kröger family? No, he felt no desire to do that. After all, were not these guardians of civic order within their right? He even agreed with them – up to a point. He shrugged his shoulders and kept quiet.

"What have you got, then?" asked the policeman. "In your portfoly, I mean?"

"Here? Nothing. Just a proof-sheet," answered Tonio Kröger.

"Proof-sheet? What's that? Let's see it."

And Tonio Kröger handed over his work. The policeman spread it out on the shelf and began reading. Herr Seehaase drew up and shared it with him. Tonio Kröger looked over their shoulders to see what they read. It was a good moment, a little effect he had worked out to a perfection. He had a sense of self-satisfaction.

"You see," he said, "there is my name. I wrote it, and it is going to be published, you understand."

"All right, that will answer," said Herr Seehaase with decision, gathered up the sheets and gave them back. "That will have to answer, Petersen," he repeated crisply, shutting his eyes and shaking his head as though to see and hear no more. "We must not keep the gentleman any longer. The carriage is waiting. I implore you to pardon the little inconvenience, sir. The officer has only done his duty, but I told him at once he was on the wrong track. . . ."

"Indeed!" thought Tonio Kröger.

The officer seemed still to have his doubts; he muttered something else about individdle and document. But Herr Seehaase, overflowing with regrets, led his guest through the vestibule, accompanied him past the two lions to the carriage, and himself, with many respectful bows, closed the door upon him. And then the funny, high, wide old cab rolled and rattled and bumped down the steep, narrow street to the quay.

And such was the manner of Tonio Kröger's visit to his ancestral home.

Night fell and the moon swam up with silver gleam as Tonio Kröger's boat reached the open sea. He stood at the prow wrapped in his cloak against a mounting wind, and looked beneath into the dark going and coming of the waves as they hovered and swayed and came on, to meet with a clap and shoot erratically away in a bright gush of foam.

He was lulled in a mood of still enchantment. The episode at the hotel, their wanting to arrest him for a swindler in his own home, had cast him down a little, even although he found it quite in order – in a certain way. But after he came on board he had watched, as he used to do as a boy with his father, the lading of goods into the deep bowels of the boat, amid shouts of mingled Danish and Plattdeutsch; not only boxes and bales, but also a Bengal tiger and a polar bear were lowered in cages with stout iron bars. They had probably come from Hamburg and were destined for a Danish menagerie. He had enjoyed these distractions. And as the boat glided along between flat river-banks he quite forgot Officer Petersen's inquisition; while all the rest – his sweet, sad, rueful dreams of the night before, the walk he had taken, the walnut tree – had welled up again in his soul. The sea opened out and he saw in the distance the beach where he as a lad had been let to listen to the ocean's summer dreams; saw the flashing of the lighthouse tower and the lights of the Kurhaus where he and his parents had lived. . . . The Baltic! He bent his head to the strong salt wind; it came sweeping on, it enfolded him, made him faintly giddy and a little deaf; and in that mild confusion of the senses all memory of evil, of anguish and error, effort and exertion of the will, sank away into joyous oblivion and were gone. The roaring, foaming, flapping, and slapping all about him came to his ears like the groan and rustle of an old walnut tree, the creaking of a garden gate. . . . More and more the darkness came on.

"The stars! Oh, by Lord, look at the stars!" a voice suddenly said, with a heavy singsong accent that seemed to come out of the inside of a tun. He recognized it. It belonged to a young man with red-blond hair who had been Tonio Kröger's neighbour at dinner in the salon. His dress was very simple, his eyes were red, and he had the moist and chilly look of a person who has just bathed. With nervous and self-conscious movements he had taken unto himself an astonishing quantity of lobster omelette. Now he leaned on the rail beside Tonio Kröger and looked up at the skies, holding his chin between thumb and forefinger. Beyond a doubt he was in one of those rare and festal and edifying moods that cause the barriers between man and man to fall; when the heart opens even to the stranger, and the mouth utters that which otherwise it would blush to speak. . . .

"Look, by dear sir, just look at the stars. There they stahd and glitter; by goodness, the whole sky is full of theb! And I ask you, when you stahd ahd look up at theb, ahd realize that bany of theb are a huddred tibes larger thad the earth, how does it bake you feel? Yes, we have idvehted the telegraph and the telephode and all the triuphs of our bodern tibes. But whed we look up there, after all we have to recogdize and uhderstad that we are worbs, biserable worbs, ahd dothing else. Ab I right, sir, or ab I wrog? Yes, we are worbs," he answered himself, and nodded meekly and abjectly in the direction of the firmament.

"Ah, no, he has no literature in his belly," thought Tonio Kröger. And he recalled something he had lately read, an essay by a famous French writer on cosmological and psychological philosophies, a very delightful *causerie*.

He made some sort of reply to the young man's feeling remarks, and they went on talking, leaning over the rail, and looking into the night with its movement and fitful lights. The young man, it seemed, was a Hamburg merchant on his holiday.

"Y'ought to travel to Copedhagen on the boat, thigks I, and so here I ab, and so far it's been fide. But they shouldn't have given us the lobster obelette, sir, for it's going to be storby – the captain said so hibself – and that's do joke with indigestible food like that in your stobach. . . ."

Tonio Kröger listed to all this engaging artlessness and was privately drawn to it.

"Yes," he said, "all the food up here is too heavy. It makes one lazy and melancholy."

"Belancholy?" repeated the young man, and looked at him, taken aback. Then he asked, suddenly: "You are a stradger up here, sir?"

"Yes, I come from a long way off," answered Tonio Kröger vaguely, waving his arm.

"But you're right," said the youth; "Lord kdows you are right about the belancholy. I am dearly always belancholy, but specially on evedings like this when there are stars in the sky." And he supported his chin again with thumb and forefinger.

"Surely this man writes verses," thought Tonio Kröger; "business man's verses, full of deep feeling and single-mindedness."

Evening drew on. The wind had grown so violent as to prevent them from talking. So they thought they would sleep a bit, and wished each other good-night.

Tonio Kröger stretched himself out on the narrow cabin bed, but he found no repose. The strong wind with its sharp tang had power to rouse him; he was strangely restless with sweet anticipations. Also he was violently sick with the motion of the ship as she glided down a steep mountain of wave and her screw vibrated as in agony, free of the water. He put on all his clothes again and went up to the deck.

Clouds raced across the moon. The sea danced. It did not come on in full-bodied, regular waves; but far out in the pale and flickering light the water was lashed, torn, and tumbled; leaped upward like great licking flames; hung in jagged and fantastic shapes above dizzy abysses, where the foam seemed to be tossed by the playful strength of colossal arms and flung upward in all directions. The ship had a heavy passage; she lurched and stamped and groaned through the welter; and far down in her bowels the tiger and the polar bear voiced their acute discomfort. A man in an oilskin, with the hood drawn over his head and a lantern strapped to his chest, went straddling painfully up and down the deck. And at the stern, leaning far out, stood the young man from Hamburg suffering the worst. "Lord!" he said in a hollow, quavering voice, when he saw Tonio Kröger. "Look at the uproar of the elebents, sir!" But he could say no more – he was obliged to turn hastily away.

Tonio Kröger clutched at a taut rope and looked abroad into the arrogance of the elements. His exultation outvied storm and wave; within himself he chanted a song to the sea, instinct with love of her: "O thou wild friend of my youth, Once more I behold thee – " But it got no further, he did not finish it. It was not fated to receive a final form nor in tranquillity to be welded to a perfect whole. For his heart was too full....

Long he stood; then stretched himself out on a bench by the pilot-house and looked up at the sky, where stars were flickering. He even slept a little. And when the cold foam splashed his face it seemed in his half-dreams like a caress.

Perpendicular chalk-cliffs, ghostly in the moonlight, came in sight. They were nearing the island of Möen. Then sleep came again, broken by salty showers of spray that bit into his face and made it stiff.... When he really roused, it was broad day, fresh and palest grey, and the sea had gone down. At breakfast he saw the young man from Hamburg again, who blushed rosy-red for shame of the poetic indiscretions he had been betrayed into by the dark, ruffled up his little red-blond moustache with all five fingers, and called out a brisk and soldierly good-morning – after that he studiously avoided him.

And Tonio Kröger landed in Denmark. He arrived in Copenhagen, gave tips to everybody who laid claim to them, took a room at a hotel, and roamed the city for three days with an open guide-book and the air of an intelligent foreigner bent on improving his mind. He looked at the king's New Market and the "Horse" in the middle of it, gazed respectfully up the columns of the Frauenkirch, stood long before Thorwaldsen's noble and beautiful statuary, climbed the round tower, visited castles, and spent two lively evenings in the Tivoli. But all this was not exactly what he saw.

The doors of the houses – so like those in his native town, with open-work gables of baroque shape – bore names known to him of old; names that had a tender and precious quality, and withal in their syllables an accent of plaintive reproach, of repining after the lost and gone. He walked, he gazed, drawing deep, lingering draughts of moist sea air, and everywhere he saw eyes as blue, hair as blond, faces as familiar, as those that had visited his rueful dreams the night he had spent in his native town. There in the open street it befell him that a glance, a ringing word, a sudden laugh would pierce him to his marrow.

He could not stand the bustling city for long. A restlessness, half memory and half hope, half foolish and half sweet, possessed him; he was moved to drop this rôle of ardently inquiring tourist and lie somewhere, quite quietly, on a beach. So he took ship once more and travelled under a cloudy sky, over a black water, northwards along the coast of Seeland towards Helsingör. Thence he drove, at once, by carriage, for three-quarters of an hour, along and above the sea, reaching at length his ultimate goal, the little white "bath-hotel" with green blinds. It stood surrounded by a settlement of cottages, and its shingled turret tower looked out on the beach and the Swedish coast. Here he left the carriage, took possession of the light room they had ready for him, filled shelves and presses with his kit, and prepared to stop awhile.

It was well on in September; not many guests were left in Aalsgaard. Meals were served on the ground floor, in the great beamed dining-room, whose lofty windows led out upon the veranda and the sea. The landlady presided, an elderly spinster with white hair and faded eyes, a faint colour in her cheek and a feeble twittering voice. She was for ever arranging her red hands to look well upon the table-cloth. There was a short-necked old gentleman, quite blue in the face, with a grey sailor beard; a fish-dealer he was, from the capital, and strong at the German. He seemed entirely congested and inclined to apoplexy; breathed in short gasps, kept putting his beringed first finger to one nostril, and snorting violently to get a passage of air through the other. Notwithstanding, he addressed himself constantly to the whisky-bottle, which stood at his place at luncheon and dinner, and breakfast as well. Besides him the company consisted only of three tall American youths with their governor or tutor, who kept adjusting his glasses in unbroken silence. All day long he played football with his charges, who had narrow, taciturn faces and reddish-yellow hair parted in the middle. "Please pass the *wurst*," said one. "That's not *wurst*, it's *schinken*," said the other, and this was the extent of their conversation, as the rest of the time they sat there dumb, drinking hot water.

Tonio Kröger could have wished himself no better table-companions. He revelled in the peace and quiet, listened to the Danish palatals, the clear and the clouded vowels in which the fish-dealer and the landlady desultorily conversed; modestly exchanged views with the fish-dealer on the state of the barometer, and then left the table to go through the veranda and on to the beach once more, where he had already spent long, long morning hours.

Sometimes it was still and summery there. The sea lay idle and smooth, in stripes of blue and russet and bottle-green, played all across with glittering silvery lights. The seaweed shrivelled in the sun and the jelly-fish lay steaming. There was a faintly stagnant smell and a whiff of tar from the fishing-boat against which Tonio Kröger leaned, so standing that he had before his eyes not the Swedish coast but the open horizon, and in his face the pure, fresh breath of the softly breathing sea.

Then grey, stormy days would come. The waves lowered their heads like bulls and charged against the beach; they ran and ramped high up the sands and left them strewn with shining wet sea-grass, driftwood, and mussels. All abroad beneath an overcast sky extended ranges of billows, and between them foaming valleys palely green; but above the spot where the sun hung behind the cloud a patch like white velvet lay on the sea.

Tonio Kröger stood wrapped in wind and tumult, sunk in the continual dull, drowsy uproar that he loved. When he turned away it seemed suddenly warm and silent all about him. But he was never unconscious of the sea at his back; it called, it lured, it beckoned him. And he smiled.

He went landward, by lonely meadow-paths, and was swallowed up in the beech-groves that clothed the rolling landscape near and far. Here he sat down on the moss, against a tree, and gazed at the strip of water he could see between the trunks. Sometimes the sound of surf came on the wind – a noise like boards collapsing at a distance. And from the tree-tops over his head a cawing – hoarse, desolate, forlorn. He held a book on his knee, but did not read a line. He enjoyed profound forgetfulness, hovered disembodied above space and time; only now and again his heart would contract with a fugitive pain, a stab of longing and regret, into whose origin he was too lazy to inquire.

Thus passed some days. He could not have said how many and had no desire to know. But then came one on which something happened; happened while the sun stood in the sky and people were about; and Tonio Kröger, even, felt no vast surprise.

The very opening of the day had been rare and festal. Tonio Kröger woke early and suddenly from his sleep, with a vague and exquisite alarm; he seemed to be looking at a miracle, a magic illumination. His room had a glass door and balcony facing the sound; a thin white gauze curtain divided it into living- and sleeping-quarters, both hung with delicately tinted paper and furnished with an airy good taste that gave them a sunny and friendly look. But now to his sleep-drunken eyes it lay bathed in a serene and roseate light, an unearthly brightness that gilded walls and furniture and turned the gauze curtain to radiant pink cloud. Tonio Kröger did not at once understand. Not until he stood at the glass door and looked out did he realize that this was the sunrise.

For several days there had been clouds and rain; but now the sky was like a piece of pale-blue silk, spanned shimmering above sea and land, and shot with light from red and golden clouds. The sun's disc rose in splendour from a crisply glittering sea that seemed to quiver and burn beneath it. So began the day. In a joyous daze Tonio Kröger flung on his clothes and, breakfasting in the veranda before everybody else, swam from the little wooden bath-house some distance out into the sound, then walked for an hour along the beach. When he came back, several omnibuses were before the door, and from the dining-room he could see people in the parlour next door where the piano was, in the veranda, and on the terrace in front; quantities of people sitting at little tables enjoying beer and sandwiches amid lively discourse. There were whole families, there were old and young, there were even a few children.

At second breakfast – the table was heavily laden with cold viands, roast, pickled, and smoked – Tonio Kröger inquired what was going on.

"Guests," said the fish-dealer. "Tourists and ball-guests from Helsingör. Lord help us, we shall get no sleep this night! There will be dancing and music, and I fear me it will keep up till late. It is a family reunion, a sort of celebration and excursion combined; they all subscribe to it and take advantage of the good weather. They came by boat and bus and they are having breakfast. After that they go on with their drive, but at night they will all come back for a dance here in the hall. Yes, damn it, you'll see we shan't get a wink of sleep."

"Oh, it will be a pleasant change," said Tonio Kröger.

After that there was nothing more said for some time. The landlady arranged her red fingers on the cloth, the fish-dealer blew through his nostril, the Americans drank hot water and made long faces.

Then all at once a thing came to pass: *Hans Hansen and Ingeborg Holm walked through the room.*

Tonio Kröger, pleasantly fatigued after his swim and rapid walk, was leaning back in his chair and eating smoked salmon on toast; he sat facing the veranda and the ocean. All at once the door opened and the two entered hand-in-hand – calmly and unhurried. Ingeborg, blonde Inge, was dressed just as she used to be at Herr Knaak's dancing-class. The light flowered frock reached down to her ankles and it had a tulle fichu draped with a pointed opening that left her soft throat free. Her hat hung by its ribbons over her arm. She, perhaps, was a little more grown up than she used to be, and her wonderful plait of hair was wound round her head; but Hans Hansen was the same as ever. He wore his sailor overcoat with gilt buttons, and his wide blue sailor collar lay across his shoulders and back; the sailor cap with its short ribbons he was dangling carelessly in his hand. Ingeborg's narrow eyes were turned away; perhaps she felt shy before the company at table. But Hans Hansen turned his head straight towards them, and measured one after another defiantly with his steel-blue eyes; challengingly, with a sort of contempt. He even dropped Ingeborg's hand and swung his cap harder than ever, to show what manner of man he was. Thus the two, against the silent, blue-dyed sea, measured the length of the room and passed through the opposite door into the parlour.

This was at half past eleven in the morning. While the guests of the house were still at table the company in the veranda broke up and went away by the side door. No one else came into the dining-room. The guests could hear them laughing and joking as they got into the omnibuses, which rumbled away one by one.... "So they are coming back?" asked Tonio Kröger.

"That they are," said the fish-dealer. "More's the pity. They have ordered music, let me tell you – and my room is right above the dining-room."

"Oh, well, it's a pleasant change," repeated Tonio Kröger. Then he got up and went away.

That day he spent as he had the others, on the beach and in the wood, holding a book on his knee and blinking in the sun. He had but one thought; they were coming back to have a dance in the hall, the fish-dealer had promised they would; and he did nothing but be glad of this, with a sweet and timorous gladness such as he had not felt through all these long dead years. Once he happened, by some chance association, to think of his friend Adalbert, the novelist, the man who had known what he wanted and betaken himself to the café to get away from the spring. Tonio Kröger shrugged his shoulders at the thought of him.

Luncheon was served earlier than usual, also supper, which they ate in the parlour because the dining-room was being got ready for the ball, and the whole house flung in disorder for the occasion. It grew dark; Tonio Kröger sitting in his room heard on the road and in the house the sounds of approaching festivity. The picnickers were coming back; from Helsingör, by bicycle and carriage, new guests were arriving; a fiddle and a nasal clarinet might be heard practising down in the dining-room. Everything promised a brilliant ball. . . .

Now the little orchestra struck up a march; he could hear the notes, faint but lively. The dancing opened with a polonaise. Tonio Kröger sat for a while and listened. But when he heard the march-time go over into a waltz he got up and slipped noiselessly out of his room.

From his corridor it was possible to go by the side stairs to the side entrance of the hotel and thence to the veranda without passing through a room. He took this route, softly and stealthily as though on forbidden paths, feeling along through the dark, relentlessly drawn by this stupid jigging music, that now came up to him loud and clear.

The veranda was empty and dim, but the glass door stood open into the hall, where shone two large oil lamps, furnished with bright reflectors. Thither he stole on soft feet; and his skin prickled with the thievish pleasure of standing unseen in the dark and spying on the dancers there in the brightly lighted room. Quickly and eagerly he glanced about for the two whom he sought. . . .

Even though the ball was only half an hour old, the merriment seemed in full swing; however, the guests had come hither already warm and merry, after a whole day of carefree, happy companionship. By bending forward a little, Tonio Kröger could see into the parlour from where he was. Several old gentlemen sat there smoking, drinking, and playing cards; others were with their wives on the plush-upholstered chairs in the foreground watching the dance. They sat with their knees apart and their hands resting on them, puffing out their cheeks with a prosperous air; the mothers, with bonnets perched on their parted hair, with their hands folded over their stomachs and their heads on one side, gazed into the whirl of dancers. A platform had been erected on the long side of the hall, and on it the musicians were doing their utmost. There was even a trumpet, that blew with a certain caution, as though afraid of its own voice, and yet after all kept breaking and cracking. Couples were dipping and circling about, others walked arm-in-arm up and down the room. No one wore ballroom clothes; they were dressed as for an outing in the summertime: the men in countrified suits which were obviously their Sunday wear; the girls in light-coloured frocks with bunches of field-flowers in their bodices. Even a few children were there, dancing with each other in their own way, even after the music stopped. There was a long-legged man in a coat with a little swallow-tail, a provincial lion with an eye-glass and frizzed hair, a post-office clerk or some such thing; he was like a comic figure stepped bodily out of a Danish novel; and he seemed to be the leader and manager of the ball. He was everywhere at once, bustling, perspiring, officious, utterly absorbed; setting down his feet, in shiny, pointed, military half-boots, in a very artificial and involved manner, toes first; waving his arms to issue an order, clapping his hands for the music to begin; here, there, and everywhere, and glancing over his shoulder in pride at his great bow of office, the streamers of which fluttered grandly in his rear.

Yes, there they were, those two, who had gone by Tonio Kröger in the broad light of day; he saw them again – with a joyful start he recognized them almost at the same moment. Here was Hans Hansen by the door, quite close; his legs apart, a little bent over, he was eating with circumspection a large piece of sponge-cake, holding his hand cupwise under his chin to catch the crumbs. And there by the wall sat Ingeborg Holm, Inge the fair; the post-office clerk was just mincing up to her with an exaggerated bow and asking her to dance. He laid one hand on his back and gracefully shoved the other into his bosom. But she was shaking her head in token that she was a little out of breath and must rest awhile, whereat the post-office clerk sat down by her side.

Tonio Kröger looked at them both, these two for whom he had in time past suffered love – at Hans and Ingeborg. They were Hans and Ingeborg not so much by virtue of individual traits and similarity of costume as by similarity of race and type. This was the blond, fair-haired breed of the steel-blue eyes, which stood to him for the pure, the blithe, the untroubled in life; for a virginal aloofness that was at once both simple and full of pride.... He looked at them. Hans Hansen was standing there in his sailor suit, lively and well built as ever, broad in the shoulders and narrow in the hips; Ingeborg was laughing and tossing her head in a certain high-spirited way she had; she carried her hand, a schoolgirl hand, not at all slender, not at all particularly aristocratic, to the back of her head in a certain manner so that the thin sleeve fell away from her elbow – and suddenly such a pang of home-sickness shook his breast that involuntarily he drew farther back into the darkness lest someone might see his features twitch.

"Had I forgotten you?" he asked. "No, never. Not thee, Hans, not thee, Inge the fair! It was always you I worked for; when I heard applause I always stole a look to see if you were there.... Did you read *Don Carlos*, Hans Hansen, as you promised me at the garden gate? No, don't read it! I do not ask it any more. What have you to do with a king who weeps for loneliness? You must not cloud your clear eyes or make them dreamy and dim by peering into melancholy poetry.... To be like you! To begin again, to grow up like you, regular like you, simple and normal and cheerful, in conformity and understanding with God and man, beloved of the innocent and happy. To take you, Ingeborg Holm, to wife, and have a son like you, Hans Hansen – to live free from the curse of knowledge and the torment of creation, live and praise God in blessed mediocrity! Begin again? But it would do no good. It would turn out the same – everything would turn out the same as it did before. For some go of necessity astray, because for them there is no such thing as a right path."

The music ceased; there was a pause in which refreshments were handed round. The post-office assistant tripped about in person with a trayful of herring salad and served the ladies; but before Ingeborg Holm he even went down on one knee as he passed her the dish, and she blushed for pleasure.

But now those within began to be aware of a spectator behind the glass door; some of the flushed and pretty faces turned to measure him with hostile glances; but he stood his ground. Ingeborg and Hans looked at him too, at almost the same time, both with that utter indifference in their eyes that looks so like contempt. And he was conscious too of a gaze resting on him from a different quarter; turned his head and met with his own the eyes that had sought him out. A girl stood not far off, with a fine, pale little face – he had already noticed her. She had not danced much, she had few partners, and he had seen her sitting there against the wall, her lips closed in a bitter line. She was standing alone now too; her dress was a thin light stuff, like the others, but beneath the transparent frock her shoulders showed angular and poor, and the thin neck was thrust down so deep between those meagre shoulders that as she stood there motionless she might almost be thought a little deformed. She was holding her hands in their thin mitts across her flat breast, with the finger-tips touching; her head was drooped, yet she was looking up at Tonio Kröger with black swimming eyes. He turned away....

Here, quite close to him, were Ingeborg and Hans. He had sat down beside her – she was perhaps his sister – and they ate and drank together surrounded by other rosy-cheeked folk; they chattered and made merry, called to each other in ringing voices, and laughed aloud. Why could he not go up and speak to them? Make some trivial remark to him or her, to which they might at least answer with a smile? It would make him happy – he longed to do it; he would go back more satisfied to his room if he might feel he had established a little contact with them. He thought out what he might say; but he had not the courage to say it. Yes, this too was just as it had been: they would not understand him, they would listen like strangers to anything he was able to say. For their speech was not his speech.

It seemed the dance was about to begin again. The leader developed a comprehensive activity. He dashed hither and thither, adjuring everybody to get partners; helped the waiters to push chairs and glasses out of the way, gave orders to the musicians, even took some awkward people by the shoulders and shoved them aside.... What was coming? They formed squares of four couples each.... A frightful memory brought the colour to Tonio Kröger's cheeks. They were forming for a quadrille.

The music struck up, the couples bowed and crossed over. The leader called off; he called off – Heaven save us – in French! And pronounced the nasals with great distinction. Ingeborg Holm danced close by, in the set nearest the glass door. She moved to and fro before him, forwards and back, pacing and turning; he caught a waft from her hair or the thin stuff of her frock, and it made him close his eyes with the old, familiar feeling, the fragrance and bitter-sweet enchantment he had faintly felt in all these days, that now filled him utterly with irresistible sweetness. And what was the feeling? Longing, tenderness? Envy? Self-contempt? ... *Moulinet des dames!* "Did you laugh, Ingeborg the blonde, did you laugh at me when I disgraced myself by dancing the *moulinet*? And would you still laugh today even after I have become something like a famous man? Yes, that you would, and you would be right to laugh. Even if I in my own person had written the nine symphonies and *The World as Will and Idea* and painted the Last Judgment, you would still be eternally right to laugh...." As he looked at her he thought of a line of verse once so familiar to him, now long forgotten: "I would sleep, but thou must dance." How well he knew it, that melancholy northern mood it evoked – its heavy inarticulateness. To sleep.... To long to be allowed to live the life of simple feeling, to rest sweetly and passively in feeling alone, without compulsion to act and achieve – and yet to be forced to dance, dance the cruel and perilous sword-dance of art; without even being allowed to forget the melancholy conflict within oneself; to be forced to dance, the while one loved....

A sudden wild extravagance had come over the scene. The sets had broken up, the quadrille was being succeeded by a gallop, and all the couples were leaping and gliding about. They flew past Tonio Kröger to a maddeningly quick tempo, crossing, advancing, retreating, with quick, breathless laughter. A couple came rushing and circling towards Tonio Kröger; the girl had a pale, refined face and lean, high shoulders. Suddenly, directly in front of him, they tripped and slipped and stumbled.... The pale girl fell, so hard and violently it almost looked dangerous; and her partner with her. He must have hurt himself badly, for he quite forgot her, and, half rising, began to rub his knee and grimace; while she, quite dazed, it seemed, still lay on the floor. Then Tonio Kröger came forward, took her gently by the arms, and lifted her up. She looked dazed, bewildered, wretched; then suddenly her delicate face flushed pink.

"*Tak, O, mange tak!*" she said, and gazed up at him with dark, swimming eyes.

"You should not dance any more, Fräulein," he said gently. Once more he looked round at *them*, at Ingeborg and Hans, and then he went out, left the ball and the veranda and returned to his own room.

He was exhausted with jealousy, worn out with the gaiety in which he had had no part. Just the same, just the same as it had always been. Always with burning cheeks he had stood in his dark corner and suffered for you, you blond, you living, you happy ones! And then quite simply gone away. Somebody *must* come now! Ingeborg *must* notice he had gone, must slip after him, lay a hand on his shoulder and say: "Come back and be happy. I love you!" But she came not at all. No, such things did not happen. Yes, all was as it had been, and he too was happy, just as he had been. For his heart was alive. But between that past and this present what had happened to make him become that which he now was? Icy desolation, solitude: mind, and art, forsooth!

He undressed, lay down, put out the light. Two names he whispered into his pillow, the few chaste northern syllables that meant for him his true and native way of love, of longing and happiness; that meant to him life and home, meant simple and heartfelt feeling. He looked back on the years that had passed. He thought of the dreamy adventures of the senses, nerves, and mind in which he had been involved; saw himself eaten up with intellect and introspection, ravaged and paralysed by insight, half worn out by the fevers and frosts of creation, helpless and in anguish of conscience between two extremes, flung to and fro between austerity and lust; *raffiné*, impoverished, exhausted by frigid and artificially heightened ecstasies; erring, forsaken, martyred, and ill – and sobbed with nostalgia and remorse.

Here in his room it was still and dark. But from below life's lulling, trivial waltz-rhythm came faintly to his ears.

Tonio Kröger sat up in the north, composing his promised letter to his friend Lisabeta Ivanovna.

"Dear Lisabeta down there in Arcady, whither I shall shortly return," he wrote: "Here is something like a letter, but it will probably disappoint you, for I mean to keep it rather general. Not that I have nothing to tell; for indeed, in my way, I have had experiences; for instance, in my native town they were even going to arrest me . . . but of that by word of mouth. Sometimes now I have days when I would rather state things in general terms than go on telling stories.

"You probably still remember, Lisabeta, that you called me a *bourgeois*, a *bourgeois manqué*? You called me that in an hour when, led on by other confessions I had previously let slip, I confessed to you my love of life, or what I call life. I ask myself if you were aware how very close you came to the truth, how much my love of 'life' is one and the same thing as my being a *bourgeois*. This journey of mine has given me much occasion to ponder the subject.

"My father, you know, had the temperament of the north: solid, reflective, puritanically correct, with a tendency to melancholia. My mother, of indeterminate foreign blood, was beautiful, sensuous, naïve, passionate, and careless at once, and, I think, irregular by instinct. The mixture was no doubt extraordinary and bore with it extraordinary dangers. The issue of it, a *bourgeois* who strayed off into art, a bohemian who feels nostalgic yearnings for respectability, an artist with a bad conscience. For surely it is my *bourgeois* conscience makes me see in the artist life, in all irregularity and all genius, something profoundly suspect, profoundly disreputable; that fills me with this lovelorn *faiblesse* for the simple and good, the comfortably normal, the average unendowed respectable human being.

"I stand between two worlds. I am at home in neither, and I suffer in consequence. You artists call me a *bourgeois*, and the *bourgeois* try to arrest me.... I don't know which makes me feel worse. The *bourgeois* are stupid; but you adorers of the beautiful, who call me phlegmatic and without aspirations, you ought to realize that there is a way of being an artist that goes so deep and is so much a matter of origins and destinies that no longing seems to it sweeter and more worth knowing than longing after the bliss of the commonplace.

"I admire those proud, cold beings who adventure upon the paths of great and daemonic beauty and despise 'mankind'; but I do not envy them. For if anything is capable of making a poet of a literary man, it is my *bourgeois* love of the human, the living and usual. It is the source of all warmth, goodness, and humour; I even almost think it is itself that love of which it stands written that one may speak with the tongues of men and of angels and yet having it not is as sounding brass and tinkling cymbals.

"The work I have so far done is nothing or not much – as good as nothing. I will do better, Lisabeta – this is a promise. As I write, the sea whispers to me and I close my eyes. I am looking into a world unborn and formless, that needs to be ordered and shaped; I see into a whirl of shadows of human figures who beckon to me to weave spells to redeem them: tragic and laughable figures and some that are both together – and to these I am drawn. But my deepest and secretest love belongs to the blond and blue-eyed, the fair and living, the happy, lovely, and commonplace.

"Do not chide this love, Lisabeta; it is good and fruitful. There is longing in it, and a gentle envy; a touch of contempt and no little innocent bliss."

THE INFANT PRODIGY

THE INFANT prodigy entered. The hall became quiet.

It became quiet and then the audience began to clap, because somewhere at the side a leader of mobs, a born organizer, clapped first. The audience had heard nothing yet, but they applauded; for a mighty publicity organization had heralded the prodigy and people were already hypnotized, whether they knew it or not.

The prodigy came from behind a splendid screen embroidered with Empire garlands and great conventionalized flowers, and climbed nimbly up the steps to the platform, diving into the applause as into a bath; a little chilly and shivering, but yet as though into a friendly element. He advanced to the edge of the platform and smiled as though he were about to be photographed; he made a shy, charming gesture of greeting, like a little girl.

He was dressed entirely in white silk, which the audience found enchanting. The little white jacket was fancifully cut, with a sash underneath it, and even his shoes were made of white silk. But against the white socks his bare little legs stood out quite brown, for he was a Greek boy.

He was called Bibi Saccellaphylaccas. And such indeed was his name. No one knew what Bibi was the pet name for, nobody but the impresario, and he regarded it as a trade secret. Bibi had smooth black hair reaching to his shoulders; it was parted on the side and fastened back from the narrow domed forehead by a little silk bow. His was the most harmless childish countenance in the world, with an unfinished nose and guileless mouth. The area beneath his pitch-black mouse-like eyes was already a little tired and visibly lined. He looked as though he were nine years old but was really eight and given out for seven. It was hard to tell whether to believe this or not. Probably everybody knew better and still believed it, as happens about so many things. The average man thinks that a little falseness goes with beauty. Where should we get any excitement out of our daily life if we were not willing to pretend a bit? And the average man is quite right, in his average brains!

The prodigy kept on bowing until the applause died down, then he went up to the grand piano, and the audience cast a last look at its programmes. First came a *Marche solennelle*, then a *Rêverie*, and then *Le Hibou et les Moineaux* – all by Bibi Saccellaphylaccas. The whole programme was by him, they were all his compositions. He could not score them, of course, but he had them all in his extraordinary little head and they possessed real artistic significance, or so it said, seriously and objectively, in the programme. The programme sounded as though the impresario had wrested these concessions from his critical nature after a hard struggle.

The prodigy sat down upon the revolving stool and felt with his feet for the pedals, which were raised by means of a clever device so that Bibi could reach them. It was Bibi's own piano, he took it everywhere with him. It rested upon wooden trestles and its polish was somewhat marred by the constant transportation – but all that only made things more interesting.

Bibi put his silk-shod feet on the pedals; then he made an artful little face, looked straight ahead of him, and lifted his right hand. It was a brown, childish little hand; but the wrist was strong and unlike a child's, with well-developed bones.

Bibi made his face for the audience because he was aware that he had to entertain them a little. But he had his own private enjoyment in the thing too, an enjoyment which he could never convey to anybody. It was that prickling delight, that secret shudder of bliss, which ran through him every time he sat at an open piano – it would always be with him. And here was the keyboard again, these seven black and white octaves, among which he had so often lost himself in abysmal and thrilling adventures – and yet it always looked as clean and untouched as a newly washed blackboard. This was the realm of music that lay before him. It lay spread out like an inviting ocean, where he might plunge in and blissfully swim, where he might let himself be borne and carried away, where he might go under in night and storm, yet keep the mastery: control, ordain – he held his right hand poised in the air.

A breathless stillness reigned in the room – the tense moment before the first note came. . . . How would it begin? It began so. And Bibi, with his index finger, fetched the first note out of the piano, a quite unexpectedly powerful first note in the middle register, like a trumpet blast. Others followed, an introduction developed – the audience relaxed.

The concert was held in the palatial hall of a fashionable first-class hotel. The walls were covered with mirrors framed in gilded arabesques, between frescoes of the rosy and fleshly school. Ornamental columns supported a ceiling that displayed a whole universe of electric bulbs, in clusters darting a brilliance far brighter than day and filling the whole space with thin, vibrating golden light. Not a seat was unoccupied, people were standing in the side aisles and at the back. The front seats cost twelve marks; for the impresario believed that anything worth having was worth paying for. And they were occupied by the best society, for it was in the upper classes, of course, that the greatest enthusiasm was felt. There were even some children, with their legs hanging down demurely from their chairs and their shining eyes staring at their gifted little white-clad contemporary.

Down in front on the left side sat the prodigy's mother, an extremely obese woman with a powdered double chin and a feather on her head. Beside her was the impresario, a man of oriental appearance with large gold buttons on his conspicuous cuffs. The princess was in the middle of the front row – a wrinkled, shrivelled little old princess but still a patron of the arts, especially everything full of sensibility. She sat in a deep, velvet-upholstered arm-chair, and a Persian carpet was spread before her feet. She held her hands folded over her grey striped-silk breast, put her head on one side, and presented a picture of elegant composure as she sat looking up at the performing prodigy. Next to her sat her lady-in-waiting, in a green striped-silk gown. Being only a lady-in-waiting she had to sit up very straight in her chair.

Bibi ended in a grand climax. With what power this wee manikin belaboured the keyboard! The audience could scarcely trust its ears. The march theme, an infectious, swinging tune, broke out once more, fully harmonized, bold and showy; with every note Bibi flung himself back from the waist as though he were marching in a triumphal procession. He ended *fortissimo*, bent over, slipped sideways off the stool, and stood with a smile awaiting the applause.

And the applause burst forth, unanimously, enthusiastically; the child made his demure little maidenly curtsy and people in the front seat thought: "Look what slim little hips he has! Clap, clap! Hurrah, bravo, little chap, Saccophylax or whatever your name is! Wait, let me take off my gloves – what a little devil of a chap he is!"

Bibi had to come out three times from behind the screen before they would stop. Some late-comers entered the hall and moved about looking for seats. Then the concert continued. Bibi's *Rêverie* murmured its numbers, consisting almost entirely of arpeggios, above which a bar of melody rose now and then, weak-winged. Then came *Le Hibou et les Moineaux*. This piece was brilliantly successful, it made a strong impression; it was an affective childhood fantasy, remarkably well envisaged. The bass represented the owl, sitting morosely rolling his filmy eyes; while in the treble the impudent, half-frightened sparrows chirped. Bibi received an ovation when he finished, he was called out four times. A hotel page with shiny buttons carried up three great laurel wreaths on to the stage and proffered them from one side while Bibi nodded and expressed his thanks. Even the princess shared in the applause, daintily and noiselessly pressing her palms together.

Ah, the knowing little creature understood how to make

people clap! He stopped behind the screen, they had to wait for him; lingered a little on the steps of the platform, admired the long streamers on the wreaths – although actually such things bored him stiff by now. He bowed with the utmost charm, he gave the audience plenty of time to rave itself out, because applause is valuable and must not be cut short. "*Le Hibou* is my drawing card," he thought – this expression he had learned from the impresario. "Now I will play the fantasy, it is a lot better than *Le Hibou*, of course, especially the C-sharp passage. But you idiots dote on the *Hibou*, though it is the first and the silliest thing I wrote." He continued to bow and smile.

Next came a *Méditation* and then an *Étude* – the programme was quite comprehensive. The *Méditation* was very like the *Rêverie* – which was nothing against it – and the *Étude* displayed all of Bibi's virtuosity, which naturally fell a little short of his inventiveness. And then the *Fantaisie*. This was his favourite; he varied it a little each time, giving himself free rein and sometimes surprising even himself, on good evenings, by his own inventiveness.

He sat and played, so little, so white and shining, against the great black grand piano, elect and alone, above that confused sea of faces, above the heavy, insensitive mass soul, upon which he was labouring to work with his individual, differentiated soul. His lock of soft black hair with the white silk bow had fallen over his forehead, his trained and bony little wrists pounded away, the muscles stood out visibly on his brown childish cheeks.

Sitting there he sometimes had moments of oblivion and solitude, when the gaze of his strange little mouselike eyes with the big rings beneath them would lose itself and stare through the painted stage into space that was peopled with strange vague life. Then out of the corner of his eye he would give a quick look back into the hall and be once more with his audience.

"Joy and pain, the heights and the depths – that is my *Fantaisie*," he thought lovingly. "Listen, here is the C-sharp passage." He lingered over the approach, wondering if they would notice anything. But no, of course not, how should they? And he cast his eyes up prettily at the ceiling so that at least they might have something to look at.

All these people sat there in their regular rows, looking at the prodigy and thinking all sorts of things in their regular brains. An old gentleman with a white beard, a seal ring on his finger and a bulbous swelling on his bald spot, a growth if you like, was thinking to himself: "Really, one ought to be shamed." He had never got any further than "Ah, thou dearest Augustin" on the piano, and here he sat now, a grey old man, looking on while this little hop-o'-my-thumb performed miracles. Yes, yes, it is a gift of God, we must remember that. God grants His gifts, or He withholds them, and there is no shame in being an ordinary man. Like with the Christ Child. – Before a child one may kneel without feeling shamed. Strange that thoughts like these should be so satisfying – he would even say so sweet, if it was not too silly for a tough old man like him to use the word. That was how he felt, anyhow.

Art . . . the business man with the parrot-nose was thinking. "Yes, it adds something cheerful to life, a little good white silk and a little tumty-ti-ti-tum. Really he does not play so badly. Fully fifty seats, twelve marks apiece, that makes six hundred marks – and everything else besides. Take off the rent of the hall, the lighting and the programmes, you must have fully a thousand marks profit. That is worth while."

That was Chopin he was just playing, thought the piano-teacher, a lady with a pointed nose; she was of an age when the understanding sharpens as the hopes decay. "But not very original – I will say that afterwards, it sounds well. And his hand position is entirely amateur. One must be able to lay a coin on the back of the hand – I would use a ruler on him."

Then there was a young girl, at that self-conscious and chlorotic time of life when the most ineffable ideas come into the mind. She was thinking to herself: "What is it he is playing? It is expressive of passion, yet he is a child. If he kissed me it would be as though my little brother kissed me – no kiss at all. Is there such a thing as passion all by itself, without any earthly object, a sort of child's-play of passion? What nonsense! If I were to say such things aloud they would just be at me with some more cod-liver oil. Such is life."

An officer was leaning against a column. He looked on at Bibi's success and thought: "Yes, you are something and I am something, each in his own way." So he clapped his heels together and paid to the prodigy the respect which he felt to be due to all the powers that be.

Then there was a critic, an elderly man in a shiny black coat and turned-up trousers splashed with mud. He sat in his free seat and thought: "Look at him, this young beggar of a Bibi. As an individual he has still to develop, but as a type he is already quite complete, the artist *par excellence*. He has in himself all the artist's exaltation and his utter worthlessness, his charlatanry and his sacred fire, his burning contempt and his secret raptures. Of course I can't write all that, it is too good. Of course, I should have been an artist myself if I had not seen through the whole business so clearly."

Then the prodigy stopped playing and a perfect storm arose in the hall. He had to come out again and again from behind his screen. The man with the shiny buttons carried up more wreaths: four laurel wreaths, a lyre made of violets, a bouquet of roses. He had not arms enough to convey all these tributes, the impresario himself mounted the stage to help him. He hung a laurel wreath round Bibi's neck, he tenderly stroked the black hair – and suddenly as though overcome he bent down and gave the prodigy a kiss, a resounding kiss, square on the mouth. And then the storm became a hurricane. That kiss ran through the room like an electric shock, it went direct to people's marrow and made them shiver down their backs. They were carried away by a helpless compulsion of sheer noise. Loud shouts mingled with the hysterical clapping of hands. Some of Bibi's commonplace little friends down there waved their handkerchiefs. But the critic thought: "Of course that kiss had to come – it's a good old gag. Yes, good Lord, if only one did not see through everything quite so clearly – "

And so the concert drew to a close. It began at half past seven and finished at half past eight. The platform was laden with wreaths and two little pots of flowers stood on the lamp-stands of the piano. Bibi played as his last number his *Rhapsodie grecque*, which turned into the Greek national hymn at the end. His fellow-countrymen in the audience would gladly have sung it with him if the company had not been so august. They made up for it with a powerful noise and hullabaloo, a hot-blooded national demonstration. And the ageing critic was thinking: "Yes, the hymn had to come too. They have to exploit every vein – publicity cannot afford to neglect any means to its end. I think I'll criticize that as inartistic. But perhaps I am wrong, perhaps that is the most artistic thing of all. What is the artist? A jack-in-the-box. Criticism is on a higher plane. But I can't say that." And away he went in his muddy trousers.

After being called out nine or ten times the prodigy did not come any more from behind the screen but went to his mother and the impresario down in the hall. The audience stood about among the chairs and applauded and pressed forward to see Bibi close at hand. Some of them wanted to see the princess too. Two dense circles formed, one round the prodigy, the other round the princess, and you could actually not tell which of them was receiving more homage. But the court lady was commanded to go over to Bibi; she smoothed down his silk jacket a bit to make it look suitable for a court function, led him by the arm to the princess, and solemnly indicated to him that he was to kiss the royal hand. "How do you do it, child?" asked the princess. "Does it come into your head of itself when you sit down?" "*Oui, madame*," answered Bibi. To himself he thought: "Oh, what a stupid old princess!" Then he turned round shyly and uncourtier-like and went back to his family.

Outside in the cloak-room there was a crowd. People held up their numbers and received with open arms furs, shawls, and galoshes. Somewhere among her acquaintances the piano-teacher stood making her critique. "He is not very original," she said audibly and looked about her.

In front of one of the great mirrors an elegant young lady was being arrayed in her evening cloak and fur shoes by her brothers, two lieutenants. She was exquisitely beautiful, with her steel-blue eyes and her clean-cut, well-bred face. A really noble dame. When she was ready she stood waiting for her brothers. "Don't stand so long in front of the glass, Adolf," she said softly to one of them, who could not tear himself away from the sight of his simple, good-looking young features. But Lieutenant Adolf thinks: What cheek! He would button his overcoat in front of the glass, just the same. Then they went out on the street where the arc-lights gleamed cloudily through the white mist. Lieutenant Adolf struck up a little nigger-dance on the frozen snow to keep warm, with his hands in his slanting overcoat pockets and his collar turned up.

A girl with untidy hair and swinging arms, accompanied by a gloomy-faced youth, came out just behind them. A child! she thought. A charming child. But in there he was an awe-inspiring . . . and aloud in a toneless voice she said: "We are all infant prodigies, we artists."

"Well, bless my soul!" thought the old gentleman who had never got further than Augustin on the piano, and whose boil was now concealed by a top hat. "What does all that mean? She sounds very oracular." But the gloomy youth understood. He nodded his head slowly.

Then they were silent and the untidy-haired girl gazed after the brothers and sister. She rather despised them, but she looked after them until they had turned the corner.

A GLEAM

HUSH! LET us look into a human soul. On the wing, as it were, and only in passing; only for a page or so, for we are very busy. We come from Florence, Florence of the old days, where we have been dealing with high and tragic and ultimate concerns. And after that – whither? To court, perhaps, a royal castle? Who knows? Strange, faint-shimmering forms are taking their place on the stage. – Anna, poor little Baroness Anna, we have little time to spare for you.

Waltz-time, tinkling glasses; smoke, steam, hubbub, voices, dance-steps. We all know these little weaknesses of ours. Do we secretly love to linger at life's silliest feasts simply because there suffering wears bigger, more childlike eyes than in other places?

"*Avantageur!*" cried Baron Harry, the cavalry captain. He stopped dancing and called the whole length of the hall, one hand on his hip, the other still holding his partner embraced. "That's not a waltz, man, it's a funeral march! You have no rhythm in your body; you just float and sway about without any sense of time. Let Lieutenant von Gelbsattel play, so that we can feel the rhythm. Come on down, *Avantageur*! Dance, if you can do that better!"

And the *Avantageur* stood up, clapped his spurs together, and without a word yielded the platform to Lieutenant von Gelbsattel, who straightaway began to make the piano ring and rattle under the blows from his sprawling white fingers.

Baron Harry, we observe, had music in him: waltz music march music. He had rhythm, joviality, hauteur, good fortune, and a conquering-hero air. His gold-braided hussar jacket suited to a T his glowing young face, unmarked by a single care, a single thought. He was burnt red, like a blond, though hair and moustache were dark – a piquant combination that appealed to the ladies – and the red scar across his right cheek gave a bold and dashing look to his open countenance. The scar might be from a wound, or a fall from a horse – in any case it was glorious. He danced divinely.

But the *Avantageur* floated and swayed – to extend the meaning of Baron Harry's phrase. His eyelids were much too large, so that he could never properly open his eyes; also his uniform fitted him rather carelessly and improbably round the waist – and God alone knew how he came to be a soldier. He had not cared much for this affair with the "Swallows" at the Casino, but even so he had come to it; he had to be careful not to give offence, for two reasons: first, because his origins were bourgeois, and second, because there was a book by him, that he had written or put together, or whatever the word is, a collection of stories, that anybody could buy in a book-shop. It must make people feel a little shy of him, of course.

The hall in the officers' Casino was long and wide – much too large for the thirty people who were disporting themselves in it. The walls and the musicians' platform were decorated with imitation draperies in red plaster, and from the ugly ceiling hung two crooked chandeliers, in which the candles stood askew and dripped hot wax. But the board floor had been scrubbed the whole forenoon by seven hussars told off for the job; and, after all, officers in a little hole like Hohendamm could not expect grandeur. Whatever was otherwise lacking to the feast was amply made up by its characteristic atmosphere; it had the sweetness of forbidden fruit, the reckless charm imparted by the presence of the "Swallows". Even the orderlies smirked knowingly as they renewed the supplies of champagne in the ice-tubs beside the white-covered tables which stood ranged along three walls of the room. They looked at each other and then down with a grin, as servants do when they assist irresponsibly at the excesses of their master. And all this with reference to the "Swallows".

The Swallows, the Swallows? Well, in short, they were the "Swallows from Vienna". Like migratory birds, thirty in the flock, they flew through the country, appearing in fifth-rate variety-theatres and music-halls, where they stood on the stage in easy, unconventional poses and chirped their famous swallows' chorus:

"When the swallows come again
See them fly, *aren't* they fly?"

It was a good song, its humour was not obscure, it was always received with warm applause from the more knowing section of the public.

Well, the Swallows came to Hohendamm and sang in Gugelfing's beer-hall. A whole regiment of hussars were in barracks at Hohendamm, and the Swallows were justified in anticipating a good reception from representative circles. But they got more, they got an enthusiastic one. Evening after evening the unmarried officers sat at the girls' feet, listened to their swallow song, and drank their health in Gugelfing's yellow beer. It was not long before the married officers were there too; one evening Colonel von Rummler appeared in person, followed the programme with the closest interest, and afterwards expressed himself with unlimited approval in various places.

So then the lieutenants and cavalry captains conceived a plan to bring about closer contact with the Swallows: to invite a select group of them – say, ten of the prettiest – to a jolly champagne supper in the Casino. The upper orders could not take any public cognizance of the affair, of course; they had to refrain, however sore at heart. Not only the unmarried lieutenants, however, but also the married first lieutenants and cavalry captains took part, and also – this was the nub of the whole matter, the thing that gave it, so to speak, its "punch" – their wives.

Obstacles and misgivings? First Lieutenant von Levzahn brushed them all away with a phrase: what else, said he, were obstacles for, if not that soldiers might triumph over them! The good citizens of Hohendamm might rage when they heard that the officers were introducing their wives to the Swallows. Of course, they could not have done such a thing themselves. But there were heights, there were aloof and untrammelled regions of existence, where things might freely come to pass that in a lower sphere could only sully and dishonour. It was not as though the worthy natives of Hohendamm were not used to expecting all sorts of unexpectednesses from their hussars. The officers would ride along the middle of the pavement, in broad daylight, if it occurred to them so to do. They had done it. One evening pistols had been fired off in the Markplatz – nobody but the officers could have done that. And had anyone dared to murmur? The following anecdote was simply vouched for:

One morning, between five and six o'clock, Captain of Cavalry Baron Harry, feeling pretty jolly, was on his way home from a party, with his friends Captain of Cavalry von Hühnemann and Lieutenants Le Maistre, Baron Truchsess, von Trautenau, and von Lichterloh. Riding across the Old Bridge, they met a baker's boy, with a great basket of rolls on his shoulder, taking his way through the fresh morning air and whistling blithely as he went. "Give me that basket!" commanded Baron Harry. He seized it by the handle, swung it three times round his head, so skilfully that not a roll fell out, and sent it flying out into the stream on a great curve that showed the strength of his arm. At first the baker's boy was scared stiff. Then as he saw his rolls swimming about, he flung up his arms with a yell and behaved as though he had gone out of his mind. The gentlemen amused themselves for a while with his childish despair; then Baron Harry tossed him a gold piece which would have paid three times over for his loss and the officers rode laughing away home. Then the boy realized that these were the nobility and ceased his outcry.

This story lost no time in going the rounds – but who would have ventured to look askance? You might gnash your teeth over the pranks of Baron Harry and his friends, outwardly you took them with a smile. They were the lords and masters of Hohendamm. And now the lords and masters were having a party for the Swallows.

The *Avantageur* seemed not to know how to dance a waltz any better than to play one. For he did not take a partner, but going up to one of the white tables made a bow and sat down near little Baroness Anna, Baron Harry's wife, to whom he addressed a few shy words. The capacity to amuse himself with a Swallow was simply beyond the poor young man. Actually he was afraid of that kind of girl; he fancied that whatever he said to one she looked at him as though she were surprised – and this hurt the *Avantageur*. But music, even the poorest, always put him into a speechless, relaxed, and dreamy mood – it is often the way with these flabby and futile characters; and as the Baroness Anna, to whom he was entirely indifferent, made only absent answers to his remarks, they soon fell silent and confined themselves to gazing into the whirling scene, with the same somewhat wry smile, strange to say, on both their faces.

The candles flickered and sputtered so much that they became quite mis-shapen with great blobs of soft wax. Beneath them the couples twisted and turned in obedience to Lieutenant von Gelbsattel's inspiring strains. They put out their feet and pointed their toes, swung round with a flourish, then glided away. The gentlemen's long legs bent and balanced and sprang again. Petticoats flew. Gay hussar jackets whirled in abandon; voluptuously the ladies inclined their heads, yielding their waists to their partners' embraces.

Baron Harry held an amazingly pretty young Swallow pressed fairly close to his braided chest, putting his face down to hers and looking unswervingly into her eyes. Baroness Anna's gaze and her smile followed the pair. The long, lanky Lichterloh was trundling along with a plump and dumpy little Swallow in an extraordinary décolletage. But Frau Cavalry Captain von Hühnemann, who loved champagne above all else in life, there she was, dancing round and round under one of the chandeliers, completely absorbed, with another Swallow, a friendly creature whose freckled face beamed all over at the unprecedented honour done her. "My dear Baroness," Frau von Hühnemann said later to Frau First Lieutenant von Truchsess, "these girls are far from ignorant. They know all the cavalry garrisons in Germany off by heart." The pair were dancing together because there were two extra ladies; they were quite unaware that the other couples had gradually left the field to them until they were performing all by themselves. At last, however, they saw what had happened and stood there together in the centre of the hall overwhelmed from all sides by laughter and applause.

Next came the champagne, and the white-gloved orderlies ran from table to table pouring out. After that the Swallows were urged to sing again – they simply had to sing, no matter how out of breath they were.

They stood on the platform that ran along the narrow side of the hall and made eyes at the company. Their shoulders and arms were bare, and they were dressed like the birds they represented, in long dark swallow-tails over pale-grey waistcoats. They wore grey clocked stockings, and slippers with very low vamps and very high heels. There were blonde and brunette, there were the fat good-natured and the interestingly lean; there were some whose cheeks were staringly rouged, others with faces chalk-white like clowns. But the prettiest was the little dark one who had almond-shaped eyes and arms like a child's – she it was with whom Baron Harry had just danced. Baroness Anna, too, found that she was the prettiest one, and continued to smile.

The Swallows sang, and Lieutenant von Gelbsattel accompanied them, flinging back his torso and twisting round his head to look, while his long arms reached out after the keys. They sang as with one voice, that they were gay birds, that they had flown the world over and always left broken hearts behind them when they flew away. They sang another very tuneful piece beginning:

"Yes, yes, the arm-y,
How we love the arm-y,"

and ending with the same. And in response to vociferous requests they repeated their Swallow song, and the officers, who knew it by now as well as they did, joined lustily in the chorus:

"When the swallows come again
See them fly – *aren't* they fly?"

The whole hall rang with laughter and song and the stamping and clinking of spurred feet beating out the time.

Baroness Anna laughed too, at all the nonsense and extravagant spirits. She had laughed so much already, all the evening, that her head and her heart ached, and she would have been glad to close her eyes in darkness and quiet had not Harry been so zealous in his pleasures. "I feel so jolly today," she had told her nieghbour, at a moment when she believed what she said; but the nieghbour had answered only by a mocking look, and she had realized that people do not say such things. If you really feel jolly, you act like it; to proclaim the fact makes it sound queer. On the other hand, it would have been quite impossible to say: "I feel so sad!"

Baroness Anna had grown up in the solitude and stillness of her father's estate by the sea; she was at all times too much inclined to leave out of consideration such home truths as the above, despite her constitutional fear of putting people out and her constitutional yearning to be like them and have them love her. She had white hands and heavy, ash-blond hair – much too heavy for her narrow face with its delicate bones. Between her light eyebrows ran a perpendicular furrow, which gave a pained expression to her smile.

The truth was, she loved her husband. You must not laugh. She loved him even for the prank with the rolls. With a cowering and miserable love, though he betrayed her and daily abused her love like a schoolboy. She suffered for love of him as a woman does who despises her own weak tenderness and knows that power and the happiness of the powerful are justified on this earth. Yes, she yielded herself to love and its torments as once she had yielded herself to him when in a brief attack of tenderness he wooed her; with the hungry yearning of a lonely and dreamy soul, that craves for life and passion and an outlet for its emotions.

Waltz-time, tinkling glasses – hurly-burly and smoke, voices and dancing steps. That was Harry's world and his kingdom. It was the kingdom of her dreams as well: the world of love and life, the happy commonplace.

Social life, harmless, jolly conviviality – what a frightful thing it is, how enervating, how degrading; what a vain, alluring poison, what an insidious enemy to our peace! There she sat, evening after evening, night after night, a martyr to the glaring contrast between the utter emptiness round about her and the feverish excitement born of wine and coffee, of sensual music and the dance. She sat and looked on while Harry exercised his arts of fascination upon gay and pretty ladies – not because of their personal charms but because it fed his vanity to have people see him with them and know what a lucky man he was, how much in the centre of things, without one single ungratified longing. His vanity hurt her – and yet she loved it! How sweet to feel how handsome he was, how young, splendid, and bewitching! The infatuation of those other women would bring her own to fever pitch. And when afterwards, at the end of an evening spent by her in suffering for his sake, he would exhaust himself in stupid and self-centred expressions of enjoyment, there would come moments when her hatred and scorn outweighed her love; in her heart she would call him a puppy and a trifler and try to punish him by not talking, by an absurd and desperate dumbness.

Are we guessing right, little Baroness Anna? Are we giving words to all that lay behind that poor little smile of yours as the Swallows sang their song? Behind that pitiable and shameful state, when you lay in bed afterwards in the grey dawn, thinking of the jests, the witticisms, the repartee, the social charms you should have displayed – and did not! Dreams come, in that grey dawn: you, quite worn with anguish, weep on his shoulder, he tries to console you with some of his empty, pleasant, commonplace phrases, and you are suddenly overcome with the mockery of your situation: you, lying on his shoulder, are shedding tears over the whole world!

Suppose he were to fall ill? Are we right in saying that some small trifling indisposition of his could call up a whole world of dreams for you, wherein you see him as your ailing child; in which he lies helpless and broken before you and at last, at last, belongs to you alone? Do not blush, do not shrink away! Trouble does sometimes make us think bad thoughts. But after all you might trouble yourself a little about the young *Avantageur* with the drooping eyelids, sitting there beside you – how gladly he would share his loneliness with you! Why do you scorn him? Why despise? Because he belongs to your own world, not to that other where pride and high spirits reign, and conscious triumph and dancing rhythm. Truly it is hard not to be at home in one world or in the other. We know. But there is no half-way house.

Applause broke in upon Lieutenant von Gelbsattel's final chords. The Swallows had finished their song. They scorned the steps of the platform and jumped down from the front, flopping or fluttering – the gentlemen rushed up to be of help. Baron Harry helped the little brunette Swallow with the childlike arms; he helped her very efficiently and with understanding for such things. He took her by the thigh and the waist, gave himself plenty of time to set her down, then almost carried her to the table, where he brimmed her glass with champagne till it overflowed, and touched his own to it, slowly, meaningfully, gazing into her eyes with a foolish, insistent smile. He had drunk a good deal, and the scar stood out on his forehead, that looked very white next his glowing face. But his mood was a free and hilarious one, unclouded by any passion.

His table stood opposite to Baroness Anna's across the hall. As she sat talking idly with her neighbour she was listening greedily to the laughter over there and sending stolen and reproachful glances to watch every moment – in that painful state of tension which enables a person to carry on a conversation that complies with all the social forms, while actually being elsewhere all the time, and in the presence of the person one is watching.

Once or twice it seemed to her that the little Swallow's eye caught her own. Did she know her? Did she know who she was? How lovely she looked! How provocative, how full of fascination and thoughtless life! If Harry had been in love with her, if he had burned and suffered for her sake, his wife could have forgiven that, she could have understood and sympathized. And suddenly she became conscious that her own feeling for the little Swallow was warmer and deeper than Harry's own.

And the little Swallow herself? Dear me, her name was Emmy, and she was fundamentally commonplace. But she was wonderful too, with black strands of hair framing a wide, sensuous face, shadowed, almond-shaped eyes, a generous mouth full of shining teeth, and those arms like a child's. Loveliest of all were the shoulders – they had a way of moving with such ineffable suppleness in their sockets. Baron Harry took great interest in these shoulders; he would not have them covered, and set up a noisy struggle for the scarf which she would have put about them. And in all this, nobody in the whole hall saw, neither Baron Harry nor his wife nor anyone else, that this poor little waif, made sentimental by the wine she had drunk, had all the evening been casting longing glances at the young *Avantageur* whose lack of feeling for rhythm had caused his demission from the piano-stool. She had been drawn by the way he played, by his drooping lids, she found him noble, poetic, a being from a different world – whereas she was familiar unto boredom with Baron Harry's sort and all its works and ways. She was saddened, she was wretched, because the *Avantageur* cast not a thought in her direction.

The candles burned low and dim in the cigarette smoke and blue wreaths drifted above the company's heads. There was a smell of coffee on the heavy air, and odours and vapours of the feast, made still more heady by the somewhat daring perfume affected by the Swallows, hung about the scene; the white tables and champagne coolers, the men and women, flirting, giggling and guffawing, weary-eyed and unrestrained.

Baroness Anna talked no more. Despair – and that frightful mixture of yearning, envy, love, and self-contempt which we call jealousy and which makes the world no good place at all to live in – had so subdued her heart that she had not power to counterfeit any more. Let him see how she felt, perhaps he would be ashamed – or at least he would have some feeling about her, of whatever kind, in his heart.

She looked across. The game over there was going rather far, everybody was watching and laughing. Harry had thought of a new kind of amorous struggle with the fair Swallow: it consisted in an exchange of rings. Bracing his knee against hers he held her fast to her chair, and snatched and tugged after her hand in a violent effort to open her little clenched fist. In the end he won. Amid noisy applause he wrenched off the narrow circlet she wore – it cost him some trouble – and triumphantly forced his own wedding ring upon her finger.

Then Baroness Anna stood up. Anger and pain, a longing to hide herself away in the dark with her sense of his so dear unworthiness; a desperate desire to punish him by making a scandal, by forcing him at all costs to acknowledge her presence – such were the emotions that overpowered her. She pushed back her chair, and pale as death she walked across the hall towards the door.

There was a great sensation. People were sobered, they looked at one another grave-faced. One or two gentlemen called out Harry's name. All at once it became still in the hall.

Then something very odd happened: the little Swallow – Emmy – suddenly and decisively espoused the Baroness's cause. Perhaps she was moved by a natural feminine instinct of pity for suffering love; perhaps her own pangs for the

Avantageur with the drooping lids made her see in the little Baroness a fellow-sufferer. In any case, she acted – to the amazement of the company.

"You are coarse!" she said loudly, in the hush, and gave the dumbfounded Harry a great push. Just these three words: "You are coarse." And all at once she was at Baroness Anna's side, where the latter stood lifting the latch of the door.

"Forgive!" she breathed – softly, as though no one else in the room were worthy to hear. "Here is the ring," and she slipped Harry's wedding ring into the Baroness's hand. And suddenly Baroness Anna felt the girl's broad, glowing face bend over this hand of hers; she felt burning on it a soft and passionate kiss. "Forgive!" whispered the little Swallow once more, and ran off.

But Baroness Anna stood outside in the darkness, still quite dazed, and waited for this unexpected event to take on shape and meaning within her. And it did: it was a joy, so warm, so sweet, so comfortable that for a moment she closed her eyes.

We stop here. No more, it is enough. Just this one priceless little detail, as it stands: there she was, quite enraptured and enchanted, simply because a little chit of a strolling chorus-girl had come and kissed her hand!

We leave you, Baroness Anna. We kiss your brow and take our leave; farewell, we must hurry away. Sleep, now. You will dream all night of the Swallow who came to you, and you will have a gleam of happiness.

For it brings happiness, it brings to the heart a little thrill and ecstasy of joy, when two worlds, between which longing plies, for one fleeting, illusory moment touch each other.

AT THE PROPHET'S

STRANGE REGIONS there are, strange minds, strange realms of the spirit, lofty and spare. At the edge of large cities, where street lamps are scarce and policemen walk by twos, are houses where you mount till you can mount no further, up and up into attics under the roof, where pale young geniuses, criminals of the dream, sit with folded arms and brood; up into cheap studios with symbolic decorations, where solitary and rebellious artists, inwardly consumed, hungry and proud, wrestle in a fog of cigarette smoke with devastatingly ultimate ideals. Here is the end: ice, chastity, null. Here is valid no compromise, no concession, no half-way, no consideration of values. Here the air is so rarefied that the mirages of life no longer exist. Here reign defiance and iron consistency, the ego supreme amid despair; here freedom, madness, and death hold sway.

It was eight o'clock of Good Friday evening. Several of those whom Daniel had invited arrived together. Their invitations, written in a peculiar script on quarto paper headed by an eagle carrying a naked dagger in its talons, had summoned them to forgather on this evening for the reading aloud of Daniel's Proclamations. Accordingly they had now met at the appointed hour, in the gloomy suburban street, in front of the cheap apartment-house wherein the prophet had his earthly dwelling.

Some of them knew each other and exchanged greetings. There were the Polish artist and the slender girl who lived with him; a lyric poet; a tall, black-bearded Semite with his heavy, pale wife, who dressed in long, flowing robes; a personage with an aspect soldierly yet somewhat sickly withal, who was a retired cavalry captain and professed spiritualist; a young philosopher who looked like a kangaroo. Finally a novelist, a man with a stiff hat and a trim moustache. He knew nobody. He belonged to quite another sphere and was present by the merest chance, being on good terms with life and having written a book which was read in middle-class circles. He wore an unassuming air, as one who knew that he was here on sufferance and was grateful. At a little distance he followed the others into the house.

They climbed the stairs, one after the other, with their hands on the cast-iron rail. There was no talking; these were folk who knew the value of the Word and were not given to light speaking. In the dim light from the little oil lamps which stood on the window-ledges of the landings they read, as they passed, the names on the doors. The homes and business premises of an insurance official, a midwife, an "agent", a *blanchisseuse du fin*, a chiropodist – they passed by all these, not contemptuous, yet remote. They mounted the narrow staircase as up a dark shaft, cautiously yet firmly; for from far above, from the very last landing, came a faint gleam, a flickering glimmer from the top-most height.

At length they arrived at their goal under the roof, in the light of six candles in divers candlesticks, burning at the head of the stairs on a little table covered with a faded altar-cloth. On the door, which seemed, as indeed it was, the entrance to an attic, was fastened a large pasteboard shield with the name of Daniel on it in Roman lettering done in black crayon. They rang. A boy in a new blue suit and shiny boots opened to them, a pleasant-looking boy with a broad forehead; he had a candle in his hand and lighted them diagonally across the narrow dark corridor into an unpapered mansard-like space, entirely bare save for a wooden hat-stand. With a gesture accompanied by gurgling and babbling sounds but no words the boy invited them to take off their things. When the novelist, inspired by vague sympathy, addressed a question to him it became evident that the lad was dumb. He lighted the guests back across the corridor to another door and ushered them in. The novelist entered last. He was wearing a frock-coat and gloves and had made up his mind to behave as though he were in church.

The moderate-sized room which they entered was pervaded by a ceremonial and flickering illumination from twenty or twenty-five candles. A young girl in a modest frock with white turn-over collar and cuffs, and with an innocent and simple face, stood near the door and gave each guest her hand in turn. This was Maria Josepha, Daniel's sister. The novelist had met her at a literary tea, where she sat bolt upright, cup in hand, and talked of her brother in a clear, earnest voice. Daniel was her adoration.

The novelist looked about for him.

"He is not here," said Maria Josepha. "He has gone out, I do not know where. But in spirit he will be with us and follow sentence by sentence the Proclamations which we shall hear read."

"Who is to read them?" asked the novelist with subdued and reverent mien. He took all this very seriously. He was a well-meaning and essentially modest man, full of respect for all the phenomena of this world, ready to learn and to esteem what was estimable.

"One of my brother's young men, whom we expect from Switzerland," Maria Josepha replied. "He is not here yet. He will be present at the right moment."

On a table opposite the door, with its upper edge resting against the slope of the mansard ceiling, was a large, hastily executed drawing. The candlelight revealed it as a picture of Napoleon, standing in a clumsy and autocratic pose warming his jack-boots at a fire. At the right of the entrance was a shrine or altar whereon, between candles in silver candelabra, was a painted figure of a saint with uplifted eyes and outstretched hands. Before the altar was a prie-dieu. A nearer view disclosed a little amateur photograph leaning at one foot of the saint: a portrait of a young man of some thirty years with pale, retreating brow and bony, vulture-like face, expressive of a ferociously concentrated intellect.

The novelist paused awhile before this picture of Daniel; then he cautiously ventured further into the room. It had a large round table with a polished yellow surface displaying in burnt-work the same design – the eagle with the dagger in its claws – which had been on the invitations. Behind the table were low wooden chairs and lording it over these one elevated seat like a throne, tall, narrow, austere, and Gothic. A long plain bench covered with cheap stuff stood under a low window, occupying the space formed by the meeting of wall and roof. The squat porcelain stove had evidently been giving out too much heat, for the window was open upon a square section of the blue night outside, in whose deeps and distances the bright yellow points of the gas street lamps made an irregular pattern that tailed off into the open country.

But opposite the window the room narrowed to form an alcove lighted more brightly than the rest and furnished half as a cabinet, half as a chapel. On the right side stood a curtained book-shelf with lighted candelabra and antique lamps on top. On the left was a white-covered table holding a crucifix, a seven-branched candlestick, a goblet of red wine, and a piece of raisin cake on a plate. But at the very front was a low platform beneath an iron chandelier; on it stood a gilded plaster column. The capital of the column was covered with an altar-cloth of blood-red silk, and on that lay a thick folio manuscript – it contained Daniel's Proclamations. A light-coloured paper with little Empire garlands covered the walls and sloping ceiling; death-masks, rose-garlands, and a great rusty sword hung against the walls, and besides the large picture of Napoleon there were about the room various reproductions of Luther, Nietzsche, Moltke, Alexander VI, Robespierre, and Savonarola.

"It is all symbolic," said Maria Josepha, searching the novelist's reserved and respectful features to see if she could tell what impression the room made on him. Meanwhile other guests had come in, silently, solemnly; they all began to take their places in suitable attitudes on the benches and chairs. Besides the earlier comers there was a designer, a fantastic creature with a wizened childish face; a lame woman, who was in the habit of introducing herself as a priestess of Eros; an unmarried young mother whose aristocratic family had cast her out, and who was admitted into the circle solely on the ground of her motherhood, since intellectual pretensions she had none; an elderly authoress and a deformed musician – in all some twelve persons. The novelist had retreated into the window-alcove, and Maria Josepha sat near the door, her hands close together on her knees. Thus they awaited the young man from Switzerland, who would be present at the right moment.

Suddenly another guest arrived – a rich woman who out of sheer amateurishness had a habit of frequenting such gatherings as this. She came from the city in her satin-lined coupé, from her splendid house with the tapestries on the walls and the giallo-antico door-jambs; she had come all the way up the stairs and in at the door, sweet-scented, luxurious, lovely, in a blue cloth frock with yellow embroidery, a Paris hat on her red-brown hair, and a smile in her Titian eyes. She came out of curiosity, out of boredom, out of craving for something different, out of amiable extravagance, out of pure universal goodwill, which is rare enough in this world. She greeted Daniel's sister, also the novelist, who had entrée at her house, and sat down on the bench under the window, between the priestess of Eros and the kangaroo-philosopher – quite as though she were used to such things.

"I was almost too late," said she softly, with her lovely mobile lips, to the novelist as he sat behind her. "I had people at tea; it was rather dragged out."

The novelist was slightly overcome; how thankful he was that he had on presentable clothes! "How beautiful she is!" thought he. "Actually she is worthy of being her daughter's mother."

"And Fräulein Sonia?" he asked over her shoulder. "You have not brought Fräulein Sonia with you?"

Sonia was the rich woman's daughter; in the novelist's eyes altogether too good to be true, a marvellous creature, a consummate cultural product, an achieved ideal. He said her name twice because it gave him an indescribable pleasure to pronounce it.

"Sonia is a little ailing," said the rich woman. "Yes, imagine, she has a bad foot. Oh, nothing – a swelling, something like a little inflammation or gathering. It has been lanced. The lancing may not have been necessary but she wanted it done."

"She wanted it done," repeated the novelist in an enraptured whisper. "How characteristic! But how may I express my sympathy for the affliction?"

"Of course, I will give her your greetings," said the rich woman. And as he was silent: "Is not that enough for you?"

"No, that is not enough for me," said he, quite low; and as she had a certain respect for his writing she replied with a smile:

"Then send her a few flowers."

"Oh, thanks!" said he. "Thanks, I will." And inwardly he thought: "A few flowers! A whole flower-shopful! Tomorrow, before breakfast. I'll go in a droshky." And he felt that life and he were on very good terms.

Just then a noise was heard outside, the door opened with a quick push and closed, and before the guests there stood in the candlelight a short, thick-set youth in a dark jacket suit – the young man from Switzerland. He glanced over the room with a threatening eye, went in an impetuous stride to the platform at the front of the alcove, and placed himself behind the plaster column – all with a certain violence, as though he wished to root himself there. He seized the top quire of the manuscript and began to read straightaway.

He was perhaps eight-and-twenty years old, short-necked and ill-favoured. His close-cropped hair grew to a point very far down on the low and wrinkled brow. His face, beardless, heavy, and morose, displayed a nose like a bulldog's, large cheek-bones, sunken cheeks, and thick protruding lips, which seemed to form words clumsily, reluctantly, and as it were with a sort of flaccid contempt. The face was coarse and yet pale. He read too loudly, in a fierce voice which nevertheless had a suppressed tremolo and sometimes faltered for lack of breath. The hand that held the manuscript was broad and red and yet it shook. The youth displayed an odd and unpleasant mixture of brutality and weakness and the matter of his reading was in remarkable consonance with its manner.

The "Proclamations" consisted of sermons, parables, theses, laws, prophecies, and exhortations resembling orders of the day, following each other in a mingled style of psalter and revelation with an endless succession of technical phrases, military and strategic as well as philosophical and critical. A fevered and frightfully irritable ego here expanded itself, a self-isolated megalomaniac flooded the world with a hurricane of violent and threatening words. *Christus imperator maximus* was his name; he enrolled troops ready to die for the subjection of the globe; he sent out embassies, gave inexorable ultimata, exacted poverty and chastity, and with a sort of morbid enjoyment reiterated his roaring demand for unconditional obedience. Buddha, Alexander, Napoleon and Jesus – their names were mentioned as his humble forerunners, not worthy to unloose the laces of their spiritual lord.

The young man read for an hour; then panting he took a swallow from the beaker of red wine and began on fresh Proclamations. Beads of sweat stood on his low brow, his thick lips quivered, and in between the words he kept expelling the air through his nose with a short, snorting sound, an exhausted roar. The solitary ego sang, raved, commanded. It would lose itself in confused pictures, go down in an eddy of logical error, to bob up again suddenly and startlingly in an entirely unexpected place. Blasphemies and hosannahs – a waft of incense and a reek of blood. In thunderings and slaughterings the world was conquered and redeemed.

It would have been hard to estimate the effect of Daniel's Proclamations upon their hearers. Some with heads tipped far back looked up to the ceiling with a blank stare; others held their heads in their hands, bowed deep over their knees. The eyes of the priestess of Eros wore a strange veiled look whenever the word "chastity" was pronounced; and the kangaroo-philosopher now and then wrote something or other with his long crooked forefinger in the air. The novelist sought in vain for a comfortable position for his aching back. At ten o'clock he had a vision of a ham sandwich but manfully put it away.

Towards half past ten the young man was seen to be holding the last sheet of paper in his red, unsteady hand. This was his peroration. "Soldiers," he cried, his voice of thunder failing for very weakness, "I deliver to you for plundering – the world!" He stepped down from the platform, looked at everybody with a threatening glance, and went out of the door, as violently as he had come in.

His audience remained a moment motionless in the last position they had taken up. Then as with a common resolve they rose and departed, each one pressing Maria Josepha's hand with a low-toned word, as she stood once more, chaste and silent, at the door.

The dumb boy was still on duty outside. He lighted the guests into the cloak-room, helped them with their overcoats, and led them down the narrow stair, with the flickering light falling upon it from up there where Daniel's kingdom was; down to the outer door, which he unlocked. One after the other the guests issued into the dismal suburban street.

The rich woman's coupé stood before the house; the coachman on the box between the two clear-shining lanterns carried the hand with the whip in it to his hat. The novelist accompanied the rich woman to her carriage.

"How are you feeling?" he inquired.

"I don't like to talk about such things," she answered. "Perhaps he really is a genius or something like that."

"Yes, after all, what is genius?" said he pensively. "In this Daniel all the conditions are present: the isolation, the freedom, the spiritual passion, the magnificent vision, the belief in his own power, yes, even the approximation to madness and crime. What is there lacking? Perhaps the human element? A little feeling, a little yearning, a little love? But of course that is just a rough hypothesis."

"Greet Sonia for me," said he, after she was seated, as she gave him her hand. He looked anxiously into her face to see how she would take his speaking simply of Sonia and not of "Fräulein Sonia" or "your daughter".

She esteemed his literary talent and so she suffered it, with a smile. "I will do so," said she.

"Thanks," said he, and a bewildering gust of hope swept over him. "Now I am as hungry as a wolf for my supper."

Yes, he and life were certainly on good terms!

FIORENZA

TIME: the afternoon of the 8th of April 1492
PLACE: the Villa Medicea, Careggi, near Florence

ACT ONE

The study of Cardinal Giovanni de' Medici, a private apartment on the top floor of the villa. Tapestries on the walls; between them book-shelves are built in, sparsely filled with books and scrolls. Windows high up in the walls, with deep sills. Entrance centre back, covered by a tapestry. On the left a table with a heavy brocade cover; on it an ink-pot, pens, and paper. Before it an arm-chair with a high back. Down stage right a sofa decorated with the Medici arms; leaning against it a lute. On the right wall a large painting with a mythological subject. In front of it an étagère with ornaments.

I

On the sofa sits the young Cardinal Giovanni – seventeen years old, in red skull-cap and mantle with broad white turn-over collar. He has a charming, whimsical, effeminate face. On a chair beside him Angelo Poliziano, in a long, dark, flowing robe with full sleeves, finished at the neck with a narrow white collar. His shrewd, sensual face, framed in grey curls, with powerful aquiline nose and a mouth with deep folds at the corners, is turned towards the Cardinal. The latter, being short-sighted, is using a lorgnon shaped like a pair of scissors. Books lie heaped on the carpet, some of them open. Poliziano holds a book in his hands.

POLIZIANO: . . . and at this point, Giovanni, my friend and son of my great and beloved friend Lorenzo, I come back to the hope, the justifiable and well-founded wish which the whole wisdom-loving world, like myself, is looking to you to gratify. Do not think I forget the respect I owe to your lofty position in the hierarchy...

GIOVANNI: Pardon me, Messer Angelo! Have you not heard that Fra Girolamo said of late in the cathedral that in the spiritual hierarchy the Christian priesthood follows after the lowest of the angels? (*He giggles.*)

POLIZIANO: What?... Perhaps...yes, I may have heard it. But no matter. What I wish to make clear to you is this: that Christ's vicar on earth, whose tiara in the course of events you will very likely be called upon to wear, does nothing incompatible with his holy office in carrying out the plan I have in mind, which is that of all lovers of wisdom. You are aware, Giovanni, that I refer to the canonization of Plato. He is divine, thus it is but obeying the dictates of reason to make him a god. Star-gazers have read in the heavens that the performance of this reasonable and meritorious act has been reserved to the enlightened dynasty of the Medicis; not only so, but it is altogether a fitting and logical thing to do. And for Christ. He Himself doubtless could but sanction the canonization of the ancient philosopher. More than once did the Sibyls explicitly prophesy the coming of Christ; I do not need to remind my pupil of Virgil's pregnant lines. Plato himself, as we have on the best authority, spoke of it in no ambiguous terms; and we read in Porphyrius that the gods recognized the rare piety and religiosity of the Nazarene; they confirmed the fact of His immortality and were on the whole favourably disposed towards Him.... In short, my dear Giovanni, I pray that the gods will let me live to see the day which will bring to fulfilment my oft-expressed hope. That day will be the ultimate fruition of our Platonic studies together. (*He sees that the Cardinal is chuckling to himself.*) Might I ask what it is that amuses you?

GIOVANNI: Nothing, nothing, Messer Angelo – really nothing at all. I was only reminded of what Fra Girolamo said of late in the cathedral: "Plato's *Symposium* is marked by an indecent pseudo-morality." That is good, isn't it? (*Laughs.*) I find it a shrewd observation. All the same...

POLIZIANO (*after a pause*): I am grieved, Giovanni, and I think justifiably. You are inattentive this afternoon, you were extremely inattentive all the time we were reading. I put it down to the unfavourable circumstances, and the care which sits heavy upon us all. Your glorious father is ill, and very ill, there are fears for his life. But we place our hopes on the costly medicine which the Jewish doctor from Pavia has administered to him; and, moreover, it seems to me that philosophy, in our hour of need, should be our loftiest and most grateful consolation. I might but too well understand it if the thought of your father should distract you from your studies. But since I am driven to realize that your mind is taken up with this absurd and fantastic mendicant friar, this Fra Girolamo –

GIOVANNI: Whose mind is not taken up with him? Forgive me, Messer Angelo! Do not be angry – look kindly at me; anger does not become you. Only the beautiful, the formal, the pellucid should be the subject of your talk. Do I love you or do I not? Who knows all your verses, and almost your whole vintage of Latin hexameters off by heart? Well, then! But this man from Ferrara – I should like to talk about him a little. You must agree that after all he is an original and arresting figure. He is the prior of a mendicant order and as such despicable. These orders are the object of general mirth and as often as I have been in Rome I have been told that they are nothing but an embarrassment to the Church. But when by reason of his own rare gifts one of these despised Frati not only overcomes the existing prejudice against his class but turns it into admiration for his person –

POLIZIANO: Admiration! Who admires him? Not I. Certainly not I. The rabble honours itself in his image.

GIOVANNI: No, no, no, Messer Angelo – he does not belong to the rabble. And not only because he comes of an old and highly respected Ferrarese family. I have heard him more than once in Santa Maria del Fiore and I assure you that he impressed me as a many-sided man. I grant you that he lacks culture and elegance to an astounding degree. But a close view shows that even so he must be constitutionally sensitive in both mind and body. Often in the pulpit he has to sit down, so shaken is he by his own passion – they say that he is so exhausted after every sermon that he has to go to bed. His voice is marvellously soft, it is only his eyes and his gestures that sometimes make it seem like crashing thunder. I will even admit to you – when I am alone, sometimes, I take up my Venetian mirror and try to imitate the way he hurls his lightnings against the clergy. (*Imitating*) "But now I will stretch out My hand, saith the Lord: I will fall upon thee, thou adulterous, thou infamous, thou shameless Church! My sword shall fall upon thy favourites, upon the places of thy shame, thy palaces and thy harlots, and I will visit My justice upon thee. . . ." So it goes – but you see I cannot do it. I should be a poor hand at preaching repentance. Florence would laugh me to scorn, pert wench that she is! Even less – though I am a cardinal and shall come to be a pope – could I foretell events like him, who is but a begging friar, Messer Angelo. More than a year ago he prophesied the coming deaths of my father the Magnifico and of the Pope; may God forfend that this prophecy be fulfilled. But even now so much has come to pass that the jovial man who with such a pretty wit took the name of Innocent has been lying for weeks in a stupor so that the whole court has at times thought him dead; and my father is so ill that this morning they gave him the sacrament. Anyhow, that seems to have revived him; he was able to make a joke about it, although in a very feeble voice. But . . .

POLIZIANO: Your father overdid during carnival, that is all. There was great excess at the artist balls, and Lorenzo loves beauty and pleasure with such a burning love that he is too ready to forget considerations of health. He plies the cup of love and joy as though his body were as puissant as his wonderful soul. But it is not. . . . A child could foretell that some day he would have to learn his lesson – and you attribute a miracle to this monk of yours? Fie, Giovanni! Either you are a fool or you want to make one of me, which is more likely. You would tell me of his visions; how now and again he sees the heavens open, hears voices, and beholds the rain of fire, of swords and arrows. I am willing to believe that this good Brother believes in his own revelations, I will not laugh at their simplicity. But I hardly think that they would visit him if he were a little more educated and disciplined, if his gifts and his learning were not so hopelessly disorderly and muddled.

GIOVANNI: I am convinced of that, it is perfectly true. All of us are far too cultured and instructed to see visions; if we did have them we would not believe in them. But he succeeds where we fail, Messer Angelo!

POLIZIANO: You cannot talk of success where only the rabble is won over, and that by flattering its miserable instincts. Otherwise Florence must blush indeed in the sight of all Italy at the success of this disgusting monk. I have been once in the Duomo when he preached, this much-admired Prior of San Marco – and, by all the Graces, Muses, and Nymphs, I will not go again! I have always flattered myself that I knew something about eloquence – but it seems I was mistaken. There was a time in Florence when a preacher was admired for his choice and measured use of gesture, word and phrase, his familiarity with the classic authors as displayed in apposite quotation; for his pregnant sayings, the clarity and elegance of his language, the masterly structure of his sentences, and for a voice of pure quality uttering harmonious cadences. But these it seems are all nothing. Real superiority is the achievement of a sickly boor with eyes like coals of fire, whose gestures are out of all compass, who sheds tears over the decay of chastity, cries down culture and the arts, vilifies the poets and philosophers, quotes exclusively from the Bible, as though the Latinity of that book were not execrable – and to cap all dares to inveigh against the life and the government of our great Lorenzo. (*He has risen and strides excitedly up and down the room, the Cardinal surveying him complacently through his lorgnon.*)

GIOVANNI: By the Holy Virgin, Messer Angelo, how splendidly wroth you are! You look at things with such conviction from a single point of view – Brother Girolamo himself could not improve upon your single-mindedness.

Go on! I listen with the utmost enjoyment. Speak even more bitingly, more crushingly. "Epicureans and swine" – he spoke of "epicureans and swine". The phrase is in everybody's mouth. He referred to my father's friends, to Ficino, to Messer Pulci, to the artists, presumably also to you. (*Laughs.*)

POLIZIANO: Hearken, my Lord Cardinal –

GIOVANNI: Now, now! What ails you? Do I love you or do I not? You are as right as you can be. . . .

POLIZIANO: I do not say that I am right, but I say that I despise this worm for imagining that he thinks he holds the truth in his hands. One little smile, ye gods! One single sly ironic word! One subtle sceptical allusion to raise him above the masses and put him in touch with the cultured among his congregation! Then I could forgive him all. But nothing, nothing, nothing of the kind. One dismal indiscriminate condemnation of unbelief, immorality, blasphemy, vice, luxury, and the lusts of the flesh –

GIOVANNI (*shaking with laughter*): *Vaccæ pingues* – oh, my God, did you hear what he said about the fat cows that graze on the hills of Samaria? He spoke of them when he was expounding Amos. "These fat cows," said he, "would you hear what they mean? They mean the courtesans, all the thousands and thousands of fat courtesans in Italy!" That is good – it is capital. Do not deny it. It takes imagination to think of a thing like that, it is a witty figure that sticks in the memory. *Vaccæ pingues*. I shall never see a fat cow again without thinking of a daughter of joy; no, nor a priestess of Venus without thinking of a fat cow. I will tell you a little discovery I have made. In wit, in the humorous point of view, lies the strongest antidote to fleshly desire. I am not a hang-dog, am I? I delight in statues, pictures, architecture, verse, music, and the jest and have no other wish than to live tranquilly in the enjoyment of these beautiful things; but I assure you that I not infrequently find the temptations of love an inconvenience. They destroy my balance, they cloud my happiness, they inflame me more than is agreeable. . . . Well, yesterday on the Piazza fat Penthesilea went past my litter, the one that lives by Porta San Gallo. I looked at her, and actually I did not feel the slightest temptation. I was simply seized with such a fit of laughter that I had to draw the curtains. She walked just like a fat cow that grazes on the hills of Samaria!

POLIZIANO (*indulgently*): What a child you are, Giovanni, you with your cows! Donna Penthesilea is a very beautiful woman, versed in the arts and humanities, who does not at all deserve the comparison. But I rejoice to hear that you can see the funny side of your exhorter to penitence.

GIOVANNI: You are wrong there. I take him with all possible seriousness. One must. He is a famous man. Our beloved Florence knows well, I should say, how to annihilate with her wit people who being without talents are so foolhardy as to expose themselves. He has made her quake. At least one must grant that in religious matters he has great gifts and much experience.

POLIZIANO: Much experience! Splendid! When a man has no knowledge, then his inner experience, his inner light, make up for everything. He disowns the ancients, he will naught of Crassus or Hortensius or Cicero. He has not even the degree of Doctor of Theology and he disdains all the wisdom of the world. He knows, recognizes, and wants only himself, himself alone; he talks of himself whatever he may be speaking of – yes, sometimes he deals with episodes out of his private life and seeks to give them deep significance – as though anybody of any education or good taste could attach significance to what happened to this black bat of a begging monk. A few days ago at Antonio Miscomini the printer's I came across a copy of his pamphlet *On Love to Jesus Christ* – there have been, absurdly enough, seven editions of it within a short time. Since our good Frate rejects the glorious dialogue of Plato, I was curious to see what he himself would have to say about love. What I read, my friend, was disgusting beyond all expectation. A perfervid and chaotic mixture of gloomy and fevered and drunken emotions, forebodings, and introspections which struggled in vain for clear expression. It made me reel, I felt actually nauseated. In all seriousness, I can well believe that this sort of study must be a wearing occupation. I understand his collapses and his fainting fits. Instead of running away from his honoured parents and taking refuge in a cloister, to sit between bare walls and stare into his own murky soul, this idiot ought to have submitted to teaching and sharpened his own perceptions of the colour and variety of the glorious material world. Then he would realize that work is not a castigation and martyrdom but a joyous thing, and that all that is good is blithely and easily accomplished. I wrote my drama *Orpheus* in a few days; and in face of the beauty of this world my songs flow from my lips as I drink, at the festal board – I do not need to go to bed after them.

GIOVANNI: Unless the wine were to blame! Yes, Messer Angelo, you are the light of the age. Who can equal you? Who sees the world so beauteous as you do? No one sings as sweetly as you. No one so sweetly sings the praises of a lovely boy. Perhaps Fra Girolamo has said to himself that an ambitious man must succeed by contrast if he wants to compete with you. . . .

POLIZIANO: Are you mocking me?

GIOVANNI: That I cannot tell. You ask too much. I never know when I am mocking and when I am serious. . . . Who is there?

AN USHER (*lifting the portière at the entrance door*): The Prince of Mirandola.

GIOVANNI: Pico! Let him come in. Shall he not, Messer Angelo? He is welcome, is he not? (*The usher withdraws.*) Come hither, do not be angry – do I love you, or do I not? You are in the right, I own myself defeated. Brother Girolamo is a bat – there, are you content? One must argue a bit, eh? If you had taken his side I should have abused him with all my strength. Here is Pico. Good day, Pico!

POLIZIANO: If you were less charming, you rogue, one might be angry with you!

2

Giovanni Pico della Mirandola enters briskly, leaving his cloak in the hands of the page and coming gaily forward. He is an exuberant youth, elegantly and capriciously dressed in silken garments, with long, well-dressed blond locks, a delicate nose, a feminine mouth, and a double chin.

PICO: How is the Magnifico? Good day, Vannino! Greeting, Messer Angelo! . . . Whew! How hot I am! If you love me, signori, get me a lemonade, cold as the waters of the Cocytus. (*The Cardinal, making a sign to Politian to remain, goes obligingly to the door and gives the order in person.*) By Bacchus, my tongue is sticking to my teeth! What a warm April! The clock at San Stephano in Pane said three, and it is as hot as ever. You must know that I come from Florence, as fast as my horse would carry me. I dined at your kinsmen's the Tornabuonis, Giovanni, and I tarried there all too long. The Tornabuonis certainly set a good table. We had fat French capons, my lad, very tender-fleshed, you would have appreciated them. Yes, life has its charms. And Lorenzo – tell me the truth, how is he since this morning?

POLIZIANO: His condition seems unchanged since you saw him, my Lord. The Cardinal and I are waiting for the court physician's report on the effect of the draught of distilled precious stones which Sor Lazzaro from Pavia has administered. To beguile the heavy time we have been giving ourselves to our studies – from which, to be sure, we were distracted by an unworthy subject – but we have had no fresh report from Messer Pierleoni. Ah, my gracious Lord, I am beginning to doubt the miraculous efficacy of this much-lauded draught. He who brewed it forsook Careggi at once – after receiving, by the by, a sinfully high fee, and left it to us to await the result of his ministrations. Would that they might be manifest! My great, my beloved Master! Did I save you, fourteen years ago in the cathedral, from the daggers of the Pazzi, that you might be torn from me by a malignant illness?

Alas, wretch that I am, whither shall I turn if you join the shades? I am but a vine which twines itself about you, the laurel, and must pine away when you do. And Florence, what will become of her? She is your mistress, I see her fading in her widow's weeds –

PICO: Messer Angelo, I beseech you! This is a dirge and comes too soon. Lorenzo lives, the while you sing his death. Your genius carries you away. . . . Tell me, has Messer Pierleoni yet expressed himself decisively as to the nature of the illness?

POLIZIANO: No, my Lord. He explains, in phrases which the lay mind finds hard to grasp, that the marrow of life is attacked by decay. A horrible thought!

PICO: The marrow of life?

POLIZIANO: And most frightful of all is the inward unrest which despite his weakness possesses the beloved patient. He refuses to remain in bed. Today he has had himself carried in a litter into the garden, into the loggia of the Platonic Academy, into various rooms in the villa, and finds nowhere rest.

PICO: Strange. Were you with your father today, Giovanni?

GIOVANNI: No, Pico. And, between ourselves, being with him is become so hard for me that I avoid it all I can. Father is so changed. He has a way of looking at you – he rolls his eyes first upwards and then turns them aside, with an agonizing expression. . . . You do not know how frightful the proximity of illness and suffering is to me. I become ill myself. No, it was Father brought us up to brush calmly aside everything ugly, sad, or painful and to keep our souls receptive only to the beautiful and the joyous. It should not surprise him now –

PICO: I understand. But you should seek to overcome your reluctance. . . . Where is your brother?

GIOVANNI: Piero? How should I know? Riding, fencing (*in an effort to strike a lighter key again*), perhaps with a fat cow –

PICO: With a – Ah, ha! Well, well, hark at little Giovanni! I shall tell my prior that the Cardinal de' Medici no longer quotes Aristotle but certain sermons. . . . (*A servant brings the lemonade and goes out.*) But now tell me, tell me! How did Lorenzo take this latest news?

POLIZIANO: Which news, my Lord?

PICO: Brother Girolamo's latest joke . . . the scandal in the cathedral.

GIOVANNI AND POLIZIANO: In the cathedral?

PICO: He doesn't know? Nor you either? So much the better. Then I can tell it to you. Let me drink and I will. – That is a beautiful spoon.

GIOVANNI: Let me see. Yes, it is charming. Ercole the goldsmith made it. Clever man.

PICO: Lovely, lovely! The golden balls – what delicate foliage! A very successful piece of work. Ercole? I'll give him an order. He has taste.

GIOVANNI: The scandal, Pico!

PICO: I'll tell you. In the first place, it is about *her.*

POLIZIANO: Ah, about *her.* . . .

GIOVANNI: Go on!

PICO: You know she attends the Frate's sermons?

POLIZIANO: I know – without comprehending why.

PICO: Oh, I comprehend it perfectly. In the first place it is the women who are his most passionate worshippers, and particularly women who have loved much are the most powerfully swayed by him – as is only natural. Besides, what do you want, our Brother has become the fashion. His success goes beyond all my expectations. And it is increasing steadily among the people as well as among the aristocracy; even the fat bourgeoisie is beginning to take notice. It is quite the fashion to attend his sermons – I find it rather fanatical of you, Messer Angelo, if you will forgive me, to keep aloof as you do. But to the point. The divine Fiore is less self-willed. She has lately been going with fair regularity to sit at the Frate's feet – which in itself would be a perfectly gratifying and even an exhilarating thing. The trouble is that she does it in such an ostentatious and challenging way. What she does is to appear in the cathedral nearly a half-hour too late, when the sermon is in full swing; and even that might pass, for, after all, she could do it quietly and unobtrusively. But here comes in the fact that our divinity enjoys making itself felt and is even more given to the pomp and splendour of a regal progress than even her great lover Lorenzo himself; she shows much less restraint. A whole brilliantly dressed cortège surrounds her litter and accompanies her ladyship into the middle of the church to make a way for her through the crowd – which they do with no great tact. I was present the first time when she made her entrance, in the middle of the sermon. Her appearance would always attract attention – but in the manner of its doing it made quite a little commotion. The crowd pushed and shoved, whispered and pointed, the people who had just been bowing to the lash of the Frate's frightful prophecies twisted their necks round to enjoy the proud and revivifying spectacle of this famous, sumptuous, divinely beautiful woman as she advanced with her imperious air. As for the Frate, I was afraid, at the moment he saw her, he would lose his poise and the thread of his discourse. The word he had on his lips took so long to utter, it seemed to be frozen. He is always pale, but his face took on a waxen pallor, and never shall I forget the uncanny flicker of his eyes, in which a flame seemed to leap up, die down, and then blaze up again.

POLIZIANO: You tell the tale well, my Lord – it is a veritable pleasure to listen to the harmonious flow of your periods.

PICO: By Hercules, Messer Angelo, in the present case what I have to tell is certainly rather more telling than the way it is told and I would pray you to fix your attention more upon the matter than upon the manner of the tale.

GIOVANNI: Matter, manner, tale, telling – bravo, Pico, bravo!

PICO: Hear me to the end. Since that day a silent, bitter struggle has gone on between the divine Fiore and Brother Girolamo. Her late appearance might seem the first time an aristocratic caprice, but she has persisted in it so obstinately as to make it obvious that she seeks to annoy the Prior and his congregation. He on his side took various measures to counteract her late appearance. He spoke louder and more emphatically to drown out the noise her retainers made. He lowered his voice to a mysterious whisper to draw attention upon himself. He paused and let the condemnation of his silence speak for him until Donna Fiore reached her place and quiet was restored, when he resumed more violently than before. The rest of us reap from the situation this advantage, that when *she* is there *he* outdoes himself. Terror and tears accompany his words; his audience quivers at the punishments he calls down upon Florence for her luxury and frivolity; after such a sermon people move about the streets half-dead and speechless. Often when he talks of the world's extremity and of pity and redemption the very scribe who takes down his words must break off in his task overcome by sobbing. The Frate has the art to touch the conscience with a single word uttered with such uncanny stress that the throng shudders as one man; it is very interesting to see this and at the same time feel the shuddering within one's proper breast. Naturally all this has made people attend the sermons in greater crowds than ever.... Our lovely mistress has not desisted from her provocative behaviour – and today things came to a climax, a catastrophe. Brother Girolamo has gone too far; I would not defend him. He was carried away by his own performance – listen to what happened. Even before dawn the cathedral was full of people who wanted to make sure of a good place. At sermon hour the crush inside and out was so great that a pin could not have fallen to the ground. At the very least, ten thousand people were present; those from outside of Florence have been reckoned at more than two thousand. From villas and from the countryside lords and peasants came by night not to miss the sermon hour – there were even people from Bologna. The crush between the Duomo and San Marco was frightful. The authorities had a hard time protecting the Prior from the demonstrations of the masses who wanted to kiss his hands and feet and cut pieces from his frock. In Via Larga, near your palace, Giovanni, a woman shrieked out that she had been healed of an issue of blood by touching the prophet's hem. There was an outcry that a miracle had happened and the crowd screamed *Misericordia*. All the Fathers of San Marco, all the brotherhoods, and all the world besides were gathered in the Duomo. There were members of the Signoria and the red-caps of the College of Eight; men and women of every rank and age, boys clambering on the pillars, workmen, poets, philosophers. At last Brother Girolamo mounted the pulpit. His gaze, that strangely fixed and burning gaze, was directed upon the throng as he began to speak amid a breathless and oppressive stillness. He spoke to Florence, addressed her with the thou and in a frightfully slow, quiet voice questioned her how she spent her days and how her nights. In chastity, in fear of sensual lusts, in the spirit, in peace? He paused, awaiting an answer. And this Florence, this thousand-headed host, bends beneath his intolerable eye that sees through all, guesses all, knows all. "Thou answerest me not?" he says.... He draws up his sickly frame and cries out in a terrible voice: "Let me tell thee!" Then begins a pitiless reckoning, a Last Judgment in words, under which the crowd writhes as under the rod. In his mouth every weakness of the flesh becomes an intolerable, abominable sin. He names them all by name, ruthlessly, with dreadful emphasis: vices which till then have never been mentioned in holy places. And all are guilty, he declares: Pope, clergy, princes, humanists, poets, artists, and makers of feasts. He lifts his arms, and lo, a hideous vision, a devilish, alluring picture rises from the maw of revelation: the whore sitting upon many waters, the woman on the beast! She is arrayed in purple and scarlet colour and decked with gold and precious stones and pearls, having a golden cup in her hand full of abominations and filthiness of her fornication. And upon her forehead was a name written, Mystery, Babylon the Great, the Mother of Harlots. "That woman art thou, Florence, thou shameless wanton and strumpet! Very delicate art thou, arrayed in fine linen, painted and scented. Thy speech is wit and elegant euphony. Thy hand rejects any instrument that bears not the mark of beauty, thine eye rests voluptuously upon costly paintings and the statues of nude heathen gods. But the Lord hath spewed thee out of His mouth. Hark! Hearest thou not the voices in the air? Hearest thou not the wings of destruction? Yea, then, the time hath come. It is past. Remorse cometh too late. Judgment is at hand. I have prophesied it unto thee a hundred times, Florence, but in thy pleasures thou wouldest not hearken to the voice of the poor, wise monk. Gone are the days of dancing, of pageantry, of obscene songs. ... Unhappy one, thou art lost. The frightful darkness falls. Thunder fills the air. The sword of the Most High flashes down.... Save thyself! Repent! Atone! ... Too late! For the Lord looses His waters over the kingdoms of the earth. The flood carries away the masks and costumes of thy carnivals, thy books of Latin and Italian poesy, thine adornments and thy tirings, thy perfumes and thy veils, thy unchaste paintings, thy heathen statuary. Seest thou the flames gleaming blood-red? Thou art overrun with savage armies. Famine stalks grinning through thy streets. The plague breathes over thee her stinking breath.... The end cometh, the end cometh! Thou shalt be rooted out, rooted out amid torments." – No, my friends, I am giving no proper picture – my words cannot make you see his face, his gestures, cannot make you hear his voice, cannot bring you under the domination of his personal dæmon. The multitudes groaned as though on the rack. I saw bearded men spring up in a panic and take to flight. A desperate, long-drawn wail for mercy was wrung from the centre of the crowd: "Have pity!" And a deathly stillness.... And then – his eyes grow dim. At the very moment of uttermost terror a miracle comes to pass. The annihilating wrath upon his countenance melts away. In overflowing love he stretches forth his arms. "The miracle of grace!" he cries. "It comes to pass! Florence, my city, my people, let me announce it unto thee, grace is vouchsafed thee if thou dost penance, if thou renouncest thy infamous revellings, if thou wilt dedicate thyself as a bride to the King of humility and suffering. Lo, He, He" – and he lifts the crucifix aloft – "He, Florence, would be thy King. Wilt thou accept Him? Ye who are tortured by sin and marked for affliction, ye poor in spirit, ye who know naught of Cicero and naught of the philosophers, ye who are cast down and rejected, ailing and wretched, He will lift you up, will comfort, refresh, and give you cheer. Did not our blessed Thomas Aquinas declare that the blessed in the heavenly kingdom will look down and see the sufferings of the damned that their bliss might be augmented? So shall it be. But the city which chooses Jesus as its King is blest already in this earthly life. No more shall some famish while others dwell among beautiful furnishings set upon floors of mosaic. Jesus will have it and I as His vicar announce that the price of meat be reduced to a minimum, to a few soldi the pound; He wills that those who must pay a penance of five measures of meal to a cloister shall give it to the poor instead. He wills that the splendid gold vessels and the paintings in the churches be turned into money and the proceeds distributed among the people. He wills" – and just at that point, Giovanni, Messer Angelo, in that moment of universal emotion, contrition, abasement – just at that moment happened the thing which will give the Florentines food for talk for many a month to come. There was a noise at the entrance, a clatter, a murmuring, a sound of feet, which echoed and increased. The slanting rays of light from the windows shone on steel, as the pike-bearers forced their way into the nave, crying to the startled crowd to make way. And into the path they opened stepped the divine Fiore with majestic tread, among her retinue. The great pearl which Lorenzo lately gave her gleamed like milk on her flawless brow. Her hands were folded before her, her eyes lowered, yet seeing all, her lips curved in an incomparable smile; she advanced slowly to her chosen position opposite the pulpit. But he, the Ferrarese, broke off his sentence abruptly, leaned his prophetic wrath far out over the pulpit, pointing down with arm outstretched straight into her face: "Behold!" he cried, "turn ye and behold! She comes, she is here, the harlot with whom kings have dallied on earth, the mother of abominations, the woman on the beast, the great Babylon!"

POLIZIANO: Terrible! The foul-mouthed wretch!

GIOVANNI: A little severe – but all's one.

PICO: No, no, do not judge, gentlemen! Since, unluckily for you, you were not present, do not try to form an idea of the tremendousness of that moment. Bear in mind that whatever he sees becomes truth and presentness when he utters it. His white hand stretching out of the dark sleeve of his habit trembled, as he gazed straight and fixedly into her face, and until he let it fall the exquisite Fiore was in very truth the apocalyptic woman, the great Babylon in all its shameless splendour. The crowd, torn to and fro by conflicting feelings, between damnation and grace, overwrought and on fire, made no doubt of it at all. Hatred, fear, and disgust spoke out of the thousand faces turned upon her. A hoarse groaning sound arose, it seemed to thirst for her blood. I too was looking at her and I swear to you, *in verbo Domini*, I felt my hair rise on my head and cold shivers run down my back.

POLIZIANO: You look for such shivers, admit it, my Lord!

GIOVANNI: And she? And she?

PICO: She stood for perhaps the space of an Ave Maria rooted to the spot. Then she drew herself up with a furious exclamation, motioned to her following, and left the church. Rumours flew about that she had ordered her people to murder him there in the pulpit, but no one dared to approach. It is said too that a secret messenger went from her to San Marco after the sermon. Certainly his frenzy led him seriously astray. I am in no wise defending him. Whatever provocation she gave, it was not the way to treat such a woman. To curse her before all the people! Is she a courtesan, then?

GIOVANNI (*with a giggle*): Yes!

PICO: By the great Eros, she is the Magnifico's mistress. That is, I mean, it is not as though she were one of those who must wear the yellow veil and live in certain streets. A flawless woman! We know that, though born abroad, she is the natural seed of a noble Florentine family. But even did we not know this, her brilliant mind, her diverse gifts, her lofty humanistic culture would daily and hourly bear witness to her origins. Her terza rimas and sonnets are ravishing, her lute-playing has moved me to tears. She knows by heart countless beautiful verses from Virgil, Ovid, and Horace; and the grace with which she recited that very free story from the *Decamerone* the other day after luncheon, in the garden – I could have worshipped her for it! And if all this be not enough to assure her of universal admiration, she is the woman to whom our great Lorenzo's love belongs.

POLIZIANO: You have said it, my Lord. And I, is it I who must teach you to interpret in the light of this fact the events you have just described? Your penetration finds out so many things in heaven and on earth, you are the phœnix of the intellect, the savant of princes, the prince of savants – and you will not see what all this means? The latest atrocity of this Ferrarese is nothing else than a new act of hostility, a fresh piece of malice and impertinence against the Magnifico himself and his house. Our divine mistress has served the monk with no more contempt than he deserves; but the unbridled character of his revenge did not follow the blind dictates of rage, it seized with intent and forethoughtedly the occasion for one of his insidious attacks on the man at whose feet Florence has for two decades been lying transported, the man whom even with his own cowardly tongue he names "the Strong". You are a great man, who could rule a city and conduct a war, did you not prefer to lead the life of a free lover of wisdom; I am but a poor poet, possessing naught on earth but my burning love for the house of the Medici, source of light, of beauty, and of joy. But this love of mine bids me speak, bids me snatch you back when in the rashness of youth you approach the snake lying hidden in the grass. The conspiracy of the Pazzi, when the beautiful Giuliano was slain in the cathedral and Lorenzo himself would have suffered the same fate had not some god given me strength at the last moment to close the door of the sacristy behind him – that conspiracy was child's-play beside the infernal machinations which – again in the same place, again in Santa Maria del

Fiore – are on foot against the Medici and their blithe sway. The cheap successes which this viper has had from laying bare the meannesses of his character to the masses have simply turned his head. His zeal for human hearts, his craving to win souls for his own ends, is daily more and more undisguised. My Lord, do not fail to understand: his lowering face is set towards power! And what if it should fall into his hands? Open your eyes to what is happening and you will shiver with fright to see how shockingly the number swells of those who throng about this sorry despot and swallow the perverted and disingenuous mildness of his doctrine. These pitiful, self-denying, beauty-hating folk have been christened by more cheerful mortals with the nick-name "The Weepers" – as one calls the paid mourners at a funeral, you know. But in their self-abasement they have taken the name as an honour, and it now forms the style of a political party, opposed to the Medici, whose head our monk reckons himself to be. But more: young sons from the first families of the city, a Gondi, a Salviati, brilliant and elegant youths, darlings of the gods like yourself, have crawled to this sorcerer's feet and applied for admission to San Marco as novices. The common folk are kept stirred up and baited with promises; it has gone so far that some good-for-nothings have stuck up lampoons in the form of sonnets against Piero de' Medici at the cathedral and the palace. Oh, my Lord, what did you do, what are you doing, calling this man to Florence and paving his way by your complaisance!

PICO: May we laugh at you a little, Messer Angelo, or will you take it amiss? If you could only see your own face! Go look at yourself in the glass! It looks as though you yourself belonged to the "Weepers", to that very political party of which you speak! Ha ha! Ye gods! A comic political party! So very important! I beg you to teach me the nature of our Florentines. I know them not, I have not studied them. They seem to me an uncommonly tough and solid folk, and with passions one would best not stir up. No, no, forgive me but I cannot take all this so seriously. For so long as my observation holds, Piero has been unloved in Florence. His brusque and domineering way makes him unpopular here; but certainly it is a bit too much to suppose a connection between the lame sonnets against him and Fra Girolamo's sermons. If Andrea Gondi and little Salviati find it the height of good taste to don the cowl – do you want to prevent them? I confess that I myself have already toyed with the idea. I believe we are living in an age free from prejudice. Is it true that here in Florence I can dress myself as I like, and express my personality as strikingly as I choose without anybody pointing the finger? Yes, it is true, true figuratively as well as literally. And if I tired of sky-blue and purple and preferred the colourless sobriety of the monk's habit? Why did you not object to the famous Procession of the Dead, in which after so many high-coloured carnivals we had corpses rising from their coffins? The effect was that of a savoury after too much sweet. What did I do when I persuaded Lorenzo to send for Fra Girolamo to Florence? I made the city the present of a great man, by Zeus, and I am proud of it! Lorenzo, I am sure, would be first to thank me. Did he not lately send to Spoleto to ask that the body of Fra Lippo Lippi be sent to our cathedral, that yet another might be added to our tombs of illustrious dead? When Brother Girolamo is once a dead body, the Ferrarese and perhaps even the Romans will send us ambassadors to beg for his ashes. But we will not surrender them. All Italy will visit the grave of the much-talked-of monk and I shall be able to say that it was I first discovered and fostered his genius. Yes, my good sirs, I have won my game. I was far from certain of it – for who can measure Fiorenza's whims? In that Dominican chapter-house where I first saw him no one paid him much heed. I sat in a circle of scholars and savants taking part in the chapter; he held aloof, among his brethren, so long as the discussion turned on scholastic matters. But when the question of discipline came up he suddenly projected himself into it and astounded the whole chapter by the almost superhuman originality of his words and point of view. The state of the Church and of public morals all at once appeared in a glaring and malefic light; I was extraordinarily shaken by the glowing enthusiasm and fanatic narrow-mindedness of his discourse. And I was not alone. Several men of superior intellect and rank, even princes, wrote to him afterwards. But I sought his personal acquaintance and only strengthened thereby my first impression. Everywhere I went I sang his praises. But then I moved to Florence and became absorbed in the stimulating observation of this mobile, cultured, sharp-tongued people, this restless little community for ever seeking after new things. And in a happy hour I conceived the plan of making my influence felt to the point of having Brother Girolamo summoned hither. His reputation was established, my praise had run before him, he would have the chance to produce his effect. It was a bold attempt, it involved a certain risk. I said to myself: "This man, in this city, will either be drowned in laughter and spitted on the point of a thousand jests – or he will have the greatest success of the century." Sirs, it is the latter that has happened. I spoke with my friend the Magnifico; the Magnifico spoke with the Fathers of San Marco. Brother Girolamo was sent for. He began by instructing the novices. But in order to gratify the curiosity of certain privileged persons he was asked to admit them to the lessons. The audience increased daily, he made no protest – my faith, he certainly did not, for he was overwhelmed with requests to mount the pulpit; connoisseurs, elegant dames, everybody implored him. He resisted at first, then he gave way. The little Church of San Marco was full to overflowing, he preached to an audience overwhelmed. His name was in every mouth. Platonists and Aristotelians laid by their quarrel for the time to dispute over these standards of Christian ethics. The monastery church became presently too small for the throngs, and he moved over to Santa Maria del Fiore. At first it was the cultivated amateur who came; but now it is the lowly who are on fire, upon whose spirits he practises with his melancholy gift of prophecy, his profound judgment of life. The monks elected him prior; and San Marco, which was no better and no worse then than other cloisters, became a sanctuary of holiness. His writings are read with eagerness. He is the talk of the town. Next to Lorenzo de' Medici he is the most famous, the most talked-of, the greatest man in Florence. And all this I behold with the liveliest satisfaction, in which, good Messer Angelo, I mean not to allow your misgivings to disturb me.

POLIZIANO: They shall not, my gracious Lord. Florence knows me too, I believe, as anything but an alarmist. Let us assume that it was merely envy whispering to me when I spoke – that I grudge you a pleasure I do not understand and cannot share. For I admit that I do not in the least grasp what is going on. Often have I given thanks to the gods that I was born in this time of dawning and new birth which seems to me as enchanting as the sunrise. The world wakes and smiles, she draws a full breath and opens her chalice to the light, she is like a flower new blossoming. All the dim, hollow-eyed spectres, the cruel and hateful prejudices which have haunted men for so long a night, melt away to nothing. Everything is born afresh. A boundless, alluring kingdom of new studies, long forgotten and undreamed-of, opens out. The labouring earth presents to us fortunate ones all the treasures of antique beauty. The individual is enlightened and set free to rejoice in his own personality. Great and ruthless deeds are crowned with glory. Art, innocent, nude, unfettered, paces through the land, and all that she touches is ennobled. All human beings are filled with the intoxication emanating from the divine; they follow their smiling leader and their jubilation makes a cult of beauty and life. And then – what happens? What next? A man, too ugly and rigid to join in the dance of the elements, embittered, churlish, full of ill will, rises to lodge a protest against our godlike state, and the poison of his zeal is such that the ranks of the joyous thin, the deserters crowd about him and behave as though what he says is something vastly new, something unheard-of. And what is it he says? What is it his whole being exhales? Morality! But morality is the oldest, the boresomest, the most exposed and exploded idea in the world. It is ridiculous. Or isn't it? Do you mean it isn't? Speak, my Lord – what is your answer?

PICO: Nothing. For the moment nothing, Messer Angelo. For I must savour in silence the after-taste of your exquisite words. Glorious, glorious, what you said of the times we live in! "Like a flower new blossoming." ... I do beseech you to put it into verse. I wonder if the ottava ... or perhaps Latin hexameters –

GIOVANNI: You must answer, Pico, or own yourself beaten.

PICO: Answer? Willingly. But it seems to me that I have already inquired whether we live in a time that is free from prejudice or whether we do not. And if we do, then shall we set limits to our freedom? Must our free-thinking become a religion and lack of morals a species of fanaticism? I would repudiate the idea. If morality has been made impossible, if it has become ridiculous – well, then! Since in Florence the ridiculous is the greatest danger of all, then the bravest man is he who does not fear it. He would startle everybody. And in Florence to startle everybody is going far towards winning the game. Ah, my friends, sin has lost much of its charm since we got rid of our consciences! Look about you: everything is permissible; at least nothing is disgraceful. There is no atrocity that could make our hair stand on end. Today the place swarms with atheists and people who assert that Christ performed His miracles by the aid of the stars. But who has dared, this long time, to make any head against beauty or art? Am I blaspheming? Pray understand me. I am full of praise for those who devoted themselves to art when it was the possession of a few, and morality sat stolidly entrenched on her throne. But since beauty has been crying aloud in the streets, the price of virtue has gone up. Let me whisper a little piece of news in your ear, Messer Angelo: morality is possible once more!

GIOVANNI (*who had been looking out of the window through his lorgnon*): Wait, Pico! I see some guests down there in the garden – you simply must say all this to them.

PICO (*looking out*): Guests? Why, so there are. They are

artists, a whole host of them. There is Aldobrandino . . . and Grifone . . . and the great Francesco Romano. Talk to them? Not to them, my dear Giovanni. It is not for them. But let us go down all the same. Come, Cardinal – and you too, singer of the glories of the house of the Medici. Let us enjoy ourselves with the brave lads.

POLIZIANO: You hear naught, you will hear naught. But I see sinister things coming to pass.

Act Two

The garden. A view of the palace, behind which the open campagna, covered with cypresses, stone pines, and olive trees, melting into the grey-green rolling horizon. A wide centre path, with smaller ones branching right and left, flanked by hermæ and potted plants, runs from the house to the front of the stage, where it opens into a rondel, with a fountain in a stone basin, where water–lilies float. Right and left front stand marble benches shaded by flat bowers of foliage like little canopies.

I

A group of eleven persons appear on the left-hand path and move forward, in lively conversation. They are the painter and sculptor Grifone, a fair man who walks with a bent, slouching gait – he wears a beard and has large bony hands; Francesco Romano, an impressive figure with a capacious forehead like a Roman portrait bronze, full, smiling mouth, and black, animal eyes which rove calmly from side to side; Ghino, blue-eyed, boyish, and sunshiny; Leone, with a round head like a fawn's, a powerful nose, little eyes set close together, and a satyr-beard through which one can see his curling lips; Aldobrandino, a noisy swaggering fellow with a red, smirking face; the embroiderer Andreuccio, a man already grey and with a gentle, feminine air; Guidantonio, the cabinet-maker; Ercole, the goldsmith; Simonetto, the architect; Pandolfo and Dioneo, of whom the one makes arabesque sculpture and the other portrait busts in wax. With the exception of Ghino, who is rather a dandy, they are negligently and comfortably dressed, with headgear of varying sorts, square, round, and peaked. As they come forward on the middle path they are discussing with some excitement, pushing each other out of the way, approaching their faces to each other, and gesticulating.

ALDOBRANDINO: We shall see, we shall see the face Lorenzo will make! I am his friend, I am justified in hoping that he will see me avenged.

GUIDANTONIO: If I were you I would not make so much noise about the beating you got.

ALDOBRANDINO: Nobody is talking about a beating, you numskull. It was a buffeting.

GRIFONE: On my soul, you are right, there. The crowd gave you such a plenty of buffets that you could drive a donkey to Rome with them.

ALDOBRANDINO: Shall I pass them on to you, you funny man, you Jack-of-all-trades? They were buffets – and even had they been a beating they could not have shaken the honour of a man like me! The silly mob had been stirred up by that owl of a Fra Girolamo, an ignoramus who knows as much about artistry as an ox does about playing the lute. What does he want anyhow? Can I paint the Madonna looking a ragged old woman as this prayer- mumbler demands? No, I must have colour, I must have brightness. And since the Holy Virgin will not do me the honour of sitting for me, I must be satisfied if a mortal maiden will serve my turn.

LEONE (*delighted*): "Serve his turn" – if a maiden will serve his turn – oh, you sly fellow!

ALDOBRANDINO: You are pleased to be very merry, my dear Leone. However, everybody knows that your pretty little Lauretta, who is sitting as your model for the Magdalena, promptly bore you a child. But you probably have some charm against beatings.

GRIFONE: Buffets, buffets! We do not speak of beatings.

LEONE: That is different. I did not take her to sit for the Magdalena and then abuse her for my own pleasure; I keep her for my pleasure and happen to be using her for a model. That is very different – the Madonna could take no exception to that.

ALDOBRANDINO: But Brother Girolamo can, you numskull, and that's enough, in these days.

ERCOLE: Yes. God keep us, he is so strict, he would give Saint Dominic himself the strappado for nothing at all. He pretends to the people that like Moses he has spoken face to face with God; since then they listen abjectly to him; he can say anything he likes.

SIMONETTO: That is true. We saw today in the Duomo how horribly he sat in judgment upon Madonna Fiore.

DIONEO: Where is she? Does anyone know where she is?

PANDOLFO: She is with the Magnifico, telling him the whole story.

GUIDANTONIO: No, she cannot be in Careggi yet. Before we came away she was seen in the city.

ALDOBRANDINO: Messer Francesco, you stand there and say nothing, as your way is, smiling as usual too. But the world knows that your house is furnished in pagan style, like an ancient Roman's, and that your paintings are a different kind from the blessed Angelico's.

GRIFONE: You are furious because it was you who received the beating.

ALDOBRANDINO: Oh, Grifone, not for nothing are you nick-named Buffone, for you are indeed but a buffoon. You can do nothing but organize pageants and wait upon princes with your jests; and so you are annoyed with me because I am a clever painter. Sew ass's ears on your cap, fool! I go now to the Magnifico.

ANDREUCCIO: No, wait, listen! Lorenzo is very ill; we may not crowd in on him as we used to, like carnival masks. When we came, I saw the Cardinal at the window. He made a sign as though he would come down. We ought to wait.

GHINO (*in a loud, clear voice*): Listen to me! We must go at the business all together. The guild of Florentine painters must lodge a protest against Brother Girolamo with the Council of Eight. And those of us who belong to Lorenzo's musical club must combine to demand that the Ferrarese's mouth be stopped.

ALDOBRANDINO: You may do as you like. But I shall appeal to Lauro alone. He is master, the priest is not. Those scoundrels who dared to lay their filthy hands on me – he will have their ears cut off, he will order them trussed up outside the palace. I am his best friend, he loves me, I came back from Rome expressly because he was ill. I came back from Rome in eight hours!

GRIFONE: What! In eight hours from Rome?

ALDOBRANDINO: Yes, in seven and a half.

GRIFONE: What, what? And Lauro's best friend? When is he supposed to have distinguished you thus? And did not I come back from Bologna and Rimini, where I have work at the court, on purpose because of his illness?

ALDOBRANDINO: Silence, buffoon! You hate me, I know, you are my deadly enemy, because you are from Pistoia, and our subject, whereas I am a Florentine and by birthright your overlord.

GRIFONE: What, what? My overlord? You are a braggart. A beaten braggart!

ALDOBRANDINO: Draw, draw, you empty-headed fool, draw the sword at your side and defend yourself or I will murder you with no more ado. I have been mortally insulted and am ready to commit a frightful deed.

ANDREUCCIO: Stop! Keep the peace! Look over there!

LEONE: By Venus! By the Mother of God! It is she – she comes!

GHINO (*rapturously*): Let us salute her! Let us all serve her!

2

A gilded and decorated litter, hung with lanterns and silken curtains, comes to a stop at the back of the stage. Fiore descends, casts a glance over her shoulder at the group of artists, and signs to the bearers to carry it away. She stands still for a moment, then comes slowly front, in the attitude Pico has described, with arms bent at right angles, hands folded before her, slender, straight, with her head back and her eyes cast down. She has a splendid and curiously artificial beauty. The impression she gives is of height, slenderness, symmetry, poise; she is almost masklike.

Her hair is confined in a thin veil, from which it flows down upon her cheeks in blond, regular curls. The brows above her rather long eyes have been artificially removed or made invisible, so that the hairless part above the drooping lids seems drawn upwards with a searching expression. The skin of her face is taut and as it were polished, her delicately chiselled lips are closed in an ambiguous smile. About her long white throat is a fine gold chain. She wears a gown of stiff brocade, with tight, dark sleeves a little slashed. It is so cut as to make the abdomen prominent and is open at the breast to display the laces of her bodice.

THE ARTISTS (*pressing towards her with loud homage, some of them even kneeling and raising their arms in greeting*): Hail, Fiore! Hail to our divine mistress! Hail!

FIORE (*still without raising her eyes, with chill authority, so quietly that all grow still as she speaks*): You will lay aside your weapons.

ALDOBRANDINO: Yes, mistress! We will put them up – see, they are gone.

FIORE: You call yourselves artists?

GRIFONE: Madama, you know well that we are artists.

FIORE: But it seems you yourselves know it not, since you are capable of taking something very different so seriously. (*Pause.*) A light art, a childish art, that leaves untasked so much blood, so much virility.

ALDOBRANDINO: Mistress, I have been mortally insulted.

FIORE (*scornfully and still very softly*): Oh, of course, then, if you were mortally insulted –

GHINO: You speak very strangely today, madama.

FIORE: Really? Do I confuse you? Do I confound your feeble brain, poor thing, poor little ... Let me see, what is your name?

GHINO (*offended*): You usually know me.

FIORE: It is true. You are Ghino, the amiable Ghino, the perfect cavalier, Ghino the dancer, who always smells so sweet. One hears that even your horse is scented when you ride out. And over there is Guidantonio, who makes the beautiful chairs. Look, and there is Leone. Good day, sir. I hope you had a delightful night....

ALDOBRANDINO (*unable to keep still*): Madonna...you too have been mortally insulted today.

FIORE: I insulted? By whom?

ALDOBRANDINO: Dear and most beautiful lady – this friar....

FIORE: What friar? A real story-book friar? Oh, I know. Did I not see you today in the cathedral? And you? And you? I went to amuse myself. You were quite a sight. I saw you go white up to your eyes.

ALDOBRANDINO: With anger, lady, with anger.

FIORE: Of course. You could not even compress your lips – you felt quite weak with the strength of your heroism. I saw.

ALDOBRANDINO: The villain! The Jew! The knave – who dared to slander you –

FIORE: Hark, what a fine flow of words! Before long you will equal your Frate himself, my stout Aldobrandino. Come, join in, you others! Do not lag behind. It will mightily relieve you to rave, for your wrath in the cathedral left you no strength for deeds.

ALDOBRANDINO: Deeds! By all the gods, madonna, you do ill to mock us. Just now before you came we were taking counsel how to put a stop to this abuse. But what can we do? Lorenzo loves us; but a word from you carries more weight than all our protestations. If you so willed, the doom of the Ferrarese would be sealed. They would cut off his tongue that slandered you, batter in his chest as he deserves – in short, they would kill him.

FIORE (*with a sudden outburst of violence*): Kill him, then! (*With a swift movement she has drawn a stiletto from her bodice and holds it out to Aldobrandino.*) Do you see this dainty little weapon? Here at the tip the blade is a little brown....Take it! The stain is from a powerful potion in which I have dipped it. One scratch is enough. Take it! Instead of standing there rolling your eyes. Take it. Ghino the *preux chevalier*! Or you, Guidantonio, maker of beautiful chairs! Or Francesco the

Roman! You that look like a butcher of antiquity. He is only a feeble priest....

ALDOBRANDINO: Madonna, we could not get to him. He stops in San Marco. And the people love him.... And he is guarded when he goes to the Duomo.

FIORE (*looking at him*): He is coming here.

THE ARTISTS (*together*): He is coming here? Who? Who?

FIORE: Brother Girolamo. Here. Today.

ALDOBRANDINO: Brother Girolamo... coming here?

FIORE (*puts away the dagger; in a changed voice*): I was jesting. I was having my joke with you. No, it is not true – a fantastic idea! Brother Girolamo – here! – Let me now take my leave of you.

ALDOBRANDINO (*still a little out of countenance*): You are going to Lorenzo?

FIORE: Lorenzo lies groaning in his bed. It goes very ill with the great Lorenzo. I feel like walking a little in the garden.

GHINO: And may we not enjoy the delights of your society?

FIORE: All praise to your courtesy. But even at the risk of seeming moody and unsocial in your eyes I would forgo the treasure of your company. (*She withdraws.*)

3

GHINO (*returning after having escorted her a little way*): She is magnificent, she is divine, she is marvellous beyond all belief!

GUIDANTONIO: Well, she was not too polite about getting rid of you.

GHINO: That is nothing. Nothing at all. One is in raptures, just seeing her.

ALDOBRANDINO: One is in raptures if she takes the smallest notice of one. And if she will not, one struggles even more to win just a single second of her attention, to lure from her one single smile, one nod of approval. If we watch ourselves we shall find that we think of her when we work. It is her beauty that moves us to create....

THE OTHERS: Yes, yes!

ALDOBRANDINO: Ye gods, how happy must he be to whom she belongs, before whom she kneels, by whom she was subdued!

ERCOLE: Did you hear how strangely she spoke of Lorenzo?

SIMONETTO: All that she said was strange to hear.

ANDREUCCIO: All that she said seemed to conceal something else.

LEONE: She asked me how I enjoyed last night. That was rather strong.

ALDOBRANDINO: She may say anything. She says the most impudent things in so charming a way that it is like angels' music.

PANDOLFO: I did not know that she was armed.

DIONEO: A dangerous mistress!

ALDOBRANDINO: She is a bold, mature, and independent woman. The weapon suits her gloriously.

ANDREUCCIO: Perhaps it was the very tool with which her father once threatened the Medici, when he was exiled, in Luca Pitti's time.

LEONE: I did not believe that story. I do not believe that she is the natural child of any exiled nobleman. When Zeus dethroned Chronos he robbed him of a member, an important one, and threw it in the sea. So strangely wed, the sea brought forth – our Lady.

GRIFONE: Not bad! In that case she would be a pretty age!

LEONE: Do you know how old she is? No one knows. If it is possible for her to age she conceals it well.

GHINO: That is true. They tell wonderful things about her beauty lotions and potions. They say she stays all day in the sun, to bleach her hair. They say that she even paints her teeth.

ALDOBRANDINO: Many people say that she uses magic. They tell it for a fact that she has bewitched Lorenzo, so that he is consuming himself with love of her. She boiled the navels of dead children in oil taken out of the sacramental lamps and gave them to him to eat.

GRIFONE: Rubbish – I don't believe any of that.

ALDOBRANDINO: You do not believe any further than the end of your nose, and you are proud of it! It is true, people are enlightened enough today not to take everything for gospel truth, as they used to. But there is such a thing as going too far. I don't believe in transubstantiation – no, it is a ridiculous doctrine, and my cousin Pasquino, who is a priest, told me expressly that he does not believe it either. But that there are witches in Fiesole and many courtesans resort to magic arts to ensnare men are proven facts.

LEONE: Proven facts! All women are witches – I know it, I!

ALDOBRANDINO: Believe me, there are miracles in the world, and if I cared to tell –

GHINO: There is our worshipful Lord Cardinal.

4

Cardinal Giovanni, Pico della Mirandola, and Angelo Poliziano walk down the centre path from the palace. Poliziano has a peaked cloth cap on one side of his head, Pico a round head-covering turned up a little in the back. There are lively greetings; on the part of the artists a sort of intimate or ironically exaggerated respect. They group themselves easily on the seats at both sides and on the border of the fountain.

GIOVANNI: Greetings, gentlemen. We find you in weighty converse?

ALDOBRANDINO: Philosophic matters, questions of faith, revered sir. We were discussing the supernatural.

PICO: About which, I trust, your views accord with the teachings of Holy Church.

ALDOBRANDINO: Absolutely, illustrious sir! In all essentials, perfectly. I think I may call myself a pious man. I observe the usages of religion and always when I finish a painting I burn a candle. I was at the sermon in the cathedral today. But I got a sorry reward, my dear sirs, let me tell you that!

GIOVANNI: A sorry reward? How so, Aldobrandino?

ALDOBRANDINO: I will tell you, worshipful sir; I will tell

you and your glorious father, for to that end I came hither. I have been mishandled.

POLIZIANO: Mishandled?

GUIDANTONIO: The populace beat him, before the cathedral, after the sermon.

POLIZIANO: After the sermon? (*Reproachfully, to Pico*) My good Lord!

PICO: They beat you, Aldobrandino *mio*? Come hither. Where have they struck you? Who has struck you? Tell me all.

ALDOBRANDINO: That will I, sir, and my own innocence will leap to the eye. Well, I was in the cathedral, where I had managed to get a small space to set my feet. It was frightfully hot in the press, I could scarce breathe and the sweat poured off me; but what will not one endure for the glory of God?

PICO: And to satisfy one's curiosity.

ALDOBRANDINO: Of course. I wept a good deal too, though I could not even see Brother Girolamo from where I was. But everyone was weeping and it was edifying to the last degree. I was most shocked at what occurred with Madonna Fiore; and I had scarce recovered from my surprise when I heard Brother Girolamo talking about art and pricked up my ears with a vengeance. His point of view is strange, it differs from mine in essentials. He said that it is wrong and wicked to paint the blessed Virgin in sumptuous robes of velvet, silk, and gold, for, so he told us angrily, she wore the garments of the poor. Very good; but what if the garments of the poor have not the faintest interest for me? What then? I have the greatest respect for the Holy Virgin – may she pray for me, poor sinner, before the throne of God! Amen, amen! But when I am at work I am less concerned with her than I am that a certain green should look well next a certain red – you can understand that, my Lord!

PICO: Certainly I can, my Aldobrandino.

ALDOBRANDINO: But he maintains that it is vicious, and a mortal sin, to paint prostitutes and dissolute women and give them out as Madonnas and Saint Sebastians as we do today. He demands that it be punished by torture and death. Well, all

Florence knows that I have just finished a Madonna for which a very beautiful girl sat to me, who lives with me for my pleasure. Laugh at me if I am boasting, sirs, but it is a glorious painting. I wrote a sonnet about it when it was done, and while I worked upon it I constantly felt that a halo of light hovered about my head.

PICO (*gravely*): You are right, Aldobrandino, your Madonna is a masterpiece.

ALDOBRANDINO: Pico Mirandola, you are a great connoisseur, I bend my knee before you. Good. Well, when the sermon was over and I was outside in the crowd that accompanied the father back to San Marco, some scoundrel looks me in the face and cries: "Here is one of those sons of Belial who paint the Madonna as a prostitute!" And at that the whole crowd turned against me in a brutish rage, struck at me with the peaks of their hoods, belaboured me with their elbows, almost trod me underfoot – I could not raise my arms, my whole body was tightly wedged in. I spat in the face of the man next me, but that was a poor defence. It is a miracle, I tell you, that I escaped with my life. God must desire me to make a few more things of beauty, since He saved me.

POLIZIANO: You see now, my Lord, to what we have come?

PICO: That I knew nothing, my Aldobrandino – that I could not come to your aid! For I cannot have been far off.

ALDOBRANDINO: Let me have my arms free, my Lord, and I need no saviour. I have a stout heart in my breast, as I have shown in more than one adventure. I have defended myself against three – it was yesterday it befell me, on my way from Rome, where I had commissions. You know that I hurried hither without stopping, on account of my patron's illness. Well, I was not far from Florence; already I could see in my mind's eye the gate of Saint Peter Gattolini. It was growing dark; I was on foot and alone. I was striding vigorously through the pass you know when two villainous-looking creatures, who had been hiding in the bushes, flung themselves upon my path, and as I turned I saw a third behind me.

Do you understand what the game was? Three rogues tall as cypress trees, fearful to behold, armed to the teeth. They may have been bravoes hired by envious rivals, or common thieves with an eye on my money – in any case my situation was desperate. "Well," thought I, "if I must die, they shall not get my life for nothing!" I drew most nimbly, set my back to the wall of the defile, struck up a *Miserere* at the top of my lungs, and when the first one made a pass at me I dealt him such a blow on the head that the sparks flew out of his eyes and he sank lifeless to the ground. The others were seized with terror at my ferocity. They crossed their arms on their breasts and begged me of my mercy to let them go – which I did, in charity, as a Christian man. So they made themselves scarce, with the corpse of their accomplice, while I continued on my journey safe and sound.

GRIFONE: Now, by all the angels, what a thumping lie!

ALDOBRANDINO: God send me my death with a plague of tumours –

PICO (*coolly*): Oh, are you there, Grifone? I overlooked you until now. Seems to me, though, you ought to be on your travels?

GRIFONE: So I have been, and in your service, my Lord. What a memory you have! I *was* on my travels. I got back only yesterday. I have been given honourable and important commissions. I have arranged a pageant for the Malatesta in honour of the name-day of his illustrious wife; also Messer Giovanni Bentivoglio found employment for my diverting talents. A witty and generous prince! He gave me a present of doubloons to sit at table and imitate all the dialects of Italy or assume the facial expression of various famous men. It is undeniable, my Lord, men like me must go a journeying to learn to set off their talents. In Florence there is already too much wit. But in Lombardy or the Romagna one can come into one's own.

PICO: I congratulate you. But tell me – you are a painter, are you not?

GRIFONE: Certainly, my Lord, that is my trade.

PICO: And it happens from time to time that you paint a picture?

GRIFONE: From time to time. Yes, my Lord, it happens. But not often, since I am active in so many fields. Lately I have been making violins, that is a joy. But first and foremost I am a designer of carnivals, the organizing of festivals is my proper sphere of art. I have hurried hither to Florence because the May-day festival in Piazza Santa Trinità is close at hand. Good God, it is the eighth of April, high time to begin! Easter is not far off either; and I must think up something new for the next carnival.

PICO: But it seems to me carnival is just over.

GRIFONE: Yes, it was a little while ago. But my friends and I are racking our brains over the next one. The carnival procession, my Lord – Orpheus with his beasts, Cæsar with the seven virtues, Perseus and Andromeda, Bacchus and Ariadne, all that is stale as nuts. The crowd whistles and boos when we serve it up such stuff. And now, after our Procession of the Dead – truly I am at a loss.

PICO: Florence counts upon your creative energy. But I was talking with Aldobrandino, and you interrupted us. Retire, my friend. – Aldobrandino, let us return to your affairs. If I understand you, you are come to complain to the Magnifico. . . .

ALDOBRANDINO: By my salvation, my Lord, that I am!

PICO: Do not, Aldobrandino, I implore you. You shall have satisfaction – or, rather, you bear your satisfaction within yourself. A man like you! So exceptional an artist knows that the esteem of all knowledgeable men is on his side. What do you care for the ephemeral hatred of the ignorant herd?

ALDOBRANDINO: Yours are glorious words, my Lord. I only –

PICO: But as for Lorenzo, he must on no account be disturbed. You know that he is ill – in what degree one dares not think, who loves him. It is essential to shield him from aught that might cloud or weaken his spirits. . . .

ALDOBRANDINO: If that is so, I gladly spare him, though

it is ill to forget an injury which one has borne in silence. But the gods know that I love him in my heart above all men.

PICO: Well said, my Aldobrandino. You are a shrewd and industrious man. Keep your word and it shall bear fruit....

POLIZIANO (*at some distance, to some other artists*): Truly, dear friends, we know nothing. We await the judgment of the doctor from Spoleto on the effect of the precious draught.

ANDREUCCIO: It is desirable that we should be able to spread good reports about the city. The people are restless.

GUIDANTONIO: Yes, they are in pessimistic mood. Evil signs have been seen.

GHINO: In the lion's cage at the palace one of the animals tore another to pieces. There are people who put a sinister interpretation on that.

ERCOLE: Some purport to have heard the saints sighing at times in the churches.

SIMONETTO: Many witness to it. And a fruit-seller in Piazza San Domenico swears that the Madonna in his shop has several times rolled her eyes.

ALDOBRANDINO: Quiet there, let me speak. All that is nothing compared to what I have seen. This morning when I was taking a walk outside the gates, it rained blood.

GRIFONE: Nonsense. It never rains blood. There is no blood in the clouds.

ALDOBRANDINO: My Lord Giovanni, will you instruct this heretic that according to our holy religion such a thing is quite possible?

GIOVANNI: Possible or not, when my father is well again it will rain good Trebbiano, a liquid which for my part I greatly prefer.

ALDOBRANDINO: To blood. Aha, that is capital! Liquid! Trebbiano is a liquid, of course, but the joke is to call it one.

ANDREUCCIO: No, no, gentlemen, the thing is that the Padre prophesied the death of the Magnifico. That is what makes the people restless.

PANDOLFO: The scoundrel! He sings the same dirge in

every sermon. And threatens war, starvation, and pestilence to boot.

ANDREUCCIO: He has a saturnine temper.

DIONEO: What rubbish! It is hatred speaks out of him, green-eyed envy.

ERCOLE: All the Ferrarese are avaricious and envious.

ANDREUCCIO: You cannot say that he is avaricious. He brought back poverty into San Marco and goes about in a worn-out habit.

LEONE: Do defend him, Brother Andreuccio the art-embroiderer. You are an old woman.

GUIDANTONIO: Easy to see he has made an impression on you. You belong to the Weepers, the bead-tellers, the head- hangers.

ANDREUCCIO: That I do not, certainly not, dear friends. But my mind is full of misgiving, and my heart is heavy. You know, gracious Prince, and you, Lord Cardinal, that I not only serve the arts with my hands, making beautiful embroideries and carpets, but also sometimes speak in public in favour of the manual arts and the beautifying of our whole life. Everything, it has seemed to me, must become art and good taste under the house of the Medici my masters. And I still think so. But there is a thorn in my flesh. You see, not long ago I was speaking to a great concourse of people about the artistic progress that has been made in the production of gingerbread; for, as you know, we now make gingerbread in all sorts of charming and amusing shapes, after the modern ideas. Well, Brother Girolamo must have got wind of my dissertation, for when I attended one of his last sermons in the Duomo he came to speak of it and looked at me as he did so. He said that whoever tried to turn higher things into common things had no conception of their significance; that it is frivolous and childish to talk about making beautiful gingerbread when thousands have not even the coarsest bread to eat to satisfy their hunger. The congregation sobbed and I hid my face. For his words are like whizzing arrows, my lords, they hit the mark! Since then I have been going about grieving and in doubt; for I know not whether my work and my activity were right all this time, or wrong.

POLIZIANO: Shame, shame, Andreuccio! You have not the heart of an artist, else you would not give ear to this creature who daily calumniates art with his vulgar hatred.

ANDREUCCIO: Does he hate art? I do not know. He speaks lovingly of the work of the blessed Angelico. Believe me, his thoughts are on fire with inward fervour. (*With an effort*) Suppose he has such reverence for art that he thinks it blasphemous to apply it to gingerbread?

ERCOLE: Whoever can understand that may! What I understand is that this loathsome mendicant friar would like to suppress all joy and light-heartedness in Florence. The feast of San Giovanni is to be abolished, the carnival –

GRIFONE: What, what? The carnival?

ERCOLE: Yes, he wants to abolish it. You would have to look to it, Grifone, how to earn your bread, after that. You will have to start painting pictures.

GIOVANNI: Come, tell me more about him. I want to hear what else he says. He is a most extraordinary man.

GUIDANTONIO: Well, I can assure your Eminence that the Frate uses some pretty strong language. He treats the Pope more scurvily than a Turk, and the Italian princes worse than heretics. He prophesies a speedy fall for you and your family; prophesies in a roundabout and uncanny way. He speaks of certain great wings which he will break. He speaks of the city of Babylon, the city of fools, which the Lord will destroy; but everybody knows that he means your father's house and his power. He describes precisely the architecture of this city: he says it is built of the twelve follies of the godless –

GRIFONE: Wait! What? Twelve follies? That would be something for my pageant. Listen! (*Pleased and excited, he draws aside another artist and begins to talk and gesticulate to him.*)

GHINO: I, your Eminence, have received the commission from the printer Antonio Miscomini to make woodcuts for the new edition of the Frate's works.

POLIZIANO: What? And you have accepted the commission?

GHINO: Certainly.

PICO: He was right, I think, Messer Angelo. The dissertations on prayer, humility, and love of Jesus Christ are capital literary performances. And they will be enhanced by Ghino's pictures.

GHINO: That last was not Brother Girolamo's view, I may say. Imagine: he protested against the adornment of his works. He wanted no pictures. Did you ever hear the like? But Signor Miscomini was shrewd enough to insist that the book have a suitably elegant appearance. I ask you: who would read a book today that has no satisfaction for the eye and only contains the bare text? I have already finished some quite good things for it, I shall cut the Frate's seal in wood –

GIOVANNI: What is his seal?

GHINO: A Madonna, your Eminence, a Virgin with the letters *F H* on either side.

LEONE: Now I know why Lorenzo cannot endure Brother Girolamo. Or at least he has always done his best not to leave any virgins in Florence. (*They all burst out laughing.*)

GIOVANNI (*slapping his knee in his relish of the joke; then, quite touched*): Come hither, Leone. That was very good. No Medici could resist it. Here, take this ducat, you long-nosed satyr. You may model me, if you wish. I like you well.

ALDOBRANDINO: That is all very fine, but after what has happened, Ghino, you must refuse the commission.

GHINO: Refuse it? A commission?

ALDOBRANDINO: Beyond any doubt. I have been insulted. In my person our whole craft is insulted, and the Frate incited to the insult. The devil can illustrate his books for him, but not one of us. You must decline.

GHINO: Not at all. Are you mad? What are you thinking of? I should refuse such a fat offer as that? Miscomini isn't stingy with his pay; he knows that he has made a tidy sum with the Frate's writings. They go everywhere. Everybody will see my woodcuts. I shall have much praise and get fresh orders. I need them, I must live. I have social obligations. And my little Ermelina wants presents, otherwise she goes with a shopkeeper behind my back. I have to bring her a silk cap, a horn of rouge and white lead if I want her to be yielding to me. I need money; I take it where I can get it.

ALDOBRANDINO: Traitor! You have no honour in your whole body. I spit on you – I despise you from the bottom of my heart.

GHINO: Ridiculous! I am an artist. A free artist. I have no opinions. I adorn with my art what is given me to adorn and would as lief illustrate Boccaccio as our holy Thomas Aquinas. There are the books, they make their impression on me, I give out again what I have received, as best I can. As for views and judgments, I leave them to Fra Girolamo.

ANDREUCCIO (*broodingly*): But hard, hard it must be, a lofty and painful task that you commit to him. To have to deal with and judge of everything, of all life and morals – seems to me it needs great courage – and freedom.

POLIZIANO: Freedom, Andreuccio? Your mind is confused. Ghino calls himself free and he is right, for the creative man is free – he over whose birth Saturn presided will always be at odds with the world in whatever state he may have found it. But truly it is better to be able to make a chair or anything of beauty than to be born to set things right.

PICO: Well, I do not know. As a collector and amateur I prize things according to their rarity. In Florence there is a legion of brave fellows who can make beautiful chairs; but only one Brother Girolamo.

POLIZIANO: You are pleased to be witty, my Lord.

PICO: No, I am serious. – Who is that coming?

5

PIERLEONI (*comes hastily through the garden from the palace, beckoning as he comes. His long robe makes him take tiny steps. He is an eccentric old man, in clothing that suggests the charlatan and magic-worker. He wears a peaked cap and has a short ivory wand in his hand.*): Lord Angelo! Messer Politian! He is asking for you.

POLIZIANO: Lorenzo! I come!

PIERLEONI: He wants you to recite to him. He has thought of a passage in your *Rusticus* and would like to hear it from your lips.

PICO: So he is awake, Messer Pierleoni? He is conscious?

PIERLEONI: He was, just a minute ago. But God knows if he will not have forgotten his wish and himself again by now.

POLIZIANO: And the draught? The healing draught of distilled precious stones? Did it help?

PIERLEONI: The draught? Very much. . . . I don't mean that it helped Lorenzo, exactly. Most likely the reverse. But the man who brewed it, Messer Lazzarro from Pavia, him it helped very much, it brought him in a fee of five hundred scudi.

(*Giovanni giggles.*)

PIERLEONI: You laugh, Lord Giovanni. You spirits are blithe. But I get red with anger when I think that this ignorant impostor from Pavia got away unpunished. Why was he called in? They did not ask me, they went over my head. He got a double handful of pearls and precious stones delivered to him out of the household treasury, among them diamonds of more than thirty-five carats; he certainly stuck half of them in his pocket, then he ground up the rest and dissolved them and gave our master the brew to drink, without even taking count of the position of the planets, for he has no knowledge of astral influences, whereas I never order a powder or apply a leech without carefully noting the position of the planets. . . .

PICO: You are a great and learned physician, Messer Pierleoni. We know that our illustrious master is well looked after in your hands. But now tell us, instruct us, remove us out of our uncertainty. What is the illness that has laid Lorenzo low? Give us its name. A name can be so consoling!

PIERLEONI: Mother of God, console us all! I can name you no name, my good Lord. This sickness is nameless, like our fears. If one give a name, it sounds short and dreadful.

PICO: You wrap yourself in silence, entrench yourself behind riddling words, and have done ever since the hour when my friend took to his bed. I insist on knowing: is there a secret here?

PIERLEONI (*breaking down*): The weightiest.

PICO: I will confess the suspicion which I have had long before today and which must overwhelm everybody who sees matters from close at hand. Lorenzo, like every strong man, has enemies.

PIERLEONI: He was never strong. He lived despite himself.

PICO: He lived like a god! His life was a triumph, an Olympian feast. His life was a great flame blazing boldly and royally to the skies. And one fine day this flame dwindles, crackles, smokes, smoulders, threatens to die down. Between ourselves we have seen the like before; such surprises are not foreign to our time. We have heard of letters, of books, the confiding receiver of which read himself over into the kingdom of the shades without knowing it; of litters wherein one sat down a joyful man and descended pining and plague-stricken; of dishes in which the hand of some generous friend had mingled diamond-dust so that the eater got an indigestion for all eternity.

GIOVANNI: Very true. Very true. My father always took these things too lightly. One should taste no banquet in the house of a friend without taking at least one's own wine and cellarer along. Certainly no good host is annoyed at that. It is a well-established custom.

PICO: In short, Pierleoni, my friend, be open with us. Speak as a man among men. Are my fears justified? Plays poison a role in the affair?

PIERLEONI (*evasively*): Poison – that depends . . . that depends, my dear sir. Will you follow me, Messer Angelo? (*He bows and withdraws. Poliziano joins him; they move quickly down the garden.*)

6

PICO: Strange old man!

GIOVANNI: Things look bad. I am afraid, I feel sad. If my father only did not roll his eyes so strangely . . .

ALDOBRANDINO: Do not grieve, your Eminence, dear Lord Giovanni. If the illness is strange, so also shall be the cure. There are extraordinary cures. Just listen what once happened to me. It will distract you. I am often ill, as sensitive people always are; but once, some years ago, I was mortally so. The trouble was in my nose, a gnawing pain inside that noble organ. No doctor knew what to do. All internal and external means had been sought in vain. I have even used the excrement of wolves with powdered cinnamon dissolved in the slime of snails and I was completely exhausted from blood-letting. But the air passages were closing and I thought there was nothing for it but I must suffocate. Then in my hour of need my friends took me to a master of the secret science, Eratosthenes of Syracuse, a marvellously skilled necromancer, alchemist, and healer. He examined me, spoke not a word, put five different kinds of powder in a pan and lighted them. He said an incantation over them and left me alone in his laboratory. Then there arose so frightful and irritating a smoke that I completely lost my breath and thought I should die upon the spot. I summoned my last ounce of strength to reach the door and escape. But when I stood up I was taken with such an immoderate sneezing as I have never had in all my life before, and as I shook and quivered from head to foot, there came out of my nose an animal, a polyp or a worm, as long as my middle finger, very ugly, hairy, striped, all slippery, with suckers and pincers. But my nose was free, I breathed in air and realized that I was entirely cured.

PICO (*looking down the garden to the right*): Listen, Vannino, I must leave you. I see your brother Piero. You know I do not love his ways. Let me avoid him. I will see if they will let me in to your father. Farewell, we shall see each other soon. Good day, my lords. (*He goes.*)

GIOVANNI: Well, and the worm, the polyp, Aldobrandino? Did you catch it?

ALDOBRANDINO: No, it got away. It ran into a crack in the floor.

GIOVANNI: Too bad. You could have tamed it and taught it to do tricks, perhaps.

7

PIERO DE' MEDICI (*comes with rapid, imperious gait along the right-hand side path. He is a tall, strong, supple youth of one-and-twenty years, with a smooth, well-proportioned, arrogant face and brown curls, falling thick and soft at the nape of his neck. He is armed with dagger and sword, and wears a velvet cap with an agraffe and plume, and a tight blue silk doublet fastened in front with quantities of little buttons. His bearing is offensive, his speech loud and commanding, his whole personality uncontrolled and violent.*): Giovanni! Where are you? I am looking for you!

GIOVANNI: And lo, you have found me out, Piero. What is the good news?

PIERO: You have company... have you been here long?

GRIFONE: About an hour, your Excellency, or thereabouts.

PIERO: Then it seems to me that at the moment you are not needed further. If you should wish to take leave you will not be hindered. (*Stamping with his foot*) You are invited to go to the devil!

ERCOLE: Your Eminence, we crave your permission.

GIOVANNI: God be with you, dear friends; do not go far off. I am convinced my father will ask for you. Farewell, Aldobrandino... Grifone... Francesco... (*He accompanies them as they go, then returning*) You do wrong, Piero, to treat such distinguished men as you did.

PIERO: I should not know how otherwise to treat buffoons and suchlike of the artist tribe.

GIOVANNI: Yes, you see, that is wrong. In every artist, it may be, there is something of the fool and the vagabond, but that is not all of him, for each is after all something of a leader who directs the taste of the many into fresh channels and, so to speak, puts in currency new coinage of pleasure.

PIERO: Glorious leaders, forsooth! This Aldobrandino –

GIOVANNI: Yes, yes, this Aldobrandino. I admit that I like best the society of his sort. The humanists are tedious and irreligious, and the poets for the most part pathetic and conceited; the artist is my man. They are cultured without being tiresome. They dress well and they have wit, originality, and a sense of fitness. And what mobility, what lively fantasy! Messer Pulci has no more, I declare. Before you can say a rosary this Aldobrandino can kill you three giants, make it rain blood and blow monsters out of his nose, without entertaining a single doubt of the truth of his boasts.

PIERO: You are welcome to all the pleasure you get out of it. But I must speak to you alone and so I made bold to send your friends packing.

GIOVANNI: You want to speak to me? I have no money, Piero!

PIERO: Don't lie! You always have money.

GIOVANNI: By the blood of Christ, I have had large expenses – for musical instruments and for a dwarf Moor, the quaintest creature on the face of the earth. Should you like to see him? Come, I will show him to you. Why stand here and talk of money –

PIERO: I need some. You must lend me for a little while.

GIOVANNI: I can't, Piero. Certainly not. The little I have I must keep together.

PIERO: Your Highness is probably saving up for the Conclave? But it is not your turn yet, most illustrious prince of the Church. You cannot vie with Roderigo Borgia. They say he sends asses laden with gold to those cardinals whom he has not yet poisoned, to attune the Holy Ghost in his favour. Your Eminence will have to have patience.

GIOVANNI: What are you talking about, Piero? Of course I shall have patience. I am hardly seventeen. But the growth of simony is a very interesting subject, which I should like to discuss with you.

PIERO: Well, I need a hundred ducats, to buy a horse to ride at our next tourney, the second day of Easter week –

GIOVANNI: A hundred ducats! You are stupid. A horse – when you have so many horses! And your silly tourneys! How you can be so mad about them! Running at each other and getting hurt – no sense in that. Did you ever read that Cæsar or Scipio rode tourneys? Such a dangerous passion! Petrarch –

PIERO: A fig for your Petrarch! I would not take advice about a knightly and elegant career from a sonnet-tinker like that. The times are past when the princes of Italy and Europe considered us shopkeepers and money-changers; they were past when we learned to wear armour and bear a lance. Our court shall lag behind none other in Europe – and what is a court without tourneys? Anyhow, will you advance me the hundred ducats or not?

GIOVANNI: No, Piero, certainly not. It's no good. Don't be angry, but giving you money is like pouring into the cask of the Danaids. You squander it all with your boon companions and your fat cows –

PIERO: What – fat cows?

GIOVANNI: A phrase all Florence knows. You do not seem to be informed about the latest witticisms. And besides, you are so far in the hands of usurers that you do not spend a florin without it costing you eight lire. Where will that end, I should like to know? The times are bad enough, anyhow. The sparrows on the house-tops know that our house has been going to the dogs since Grandfather died. They say that our banks in Lyons and Bruges are shaky. People are whispering that the bank of deposit for the dowries of burghers' daughters has had to limit its payments because Father spent a lot of the money for works of art and festivals. Many people have taken that amiss.

PIERO: Taken it amiss! Who dares grumble? The factions are scattered, the refractory have been consigned to exile or a dungeon. We are masters. Today it is Lorenzo, tomorrow or day after it is myself. Then, trust me, there will be an end of small shopkeeping. If the banks crash, let them. I'll give them a kick to finish them. The important thing is landownership. We must get more and more property. We are princes. Charles of France called my father his favourite cousin – he must call me his brother! Just let me be master once! Not a law shall be left that gives the people the shadow of a right or even seems to set limits to our will. We will have no nobility near the throne. There will be confiscations, condemnations.

Lorenzo has never gone about this matter firmly enough. He has been too poor-spirited to give our position the title it deserves. I do not care to be the first citizen of Florence; duke and king is what they shall call me throughout Tuscany.

GIOVANNI: Ah, your Grace, your Majesty! – You are a braggart. Is that all your political theory you are showing off? Are you so sure that Madonna Fiorenza will take you for her lord and lover, when our father – which may God forbid – is dead? You have a wonderful understanding of physical exercise and affairs of gallantry; but your knowledge of public matters is to seek. Did you know that Brother Girolamo preaches against you? That the people cannot stand you? That they stick up lampoons against you on the palace?

PIERO: Listen, my lad, I advise you not to make me angry. Give me the hundred ducats I need and keep your political dissertations to yourself.

GIOVANNI: No, Piero. I gladly give you my blessing; receive it, dear brother, I pray you. But I lend you no more money. Finis, signed and sealed.

PIERO: You mule! You Sodomite! Sanctified son of a pig! What prevents me from boxing your ears, you purple ape!

GIOVANNI: Nothing prevents you, you are quite vulgar and ungentle enough. So I will go away and withdraw myself from the vicinity of your bad manners. You will find me with our father if you should be looking for me to beg my pardon. Farewell. (*He goes off up the centre path.*)

PIERO: Go, go, you weakling! Red hat on your head, wet swaddling-clouts on your breech! I do not need you. Soon I shall be master; then the rejoicing world will see a prince to make its teeth chatter! Wagons... wagons... towers on wheels... a swaying, shimmering purple progress in the dust, between carpets, under awnings, through the heart of the yelling mob! Youths poising lances, on prancing, whinnying steeds... flying genii strewing roses... Scipio, Hannibal, the Olympian gods descending to pay homage, rolling up to the triumph of Piero the divine!... And on a gilded car high as a house – I, I! The orb of the earth revolving at my feet,

Cæsar's laurel wreath on my brow, and in my arms she . . . my creature, my handmaid, my blissfully blushing slave . . . Fiorenza. . . . Ah! . . . You are there, madonna?

8

Fiore has appeared on the right-hand path and now stands in the centre one, her hands folded on her advanced abdomen, her head thrown back, and her eyes cast down, calmly symmetrical, in mute and mysterious loveliness.

PIERO: (*going up to her*): Is it you, madonna?

FIORE: You behold me in the flesh, noble sir.

PIERO: I was unaware of your nearness. I was busy with my thoughts.

FIORE: Thoughts?

PIERO: Still I will say that I am glad, that I am inexpressibly rejoiced, to meet you.

FIORE: I beg you, spare me. I am a woman, and such words in the mouth of the glorious Piero must abash any woman. . . .

PIERO: Most gracious Fiore! Ravishing Anadyomene!

FIORE: Audacious flatterer! The Grand Turk sent us some of his sweets, and when I ate of them after the meal I thought there was nothing sweeter on earth. I think so no more, now I have heard your words.

PIERO: Sweet simpleton! Come, we shall chat, you and I. . . . What would I say? . . . It grows cool. . . . You have been walking in the garden, lovely Fiore?

FIORE: Your keen perceptions have told you as much. I walked between the hedgerows. And gazed sometimes out into the country, to see if guests were coming from the town, one guest perhaps, to bring a little diversion to the villa. . . .

PIERO: Yes, yes . . . I quite understand your longing for variety, beautiful lady! Nothing more fatiguing than a country sojourn, since Lorenzo got the bad idea of stopping in bed. Just between us, I am surprised that you have not sooner thought of having a change.

FIORE: What do you mean, my Lord?

PIERO: I mean – I mean, sweet Fiore, that you would not have far to seek to find people downright willing to take over the sweet duties of which my father has seemed now for a while no longer capable. Your beauty blooms untasted, your mouth, your bosom orphaned.... Be assured, not you alone are vexed. Look up and see a man who yearns immoderately to be in every way of service to you.

FIORE: Forgive me, the sight is not novel enough to lure my gaze from the ground. All long for me; do you say it of yourself in hope to win me?

PIERO: In hope? Am I a boy? Am I a tyro in the lists of love? I would and shall possess thee, divine creature....

FIORE (*slowly lifting her eyes and looking with inexpressibly languid contempt into his face*): If you knew how you weary me!

PIERO: What are you saying? In my arms you would forget your weariness.

FIORE (*repulsing him scornfully*): I will not belong to you, Piero de' Medici!

PIERO: Not to me? Why not? I am strong, you would have naught to complain of. I control the wildest stallion with my thighs, needing no saddle nor bridle. I have challenged the best players in Italy to wrestling, to ball, to boxing, and you have seen that I was victor. If you will lie with me, sweet Fiore, I will tell you of my triumphs in the gymnasia of Eros.

FIORE: I will not belong to you, Piero de' Medici.

PIERO: Hell and Hades, does that mean that you scorn me?

FIORE: It means that you bore me inexpressibly.

PIERO: Hearken, madama, I speak to you as to a lady whose charm and culture one considers, but I am not minded to whimper after your love as though you were a bashful and dutiful burgher's wife. If you would play the prude, it will but sweeten my love; but I beg you not to ask me to take your cruelty to heart. Who are you, to give yourself the air of repelling my advances? You are of noble Florentine blood, but your father begot you without priestly blessing and died in exile as a reward for his bargain with Luca Pitti. You live and confer your favours in the service of Aphrodite; and Lorenzo conceived you as a partner of his pleasures when they were feasting him in Ferrara. You need not doubt that Piero will know how to reward you for your caresses as richly as Lorenzo.

FIORE: I will not belong to you, Piero de' Medici.

PIERO (*furiously*): To whom, then? To whom? You have another lover already, you shameless courtesan?

FIORE: I will not belong to you, Piero de' Medici.

PIERO: To a hero? I am a hero! Italy knows it.

FIORE: You are no hero; you are only strong. And you bore me.

PIERO: Only strong? Only strong? And is not the strong man a hero?

FIORE: No. He who is weak, but of so glowing a spirit that even so he wears the garland – he is a hero.

PIERO: You gave yourself to my father – is he a hero?

FIORE: He is one. But another has arisen, to tear the garland from him.

PIERO: You? You? I will have you. Who is he, who is he, the weakling with the glowing soul, that I may flout him, and choke him with two of my fingers?

FIORE: He is coming. I have seen to it that he should come. They shall confront each other. But as for you – withdraw, when heroes quarrel!

PIERO (*raging*): I will have you, I will have you, sweet insolence, flower of all the world –

FIORE: You will not have me. You bore me. Make way, that I may go and await your father's rival.

ACT THREE

A room adjoining the sleeping-chamber of the Magnifico. In the background, left, between heavy half-open portières, a view of the bedchamber; steps occupy the rest of the rear of the stage, leading up to a gallery. Centre left a splendid marble chimney-piece with a relief supported by columns, and the Medici arms. In front of it chairs. Left front an étagère with antique vases. Right front a door hung with a gold-embroidered tapestry. Right back a curtained window. Between door and windows, drawn a little forward, a bust of Julius Cæsar on a pedestal. Smaller busts, without pedestals, on the chimney-piece and above the doors. Slender columns are let into the walls. The subdued light of the late afternoon sun filters through the window curtain.

I

Lorenzo de' Medici sits in a high-backed arm-chair in front of the fire, asleep, with his head on his chest, a cushion at his back, and a rug over his knees. He is ugly; with a yellowish-olive complexion and a sinister expression due to the wrinkles in his brow. He has a broad, flat face with a flattened nose and a large projecting mouth with flabby wrinkles round it. His cheeks are marked from nose to fleshless chin by two deep slack furrows; these are the more prominent because he cannot breathe through his nose but must keep his mouth open. Yet his eyes as he awakes are clear and full of fire despite his weakness and seem to seize upon men and things with vigour and avidity. His lofty and speaking brow triumphs over the rest of his facial ugliness; his motions are the perfection of aristocracy. Sometimes a charming expression of fascinatingly innocent merriment comes out upon his ravaged features, seeming to purify them entirely and give them a childlike look. He wears a voluminous fur-bordered garment like a dressing-gown, closed high round his short neck. His hair is brown, with white threads; it is parted in the middle and waves against his cheek and neck. He speaks with studied clarity, in a nasal voice. – Watching his uneasy sleep are Pico della Mirandola, Poliziano, Pierleoni, Marsilio Ficino, and Luigi Pulci. Old Ficino has the worn face of a scholar, a withered neck, and scant white locks coming out beneath his pointed cap; he wears the usual voluminous garment closed to the throat and sits in the centre of the room, surrounded by the others. Pulci, a comic type, with little red-rimmed eyes and inflamed pockets beneath them, a pointed nose, prominent ears, and a mole on his cheek, is pressing his finger to his lips as he gazes with the others into Lorenzo's face.

PIERLEONI (*going cautiously up to the invalid and feeling his pulse*): It is very irregular. I am considering whether this is not the time to bleed him once more.

PICO: You will kill him with your blood-lettings. It is not twelve hours since you took a basinful from him.

PIERLEONI: The man does not need a tenth of the blood he carries round with him.

POLIZIANO: Where is his spirit? It seems to move upon strange paths far from ours. I would gladly hear your opinion of its experiences, dear Marsilius.

FICINO: It is likely that at this hour contact with the divine unity is established in his brain.

PULCI (*lowering his strident and comically cracked voice*): Look, look, all that is mirrored upon his countenance! I wager that he is dreaming the most extraordinary things. If he feels no pain, then I envy him. The fever causes the strangest fancies, far better than are produced by strong wine. Sometimes one may dream in verse, but is prone to forget it.

PIERLEONI: This sleep is not the sort that feeds the natural resources of the man. If his faintness continue, then I must hold the little fingers and toes of His Magnificence while I anoint his heart and his pulse with the oil which I have ready here.

PICO: Hush! He is stirring, he wakes.

PULCI: He will tell us of his adventures.

FICINO: Do you know us, Laurentius, my dear pupil?

LORENZO: Water.... (*They give him to drink.*)

LORENZO: The water-seller had a skull....

POLIZIANO: What water-seller, my Lauro?

LORENZO: Angelo... is it you? Good, good, I will control myself. Shall not one master this madness? I met a water-seller with his laden ass and full jugs; but when he put a wooden goblet to my parched lips there was fire in it and on the villain's shoulders sat a grinning death's-head.

PULCI: Well, that is a modest invention.

LORENZO (*recognizing him*): Good day, Morgante. Are you there, old good-for-nothing? And my Pico with the ambrosial locks? And even great Marsilius, wooer and messenger between me and wisdom – you are all with me, friends. The frightful old man was only in my own blood.

PULCI: A frightful old man?

LORENZO: Rubbish! Worthless rubbish! I dreamed so hard of a bald-headed old man who wanted me to ride in his rotten bark...

POLIZIANO (*shaken*): Charon?

LORENZO: I was asleep.... What time is it?

PICO: You slept about an hour. It is three o'clock. The sun has begun to set.

LORENZO: Already? (*Seized by sudden unrest*) Listen, my friends, I should like my carrying-chair. The air here is stifling.... Carry me... carry me into the loggia; take me up on the battlements....

PIERLEONI: Dear and gracious Lord, that would be folly. You need rest.

LORENZO: Rest? I cannot rest. Why can I not rest, doctor? Why do I feel that I must strain myself to think and arrange manifold matters before it is too late?

PIERLEONI: You have a little fever, my Lord.

LORENZO: I do not deny it. But I would say that the fever is no ground for my being tortured by these ridiculous fears. You see, I think logically. But I do not conceal that I am heavy with cares. I have never pretended – Pico, there are no more Pazzi in Florence, are there? And the Nieroni Diotisalvi are either in exile or put safely away?

PULCI: Save those you sent to hear the grass grow!

LORENZO: Yes, come here, Margutte! Make jokes, you wild rhapsodist! Yes, in truth, much blood has flowed. It had to. – I implore you, Pico, for the time I am not able, to keep an eye on the collections in Via Larga and the villas. You will do it for me? A couple of lovely little trifles, two terracottas and a medallion, have just been acquired; they must be kept in Poggio a Cajano, you know, my dear fellow? And the Sforza has presented me with a glorious antique from Pesaro, an Ares with breastplate. It should be set up in my public garden and serve the young sculptors as a model. Will you see to it? Thanks. That is all that was troubling me. – Is Angelo here still?

POLIZIANO: Here, my Lauro.

LORENZO: Angelo, the Pliny which my grandfather got from a cloister in Lübeck is in the Signoria, is it not? I should like to see it. It is bound in red velvet with silver mountings. Let a responsible person go at once – no, wait. That seems to me less important than something else on my mind. Wait. One of my searchers has been offered a Cato manuscript for five hundred gulden. I am in doubt over the genuineness of the script. There are cases where some rascal has made up something out of his own head and put it on the market under an ancient name. I beg you to test the manuscript very carefully and if it be genuine procure it for me without bargaining. They must not say that I let a Cato escape me. May I burden you with this? – You lift a load from my heart. Come, my friends, now I feel easier. I can think of nothing to depress me. Let us talk. Let us discuss. Who was greater, Mirandola, Cæsar or Scipio? I say Cæsar, and ye shall see how I defend my thesis! But our great Marsilius Ficinus wants an abstract theme, of course!

FICINO: Let your mind have repose, Laurentius! You will wear yourself out.

LORENZO: Wisdom is worthy the sacrifice of one's last strength. There is so much to clear up! It often used to seem to me as though everything lay clear and open before me; but now I see only darkness and confusion. How is it with the immortality of the soul? Tell me!

PULCI: An old, a treacherous question – and not to be answered *ex abrupto* like that. They say that Aristotle himself, even in the kingdom of the shades, was still going about with equivocal phrases, in order not to commit himself – though he was as dead as a door-nail and yet alive. Let anyone try to make it out from his writings!

LORENZO (*laughing heartily*): Good! But now, Angelo, say something serious.

POLIZIANO: You are immortal, my Lauro! Must I tell you so? Not everybody is. Not the masses, not the small and unknown man. But you shall share the enlightened society of the laurel-crowned spirits.

LORENZO: And why I?

PICO: Now, by the blue-eyed Athene! You have written carnival songs which I have not scrupled to place above Alighieri's great poem!

FICINO: You have divine origins, forget it not. The six balls in your arms signify the apples of the Hesperides, where your stock had its rise.

POLIZIANO: They will know how to welcome you, singer of the "Rencia", *pater patriæ*! They will celebrate your coming. Cicero, the Fabians, Curius, Fabricius, and all the others will surround you and lead you into the hall of fame, which echoes with the music of the spheres.

LORENZO: That is poesy, poesy, my friend! That is beauty, beauty – but neither knowledge nor consolation!

PULCI: Yes, yes, it is a little thin, your music of the spheres, Messer Politian. It is small comfort. Do not die, Lauro, it would be stupid. You know Achilles' answer, when Odysseus visited him in Hades and asked how he fared. "I assure you," said he, "that we departed have the strongest desire to return to life." The body, lad! The body is the main thing. The body cannot be substituted for by any music of the spheres! Oh, forgive me! Are you worse?

LORENZO (*very pale*): Doctor – a coldness is coming round my heart – do you hear? A horror seizes upon me – help! It is death.... What does it mean, that suddenly all power is gone from my brain and my entrails? I am lost... I am forsaken.... Dry the sweat from my brow.... Do not despise me. My spirit is steadfast, this fear is in my body.

PIERLEONI: It is nothing. Drink this good beaker of Greek wine. I have been begging your Magnificence to go to bed.

LORENZO: If you want me to be able to breathe, let me sit in a chair. I must see about me all you who love me. I must hear your voices. Death is horrible, Pico. You cannot grasp it. No one here can grasp it, save myself, who must die. I have so dearly loved life that I held death to be the triumph of life. That was poetry and extravagance. It is gone, it fails one at the pinch. For I have seen dissolution unroll before me, the decay of the tomb. – Quick, Ficino, quick, dear, wise old Ficino! What have you taught me, that I might face death with fortitude? I have forgotten. What is your uttermost wisdom, Ficino?

FICINO: I taught you that Plato's "Idea" and the "First Form" of Aristotle are one and the same; that is, the sensitive soul, the *tertia essentia* of bodies, which in man, the microcosm of creation, is distinguished from the intellectual soul in that it –

LORENZO: Stop, wait a minute. I am confused. I understood that once; perhaps I felt it. But now I struggle in vain to do so. I am tired. I long to have something simple to hold fast to. Purgatory is simpler than Plato; you will have to admit that, Marsilius. Was it not a Franciscan father who came to me today?

POLIZIANO: Yes, beloved, a confessor came from that order.

LORENZO: A rascal. A clever head. I was ashamed to take the business seriously before him. I turned a few good Florentine phrases when he waited on me with his sacraments and he smiled like the man of the world he was. I confess that the ceremony did not soothe me much. The Father's morals were all too complaisant. He forgave me my sins as though they were boyish pranks. But I doubt if such absolution be quite valid in high places. I might have confessed that I had murdered my father and mother and he would have signed the cross over me with the greatest obligingness. No wonder. I am the master. But when the end comes, there are drawbacks about being the master whom nobody dare offend. I need a confessor who would be as priest what I have been as mocker and sinner.... What is it your eyes say, Pico? You have something in your mind. You are hiding your thoughts.

PICO: What thoughts, my Lorenzo?

LORENZO: You are thinking of a priest who would be fit to be my confessor, who would dare to damn me, who has already dared, Pico....

PICO: What priest –?

LORENZO: *The* priest. What say, Marsilius? The Platonic idea of the priest, become person and will –

POLIZIANO: I implore you, my dear Lord, turn your thoughts to gayer pictures! You cloud your spirits with thoughts unworthy for you to think. Do not forget yourself, Lorenzo de' Medici!

LORENZO: Truly, that will I not. Thanks, my Angelo. I feel better. We will be gay. We will laugh. Laughter is a sunbeam of the soul, so says a classic. We will let our souls shine in the recollection of what has been.

PICO: And what will be again.

LORENZO: Enough that it has been. This was wont to be the hour when we walked together to a spring. You remember? We lay in a ring upon the rolling sward, with the childlike prattle of the water in our midst. And we spent the time till the evening meal with each of us telling a tale.

PICO: What a charming hour! And how we admired you! Perhaps in the forenoon you may have been working out a new law for the statutes, designed to give power more fully into your hands, that you might be in a position to bless Florence still more freely with beauty and joy; perhaps uttered the death sentence upon some noble adversary; argued in the Platonic Academy upon virtue; presided over a symposium in a group of artists and lovely women; at table solved theoretic questions in art and poetry – and in all that you had brought your whole mind to bear and now were sharing the evening play of our minds, as fresh and detached as though you had not given out any part of your vital energy.

PIERLEONI: Yes, you were never niggard with your strength, my gracious Lord.

LORENZO: Was I not, my astronomical doctor? Did I not bend them to my will, despite stars and portents, which had destined me to your careful charge? Yes, I have lived. Come, let us remember. Remember with me, my friends. Remember the drunken starry nights, when we rose from our wine, you, Pico, Luigi, Angelo, you, mad Ugolino, Cardiere the ecstatic musician, and all the rest – when singing and twanging the lute we stormed the sleeping streets and inflamed maidens in their chambers by the verses we sent up to them.

POLIZIANO (*rapturously*): Alcibiades!

LORENZO: And the carnival, remember the carnival! When pleasure like a torrent overflowed the bounds of everyday, when wine ran in the streets and the populace in the squares danced and shouted the songs I composed for them; when Florence surrendered to the god of love, and men's dignity and women's modesty reeled in one intoxicated shout: Evoe! When the holy madness seized even children and kindled their senses to love before its time.

POLIZIANO: You were Dionysus.

LORENZO: And the kingdom was mine! And the sway of my soul went abroad! And the fire of my longing kindled the woman's breast, so that she fell to me, and the ugly weakling became lord of her beauty –

PICO: Lord of beauty – in that name we salute you! Speak not as though you *had been* all that!

LORENZO (*after a moment of silence, gesturing with his head behind him*): Someone wants to come in.

A PAGE (*half-way down the stairs*): Signor Niccolo Cambi has come from Florence and begs to be admitted to your Grace.

PIERLEONI: The Magnifico is receiving nobody.

LORENZO: Why not? Signor Niccolo is my friend. He comes from Florence – I feel quite well. I want to see him.

2

The page conducts the merchant Niccolo Cambi from the gallery down the steps into the room, leads him to Lorenzo, and withdraws with a low bow. Cambi is a citizen, respectable, well dressed, already a little stout, with a lively Florentine face. His shoes and stockings are dusty. He wears a light-grey cloak over darker undergarments.

LORENZO: A welcome visit, Messer Niccolo. Do not take it for discourtesy that I remain seated. I am a little unwell these days.

CAMBI: Enough to see you! To hear your voice again! My

heart is lightened thereby. Good evening, gentlemen. You in particular, illustrious Prince, you, Messer Pulci, Master Poliziano! My faith, the great translator of Plato too! Messer Pierleoni! To see you again, Magnifico! To hear you speak! To feel the living pressure of your hand!

LORENZO: Then you had not expected it?

CAMBI: Why not? Certainly, of course.

LORENZO: Sit down. Push your chair close to mine. You rode up? You are over-heated; did you ride so fast, then? Are you on business? Messages from Florence?

CAMBI: But why? Must one always have business with you, messages for you, in order to feel impelled to see you? My business is to look you a little while in the eye, witness my love to you, and assure myself afresh of yours. My message, to tell in all the streets of Florence that you are of good cheer, that soon we shall be able to celebrate your return to health.

LORENZO: So Florence busies itself about my illness?

CAMBI: It certainly does! One cannot say that it is exactly indifferent to it, ha ha! The Magnifico is naïve in his question. But I mean to give those rascals the lie who disquiet the people without reason and make them prey to sinister rumours.

LORENZO: There are such rascals, then?

CAMBI: There are, there are! And, Magnifico, you would do well, you would do very well, to put a stop to their activities without delay. I see you up, I see you out of bed – could you not come to Florence? Even for an hour? Just to show yourself five seconds long at a window?

LORENZO: Master Niccolo Cambi, what is going on in Florence?

CAMBI: Nothing, nothing. God keep me! Messer Pierleoni – my visit is untimely. Shall I withdraw?

LORENZO: My desire, my will, are what count here. (*With an effort at gentleness*) You will oblige me very much, honest Messer Niccolo, by speaking briefly and without reserve.

CAMBI: Then I will do so. To whom should one speak, to whom bring these fears and cares, if not to you? Things are not in Florence as they were, Magnifico! Vile machinations are afoot. The source whence these rumours are disseminated is known, which report you to be either already dead or sickened beyond cure: they come from the monkish party, from the "Weepers", from the party of the Ferrarese....

LORENZO (*who has started at mention of the Ferrarese, with forced lightness*): You hear, Pico? They come from your discovery, our monk.

CAMBI: Pardon me, illustrious Prince, it is the truth. I know that you fostered him, that you first drew attention to his strange new works, I know it. And I would not assert, either, that I do not know how to value his gifts. I am not so behind the times. His performances are titbits for a spoilt and licensed taste, that is beyond a doubt. I am not speaking of him. I am speaking of the influence he wields, which is – it is possible – independent of his intentions.

POLIZIANO: Do you think so?

CAMBI: The people, Magnifico, the people! We can afford to smile when young sprigs of the nobility forswear dancing, singing and all frivolity, and enter a cloister. But the people! All day they run irresolute through the streets, they look darkly at the beautiful houses of the rich and know nothing better to do than to throng the cathedral to hear the sermons – a dense, silent crowd, inwardly distraught, a great acreage of muddled heads, all turned in his direction, in the direction of the lean little monk up above them. When the Frate is carried back in triumph to San Marco, the masses choke the streets again and resume their obstinate, mischief-breeding activities. Before the house of Guidi, chancellor of the city archives, and in front of Miniati's the administrator of municipal debts, they have been disorderly and insulting; for Brother Girolamo designated both of these citizens as your tools, Magnifico, as people who connived with you how to squeeze new taxes from the poor for your festivities. Barbarous, insane things are happening. Before I left Florence I heard that a group of mechanics forced themselves into the house of a wealthy and art-loving citizen and broke a statue in the vestibule –

(*Pained exclamations from his audience.*)

LORENZO: Hush! An antique?

CAMBI: No, it seems to have been new and not very valuable. But, O Magnifico, it is not that which you must hear! There have been noisy demonstrations before the palace all day. I was in the Piazza, I was present. There were shouts from the people, which I could have wished not to hear, not to understand. It sounded like "Down with the golden balls!"

POLIZIANO: That is treason! That is ingratitude and treachery!

PICO: It is the childish love of the populace for political cries – and nothing more! They should be dispersed with the pikes.

CAMBI: And yet another cry rose above these – a strange cry, never heard before – once, twice, and again. I did not understand, I am as you know a little deaf in one ear. But when I listened very carefully, I heard it clear and plain: "*Evviva Christo!*"

(*Silence*)

CAMBI: You are silent, Magnifico.

LORENZO: What was the cry?

CAMBI: The one against your arms?

LORENZO: The other.

CAMBI: *Evviva Christo!*

(*Silence. Lorenzo has collapsed into the cushions; his eyes are closed.*)

PIERLEONI: Go, gentlemen! In God's name, go! You see, he is exhausted.

CAMBI: Magnifico, I wish you good repose. I have done my mission. You had to know how things stand with us. You are not angry?

LORENZO: Go, friend. . . . No, I am not angry with you. Go. . . . Tell Florence – no, tell her nothing. She is a woman, one must take care what one says or has said to her. She runs after you with burning desire when you seem cool and strong and despises you when you betray that you are lost in love for her. Go, friend, say nothing. Say that I am well and that I laugh at what I have heard.

CAMBI: That will I. By Bacchus, that will I say. That is a good message, by my faith. And so be in good health, Laurentius Medici. And come to Florence so soon as you can. Farewell! (*He hurries off.*)

3

LORENZO (*after a pause*): Pico!

PICO: I am at your side, my Lorenzo.

LORENZO: Look at me. Seems to me you look a little embarrassed, eh, my subtle Pico? What have you to say now?

PICO: Nothing at all. What should I say? The people are drunk – with drunkenness of a sort different from that you have known so long how to cause in them. Tell the Bargello, it will know how to sober them.

LORENZO: Pico! Mæcenas! My subtle innovator! To call in the hangman's services against the spirit? That was not subtle!

PICO: One counsel or the other. Call *him* in, then. Bewitch him. Do you think this petty and solitary soul can withstand the brilliant allurement of your offers of friendliness?

LORENZO: It will, my Pico, it will! I know it better than do you, whose inquiring spirit discovered it for us. It is full of hate and mean opposition. Its gifts do not make it blithe or friendly – only more obstinate. Do you understand that? He did not come to me when he became prior – prior in that San Marco which my own grandfather built. He stuck dumbly to his priestly independence. See, thought I to myself, a stranger enters my house and has not even the decency to pay me a visit. But I was silent. I shrugged my shoulders at the little man's incivility. He reviled me from the pulpit, indirectly and by name. I went – you did not know it – to seek him out. More than once I attended mass at San Marco and afterward stopped some hour in the cloister garden, awaiting his summons. Do you think he paused in his literary labours to be hospitable to a guest who was after all more than a guest?

I went further. I am not used to have men deny themselves to me. I sent presents to the cloister and gifts to charity. He took them as signs of yielding and never once thanked me. I let them find gold coins in the offertory boxes. He gave them to the poor-wardens of San Martino; the copper and silver, he said, were enough for the needs of the cloister. Do you understand? He wants war. He wants hostility. Approaches, homage, he pockets, and gives nothing in return. He cannot be shamed. Success does not soften him nor his mood. He came a nothing, a beggar, to Florence. What he is after today is a decision between me and him.

PICO: Dear friend, what fancies! He is ill and wretched. His digestion is ruined, from watching, from ecstasies. He lives on salad and water. May he enjoy them! Is he Lorenzo, who even in suffering is courteous and full of charm? Do you expect pleasant social intercourse with a father confessor? Let him have his way. And let the childish populace have theirs. Any measures you would take would give the situation a serious complexion which it has not got. Only get well, only show your face again to your city.

(*There is a general backward movement. A pale and breathless youth, in a distracted condition, appears rushing down the steps. It is Ognibene, a young painter. He leans on the balustrade a moment, quite exhausted, one foot a step lower than the other.*)

OGNIBENE: Lorenzo! You are here. Thank God, I have found him. Your Excellency, dear and gracious Lord, forgive me for my urgent haste; I pressed onwards, I would not let them bar the way to you. I must speak to you. I ran – Oh, my God! (*He kneels beside the Magnifico and takes his hand imploringly in both his own.*)

LORENZO: Ognibene! Indeed, you alarm me. No, let him lie where he is. He has audience. He is a gifted youth and moreover Botticelli's pupil. What is it, Ognibene?

OGNIBENE: I ran – I came – from Florence, from my master's shop. Ah, my master! Ah, the picture! The wonderful, beautiful new picture! Forgive me! I had not time to put on my cloak. I ran as I was. The monk! My master! Lauro, win him back to you!

LORENZO (*in alarm, threateningly*): Pico! . . . Hush! I will hear nothing. I will not hear it. Withdraw. . . . Speak, boy, speak low. What of Botticelli?

OGNIBENE: You know that he was painting a new picture. What am I asking – he was painting it for you! I was allowed to help him . . . and trembled for joy as I saw it grow. Often I slipped alone into the workshop and knelt down in the stillness where it stood and gleamed – it was more beautiful than the Primavera, more beautiful than the Pallas, lovelier than the Birth of Aphrodite. It was youth, it was bliss, it was ravishment, painted with sunshine –

LORENZO: And now? You must part?

OGNIBENE: Since he first heard Brother Girolamo in the cathedral he has worked heavily and without joy. Often he sat silent on a stool with his head in both hands and brooded. And when he raised his head he stared at the picture with eyes full of conflicting horrors. And today –

LORENZO: And today?

OGNIBENE: Today he was in San Marco after the sermon. In the Frate's cell. Two hours or three, I do not know. And when he came home he was as though dead – full of peace, but dead. "Ognibene," he said, "God has called me with a frightful voice. There is no healing in beauty and in the delight of the eyes. Tell the Magnifico that I served Satan and that from now I will serve Jesus the King, whose representative in Florence is His prophet Girolamo. When I take my brush now I will paint in deep humility the Mother of Sorrows – tell the Medici that. Now will I save my soul." And as he said that he took a knife from the colour table and cut and slashed it across and across so that the tatters hung down. . . . (*He sobs with his head in his hands, as though his heart would break.*)

LORENZO (*with clenched fists, rigid with pain and rage*): Sandro. . . .

OGNIBENE: Lauro, Lauro, what shall we do? I mean – what does your Excellency command? Will you summon him? Will you speak to him? I think if he saw you – Command me, order me what to do. I will run back. I will bring my master to you despite the darkness. You can do anything. You will lighten and set free his spirit.

LORENZO (*gloomy and exhausted*): No. Let it go. It is too late, for today. I mean, it is too late in the afternoon. Be brave and go. Go to your work. Or to your wine. Take a girl – forget. I would be alone. Go, till I call you. No, Pico, you too. And listen: send me the boys. I want to talk to Gino and Piero. They may come in now. And then go.

(*They all leave, some by the stairs, some by the door front right. Lorenzo remains alone, sunk in his chair, clutching the lions' heads on the arms with his emaciated hands. His chin rests on his breast, his gaze seems to burrow deep into his own thoughts.*)

4

LORENZO (*dully and brokenly, between pauses*): Jealousy – I have never known what it was. – I was alone. Where was there a purpose like to mine . . . a knowledge of power? Here! – Often I marvelled. – And I made it serve. – It was beautiful, here within me. – Distraction – suffering – burning – smiling? All in vain. I hate him. I hate him too. He triumphs. For he is upright. He is effective. He wasted himself, like me, he was not wise. But he had enough left – just enough left, to do it. Perhaps because he is of commoner stuff. – The picture? Let it go. A small matter here – where we are dealing with souls. We are dealing with the kingdom. (*His eyes rest on the bust between the door and the window. He continues to muse. Piero and Giovanni come cautiously through the portières of the door right front, approach him, and kiss his hands.*)

GIOVANNI (*kneeling*): How are you, Father?

LORENZO: Oh, so it is you. You don't often come,

gentlemen. Why has one sons? For show? To make an appearance? To make one look more imposing? Just as one marries a wife, of noble Roman blood, marries her in Rome by proxy and gets children with her hardly knowing her, for reasons of state? Is that the way?

GIOVANNI: Father, you have been sincerely in our thoughts.

PIERO: We were impatiently awaiting your summons.

LORENZO: You are most courteous. Very well brought up. It would be exacting to ask more, I suppose. How true it is that father and son are furthest of all from each other. Relations between them are stranger and more uncomfortable than between man and wife. Well, let that be. One must not give anything away. Must not seek love too eagerly. Still, I confess, I have had you in my mind, I have thought of your welfare. That is why I had you summoned.... It seemed to me I had a few words to say to you, and that I should like to have you stand before me. You look at me searchingly – how do you find me?

GIOVANNI: Better, Father, much better. You have a little colour.

LORENZO: Really? My friendly little Giovanni. See, I lift my hand. I will to do it, and do it. It trembles – and falls. And falls. There it lies; quite white. I could not hold it up. Come here, Nino; bend over, Piero. I stand with one foot in Charon's bark.

GIOVANNI: No, no, Father! Do not speak like that. Pierleoni –

LORENZO: Pierleoni is a ninny. He and his rival with his draught of precious stones. I am at my last hour. I am going to hear the grass grow, as Pulci says. I am going, and you remain. Now, Piero, what have you to say to that?

PIERO: God grant you a long life, Father.

LORENZO: Very polite. But to come to the point: Are you ready to step into my shoes?

PIERO: If it must be so, yes, Father.

LORENZO: Fiorenza – you love her? Patience a little. My

thoughts are confused, that I admit. I see everything in a lurid light, as in a conflagration; one thing flows into another in my mind.

GIOVANNI: Perhaps we ought to go, Father?

LORENZO: Ah, the little one is afraid. No, stay here, Nino. The fever gives me courage to speak out my feelings boldly. What I say sounds odd. But reason is at work. Piero, I speak to you. Your expectancy of power is great, and well founded – but it is not sure, not unimpeachable. You cannot rest idly upon it. We are not kings, not princes in Florence. We have no document on which our power is secured. We rule without a crown, by natural right, by our own strength. We became great of ourselves, by industry, by struggle, by self-discipline; the idle throng stood amazed and then submitted. But such power, my son, must daily be won afresh. Glory, love, the submission of others – these are all false and fickle things. If you think to rule, to shine without shining deeds, Florence will be lost to you. You will hear your name cried aloud, they will strew the laurel at your feet, they will lift you on their shields, recount your great deeds with slavish exaggeration; that is but for the moment, for what you have done up to now; it secures not a single morrow, promises no future like the past – even as they shout you may be losing ground. Be on your guard. Be cool-headed. Be aloof. They think only of themselves. They need to pay homage – homage is so easy to pay! But no one will think of sharing your struggles, your pains, your cares, your own deep fears. Guard yourself from the injurious contempt of these same idle acclamations. You stand alone, you stand entirely by yourself. Do you understand? Be stern with yourself. Do not be rendered soft and careless, for if you do, Florence will be lost to you. Do you understand?

PIERO: Yes, Father.

LORENZO: Count as nothing the outward glitter of power. Cosimo the Great shunned the eyes and the homage of the crowd, that its love might not exhaust itself in acclamations. Oh, how wise he was! How much shrewdness passion needs, to be creative! And you are foolish – I know you. You are too much like your mother. You have too much Orsini blood in your veins. You want to be painted in armour, play the prince in all the streets of Florence. Do not be a fool. Take care! Florence is sharp-eyed and loose-tongued. Be reserved – and reign! . . . Remember, too, that we are of burgher, not noble stock; that we are what we are only because of the people; that our only foe is he who would estrange the people from us – do you understand?

PIERO: Yes, Father.

LORENZO: "Yes, Father." Polite, soothing, knowing better. A perfect son. I am certain you do not believe a syllable. Hearken, Piero, things may turn out badly, I foresee it. We might fall, be driven out, when I am gone. It might be so – be quiet. Florence is false; she is a strumpet. Lovely, indeed – ah, lovely, but a strumpet. She might come to give herself to a wooer who wooed her with scorpions. So, if that should hap, Piero, if the foolish people should rise in wrath against us, then, Piero, listen, save our treasure, save the treasure of beauty which through three generations we have gathered together. I see it spread out in the palace, in the villas. I could touch the marble limbs, drink in with my eyes the glowing colour of the paintings – put my hands on the splendid vases, the gems, the inlay work, the coins, the gay majolica. You see, my children, it was not only my money and my zeal, it was my worth as a citizen I spent upon them. Who does not understand me would condemn. I made no scruple to seize the property of the state when I needed money to pay for my collections and my feasts. Unrighteous goods? Rubbish! I was the state. The state was I. Pericles himself took public money unhesitatingly when he needed it. And beauty is above law and virtue. Enough. But when they rave against it, then, Piero, save our treasures of beauty. Rescue them. Let all else go, but protect them with your life. This is my last will. You promise me?

PIERO: Be without care, Father.

LORENZO: But have a care yourself! Be shrewd. I do not believe you will be shrewd, but that is my advice. – And you,

Vannino, my friendly little Giovanni! With a quiet heart I leave you. For you I have no misgivings. Your path is marked out. It will lead you to the throne of Saint Peter. You will add to our arms the triple tiara and the crossed keys. Have you any idea what that means? Why I put that in train with all my skill? A Medici in the seat of Christ? Do you understand? Do not speak. But if you understand, smile with your eyes into mine. He smiles – see, he smiles. Come, let me kiss you on your brow. Farewell. Live joyously. I summon you to no great deeds. You are not made for bearing heavy burdens of guilt and greatness. Keep yourself free of deeds of violence and crime too great for you. Be innocent, be undisturbed. Cover yourself not with blood. Be a happy father to the populace. Let the Vatican ring with merriment and the sound of lutes. Let jests and jollity be the lightnings that flash from the throne of this son of Zeus. May beauty and the arts flourish beneath your staff of power, and joy go out from your throne into all the lands. I have your promise?

GIOVANNI: I will ever be dutifully mindful of your words, dear Father.

LORENZO: Then leave me now. And thanks to you both – go now. I am very weary. My soul yearns for deep stillness. Farewell, my sons. Love one another. Think of me, and farewell.

(*The brothers quietly leave the room by the same door. Giovanni with a charming gesture makes way for Piero to pass.*)

5

LORENZO (*alone*): "Yes, Father." He understood not a word. I was talking to myself. It has not eased my mind. There is one to whom to speak out all one's mind would avail. Impossible. Ah, Florence, Florence! If she were to yield herself to him, this frightful Christian! She loved me, she for whom we wrestle, this sombre monk and I. O world! O deep desire! O love-dream of power, sweeter, more consuming – one must not possess. Longing is a giant's power, owning unmans. Our bliss was mutual so long as my slender strength sufficed. The wanton responds to the hero's mighty charms. Now that I am broken, she despises me.... She is vulgar, boundlessly vulgar and cruel. Why do we vie for her favour? Ah, I am weary unto death!

(*Fiore appears in the background, at the top of the steps; her hands crossed over her abdomen, artificial, symmetrical, mysterious. From where she stands she flashes a quick glance across at Lorenzo from beneath her lowered lids, then descends slowly into the room, with a smile.*)

FIORE: How goes it with the Lord of Florence?

LORENZO (*starts and struggles to sit upright. A painful, pathetic smile spreads over his features*): Well, very well, excellently well, my beauty! Is it you? I am well. Why should I not be so? Did I seem a little absorbed in thought as I sat here? I was composing a poem. I was conceiving a little sonnet to the exquisiteness of your nostrils when they dilate in mockery. And since I was composing poetry, it follows I am well; I am as sound as a fish swimming in its native element. For he who versifies thereby evinces a plenitude of fancy.

FIORE: Then I congratulate you.

LORENZO: And I thank you, my gracious goddess. I do not see you; yet your sweet, cool voice laves and refreshes my heart. And now, now I will see you; ah, your loveliness! Will you sit down beside me? Here on this stool? Though it would be more fitting were I to take my place at your feet. You see, they have left me alone – and I complain not. Indeed, I may have sent them on their way, I needed them not. I could meditate more profoundly upon your charms, and love you better, being alone.

FIORE: So you still love me, Lorenzo de' Medici?

LORENZO: Love you still? I should perhaps love you no more. You do not know that all the strength of my being and my understanding are consumed in love of you?

FIORE: Then I do not understand why you do not stir out of your cushions to make fêtes for me.

LORENZO: Fêtes? Certainly. But – fêtes – you see, I am a little tired.

FIORE: Of me?

LORENZO: Sharp and sweet! I love your scorn.

FIORE: How should you be tired, if not of me?

LORENZO: Permit me to lay my hand upon your brow. It is hot, is it not? This fever – Pierleoni says it comes from the unfavourable position of Jupiter and Venus with respect to the sun and to each other, which is harmful to me. Pierleoni knows nothing. This fever inflamed my blood when I first caught sight of you, when my soul first comprehended all your charms. Since that hour it has not ceased to glow. Do you remember? Ferrara? The Duke came to meet me on the Po in a gilded gondola, surrounded by gay little barks where banners fluttered, music sounded, and I was greeted by a choir of singers. The shores were strewn with flowers, the statues of the joyous gods gleamed white; and between them stood slender boys holding garlands in their hands. But every bark bore a lovely woman, adorned each differently, for these were the cities of Italy, who came to meet me. And one, one I saw among them all, laurel in her hair and lilies in her hand; and the minstrels sang to me in saucy strophes: "Thou art Fiorenza, thou, the only one, the sweet one, the glory and the brilliance, the love and the power, the goal of yearning, thou the flower of the world, thou wilt be mine. . . ." I looked at you and pain seized my heart, an ache, a deep oppression and a stubborn grief – what shall I call it? A longing for thee! For thee! To possess thee, thou flower of the world, thou many-hued seduction, and of thee to die!

FIORE: Poor victor! What would you not give to receive this pain back again for your weariness!

LORENZO: I feel it. It never left me again. Does one possess you? Does the struggle to win you ever end? Is there ever repose in your arms? . . . You came to me, you wonderful creature. Do you remember the evening after the fête? You came. . . . You came in to me through the marble doorway. And when for the first time I embraced you in the golden darkness of the room and won your lips with my mouth – then I felt the dagger you carry in your bodice and thought of

Judith. Your father hated us Medici. He joined the Pitti, we sent him away to misery, and his exile saw your beauty reach its flower. Perhaps you only gave yourself to be revenged? Perhaps in the moment of deepest desire the poisoned death found its mark? How often, let us be never so drunken with love, I searched your unfathomable eyes, listened to what lay behind your cool and polished words.... Have you ever loved me? Ever loved anyone to whom you gave yourself? Or do you only out of curiosity obey the power of desire, which may never slumber satiated, which having once possessed must ever be born anew, if it will not lose you ignominiously? For him, madonna, who has once tasted of your charms, there can be no more repose, in conning either memories of the past or dreams of the future. Only a constant, piercing present, wakeful, fateful, perilous, and – consuming.

FIORE: Hearken, my Lord Lorenzo. I am not come to argue with you about the art of love. I am a woman; yet it often seemed that you laid stress upon my view and voice even in serious matters?

LORENZO: Speak, I beg you.

FIORE: Well, then, I came to express to you my astonishment at the negligence with which you look on at the evil course which public affairs are taking.... You have never heard of a monk, Hieronymus Ferrarensis by name and Prior of San Marco?

LORENZO (*looking at her*): I have heard of him.

FIORE: And heard that he subdues the city to himself with words, brings youth to his feet, makes artists repent in sackcloth and ashes, stirs up the populace against you and your rule, and lets himself be the object of worship as envoy of the Crucified?

LORENZO: I have heard of it.

FIORE: Indeed – and you suffer all this mildly, sitting in weakness amid your cushions?

LORENZO: If Florence loves him, I cannot and I will not hinder it.

FIORE: He insults Florence.

LORENZO: And Florence loves him for it.

FIORE: Would you endure to have him insult me too?

LORENZO: Did he do so?

FIORE: I will tell you all the tale from the beginning. It lies further back than events in Santa Maria del Fiore.

LORENZO: You were in the cathedral?

FIORE: Like the rest of the world.

LORENZO: You went often to the cathedral?

FIORE: As often as it pleased me. And from a curiosity better grounded than that of others. I know this monk from early days.

LORENZO: From early days?

FIORE: From days when your glory's crown still hovered invisible high above your head. It is quickly told. At Ferrara, near the hut where my father and I found refuge from your bravoes, there lived a citizen named Niccolo, learned, wealthy, and of ancient lineage, in favour at court. He lived there with his wife, Monna Helena, and two daughters and four sons. The eldest son had gone for a soldier. I was a child still, or almost a child, twelve years, thirteen – yet I was already beautiful (if you can believe it) and youths gazed after me. I was on friendly terms with my neighbours. We visited each other, we talked at the windows, walked together in summer outside the city walls, played games in the fields, wove wreaths for each other's heads. But one of our neighbour's sons shut himself away from our merry company, the second eldest, about eighteen years old, I think: small, weak, ugly as darkness. He feared people. When all Ferrara streamed out of doors to the public festivals, he buried himself in his books, played mournful melodies upon his lute, and wrote what no one was allowed to read. They thought to make a physician of him, and he applied himself to the study of philosophy, sitting in his little chamber bowed over Thomas Aquinas and the expounders of Aristotle. Often we teased him and threw orange-peel through the window on his writing-desk; he would look up with an uneasy and contemptuous smile. Between us two, things stood very strangely. He seemed to flee the sight of me with fear and loathing, yet to be condemned to meet me for ever, indoors and out and everywhere I went. Then he seemed to play the coward and avoid me, yet he would force himself, pressing his thick lips together as he came towards me, passed and greeted me, blushing red and bending on me a sour and injured gaze. In this wise I came to understand that he was in love with me, and I rejoiced in the power I had over his gloomy arrogance. I played with him and led him on, I gave him hope and dashed it with a look. It thrilled me to know that my eyes could control the flow of his blood. He grew more lean and silent still, he began a fast that hollowed out the caverns of his eyes; one saw him sitting long hours in church, bruising his brow against the altar step. But one day, out of curiosity, I brought it about that he was alone with me in a room at twilight. I sat silent and waited. Then he groaned and was as though pulled towards me, and whispered and confessed. I made as though astonished and repulsed him; he seemed then to rave, almost like an animal, begging me with gasps and panting with parched lips to yield me to him. With horror and disgust I thrust him from me – it may even be I struck at him, since he would not leave his avid clinging. And when I did so, he tore himself away and stood up with a shriek, inarticulate and hoarse, and rushed off, his fists before his eyes.

LORENZO: I understand, I understand.

FIORE: He was named Girolamo. That night he fled to Bologna, and entered a cloister of Dominicans. He preached repentance in unheard-of accents. Folk laughed, they stared, they were subdued. His name went through all Italy. And your spoilt curiosity, gentlemen of Florence, drew him hither. And he waxes great in this Florence.

LORENZO: You have made him great.

FIORE: I – have made him? Then hear how he rewards me. He has insulted me before the populace, today, in the cathedral... pointed at me with his finger, spat upon me with words, compared me to the great Babylon, with whom kings have commerce!

LORENZO: Kings! You made him great. Greater than I, to whom you gave yourself.

FIORE: Greater than you? That I find still undecided; it will be decided. Hearken, my friend – if you summoned him? Here before you? Be it only to see how the poor little monk stumbles over the carpet when in the presence of the Magnifico. For his Rhodus would be here. Hear him, answer him. Let him measure himself against you. And if you see his worthlessness, then send him back to his cell, back to his pulpit. Let him insult you further as he will, you – and me. And if you feel his power predominant, then it lies with you to deny it out of existence with arguments of the sternest and coldest. He is in your grasp; if you are a man he will never escape from it. . . .

LORENZO: And if I should shame to employ such arguments? You know that I should thus shame.

FIORE: I know nothing. I wait. I wait to see how each one shows himself. I await the event. From me, indeed, expect no thanks if you feel shame to show yourself the stronger!

LORENZO: He would not come. On what pretext could one call him hither?

FIORE: Indeed, you are very ailing. Have you never lied? You call the priest. You feel ill. You want to confess. You seek for spiritual counsel.

LORENZO: In very truth I seek it. I yearn for it. Emptiness and horror are all about me at this moment. I see you not, madonna. I see not that you are beautiful. No longer do I understand what desire is. I should like to despise you, but I only shudder at you. Whither shall I turn? Call Ficino! Ah, that is naught. Call Brother Girolamo. You are right. Let him come.

FIORE: He is coming.

LORENZO: How then – he is coming?

FIORE: I sent for him to you. I knew you desired him. I sent for him today after the sermon. After he had insulted me. He is on the way. He may be here at any moment.

LORENZO: At any moment. By God, you know how to

act! Your zeal for this meeting is great. At any moment . . . the enemy in Careggi! Today, at once. Good, then, let him come. Am I afraid? If he comes I will not send him away. If I will still hear him; it may be the time has come. But first call someone about me. Summon my companions. Have Pico come and the others. (*Fiore touches a bell.*) Thank you, madonna. I love you. I were ill armed against this prophet did I not love you. . . . Ah, there you are, my friends! Lend me yet awhile the pleasure of your blithe company!

6

Pico, Ficino, Poliziano, Pulci, and Pierleoni come down the steps.

PICO: Ah, Lauro! We thought you resting quietly and alone, and you have just finished, so it seems, an appointment and a love-scene. Humble good day, madonna. But, Lauro, seriously: then you must not deny yourself to the jovial youth who have been hours long awaiting your pleasure: a group of artists, with Francesco Romano at their head, Aldobrandino –

LORENZO: He too? Good, good, I will see them. I need them. Let them come. (*A message is sent out by the gallery.*) I am in a good mood, gentlemen. I have had good news. I am receiving a visit. I expect today a charming and famous guest. No, you could not guess. Not even you, Pico. But I await him with impatience and am highly gratified that my artists have come to shorten the time before his entrance to my chamber. There they are. See Aldobrandino's innocent red face. And Leone's amorous nose. And Ghino, the bright darling of the gods. Welcome, children!

(*The eleven artists come in, making low bows.*)

ALDOBRANDINO: Health and blessings to your Excellency!

GRIFONE: Healing and joy to the godlike Laurentius Medici!

(*They press round him, kneel down, or bend over his hand.*)

LORENZO: I thank you. Be sure that I rejoice to see you all. Let me see, who are there here? Ercole, my brave goldsmith, and Guidantonio, who makes the beautiful chairs.... Yes, and I see Simonetto, the glorious architect, and Dioneo, who shapes wax in men's images. How is it with art, Pandolfo? I have not said, but I saw Messer Francesco at first glance.

ALDOBRANDINO: Truly, your Excellency, Messer Francesco is a great painter, and despite the closeness of his mouth far ahead of us all in his art; yet in love to you, gracious Lord, not one of us stands behind him, and some, perhaps, might even be before. May I mention, since it just occurs to me, that I have not long since come back to breathe my native air?

LORENZO: Yes, yes, my good Aldobrandino, you are right. You were away. You were in Rome. I remember quite clearly. You had work there, did you not?

ALDOBRANDINO: I did indeed, sir, and for lovers of art in high places, if I may say so. But then I heard a report that Lorenzo de' Medici, my good and great patron, was not well, and I dropped everything where it was and hastened to Florence with such zeal that I covered the ground in less than eight hours.

GRIFONE: He is only boasting, my Lord; it is shameless of him, I say. Nobody could cover that distance in eight hours; it is a lie.

ALDOBRANDINO: You hear, my gracious Lord, how this man tries to harm me before you and in your eyes.

LORENZO: Peace, children, there is no cause for hard words. Even if it is impossible to come hither from Rome in eight hours, Aldobrandino in saying so merely shows that he wants to give evidence of his love to me, and that in some vivid and poetical way. I cannot chide him for it.

ALDOBRANDINO: That is a splendid setting out, my Lord. But yet you do not know the depth of my devotion, nor what I am ready to do and suffer in silence for you.... So much I must be allowed to say, your Excellency. Good, good, I don't want to make a fuss.

GRIFONE: You are right there. We came here on a more important errand. We must discuss the festivities to be arranged in honour of your recovery, Magnifico.

LORENZO: My recovery –

GRIFONE: That is my suggestion – with your magnanimous permission I ask leave to suggest it. We must consider what a fine opportunity Lorenzo's restoration to health gives us for organizing a beautiful pageant and a ball and public banquet afterwards. My head is full of ideas. Let me manage the whole thing and you shall see a fête the printed descriptions of which will spread throughout Italy.

LORENZO: Good, good, Grifone. Thank you, my lad. I will count on you. We will take up the matter together later. Now I must ask what Ercole has been doing since I saw him last.... What are you peering about the room like that for, Guidantonio?

GUIDANTONIO: Pardon, my Lord, I was looking at the furnishing. Some of it is good. The chair your Excellency is sitting on at this minute was made by me. A fine piece. But the other things are quite out of fashion and not the height of good taste. I am working on a room for you which shall most wonderfully combine the classic motifs with the most modern comfort. May I bring you the drawings?

LORENZO: Pray do so one of these days. I shall not be able to resist ordering the room, if it is a genuine Guidantonio in taste and comfort. And now, Ercole, let me hear from you.

ERCOLE: I have done only trifles, sir; still, there are pretty conceits among them. A charming set for salt and pepper, with figures and foliage, I made especially for your table. You will pay me anything I ask, so soon as you see it. Also I have made a medallion with your likeness, with Moses on the reverse striking water from the rock. The inscription runs: *Ut bibat populus*.

LORENZO: And it has drunk, the people! Cast me the medal, my Ercole. Cast it in silver and in copper. I must praise it without even having seen it. You have chosen your motto well – *Ut bibat populus*.

ERCOLE: But the finest of all is a little breviary to the honour of God's Mother, with covers in heavy gold most richly worked. There is an image of the Mother of God on the front, you see, in precious stones – they alone are worth six thousand scudi.

ALDOBRANDINO: Pack up, Ercole! Lorenzo will not buy your breviary.

LORENZO: And why will he not?

ALDOBRANDINO: Because he does not care for the sign of the Virgin. At least he has done his best to have as few as possible of them in Florence. (*Laughter and applause.*)

LEONE: What cheek, Magnifico! That is a shameless piece of plagiarism. I made that joke myself an hour ago, down in the garden. I call these gentlemen to witness.

ALDOBRANDINO: You should not make such an ugly display of your envy, Leone. You may have said something of the sort, I admit it. But it was in quite a different connection, and anyhow it shows a bad character to grudge me the applause these gentlemen would pay to my quickwittedness.

LEONE: If Lauro were not sitting here, and Madonna Fiore, you braggart, you, I would tell you to your face that you are an empty-headed rattlepate.

ALDOBRANDINO: And I would counter with the absolute truth that you are like nothing so much as a stinking billy-goat.

LORENZO: Aldobrandino! Leone! Enough! I declare the subject closed. I know that you are both of you very witty. Come here, Leone. Tell us a story. Tell us one of your adventures, you jokesmith, you! We will make up for your lost applause. Look how our mistress prays you with her eyes. She loves your historiettes. And our Messer Francesco – his wishes are written on his face. Would you like Leone to tell us a tender tale – yes or no?

FRANCESCO ROMANO (*rolls his black eyes, simpers, then opens his mouth for the first time and says in a loud, naïve voice*): Yes.

LORENZO (*much diverted*): Did you hear, Leone? The

master understands painting better than making words; but what he says is weighty and solid. Impossible to refuse. Begin! Madonna is queen of the day. She summons you, and this noble circle waits to hear.

LEONE: Well, then, listen. But I must beg the learned gentlemen to bear one thing in mind. I talk as it comes to me, without art. I am no tale-writer, I make no fables, nor need to fable as a poet does. A poet, it is well known, loves and enjoys only with his inky goose-quill – but I do it with another kind of productive stub. (*Hilarity, cries of "Bravo!"*) And accordingly I will tell you truly how Dan Cupid has favoured me of late. Listen: I was of late in Lombardy, at the house of a friend, which neighbours a convent famed for its abbess, who lives in great piety and in the odour of sanctity. Now, my friend's cousin, named Fiammetta, was a nun in this abbey, and I went with him to visit her one day at the grating. Hardly had I set eyes on her when I was enflamed by love for her youth and beauty and in her eyes I read that I was no less attractive to her. From then on I bent all my powers to see how I could gain her intimacy, and as I am not inexperienced in these matters I had soon conceived a plan to take advantage of the fact that a gardener was needed for the convent gardens. I took the precaution of changing my appearance a little, shaved my beard, put on ragged clothing, and applied to the holy and austere abbess for the vacant place. I made out that I was dumb, a capital idea, since it reassured the chaste madame that I was completely harmless to her flock. I was taken on and went at once to work. And it soon fell out that I met the lovely Fiammetta in the garden, made myself known and explained to her that I was not only not dumb but also not suffering from any other physical lacks – the which she begged me to demonstrate to her more convincingly. And since her desire most fully coincided with mine, she took me into her cell on the first evening that offered, and I remained there the night. And I assure you that whatever skill I lacked in my tasks by day, I was most punctual and adroit at my nightly ones. Yes, the charms of my lovely Fiammetta roused me on more than one night to heroic deeds, and would have gone on doing so, had not envy made an end to our joys. There were two ugly little nuns who had no lovers and had privately to go about as best they could to satisfy their needs. They made the discovery that here in the cloister the goat had been made the gardener; filled with ill will against their sweet sister, they scrupled not to bring their suspicions to the ear of the abbess. In order that no doubt remain, it was decided to take us in the act. They watched; and one evening late, when Fiammetta had opened her door to me, the two envious nuns hastened to the cell of the abbess, pounded on the door, and announced that the fox was in the trap. It may have disturbed the abbess's rest to be thus summoned in the night – as the sequel will show. But at all events she sprang from her bed, flung on her clothes, and rushed with the two spies to Fiammetta's cell. They burst open the door, brought lights, and exposed our embraces to the public eye. Fiammetta and I were stiff with fright. But when I had pulled myself together and looked at the abbess, who was exhausting all the curses and vile names in her vocabulary, I noticed an extraordinary circumstance. The holy female, that is, when she had thought in the darkness to set her hood on her head, had stuck on a priest's small-clothes instead, so that the kneebands hung down on her shoulders in the most singular way. "Madonna," said I, interrupting the stream of her cursings, "will perhaps first button up her headgear and then say on what pleases her to say." Then she noticed what she had done and stood crimson with blushes, for she knew where he was to whom the garment belonged. She rushed off in a fury and with her the two spies, and my Fiammetta and I were left alone to enjoy once more unvexed all the bliss of heaven.

(The general merriment has increased as he talks, certain places being warmly applauded by the artists and humanists. Even Fiore joins in. Lorenzo, completely diverted, has followed the tale with childlike enjoyment. Towards the end of it the whole room resounds with tumultuous mirth. Lorenzo laughs heartily; the artists fit to split themselves. But suddenly the narrator breaks off and there comes an abrupt silence.)

A PAGE (*entering through the curtained door front right, announces in a clear, very audible voice*): The Prior of San Marco. (*Pause.*)

POLIZIANO (*horrified, not trusting his ears*): What did you say, boy?

PAGE (*abashed*): The Prior of San Marco.

(*Stillness. All present seek Lorenzo helplessly with their eyes. All mouths are open, all eyebrows raised.*)

LORENZO (*to the page*): Come nearer. What do they call-you?

PAGE: My name is Gentile, gracious Lord.

LORENZO: Gentile. That is pretty. Go back to the door, Gentile, and come in again. I like to look at you, you walk so well. You have pretty hips. Stand so, as you are. Aldobrandino, notice the line. Take this ring, Gentile, because you have pleased my eyes. And him whom you have announced, let him now come in.

POLIZIANO: You would not!

LORENZO: I will.

(*The page goes out. Deathlike stillness reigns. The portière is lifted. The sallow, woebegone, fanatical profile of the Ferrarese is projected slowly into the room. It is irredeemably ugly; its savage expression and large bony structure are in startling contrast to the smallness and sickliness of the rest of his figure. His head is framed in the cowl of the black mantle he wears over his white habit. There is an abrupt depression between the great hooked nose and the narrow peaked forehead. The thick lips are compressed with a sort of finality, emphasized still more by the hollow ashen cheeks. The eyebrows are thick and grow together over the nose, also they are perpetually raised, making horizontal wrinkles in the forehead and giving the little eyes, ringed with the black shadows of exhaustion, a staring and yet vacant expression. He is out of breath from walking at a quick pace through the long passages, but tries to conceal the fact. His hands, now hanging down inside his mantle, look waxen and shake when he raises them. His voice has a nervous, frightened note, yet sometimes inexplicably takes on a hard and savage power.*

As he enters, the artists retreat backwards, giving him more than enough room. They form a group; one of them takes his neighbour's arm, turns half round, and stares over his shoulder at the monk, with lifted brows, his lips distorted with amazement, disgust, and fear. They retreat gradually leftwards up the steps and through the gallery, and with them the humanists. Pico is the last to go, casting inquisitive glances back at the group of three persons who remain. At last he goes off, treading softly.

The Ferrarese looks straight ahead and his gaze meets Fiore as she sits in her composed and studied posture at Lorenzo's feet. He starts back, for a moment his face is visited by a tormented expression; then he straightens himself, fixes his eye on Lorenzo, and with his head and the upper part of his body makes a vague gesture of salutation.)

FIORE (*has risen. Her hands are folded on her prominent abdomen, her eyes are lowered as she moves towards the Ferrarese and speaks in a high, monotonous murmur*): Welcome to Careggi, Master Prior. May I congratulate you on your sermon today? I was a little late, yet not too late to hear the best of it. Be assured that I was highly edified. Your performance is very powerful indeed. – Well? Why are you so silent? It is not fitting that an artist should so stiffly and haughtily pocket the praise he gets, without even the tribute of a disclaiming smile.

THE PRIOR (*still breathless, tormented and harsh*): I spoke to you in the Duomo. I will speak to you only from my pulpit.

FIORE (*affecting a pout*): Not everybody is so stern. From the cathedrals of all the arts they speak to me – they make me smile or I give them my ear – and still have enough flesh and blood left over to treat me as a human being.

THE PRIOR: I live only in my pulpit.

FIORE (*pretending to shudder*): So down here you are dead? Ha, yes, so you are. You are pale and cold. I am here in this room with a sick man and a dead man. But once on a time, Mr Dead Man, a long time ago, you were alive, were you not, and spoke to me here below.

THE PRIOR: I spoke. I shrieked. You smiled. You laughed. You lashed me with opprobrium. You drove me up – up to my pulpit. And now you pay me homage.

FIORE: You use large words. That is the orator's art. I pay you homage? People pay me homage, and I incline to him who knows how to pay it in the best and finest way.

THE PRIOR: I pay you no homage. I revile you. I call you abandoned and an abomination. I call you the bait of Satan, the poison, of the spirit, the sword of souls, wolf's milk for him who drinks it, occasion of destruction, nymph, witch, Diana I call you.

FIORE: And you say well. It takes as much talent to revile as to praise. And what if all that seems to me but the last and extremest kind of homage? Can you imagine that? Tell me! You felt it yourself!

THE PRIOR: I understand you not. You heard me in the Duomo. I am unskilled and cannot trifle. But you heard me in the Duomo. The Word is hard and it is holy. He who closes his lips with his finger, Peter Martyr, he is my master.

FIORE: Work and be silent. . . . I find, Magnifico, much resemblance between your guest and Messer Francesco Romano. But, Mr Dead Man, you came to talk to this sick man here. So I will go, wishing the gentlemen the pleasantest entertainment. I wish you good accord and rich experience. It would seem that it cannot lack.

(*She goes up the steps and disappears through the gallery. During the following scene it grows dark.*)

7

LORENZO (*seems entirely to have forgotten the Ferrarese, who keeps his burning gaze directed upon him. With bowed head the Magnifico gazes up into space. At length, coming back to himself, he makes a charming effort to assume his man-of-the-world manner and says*): Will you not sit down, Padre?

THE PRIOR (*tempted by weariness to sink down upon a chair near the door, but recovering himself and standing stiffly erect*): Let me tell you this one thing, Lorenzo de' Medici! I have seen the world. I know the treachery of princes, their accustomed practice of bloody violence. If this is a snare, if I have been lured higher to be enforced and done away with – then have a care. I am beloved. My words have won souls to me. The people stand behind me. You dare not touch me.

LORENZO (*suppressing a smile*): You are afraid? But no! Have no fear. It would be far from my mind to lay traitorous hands on a man so extraordinary as yourself. Am I a Malatesta, a Baglioni? You do me less than justice to compare me with these. I am not savage, not without honour. I know how to value your life and work as well as any of your own flock. May I not ask in return that you will look upon mine as direct and fairly?

THE PRIOR: What have you to say to me?

LORENZO: Oh, I have already said some of it. But you speak grudgingly. And you look worn and weary. I do not deceive myself. My eye is sharp for such signs. (*With genuine sympathy*) You are not well?

THE PRIOR: I preached in the cathedral today. Afterwards I was ill. I lay abed. I left my bed only on your summons.

LORENZO: On my – yes, yes, quite right. I am sorry. So your work consumes you, then, so much?

THE PRIOR: My life is tortured. Fever, dysentery, and continuous mental labour for the weal of this city have so weakened all my internal organs that I can no longer bear the least hardship.

LORENZO: By God, you should spare yourself – you ought to rest.

THE PRIOR (*scornfully*): I know no rest. Rest the many know who have no mission. For them it is easy. But an inward fire burns in my limbs and urges me to the pulpit.

LORENZO: An inward fire – I know, I know! I know this fire. I have called it daemon, will, frenzy – but it has no name. It is the madness of him who offers himself up to an unknown god. He despises the base, cautious, home-keeping folk and lets them stare amazed at one for choosing a wild, brief, burning life instead of their long, wretched, frightened one.

THE PRIOR: Choosing? I have not chosen. God summoned me to greatness and to pain and I obeyed.

LORENZO: God – or passion. Ah, Padre, we understand each other. We shall understand each other.

THE PRIOR: You and I? You blaspheme. Why did you send for the priest? You who have worked evil all your life long!

LORENZO: What do you call evil?

THE PRIOR: All that is against spirit – within us and without.

LORENZO: Against spirit.... I will gladly follow you. I called you to listen to you. I beg you, Brother, have faith in my goodwill. Tell me, pray: What do you mean by spirit?

THE PRIOR: The power, Lorenzo Medici, which makes for purity and freedom.

LORENZO: That sounds strong – and mild. And yet – why do I shudder? But I will hear you. In us, you say? And so in you as well? You struggle also with yourself?

THE PRIOR: I am born of woman. No flesh is pure. One must know sin, feel it, understand it, in order to hate it. The angels do not hate sin. They are ignorant of it. There have been hours when I rebelled against the order of spirits. It seemed to me that I was higher than the angels.

LORENZO (*with unaccustomed light irony*): A question so daring, so enthralling, that it is worthy being put by you. Yet, dear Brother, a question concerning you alone, and so today we can put it aside. See, I am ill, and fear is in my heart – I make no bones of telling you this. Fear for the world, for myself – who knows? – for truth. I have sought consolation with my Platonists, my artists – and I have found none. Why not? Because they are none of them my sort. They admire me, perhaps, they love me, and they know nothing of me. Courtiers, orators, children – what use is all that to me? You see, I count on you, Padre. I must hear you – about you and about me; I must compare myself, must come to terms with you; then I should have peace – I feel it. You are not like the others. You do not crawl prattling to my feet. You have risen up beside me, you breathe the same air as myself. You hate me, you repulse me, you work against me with all your art – and see, I am in my soul not far from calling you brother.

THE PRIOR (*whose lank cheeks, at the words, have taken on a glow*): I will not be your brother. I am not your brother. There you have it. I am a poor monk, a priest, scorned and despised like all my kind by the whole insolent world of the flesh, and yet I have raised myself and through me my kind to honour, so that I throw your brotherliness in your face, Magnifico though you be and a lord of this earth.

LORENZO: You see me inclined to admire you for it.

THE PRIOR: You shall not admire me, you shall hate me. And as I must be frightful to you, so must you fear me. I have heard much of your charm, Lorenzo Medici. It shall not ensnare me. Once more: why did you send for me? You shuddered before the heaped-up measure of your sins, and fear urges you to treat with God – you thirst to learn the conditions of grace. Am I not right?

LORENZO: Not quite – perhaps almost. And treat – yes, you see, that is what I want to do, that is what I am doing. But you are impatient. Let me understand you. You say I have all my life worked against the spirit?

THE PRIOR: Do you ask? Is your soul utterly insensitive, then, as they say your nose is? You have made more the temptations of this earth, the allurements of Satan which he makes run through the flesh like a luscious torment. You have set up the pride of the eye as a god, you have made pleasure spurt from the very walls of Florence – and called it beauty. You have beguiled the masses to believe the rankest lies which paralyse the desire for salvation; you have instigated feasts of gallantry in honour of the glistening surface of life – and called that art.

LORENZO: I perceive a strange contradiction here: You are zealous against art, and yet, Brother, you yourself – you too are an artist!

THE PRIOR: The people see more clearly – they call me a prophet.

LORENZO: What is a prophet, then?

THE PRIOR: An artist who is at the same time a saint. – I have nothing in common with your art of the eyes, Lorenzo de' Medici. My art is holy, for it is knowledge and a flaming denial. Long ago, when I suffered agony, I dreamed of a torch which should light up with mercy all the frightful depths, all the shameful and sorrowful abysses of being, of a divine fire which should be laid to all the world that it might blaze up and perish, together with all its shame and martyrdom in redeeming pity. It was art of which I dreamt.

LORENZO (*musing*): The earth seemed fair to me.

THE PRIOR: I saw! I saw through the fairness and the appearance! I suffered too much not to insist proudly upon my vision. Shall I tell you a parable? It was in Ferrara. Once my father took me to court with him. I saw the castle of the Estes. I saw the prince with his companions – women, dwarfs, jesters, and enlightened spirits – revelling at table. Music and the dance, sweet odours and feasting were all. Yet sometimes, very low, awesomely faint, another and strange sound rose above the tumult and the luxury: a sound of torment, a groaning and moaning – it came from below, out of frightful dungeons, where the prisoners lay and languished. I saw them too, I asked and was taken down below whence the howling and the horror came. And the sound of the feasting came down to them below; and I knew that those above felt no shame, that not one conscience was even uneasy. And suddenly it seemed as though I must choke with hatred and resistance.... And I saw a great bird in the air, beautiful, bold, and blithe of spirit it hovered there. And my heart was gripped by a pain, an aching, a defiance and a profound urge, a fervid wish, a gigantic resolve: could I but break those great pinions!

LORENZO: So that was your one desire?

THE PRIOR: I looked into the heart of the time and saw its forehead with the mark of the whore; shameless was she, gladsome and shameless – can you understand? She would not be ashamed. She took the tapers from the altar of the

Crucified and bore them to the sepulchre of one who had created beauty. Beauty – what is beauty? Is it possible not to fathom what she is? If not – who could realize a state of things on earth without being prevented by pain and disgust from still willing it to be? Who? Who? The time! All of you! But not I – I alone! I fled, fled from the abominable sight of such complacency, which laughed at feeling and suffering and redemption. I fled into the monastery, I saved myself in the austere twilight of Holy Church. Here, thought I, in the sanctified precincts of the Cross, here suffering has power to move. Here, so I thought, holiness and wisdom reign, the *sacræ litteræ*. What did I see? Here too I saw the Cross betrayed. The wearers of stole and cowl, whom I thought to be my brothers in the company of suffering – I saw them fallen away from the majesty of the spirit. They had compounded with the foe, with the great Babylon. Here also I was alone. Lo, I understood this too: I had to make myself, my very self, great in opposition against the world – for I was chosen Christ's vicar. The spirit was born again in me!

LORENZO: Against beauty? Brother, Brother, you are leading me astray. Must there be conflict here too? Must one see the world divided in two hostile camps? Are spirit and beauty opposed to each other?

THE PRIOR: They are. I speak the truth, learnt in suffering. (*A pause. It has grown dark.*) Would you know a sign, manifest when two worlds are eternally strange to each other and may not be reconciled? Longing is this sign. Where abysses yawn, she spans her rainbow, and where she is, are abysses. Learn, learn, Lorenzo de' Medici: The spirit can yearn towards beauty. In hours of weakness and self-betrayal, in the sweetness of shame, then it happens. For she, who is blithe and lovely and strong, she who is life, she can never understand spirit, she shrinks from it, perhaps would fear it and put it away from her; even mock it pitilessly and drive it back upon itself. But then, Lorenzo de' Medici, it can renounce, it can grow hard under torture and great in solitude and return in power so that she gives herself.

LORENZO: Why do you stop? I am listening – I am closing my eyes to hear. I am hearing the melody of my life. Will you stop so soon? It is so sweet to listen thus, without an effort, to oneself. I scarcely see you. Perhaps it is darkness, perhaps my sight is failing, but my spirit is awake, I listen. And I hear a song: my own song, the deep low song of longing. Girolamo, yet do you not know me? Whither the longing urges, there one is not, that one is not – you know? And yet man likes to confuse himself with his longing. You have heard that people call me the lord of beauty? But I myself am ugly. Yellow, ugly and weak. I adore the senses – and one lacks me, a precious one. I have no sense of smell. I know not the scent of the rose nor of a woman. I am a cripple, a deformed object. Is that only my body? Nature thrust me forth in a contortion; but I have compelled the frenzy and the staggering to measure and rhythm. My soul was a smouldering torment of desire and a flame of lust; I have fanned it to a clear flame. Without my longing I should be but a satyr; and when my poets put me with the company of the Olympians, not one of them dreams of the long, stern discipline which went to bridle my wild nature. It was well so. Had I been born beautiful, I had never made myself the lord of beauty. Hindrance is the will's best friend. To whom do I say that? To you, who know so painfully well that the hero's garland is not won by him who is merely strong. Are we foes? Well, then, I say that we are warring brothers.

THE PRIOR: I am not your brother. Have you not heard me say it? Let lights be brought, if the darkness weakens you. I hate this contemptible balancing, this lewd intellectuality, this blasphemous toleration of extremes! It shall not move me. Let them be still. I know it, this spirit – too well, too well! I put it behind me. I hear Florence, I hear your time – subtle, daring, easy-going – but it shall not weaken my powers, shall not disarm me, not me, not me – know that once and for all!

LORENZO: You hate the time, it understands you. Which is greater?

THE PRIOR (*savagely*): I am, I am!

LORENZO: Perhaps. You, then. I did not summon you to quarrel with you. And yet – forgive me: I would gladly see you at one with yourself. You rave at the spirit by which you rose to greatness, by which you *let* yourself be borne upwards – am I right? I cannot see your face. But this is how things seem to me: in times like these, such as you have said they are – subtle, sceptical, tolerant, inquisitive, vacillating, manifold, without clear limits – in such a time limitation can seem like genius. Forgive me. I am not fencing, I seek not to offend, I seek but clarity as between you and me. A power that resolutely holds itself aloof from the general scepticism can work wonders. All these subtle little people – they have no faith, do not believe it – they feel a *power* and they bow before it. Once more, forgive me! And again: you revile art, yet use it for your ends. Your name and fame are cried aloud because the city and our time worship the man who proudly dares to be himself. Never, anywhere, has there been such rich reward, so much response, for him who strives in his own way after fame. That you grew great in Florence was only because this Florence is so free, such a spoilt child of art, as to take you as her lord. Were it less so, were it only a very little less lapped in art, it would tear you to pieces instead of paying you homage. You are aware of that?

THE PRIOR: I will not be aware of it.

LORENZO: May one will not to be aware? You rail at the indifference, at the refusal to see, at the shamelessness. But are you not yourself ashamed to win such power, knowing by what means you win it?

THE PRIOR: I am chosen. I may know and still do it. For I must be strong. God performs miracles. You see the miracle of detachment regained. (*Looking at the bust of Cæsar*) Did *he* ask by what means he climbed?

LORENZO: Cæsar? You are a monk. And you have ambition!

THE PRIOR: How could I not have, I that suffered so? Ambition says: My sufferings must not have been in vain. They must bring me fame.

LORENZO: By God, that is it! Have I not known it? You have understood all that to a miracle. We rulers of men are egoist, and they blame us for it, not knowing that it comes of our suffering. They call us hard and understand not it was pain made us so. We may justly say: Look at yourselves, who have had so much easier a time on this earth. To myself I am torment and joy sufficient.

THE PRIOR: But they do not rail. They marvel. They reverence. See them come to the strong ego, the many who are only *we*, see them serve, see them tirelessly do his will –

LORENZO: Although his own advantage is plain to any eye –

THE PRIOR: Although he leave their services quite unrewarded and take them for granted –

LORENZO: Cosimo my forebear – I was old enough to know him; he was a cold and clever tyrant. They gave him the title *pater patriæ*. He took it with a smile and never a word of thanks. I shall never forget it. How he must despise them, I thought. And since then I have despised the folk.

THE PRIOR: Fame is the school of scorn.

LORENZO: Ah, the worthlessness of the masses! They are so poor, so empty, so selflessly self-forgetful.

THE PRIOR: So simple, so easy to dominate.

LORENZO: They know nothing better than to be dominated.

THE PRIOR: They write to me from all the quarters of the earth, they come from far to kiss the hem of my robe, they spread my fame to the four winds. Do I ever ask them for it, have I ever thanked them?

LORENZO: It is amazing.

THE PRIOR: Quite amazing is it. Are you so futile, one thinks, so vacant yourselves, that you know nothing prouder than to serve another?

LORENZO: Just so, just so! One cannot believe one's eyes, to see them bowing low and willingly – so satisfied.

THE PRIOR: One might laugh at the docility of the world . . .

LORENZO: And laughing, laughing, one takes the world as willing instrument on which to play.

THE PRIOR: To play one's own tune.

LORENZO (*feverishly*): Oh, my dreams! My power and art! Florence was my lyre. Did it not resound? Sweetly? It sang of my longing. It sang of beauty, it sang of great desire, it sang, it sang the great song of life.... Hush! On your knees.... There! I see her. She comes, she draws near to me, all the veils fall and all my blood flows out to meet her naked beauty. Oh, joy! Oh, sweet and fearful thrill! Am I chosen to look upon you, Venus Genetrix, you who are life, the sweet world?... Creative beauty, mighty impulse of art! Venus Fiorenza! Dost thou know what I would? The perpetual feast – that was my sovereign will!... Oh, stay! Dost thou turn away? Dost pale? I see no more.... Red waves come...and a horror...a yawning abyss. (*Fainting*) Are you still there, by whom I have understood myself? Speak to me! Fear! Anguish! Volterra! Blood! I emptied the treasury of the dowries, I drove the virgins to unchastity.... Speak quickly. Speak quickly. The conditions of grace...?

THE PRIOR (*beside him, low, eagerly*): *Misericordiam volo*.... There are three. The first, repentance.

LORENZO (*in the same tone*): I will repent the plundering of Volterra and the theft of moneys....

THE PRIOR: The second: That you return all unjustly owned property to the state.

LORENZO: My son shall do so. Then?

THE PRIOR (*in an awesome whisper, with a gesture of command*): The third: That you make Florence free – at once for ever – free from the lordship of your house.

LORENZO (*as softly; there is a silent, passionate struggle between the two*): Free – for you!

THE PRIOR: Free for the King who died on the Cross.

LORENZO: For you. For you! Why do you lie? We understood each other. Fiorenza, my city! Do you love her, then? Say quickly. You love her?

THE PRIOR: Fool! Child! Lay yourself to bed in the grave

with the ideas which are your playthings. A torrential love, a hate all-embracingly sweet – I am this complex, and this complex wills that I be lord in Florence!

LORENZO: Unhappy one – to what end? What can be your purpose?

THE PRIOR: Eternal peace. The triumph of the spirit. I will break them, these great wings –

LORENZO (*anguished, desperate*): You shall not. Wretch! You shall not. I forbid you – I, the Magnifico. Oh, I know you now, you have betrayed yourself to me. It is the wings of life you mean. It is death whom you proclaim as spirit, and all the life of life is art. I will prevent you. I am still master.

THE PRIOR: I laugh at you. You are dying, I am on my feet. My art won the people. Florence is mine.

LORENZO (*in a paroxysm*): Ah, monster! Evil spirit! Then you shall see me strong and ruthless. (*He shrieks, pulling himself up in the chair by both hands on the arms*) To me, to me! Come, come! Seize him! Bind him! He will break the great wings. Dungeon and chains! The lions' den! Kill him, he would slay all! Florence is mine . . . Florence . . . Florence! (*He collapses, his head rolls upon his neck. His eyeballs turn in, his arms describe a last all-embracing motion. Several servants with wax torches come from the right along the gallery into the room. The stage is suddenly full of flickering light. Pico, Ficino, Poliziano, Pulci, Pierleoni, and the artists hasten in horror down the steps.*)

PICO: Lorenzo!

PIERLEONI: He is gone.

POLIZIANO (*in despair*): My Lauro, my Lauro!

(*A new movement in the gallery. Four or five men, dust-covered, make their way hastily in.*)

ONE OF THEM: Hear ye, hear ye! We are sent by the high and noble Signoria. The city is in an uproar. It is reported that the Prophet Girolamo has been betrayed, taken, murdered. The populace are on their way to Careggi. They demand to see the Frate.

THE PRIOR (*looking down at the body of his foe*): Here am I.

FIORE (*appearing like a vision in the torchlight, at the top of the steps*): Monk, do you hear me?

THE PRIOR (*stiffly upright, without turning round*): I hear.

FIORE: Then hear this: Descend! The fire you have fanned will consume you, you yourself, to purify you and the world of you. Shudder before it – and descend. Cease to will, instead of willing nothingness. Void the power! Renounce! Be a monk!

THE PRIOR: I love the fire.

(*He turns. They make way. A lane opens for him, timidly. He strides slowly through it in the torchlight, upwards, away, into his destiny.*)

A WEARY HOUR

HE GOT up from the table, his little, fragile writing-desk; got up as though desperate, and with hanging head crossed the room to the tall, thin, pillar-like stove in the opposite corner. He put his hands to it; but the hour was long past midnight and the tiles were nearly stone-cold. Not getting even this little comfort that he sought, he leaned his back against them and, coughing, drew together the folds of his dressing-gown, between which a draggled lace shirt-frill stuck out; he snuffed hard through his nostrils to get a little air, for as usual he had a cold.

It was a particular, a sinister cold, which scarcely ever quite disappeared. It inflamed his eyelids and made the flanges of his nose all raw; in his head and limbs it lay like a heavy, sombre intoxication. Or was this cursed confinement to his room, to which the doctor had weeks ago condemned him, to blame for all his languor and flabbiness? God knew if it was the right thing – perhaps so, on account of his chronic catarrh and the spasms in his chest and belly. And for weeks on end now, yes, weeks, bad weather had reigned in Jena – hateful, horrible weather, which he felt in every nerve of his body – cold, wild, gloomy. The December wind roared in the stove-pipe with a desolate god-forsaken sound – he might have been wandering on a heath, by night and storm, his soul full of unappeasable grief. Yet this close confinement – that was not good either; not good for thought, nor for the rhythm of the blood, where thought was engendered.

The six-sided room was bare and colourless and devoid of cheer: a whitewashed ceiling wreathed in tobacco smoke, walls covered with trellis-patterned paper and hung with silhouettes in oval frames, half a dozen slender-legged pieces of furniture; the whole lighted by two candles burning at the head of the manuscript on the writing-table. Red curtains draped the upper part of the window-frames; mere festooned wisps of cotton they were, but red, a warm, sonorous red, and he loved them and would not have parted from them; they gave a little air of ease and charm to the bald unlovely poverty of his surroundings. He stood by the stove and blinked repeatedly, straining his eyes across at the work from which he had just fled: that load, that weight, that gnawing conscience, that sea which to drink up, that frightful task which to perform, was all his pride and all his misery, at once his heaven and his hell. It dragged, it stuck, it would not budge – and now again . . . ! It must be the weather; or his catarrh, or his fatigue. Or was it the work? Was the thing itself an unfortunate conception, doomed from its beginning to despair?

He had risen in order to put a little space between him and his task, for physical distance would often result in improved perspective, a wider view of his material and a better chance of conspectus. Yes, the mere feeling of relief on turning away from the battlefield had been known to work like an inspiration. And a more innocent one than that purveyed by alcohol or strong, black coffee.

The little cup stood on the side-table. Perhaps it would help him out of the impasse? No, no, not again! Not the doctor only, but somebody else too, a more important somebody, had cautioned him against that sort of thing – another person, who lived over in Weimar and for whom he felt a love which was a mixture of hostility and yearning. That was a wise man. He knew how to live and create; did not abuse himself; was full of self-regard.

Quiet reigned in the house. There was only the wind, driving down the Schlossgasse and dashing the rain in gusts against the panes. They were all asleep – the landlord and his family, Lotte and the children. And here he stood by the cold stove, awake, alone, tormented; blinking across at the work in which his morbid self-dissatisfaction would not let him believe.

His neck rose long and white out of his stock and his knock-kneed legs showed between the skirts of his dressing-gown. The red hair was smoothed back from a thin, high forehead; it retreated in bays from his veined white temples and hung down in thin locks over the ears. His nose was aquiline, with an abrupt whitish tip; above it the well-marked line of the brows almost met. They were darker than his hair and gave the deep-set, inflamed eyes a tragic, staring look. He could not breathe through his nose; so he opened his thin lips and made the freckled, sickly cheeks look even more sunken thereby.

No, it was a failure, it was all hopelessly wrong. The army ought to have been brought in! The army was the root of the whole thing. But it was impossible to present it before the eyes of the audience – and was art powerful enough thus to enforce the imagination? Besides, his hero was no hero; he was contemptible, he was frigid. The situation was wrong, the language was wrong; it was a dry pedestrian lecture, good for a history class, but as drama absolutely hopeless!

Very good, then, it was over. A defeat. A failure. Bankruptcy. He would write to Körner, the good Körner, who believed in him, who clung with childlike faith to his genius. He would scoff, scold, beseech – this friend of his; would remind him of the *Carlos*, which likewise had issued out of doubts and pains and rewritings and after all the anguish turned out to be something really fine, a genuine masterpiece. But times were changed. Then he had been a man still capable of taking a strong, confident grip on a thing and giving it triumphant shape. Doubts and struggles? Yes. And ill he had been, perhaps more ill than now; a fugitive, oppressed and hungry, at odds with the world; humanly speaking, a beggar. But young, still young! Each time, however low he had sunk, his resilient spirit had leaped up anew; upon the hour of affliction had followed the feeling of triumphant self-confidence. That came no more, or hardly ever, now. There might be one night of glowing exaltation – when the fires of his genius lighted up an impassioned vision of all that he might do if only they burned on; but it had always to be paid for with a week of enervation and gloom. Faith in the future, his guiding star in times of stress, was dead. Here was the despairing truth: the years of need and nothingness, which he had thought of as the painful testing-time, turned out to have been the rich and fruitful ones; and now that a little happiness had fallen to his lot, now that he had ceased to be an intellectual freebooter and occupied a position of civic dignity, with office and honours, wife and children – now he was exhausted, worn out. To give up, to own himself beaten – that was all there was left to do. He groaned; he pressed his hands to his eyes and dashed up and down the room like one possessed. What he had just thought was so frightful that he could not stand still on the spot where he had thought it. He sat down on a chair by the further wall and stared gloomily at the floor, his clasped hands hanging down between his knees.

His conscience . . . how loudly his conscience cried out! He had sinned, sinned against himself all these years, against the delicate instrument that was his body. Those youthful excesses, the nights without sleep, the days spent in close, smoke-laden air, straining his mind and heedless of his body; the narcotics with which he had spurred himself on – all that was now taking its revenge.

And if it did – then he would defy the gods, who decreed the guilt and then imposed the penalties. He had lived as he had to live, he had not had time to be wise, not time to be careful. Here in this place in his chest, when he breathed, coughed, yawned, always in the same spot came this pain, this piercing, stabbing, diabolical little warning; it never left him, since that time in Erfurt five years ago when he had catarrhal fever and inflammation of the lungs. What was it warning him of? Ah, he knew only too well what it meant – no matter how the doctor chose to put him off. He had not time to be wise and spare himself, no time to save his strength by submission to moral laws. What he wanted to do he must do soon, do quickly, do today.

And the moral laws? . . . Why was it that precisely sin,

surrender to the harmful and the consuming, actually seemed to him more moral than any amount of wisdom and frigid self-discipline? Not that constituted morality: not the contemptible knack of keeping a good conscience – rather the struggle and compulsion, the passion and pain.

Pain . . . how his breast swelled at the word! He drew himself up and folded his arms; his gaze, beneath the close-set auburn brows, was kindled by the nobility of his suffering. No man was utterly wretched so long as he could still speak of his misery in high-sounding and noble words. One thing only was indispensable: the courage to call his life by large and fine names. Not to ascribe his sufferings to bad air and constipation; to be well enough to cherish emotions, to scorn and ignore the material. Just on this one point to be naïve, though in all else sophisticated. To believe, to have strength to believe, in suffering. . . . But he *did* believe in it; so profoundly, so ardently, that nothing which came to pass with suffering could seem to him either useless or evil. His glance sought the manuscript, and his arms tightened across his chest. Talent itself – was that not suffering? And if the manuscript over there, his unhappy effort, made him suffer, was not that quite as it should be – a good sign, so to speak? His talents had never been of the copious, ebullient sort; were they to become so he would feel mistrustful. That only happened with beginners and bunglers, with the ignorant and easily satisfied, whose life was not shaped and disciplined by the possession of a gift. For a gift, my friends down there in the audience, a gift is not anything simple, not anything to play with; it is not mere ability. At bottom it is a compulsion; a critical knowledge of the ideal, a permanent dissatisfaction, which rises only through suffering to the height of its powers. And it is to the greatest, the most unsatisfied, that their gift is the sharpest scourge. Not to complain, not to boast; to think modestly, patiently of one's pain; and if not a day in the week, not even an hour, be free from it – what then? To make light and little of it all, of suffering and achievement alike – that was what made a man great.

He stood up, pulled out his snuff-box and sniffed eagerly, then suddenly clasped his hands behind his back and strode so briskly through the room that the flames of the candles flickered in the draught. Greatness, distinction, world conquest and an imperishable name! To be happy and unknown, what was that by comparison? To be known – known and loved by all the world – ah, they might call that egotism, those who knew naught of the urge, naught of the sweetness of this dream! Everything out of the ordinary is egotistic, in proportion to its suffering. "Speak for yourselves," it says, "ye without mission on this earth, ye whose life is so much easier than mine!" And Ambition says: "Shall my sufferings be vain? No, they must make me great!"

The nostrils of his great nose dilated, his gaze darted fiercely about the room. His right hand was thrust hard and far into the opening of his dressing-gown, his left arm hung down, the fist clenched. A fugitive red played in the gaunt cheeks – a glow thrown up from the fire of his artistic egoism: that passion for his own ego, which burnt unquenchably in his being's depths. Well he knew it, the secret intoxication of this love! Sometimes he needed only to contemplate his own hand, to be filled with the liveliest tenderness towards himself, in whose service he was bent on spending all the talent, all the art that he owned. And he was right so to do, there was nothing base about it. For deeper still than his egoism lay the knowledge that he was freely consuming and sacrificing himself in the service of a high ideal, not as a virtue, of course, but rather out of sheer necessity. And this was his ambition: that no one should be greater than he who had not also suffered more for the sake of the high ideal. No one. He stood still, his hand over his eyes, his body turned aside in a posture of shrinking and avoidance. For already the inevitable thought had stabbed him: the thought of that other man, that radiant being, so sense-endowed, so divinely unconscious, that man over there in Weimar, whom he loved and hated. And once more, as always, in deep disquiet, in feverish haste, there began working within him the inevitable sequence of his thoughts: he must assert and define his own nature, his own art, against that other's. Was that other greater? Wherein, then, and why? If he won, would he have sweated blood to do so? If he lost, would his downfall be a tragic sight? He was no hero, no; a god, perhaps. But it was easier to be a god than a hero. Yes, things were easier for him. He was wise, he was deft, he knew how to distinguish between knowing and creating; perhaps that was why he was so blithe and carefree, such an effortless and gushing spring! But if creation was divine, knowledge was heroic, and he who created in knowledge was hero as well as god.

The will to face difficulties.... Did anyone realize what discipline and self-control it cost him to shape a sentence or follow out a hard train of thought? For after all he was ignorant, undisciplined, a slow, dreamy enthusiast. One of Cæsar's letters was harder to write than the most effective scene – and was it not almost for that very reason higher? From the first rhythmical urge of the inward creative force towards matter, towards the material, towards casting in shape and form – from that to the thought, the image, the word, the line – what a struggle, what a Gethsemane! Everything that he wrote was a marvel of yearning after form, shape, line, body; of yearning after the sunlit world of that other man who had only to open his godlike lips and straightaway call the bright unshadowed things he saw by name!

And yet – and despite that other man. Where was there an artist, a poet, like himself? Who like him created out of nothing, out of his own breast? A poem was born as music in his soul, as pure, primitive essence, long before it put on a garment of metaphor from the visible world. History, philosophy, passion were no more than pretexts and vehicles for something which had little to do with them, but was at home in orphic depths. Words and conceptions were keys upon which his art played and made vibrate the hidden strings. No one realized. The good souls praised him, indeed, for the power of feeling with which he struck one note or another. And his favourite note, his final emotional appeal, the great bell upon which he sounded his summons to the highest feasts of the soul – many there were who responded to its sound. Freedom! But in all their exaltation, certainly he meant by the word both more and less than they did. Freedom – what was it? A self-respecting middle-class attitude towards thrones and princes? Surely not that. When one thinks of all that the spirit of man has dared to put into the word! Freedom from what? After all, from what? Perhaps, indeed, even from human happiness, that silken bond, that tender, sacred tie. . . .

From happiness. His lips quivered. It was as though his glance turned inward upon himself; slowly his face sank into his hands. . . . He stood by the bed in the next room, where the flowered curtains hung in motionless folds across the window, and the lamp shed a bluish light. He bent over the sweet head on the pillow . . . a ringlet of dark hair lay across her cheek, that had the paleness of pearl; the childlike lips were open in slumber. "My wife! Beloved, didst thou yield to my yearning and come to me to be my joy? And that thou art. . . . Lie still and sleep; nay, lift not those sweet shadowy lashes and gaze up at me, as sometimes with thy great, dark, questioning, searching eyes. I love thee so! By God I swear it. It is only that sometimes I am tired out, struggling at my self-imposed task, and my feelings will not respond. And I must not be too utterly thine, never utterly happy in thee, for the sake of my mission."

He kissed her, drew away from her pleasant, slumbrous warmth, looked about him, turned back to the outer room. The clock struck; it warned him that the night was already far spent; but likewise it seemed to be mildly marking the end of a weary hour. He drew a deep breath, his lips closed firmly; he went back and took up his pen. No, he must not brood, he was too far down for that. He must not descend into chaos; or at least he must not stop there. Rather out of chaos, which is fullness, he must draw up to the light whatever he found there fit and ripe for form. No brooding! Work! Define, eliminate, fashion, complete!

And complete it he did, that effort of a labouring hour. He

brought it to an end, perhaps not to a good end, but in any case to an end. And being once finished, lo, it was also good. And from his soul, from music and idea, new works struggled upward to birth and, taking shape, gave out light and sound, ringing and shimmering, and giving hint of their infinite origin – as in a shell we hear the sighing of the sea whence it came.

THE BLOOD OF THE WALSUNGS

IT WAS seven minutes to twelve. Wendelin came into the first-floor entrance-hall and sounded the gong. He straddled in his violet knee-breeches on a prayer-rug pale with age and belaboured with his drumstick the metal disc. The brazen din, savage and primitive out of all proportion to its purport, resounded through the drawing-rooms to left and right, the billiard-room, the library, the winter-garden, up and down through the house; it vibrated through the warm and even atmosphere, heavy with exotic perfume. At last the sound ceased, and for another seven minutes Wendelin went about his business while Florian in the dining-room gave the last touches to the table. But on the stroke of twelve the cannibalistic summons sounded a second time. And the family appeared.

Herr Aarenhold came in his little toddle out of the library where he had been busy with his old editions. He was continually acquiring old books, first editions, in many languages, costly and crumbling trifles. Gently rubbing his hands he asked in his slightly plaintive way:

"Beckerath not here yet?"

"No, but he will be. Why shouldn't he? He will be saving a meal in a restaurant," answered Frau Aarenhold, coming noiselessly up the thick-carpeted stairs, on the landing of which stood a small, very ancient church organ.

Herr Aarenhold blinked. His wife was impossible. She was small, ugly, prematurely aged, and shrivelled as though by tropic suns. A necklace of brilliants rested upon her shrunken breast. She wore her hair in complicated twists and knots to form a lofty pile, in which, somewhere on one side, sat a great jewelled brooch, adorned in its turn with a bunch of white aigrettes. Herr Aarenhold and the children had more than once, as diplomatically as possible, advised against this style of coiffure. But Frau Aarenhold clung stoutly to her own taste.

The children came: Kunz and Märit, Siegmund and Sieglinde. Kunz was in a braided uniform, a stunning tanned creature with curling lips and a killing scar. He was doing six weeks' service with his regiment of hussars. Märit made her appearance in an uncorseted garment. She was an ashen, austere blonde of twenty-eight, with a hooked nose, grey eyes like a falcon's, and a bitter, contemptuous mouth. She was studying law and went entirely her own way in life.

Siegmund and Sieglinde came last, hand in hand, from the second floor. They were twins, graceful as young fawns, and with immature figures despite their nineteen years. She wore a Florentine cinquecento frock of claret-coloured velvet, too heavy for her slight body. Siegmund had on a green jacket suit with a tie of raspberry shantung, patent-leather shoes on his narrow feet, and cuff-buttons set with small diamonds. He had a strong growth of black beard but kept it so close-shaven that his sallow face with the heavy gathered brows looked no less boyish than his figure. His head was covered with thick black locks parted far down on one side and growing low on his temples. Her dark-brown hair was waved in long, smooth undulations over her ears, confined by a gold circlet. A large pearl – his gift – hung down upon her brow. Round one of his boyish wrists was a heavy gold chain – a gift from her. They were very like each other, with the same slightly drooping nose, the same full lips lying softly together, the same prominent cheek-bones and black, bright eyes. Likest of all were their long slim hands, his no more masculine than hers, save that they were slightly redder. And they went always hand in hand, heedless that the hands of both inclined to moisture.

The family stood about awhile in the lobby, scarcely speaking. Then Beckerath appeared. He was engaged to Sieglinde. Wendelin opened the door to him and as he entered in his black frock-coat he excused himself for his tardiness. He was a government official and came of a good family. He was short of stature, with a pointed beard and a very yellow complexion, like a canary. His manners were punctilious. He began every sentence by drawing his breath in quickly through his mouth and pressing his chin on his chest.

He kissed Sieglinde's hand and said:

"And you must excuse me too, Sieglinde – it is so far from the Ministry to the Zoo –"

He was not allowed to say thou to her – she did not like it. She answered briskly:

"Very far. Supposing that, in consideration of the fact, you left your office a bit earlier."

Kunz seconded her, his black eyes narrowing to glittering cracks:

"It would no doubt have a most beneficial effect upon our household economy."

"Oh, well – business, you know what it is," von Beckerath said dully. He was thirty-five years old.

The brother and sister had spoken glibly and with point. They may have attacked out of a habitual inward posture of self-defence; perhaps they deliberately meant to wound – perhaps again their words were due to the sheer pleasure of turning a phrase. It would have been unreasonable to feel annoyed. They let his feeble answer pass, as though they found it in character; as though cleverness in him would have been out of place. They went to table; Herr Aarenhold led the way, eager to let von Beckerath see that he was hungry.

They sat down, they unfolded their stiff table-napkins. The immense room was carpeted, the walls were covered with eighteenth-century panelling, and three electric lustres hung from the ceiling. The family table, with its seven places, was lost in the void. It was drawn up close to the large French window, beneath which a dainty little fountain spread its silver spray behind a low lattice. Outside was an extended view of the still wintry garden. Tapestries with pastoral scenes covered the upper part of the walls; they, like the panelling, had been part of the furnishings of a French château. The dining-chairs were low and soft and cushioned with tapestry. A tapering glass vase holding two orchids stood at each place, on the glistening, spotless, faultlessly ironed damask cloth. With careful, skinny hands Herr Aarenhold settled the pince-nez halfway down his nose and with a mistrustful air read the menu, three copies of which lay on the table. He suffered from a weakness of the solar plexus, that nerve centre which lies at the pit of the stomach and may give rise to serious distress. He was obliged to be very careful what he ate.

There was bouillon with beef marrow, sole *au vin blanc*, pheasant, and pineapple.

Nothing else. It was a simple family meal. But it satisfied Herr Aarenhold. It was good, light, nourishing food. The soup was served: a dumb-waiter above the sideboard brought it noiselessly down from the kitchen and the servants handed it round, bending over assiduously, in a very passion of service. The tiny cups were of translucent porcelain, whitish morsels of marrow floated in the hot golden liquid.

Herr Aarenhold felt himself moved to expand a little in the comfortable warmth thus purveyed. He carried his napkin cautiously to his mouth and cast after a means of clothing his thought in words.

"Have another cup, Beckerath," said he. "A working-man has a right to his comforts and his pleasures. Do you really like to eat – really enjoy it, I mean? If not, so much the worse for you. To me every meal is a little celebration. Somebody said that life is pretty nice after all – being arranged so that we can eat four times a day. He's my man! But to do justice to the arrangement one has to preserve one's youthful receptivity – and not everybody can do that. We get old – well, we can't help it. But the thing is to keep things fresh and not get used to them. For instance," he went on putting a bit of marrow on a piece of roll and sprinkling salt on it, "you are about to change your estate, the plane on which you live is going to be a good deal elevated" (von Beckerath smiled), "and if you want to enjoy your new life, really enjoy it, consciously and artistically, you must take care never to get used to your new situation. Getting used to things is death. It is ennui. Don't live into it, don't let anything become a matter of course, preserve a childlike taste for the sweets of life. You see . . . for some years now I have been able to command some of the amenities of life" (von Beckerath smiled), "and yet I assure you, every morning that God lets me wake up I have a little thrill because my bed-cover is made of silk. That is what it is to be young. I know perfectly well how I did it; and yet I can look round me and feel like an enchanted prince."

The children exchanged looks, so openly that Herr Aarenhold could not help seeing it; he became visibly embarrassed. He knew that they were united against him, that they despised him: for his origins, for the blood which flowed in his veins and through him in theirs; for the way he had earned his money; for his fads, which in their eyes were unbecoming: for his valetudinarianism, which they found equally annoying; for his weak and whimsical loquacity, which in their eyes traversed the bounds of good taste. He knew all this – and in a way conceded that they were right. But after all he had to assert his personality, he had to lead his own life; and above all he had to be able to talk about it. That was only fair – he had proved that it was worth talking about. He had been a worm, a louse if you like. But just his capacity to realize it so fully, with such vivid self-contempt, had become the ground of that persistent, painful, never-satisfied striving which had made him great. Herr Aarenhold had been born in a remote village in East Prussia, had married the daughter of a well-to-do tradesman, and by means of a bold and shrewd enterprise, of large-scale schemings which had as their object a new and productive coal-bed, he had diverted a large and inexhaustible stream of gold into his coffers.

The fish course came on. The servants hurried with it from the sideboard through the length of the room. They handed round with it a creamy sauce and poured out a Rhine wine that prickled on the tongue. The conversation turned to the approaching wedding.

It was very near, it was to take place in the following week. They talked about the dowry, about plans for the wedding journey to Spain. Actually it was only Herr Aarenhold who talked about them, supported by von Beckerath's polite acquiescence. Frau Aarenhold ate greedily, and as usual contributed nothing to the conversation save some rather pointless questions. Her speech was interlarded with guttural words and phrases from the dialect of her childhood days. Märit was full of silent opposition to the church ceremony which they planned to have; it affronted her highly enlightened convictions. Herr Aarenhold also was privately opposed to the ceremony. Von Beckerath was a Protestant and in Herr Aarenhold's view Protestant ceremonial was without any æsthetic value. It would be different if von Beckerath belonged to the Roman confession. Kunz said nothing, because when von Beckerath was present he always felt annoyed with his mother. And neither Siegmund nor Sieglinde displayed any interest. They held each other's narrow hands between their chairs. Sometimes their gaze sought each other's, melting together in an understanding from which everybody else was shut out. Von Beckerath sat next to Sieglinde on the other side.

"Fifty hours," said Herr Aarenhold, "and you are in Madrid, if you like. That is progress. It took me sixty by the shortest way. I assume that you prefer the train to the sea route via Rotterdam?"

Von Beckerath hastily expressed his preference for the overland route.

"But you won't leave Paris out. Of course, you could go direct to Lyons. And Sieglinde knows Paris. But you should not neglect the opportunity... I leave it to you whether or not to stop before that. The choice of the place where the honeymoon begins should certainly be left to you."

Sieglinde turned her head, turned it for the first time towards her betrothed, quite openly and unembarrassed, careless of the lookers-on. For quite three seconds she bent upon the courteous face beside her the wide-eyed, questioning, expectant gaze of her sparkling black eyes – a gaze as vacant of thought as any animal's. Between their chairs she was holding the slender hand of her twin; and Siegmund drew his brows together till they formed two black folds at the base of his nose.

The conversation veered and tacked to and fro. They talked of a consignment of cigars which had just come by Herr Aarenhold's order from Havana, packed in zinc. Then it circled round a point of purely abstract interest, brought up by Kunz: namely, whether if *a* were the necessary and sufficient conditon for *b*, *b* must also be the necessary and sufficient condition for *a*. They argued the matter, they analysed it with great ingenuity, they gave examples; they talked nineteen to the dozen, attacked each other with steely and abstract dialectic, and got no little heated. Märit had introduced a philosophical distinction, that between the actual and the causal principle. Kunz told her, with his nose in the air, that "causal principle" was a pleonasm. Märit, in some annoyance, insisted upon her terminology. Herr Aarenhold straightened himself, with a bit of bread between thumb and forefinger, and prepared to elucidate the whole matter. He suffered a complete rout, the children joined forces to laugh him down. Even his wife jeered at him. "What are you talking about?" she said. "Where did you learn that – you didn't learn much!" Von Beckerath pressed his chin on his breast, opened his mouth, and drew in breath to speak – but they had already passed on, leaving him hanging.

Siegmund began, in a tone of ironic amusement, to speak of an acquaintance of his, a child of nature whose simplicity was such that he abode in ignorance of the difference between dress clothes and dinner jacket. This Parsifal actually talked about a checked dinner jacket. Kunz knew an even more pathetic case – a man who went out to tea in dinner clothes.

"Dinner clothes in the afternoon!" Sieglinde said, making a face. "It isn't even human!"

Von Beckerath laughed sedulously. But inwardly he was remembering that once he himself had worn a dinner coat before six o'clock. And with the game course they passed on to matters of more general cultural interest: to the plastic arts, of which von Beckerath was an amateur, to literature and the theatre, which in the Aarenhold house had the preference – though Siegmund did devote some of his leisure to painting.

The conversation was lively and general and the young people set the key. They talked well, their gestures were nervous and self-assured. They marched in the van of taste, the best was none too good for them. For the vision, the intention, the labouring will, they had no use at all; they ruthlessly insisted upon power achievement, success in the cruel trial of strength. The triumphant work of art they recognized – but they paid it no homage. Herr Aarenhold himself said to von Beckerath:

"You are very indulgent, my dear fellow; you speak up for intentions – but results, *results* are what we are after! You say: 'Of course his work is not much good – but he was only a peasant before he took it up, so his performance is after all astonishing.' Nothing in it. Accomplishment is absolute, not relative. There are no mitigating circumstances. Let a man do first-class work or let him shovel coals. How far should I have got with a good-natured attitude like that? I might have said to myself: 'You're only a poor fish, originally – it's wonderful if you get to be the head of your office.' Well, I'd not be sitting here! I've had to force the world to recognize me, so now I won't recognize anything unless I am forced to!"

The children laughed. At that moment they did not look down on him. They sat there at table, in their low, luxuriously cushioned chairs, with their spoilt, dissatisfied faces. They sat in splendour and security, but their words rang as sharp as though sharpness, hardness, alertness, and pitiless clarity were demanded of them as survival values. Their highest praise was a grudging acceptance, their criticism deft and ruthless; it snatched the weapons from one's hand, it paralysed enthusiasm, made it a laughing-stock. "Very good," they would say of some masterpiece whose lofty intellectual plane would seem to have put it beyond the reach of critique. Passion was a blunder – it made them laugh. Von Beckerath, who tended to be disarmed by his enthusiasms, had hard work holding his own – also his age put him in the wrong. He got smaller and smaller in his chair, pressed his chin on his breast, and in his excitement breathed through his mouth – quite unhorsed by the brisk arrogance of youth. They contradicted everything – as though they found it impossible, discreditable, lamentable, not to contradict. They contradicted most efficiently, their eyes narrowing to gleaming cracks. They fell upon a single word of his, they worried it, they tore it to bits and replaced it by another so telling and deadly that it went straight to the mark and sat in the wound with quivering shaft. Towards the end of luncheon von Beckerath's eyes were red and he looked slightly deranged.

Suddenly – they were sprinkling sugar on their slices of pineapple – Siegmund said, wrinkling up his face in the way he had, as though the sun were making him blink:

"Oh, by the by, von Beckerath, something else, before we forget it. Sieglinde and I approach you with a request – metaphorically speaking, you see us on our knees. They are giving the *Walküre* tonight. We should like, Sieglinde and I, to hear it once more together – may we? We are of course aware that everything depends upon your gracious favour – "

"How thoughtful!" said Herr Aarenhold.

Kunz drummed the Hunding motif on the cloth.

Von Beckerath was overcome at anybody asking his permission about anything. He answered eagerly:

"But by all means, Siegmund – and you too, Sieglinde; I find your request very reasonable – do go, of course; in fact, I shall be able to go with you. There is an excellent cast tonight."

All the Aarenholds bowed over their plates to hide their laughter. Von Beckerath blinked with his effort to be one of them, to understand and share their mirth.

Siegmund hastened to say:

"Oh, well, actually, it's a rather poor cast, you know. Of

course, we are just as grateful to you as though it were good. But I am afraid there is a slight misunderstanding. Sieglinde and I were asking you to permit us to hear the *Walküre* once more *alone* together before the wedding. I don't know if you feel now that – "

"Oh, certainly. I quite understand. How charming! Of course you *must* go!"

"Thanks, we are most grateful indeed. Then I will have Percy and Leiermann put in for us. . . ."

"Perhaps I may venture to remark," said Herr Aarenhold, "that your mother and I are driving to dinner with the Erlangers and using Percy and Leiermann. You will have to condescend to the brown coupé and Baal and Lampa."

"And your box?" asked Kunz.

"I took it long ago," said Siegmund, tossing back his head.

They all laughed, all staring at the bridegroom.

Herr Aarenhold unfolded with his finger-tips the paper of a belladonna powder and shook it carefully into his mouth. Then he lighted a fat cigarette, which presently spread abroad a priceless fragrance. The servants sprang forward to draw away his and Frau Aarenhold's chairs. The order was given to serve coffee in the winter-garden. Kunz in a sharp voice ordered his dog-cart brought round; he would drive to the barracks.

Siegmund was dressing for the opera; he had been dressing for an hour. He had so abnormal and constant a need for purification that actually he spent a considerable part of his time before the wash-basin. He stood now in front of his large Empire mirror with the white enamelled frame; dipped a powder-puff in its embossed box and powdered his freshly shaven chin and cheeks. His beard was so strong that when he went out in the evening he was obliged to shave a second time.

He presented a colourful picture as he stood there, in rose-tinted silk drawers and socks, red morocco slippers, and a wadded house-jacket in a dark pattern with revers of grey fur. For background he had his large sleeping-chamber, full of all sorts of elegant and practical white-enamelled devices. Beyond the windows was a misty view over the tree-tops of the Tiergarten.

It was growing dark. He turned on the circular arrangement of electric bulbs in the white ceiling – they filled the room with soft milky light. Then he drew the velvet curtains across the darkening panes. The light was reflected from the liquid depths of the mirrors in wardrobe, washing-stand, and toilet-table, it flashed from the polished bottles on the tile-inlaid shelves. And Siegmund continued to work on himself. Now and then some thought in his mind would draw his brows together till they formed two black folds over the base of the nose.

His day had passed as his days usually did, vacantly and swiftly. The opera began at half past six and he had begun to change at half past five, so there had not been much afternoon. He had rested on his chaise-longue from two to three, then drunk tea and employed the remaining hour sprawled in a deep leather arm-chair in the study which he shared with Kunz, reading a few pages in each of several new novels. He had found them pitiably weak on the whole; but he had sent a few of them to the binder's to be artistically bound in choice bindings, for his library.

But in the forenoon he had worked. He had spent the hour from ten to eleven in the atelier of his professor, an artist of European repute, who was developing Siegmund's talent for drawing and painting, and receiving from Herr Aarenhold two thousand marks a month for his services. But what Siegmund painted was absurd. He knew it himself; he was far from having any glowing expectations on the score of his talent in this line. He was too shrewd not to know that the conditions of his existence were not the most favourable in the world for the development of a creative gift. The accoutrements of life were so rich and varied, so elaborated, that almost no place at all was left for life itself. Each and every single accessory was so costly and beautiful that it had an existence above and beyond the purpose it was meant to serve – until one's attention was first confused and then exhausted. Siegmund had been born into superfluity, he was perfectly adjusted to it. And yet it was the fact that this superfluity never ceased to thrill and occupy him, to give him constant pleasure. Whether consciously or not, it was with him as with his father, who practised the art of never getting used to anything.

Siegmund loved to read, he strove after the word and the spirit as after a tool which a profound instinct urged him to grasp. But never had he lost himself in a book as one does when that single work seems the most important in the world; unique, a little, all-embracing universe, into which one plunges and submerges oneself in order to draw nourishment out of every syllable. The books and magazines streamed in, he could buy them all, they heaped up about him and even while he read, the number of those still to be read disturbed him. But he had the books bound in stamped leather and labelled with Siegmund Aarenhold's beautiful book-plate; they stood in rows, weighing down his life like a possession which he did not succeed in subordinating to his personality.

The day was his, it was given to him as a gift with all its hours from sunrise to sunset; and yet Siegmund found in his heart that he had no time for a resolve, how much less then for a deed. He was no hero, he commanded no giant powers. The preparation, the lavish equipment for what should have been the serious business of life used up all his energy. How much mental effort had to be expended simply in making a proper toilette! How much time and attention went to his supplies of cigarettes, soaps, and perfumes; how much occasion for making up his mind lay in that moment, recurring two or three times daily, when he had to select his cravat! And it was worth the effort. It was important. The blond-haired citizenry of the land might go about in elastic-sided boots and turn-over collars, heedless of the effect. But he – and most explicitly he – must be unassailable and blameless of exterior from head to foot.

And in the end no one expected more of him. Sometimes

there came moments when he had a feeble misgiving about the nature of the "actual"; sometimes he felt that this lack of expectation lamed and dislodged his sense of it. . . . The household arrangements were all made to the end that the day might pass quickly and no empty hour be perceived. The next mealtime always came promptly on. They dined before seven; the evening, when one can idle with a good conscience, was long. The days disappeared, swiftly the seasons came and went. The family spent two summer months at their little castle on the lake, with its large and splendid grounds and many tennis courts, its cool paths through the parks, and shaven lawns adorned by bronze statuettes. A third month was spent in the mountains, in hotels where life was even more expensive than at home. Of late, during the winter, he had had himself driven to school to listen to a course of lectures in the history of art which came at a convenient time. But he had had to leave off because his sense of smell indicated that the rest of the class did not wash often enough.

He spent the hour walking with Sieglinde instead. Always she had been at his side since the very first; she had clung to him since they lisped their first syllables, taken their first steps. He had no friends, never had had one but this, his exquisitely groomed, darkly beautiful counterpart, whose moist and slender hand he held while the richly gilded, empty-eyed hours slipped past. They took fresh flowers with them on their walks, a bunch of violets or lilies of the valley, smelling them in turn or sometimes both together, with languid yet voluptuous abandon. They were like self-centred invalids who absorb themselves in trifles, as narcotics to console them for the loss of hope. With an inward gesture of renunciation they doffed aside the evil-smelling world and loved each other alone, for the priceless sake of their own rare uselessness. But all that they uttered was pointed, neat, and brilliant; it hit off the people they met, the things they saw, everything done by somebody else to the end that it might be exposed to the unerring eye, the sharp tongue, the witty condemnation.

Then von Beckerath had appeared. He had a post in the

government and came of a good family. He had proposed for Sieglinde. Frau Aarenhold had supported him, Herr Aarenhold had displayed a benevolent neutrality, Kunz the hussar was his zealous partisan. He had been patient, assiduous, endlessly good-mannered and tactful. And in the end, after she had told him often enough that she did not love him, Sieglinde had begun to look at him searchingly, expectantly, mutely, with her sparkling black eyes – a gaze as speaking and as vacant of thought as an animal's – and had said yes. And Siegmund, whose will was her law, had taken up a position too; slightly to his own disgust he had not opposed the match; was not von Beckerath in the government and a man of good family too? Sometimes he wrinkled his brows over his toilette until they made two heavy black folds at the base of his nose.

He stood on the white bearskin which stretched out its claws beside the bed; his feet were lost in the long soft hair. He sprinkled himself lavishly with toilet water and took up his dress shirt. The starched and shining linen glided over his yellowish torso, which was as lean as a young boy's and yet shaggy with black hair. He arrayed himself further in black silk drawers, black silk socks, and heavy black silk garters with silver buckles, put on the well-pressed trousers of silky black cloth, fastened the white silk braces over his narrow shoulders, and with one foot on a stool began to button his shoes. There was a knock on the door.

"May I come in, Gigi?" asked Sieglinde.

"Yes, come in," he answered.

She was already dressed, in a frock of shimmering sea-green silk, with a square neck outlined by a wide band of beige embroidery. Two embroidered peacocks facing each other above the girdle held a garland in their beaks. Her dark brown hair was unadorned; but a large egg-shaped precious stone hung on a thin pearl chain against her bare skin, the colour of smoked meerschaum. Over her arm she carried a scarf heavily worked with silver.

"I am unable to conceal from you," she said, "that the carriage is waiting." He parried at once:

"And I have no hesitation in replying that it will have to wait patiently two minutes more." It was at least ten. She sat down on the white velvet chaise-longue and watched him at his labours.

Out of a rich chaos of ties he selected a white piqué band and began to tie it before the glass.

"Beckerath," said she, "wears coloured cravats, crossed over the way they wore them last year."

"Beckerath," said he, "is the most trivial existence I have ever had under my personal observation." Turning to her quickly he added: "Moreover, you will do me the favour of not mentioning that German's name to me again this evening."

She gave a short laugh and replied: "You may be sure it will not be a hardship."

He put on the low-cut piqué waistcoat and drew his dress coat over it, the white silk lining caressing his hands as they passed through the sleeves.

"Let me see which buttons you chose," said Sieglinde. They were the amethyst ones; shirt-studs, cuff-links, and waistcoat buttons, a complete set.

She looked at him admiringly, proudly, adoringly, with a world of tenderness in her dark, shining eyes. He kissed the lips lying so softly on each other. They spent another minute on the chaise-longue in mutual caresses.

"Quite, quite soft you are again," said she, stroking his shaven cheeks.

"Your little arm feels like satin," said he, running his hand down her tender forearm. He breathed in the violet odour of her hair.

She kissed him on his closed eyelids; he kissed her on the throat where the pendant hung. They kissed one another's hands. They loved one another sweetly, sensually, for sheer mutual delight in their own well-groomed, pampered, expensive smell. They played together like puppies, biting each other with their lips. Then he got up.

"We mustn't be too late today," said he. He turned the top

of the perfume bottle upside down on his handkerchief one last time, rubbed a drop into his narrow red hands, took his gloves, and declared himself ready to go.

He put out the light and they went along the red-carpeted corridor hung with dark old oil paintings and down the steps past the little organ. In the vestibule on the ground floor Wendelin was waiting with their coats, very tall in his long yellow paletot. They yielded their shoulders to his ministrations; Sieglinde's dark head was half lost in her collar of silver fox. Followed by the servant they passed through the stone-paved vestibule into the outer air. It was mild, and there were great ragged flakes of snow in the pearly air. The coupé awaited them. The coachman bent down with his hand to his cockaded hat while Wendelin ushered the brother and sister to their seats; then the door banged shut, he swung himself up to the box, and the carriage was at once in swift motion. It crackled over the gravel, glided through the high, wide gate, curved smoothly to the right, and rolled away.

The luxurious little space in which they sat was pervaded by a gentle warmth. "Shall I shut us in?" Siegmund asked. She nodded and he drew the brown silk curtains across the polished panes.

They were in the city's heart. Lights flew past behind the curtains. Their horses' hoofs rhythmically beat the ground, the carriage swayed noiselessly over the pavement, and round them roared and shrieked and thundered the machinery of urban life. Quite safe and shut away they sat among the wadded brown silk cushions, hand in hand. The carriage drew up and stopped. Wendelin was at the door to help them out. A little group of grey-faced shivering folk stood in the brilliance of the arc-lights and followed them with hostile glances as they passed through the lobby. It was already late, they were the last. They mounted the staircase, threw their cloaks over Wendelin's arms, paused a second before a high mirror, then went through the little door into their box. They were greeted by the last sounds before the hush – voices and the slamming of seats. The lackey pushed their plush-upholstered chairs beneath them; at that moment the lights went down and below their box the orchestra broke into the wild pulsating notes of the prelude.

Night, and tempest.... And they, who had been wafted hither on the wings of ease, with no petty annoyances on the way, were in exactly the right mood and could give all their attention at once. Storm, a raging tempest, without in the wood. The angry god's command resounded, once, twice repeated in its wrath, obediently the thunder crashed. The curtain flew up as though blown by the storm. There was the rude hall, dark save for a glow on the pagan hearth. In the centre towered up the trunk of the ash tree. Siegmund appeared in the doorway and leaned against the wooden post beaten and harried by the storm. Draggingly he moved forwards on his sturdy legs wrapped round with hide and thongs. He was rosy-skinned, with a straw-coloured beard; beneath his blond brows and the blond forelock of his wig his blue eyes were directed upon the conductor, with an imploring gaze. At last the orchestra gave way to his voice, which rang clear and metallic, though he tried to make it sound like a gasp. He sang a few bars, to the effect that no matter to whom the hearth belonged he must rest upon it; and at the last word he let himself drop heavily on the bearskin rug and lay there with his head cushioned on his plump arms. His breast heaved in slumber. A minute passed, filled with the singing, speaking flow of the music, rolling its waves at the feet of the events on the stage.... Sieglinde entered from the left. She had an alabaster bosom which rose and fell marvellously beneath her muslin robe and deerskin mantle. She displayed surprise at sight of the strange man; pressed her chin upon her breast until it was double, put her lips in position and expressed it, this surprise, in tones which swelled soft and warm from her white throat and were given shape by her tongue and her mobile lips. She tended the stranger; bending over him so that he could see the white flower of her bosom rising from the rough skins, she gave him with both hands the drinking-horn. He drank. The music spoke movingly to him of cool refreshment and cherishing care. They looked at each other with the beginning of enchantment, a first dim recognition, standing rapt while the orchestra interpreted in a melody of profound enchantment.

She gave him mead, first touching the horn with her lips, then watching while he took a long draught. Again their glances met and mingled, while below, the melody voiced their yearning. Then he rose, in deep dejection, turning away painfully, his arms hanging at his sides, to the door, that he might remove from her sight his affliction, his loneliness, his persecuted, hated existence and bear it back into the wild. She called upon him but he did not hear; heedless of self she lifted up her arms and confessed her intolerable anguish. He stopped. Her eyes fell. Below them the music spoke darkly of the bond of suffering that united them. He stayed. He folded his arms and remained by the hearth, awaiting his destiny.

Announced by his pugnacious motif, Hunding entered, paunchy and knock-kneed, like a cow. His beard was black with brown tufts. He stood there frowning, leaning heavily on his spear, and staring ox-eyed at the stranger guest. But as the primitive custom would have it he bade him welcome, in an enormous, rusty voice.

Sieglinde laid the evening meal, Hunding's slow, suspicious gaze moving to and fro between her and the stranger. Dull lout though he was, he saw their likeness: the selfsame breed, that odd, untrammelled rebellious stock, which he hated, to which he felt inferior. They sat down, and Hunding, in two words, introduced himself and accounted for his simple, regular, and orthodox existence. Thus he forced Siegmund to speak of himself – and that was incomparably more difficult. Yet Siegmund spoke, he sang clearly and with wonderful beauty of his life and misfortunes. He told how he had been born with a twin sister – and as people do who dare not speak out, he called himself by a false name. He gave a moving account of the hatred and envy which had been the bane of his life and his strange father's life, how their hall had been burnt, his sister carried off, how they had led in the forest a horrid, persecuted, outlawed life; and how finally he had mysteriously lost his father as well.... And then Siegmund sang the most painful thing of all: he told of his yearning for human beings, his longing and ceaseless loneliness. He sang of men and women, of friendship and love he had sometimes won, only to be thrust back again into the dark. A curse had lain upon him for ever, he was marked by the brand of his strange origins. His speech had not been as others' speech nor theirs as his. What he found good was vexation to them, he was galled by the ancient laws to which they paid honour. Always and everywhere he had lived amid anger and strife, he had borne the yoke of scorn and hatred and contempt – all because he was strange, of a breed and kind hopelessly different from them.

Hunding's reception of all this was entirely characteristic. His reply showed no sympathy and no understanding, but only a sour disgust and suspicion of all Siegmund's story. And finally understanding that the stranger standing here on his own hearth was the very man for whom the hunt had been called up today, he behaved with the four-square pedantry one would have expected of him. With a grim sort of courtesy he declared that for tonight the guest-right protected the fugitive; tomorrow he would have the honour of slaying him in battle. Gruffly he commanded Sieglinde to spice his night-drink for him and to await him in bed within; then after a few more threats he followed her, taking all his weapons with him and leaving Siegmund alone and despairing by the hearth.

Up in the box Siegmund bent over the velvet ledge and leaned his dark boyish head on his narrow red hand. His brows made two black furrows, and one foot, resting on the heel of his patent-leather shoe, was in constant nervous motion. But it stopped as he heard a whisper close to him.

"Gigi!"

His mouth, as he turned, had an insolent line.

Sieglinde was holding out to him a mother-of-pearl box with maraschino cherries.

"The brandy chocolates are underneath," she whispered. But he accepted only a cherry, and as he took it out of the waxed paper she said in his ear:

"She will come back to him again at once."

"I am not entirely unaware of the fact," he said, so loud that several heads were jerked angrily in his direction. . . . Down in the darkness big Siegmund was singing alone. From the depths of his heart he cried out for the sword – for a shining haft to swing on that day when there burst forth at last the bright flame of his anger and rage, which so long had smouldered deep in his heart. He saw the hilt glitter in the tree, saw the embers fade on the hearth, sank back in gloomy slumber – and started up in joyful amaze when Sieglinde glided back to him in the darkness.

Hunding slept like a stone, a deafened, drunken sleep. Together they rejoiced at the outwitting of the clod; they laughed, and their eyes had the same way of narrowing as they laughed. Then Sieglinde stole a look at the conductor, received her cue, and putting her lips in position sang a long recitative: related the heart-breaking tale of how they had forced her, forsaken, strange and wild as she was, to give herself to the crude and savage Hunding and to count herself lucky in an honourable marriage which might bury her dark origins in oblivion. She sang too, sweetly and soothingly, of the strange old man in the hat and how he had driven the sword-blade into the trunk of the ash tree, to await the coming of him who was destined to draw it out. Passionately she prayed in song that it might be he whom she meant, whom she knew and grievously longed for, the consoler of her sorrows, the friend who should be more than friend, the avenger of her shame, whom once she had lost, whom in her abasement she wept for, her brother in suffering, her saviour, her rescuer. . . .

But at this point Siegmund flung about her his two rosy arms. He pressed her cheek against the pelt that covered his breast and, holding her so, sang above her head – sang out his exultation to the four winds, in a silver trumpeting of sound. His breast glowed hot with the oath that bound him to his mate. All the yearning of his hunted life found assuagement in her; all that love which others had repulsed, when in conscious shame of his dark origins he forced it upon them – in her it found its home. She suffered shame as did he, dishonoured was she like to himself – and now, now their brother-and-sister love should be their revenge!

The storm whistled, a gust of wind burst open the door, a flood of white electric light poured into the hall. Divested of darkness they stood and sang their song of spring and spring's sister, love!

Crouching on the bearskin they looked at each other in the white light, as they sang their duet of love. Their bare arms touched each other's as they held each other by the temples and gazed into each other's eyes, and as they sang their mouths were very near. They compared their eyes, their foreheads, their voices – they were the same. The growing, urging recognition wrung from his breast his father's name; she called him by his: Siegmund! Siegmund! He freed the sword, he swung it above his head, and submerged in bliss she told him in song who she was: his twin sister, Sieglinde. In ravishment he stretched out his arms to her, his bride, she sank upon his breast – the curtain fell as the music swelled into a roaring, rushing, foaming whirlpool of passion – swirled and swirled and with one mighty throb stood still.

Rapturous applause. The lights went on. A thousand people got up, stretched unobtrusively as they clapped, then made ready to leave the hall, with heads still turned towards the stage, where the singers appeared before the curtain, like masks hung out in a row at a fair. Hunding too came out and smiled politely, despite all that had just been happening.

Siegmund pushed back his chair and stood up. He was hot; little red patches showed on his cheek-bones, above the lean, sallow, shaven cheeks.

"For my part," said he, "what I want now is a breath of fresh air. Siegmund was pretty feeble, wasn't he?"

"Yes," answered Sieglinde, "and the orchestra saw fit to drag abominably in the Spring Song."

"Frightfully sentimental," said Siegmund, shrugging his narrow shoulders in his dress coat. "Are you coming out?" She lingered a moment, with her elbows on the ledge, still gazing at the stage. He looked at her as she rose and took up her silver scarf. Her soft, full lips were quivering.

They went into the foyer and mingled with the slow-moving throng, downstairs and up again, sometimes holding each other by the hand.

"I should enjoy an ice," said she, "if they were not in all probability uneatable."

"Don't think of it," said he. So they ate bonbons out of their box – maraschino cherries and chocolate beans filled with cognac.

The bell rang and they looked on contemptuously as the crowds rushed back to their seats, blocking the corridors. They waited until all was quiet, regaining their places just as the lights went down again and silence and darkness fell soothingly upon the hall. There was another little ring, the conductor raised his arms and summoned up anew the wave of splendid sound.

Siegmund looked down into the orchestra. The sunken space stood out bright against the darkness of the listening house; hands fingered, arms drew the bows, cheeks puffed out – all these simple folk laboured zealously to bring to utterance the work of a master who suffered and created; created the noble and simple visions enacted above on the stage. Creation? How did one create? Pain gnawed and burned in Siegmund's breast, a drawing anguish which yet was somehow sweet, a yearning – whither, for what? It was all so dark, so shamefully unclear! Two thoughts, two words he had: creation, passion. His temples glowed and throbbed, and it came to him as in a yearning vision that creation was born of passion and was reshaped anew as passion. He saw the pale, spent woman hanging on the breast of the fugitive to whom she gave herself, he saw her love and her destiny and knew that so life must be to be creative. He saw his own life, and knew its contradictions, its clear understanding and spoilt voluptuousness, its splendid security and idle spite, its weakness and wittiness, its languid contempt; his life, so full of words, so void of acts, so full of cleverness, so empty of emotion – and he felt again the burning, the drawing anguish which yet was sweet – whither, and to what end? Creation? Experience? Passion?

The finale of the act came, the curtain fell. Light, applause, general exit. Sieglinde and Siegmund spent the interval as before. They scarcely spoke, as they walked hand-in-hand through the corridors and up and down the steps. She offered him cherries but he took no more. She looked at him, but withdrew her gaze as his rested upon her, walking rather constrained at his side and enduring his eye. Her childish shoulders under the silver web of her scarf looked like those of an Egyptian statue, a little too high and too square. Upon her cheeks burned the same fire he felt in his own.

Again they waited until the crowd had gone in and took their seats at the last possible moment. Storm and wind and driving cloud; wild, heathenish cries of exultation. Eight females, not exactly stars in appearance, eight untrammelled, laughing maidens of the wild, were disporting themselves amid a rocky scene. Brünnhilde broke in upon their merriment with her fears. They skimmed away in terror before the approaching wrath of Wotan, leaving her alone to face him. The angry god nearly annihilated his daughter – but his wrath roared itself out, by degrees grew gentle and dispersed into a mild melancholy, on which note it ended. A noble prospect opened out, the scene was pervaded with epic and religious splendour. Brünnhilde slept. The god mounted the rocks. Great, full-bodied flames, rising, falling, and flickering, glowed all over the boards. The Walküre lay with her coat of mail and her shield on her mossy couch ringed round with fire and smoke, with leaping, dancing tongues, with the magic sleep-compelling fire-music. But she had saved Sieglinde, in whose womb there grew and waxed the seed of that hated unprized race, chosen of the gods, from which the twins had sprung, who had mingled their misfortunes and their afflictions in free and mutual bliss.

Siegmund and Sieglinde left their box; Wendelin was outside, towering in his yellow paletot and holding their cloaks for them to put on. Like a gigantic slave he followed the two dark, slender, fur-mantled, exotic creatures down the stairs to where the carriage waited and the pair of large finely glossy thoroughbreds tossed their proud heads in the winter night. Wendelin ushered the twins into their warm little silken-lined retreat, closed the door, and the coupé stood poised for yet a second, quivering slightly from the swing with which Wendelin agilely mounted the box. Then it glided swiftly away and left the theatre behind. Again they rolled noiselessly and easefully to the rhythmic beat of the horses' hoofs, over all the unevennesses of the road, sheltered from the shrill harshness of the bustling life through which they passed. They sat as silent and remote as they had sat in their opera-box facing the stage – almost, one might say, in the same atmosphere. Nothing was there which could alienate them from the extravagant and stormily passionate world which worked upon them with its magic power to draw them to itself.

The carriage stopped; they did not at once realize where they were, or that they had arrived before the door of their parents' house. Then Wendelin appeared at the window, and the porter came out of his lodge to open the door.

"Are my father and mother at home?" Siegmund asked, looking over the porter's head and blinking as though he were staring into the sun.

No, they had not returned from dinner at the Erlangers'. Nor was Kunz at home; Märit too was out, no one knew where, for she went entirely her own way.

In the vestibule they paused to be divested of their wraps; then they went up the stairs and through the first-floor hall into the dining-room. Its immense and splendid spaces lay in darkness save at the upper end, where one lustre burned above a table and Florian waited to serve them. They moved noiselessly across the thick carpet, and Florian seated them in their softly upholstered chairs. Then a gesture from Siegmund dismissed him, they would dispense with his services.

The table was laid with a dish of fruit, a plate of sandwiches, and a jug of red wine. An electric tea-kettle hummed upon a great silver tray, with all appliances about it.

Siegmund ate a caviar sandwich and poured out wine into a slender glass where it glowed a dark ruby red. He drank in quick gulps, and grumblingly stated his opinion that red wine and caviar were a combination offensive to good taste. He drew out his case, jerkily selected a cigarette, and began to smoke, leaning back with his hands in his pockets, wrinkling up his face and twitching his cigarette from one corner of his mouth to the other. His strong growth of beard was already beginning to show again under the high cheek-bones; the two black folds stood out on the base of his nose.

Sieglinde had brewed the tea and added a drop of burgundy. She touched the fragile porcelain cup delicately with her full, soft lips and as she drank she looked across at Siegmund with her great humid black eyes.

She set down her cup and leaned her dark, sweet little head upon her slender hand. Her eyes rested full upon him, with such liquid, speechless eloquence that all she might have said could be nothing beside it.

"Won't you have any more to eat, Gigi?"

"One would not draw," said he, "from the fact that I am smoking, the conclusion that I intend to eat more."

"But you have had nothing but bonbons since tea. Take a peach, at least."

He shrugged his shoulders – or rather he wriggled them like a naughty child, in his dress coat.

"This is stupid. I am going upstairs. Good night."

He drank out his wine, tossed away his table-napkin, and lounged away, with his hands in his pockets, into the darkness at the other end of the room.

He went upstairs to his room, where he turned on the light – not much, only two or three bulbs, which made a wide white circle on the ceiling. Then he stood considering what to do next. The good-night had not been final; this was not how they were used to take leave of each other at the close of the day. She was sure to come to his room. He flung off his coat, put on his fur-trimmed house-jacket, and lighted another cigarette. He lay down on the chaise-longue; sat up again, tried another posture, with his cheek in the pillow; threw himself on his back again and so remained awhile, with his hands under his head.

The subtle, bitterish scent of the tobacco mingled with that of cosmetics, the soaps, and the toilet waters; their combined perfume hung in the tepid air of the room and Siegmund breathed it in with conscious pleasure, finding it sweeter than ever. Closing his eyes he surrendered to this atmosphere, as a man will console himself with some delicate pleasure of the senses for the extraordinary harshness of his lot.

Then suddenly he started up again, tossed away his cigarette and stood in front of the white wardrobe, which had long mirrors let into each of its three divisions. He moved very close to the middle one and eye to eye he studied himself, conned every feature of his face. Then he opened the two side wings and studied both profiles as well. Long he looked at each mark of his race: the slightly drooping nose, the full lips that rested so softly on each other; the high cheek-bones, the thick black, curling hair that grew far down on the temples and parted so decidedly on one side; finally the eyes under the knit brows, those large black eyes that glowed like fire and had an expression of weary sufferance.

In the mirror he saw the bearskin lying behind him, spreading out his claws beside the bed. He turned round, and there was tragic meaning in the dragging step that bore him towards it – until after a moment more of hesitation he lay down all its length and buried his head in his arm.

For a while he lay motionless, then propped his head on his elbows, with his cheeks resting on his slim reddish hands, and fell again into contemplation of his image opposite him in the mirror. There was a knock on the door. He started, reddened, and moved as though to get up – but sank back again, his head against his outstretched arm, and stopped there, silent.

Sieglinde entered. Her eyes searched the room, without finding him at once. Then with a start she saw him lying on the rug.

"Gigi, whatever are you doing there? Are you ill?" She ran to him, bending over with her hand on his forehead, stroking his hair as she repeated: "You are not ill?"

He shook his head, looking up at her under his brow as she continued to caress him.

She was half ready for bed, having come over in slippers from her dressing-room, which was opposite to his. Her loosened hair flowed down over her open white dressing-jacket; beneath the lace of her chemise Siegmund saw her little breasts, the colour of smoked meerschaum.

"You were so cross," she said. "It was beastly of you to go away like that. I thought I would not come. But then I did, because that was not a proper good-night at all. . . . "

"I was waiting for you," said he.

She was still standing bent over, and made a little moue which brought out markedly the facial characteristics of her race. Then, in her ordinary tone:

"Which does not prevent my present position from giving me a crick in the back."

He shook her off.

"Don't, don't – we must not talk like that – not that way, Sieglinde." His voice was strange, he himself noticed it. He felt parched with fever, his hands and feet were cold and clammy. She knelt beside him on the skin, her hand in his hair. He lifted himself a little to fling one arm round her neck and so looked at her, looked as he had just been looking at himself – at eyes and temples, brow and cheeks.

"You are just like me," said he, haltingly, and swallowed to moisten his dry throat. "Everything about you is just like me – and so – what you have – with Beckerath – the experience – is for me too. That makes things even, Sieglinde – and anyhow, after all, it is, for that matter – it is a revenge, Sieglinde – "

He was seeking to clothe in reason what he was trying to say – yet his words sounded as though he uttered them out of some strange, rash, bewildered dream.

But to her it had no quality of strangeness. She did not blush at his half-spoken, turbid, wild imaginings; his words enveloped her senses like a mist, they drew her down whence they had come, to the borders of a kingdom she had never entered, though sometimes, since her betrothal, she had been carried thither in expectant dreams.

She kissed him on his closed eyelids; he kissed her on her throat, beneath the lace she wore. They kissed each other's hands. They loved each other with all the sweetness of the senses, each for the other's spoilt and costly well-being and delicious fragrance. They breathed it in, this fragrance, with languid and voluptuous abandon, like self-centred invalids, consoling themselves for the loss of hope. They forgot themselves in caresses, which took the upper hand, passing over into a tumult of passion, dying away into a sobbing. . . .

She sat there on the bearskin, with parted lips, supporting herself with one hand, and brushed the hair out of her eyes. He leaned back on his hands against the white dressing-chest, rocked to and fro on his hips, and gazed into the air.

"But Beckerath," said she, seeking to find some order in her thoughts, "Beckerath, Gigi . . . what about him, now?"

"Oh," he said – and for a second the marks of his race stood out strong upon his face – "he ought to be grateful to us. His existence will be a little less trivial, from now on."

RAILWAY ACCIDENT

TELL YOU a story? But I don't know any. Well, yes, after all, here is something I might tell.

Once, two years ago now it is, I was in a railway accident; all the details are clear in my memory.

It was not really a first-class one – no wholesale telescoping or "heaps of unidentifiable dead" – not that sort of thing. Still, it was a proper accident, with all the trimmings, and on top of that it was at night. Not everybody has been through one, so I will describe it the best I can.

I was on my way to Dresden, whither I had been invited by some friends of letters: it was a literary and artistic pilgrimage, in short, such as, from time to time, I undertake not unwillingly. You make appearances, you attend functions, you show yourself to admiring crowds – not for nothing is one a subject of William II. And certainly Dresden is beautiful, especially the Zwinger; and afterwards I intended to go for ten days or a fortnight to the White Hart to rest, and if, thanks to the treatments, the spirit should come upon me, I might do a little work as well. To this end I had put my manuscript at the bottom of my trunk, together with my notes – a good stout bundle done up in brown paper and tied with string in the Bavarian colours. I like to travel in comfort, especially when my expenses are paid. So I patronized the sleeping-cars, reserving a place days ahead in a first-class compartment. All was in order; nevertheless I was excited, as I always am on such occasions, for a journey is still an adventure to me, and where travelling is concerned I shall never manage to feel properly blasé. I perfectly well know that the night train for Dresden leaves the central station at Munich regularly every evening, and every morning is in Dresden. But when I am travelling with it, and linking my momentous destiny to its own, the matter assumes importance. I cannot rid myself of the notion that it is making a special trip today, just on my account, and the unreasoning and mistaken conviction sets up in me a deep and speechless unrest, which does not subside until all the formalities of departure are behind me – the packing, the drive in the loaded cab to the station, the arrival there, and the registration of luggage – and I can feel myself finally and securely bestowed. Then, indeed, a pleasing relaxation takes place, the mind turns to fresh concerns, the unknown unfolds itself beyond the expanse of window-pane, and I am consumed with joyful anticipations.

And so on this occasion. I had tipped my porter so liberally that he pulled his cap and gave me a pleasant journey; and I stood at the corridor window of my sleeping-car smoking my evening cigar and watching the bustle on the platform. There were whistlings and rumblings, hurryings and farewells, and the singsong of newspaper and refreshment vendors, and over all the great electric moons glowed through the mist of the October evening. Two stout fellows pulled a hand-cart of large trunks along the platform to the baggage car in front of the train. I easily identified, by certain unmistakable features, my own trunk; one among many there it lay, and at the bottom of it reposed my precious package. "There," thought I, "no need to worry, it is in good hands. Look at that guard with the leather cartridge-belt, the prodigious sergeant-major's moustache, and the inhospitable eye. Watch him rebuking the old woman in the threadbare black cape – for two pins she would have got into a second-class carriage. He is security, he is authority, he is our parent, he is the State. He is strict, not to say gruff, you would not care to mingle with him; but reliability is writ large upon his brow, and in his care your trunk reposes as in the bosom of Abraham."

A man was strolling up and down the platform in spats and a yellow autumn coat, with a dog on a leash. Never have I seen a handsomer dog: a small, stocky bull, smooth-coated, muscular, with black spots; as well groomed and amusing as the dogs one sees in circuses, who make the audience laugh by dashing round and round the ring with all the energy of their small bodies. This dog had a silver collar, with a plaited leather leash. But all this was not surprising, considering his master, the gentleman in spats, who had beyond a doubt the noblest origins. He wore a monocle, which accentuated without distorting his general air; the defiant perch of his moustache bore out the proud and stubborn expression of his chin and the corners of his mouth. He addressed a question to the martial guard, who knew perfectly well with whom he was dealing and answered hand to cap. My gentleman strolled on, gratified with the impression he had made. He strutted in his spats, his gaze was cold, he regarded men and affairs with penetrating eye. Certainly he was far above feeling journey-proud; travel by train was no novelty to him. He was at home in life, without fear of authority or regulations; he was an authority himself – in short, a nob. I could not look at him enough. When he thought the time had come, he got into the train (the guard had just turned his back). He came along the corridor behind me, bumped into me, and did not apologize. What a man! But that was nothing to what followed. Without turning a hair he took his dog with him into the sleeping-compartment! Surely it was forbidden to do that. When should I presume to take a dog with me into a sleeping-compartment? But he did it, on the strength of his prescriptive rights as a nob, and shut the door behind him.

There came a whistle outside, the locomotive whistled in response, gently the train began to move. I stayed awhile by the window watching the hand-waving and the shifting lights. . . . I retired inside the carriage.

The sleeping-car was not very full, a compartment next to mine was empty and had not been got ready for the night; I decided to make myself comfortable there for an hour's peaceful reading. I fetched my book and settled in. The sofa had a silky salmon-pink covering, an ash-tray stood on the folding table, the light burned bright. I read and smoked.

The sleeping-car attendant entered in pursuance of his duties and asked for my ticket for the night. I delivered it into his grimy hands. He was polite but entirely official, did not even vouchsafe me a good-night as from one human being to another, but went out at once and knocked on the door of the next compartment. He would better have left it alone, for my gentleman of the spats was inside; and perhaps because he did not wish anyone to discover his dog, but possibly because he had really gone to bed, he got furious at anyone daring to disturb him. Above the rumbling of the train I heard his immediate and elemental burst of rage. "What do you want?" he roared. "Leave me alone, you swine." He said "swine". It was a lordly epithet, the epithet of a cavalry officer – it did my heart good to hear it. But the sleeping-car attendant must have resorted to diplomacy – of course he had to have the man's ticket – for just as I stepped into the corridor to get a better view the door of the compartment abruptly opened a little way and the ticket flew out into the attendant's face; yes, it was flung with violence straight in his face. He picked it up with both hands, and though he had got the corner of it in one eye, so that the tears came, he thanked the man, saluting and clicking his heels together. Quite overcome, I returned to my book.

I considered whether there was anything against my smoking another cigar and concluded that there was little or nothing. So I did it, rolling onward and reading; I felt full of contentment and good ideas. Time passed, it was ten o'clock, half past ten, all my fellow-travellers had gone to bed, at last I decided to follow them. I got up and went into my own compartment. A real little bedroom, most luxurious, with stamped leather wall hangings, clothes-hooks, a nickel-plated wash-basin. The lower berth was snowily prepared, the covers invitingly turned back. Oh, triumph of modern times! I thought. One lies in this bed as though at home, it rocks a little all night, and the result is that next morning one is in Dresden. I took my suitcase out of the rack to get ready for bed; I was holding it above my head, with my arms stretched up.

It was at this moment that the railway accident occurred. I remember it like yesterday.

We gave a jerk – but jerk is a poor word for it. It was a jerk of deliberately foul intent, a jerk with a horrid reverberating crash, and so violent that my suitcase leaped out of my hands I knew not whither, while I was flung forcibly with my shoulder against the wall. I had no time to stop and think. But now followed a frightful rocking of the carriage, and while that went on, one had plenty of leisure to be frightened. A railway carriage rocks going over switches or on sharp curves, that we know; but this rocking would not let me stand up, I was thrown from one wall to the other as the carriage careened. I had only one simple thought, but I thought it with concentration, exclusively. I thought: "Something is the matter, something is the matter, something is *very much* the matter!" Just in those words. But later I thought: "Stop, stop, stop!" For I knew that it would be a great help if only the train could be brought to a halt. And lo, at this my unuttered but fervent behest, the train did stop.

Up to now a deathlike stillness had reigned in the carriage, but at this point found tongue. Shrill feminine screams mingled with deeper masculine cries of alarm. Next door someone was shouting "Help!" No doubt about it, this was the very same voice which, just previously, had uttered the lordly epithet – the voice of the man in spats, his very voice, though distorted by fear. "Help!" it cried; and just as I stepped into the corridor, where the passengers were collecting, he burst out of his compartment in a silk sleeping-suit and halted, looking wildly round him. "Great God!" he exclaimed, "Almighty God!" and then, as though to abase himself utterly, perhaps in hope to avert destruction, he added in a deprecating tone: "*Dear* God!" But suddenly he thought of something else, of trying to help himself. He threw himself upon the case on the wall where an axe and saw are kept for emergencies, and broke the glass with his fist. But finding that he could not release the tools at once, he abandoned them, buffeted his way through the crowd of passengers, so that the half-dressed women screamed afresh, and leaped out of the carriage.

All that was the work of a moment only. And then for the first time I began to feel the shock: in a certain weakness of the spine, a passing inability to swallow. The sleeping-car attendant, red-eyed, grimy-handed, had just come up; we all pressed round him; the women, with bare arms and shoulders, stood wringing their hands.

The train, he explained, had been derailed, we had run off the track. That, as it afterwards turned out, was not true. But behold, the man in his excitement had become voluble, he abandoned his official neutrality; events had loosened his tongue and he spoke to us in confidence, about his wife. "I told her today, I did. 'Wife,' I said, 'I feel in my bones somethin's goin' to happen.'" And sure enough, hadn't something happened? We all felt how right he had been. The carriage had begun to fill with smoke, a thick smudge; nobody knew where it came from, but we all thought it best to get out into the night.

That could only be done by quite a big jump from the footboard on to the line, for there was no platform, of course, and besides our carriage was canted a good deal towards the opposite side. But the ladies – they had hastily covered their nakedness – jumped in desperation and soon we were all standing there between the lines.

It was nearly dark, but from where we were we could see that no damage had been done at the rear of the train, though all the carriages stood at a slant. But farther forward – fifteen or twenty paces farther forward! Not for nothing had the jerk we felt made such a horrid crash. There lay a waste of wreckage; we could see the margins of it, with the little lights of the guards' lanterns flickering across and to and fro.

Excited people came towards us, bringing reports of the situation. We were close by a small station not far beyond Regensburg, and as a result of a defective point our express had run on to the wrong line, had crashed at full speed into a stationary freight train, hurling it out of the station, annihilating its rear carriages, and itself sustaining serious damage. The great express engine from Maffei's in Munich lay smashed up and done for. Price seventy thousand marks. And in the forward coaches, themselves lying almost on one side, many of the seats were telescoped. No, thank goodness, there were no lives lost. There was talk of an old woman having been "taken out", but nobody had seen her. At least, people had been thrown in all directions, children buried under luggage, the shock had been great. The baggage car was demolished. Demolished – the baggage car? Demolished.

There I stood.

A bareheaded official came running along the track. The station-master. He issued wild and tearful commands to the passengers, to make them behave themselves and get back into the coaches. But nobody took any notice of him, he had no cap and no self-control. Poor wretch! Probably the responsibility was his. Perhaps this was the end of his career, the wreck of his prospects. I could not ask him about the baggage car – it would have been tactless.

Another official came up – he *limped* up. I recognized him by the sergeant-major's moustache: it was the stern and vigilant guard of the early evening – our Father, the State. He limped along, bent over with his hand on his knee, thinking about nothing else. "Oh, dear!" he said, "oh, dear, oh, dear me!" I asked him what was the matter. "I got stuck, sir, jammed me in the chest, I made my escape through the roof." This "made my escape through the roof" sounded like a newspaper report. Certainly the man would not have used the phrase in everyday life; he had experienced not so much an accident as a newspaper account of it – but what was that to me? He was in no state to give me news of my manuscript. So I accosted a young man who came up bustling and self-important from the waste of wreckage, and asked him about the heavy luggage.

"Well, sir, nobody can say anything as to that" – his tone implied that I ought to be grateful to have escaped unhurt. "Everything is all over the place. Women's shoes – " he said with a sweeping gesture to indicate the devastation, and wrinkled his nose. "When they start the clearing operations we shall see.... Women's shoes.... "

There I stood. All alone I stood there in the night and searched my heart. Clearing operations. Clearing operations were to be undertaken with my manuscript. Probably it was destroyed, then, torn up, demolished. My honeycomb, my spider-web, my nest, my earth, my pride and pain, my all, the best of me – what should I do if it were gone? I had no copy of what had been welded and forged, of what already was a living, speaking thing – to say nothing of my notes and drafts, all that I had saved and stored up and overheard and sweated over for years – my squirrel's hoard. What should I do? I inquired of my own soul and I knew that I should begin over again from the beginning. Yes, with animal patience, with the tenacity of a primitive creature the curious and complex product of whose little ingenuity and industry has been destroyed; after a moment of helpless bewilderment I should set to work again – and perhaps this time it would come easier!

But meanwhile a fire brigade had come up, their torches cast a red light over the wreck; when I went forward and looked for the baggage car, behold it was almost intact, the luggage quite unharmed. All the things that lay strewn about came out of the freight train: among the rest a quantity of balls of string – a perfect sea of string covered the ground far and wide.

A load was lifted from my heart. I mingled with the people who stood talking and fraternizing in misfortune – also showing off and being important. So much seemed clear, that the engine-driver had acted with great presence of mind. He had averted a great catastrophe by pulling the emergency brake at the last moment. Otherwise, it was said, there would have been a general smash and the whole train would have gone over the steep embankment on the left. Oh, praiseworthy engine-driver! He was not about, nobody had seen him, but his fame spread down the whole length of the train and we all lauded him in his absence. "That chap," said one man, and pointed with one hand somewhere off into the night, "that chap saved our lives." We all agreed.

But our train was standing on a track where it did not belong, and it behoved those in charge to guard it from behind so that another one did not run into it. Firemen perched on the rear carriage with torches of flaming pitch, and the excited young man who had given me such a fright with his "women's shoes" seized upon a torch too and began signalling with it, though no train was anywhere in sight.

Slowly and by degrees something like order was produced, the State our Father regained pose and presence. Steps had been taken, wires sent, presently a breakdown train from Regensburg steamed cautiously into the station and great gas flares with reflectors were set up about the wreck. We passengers were now turned off and told to go into the little station building to wait for our new conveyance. Laden with our hand luggage, some of the party with bandaged heads, we passed through a lane of inquisitive natives into the tiny waiting-room, where we herded together as best we could. And inside of an hour we were all stowed higgledy-piggledy into a special train.

I had my first-class ticket – my journey being paid for – but it availed me nothing, for everybody wanted to ride first and my carriage was more crowded than the others. But just as I found me a little niche, whom do I see diagonally opposite to me, huddled in the corner? My hero, the gentleman with the spats and the vocabulary of a cavalry officer. He did not have his dog, it had been taken away from him in defiance of his rights as a nob and now sat howling in a gloomy prison just behind the engine. His master, like myself, held a yellow ticket which was no good to him, and he was grumbling, he was trying to make head against this communistic levelling of rank in the face of general misfortune. But another man answered him in a virtuous tone: "You ought to be thankful that you can sit down." And with a sour smile my gentleman resigned himself to the crazy situation.

And now who got in, supported by two firemen? A wee

little old grandmother in a tattered black cape, the very same who in Munich would for two pins have got into a second-class carriage. "Is this the first class?" she kept asking. And when we made room and assured her that it was, she sank down with a "God be praised!" on to the plush cushions as though only now was she safe and sound.

By Hof it was already five o'clock and light. There we breakfasted; an express train picked me up and deposited me with my belongings, three hours late, in Dresden.

Well, that was the railway accident I went through. I suppose it had to happen once; but whatever mathematicians may say, I feel that I now have every chance of escaping another.

THE FIGHT BETWEEN JAPPE AND DO ESCOBAR

I WAS very much taken aback when Johnny Bishop told me that Jappe and Do Escobar were going to fight each other and that we must go and watch them do it.

It was in the summer holidays at Travemünde, on a sultry day with a slight land breeze and a flat sea ever so far away across the sands. We had been some three-quarters of an hour in the water and were lying on the hard sand under the props of the bathing-cabins – we two and Jürgen Brattström the shipowner's son. Johnny and Brattström were lying on their backs entirely naked; I felt more comfortable with my towel wrapped round my hips. Brattström asked me why I did it and I could not think of any sensible answer; so Johnny said with his winning smile that I was probably too big now to lie naked. I really was larger and more developed than Johnny and Brattström; also a little older, about thirteen; so I accepted Johnny's explanation in silence, although with a certain feeling of mortification. For in Johnny Bishop's presence you actually felt rather out of it if you were any less small, fine, and physically childlike than he, who was all these things in such a very high degree. He knew how to look up at you with his pretty, friendly blue eyes, which had a certain mocking smile in them too, with an expression that said: "What a great, gawky thing you are, to be sure!" The ideal of manliness and long trousers had no validity in his presence – and that at a time, not long after the war, when strength, courage, and every hardy virtue stood very high among us youth and all sorts of conduct were banned as effeminate. But Johnny, as a foreigner – or half-foreigner – was exempt from this atmosphere. He was a little like a woman who preserves her youth and looks down on other women who are less successful at the feat. Besides he was far and away the best-dressed boy in town, distinctly aristocratic and elegant in his real English sailor suit with the linen collar, sailor's knot, laces, a silver whistle in his pocket, and an anchor on the sleeves that narrowed round his wrists. Anyone else would have been laughed at for that sort of thing – it would have been jeered at as "girls' clothes". But he wore them with such a disarming and confident air that he never suffered in the least.

He looked rather like a thin little cupid as he lay there, with his pretty, soft blond curls and his arms up over the narrow English head that rested on the sand. His father had been a German business man who had been naturalized in England and died some years since. His mother was English by blood, a long-featured lady with quiet, gentle ways, who had settled in our town with her two children, Johnny and a mischievous little girl just as pretty as he. She still wore black for her husband, and she was probably honouring his last wishes when she brought the children to grow up in Germany. Obviously they were in easy circumstances. She owned a spacious house outside the city and a villa at the sea and from time to time she travelled with Johnny and Sissie to more distant resorts. She did not move in society, although it would have been open to her. Whether on account of her mourning or perhaps because the horizon of our best families was too narrow for her, she herself led a retired life, but she managed that her children should have social intercourse. She invited other children to play with them and sent them to dancing and deportment lessons, thus quietly arranging that Johnny and Sissie should associate exclusively with the children of well-to-do families – of course not in pursuance of any well-defined principle, but just as a matter of course. Mrs Bishop contributed, remotely, to my own education: it was from her I learned that to be well thought of by others no more is needed than to think well of yourself. Though deprived of its male head the little family showed none of the marks of neglect or disruption which often in such cases make people fight shy. Without further family connection, without title, tradition, influence, or public office, and living a life apart, Mrs Bishop by no means lacked social security or pretensions. She was definitely accepted at her own valuation and the friendship of her children was much sought after by their young contemporaries.

As for Jürgen Brattström, I may say in passing that his father had made his own money, achieved public office, and built for himself and his family the red sandstone house on the Burgfeld, next to Mrs Bishop's. And that lady had quietly accepted his son as Johnny's playmate and let the two go to school together. Jürgen was a decent, phlegmatic, short-legged lad without any prominent characteristics. He had begun to do a little private business in licorice sticks.

As I said, I was extremely shocked when Johnny told me about the impending meeting between Jappe and Do Escobar which was to take place at twelve o'clock that day on the Leuchtenfeld. It was dead earnest – might have a serious outcome, for Jappe and Do Escobar were both stout and reckless fellows and had strong feelings about knightly honour. The issue might well be frightful. In my memory they still seem as tall and manly as they did then, though they could not have been more than fifteen at the time. Jappe came from the middle class of the city; he was not much looked after at home, he was already almost his own master, a combination of loafer and man-about-town. Do Escobar was an exotic and bohemian foreigner, who did not even come regularly to school but only attended lectures now and then – an irregular but paradisial existence! He lived *en pension* with some middle-class people and rejoiced in complete independence. Both were people who went late to bed, visited public houses, strolled of evenings in the Broad Street, followed girls about, performed crazy "stunts" – in short, were regular blades. Although they did not live in the Kurhotel at Travemünde – where they would scarcely have been acceptable – but somewhere in the village, they frequented the Kurhaus and garden and were at home there as cosmopolitans. In the evening, especially on a Sunday, when I had long since been in my bed in one of the chalets and gone off to sleep to the pleasant sound of the Kurhaus band, they, and other members of the young generation – as I was aware – still sauntered up and down in the stream of tourists and guests, loitered in front of the long awning of the café, and sought and found grown-up entertainment. And here they had come to blows, goodness knows how and why. It is possible that they had only brushed against each other in passing and in the sensitiveness of their knightly honour had made a fighting matter of the encounter. Johnny, who of course had been long since in bed too and was instructed only by hearsay in what happened, expressed himself in his pleasant, slightly husky childish voice, that the quarrel was probably about some "gal" – an easy assumption, considering Jappe's and Do Escobar's precocity and boldness. In short, they had made no scene among the guests, but in few and biting words agreed upon hour and place and witnesses for the satisfaction of their honour. The next day, at twelve, rendezvous at such and such a spot on the Leuchtenfeld. Good evening. – Ballet-master Knaak from Hamburg, master of ceremonies and leader of the Kurhaus cotillions, had been on the scene and promised his presence at the appointed hour and place.

Johnny rejoiced wholeheartedly in the fray – I think that neither he nor Brattström would have shared my apprehensions. Johnny repeatedly assured me, forming the *r* far forward on his palate, with his pretty enunciation, that they were both "in dead eahnest" and certainly meant business. Complacently and with a rather ironic objectivity he weighed the chances of victory for each. They were both frightfully strong, he grinned; both of them great fighters – it would be fun to have it settled which of them was the greater. Jappe, Johnny thought, had a broad chest and capital arm and leg muscles, he could tell that from seeing him swimming. But Do Escobar was uncommonly wiry and savage – hard to tell beforehand who would get the upper hand. It was strange to hear Johnny discourse so sovereignly upon Jappe's and Do Escobar's qualifications, looking at his childish arms, which could never have given or warded off a blow. As for me, I was indeed far from absenting myself from the spectacle. That would have been absurd and moreover the proceedings had a great fascination for me. Of course I must go, I must see it all, now that I knew about it. I felt a certain sense of duty, along with other and conflicting emotions: a great shyness and shame, all unwarlike as I was, and not at all minded to trust myself upon the scene of manly exploits. I had a nervous dread of the shock which the sight of a duel *à outrance*, a fight for life and death, as it were, would give me. I was cowardly enough to ask myself whether, once on the field, I might not be caught up in the struggle and have to expose my own person to a proof of valour which I knew in my inmost heart I was far from being able or willing to give. On the other hand I kept putting myself in Jappe's and Do Escobar's place and feeling consuming sensations which I assumed to be what they were feeling. I visualized the scene of the insult and the challenge, summoned my sense of good form and with Jappe and Do Escobar resisted the impulse to fall to there and then. I experienced the agony of an overwrought passion for justice, the flaring, shattering hatred, the attacks of raving impatience for revenge, in which they must have passed the night. Arrived at the last ditch, lost to all sense of fear, I fought myself blind and bloody with an adversary just as inhuman, drove my fist into his hated jaw with all the strength of my being, so that all his teeth were broken, received in exchange a brutal kick in the stomach and went under in a sea of blood. After which I woke in my bed with ice-bags, quieted nerves, and a chorus of mild reproaches from my family. In short, when it was half past twelve and we got up to dress I was half worn out with my apprehensions. In the cabin and afterwards when we were dressed and went outdoors, my heart throbbed exactly as though it was I myself who was to fight with Jappe or Do Escobar, in public and with all the rigours of the game.

I still remember how we took the narrow wooden bridge which ran diagonally up from the beach to the cabins. Of course we jumped, in order to make it sway as much as possible, so that we bounced as though on a spring-board. But once below we did not follow the board walk which led along the beach past the tents and the basket chairs; but held inland in the general direction of the Kurhaus but rather more leftwards. The sun brooded over the dunes and sucked a dry, hot odour from the sparse and withered vegetation, the reeds and thistles that stuck into our legs. There was no sound but the ceaseless humming of the blue-bottle flies which hung apparently motionless in the heavy warmth, suddenly to shift to another spot and begin afresh their sharp, monotonous whine. The cooling effect of the bath was long since spent. Brattström and I kept lifting our hats, he his Swedish sailor cap with the oilcloth visor, I my round Heligoland woollen bonnet – the so-called tam-o'-shanter – to wipe our brows. Johnny suffered little from heat, thanks to his slightness and also because his clothing was more elegantly adapted than ours to the summer day. In his light and comfortable sailor suit of striped washing material which left bare his throat and legs, the blue, short-ribboned cap with English lettering on his pretty little head, the long slender feet in fine, almost heelless white leather shoes, he walked with mounting strides and somewhat bent knees between Brattström and me and sang with his charming accent "Little Fisher Maiden" – a ditty which was then the rage. He sang it with some vulgar variation in the words, such as boys like to invent. Curiously enough, in all his childishness he knew a good deal about various matters and was not at all too prudish to take them in his mouth. But always he would make a sanctimonious little face and say: "Fie! Who would sing such dirty songs?" – as though Brattström and I had been the ones to make indecent advances to the little fisher maiden.

I did not feel at all like singing, we were too near the fatal spot. The prickly grass of the dunes had changed to the sand and sea moss of a barren meadow; this was the Leuchtenfeld, so called after the yellow lighthouse towering up in the far distance. We soon found ourselves at our goal.

It was a warm, peaceful spot, where almost nobody ever came: protected from view by scrubby willow trees. On the free space among the bushes a crowd of youths lay or sat in a circle. They were almost all older than we and from various strata of society. We seemed to be the last spectators to arrive. Everybody was waiting for Knaak the dancing-master, who was needed in the capacity of neutral and umpire. Both Jappe and Do Escobar were there – I saw them at once. They were sitting far apart in the circle and pretending not to see each other. We greeted a few acquaintances with silent nods and squatted in our turn on the sun-warmed ground.

Some of the group were smoking. Both Jappe and Do Escobar held cigarettes in the corners of their mouths. Each kept one eye shut against the smoke and I instantly felt and knew that they were aware how grand it was to sit there and smoke before entering the ring. They were both dressed in grown-up clothes, but Do Escobar's were more gentlemanly than Jappe's. He wore yellow shoes with pointed toes, a light-grey summer suit, a rose-coloured shirt with cuffs, a coloured silk cravat, and a round, narrow-brimmed straw hat sitting far back on his head, so that his mop of shiny black hair showed on one side beneath it, in a big hummock. He kept raising his right hand to shake back the silver bangle he wore under his cuff. Jappe's appearance was distinctly less pretentious. His legs were encased in tight trousers of a lighter colour than his coat and waistcoat and fastened with straps under his waxed black boots. A checked cap covered his curly blond hair; in contrast to Do Escobar's jaunty headgear he wore it pulled down over his forehead. He sat with his arms clasped round one knee; you could see that he had on loose cuffs over his shirt-sleeves, also that his finger-nails were either cut too short or else that he indulged in the vice of biting them. Despite the smoking and the assumed nonchalance, the whole circle was serious and silent, restraint was in the air. The only one to make head against it was Do Escobar, who talked without stopping to his neighbours, in a loud, strained voice, rolling his *r*'s and blowing smoke out of his nose.

I was rather put off by his volubility; it inclined me, despite the bitten finger-nails, to side with Jappe, who at most addressed a word or two over his shoulder to his neighbour and for the rest gazed in apparent composure at the smoke of his cigarette.

Then came Herr Knaak – I can still see him, in his blue striped flannel morning suit, coming with winged tread from the direction of the Kurhaus and lifting his hat as he paused outside the circle. That he wanted to come I do not believe; I am convinced rather that he had made a virtue of necessity when he honoured the fight with his presence. And the necessity, the compulsion, was due to his equivocal position in the eyes of martially- and masculinely-minded youth. Dark-skinned and comely, plump, particularly in the region of the hips, he gave us dancing and deportment lessons in the wintertime – private, family lessons as well as public classes in the Casino; and in the summer he acted as bathing-master and social manager at Travemünde. He rocked on his hips and weaved in his walk, turning out his toes very much and setting them first on the ground as he stepped. His eyes had a vain expression, his speech was pleasant but affected, and his way of entering a room as though it were a stage, his extraordinary and fastidious mannerisms charmed all the female sex, while the masculine world, and especially critical youth, viewed him with suspicion. I have often pondered over the position of François Knaak in life and always I have found it strange and fantastic. He was of humble origins, his parents were poor, and his taste for the social graces left him as it were hanging in the air – not a member of society, yet paid by it as a guardian and instructor of its conventions. Jappe and Do Escobar were his pupils too; not in private lessons, like Johnny, Brattström, and me, but in the public classes in the Casino. It was in these that Herr Knaak's character and position were most sharply criticized. We of the private classes were less austere. A fellow who taught you the proper deportment towards little girls, who was thrillingly reported to wear a corset, who picked up the edge of his frock-coat with his finger-tips, curtsied, cut capers, leaped suddenly into the air, where he twirled his toes before he came down again – what sort of chap was he, after all? These were the suspicions harboured by militant youth on the score of Herr Knaak's character and mode of life, and his exaggerated airs did nothing to allay them. Of course, he was a grown-up man (he was even, comically enough, said to have a wife and children in Hamburg); and his advantage in years and the fact that he was never seen except officially and in the dance-hall prevented him from being convicted and unmasked. Could he do gymnastics? Had he ever been able to? Had he courage? Had he parts? In short, could one accept him as an equal? He was never in a position to display the soldier characteristics which might have balanced his salon arts and made him a decent chap. So there were youths who made no bones of calling him straight out a coward and a jackanapes. All this he knew and therefore he was here today to manifest his interest in a good stand-up fight and to put himself on terms with the young, though in his official position he should not have countenanced such goings-on. I am convinced, however, that he was not comfortable – he knew he was treading on thin ice. Some of the audience looked coldly at him and he himself gazed uneasily round to see if anybody was coming.

He politely excused his late arrival, saying that he had been kept by a consultation with the management of the Kurhaus about the next Sunday's ball. "Are the combatants present?" he next inquired in official tones. "Then we can begin." Leaning on his stick with his feet crossed he gnawed his soft brown moustache with his under lip and made owl eyes to look like a connoisseur.

Jappe and Do Escobar stood up, threw away their cigarettes, and began to prepare for the fray. Do Escobar did it in a hurry, with impressive speed. He threw hat, coat, and waistcoat on the ground, unfastened tie, collar, and braces and added them to the pile. He even drew his rose-coloured shirt out of his trousers, pulled his arms briskly out of the sleeves, and stood up in a red and white striped undershirt which exposed the larger part of his yellow arms, already covered with a thick black fell. "At your service, sir," he said, with a rolling *r*, stepping into the middle of the ring, expanding his chest and throwing back his shoulders. He still wore the silver bangle.

Jappe was not ready yet. He turned his head, elevated his brows, and looked at Do Escobar's feet a moment with narrowed eyes – as much as to say: "Wait a bit – I'll get there too, even if I don't swagger so much." He was broader in the shoulder; but as he took his place beside Do Escobar he seemed nowhere near so fit or athletic. His legs in the tight strapped boots inclined to be knock-kneed and his fit-out was not impressive – grey braces over a yellowed white shirt with loose buttoned sleeves. By contrast Do Escobar's striped tricot and the black hair on his arms looked uncommonly grim and businesslike. Both were pale but it showed more in Jappe as he was otherwise blond and red-cheeked, with jolly, not-too-refined features including a rather turned-up nose with a saddle of freckles. Do Escobar's nose was short, straight, and drooping and there was a downy black growth on his full upper lip.

They stood with hanging arms almost breast to breast, and looked at one another darkly and haughtily in the region of the stomach. They obviously did not know how to begin – and how well I could understand that! A night and half a day had intervened since the unpleasantness. They had wanted to fly at each other's throats and had only been held in check by the rules of the game. But they had had time to cool off. To do to order, as it were, before an audience, by appointment, in cold blood, what they had wanted to do yesterday when the fit was on them – it was not the same thing at all. After all, they were not gladiators. They were civilized young men. And in possession of one's senses one has a certain reluctance to smash a sound human body with one's fists. So I thought, and so, very likely, it was.

But something had to be done, that honour might be satisfied, so each began to work the other up by hitting him contemptuously with the finger-tips on the breast, as though that would be enough to finish him off. And, indeed, Jappe's face began to be distorted with anger – but just at that moment Do Escobar broke off the skirmish.

"Pardon," said he, taking two steps backwards and turning aside. He had to tighten the buckle at the back of his trousers, for he was narrow-hipped and in the absence of braces they had begun to slip. He took his position again almost at once, throwing out his chest and saying something in guttural and rattling Spanish, probably to the effect that he was again at Jappe's service. It was clear that he was inordinately vain.

The skirmishing with shoulders and buffeting with palms began again. Then unexpectedly there ensued a blind and raging hand-to-hand scuffle with the fists, which lasted three seconds and broke off without notice.

"Now they are warming up," said Johnny, sitting next to me with a dry grass in his mouth. "I'll wager Jappe beats him. Look how he keeps squinting over at us – Jappe keeps his mind on his job. Will you bet he won't give him a good hiding?"

They had now recoiled and stood, fists on hips, their chests heaving. Both had doubtless taken some punishment, for they both looked angry, sticking out their lips furiously as much as to say: "What do you mean by hurting me like that?" Jappe was red-eyed and Do Escobar showed his white teeth as they fell to again.

They were hitting out now with all their strength on shoulders, forearms, and breasts by turns and in quick succession. "That's nothing," Johnny said, with his charming accent. "They won't get anywhere that way, either of them. They must go at it under the chin, with an uppercut to the jaw. That does it." But meanwhile Do Escobar had caught both Jappe's arms with his left arm, pressed them as in a vice against his chest, and with his right went on pummelling Jappe's flanks.

There was great excitement. "No clinching!" several voices cried out, and people jumped up. Herr Knaak hastened between the combatants, in horror. "You are holding him fast, my dear friend. That is against all the rules." He separated them and again instructed Do Escobar in the regulations. Then he withdrew once more outside the ring.

Jappe was obviously in a fury. He was quite white, rubbing his side and looking at Do Escobar with a slow nod that boded no good. When the next round began, his face looked so grim that everybody expected him to deliver a decisive blow.

And actually as soon as contact had been renewed Jappe carried out a coup – he practised a feint which he had probably planned beforehand. A thrust with his left caused Do Escobar to protect his head; but as he did so Jappe's right hit him so hard in the stomach that he crumpled forwards and his face took on the colour of yellow wax.

"That went home," said Johnny. "That's where it hurts. Maybe now he will pull himself together and take things seriously, so as to pay it back." But the blow to the stomach had been too telling, Do Escobar's nerve was visibly shaken. It was clear he could not even clench his fists properly, and his eyes took on a glazed look. However, finding his muscles thus affected, his vanity counselled him to play the agile southron, dancing round the German bear and rendering him desperate by his own dexterity. He took tiny steps and made all sorts of useless passes, moving round Jappe in little circles and trying to assume an arrogant smile – which in his reduced condition struck me as really heroic. But it did not upset Jappe at all – he simply turned round on his heel and got in many a good blow with his right while with his left he warded off Do Escobar's feeble attack. But what sealed Do Escobar's fate was that his trousers kept slipping. His tricot shirt even came outside and rucked up, showing a little strip of his bare yellow skin – some of the audience sniggered. But why had he taken off his braces? He would have done better to leave æsthetic considerations on one side. For now his trousers bothered him, they had bothered him during the whole fight. He kept wanting to pull them up and stuff in his shirt, for however much he was punished he could bear it better than the thought that he might be cutting a ridiculous figure. In the end he was fighting with one hand while with the other he tried to put himself to rights; and thus Jappe was able to land such a blow on his nose that to this day I do not understand why it was not broken.

But the blood poured out, and Do Escobar turned and went apart from Jappe, trying with his right hand to stop the bleeding and with his left making an eloquent gesture behind him as he went. Jappe stood there with his knock-kneed legs spread out and waited for Do Escobar to come back. But Do Escobar was finished with the business. If I interpret him aright he was the more civilized of the two and felt that it was high time to call a halt. Jappe would beyond doubt have fought on with his nose bleeding; but almost as certainly Do Escobar would equally have refused to go on, and he did so with even more conviction in that it was himself that bled. They had made the claret run out of his nose – in his view things should never have been allowed to go so far, devil take it! The blood ran between his fingers on to his clothes, it soiled his light trousers and dripped on his yellow shoes. It was beastly and nothing but beastly – and under such circumstances he declined to take part in more fighting. It would be inhuman.

And his attitude was accepted by the majority of the spectators. Herr Knaak came into the ring and declared that the fight was over. Both sides had behaved with distinction. You could see how relieved he felt that the affair had gone off so smoothly.

"But neither of them was brought to a fall," said Johnny, surprised and disappointed. However, even Jappe was quite satisfied to consider the affair as settled. Drawing a long breath he went to fetch his clothes. Everybody generally accepted Herr Knaak's delicate fiction that the issue was a draw. Jappe was congratulated, but only surreptitiously; on the other hand some people lent Do Escobar their handkerchiefs, as his own was soon drenched. And now the cry was for more. Let two other fellows fight. That was the sense of the meeting; Jappe's and Do Escobar's business had taken so little time, hardly ten minutes; since they were all there and it was still quite early something more ought to come. Another pair must enter the arena – whoever wanted to show that he deserved being called a lad of parts.

Nobody offered. But why at this summons did my heart begin to beat like a little drum? What I had feared had come to pass: the challenge had become general. Why did I feel as though I had all the time been awaiting this very moment with shivers of delicious anticipation and now when it had come why was I plunged into a whirl of conflicting emotions? I looked at Johnny. Perfectly calm and detached he sat beside me, turned his straw about in his mouth and looked about the ring with a frankly curious air, to see whether a couple of stout chaps would not be found to let their noses be broken for his amusement. Why was it that I had to feel personally challenged to conquer my nervous timidity, to make an unnatural effort and draw all eyes upon myself by heroically stepping into the ring? In an access of self-consciousness mingled with vanity I was about to raise my hand and offer myself for combat when somewhere in the circle the shout arose:

"Herr Knaak ought to fight!"

All eyes fastened themselves upon Herr Knaak. I have said that he was walking upon slippery ice in exposing himself to the danger of such a test of his kidney. But he simply answered:

"No, thanks very much – I had enough beatings when I was young."

He was safe. He had slipped like an eel out of the trap. How astute of him, to bring in his superiority in years, to imply that at our age he would not have avoided an honourable fight – and that without boasting at all, even making his words carry irresistible conviction by admitting with a disarming laugh at himself that he too had taken beatings in his time. They let him alone. They perceived that it was hard, if not impossible, to bring him to book.

"Then somebody must wrestle!" was the next cry. This suggestion was not taken up either; but in the midst of the discussion over it (and I shall never forget the painful impression it made) Do Escobar said in his hoarse Spanish voice from behind his gory handkerchief: "Wrestling is for cowards. Only Germans wrestle." It was an unheard-of piece of tactlessness, coming from him, and got its reward at once in the capital retort made by Herr Knaak: "Possibly," said he. "But it looks as though the Germans know how to give pretty good beatings sometimes too!" He was rewarded by shouts of approving laughter; his whole position was improved, and Do Escobar definitely put down for the day.

But it was the general opinion that wrestling was a good deal of a bore, and so various athletic feats were resorted to instead: leap-frog, standing on one's head, handsprings and so on, to fill in the time.

"Come on, let's go," said Johnny to Brattström and me, and got up. That was Johnny Bishop for you. He had come to see something real, with the possibility of a bloody issue. But the thing had petered out and so he left.

He gave me my first impression of the peculiar superiority of the English character, which later on I came so greatly to admire.

DEATH IN VENICE

GUSTAVE ASCHENBACH – or von Aschenbach, as he had been known officially since his fiftieth birthday – had set out alone from his house in Prince Regent Street, Munich, for an extended walk. It was a spring afternoon in that year of grace 19–, when Europe sat upon the anxious seat beneath a menace that hung over its head for months. Aschenbach had sought the open soon after tea. He was overwrought by a morning of hard, nerve-taxing work, work which had not ceased to exact his uttermost in the way of sustained concentration, conscientiousness, and tact; and after the noon meal found himself powerless to check the onward sweep of the productive mechanism within him, that *motus animi continuus* in which, according to Cicero, eloquence resides. He had sought but not found relaxation in sleep – though the wear and tear upon his system had come to make a daily nap more and more imperative – and now undertook a walk, in the hope that air and exercise might send him back refreshed to a good evening's work.

May had begun, and after weeks of cold and wet a mock summer had set in. The English Gardens, though in tenderest leaf, felt as sultry as in August and were full of vehicles and pedestrians near the city. But towards Aumeister the paths were solitary and still, and Aschenbach strolled thither, stopping awhile to watch the lively crowds in the restaurant garden with its fringe of carriages and cabs. Thence he took his homeward way outside the park and across the sunset fields. By the time he reached the North Cemetery, however, he felt tired, and a storm was brewing above Föhring; so he waited at the stopping-place for a tram to carry him back to the city.

He found the neighbourhood quite empty. Not a wagon in sight, either on the paved Ungererstrasse, with its gleaming tramlines stretching off towards Schwabing, nor on the Föhring highway. Nothing stirred behind the hedge in the stonemason's yard, where crosses, monuments, and commemorative tablets made a supernumerary and untenanted graveyard opposite the real one. The mortuary chapel, a structure in Byzantine style, stood facing it, silent in the gleam of the ebbing day. Its façade was adorned with Greek crosses and tinted hieratic designs, and displayed a symmetrically arranged selection of scriptural texts in gilded letters, all of them with a bearing upon the future life, such as: "They are entering into the House of the Lord" and "May the Light Everlasting shine upon them." Aschenbach beguiled some minutes of his waiting with reading these formulas and letting his mind's eye lose itself in their mystical meaning. He was brought back to reality by the sight of a man standing in the portico, above the two apocalyptic beasts that guarded the staircase, and something not quite usual in this man's appearance gave his thoughts a fresh turn.

Whether he had come out of the hall through the bronze doors or mounted unnoticed from outside, it was impossible to tell. Aschenbach casually inclined to the first idea. He was of medium height, thin, beardless, and strikingly snub-nosed; he belonged to the red-haired type and possessed its milky, freckled skin. He was obviously not Bavarian; and the broad, straight-brimmed straw hat he had on even made him look distinctly exotic. True, he had the indigenous rucksack buckled on his back, wore a belted suit of yellowish woollen stuff, apparently frieze, and carried a grey mackintosh cape across his left forearm, which was propped against his waist. In his right hand, slantwise to the ground, he held an iron-shod stick, and braced himself against its crook, with his legs crossed. His chin was up, so that the Adam's apple looked very bald in the lean neck rising from the loose shirt; and he stood there sharply peering up into space out of colourless, red-lashed eyes, while two pronounced perpendicular furrows showed on his forehead in curious contrast to his little turned-up nose. Perhaps his heightened and heightening position helped out the impression Aschenbach received. At any rate, standing there as though at survey, the man had a bold and domineering, even a ruthless, air, and his lips completed the picture by seeming to curl back, either by reason of some deformity or else because he grimaced, being blinded by the sun in his face; they laid bare the long, white, glistening teeth to the gums.

Aschenbach's gaze, though unawares, had very likely been inquisitive and tactless; for he became suddenly conscious that the stranger was returning it, and indeed so directly, with such hostility, such plain intent to force the withdrawal of the other's eyes, that Aschenbach felt an unpleasant twinge and, turning his back, began to walk along the hedge, hastily resolving to give the man no further heed. He had forgotten him the next minute. Yet whether the pilgrim air the stranger wore kindled his fantasy or whether some other physical or psychical influence came in play, he could not tell; but he felt the most surprising consciousness of a widening of inward barriers, a kind of vaulting unrest, a youthfully ardent thirst for distant scenes – a feeling so lively and so new, or at least so long ago outgrown and forgot, that he stood there rooted to the spot, his eyes on the ground and his hands clasped behind him, exploring these sentiments of his, their bearing and scope.

True, what he felt was no more than a longing to travel; yet coming upon him with such suddenness and passion as to resemble a seizure, almost an hallucination. Desire projected itself visually: his fancy, not quite yet lulled since morning, imaged the marvels and terrors of the manifold earth. He saw. He beheld a landscape, a tropical marshland, beneath a reeking sky, steaming, monstrous, rank – a kind of primeval wilderness-world of islands, morasses, and alluvial channels. Hairy palm-trunks rose near and far out of lush brakes of fern, out of bottoms of crass vegetation, fat, swollen, thick with incredible bloom. There were trees, mis-shapen as a dream, that dropped their naked roots straight through the air into the ground or into water that was stagnant and shadowy and glassy-green, where mammoth milk-white blossoms floated, and strange high-shouldered birds with curious bills stood gazing sidewise without sound or stir. Among the knotted joints of a bamboo thicket the eyes of a crouching tiger gleamed – and he felt his heart throb with terror, yet with a longing inexplicable. Then the vision vanished. Aschenbach, shaking his head, took up his march once more along the hedge of the stonemason's yard.

He had, at least ever since he commanded means to get about the world at will, regarded travel as a necessary evil, to be endured now and again willy-nilly for the sake of one's health. Too busy with the tasks imposed upon him by his own ego and the European soul, too laden with the care and duty to create, too preoccupied to be an amateur of the gay outer world, he had been content to know as much of the earth's surface as he could without stirring far outside his own sphere – had, indeed, never even been tempted to leave Europe. Now more than ever, since his life was on the wane, since he could no longer brush aside as fanciful his artist fear of not having done, of not being finished before the works ran down, he had confined himself to close range, had hardly stepped outside the charming city which he had made his home and the rude country house he had built in the mountains, whither he went to spend the rainy summers.

And so the new impulse which thus late and suddenly swept over him was speedily made to conform to the pattern of self-discipline he had followed from his youth up. He had meant to bring his work, for which he lived, to a certain point before leaving for the country, and the thought of a leisurely ramble across the globe, which should take him away from his desk for months, was too fantastic and upsetting to be seriously entertained. Yet the source of the unexpected contagion was known to him only too well. This yearning for new and distant scenes, this craving for freedom, release, forgetfulness – they were, he admitted to himself, an impulse towards flight, flight from the spot which was the daily theatre of a rigid, cold, and passionate service. That service he loved, had even almost come to love the enervating daily struggle between a proud, tenacious, well-tried will and this growing fatigue, which no one must suspect, nor the finished product betray by any faintest sign that his inspiration could ever flag or miss fire. On the other hand, it seemed the part of common sense not to span the bow too far, not to suppress summarily a need that so unequivocally asserted itself. He thought of his work, and the place where yesterday and again today he had been forced to lay it down, since it would not yield either to patient effort or a swift *coup de main*. Again and again he had tried to break or untie the knot – only to retire at last from the attack with a shiver of repugnance. Yet the difficulty was actually not a great one; what sapped his strength was distaste for the task, betrayed by a fastidiousness he could no longer satisfy. In his youth, indeed, the nature and inmost essence of the literary gift had been, to him, this very scrupulosity; for it he had bridled and tempered his sensibilities, knowing full well that feeling is prone to be content with easy gains and blithe half-perfection. So now, perhaps, feeling, thus tyrannized, avenged itself by leaving him, refusing from now on to carry and wing his art and taking away with it all the ecstasy he had known in form and expression. Not that he was doing bad work. So much, at least, the years had brought him, that at any moment he might feel tranquilly assured of mastery. But he got no joy of it – not though a nation paid it homage. To him it seemed his work had ceased to be marked by that fiery play of fancy which is the product of joy, and more, and more potently, than any intrinsic content, forms in turn the joy of the receiving world. He dreaded the summer in the country, alone with the maid who prepared his food and the man who served him; dreaded to see the familiar mountain peaks and walls that would shut him up again with his heavy discontent. What he needed was a break, an interim existence, a means of passing time, other air and a new stock of blood, to make the summer tolerable and productive. Good, then, he would go a journey. Not far – not all the way to the tigers. A night in a *wagon-lit*, three or four weeks of lotus-eating at some one of the gay world's playgrounds in the lovely south. . . .

So ran his thoughts, while the clang of the electric tram drew nearer down the Ungererstrasse; and as he mounted the platform he decided to devote the evening to a study of maps and railway guides. Once in, he bethought him to look back after the man in the straw hat, the companion of this brief interval which had after all been so fruitful. But he was not in his former place, nor in the tram itself, nor yet at the next stop; in short, his whereabouts remained a mystery.

Gustave Aschenbach was born at L–, a country town in the province of Silesia. He was the son of an upper official in the judicature, and his forebears had all been officers, judges, departmental functionaries – men who lived their strict, decent, sparing lives in the service of king and state. Only once before had a livelier mentality – in the quality of a clergyman – turned up among them; but swifter, more perceptive blood had in the generation before the poet's flowed into the stock from the mother's side, she being the daughter of a Bohemian musical conductor. It was from her he had the foreign traits that betrayed themselves in his appearance. The union of dry, conscientious officialdom and ardent, obscure impulse, produced an artist – and this particular artist: author of the lucid and vigorous prose epic on the life of Frederick the Great; careful, tireless weaver of the richly patterned tapestry entitled *Maia*, a novel that gathers up the threads of many human destinies in the warp of a single idea; creator of that powerful narrative *The Abject*, which taught a whole grateful generation that a man can still be capable of moral resolution even after he has plumbed the depths of knowledge; and lastly – to complete the tale of works of his mature period – the writer of that impassioned discourse on the theme of Mind and Art whose ordered force and antithetic eloquence led serious critics to rank it with Schiller's *Simple and Sentimental Poetry*.

Aschenbach's whole soul, from the very beginning, was bent on fame – and thus, while not precisely precocious, yet thanks to the unmistakable trenchancy of his personal accent he was early ripe and ready for a career. Almost before he was out of high school he had a name. Ten years later he had learned to sit at his desk and sustain and live up to his growing reputation, to write gracious and pregnant phrases in letters that must needs be brief, for many claims press upon the solid and successful man. At forty, worn down by the strains and stresses of his actual task, he had to deal with a daily post heavy with tributes from his own and foreign countries.

Remote on one hand from the banal, on the other from the eccentric, his genius was calculated to win at once the adhesion of the general public and the admiration, both sympathetic and stimulating, of the connoisseur. From childhood up he was pushed on every side to achievement, and achievement of no ordinary kind; and so his young days never knew the sweet idleness and blithe *laissez aller* that belong to youth. A nice observer once said of him in company – it was at the time when he fell ill in Vienna in his thirty-fifth year: "You see, Aschenbach has always lived like this" – here the speaker closed the fingers of his left hand to a fist – "never like this" – and he let his open hand hang relaxed from the back of his chair. It was apt. And this attitude was the more morally valiant in that Aschenbach was not by nature robust – he was only called to the constant tension of his career, not actually born to it.

By medical advice he had been kept from school and educated at home. He had grown up solitary, without comradeship; yet had early been driven to see that he belonged to those whose talent is not so much out of the common as is the physical basis on which talent relies for its fulfilment. It is a seed that gives early of its fruit, whose powers seldom reach a ripe old age. But his favourite motto was "Hold fast"; indeed, in his novel on the life of Frederick the Great he envisaged nothing else than the apotheosis of the old hero's word of command, "*Durchhalten*", which seemed to him the epitome of fortitude under suffering. Besides, he deeply desired to live to a good old age, for it was his conviction that only the artist to whom it has been granted to be fruitful on all stages of our human scene can be truly great, or universal, or worthy of honour.

Bearing the burden of his genius, then, upon such slender shoulders and resolved to go so far, he had the more need of discipline – and discipline, fortunately, was his native inheritance from the father's side. At forty, at fifty, he was still living as he had commenced to live in the years when others are prone to waste and revel, dream high thoughts and postpone fulfilment. He began his day with a cold shower over chest and back; then, setting a pair of tall wax candles in silver holders at the head of his manuscript, he sacrificed to art, in two or three hours of almost religious fervour, the powers he had assembled in sleep. Outsiders might be pardoned for believing that his *Maia* world and the epic amplitude revealed by the life of Frederick were a manifestation of great power working under high pressure, that they came forth, as it were, all in one breath. It was the more triumph for his morale; for the truth was that they were heaped up to greatness in layer after layer, in long days of work, out of hundreds and hundreds of single inspirations; they owed their excellence, both of mass and detail, to one thing and one alone: that their creator could hold out for years under the strain of the same piece of work, with an endurance and a tenacity of purpose like that which had conquered his native province of Silesia, devoting to actual composition none but his best and freshest hours.

For an intellectual product of any value to exert an immediate influence which shall also be deep and lasting, it must rest on an inner harmony, yes, an affinity, between the personal destiny of its author and that of his contemporaries in general. Men do not know why they award fame to one work of art rather than another. Without being in the faintest connoisseurs, they think to justify the warmth of their commendations by discovering in it a hundred virtues, whereas the real ground of their applause is inexplicable – it is sympathy. Aschenbach had once given direct expression – though in an unobtrusive place – to the idea that almost everything conspicuously great is great in despite: has come into being in defiance of affliction and pain, poverty, destitution, bodily weakness, vice, passion, and a thousand other obstructions. And that was more than observation – it was the fruit of experience, it was precisely the formula of his life and fame, it was the key to his work. What wonder, then, if it was also the fixed character, the outward gesture, of his most individual figures?

The new type of hero favoured by Aschenbach, and recurring many times in his works, had early been analysed by a shrewd critic: "The conception of an intellectual and virginal manliness, which clenches its teeth and stands in modest defiance of the swords and spears that pierce its side." That was beautiful, it was *spirituel*, it was exact, despite the suggestion of too great passivity it held. Forbearance in the face of fate, beauty constant under torture, are not merely passive. They are a positive achievement, an explicit triumph; and the figure of Sebastian is the most beautiful symbol, if not of art as a whole, yet certainly of the art we speak of here. Within that world of Aschenbach's creation were exhibited many phases of this theme: there was the aristocratic self-command that is eaten out within and for as long as it can conceals its biologic decline from the eyes of the world; the sere and ugly outside, hiding the embers of smouldering fire – and having power to fan them to so pure a flame as to challenge supremacy in the domain of beauty itself; the pallid languors of the flesh, contrasted with the fiery ardours of the spirit within, which can fling a whole proud people down at the foot of the Cross, at the feet of its own sheer self-abnegation; the gracious bearing preserved in the stern, stark service of form; the unreal, precarious existence of the born intriguant with its swiftly enervating alternation of schemes and desires – all these human fates and many more of their like one read in Aschenbach's pages, and reading them might doubt the existence of any other kind of heroism than the heroism born of weakness. And, after all, what kind could be truer to the spirit of the times? Gustave Aschenbach was the poet-spokesman of all those who labour at the edge of exhaustion; of the over-burdened, of those who are already worn out but still hold themselves upright; of all our modern moralizers of accomplishment, with stunted growth and scanty resources, who yet contrive by skilful husbanding and prodigious spasms of will to produce, at least for a while, the effect of greatness. There are many such, they are the heroes of the age. And in Aschenbach's pages they saw themselves; he justified, he exalted them, he sang their praise – and they, they were grateful, they heralded his fame.

He had been young and crude with the times and by them badly counselled. He had taken false steps, blundered, exposed himself, offended in speech and writing against tact and good sense. But he had attained to honour, and honour, he used to say, is the natural goal towards which every considerable talent presses with whip and spur. Yes, one might put it that his whole career had been one conscious and overweening ascent to honour, which left in the rear all the misgivings or self-derogation which might have hampered him.

What pleases the public is lively and vivid delineation which makes no demands on the intellect; but passionate and absolutist youth can only be enthralled by a problem. And Aschenbach was as absolute, as problematist, as any youth of them all. He had done homage to intellect, had overworked the soil of knowledge and ground up her seed-corn; had turned his back on the "mysteries", called genius itself in question, held up art to scorn – yes, even while his faithful following revelled in the characters he created, he, the young artist, was taking away the breath of the twenty-year-olds with his cynic utterances on the nature of art and the artist life.

But it seems that a noble and active mind blunts itself against nothing so quickly as the sharp and bitter irritant of knowledge. And certain it is that the youth's constancy of purpose, no matter how painfully conscientious, was shallow beside the mature resolution of the master of his craft, who made a right-about-face, turned his back on the realm of knowledge, and passed it by with averted face, lest it lame his will or power of action, paralyse his feelings or his passions, deprive any of these of their conviction or utility. How else interpret the oft-cited story of *The Abject* than as a rebuke to the excesses of a psychology-ridden age, embodied in the delineation of the weak and silly fool who manages to lead fate by the nose; driving his wife, out of sheer innate pusillanimity, into the arms of a beardless youth, and making this disaster an excuse for trifling away the rest of his life?

With rage the author here rejects the rejected, casts out the outcast – and the measure of his fury is the measure of his condemnation of all moral shilly-shallying. Explicitly he renounces sympathy with the abyss, explicitly he refutes the flabby humanitarianism of the phrase: "*Tout comprendre c'est tout pardonner.*" What was here unfolding, or rather was already in full bloom, was the "miracle of regained detachment", which a little later became the theme of one of the author's dialogues, dwelt upon not without a certain oracular emphasis. Strange sequence of thought! Was it perhaps an intellectual consequence of this rebirth, this new austerity, that from now on his style showed an almost exaggerated sense of beauty, a lofty purity, symmetry, and simplicity, which gave his productions a stamp of the classic, of conscious and deliberate mastery? And yet: this moral fibre, surviving the hampering and disintegrating effect of knowledge, does it not result in its turn in a dangerous simplification, in a tendency to equate the world and the human soul, and thus to strengthen the hold of the evil, the forbidden, and the ethically impossible? And has not form two aspects? Is it not moral and immoral at once: moral in so far as it is the expression and result of discipline; immoral – yes, actually hostile to morality – in that of its very essence it is indifferent to good and evil, and deliberately concerned to make the moral world stoop beneath its proud and undivided sceptre?

Be that as it may. Development is destiny; and why should a career attended by the applause and adulation of the masses necessarily take the same course as one which does not share the glamour and the obligations of fame? Only the incorrigible bohemian smiles or scoffs when a man of transcendent gifts outgrows his carefree prentice stage, recognizes his own worth and forces the world to recognize it too and pay it homage, though he puts on a courtly bearing to hide his bitter struggles and his loneliness. Again, the play of a developing talent must give its possessor joy, if of a wilful, defiant kind. With time, an official note, something almost expository, crept into Gustave Aschenbach's method. His later style gave up the old sheer audacities, the fresh and subtle nuances – it became fixed and exemplary, conservative, formal, even formulated. Like Louis XIV – or as tradition has it of him – Aschenbach, as he went on in years, banished from his style every common word. It was at this time that the school authorities adopted selections from his works into their textbooks. And he found it only fitting – and had no thought but to accept – when a German prince signalized his accession to the throne by conferring upon the poet-author of the life of Frederick the Great on his fiftieth birthday the letters-patent of nobility.

He had roved about for a few years, trying this place and that as a place of residence, before choosing, as he soon did, the city of Munich for his permanent home. And there he lived, enjoying among his fellow-citizens the honour which is in rare cases the reward of intellectual eminence. He married young, the daughter of a university family; but after a brief term of wedded happiness his wife had died. A daughter, already married, remained to him. A son he never had.

Gustave von Aschenbach was somewhat below middle height, dark and smooth-shaven, with a head that looked rather too large for his almost delicate figure. He wore his hair brushed back; it was thin at the parting, bushy and grey on the temples, framing a lofty, rugged, knotty brow – if one may so characterize it. The nose-piece of his rimless gold spectacles cut into the base of his thick, aristocratically hooked nose. The mouth was large, often lax, often suddenly narrow and tense; the cheeks lean and furrowed, the pronounced chin slightly cleft. The vicissitudes of fate, it seemed, must have passed over this head, for he held it, plaintively, rather on one side; yet it was art, not the stern discipline of an active career, that had taken over the office of modelling these features. Behind this brow were born the flashing thrust and parry of the dialogue between Frederick and Voltaire on the theme of war; these eyes, weary and sunken, gazing through their glasses, had beheld the blood-stained inferno of the hospitals in the Seven Years' War. Yes, personally speaking too, art heightens life. She gives deeper joy, she consumes more swiftly. She engraves adventures of the spirit and the mind in the faces of her votaries; let them lead outwardly a life of the most cloistered calm, she will in the end produce in them a fastidiousness, an over-refinement, a nervous fever and exhaustion, such as a career of extravagant passions and pleasures can hardly show.

Eager though he was to be off, Aschenbach was kept in Munich by affairs both literary and practical for some two weeks after that walk of his. But at length he ordered his country home put ready against his return within the next few weeks, and on a day between the middle and the end of May took the evening train for Trieste, where he stopped only twenty-four hours, embarking for Pola the next morning but one.

What he sought was a fresh scene, without associations, which should yet be not too out-of-the-way; and accordingly he chose an island in the Adriatic, not far off the Istrian coast. It had been well known some years, for its splendidly rugged cliff formations on the side next the open sea, and its population, clad in a bright flutter of rags and speaking an outlandish tongue. But there was rain and heavy air; the society at the hotel was provincial Austrian, and limited; besides, it annoyed him not to be able to get at the sea – he missed the close and soothing contact which only a gentle sandy slope affords. He could not feel this was the place he sought; an inner impulse made him wretched, urging him on he knew not whither; he racked his brains, he looked up boats, then all at once his goal stood plain before his eyes. But of course! When one wanted to arrive overnight at the incomparable, the fabulous, the like-nothing-else-in-the-world, where was it one went? Why, obviously; he had intended to go there, whatever was he doing here? A blunder. He made all haste to correct it, announcing his departure at once. Ten days after his arrival on the island a swift motor-boat bore him and his luggage in the misty dawning back across the water to the naval station, where he landed only to pass over the landing-stage and on to the wet decks of a ship lying there with steam up for the passage to Venice.

It was an ancient hulk belonging to an Italian line, obsolete, dingy, grimed with soot. A dirty hunchbacked sailor, smirkingly polite, conducted him at once belowships to a cavernous, lamplit cabin. There behind a table sat a man with a beard like a goat's; he had his hat on the back of his head, a cigar-stump in the corner of his mouth; he reminded Aschenbach of an old-fashioned circus-director. This person put the usual questions and wrote out a ticket to Venice, which he issued to the traveller with many commercial flourishes.

"A ticket for Venice," repeated he, stretching out his arm to dip the pen into the thick ink in a tilted ink-stand. "One first-class to Venice! Here you are, *signore mio*." He made some scrawls on the paper, strewed bluish sand on it out of a box, thereafter letting the sand run off into an earthen vessel, folded the paper with bony yellow fingers, and wrote on the outside. "An excellent choice," he rattled on. "Ah, Venice! What a glorious city! Irresistibly attractive to the cultured man for her past history as well as her present charm." His copious gesturings and empty phrases gave the odd impression that he feared the traveller might alter his mind. He changed Aschenbach's note, laying the money on the spotted table-cover with the glibness of a croupier. "A pleasant visit to you, signore," he said, with a melodramatic bow. "Delighted to serve you." Then he beckoned and called out: "Next" as though a stream of passengers stood waiting to be served, though in point of fact there was not one. Aschenbach returned to the upper deck.

He leaned an arm on the railing and looked at the idlers lounging along the quay to watch the boat go out. Then he turned his attention to his fellow-passengers. Those of the second class, both men and women, were squatted on their bundles of luggage on the forward deck. The first cabin consisted of a group of lively youths, clerks from Pola, evidently, who had made up a pleasure excursion to Italy and were not a little thrilled at the prospect, bustling about and laughing with satisfaction at the stir they made. They leaned over the railings and shouted, with a glib command of epithet, derisory remarks at such of their fellow-clerks as they saw going to business along the quay; and these in turn shook their sticks and shouted as good back again. One of the party, in a dandified buff suit, a rakish panama with a coloured scarf, and a red cravat, was loudest of the loud: he outcrowed all the rest. Aschenbach's eye dwelt on him, and he was shocked to see that the apparent youth was no youth at all. He was an old man, beyond a doubt, with wrinkles and crow's-feet round eyes and mouth; the dull carmine of the cheeks was rouge, the brown hair a wig. His neck was shrunken and sinewy, his turned-up moustaches and small imperial were dyed, and the unbroken double row of yellow teeth he showed when he laughed were but too obviously a cheapish false set. He wore a seal ring on each forefinger, but the hands were those of an old man. Aschenbach was moved to shudder as he watched the creature and his association with the rest of the group. Could they not see he was old, that he had no right to wear the clothes they wore or pretend to be one of them? But they were used to him, it seemed; they suffered him among them, they paid back his jokes in kind and the playful pokes in the ribs he gave them. How could they? Aschenbach put his hand to his brow, he covered his eyes, for he had slept little, and they smarted. He felt not quite canny, as though the world were suffering a dreamlike distortion of perspective which he might arrest by shutting it all out for a few minutes and then looking at it afresh. But instead he felt a floating sensation, and opened his eyes with unreasoning alarm to find that the ship's dark sluggish bulk was slowly leaving the jetty. Inch by inch, with the to-and-fro motion of her machinery, the strip of iridescent dirty water widened, the boat manoeuvred clumsily and turned her bow to the open sea. Aschenbach moved over to the starboard side, where the hunchbacked sailor had set up a deck-chair for him, and a steward in a greasy dress-coat asked for orders.

The sky was grey, the wind humid. Harbour and island dropped behind, all sight of land soon vanished in mist. Flakes of sodden, clammy soot fell upon the still undried deck. Before the boat was an hour out a canvas had to be spread as a shelter from the rain.

Wrapped in his cloak, a book in his lap, our traveller rested; the hours slipped by unawares. It stopped raining, the canvas was taken down. The horizon was visible right round: beneath the sombre dome of the sky stretched the vast plain of empty sea. But immeasurable unarticulated space weakens our power to measure time as well: the time-sense falters and grows dim. Strange, shadowy figures passed and repassed – the elderly coxcomb, the goat-bearded man from the bowels of the ship – with vague gesturings and mutterings through the traveller's mind as he lay. He fell asleep.

At mid-day he was summoned to luncheon in a corridor-like saloon with the sleeping-cabins giving off it. He ate at the head of the long table; the party of clerks, including the old man, sat with the jolly captain at the other end, where they had been carousing since ten o'clock. The meal was wretched, and soon done. Aschenbach was driven to seek the open and look at the sky – perhaps it would lighten presently above Venice.

He had not dreamed it could be otherwise, for the city had ever given him a brilliant welcome. But sky and sea remained leaden, with spurts of fine, mistlike rain; he reconciled himself to the idea of seeing a different Venice from that he had always approached on the landward side. He stood by the foremast, his gaze on the distance, alert for the first glimpse of the coast. And he thought of the melancholy and susceptible poet who had once seen the towers and turrets of his dreams rise out of these waves; repeated the rhythms born of his awe, his mingled emotions of joy and suffering – and easily susceptible to a prescience already shaped within him, he asked his own sober, weary heart if a new enthusiasm, a new preoccupation, some late adventure of the feelings could still be in store for the idle traveller.

The flat coast showed on the right, the sea was soon populous with fishing-boats. The Lido appeared and was left behind as the ship glided at half speed through the narrow harbour of the same name, coming to a full stop on the lagoon in sight of garish, badly built houses. Here it waited for the boat bringing the sanitary inspector.

An hour passed. One had arrived – and yet not. There was no conceivable haste – yet one felt harried. The youths from Pola were on deck, drawn hither by the martial sound of horns coming across the water from the direction of the Public Gardens. They had drunk a good deal of Asti and were moved to shout and hurrah at the drilling *bersaglieri*. But the young-old man was a truly repulsive sight in the condition to which his company with youth had brought him. He could not carry his wine like them: he was pitiably drunk. He swayed as he stood – watery-eyed, a cigarette between his shaking fingers, keeping upright with difficulty. He could not have taken a step without falling and knew better than to stir, but his spirits were deplorably high. He buttonholed anyone who came within reach, he stuttered, he giggled, he leered, he fatuously shook his beringed old forefinger; his tongue kept seeking the corner of his mouth in a suggestive motion ugly to behold. Aschenbach's brow darkened as he looked, and there came over him once more a dazed sense, as though things about him were just slightly losing their ordinary perspective, beginning to show a distortion that might merge into the grotesque. He was prevented from dwelling on the feeling, for now the machinery began to thud again, and the ship took up its passage through the Canale di San Marco which had been interrupted so near the goal.

He saw it once more, that landing-place that takes the breath away, that amazing group of incredible structures the Republic set up to meet the awe-struck eye of the approaching seafarer: the airy splendour of the palace and Bridge of Sighs, the columns of lion and saint on the shore, the glory of the projecting flank of the fairy temple, the vista of gateway and clock. Looking, he thought that to come to Venice by the station is like entering a palace by the back door. No one should approach, save by the high seas as he was doing now, this most improbable of cities.

The engines stopped. Gondolas pressed alongside, the landing-stairs were let down, customs officials came on board and did their office, people began to go ashore. Aschenbach ordered a gondola. He meant to take up his abode by the sea and needed to be conveyed with his luggage to the landing-stage of the little steamers that ply between the city and the Lido. They called down his order to the surface of the water where the gondoliers were quarrelling in dialect. Then came another delay while his trunk was worried down the ladderlike stairs. Thus he was forced to endure the importunities of the ghastly young-old man, whose drunken state obscurely urged him to pay the stranger the honour of a formal farewell. "We wish you a very pleasant sojourn," he babbled, bowing and scraping. "Pray keep us in mind. *Au revoir, excusez et bon jour, votre Excellence.*" He drooled, he blinked, he licked the corner of his mouth, the little imperial bristled on his elderly chin. He put the tips of two fingers to his mouth and said thickly: "Give her our love, will you, the p-pretty little dear" – here his upper plate came away and fell down on the lower one.... Aschenbach escaped. "Little sweety-sweety-sweetheart" he heard behind him, gurgled and stuttered, as he climbed down the rope stair into the boat.

Is there anyone but must repress a secret thrill, on arriving in Venice for the first time – or returning thither after long absence – and stepping into a Venetian gondola? That singular conveyance, come down unchanged from ballad times, black as nothing else on earth except a coffin – what pictures it calls up of lawless, silent adventures in the plashing night; or even more, what visions of death itself, the bier and solemn rites and last soundless voyage! And has anyone remarked that the seat in such a bark, the arm-chair lacquered in coffin-black and dully black-upholstered, is the softest, most luxurious, most relaxing seat in the world? Aschenbach realized it when he had let himself down at the gondolier's feet, opposite his luggage, which lay neatly composed on the vessel's beak. The rowers still gestured fiercely; he heard their harsh, incoherent tones. But the strange stillness of the water-city seemed to take up their voices gently, to disembody and scatter them over the sea. It was warm here in the harbour. The lukewarm air of the sirocco breathed upon him, he leaned back among his cushions and gave himself to the yielding element, closing his eyes for very pleasure in an indolence as unaccustomed as sweet. "The trip will be short," he thought, and wished it might last for ever. They gently swayed away from the boat with its bustle and clamour of voices.

It grew still and stiller all about. No sound but the splash of the oars, the hollow slap of the wave against the steep, black, halbert-shaped beak of the vessel, and one sound more – a muttering by fits and starts, expressed as it were by the motion of his arms, from the lips of the gondolier. He was talking to himself, between his teeth. Aschenbach glanced up and saw with surprise that the lagoon was widening, his vessel was headed for the open sea. Evidently it would not do to give himself up to sweet *far niente*; he must see his wishes carried out.

"You are to take me to the steamboat landing, you know,"

he said, half turning round towards it. The muttering stopped. There was no reply.

"Take me to the steamboat landing," he repeated, and this time turned quite round and looked up into the face of the gondolier as he stood there on his little elevated deck, high against the pale grey sky. The man had an unpleasing, even brutish face, and wore blue clothes like a sailor's, with a yellow sash; a shapeless straw hat with the braid torn at the brim perched rakishly on his head. His facial structure, as well as the curling blond moustache under the short snub nose, showed him to be of non-Italian stock. Physically rather under-sized, so that one would not have expected him to be very muscular, he pulled vigorously at the oar, putting all his body-weight behind each stroke. Now and then the effort he made curled back his lips and bared his white teeth to the gums. He spoke in a decided, almost curt voice, looking out to sea over his fare's head: "The signore is going to the Lido."

Aschenbach answered: "Yes, I am. But I only took the gondola to cross over to San Marco. I am using the *vaporetto* from there."

"But the signore cannot use the *vaporetto*."

"And why not?"

"Because the *vaporetto* does not take luggage."

It was true. Aschenbach remembered it. He made no answer. But the man's gruff, overbearing manner, so unlike the usual courtesy of his countrymen towards the stranger, was intolerable. Aschenbach spoke again: "That is my own affair. I may want to give my luggage in deposit. You will turn round."

No answer. The oar splashed, the wave struck dull against the prow. And the muttering began anew, the gondolier talked to himself, between his teeth.

What should the traveller do? Alone on the water with this tongue-tied, obstinate, uncanny man, he saw no way of enforcing his will. And if only he did not excite himself, how pleasantly he might rest! Had he not wished the voyage might last for ever? The wisest thing – and how much the pleasantest! – was to let matters take their own course. A spell of indolence was upon him; it came from the chair he sat in – this low, black-upholstered arm-chair, so gently rocked at the hands of the despotic boatman in his rear. The thought passed dreamily through Aschenbach's brain that perhaps he had fallen into the clutches of a criminal; it had not power to rouse him to action. More annoying was the simpler explanation: that the man was only trying to extort money. A sense of duty, a recollection, as it were, that this ought to be prevented, made him collect himself to say:

"How much do you ask for the trip?"

And the gondolier, gazing out over his head, replied: "The signore will pay."

There was an established reply to this; Aschenbach made it, mechanically:

"I will pay nothing whatever if you do not take me where I want to go."

"The signore wants to go to the Lido."

"But not with you."

"I am a good rower, signore. I will row you well."

"So much is true," thought Aschenbach, and again he relaxed. "That is true, you row me well. Even if you mean to rob me, even if you hit me in the back with your oar and send me down to the kingdom of Hades, even then you will have rowed me well."

But nothing of the sort happened. Instead, they fell in with company: a boat came alongside and waylaid them, full of men and women singing to guitar and mandolin. They rowed persistently bow for bow with the gondola and filled the silence that had rested on the waters with their lyric love of gain. Aschenbach tossed money into the hat they held out. The music stopped at once, they rowed away. And once more the gondolier's mutter became audible as he talked to himself in fits and snatches.

Thus they rowed on, rocked by the wash of a steamer returning citywards. At the landing two municipal officials were walking up and down with their hands behind their backs and their faces turned towards the lagoon. Aschenbach was helped on shore by the old man with a boat-hook who is the permanent feature of every landing-stage in Venice; and having no small change to pay the boatman, crossed over into the hotel opposite. His wants were supplied in the lobby; but when he came back his possessions were already on a hand-cart on the quay, and gondola and gondolier were gone.

"He ran away, signore," said the old boatman. "A bad lot, a man without a licence. He is the only gondolier without one. The others telephoned over, and he knew we were on the look-out, so he made off."

Aschenbach shrugged.

"The signore has had a ride for nothing," said the old man, and held out his hat. Aschenbach dropped some coins. He directed that his luggage be taken to the Hôtel des Bains and followed the hand-cart through the avenue, that white-blossoming avenue with taverns, booths, and pensions on either side it, which runs across the island diagonally to the beach.

He entered the hotel from the garden terrace at the back and passed through the vestibule and hall into the office. His arrival was expected, and he was served with courtesy and dispatch. The manager, a small, soft, dapper man with a black moustache and a caressing way with him, wearing a French frock-coat, himself took him up in the lift and showed him his room. It was a pleasant chamber, furnished in cherry-wood, with lofty windows looking out to sea. It was decorated with strong-scented flowers. Aschenbach, as soon as he was alone, and while they brought in his trunk and bags and disposed them in the room, went up to one of the windows and stood looking out upon the beach in its afternoon emptiness, and at the sunless sea, now full and sending long, low waves with rhythmic beat upon the sand.

A solitary, unused to speaking of what he sees and feels, has mental experiences which are at once more intense and less articulate than those of a gregarious man. They are sluggish, yet more wayward, and never without a melancholy tinge. Sights and impressions which others brush aside with a glance, a light comment, a smile, occupy him more than their due; they sink silently in, they take on meaning, they become experience, emotion, adventure. Solitude gives birth to the original in us, to beauty unfamiliar and perilous – to poetry. But also, it gives birth to the opposite: to the perverse, the illicit, the absurd. Thus the traveller's mind still dwelt with disquiet on the episodes of his journey hither: on the horrible old fop with his drivel about a mistress, on the outlaw boatman and his lost tip. They did not offend his reason, they hardly afforded food for thought; yet they seemed by their very nature fundamentally strange, and thereby vaguely disquieting. Yet here was the sea; even in the midst of such thoughts he saluted it with his eyes, exulting that Venice was near and accessible. At length he turned round, disposed his personal belongings and made certain arrangements with the chambermaid for his comfort, washed up, and was conveyed to the ground floor by the green-uniformed Swiss who ran the lift.

He took tea on the terrace facing the sea and afterwards went down and walked some distance along the shore promenade in the direction of Hôtel Excelsior. When he came back it seemed to be time to change for dinner. He did so, slowly and methodically as his way was, for he was accustomed to work while he dressed; but even so found himself a little early when he entered the hall, where a large number of guests had collected – strangers to each other and affecting mutual indifference, yet united in expectancy of the meal. He picked up a paper, sat down in a leather arm-chair, and took stock of the company, which compared most favourably with that he had just left.

This was a broad and tolerant atmosphere, of wide horizons. Subdued voices were speaking most of the principal European tongues. That uniform of civilization, the conventional evening dress, gave outward conformity to the varied types. There were long, dry Americans, large-familied Russians, English ladies, German children with French *bonnes*. The Slavic element predominated it seemed. In Aschenbach's neighbourhood Polish was being spoken.

Round a wicker table next him was gathered a group of young folk in charge of a governess or companion – three young girls, perhaps fifteen to seventeen years old, and a long-haired boy of about fourteen. Aschenbach noticed with astonishment the lad's perfect beauty. His face recalled the noblest moment of Greek sculpture – pale, with a sweet reserve, with clustering honey-coloured ringlets, the brow and nose descending in one line, the winning mouth, the expression of pure and godlike serenity. Yet with all this chaste perfection of form it was of such unique personal charm that the observer thought he had never seen, either in nature or art, anything so utterly happy and consummate. What struck him further was the strange contrast the group afforded, a difference in educational method, so to speak, shown in the way the brother and sisters were clothed and treated. The girls, the eldest of whom was practically grown up, were dressed with an almost disfiguring austerity. All three wore half-length slate-coloured frocks of cloister-like plainness, arbitrarily unbecoming in cut, with white turn-over collars as their only adornment. Every grace of outline was wilfully suppressed; their hair lay smoothly plastered to their heads, giving them a vacant expression, like a nun's. All this could only be by the mother's orders; but there was no trace of the same pedagogic severity in the case of the boy. Tenderness and softness, it was plain, conditioned his existence. No scissors had been put to the lovely hair that (like the Spinnario's) curled about his brows, above his ears, longer still in the neck. He wore an English sailor suit, with quilted sleeves that narrowed round the delicate wrists of his long and slender though still childish hands. And this suit, with its breast-knot, lacings, and embroideries, lent the slight figure something "rich and strange", a spoilt, exquisite air. The observer saw him in half profile, with one foot in its black patent leather advanced, one elbow resting on the arm of his basket-chair, the cheek nestled into the closed hand in a pose of easy grace, quite unlike the stiff subservient mien which was evidently habitual to his sisters. Was he delicate? His facial tint was ivory-white against the golden darkness of his clustering locks. Or was he simply a pampered darling, the object of a self-willed and partial love? Aschenbach inclined to think the latter. For in almost every artist's nature is inborn a wanton and treacherous proneness to side with the beauty that breaks hearts, to single out aristocratic pretensions and pay them homage.

A waiter announced, in English, that dinner was served. Gradually the company dispersed through the glass doors into the dining-room. Late-comers entered from the vestibule or the lifts. Inside, dinner was being served; but the young Poles still sat and waited about their wicker table. Aschenbach felt comfortable in his deep arm-chair, he enjoyed the beauty before his eyes, he waited with them.

The governess, a short, stout, red-faced person, at length gave the signal. With lifted brows she pushed back her chair and made a bow to the tall woman, dressed in palest grey, who now entered the hall. This lady's abundant jewels were pearls, her manner was cool and measured; the fashion of her gown and the arrangement of her lightly powdered hair had the simplicity prescribed in certain circles whose piety and aristocracy are equally marked. She might have been, in Germany, the wife of some high official. But there was something faintly fabulous, after all, in her appearance, though lent it solely by the pearls she wore: they were well-nigh priceless, and consisted of ear-rings and a three-stranded necklace, very long, with gems the size of cherries.

The brother and sisters had risen briskly. They bowed over their mother's hand to kiss it, she turning away from them, with a slight smile on her face, which was carefully preserved but rather sharp-nosed and worn. She addressed a few words in French to the governess, then moved towards the glass door. The children followed, the girls in order of age, then the governess, and last the boy. He chanced to turn before he crossed the threshold, and as there was no one else in the room, his strange, twilit grey eyes met Aschenbach's, as our traveller sat there with the paper on his knee, absorbed in looking after the group.

There was nothing singular, of course, in what he had seen. They had not gone in to dinner before their mother, they had waited, given her a respectful salute, and but observed the right and proper forms on entering the room. Yet they had done all this so expressly, with such self-respecting dignity, discipline, and sense of duty that Aschenbach was impressed. He lingered still a few minutes, then he, too, went into the dining-room, where he was shown a table far off the Polish family, as he noted at once, with a stirring of regret.

Tired, yet mentally alert, he beguiled the long, tedious meal with abstract, even with transcendent matters: pondered the mysterious harmony that must come to subsist between the individual human being and the universal law, in order that human beauty may result; passed on to general problems of form and art, and came at length to the conclusion that what seemed to him fresh and happy thoughts were like the flattering inventions of a dream, which the waking sense proves worthless and insubstantial. He spent the evening in the park, that was sweet with the odours of evening – sitting, smoking, wandering about; went to bed betimes, and passed the night in deep, unbroken sleep, visited, however, by varied and lively dreams.

The weather next day was no more promising. A land breeze blew. Beneath a colourless, overcast sky the sea lay sluggish, and as it were shrunken, so far withdrawn as to leave bare several rows of long sand-banks. The horizon looked close and prosaic. When Aschenbach opened his window he thought he smelt the stagnant odour of the lagoons.

He felt suddenly out of sorts and already began to think of leaving. Once, years before, after weeks of bright spring weather, this wind had found him out; it had been so bad as to force him to flee from the city like a fugitive. And now it seemed beginning again – the same feverish distaste, the pressure on his temples, the heavy eyelids. It would be a nuisance to change again; but if the wind did not turn, this was no place for him. To be on the safe side, he did not entirely unpack. At nine o'clock he went down to the buffet, which lay between the hall and the dining-room and served as a breakfast-room.

A solemn stillness reigned here, such as it is the ambition of all large hotels to achieve. The waiters moved on noiseless feet. A rattling of tea-things, a whispered word – and no other sounds. In a corner diagonally to the door, two tables off his own, Aschenbach saw the Polish girls with their governess. They sat there very straight, in their stiff blue linen frocks with little turn-over collars and cuffs, their ash-blond hair newly brushed flat, their eyelids red from sleep; and handed each other the marmalade. They had nearly finished their meal. The boy was not there.

Aschenbach smiled. "Aha, little Phæax," he thought. "It seems you are privileged to sleep yourself out." With sudden gaiety he quoted:

"*Oft veränderten Schmuck und warme Bäder und Ruhe.*"

He took a leisurely breakfast. The porter came up with his braided cap in his hand, to deliver some letters that had been sent on. Aschenbach lighted a cigarette and opened a few letters and thus was still seated to witness the arrival of the sluggard.

He entered through the glass doors and passed diagonally across the room to his sisters at their table. He walked with extraordinary grace – the carriage of the body, the action of the knee, the way he set down his foot in its white shoe – it was all so light, it was at once dainty and proud, it wore an added charm in the childish shyness which made him twice turn his head as he crossed the room, made him give a quick glance and then drop his eyes. He took his seat, with a smile and a murmured word in his soft and blurry tongue; and Aschenbach, sitting so that he could see him in profile, was astonished anew, yes, startled, at the godlike beauty of the human being. The lad had on a light sailor suit of blue and white striped cotton, with a red silk breast-knot and a simple white standing collar round the neck – a not very elegant effect – yet above this collar the head was poised like a flower, in incomparable loveliness. It was the head of Eros, with the yellowish bloom of Parian marble, with fine serious brows, and dusky clustering ringlets standing out in soft plenteousness over temples and ears.

"Good, oh, very good indeed!" thought Aschenbach, assuming the patronizing air of the connoisseur to hide, as artists will, their ravishment over a masterpiece. "Yes," he went on to himself, "if it were not that sea and beach were waiting for me, I should sit here as long as you do." But he went out on that, passing through the hall, beneath the watchful eye of the functionaries, down the steps and directly across the board walk to the section of the beach reserved for the guests of the hotel. The bathing-master, a barefoot old man in linen trousers and sailor blouse, with a straw hat, showed him the cabin that had been rented for him, and Aschenbach had him set up table and chair on the sandy platform before it. Then he dragged the reclining-chair through the pale yellow sand, closer to the sea, sat down, and composed himself.

He delighted, as always, in the scene on the beach, the sight of sophisticated society giving itself over to a simple life at the edge of the element. The shallow grey sea was already gay with children wading, with swimmers, with figures in bright colours lying on the sand-banks with arms behind their heads. Some were rowing in little keelless boats painted red and blue, and laughing when they capsized. A long row of *capanne* ran down the beach, with platforms, where people sat as on verandas, and there was social life, with bustle and with indolent repose; visits were paid, amid much chatter, punctilious morning *toilettes* hob-nobbed with comfortable and privileged dishabille. On the hard wet sand close to the sea figures in white bath-robes or loose wrappings in garish colours strolled up and down. A mammoth sand-hill had been built up on Aschenbach's right, the work of children, who had stuck it full of tiny flags. Vendors of sea-shells, fruit, and cakes knelt beside their wares spread out on the sand. A row of cabins on the left stood obliquely to the others and to the sea, thus forming the boundary of the enclosure on this side; and on the little veranda in front of one of these a Russian family was encamped; bearded men with strong white teeth, ripe, indolent women, a Fräulein from the Baltic provinces, who sat at an easel painting the sea and tearing her hair in despair; two ugly but good-natured children and an old maidservant in a head-cloth, with the caressing, servile manner of the born dependant. There they sat together in grateful enjoyment of their blessings: constantly shouting at their romping children, who paid not the slightest heed; making jokes in broken Italian to the funny old man who sold them sweetmeats, kissing each other on the cheeks – no jot concerned that their domesticity was overlooked.

"I'll stop," thought Aschenbach. "Where could it be better than here?" With his hands clasped in his lap he let his eyes swim in the wideness of the sea, his gaze lose focus, blur, and grow vague in the misty immensity of space. His love of the ocean had profound sources: the hard-worked artist's longing for rest, his yearning to seek refuge from the thronging manifold shapes of his fancy in the bosom of the simple and vast; and another yearning, opposed to his art and perhaps for that very reason a lure, for the unorganized, the immeasurable, the eternal – in short, for nothingness. He whose preoccupation is with excellence longs fervently to find rest in perfection; and is not nothingness a form of perfection? As he sat there dreaming thus, deep, deep into the void, suddenly the margin line of the shore was cut by a human form. He gathered up his gaze and withdrew it from the illimitable, and lo, it was the lovely boy who crossed his vision coming from the left along the sand. He was barefoot, ready for wading, the slender legs uncovered above the knee, and moved slowly, yet with such a proud, light tread as to make it seem he had never worn shoes. He looked towards the diagonal row of cabins; and the sight of the Russian family, leading their lives there in joyous simplicity, distorted his features in a spasm of angry disgust. His brow darkened, his lips curled, one corner of the mouth was drawn down in a harsh line that marred the curve of the cheek, his frown was so heavy that the eyes seemed to sink in as they uttered beneath the black and vicious language of hate. He looked down, looked threateningly back once more; then giving it up with a violent and contemptuous shoulder-shrug, he left his enemies in the rear.

A feeling of delicacy, a qualm, almost like a sense of shame, made Aschenbach turn away as though he had not seen; he felt unwilling to take advantage of having been, by chance, privy to this passionate reaction. But he was in truth both moved and exhilarated – that is to say, he was delighted. This childish exhibition of fanaticism, directed against the good-naturedest simplicity in the world – it gave to the godlike and inexpressive the final human touch. The figure of the half-grown lad, a masterpiece from nature's own hand, had been significant enough when it gratified the eye alone; and now it evoked sympathy as well – the little episode had set it off, lent it a dignity in the onlooker's eyes that was beyond its years.

Aschenbach listened with still averted head to the boy's voice announcing his coming to his companions at the sand-heap. The voice was clear, though a little weak, but they answered, shouting his name – or his nick-name – again and again. Aschenbach was not without curiosity to learn it, but could make out nothing more exact than two musical syllables, something like Adgio – or, oftener still, Adjiu, with a long-drawn-out *u* at the end. He liked the melodious sound, and found it fitting; said it over to himself a few times and turned back with satisfaction to his papers.

Holding his travelling-pad on his knees, he took his fountain-pen and began to answer various items of his correspondence. But presently he felt it too great a pity to turn his back, and the eyes of his mind, for the sake of mere commonplace correspondence, to this scene which was, after all, the most rewarding one he knew. He put aside his papers and swung round to the sea; in no long time, beguiled by the voices of the children at play, he had turned his head and sat resting it against the chair-back, while he gave himself up to contemplating the activities of the exquisite Adgio.

His eye found him out at once, the red breast-knot was

unmistakable. With some nine or ten companions, boys and girls of his own age and younger, he was busy putting in place an old plank to serve as a bridge across the ditches between the sand-piles. He directed the work by shouting and motioning with his head, and they were all chattering in many tongues – French, Polish, and even some of the Balkan languages. But his was the name oftenest on their lips, he was plainly sought after, wooed, admired. One lad in particular, a Pole like himself, with a name that sounded something like Jaschiu, a sturdy lad with brilliantined black hair, in a belted linen suit, was his particular liegeman and friend. Operations at the sand-pile being ended for the time, the two walked away along the beach, with their arms round each other's waists, and once the lad Jaschiu gave Adgio a kiss.

Aschenbach felt like shaking a finger at him. "But you, Critobulus," he thought with a smile, "you I advise to take a year's leave. That long, at least, you will need for complete recovery." A vendor came by with strawberries, and Aschenbach made his second breakfast of the great luscious, dead-ripe fruit. It had grown very warm, although the sun had not availed to pierce the heavy layer of mist. His mind felt relaxed, his senses revelled in this vast and soothing communion with the silence of the sea. The grave and serious man found sufficient occupation in speculating what name it could be that sounded like Adgio. And with the help of a few Polish memories he at length fixed on Tadzio, a shortened form of Thaddeus, which sounded, when called, like Tadziu or Adziu.

Tadzio was bathing. Aschenbach had lost sight of him for a moment, then descried him far out in the water, which was shallow a very long way – saw his head, and his arm striking out like an oar. But his watchful family were already on the alert; the mother and governess called from the veranda in front of their bathing-cabin, until the lad's name, with its softened consonants and long-drawn *u*-sound, seemed to possess the beach like a rallying-cry; the cadence had something sweet and wild: "Tadziu! Tadziu!" He turned and ran back against the water, churning the waves to a foam, his head flung high. The sight of this living figure, virginally pure and austere, with dripping locks, beautiful as a tender young god, emerging from the depths of sea and sky, outrunning the element – it conjured up mythologies, it was like a primeval legend, handed down from the beginning of time, of the birth of form, of the origin of the gods. With closed lids Aschenbach listened to this poesy hymning itself silently within him, and anon he thought it was good to be here and that he would stop awhile.

Afterwards Tadzio lay on the sand and rested from his bathe, wrapped in his white sheet, which he wore drawn underneath the right shoulder, so that his head was cradled on his bare right arm. And even when Aschenbach read, without looking up, he was conscious that the lad was there; that it would cost him but the slightest turn of the head to have the rewarding vision once more in his purview. Indeed, it was almost as though he sat there to guard the youth's repose; occupied, of course, with his own affairs, yet alive to the presence of that noble human creature close at hand. And his heart was stirred, it felt a father's kindness: such an emotion as the possessor of beauty can inspire in one who has offered himself up in spirit to create beauty.

At mid-day he left the beach, returned to the hotel, and was carried up in the lift to his room. There he lingered a little time before the glass and looked at his own grey hair, his keen and weary face. And he thought of his fame, and how people gazed respectfully at him in the streets, on account of his unerring gift of words and their power to charm. He called up all the worldly successes his genius had reaped, all he could remember, even his patent of nobility. Then went to luncheon down in the dining-room, sat at his little table and ate. Afterwards he mounted again in the lift, and a group of young folk, Tadzio among them, pressed with him into the little compartment. It was the first time Aschenbach had seen him close at hand, not merely in perspective, and could see and take account of the details of his humanity. Someone spoke to the lad, and he, answering, with indescribably lovely smile, stepped out again, as they had come to the first floor, backwards, with his eyes cast down. "Beauty makes people self-conscious," Aschenbach thought, and considered within himself imperatively why this should be. He had noted, further, that Tadzio's teeth were imperfect, rather jagged and bluish, without a healthy glaze, and of that peculiar brittle transparency which the teeth of chlorotic people often show. "He is delicate, he is sickly," Aschenbach thought. "He will most likely not live to grow old." He did not try to account for the pleasure the idea gave him.

In the afternoon he spent two hours in his room, then took the *vaporetto* to Venice, across the foul-smelling lagoon. He got out at San Marco, had his tea in the Piazza, and then, as his custom was, took a walk through the streets. But this walk of his brought about nothing less than a revolution in his mood and an entire change in all his plans.

There was a hateful sultriness in the narrow streets. The air was so heavy that all the manifold smells wafted out of houses, shops, and cook-shops – smells of oil, perfumery, and so forth – hung low, like exhalations, not dissipating. Cigarette smoke seemed to stand in the air, it drifted so slowly away. Today the crowd in these narrow lanes oppressed the stroller instead of diverting him. The longer he walked, the more was he in tortures under that state, which is the product of the sea air and the sirocco and which excites and enervates at once. He perspired painfully. His eyes rebelled, his chest was heavy, he felt feverish, the blood throbbed in his temples. He fled from the huddled, narrow streets of the commercial city, crossed many bridges, and came into the poor quarter of Venice. Beggars waylaid him, the canals sickened him with their evil exhalations. He reached a quiet square, one of those that exist at the city's heart, forsaken of God and man; there he rested awhile on the margin of a fountain, wiped his brow, and admitted to himself that he must be gone.

For the second time, and now quite definitely, the city proved that in certain weathers it could be directly inimical to his health. Nothing but sheer unreasoning obstinacy would linger on, hoping for an unprophesiable change in the wind. A quick decision was in place. He could not go home at this stage, neither summer nor winter quarters would be ready. But Venice had not a monopoly of sea and shore: there were other spots where these were to be had without the evil concomitants of lagoon and fever-breeding vapours. He remembered a little bathing-place not far from Trieste of which he had had a good report. Why not go thither? At once, of course, in order that this second change might be worth the making. He resolved, he rose to his feet and sought the nearest gondola-landing, where he took a boat and was conveyed to San Marco through the gloomy windings of many canals, beneath balconies of delicate marble traceries flanked by carven lions; round slippery corners of wall, past melancholy façades with ancient business shields reflected in the rocking water. It was not too easy to arrive at his destination, for his gondolier, being in league with various lace-makers and glass-blowers, did his best to persuade his fare to pause, look, and be tempted to buy. Thus the charm of this bizarre passage through the heart of Venice, even while it played upon his spirit, yet was sensibly cooled by the predatory commercial spirit of the fallen queen of the seas.

Once back in his hotel, he announced at the office, even before dinner, that circumstances unforeseen obliged him to leave early next morning. The management expressed its regret, it changed his money and receipted his bill. He dined, and spent the lukewarm evening in a rocking-chair on the rear terrace, reading the newspapers. Before he went to bed, he made his luggage ready against the morning.

His sleep was not of the best, for the prospect of another journey made him restless. When he opened his window next morning, the sky was still overcast, but the air seemed fresher – and there and then his rue began. Had he not given notice too soon? Had he not let himself be swayed by a slight and momentary indisposition? If he had only been patient, not lost heart so quickly, tried to adapt himself to the climate, or even waited for a change in the weather before deciding! Then, instead of the hurry and flurry of departure, he would have before him now a morning like yesterday's on the beach. Too late! He must go on wanting what he had wanted yesterday. He dressed and at eight o'clock went down to breakfast.

When he entered the breakfast-room it was empty. Guests came in while he sat waiting for his order to be filled. As he sipped his tea he saw the Polish girls enter with their governess, chaste and morning-fresh, with sleep-reddened eyelids. They crossed the room and sat down at their table in the window. Behind them came the porter, cap in hand, to announce that it was time for him to go. The car was waiting to convey him and other travellers to the Hôtel Excelsior, whence they would go by motor-boat through the company's private canal to the station. Time passed. But Aschenbach found it did nothing of the sort. There still lacked more than an hour of train-time. He felt irritated at the hotel habit of getting the guests out of the house earlier than necessary; and requested the porter to let him breakfast in peace. The man hesitated and withdrew, only to come back again five minutes later. The car could wait no longer. Good, then it might go, and take his trunk with it, Aschenbach answered with some heat. He would use the public conveyance, in his own time; he begged them to leave the choice of it to him. The functionary bowed. Aschenbach, pleased to be rid of him, made a leisurely meal, and even had a newspaper off the waiter. When at length he rose, the time was grown very short. And it so happened that at that moment Tadzio came through the glass doors into the room.

To reach his own table he crossed the traveller's path, and modestly cast down his eyes before the grey-haired man of the lofty brows – only to lift them again in that sweet way he had and direct his full soft gaze upon Aschenbach's face. Then he was past. "For the last time, Tadzio," thought the elder man. "It was all too brief!" Quite unusually for him, he shaped a farewell with his lips, he actually uttered it, and added: "May God bless you!" Then he went out, distributed tips, exchanged farewells with the mild little manager in the frock-coat, and, followed by the porter with his hand-luggage, left the hotel. On foot as he had come, he passed through the white-blossoming avenue, diagonally across the island to the boat-landing. He went on board at once – but the tale of his journey across the lagoon was a tale of woe, a passage through the very valley of regrets.

It was the well-known route: through the lagoon, past San Marco, up the Grand Canal. Aschenbach sat on the circular bench in the bows, with his elbow on the railing, one hand shading his eyes. They passed the Public Gardens, once more the princely charm of the Piazzetta rose up before him and then dropped behind, next came the great row of palaces, the canal curved, and the splendid marble arches of the Rialto came in sight. The traveller gazed – and his bosom was torn. The atmosphere of the city, the faintly rotten scent of swamp and sea, which had driven him to leave – in what deep, tender, almost painful draughts he breathed it in! How was it he had not known, had not thought, how much his heart was set upon it all? What this morning had been slight regret, some little doubt of his own wisdom, turned now to grief, to actual wretchedness, a mental agony so sharp that it repeatedly brought tears to his eyes, while he questioned himself how he could have foreseen it. The hardest part, the part that more than once it seemed he could not bear, was the thought that he should never more see Venice again. Since now for the second time the place had made him ill, since for the second time he had had to flee for his life, he must henceforth regard it as a forbidden spot, to be for ever shunned; senseless to try it again, after he had proved himself unfit. Yes, if he fled it now, he felt that wounded pride must prevent his return to this spot where twice he had made actual bodily surrender. And this conflict between inclination and capacity all at once assumed, in this middle-aged man's mind, immense weight and importance; the physical defeat seemed a shameful thing, to be avoided at whatever cost; and he stood amazed at the ease with which on the day before he had yielded to it.

Meanwhile the steamer neared the station landing; his

anguish of irresolution amounted almost to panic. To leave seemed to the sufferer impossible, to remain not less so. Torn thus between two alternatives, he entered the station. It was very late, he had not a moment to lose. Time pressed, it scourged him onward. He hastened to buy his ticket and looked round in the crowd to find the hotel porter. The man appeared and said that the trunk had already gone off. "Gone already?" "Yes, it has gone to Como." "To Como?" A hasty exchange of words – angry questions from Aschenbach, and puzzled replies from the porter – at length made it clear that the trunk had been put with the wrong luggage even before leaving the hotel, and in company with other trunks was now well on its way in precisely the wrong direction.

Aschenbach found it hard to wear the right expression as he heard this news. A reckless joy, a deep incredible mirthfulness shook him almost as with a spasm. The porter dashed off after the lost trunk, returning very soon, of course, to announce that his efforts were unavailing. Aschenbach said he would not travel without his luggage; that he would go back and wait at the Hôtel des Bains until it turned up. Was the company's motor-boat still outside? The man said yes, it was at the door. With his native eloquence he prevailed upon the ticket-agent to take back the ticket already purchased; he swore that he would wire, that no pains should be spared, that the trunk would be restored in the twinkling of an eye. And the unbelievable thing came to pass: the traveller, twenty minutes after he had reached the station, found himself once more on the Grand Canal on his way back to the Lido.

What a strange adventure indeed, this right-about face of destiny – incredible, humiliating, whimsical as any dream! To be passing again, within the hour, these scenes from which in profoundest grief he had but now taken leave for ever! The little swift-moving vessel, a furrow of foam at its prow, tacking with droll agility between steamboats and gondolas, went like a shot to its goal; and he, its sole passenger, sat hiding the panic and thrills of a truant schoolboy beneath a mask of forced resignation. His breast still heaved from time to time with a burst of laughter over the contretemps. Things could not, he told himself, have fallen out more luckily. There would be the necessary explanations, a few astonished faces – then all would be well once more, a mischance prevented, a grievous error set right; and all he had thought to have left for ever was his own once more, his for as long as he liked.... And did the boat's swift motion deceive him, or was the wind now coming from the sea?

The waves struck against the tiled sides of the narrow canal. At Hôtel Excelsior the automobile omnibus awaited the returned traveller and bore him along by the crisping waves back to the Hôtel des Bains. The little mustachioed manager in the frock-coat came down the steps to greet him.

In dulcet tones he deplored the mistake, said how painful it was to the management and himself; applauded Aschenbach's resolve to stop on until the errant trunk came back; his former room, alas, was already taken, but another as good awaited his approval. "*Pas de chance, monsieur,*" said the Swiss lift-porter, with a smile, as he conveyed him upstairs. And the fugitive was soon quartered in another room which in situation and furnishings almost precisely resembled the first.

He laid out the contents of his hand-bag in their wonted places; then, tired out, dazed by the whirl of the extraordinary forenoon, subsided into the arm-chair by the open window. The sea wore a pale-green cast, the air felt thinner and purer, the beach with its cabins and boats had more colour, notwithstanding the sky was still grey. Aschenbach, his hands folded in his lap, looked out. He felt rejoiced to be back, yet displeased with his vacillating moods, his ignorance of his own real desires. Thus for nearly an hour he sat, dreaming, resting, barely thinking. At mid-day he saw Tadzio, in his striped sailor suit with red breast-knot, coming up from the sea, across the barrier and along the board walk to the hotel. Aschenbach recognized him, even at this height, knew it was he before he actually saw him, had it in mind to say to himself: "Well, Tadzio, so here you are again too!" But the casual greeting died away before it reached his lips, slain by the truth in his heart. He felt the rapture of his blood, the poignant pleasure, and realized that it was for Tadzio's sake the leavetaking had been so hard.

He sat quite still, unseen at his high post, and looked within himself. His features were lively, he lifted his brows; a smile, alert, inquiring, vivid, widened the mouth. Then he raised his head, and with both hands, hanging limp over the chair-arms, he described a slow motion, palms outward, a lifting and turning movement, as though to indicate a wide embrace. It was a gesture of welcome, a calm and deliberate acceptance of what might come.

Now daily the naked god with cheeks aflame drove his four fire-breathing steeds through heaven's spaces; and with him streamed the strong east wind that fluttered his yellow locks. A sheen, like white satin, lay over all the idly rolling sea's expanse. The sand was burning hot. Awnings of rust-coloured canvas were spanned before the bathing-huts, under the ether's quivering silver-blue; one spent the morning hours within the small, sharp square of shadow they purveyed. But evening too was rarely lovely: balsamic with the breath of flowers and shrubs from the near-by park, while overhead the constellations circled in their spheres, and the murmuring of the night-girted sea swelled softly up and whispered to the soul. Such nights as these contained the joyful promise of a sunlit morrow, brim-full of sweetly ordered idleness, studded thick with countless precious possibilities.

The guest detained here by so happy a mischance was far from finding the return of his luggage a ground for setting out anew. For two days he had suffered slight inconvenience and had to dine in the large salon in his travelling-clothes. Then the lost trunk was set down in his room, and he hastened to unpack, filling presses and drawers with his possessions. He meant to stay on – and on; he rejoiced in the prospect of wearing a silk suit for the hot morning hours on the beach and appearing in acceptable evening dress at dinner.

He was quick to fall in with the pleasing monotony of this manner of life, readily enchanted by its mild soft brilliance and ease. And what a spot it is, indeed! – uniting the charms of a luxurious bathing-resort by a southern sea with the immediate nearness of a unique and marvellous city. Aschenbach was not pleasure-loving. Always, wherever and whenever it was the order of the day to be merry, to refrain from labour and make glad the heart, he would soon be conscious of the imperative summons – and especially was this so in his youth – back to the high fatigues, the sacred and fasting service that consumed his days. This spot and this alone had power to beguile him, to relax his resolution, to make him glad. At times – of a forenoon perhaps, as he lay in the shadow of his awning, gazing out dreamily over the blue of the southern sea, or in the mildness of the night, beneath the wide starry sky, ensconced among the cushions of the gondola that bore him Lido-wards after an evening on the Piazza, while the gay lights faded and the melting music of the serenades died away on his ear – he would think of his mountain home, the theatre of his summer labours. There clouds hung low and trailed through the garden, violent storms extinguished the lights of the house at night, and the ravens he fed swung in the tops of the fir trees. And he would feel transported to Elysium, to the ends of the earth, to a spot most carefree for the sons of men, where no snow is, and no winter, no storms or downpours of rain; where Oceanus sends a mild and cooling breath, and days flow on in blissful idleness, without effort or struggle, entirely dedicated to the sun and the feasts of the sun.

Aschenbach saw the boy Tadzio almost constantly. The narrow confines of their world of hotel and beach, the daily round followed by all alike, brought him in close, almost uninterrupted touch with the beautiful lad. He encountered him everywhere – in the salons of the hotel, on the cooling rides to the city and back, among the splendours of the Piazza, and besides all this in many another going and coming as chance vouchsafed. But it was the regular morning hours on the beach which gave him his happiest opportunity to study and admire the lovely apparition. Yes, this immediate happiness, this daily recurring boon at the hand of circumstance, this it was that filled him with content, with joy in life, enriched his stay, and lingered out the row of sunny days that fell into place so pleasantly one behind the other.

He rose early – as early as though he had a panting press of work – and was among the first on the beach, when the sun was still benign and the sea lay dazzling white in its morning slumber. He gave the watchman a friendly good-morning and chatted with the barefoot, white-haired old man who prepared his place, spread the awning, trundled out the chair and table on to the little platform. Then he settled down; he had three or four hours before the sun reached its height and the fearful climax of its power; three or four hours while the sea went deeper and deeper blue; three or four hours in which to watch Tadzio.

He would see him come up, on the left, along the margin of the sea; or from behind, between the cabins; or, with a start of joyful surprise, would discover that he himself was late, and Tadzio already down, in the blue and white bathing-suit that was now his only wear on the beach; there and engrossed in his usual activities in the sand, beneath the sun. It was a sweetly idle, trifling, fitful life, of play and rest, of strolling, wading, digging, fishing, swimming, lying on the sand. Often the women sitting on the platform would call out to him in their high voices: "Tadziu! Tadziu!" and he would come running and waving his arms, eager to tell them what he had done, show them what he had found, what caught – shells, seahorses, jelly-fish, and sidewards-running crabs. Aschenbach understood not a word he said; it might be the sheerest commonplace, in his ear it became mingled harmonies. Thus the lad's foreign birth raised his speech to music; a wanton sun showered splendour on him, and the noble distances of the sea formed the background which set off his figure.

Soon the observer knew every line and pose of this form that limned itself so freely against sea and sky; its every loveliness, though conned by heart, yet thrilled him each day afresh; his admiration knew no bounds, the delight of his eye was unending. Once the lad was summoned to speak to a guest who was waiting for his mother at their cabin. He ran up, ran dripping wet out of the sea, tossing his curls, and put out his hand, standing with his weight on one leg, resting the other foot on the toes; as he stood there in a posture of suspense the turn of his body was enchanting, while his features wore a look half shamefaced, half conscious of the duty breeding laid upon him to please. Or he would lie at full length, with his bath-robe around him, one slender young arm resting on the sand, his chin in the hollow of his hand; the lad they called Jaschiu squatting beside him, paying him court. There could be nothing lovelier on earth than the smile and look with which the playmate thus singled out rewarded his humble friend and vassal. Again, he might be at the water's edge, alone, removed from his family, quite close to Aschenbach; standing erect, his hands clasped at the back of his neck, rocking slowly on the balls of his feet, day-dreaming away into blue space, while little waves ran up and bathed his toes. The ringlets of honey-coloured hair clung to his temples and neck, the fine down along the upper vertebræ was yellow in the sunlight; the thin envelope of flesh covering the torso betrayed the delicate outlines of the ribs and the symmetry of the breast-structure. His armpits were still as smooth as a statue's, smooth the glistening hollows behind the knees, where the blue network of veins suggested that the body was formed of some stuff more transparent than mere flesh. What discipline, what precision of thought were expressed by the tense youthful perfection of this form! And yet the pure, strong will which had laboured in darkness and succeeded in bringing this godlike work of art to the light of day – was it not known and familiar to him, the artist? Was not the same force at work in himself when he strove in cold fury to liberate from the marble mass of language the slender forms of his art which he saw with the eye of his mind and would body forth to men as the mirror and image of spiritual beauty?

Mirror and image! His eyes took in the proud bearing of that figure there at the blue water's edge; with an outburst of rapture he told himself that what he saw was beauty's very essence; form as divine thought, the single and pure perfection which resides in the mind, of which an image and likeness, rare and holy, was here raised up for adoration. This was very frenzy – and without a scruple, nay, eagerly, the ageing artist bade it come. His mind was in travail, his whole mental background in a state of flux. Memory flung up in him the primitive thoughts which are youth's inheritance, but which with him had remained latent, never leaping up into a blaze. Has it not been written that the sun beguiles our attention from things of the intellect to fix it on things of the sense? The sun, they say, dazzles; so bewitching reason and memory that the soul for very pleasure forgets its actual state, to cling with doting on the loveliest of all the objects she shines on. Yes, and then it is only through the medium of some corporeal being that it can raise itself again to contemplation of higher things. Amor, in sooth, is like the mathematician who in order to give children a knowledge of pure form must do so in the language of pictures; so, too, the god, in order to make visible the spirit, avails himself of the forms and colours of human youth, gilding it with all imaginable beauty that it may serve memory as a tool, the very sight of which then sets us afire with pain and longing.

Such were the devotee's thoughts, such the power of his emotions. And the sea, so bright with glancing sunbeams, wove in his mind a spell and summoned up a lovely picture: there was the ancient plane-tree outside the walls of Athens, a hallowed, shady spot, fragrant with willow-blossom and adorned with images and votive offerings in honour of the nymphs and Achelous. Clear ran the smooth-pebbled stream at the foot of the spreading tree. Crickets were fiddling. But on the gentle grassy slope, where one could lie yet hold the head erect, and shelter from the scorching heat, two men reclined, an elder with a younger, ugliness paired with beauty and wisdom with grace. Here Socrates held forth to youthful

Phædrus upon the nature of virtue and desire, wooing him with insinuating wit and charming turns of phrase. He told him of the shuddering and unwonted heat that come upon him whose heart is open, when his eye beholds an image of eternal beauty; spoke of the impious and corrupt, who cannot conceive beauty though they see its image, and are incapable of awe; and of the fear and reverence felt by the noble soul when he beholds a godlike face or a form which is a good image of beauty: how as he gazes he worships the beautiful one and scarcely dares to look upon him, but would offer sacrifice as to an idol or a god, did he not fear to be thought stark mad. "For beauty, my Phædrus, beauty alone, is lovely and visible at once. For, mark you, it is the sole aspect of the spiritual which we can perceive through our senses, or bear so to perceive. Else what should become of us, if the divine, if reason and virtue and truth, were to speak to us through the senses? Should we not perish and be consumed by love, as Semele aforetime was by Zeus? So beauty, then, is the beauty-lover's way to the spirit – but only the way, only the means, my little Phædrus." . . . And then, sly arch-lover that he was, he said the subtlest thing of all: that the lover was nearer the divine than the beloved; for the god was in the one but not in the other – perhaps the tenderest, most mocking thought that ever was thought, and source of all the guile and secret bliss the lover knows.

Thought that can merge wholly into feeling, feeling that can merge wholly into thought – these are the artist's highest joy. And our solitary felt in himself at this moment power to command and wield a thought that thrilled with emotion, an emotion as precise and concentrated as thought: namely, that nature herself shivers with ecstasy when the mind bows down in homage before beauty. He felt a sudden desire to write. Eros, indeed, we are told, loves idleness, and for idle hours alone was he created. But in this crisis the violence of our sufferer's seizure was directed almost wholly towards production, its occasion almost a matter of indifference. News had reached him on his travels that a certain problem had been raised, the intellectual world challenged for its opinion on a great and burning question of art and taste. By nature and experience the theme was his own; and he could not resist the temptation to set it off in the glistering foil of his words. He would write, and moreover he would write in Tadzio's presence. This lad should be in a sense his model, his style should follow the lines of this figure that seemed to him divine; he would snatch up this beauty into the realms of the mind, as once the eagle bore the Trojan shepherd aloft. Never had the pride of the word been so sweet to him, never had he known so well that Eros is in the word, as in those perilous and precious hours when he sat at his rude table, within the shade of his awning, his idol full in his view and the music of his voice in his ears, and fashioned his little essay after the model Tadzio's beauty set: that page and a half of choicest prose, so chaste, so lofty, so poignant with feeling, which would shortly be the wonder and admiration of the multitude. Verily it is well for the world that it sees only the beauty of the completed work and not its origins nor the conditions whence it sprang; since knowledge of the artist's inspiration might often but confuse and alarm and so prevent the full effect of its excellence. Strange hours, indeed, these were, and strangely unnerving the labour that filled them! Strangely fruitful intercourse this, between one body and another mind! When Aschenbach put aside his work and left the beach he felt exhausted, he felt broken – conscience reproached him, as it were after a debauch.

Next morning on leaving the hotel he stood at the top of the stairs leading down from the terrace and saw Tadzio in front of him on his way to the beach. The lad had just reached the gate in the railings, and he was alone. Aschenbach felt, quite simply, a wish to overtake him, to address him and have the pleasure of his reply and answering look; to put upon a blithe and friendly footing his relation with this being who all unconsciously had so greatly heightened and quickened his emotions. The lovely youth moved at a loitering pace – he might easily be overtaken; and Aschenbach hastened his own step. He reached him on the board walk that ran behind the bathing-cabins, and all but put out his hand to lay it on shoulder or head, while his lips parted to utter a friendly salutation in French. But – perhaps from the swift pace of his last few steps – he found his heart throbbing unpleasantly fast, while his breath came in such quick pants that he could only have gasped had he tried to speak. He hesitated, sought after self-control, was suddenly panic-stricken lest the boy notice him hanging there behind him and look round. Then he gave up, abandoned his plan, and passed him with bent head and hurried step.

"Too late! Too late!" he thought as he went by. But was it too late? This step he had delayed to take might so easily have put everything in a lighter key, have led to a sane recovery from his folly. But the truth may have been that the ageing man did not want to be cured, that his illusion was far too dear to him. Who shall unriddle the puzzle of the artist nature? Who understands that mingling of discipline and licence in which it stands so deeply rooted? For not to be able to want sobriety is licentious folly. Aschenbach was no longer disposed to self-analysis. He had no taste for it; his self-esteem, the attitude of mind proper to his years, his maturity and single-mindedness, disinclined him to look within himself and decide whether it was constraint or puerile sensuality that had prevented him from carrying out his project. He felt confused, he was afraid someone, if only the watchman, might have been observing his behaviour and final surrender – very much he feared being ridiculous. And all the time he was laughing at himself for his serio-comic seizure. "Quite crestfallen," he thought. "I was like the gamecock that lets his wings droop in the battle. That must be the Love-God himself, that makes us hang our heads at sight of beauty and weighs our proud spirits low as the ground." Thus he played with the idea – he embroidered upon it, and was too arrogant to admit fear of an emotion.

The term he had set for his holiday passed by unheeded; he had no thought of going home. Ample funds had been sent him. His sole concern was that the Polish family might leave, and a chance question put to the hotel barber elicited the information that they had come only very shortly before himself. The sun browned his face and hands, the invigorating salty air heightened his emotional energies. Heretofore he had been wont to give out at once, in some new effort, the powers accumulated by sleep or food or outdoor air; but now the strength that flowed in upon him with each day of sun and sea and idleness he let go up in one extravagant gush of emotional intoxication.

His sleep was fitful; the priceless, equable days were divided one from the next by brief nights filled with happy unrest. He went, indeed, early to bed, for at nine o'clock, with the departure of Tadzio from the scene, the day was over for him. But in the faint greyness of the morning a tender pang would go through him as his heart was minded of its adventure; he could no longer bear his pillow and, rising, would wrap himself against the early chill and sit down by the window to await the sunrise. Awe of the miracle filled his soul new-risen from its sleep. Heaven, earth, and its waters yet lay enfolded in the ghostly, glassy pallor of dawn; one paling star still swam in the shadowy vast. But there came a breath, a winged word from far and inaccessible abodes, that Eos was rising from the side of her spouse; and there was that first sweet reddening of the farthest strip of sea and sky that manifests creation to man's sense. She neared, the goddess, ravisher of youth, who stole away Cleitos and Cephalus and, defying all the envious Olympians, tasted beautiful Orion's love. At the world's edge began a strewing of roses, a shining and a blooming ineffably pure; baby cloudlets hung illumined, like attendant amoretti, in the blue and blushful haze; purple effulgence fell upon the sea, that seemed to heave it forward on its welling waves; from horizon to zenith went great quivering thrusts like golden lances, the gleam became a glare; without a sound, with godlike violence, glow and glare and rolling flames streamed upwards, and with flying hoof-beats the steeds of the sun-god mounted the sky. The lonely watcher sat, the splendour of the god shone on him, he closed his eyes and let the glory kiss his lids. Forgotten feelings, precious pangs of his youth, quenched long since by the stern service that had been his life and now returned so strangely metamorphosed – he recognized them with a puzzled, wondering smile. He mused, he dreamed, his lips slowly shaped a name; still smiling, his face turned seawards and his hands lying folded in his lap, he fell asleep once more as he sat.

But that day, which began so fierily and festally, was not like other days; it was transmuted and gilded with mythical significance. For whence could come the breath, so mild and meaningful, like a whisper from higher spheres, that played about temple and ear? Troops of small feathery white clouds ranged over the sky, like grazing herds of the gods. A stronger wind arose, and Poseidon's horses ran up, arching their manes, among them too the steers of him with the purpled locks, who lowered their horns and bellowed as they came on; while like prancing goats the waves on the farther strand leaped among the craggy rocks. It was a world possessed, peopled by Pan, that closed round the spellbound man, and his doting heart conceived the most delicate fancies. When the sun was going down behind Venice, he would sometimes sit on a bench in the park and watch Tadzio, white-clad, with gay-coloured sash, at play there on the rolled gravel with his ball; and at such times it was not Tadzio whom he saw, but Hyacinthus, doomed to die because two gods were rivals for his love. Ah, yes, he tasted the envious pangs that Zephyr knew when his rival, bow and cithara, oracle and all forgot, played with the beauteous youth; he watched the discus, guided by torturing jealousy, strike the beloved head; paled as he received the broken body in his arms, and saw the flower spring up, watered by that sweet blood and signed for evermore with his lament.

There can be no relation more strange, more critical, than that between two beings who know each other only with their eyes, who meet daily, yes, even hourly, eye each other with a fixed regard, and yet by some whim or freak of convention feel constrained to act like strangers. Uneasiness rules between them, unslaked curiosity, a hysterical desire to give rein to their suppressed impulse to recognize and address each other; even, actually, a sort of strained but mutual regard. For one human being instinctively feels respect and love for another human being so long as he does not know him well enough to judge him; and that he does not, the craving he feels is evidence.

Some sort of relation and acquaintanceship was perforce set up between Aschenbach and the youthful Tadzio; it was with a thrill of joy the older man perceived that the lad was not entirely unresponsive to all the tender notice lavished on him. For instance, what should move the lovely youth, nowadays when he descended to the beach, always to avoid the board walk behind the bathing-huts and saunter along the sand, passing Aschenbach's tent in front, sometimes so unnecessarily close as almost to graze his table or chair? Could the power of an emotion so beyond his own so draw, so fascinate its innocent object? Daily Aschenbach would wait for Tadzio. Then sometimes, on his approach, he would pretend to be preoccupied and let the charmer pass unregarded by. But sometimes he looked up, and their glances met; when that happened both were profoundly serious. The elder's dignified and cultured mien let nothing appear of his inward state; but in Tadzio's eyes a question lay – he faltered in his step, gazed on the ground, then up again with that ineffably sweet look he had; and when he was past, something in his bearing seemed to say that only good breeding hindered him from turning round.

But once, one evening, it fell out differently. The Polish brother and sisters, with their governess, had missed the evening meal, and Aschenbach had noted the fact with concern. He was restive over their absence, and after dinner walked up and down in front of the hotel, in evening dress and a straw hat; when suddenly he saw the nunlike sisters with their companion appear in the light of the arc-lamps, and four paces behind them Tadzio. Evidently they came from the steamer-landing, having dined for some reason in Venice. It had been chilly on the lagoon, for Tadzio wore a dark-blue reefer-jacket with gilt buttons, and a cap to match. Sun and sea air could not burn his skin, it was the same creamy marble hue as at first – though he did look a little pale, either from the cold or in the bluish moonlight of the arc-lamps. The shapely brows were so delicately drawn, the eyes so deeply dark – lovelier he was than words could say, and as often the thought visited Aschenbach, and brought its own pang, that language could but extol, not reproduce, the beauties of the sense.

The sight of that dear form was unexpected, it had appeared unhoped-for, without giving him time to compose his features. Joy, surprise, and admiration might have painted themselves quite openly upon his face – and just at this second it happened that Tadzio smiled. Smiled at Aschenbach, unabashed and friendly, a speaking, winning, captivating smile, with slowly parting lips. With such a smile it might be that Narcissus bent over the mirroring pool, a smile profound, infatuated, lingering, as he put out his arms to the reflection of his own beauty; the lips just slightly pursed, perhaps half-realizing his own folly in trying to kiss the cold lips of his shadow – with a mingling of coquetry and curiosity and a faint unease, enthralling and enthralled.

Aschenbach received that smile and turned away with it as though entrusted with a fatal gift. So shaken was he that he had to flee from the lighted terrace and front gardens and seek out with hurried steps the darkness of the park at the rear. Reproaches strangely mixed of tenderness and remonstrance burst from him: "How dare you smile like that! No one is allowed to smile like that!" He flung himself on a bench, his composure gone to the winds, and breathed in the nocturnal fragrance of the garden. He leaned back, with hanging arms, quivering from head to foot, and quite unmanned he whispered the hackneyed phrase of love and longing – impossible in these circumstances, absurd, abject, ridiculous enough, yet sacred too, and not unworthy of honour even here: "I love you!"

In the fourth week of his stay on the Lido, Gustave von Aschenbach made certain singular observations touching the world about him. He noticed, in the first place, that though the season was approaching its height, yet the number of guests declined and, in particular, that the German tongue had suffered a rout, being scarcely or never heard in the land. At table and on the beach he caught nothing but foreign words. One day at the barber's – where he was now a frequent visitor – he heard something rather startling. The barber mentioned a German family who had just left the Lido after a brief stay, and rattled on in his obsequious way: "The signore is not leaving – he has no fear of the sickness, has he?" Aschenbach looked at him. "The sickness?" he repeated. Whereat the prattler fell silent, became very busy all at once, affected not to hear. When Aschenbach persisted he said he really knew nothing at all about it, and tried in a fresh burst of eloquence to drown the embarrassing subject.

That was one forenoon. After luncheon Aschenbach had himself ferried across to Venice, in a dead calm, under a burning sun; driven by his mania, he was following the Polish young folk, whom he had seen with their companion, taking the way to the landing-stage. He did not find his idol on the Piazza. But as he sat there at tea, at a little round table on the shady side, suddenly he noticed a peculiar odour, which, it seemed to him now, had been in the air for days without his being aware: a sweetish, medicinal smell, associated with wounds and disease and suspect cleanliness. He sniffed and pondered and at length recognized it; finished his tea and left the square at the end facing the cathedral. In the narrow space the stench grew stronger. At the street corners placards were stuck up, in which the city authorities warned the population against the danger of certain infections of the gastric system, prevalent during the heated season; advising them not to eat oysters or other shell-fish and not to use the canal waters. The ordinance showed every sign of minimizing an existing situation. Little groups of people stood about silently in the squares and on the bridges; the traveller moved among them, watched and listened and thought.

He spoke to a shopkeeper lounging at his door among dangling coral necklaces and trinkets of artificial amethyst, and asked him about the disagreeable odour. The man looked at him, heavy-eyed, and hastily pulled himself together. "Just a formal precaution, signore," he said, with a gesture. "A police regulation we have to put up with. The air is sultry – the sirocco is not wholesome, as the signore knows. Just a precautionary measure, you understand – probably unnecessary. . . ." Aschenbach thanked him and passed on. And on the boat that bore him back to the Lido he smelt the germicide again.

On reaching his hotel he sought the table in the lobby and buried himself in the newspapers. The foreign-language sheets had nothing. But in the German papers certain rumours were mentioned, statistics given, then officially denied, then the good faith of the denials called in question. The departure of the German and Austrian contingent was thus made plain. As for other nationals, they knew or suspected nothing – they were still undisturbed. Aschenbach tossed the newspapers back on the table. "It ought to be kept quiet," he thought, aroused. "It should not be talked about." And he felt in his heart a curious elation at these events impending in the world about him. Passion is like crime: it does not thrive on the established order and the common round; it welcomes every blow dealt the bourgeois structure, every weakening of the social fabric, because therein it feels a sure hope of its own advantage. These things that were going on in the unclean alleys of Venice, under cover of an official hushing-up policy – they gave Aschenbach a dark satisfaction. The city's evil secret mingled with the one in the depths of his heart – and he would have staked all he possessed to keep it, since in his infatuation he cared for nothing but to keep Tadzio here, and owned to himself, not without horror, that he could not exist were the lad to pass from his sight.

He was no longer satisfied to owe his communion with his charmer to chance and the routine of hotel life; he had begun to follow and waylay him. On Sundays, for example, the Polish family never appeared on the beach. Aschenbach guessed they went to mass at San Marco and pursued them thither. He passed from the glare of the Piazza into the golden twilight of the holy place and found him he sought bowed in worship over a prie-dieu. He kept in the background, standing on the fissured mosaic pavement among the devout populace, that knelt and muttered and made the sign of the cross; and the crowded splendour of the oriental temple weighed voluptuously on his sense. A heavily ornate priest intoned and gesticulated before the altar, where little candle-flames flickered helplessly in the reek of incense-breathing smoke; and with that cloying sacrificial smell another seemed to mingle – the odour of the sickened city. But through all the glamour and glitter Aschenbach saw the exquisite creature there in front turn his head, seek out and meet his lover's eye.

The crowd streamed out through the portals into the brilliant square thick with fluttering doves, and the fond fool stood aside in the vestibule on the watch. He saw the Polish family leave the church. The children took ceremonial leave of their mother, and she turned towards the Piazzetta on her way home, while his charmer and the cloistered sisters, with their governess, passed beneath the clock tower into the Merceria. When they were a few paces on, he followed – he stole behind them on their walk through the city. When they paused, he did so too; when they turned round, he fled into inns and courtyards to let them pass. Once he lost them from view, hunted feverishly over bridges and in filthy *culs-de-sac*, only to confront them suddenly in a narrow passage whence there was no escape, and experienced a moment of panic fear. Yet it would be untrue to say he suffered. Mind and heart were drunk with passion, his footsteps guided by the dæmonic power whose pastime it is to trample on human reason and dignity.

Tadzio and his sisters at length took a gondola. Aschenbach hid behind a portico or fountain while they embarked, and directly they pushed off did the same. In a furtive whisper he told the boatman he would tip him well to follow at a little distance the other gondola, just rounding a corner, and fairly sickened at the man's quick, sly grasp and ready acceptance of the go-between's role.

Leaning back among soft, black cushions he swayed gently in the wake of the other black-snouted bark, to which the strength of his passion chained him. Sometimes it passed from his view, and then he was assailed by an anguish of unrest. But his guide appeared to have long practice in affairs like these; always, by dint of short cuts or deft manoeuvres, he contrived to overtake the coveted sight. The air was heavy and foul, the sun burned down through a slate-coloured haze. Water slapped gurgling against wood and stone. The gondolier's cry, half warning, half salute, was answered with singular accord from far within the silence of the labyrinth. They passed little gardens, high up the crumbling wall, hung with clustering white and purple flowers that sent down an odour of almonds. Moorish lattices showed shadowy in the gloom. The marble steps of a church descended into the canal, and on them a beggar squatted, displaying his misery to view, showing the whites of his eyes, holding out his hat for alms. Farther on a dealer in antiquities cringed before his lair, inviting the passer-by to enter and be duped. Yes, this was Venice, this the fair frailty that fawned and that betrayed, half fairy-tale, half snare; the city in whose stagnating air the art of painting once put forth so lusty a growth, and where musicians were moved to accords so weirdly lulling and lascivious. Our adventurer felt his senses wooed by this voluptuousness of sight and sound, tasted his secret knowledge that the city sickened and hid its sickness for love of gain, and bent an ever more unbridled leer on the gondola that glided on before him.

It came at last to this – that his frenzy left him capacity for nothing else but to pursue his flame; to dream of him absent, to lavish, loverlike, endearing terms on his mere shadow. He was alone, he was a foreigner, he was sunk deep in this belated bliss of his – all which enabled him to pass unblushing through experiences well-nigh unbelievable. One night, returning late from Venice, he paused by his beloved's chamber door in the second storey, leaned his head against the panel, and remained there long, in utter drunkenness, powerless to tear himself away, blind to the danger of being caught in so mad an attitude.

And yet there were not wholly lacking moments when he paused and reflected, when in consternation he asked himself what path was this on which he had set his foot. Like most other men of parts and attainments, he had an aristocratic interest in his forebears, and when he achieved a success he liked to think he had gratified them, compelled their admiration and regard. He thought of them now, involved as he was in this illicit adventure, seized of these exotic excesses of feeling; thought of their stern self-command and decent manliness, and gave a melancholy smile. What would they have said? What, indeed, would they have said to his entire life, that varied to the point of degeneracy from theirs? This life in the bonds of art, had not he himself, in the days of his youth and in the very spirit of those bourgeois forefathers, pronounced mocking judgment upon it? And yet, at bottom, it had been so like their own! It had been a service, and he a soldier, like some of them; and art was war – a grilling, exhausting struggle that nowadays wore one out before one could grow old. It had been a life of self-conquest, a life against odds, dour, steadfast, abstinent; he had made it symbolical of the kind of overstrained heroism the time admired, and he was entitled to call it manly, even courageous. He wondered if such a life might not be somehow specially pleasing in the eyes of the god who had him in his power. For Eros had received most countenance among the most valiant nations – yes, were we not told that in their cities prowess made him flourish exceedingly? And many heroes of olden time had willingly borne his yoke, not counting any humiliation such if it happened by the god's decree; vows, prostrations, self-abasements, these were no source of shame to the lover; rather they reaped him praise and honour.

Thus did the fond man's folly condition his thoughts; thus did he seek to hold his dignity upright in his own eyes. And all the while he kept doggedly on the traces of the disreputable secret the city kept hidden at its heart, just as he kept his own – and all that he learned fed his passion with vague, lawless hopes. He turned over newspapers at cafés, bent on finding a report on the progress of the disease; and in the German sheets, which had ceased to appear on the hotel table, he found a series of contradictory statements. The deaths, it was variously asserted, ran to twenty, to forty, to a hundred or more; yet in the next day's issue the existence of the pestilence was, if not roundly denied, reported as a matter of a few sporadic cases such as might be brought into a seaport town. After that the warnings would break out again, and the protests against the unscrupulous game the authorities were playing. No definite information was to be had.

And yet our solitary felt he had a sort of first claim on a share in the unwholesome secret; he took a fantastic satisfaction in putting leading questions to such persons as were interested to conceal it, and forcing them to explicit untruths by way of denial. One day he attacked the manager, that small, soft-stepping man in the French frock-coat, who was moving about among the guests at luncheon, supervising the service and making himself socially agreeable. He paused at Aschenbach's table to exchange a greeting, and the guest put a question, with a negligent, casual air: "Why in the world are they forever disinfecting the city of Venice?" "A police regulation," the adroit one replied; "a precautionary measure, intended to protect the health of the public during this unseasonably warm and sultry weather." "Very praiseworthy of the police," Aschenbach gravely responded. After a further exchange of meteorological commonplaces the manager passed on.

It happened that a band of street musicians came to perform in the hotel gardens that evening after dinner. They grouped themselves beneath an iron stanchion supporting an arc-light, two women and two men, and turned their faces, that shone white in the glare, up towards the guests who sat on the hotel terrace enjoying this popular entertainment along with their coffee and iced drinks. The hotel lift-boys, waiters, and office staff stood in the doorway and listened; the Russian family displayed the usual Russian absorption in their enjoyment – they had their chairs put down into the garden to be nearer the singers and sat there in a half-circle with gratitude painted on their features, the old serf in her turban erect behind their chairs.

These strolling players were adepts at mandolin, guitar, harmonica, even compassing a reedy violin. Vocal numbers alternated with instrumental, the younger woman, who had a high shrill voice, joining in a love-duet with the sweetly falsettoing tenor. The actual head of the company, however, and incontestably its most gifted member, was the other man, who played the guitar. He was a sort of baritone buffo; with no voice to speak of, but possessed of a pantomimic gift and remarkable burlesque *élan*. Often he stepped out of the group and advanced towards the terrace, guitar in hand, and his audience rewarded his sallies with bursts of laughter. The Russians in their parterre seats were beside themselves with delight over this display of southern vivacity; their shouts and screams of applause encouraged him to bolder and bolder flights.

Aschenbach sat near the balustrade, a glass of pomegranate-juice and soda-water sparkling ruby-red before him, with which he now and then moistened his lips. His nerves drank in thirstily the unlovely sounds, the vulgar and sentimental tunes, for passion paralyses good taste and makes its victim accept with rapture what a man in his senses would either laugh at or turn from with disgust. Idly he sat and watched the antics of the buffoon with his face set in a fixed and painful smile, while inwardly his whole being was rigid with the intensity of the regard he bent on Tadzio, leaning over the railing six paces off.

He lounged there, in the white belted suit he sometimes wore at dinner, in all his innate, inevitable grace, with his left arm on the balustrade, his legs crossed, the right hand on the supporting hip; and looked down on the strolling singers with an expression that was hardly a smile, but rather a distant curiosity and polite toleration. Now and then he straightened himself and with a charming movement of both arms drew down his white blouse through his leather belt, throwing out his chest. And sometimes – Aschenbach saw it with triumph, with horror, and a sense that his reason was tottering – the lad would cast a glance, that might be slow and cautious, or might be sudden and swift, as though to take him by surprise, to the place where his lover sat. Aschenbach did not meet the glance. An ignoble caution made him keep his eyes in leash. For in the rear of the terrace sat Tadzio's mother and governess; and matters had gone so far that he feared to make himself conspicuous. Several times, on the beach, in the hotel lobby, on the Piazza, he had seen, with a stealing numbness, that they called Tadzio away from his neighbourhood. And his pride revolted at the affront, even while conscience told him it was deserved.

The performer below presently began a solo, with guitar accompaniment, a street song in several stanzas, just then the rage all over Italy. He delivered it in a striking and dramatic recitative, and his company joined in the refrain. He was a man of slight build, with a thin, undernourished face; his shabby felt hat rested on the back of his neck, a great mop of red hair sticking out in front; and he stood there on the gravel in advance of his troupe, in an impudent, swaggering posture, twanging the strings of his instrument and flinging a witty and rollicking recitative up to the terrace, while the veins on his forehead swelled with the violence of his effort. He was scarcely a Venetian type, belonging rather to the race of Neapolitan jesters, half bully, half comedian, brutal, blustering, an unpleasant customer, and entertaining to the last degree. The words of his song were trivial and silly, but on his lips, accompanied with gestures of head, hands, arms, and body, with leers and winks and the loose play of the tongue in the corner of his mouth, they took on meaning; an equivocal meaning, yet vaguely offensive. He wore a white sports shirt with a suit of ordinary clothes, and a strikingly large and naked-looking Adam's apple rose out of the open collar. From that pale, snub-nosed face it was hard to judge of his age; vice sat on it, it was furrowed with grimacing, and two deep wrinkles of defiance and self-will, almost of desperation, stood oddly between the red brows, above the grinning, mobile mouth. But what more than all drew upon him the profound scrutiny of our solitary watcher was that this suspicious figure seemed to carry with it its own suspicious odour. For whenever the refrain occurred and the singer, with waving arms and antic gestures, passed in his grotesque march immediately beneath Aschenbach's seat, a strong smell of carbolic was wafted up to the terrace.

After the song he began to take up money, beginning with the Russian family, who gave liberally, and then mounting the steps to the terrace. But here he became as cringing as he had before been forward. He glided between the tables, bowing and scraping, showing his strong white teeth in a servile smile, though the two deep furrows on the brow were still very marked. His audience looked at the strange creature as he went about collecting his livelihood, and their curiosity was not unmixed with disfavour. They tossed coins with their finger-tips into his hat and took care not to touch it. Let the enjoyment be never so great, a sort of embarrassment always comes when the comedian oversteps the physical distance between himself and respectable people. This man felt it and sought to make his peace by fawning. He came along the railing to Aschenbach, and with him came that smell no one else seemed to notice.

"Listen!" said the solitary, in a low voice, almost mechanically; "they are disinfecting Venice – why?" The mountebank answered hoarsely: "Because of the police. Orders, signore. On account of the heat and the sirocco. The sirocco is oppressive. Not good for the health." He spoke as though surprised that anyone could ask, and with the flat of his hand he demonstrated how oppressive the sirocco was. "So there is no plague in Venice?" Aschenbach asked the question between his teeth, very low. The man's expressive face fell, he put on a look of comical innocence. "A plague? What sort of plague? Is the sirocco a plague? Or perhaps our police are a plague! You are making fun of us, signore! A plague! Why should there be? The police make regulations on account of the heat and the weather...." He gestured. "Quite," said Aschenbach, once more, soft and low; and dropping an unduly large coin into the man's hat dismissed him with a sign. He bowed very low and left. But he had not reached the steps when two of the hotel servants flung themselves on him and began to whisper, their faces close to his. He shrugged, seemed to be giving assurances, to be swearing he had said nothing. It was not hard to guess the import of his words. They let him go at last and he went back into the garden, where he conferred briefly with his troupe and then stepped forward for a farewell song.

It was one Aschenbach had never to his knowledge heard before, a rowdy air, with words in impossible dialect. It had a laughing-refrain in which the other three artists joined at the top of their lungs. The refrain had neither words nor accompaniment, it was nothing but rhythmical, modulated, natural laughter, which the soloist in particular knew how to render with most deceptive realism. Now that he was farther off his audience, his self-assurance had come back, and this laughter of his rang with a mocking note. He would be overtaken, before he reached the end of the last line of each stanza; he would catch his breath, lay his hand over his mouth, his voice would quaver and his shoulders shake, he would lose power to contain himself longer. Just at the right moment each time, it came whooping, bawling, crashing out of him, with a verisimilitude that never failed to set his audience off in profuse and unpremeditated mirth that seemed to add gusto to his own. He bent his knees, he clapped his thigh, he held his sides, he looked ripe for bursting. He no longer laughed, but yelled, pointing his finger at the company there above as though there could be in all the world nothing so comic as they; until at last they laughed in hotel, terrace, and garden, down to the waiters, lift-boys, and servants – laughed as though possessed.

Aschenbach could no longer rest in his chair, he sat poised for flight. But the combined effect of the laughing, the hospital odour in his nostrils, and the nearness of the beloved was to hold him in a spell; he felt unable to stir. Under cover of the general commotion he looked across at Tadzio and saw that the lovely boy returned his gaze with a seriousness that seemed the copy of his own; the general hilarity, it seemed to say, had no power over him, he kept aloof. The grey-haired man was overpowered, disarmed by this docile, childlike deference; with difficulty he refrained from hiding his face in his hands. Tadzio's habit, too, of drawing himself up and taking a deep sighing breath struck him as being due to an oppression of the chest. "He is sickly, he will never live to grow up," he thought once again, with that dispassionate vision to which his madness of desire sometimes so strangely gave way. And compassion struggled with the reckless exultation of his heart.

The players, meanwhile, had finished and gone; their leader bowing and scraping, kissing his hands and adorning his leave-taking with antics that grew madder with the applause they evoked. After all the others were outside, he pretended to run backwards full tilt against a lamp-post and slunk to the gate apparently doubled over with pain. But there he threw off his buffoon's mask, stood erect, with an elastic straightening of his whole figure, ran out his tongue impudently at the guests on the terrace, and vanished in the night. The company dispersed. Tadzio had long since left the balustrade. But he, the lonely man, sat for long, to the waiters' great annoyance, before the dregs of pomegranate-juice in his glass. Time passed, the night went on. Long ago, in his parental home, he had watched the sand filter through an hour-glass – he could still see, as though it stood before him, the fragile, pregnant little toy. Soundless and fine the rust-red streamlet ran through the narrow neck, and made, as it declined in the upper cavity, an exquisite little vortex.

The very next afternoon the solitary took another step in pursuit of his fixed policy of baiting the outer world. This time he had all possible success. He went, that is, into the English travel bureau in the Piazza, changed some money at the desk, and posing as the suspicious foreigner, put his fateful question. The clerk was a tweed-clad young Britisher, with his eyes set close together, his hair parted in the middle, and radiating that steady reliability which makes his like so strange a phenomenon in the *gamin*, agile-witted south. He began: "No ground for alarm, sir. A mere formality. Quite regular in view of the unhealthy climatic conditions." But then, looking up, he chanced to meet with his own blue eyes the stranger's weary, melancholy gaze, fixed on his face. The Englishman coloured. He continued in a lower voice, rather confused: "At least, that is the official explanation, which they see fit to stick to. I may tell you there's a bit more to it than that." And then, in his good, straightforward way, he told the truth.

For the past several years Asiatic cholera had shown a strong tendency to spread. Its source was the hot, moist swamps of the delta of the Ganges, where it bred in the mephitic air of that primeval island-jungle, among whose bamboo thickets the tiger crouches, where life of every sort flourishes in rankest abundance, and only man avoids the spot. Thence the pestilence had spread throughout Hindustan, raging with great violence; moved eastward to China, westward to Afghanistan and Persia; following the great caravan routes, it brought terror to Astrakhan, terror to Moscow. Even while Europe trembled lest the spectre be seen striding westward across country, it was carried by sea from Syrian ports and appeared simultaneously at several points on the Mediterranean littoral; raised its head in Toulon and Malaga, Palermo and Naples, and soon got a firm hold in Calabria and Apulia. Northern Italy had been spared – so far. But in May the horrible vibrions were found on the same day in two bodies:

the emaciated, blackened corpses of a bargee and a woman who kept a greengrocer's shop. Both cases were hushed up. But in a week there were ten more – twenty, thirty in different quarters of the town. An Austrian provincial, having come to Venice on a few days' pleasure trip, went home and died with all the symptoms of the plague. Thus was explained the fact that the German-language papers were the first to print the news of the Venetian outbreak. The Venetian authorities published in reply a statement to the effect that the state of the city's health had never been better; at the same time instituting the most necessary precautions. But by that time the food supplies – milk, meat or vegetables – had probably been contaminated, for death unseen and unacknowledged was devouring and laying waste in the narrow streets, while a brooding, unseasonable heat warmed the waters of the canals and encouraged the spread of the pestilence. Yes, the disease seemed to flourish and wax strong, to redouble its generative powers. Recoveries were rare. Eighty out of every hundred died, and horribly, for the onslaught was of the extremest violence, and not infrequently of the "dry" type, the most malignant form of the contagion. In this form the victim's body loses power to expel the water secreted by the blood-vessels, it shrivels up, he passes with hoarse cries from convulsion to convulsion, his blood grows thick like pitch, and he suffocates in a few hours. He is fortunate indeed, if, as sometimes happens, the disease, after a slight *malaise*, takes the form of a profound unconsciousness, from which the sufferer seldom or never rouses. By the beginning of June the quarantine buildings of the *ospedale civico* had quietly filled up, the two orphan asylums were entirely occupied, and there was a hideously brisk traffic between the *Nuovo Fundamento* and the island of San Michele, where the cemetery was. But the city was not swayed by high-minded motives or regard for international agreements. The authorities were more actuated by fear of being out of pocket, by regard for the new exhibition of paintings just opened in the Public Gardens, or by apprehension of the large losses the hotels and the shops that catered to foreigners would suffer in case of panic and blockade. And the fears of the people supported the persistent official policy of silence and denial. The city's first medical officer, an honest and competent man, had indignantly resigned his office and been privily replaced by a more compliant person. The fact was known; and this corruption in high places played its part, together with the suspense as to where the walking terror might strike next, to demoralize the baser elements in the city and encourage those antisocial forces which shun the light of day. There was intemperance, indecency, increase of crime. Evenings one saw many drunken people, which was unusual. Gangs of men in surly mood made the streets unsafe, theft and assault were said to be frequent, even murder; for in two cases persons supposedly victims of the plague were proved to have been poisoned by their own families. And professional vice was rampant, displaying excesses heretofore unknown and only at home much farther south and in the east.

Such was the substance of the Englishman's tale. "You would do well," he concluded, "to leave today instead of tomorrow. The blockade cannot be more than a few days off."

"Thank you," said Aschenbach, and left the office.

The Piazza lay in sweltering sunshine. Innocent foreigners sat before the cafés or stood in front of the cathedral, the centre of clouds of doves that, with fluttering wings, tried to shoulder each other away and pick the kernels of maize from the extended hand. Aschenbach strode up and down the spacious flags, feverishly excited, triumphant in possession of the truth at last, but with a sickening taste in his mouth and a fantastic horror at his heart. One decent, expiatory course lay open to him; he considered it. Tonight, after dinner, he might approach the lady of the pearls and address her in words which he precisely formulated in his mind: "Madame, will you permit an entire stranger to serve you with a word of advice and warning which self-interest prevents others from uttering? Go away. Leave here at once, without delay, with Tadzio and your daughters. Venice is in the grip of pestilence." Then might he lay his hand in farewell upon the head of that instrument of a mocking deity; and thereafter himself flee the accursed morass. But he knew that he was far indeed from any serious desire to take such a step. It would restore him, would give him back himself once more; but he who is beside himself revolts at the idea of self-possession. There crossed his mind the vision of a white building with inscriptions on it, glittering in the sinking sun – he recalled how his mind had dreamed away into their transparent mysticism; recalled the strange pilgrim apparition that had wakened in the ageing man a lust for strange countries and fresh sights. And these memories, again, brought in their train the thought of returning home, returning to reason, self-mastery, an ordered existence, to the old life of effort. Alas! the bare thought made him wince with a revulsion that was like physical nausea. "It must be kept quiet," he whispered fiercely. "I will not speak!" The knowledge that he shared the city's secret, the city's guilt – it put him beside himself, intoxicated him as a small quantity of wine will a man suffering from brain-fag. His thoughts dwelt upon the image of the desolate and calamitous city, and he was giddy with fugitive, mad, unreasoning hopes and visions of a monstrous sweetness. That tender sentiment he had a moment ago evoked, what was it compared with such images as these? His art, his moral sense, what were they in the balance beside the boons that chaos might confer? He kept silence, he stopped on.

That night he had a fearful dream – if dream be the right word for a mental and physical experience which did indeed befall him in deep sleep, as a thing quite apart and real to his senses, yet without his seeing himself as present in it. Rather its theatre seemed to be his own soul, and the events burst in from outside, violently overcoming the profound resistance of his spirit; passed him through and left him, left the whole cultural structure of a lifetime trampled on, ravaged, and destroyed.

The beginning was fear; fear and desire, with a shuddering

curiosity. Night reigned, and his senses were on the alert; he heard loud, confused noises from far away, clamour and hubbub. There was a rattling, a crashing, a low dull thunder; shrill halloos and a kind of howl with a long-drawn *u*-sound at the end. And with all these, dominating them all, flute-notes of the cruellest sweetness, deep and cooing, keeping shamelessly on until the listener felt his very entrails bewitched. He heard a voice, naming, though darkly, that which was to come: "The stranger god!" A glow lighted up the surrounding mist and by it he recognized a mountain scene like that about his country home. From the wooded heights, from among the tree-trunks and crumbling moss-covered rocks, a troop came tumbling and raging down, a whirling rout of men and animals, and overflowed the hillside with flames and human forms, with clamour and the reeling dance. The females stumbled over the long, hairy pelts that dangled from their girdles; with heads flung back they uttered loud hoarse cries and shook their tambourines high in air; brandished naked daggers or torches vomiting trails of sparks. They shrieked, holding their breasts in both hands; coiling snakes with quivering tongues they clutched about their waists. Horned and hairy males, girt about the loins with hides, drooped heads and lifted arms and thighs in unison, as they beat on brazen vessels that gave out droning thunder, or thumped madly on drums. There were troops of beardless youths armed with garlanded staves; these ran after goats and thrust their staves against the creatures' flanks, then clung on the plunging horns and let themselves be borne off with triumphant shouts. And one and all the mad rout yelled that cry, composed of soft consonants with a long-drawn *u*-sound at the end, so sweet and wild it was together, and like nothing ever heard before! It would ring through the air like the bellow of a challenging stag, and be given back many-tongued; or they would use it to goad each other on to dance with wild excess of tossing limbs – they never let it die. But the deep, beguiling notes of the flute wove in and out and over all. Beguiling too it was to him who struggled in the grip of these sights and sounds, shamelessly awaiting the coming feast and the uttermost surrender. He trembled, he shrank, his will was steadfast to preserve and uphold his own god against this stranger who was sworn enemy to dignity and self-control. But the mountain wall took up the noise and howling and gave it back manifold; it rose high, swelled to a madness that carried him away. His senses reeled in the steam of panting bodies, the acrid stench from the goats, the odour as of stagnant waters – and another, too familiar smell – of wounds, uncleanness, and disease. His heart throbbed to the drums, his brain reeled, a blind rage seized him, a whirling lust, he craved with all his soul to join the ring that formed about the obscene symbol of the godhead, which they were unveiling and elevating, monstrous and wooden, while from full throats they yelled their rallying-cry. Foam dripped from their lips, they drove each other on with lewd gesturings and beckoning hands. They laughed, they howled, they thrust their pointed staves into each other's flesh and licked the blood as it ran down. But now the dreamer was in them and of them, the stranger god was his own. Yes, it was he who was flinging himself upon the animals, who bit and tore and swallowed smoking gobbets of flesh – while on the trampled moss there now began the rites in honour of the god, an orgy of promiscuous embraces – and in his very soul he tasted the bestial degradation of his fall.

The unhappy man woke from this dream shattered, unhinged, powerless in the demon's grip. He no longer avoided men's eyes nor cared whether he exposed himself to suspicion. And anyhow, people were leaving; many of the bathing-cabins stood empty, there were many vacant places in the dining-room, scarcely any foreigners were seen in the streets. The truth seemed to have leaked out; despite all efforts to the contrary, panic was in the air. But the lady of the pearls stopped on with her family; whether because the rumours had not reached her or because she was too proud and fearless to heed them. Tadzio remained; and it seemed at times to Aschenbach, in his obsessed state, that death and fear together might clear the island of all other souls and leave him there alone with him he coveted. In the long mornings on the beach his heavy gaze would rest, a fixed and reckless stare, upon the lad; towards nightfall, lost to shame, he would follow him through the city's narrow streets where horrid death stalked too, and at such time it seemed to him as though the moral law were fallen in ruins and only the monstrous and perverse held out a hope.

Like any lover, he desired to please; suffered agonies at the thought of failure, and brightened his dress with smart ties and handkerchiefs and other youthful touches. He added jewellery and perfumes and spent hours each day over his *toilette*, appearing at dinner elaborately arrayed and tensely excited. The presence of the youthful beauty that had bewitched him filled him with disgust of his own ageing body; the sight of his own sharp features and grey hair plunged him in hopeless mortification; he made desperate efforts to recover the appearance and freshness of his youth and began paying frequent visits to the hotel barber. Enveloped in the white sheet, beneath the hands of that garrulous personage, he would lean back in the chair and look at himself in the glass with misgiving.

"Grey," he said, with a grimace.

"Slightly," answered the man. "Entirely due to neglect, to a lack of regard for appearances. Very natural, of course, in men of affairs, but, after all, not very sensible, for it is just such people who ought to be above vulgar prejudice in matters like these. Some folk have very strict ideas about the use of cosmetics; but they never extend them to the teeth, as they logically should. And very disgusted other people would be if they did. No, we are all as old as we feel, but no older, and grey hair can misrepresent a man worse than dyed. You, for instance, signore, have a right to your natural colour. Surely you will permit me to restore what belongs to you?"

"How?" asked Aschenbach.

For answer the oily one washed his client's hair in two waters, one clear and one dark, and lo, it was as black as in the days of his youth. He waved it with the tongs in wide, flat undulations, and stepped back to admire the effect.

"Now if we were just to freshen up the skin a little," he said.

And with that he went on from one thing to another, his enthusiasm waxing with each new idea. Aschenbach sat there comfortably; he was incapable of objecting to the process – rather as it went forward it roused his hopes. He watched it in the mirror and saw his eyebrows grow more even and arching, the eyes gain in size and brilliance, by dint of a little application below the lids. A delicate carmine glowed on his cheeks where the skin had been so brown and leathery. The dry, anæmic lips grew full, they turned the colour of ripe strawberries, the lines round eyes and mouth were treated with a facial cream and gave place to youthful bloom. It was a young man who looked back at him from the glass – Aschenbach's heart leaped at the sight. The artist in cosmetic at last professed himself satisfied; after the manner of such people, he thanked his client profusely for what he had done himself. "The merest trifle, the merest, signore," he said as he added the final touches. "Now the signore can fall in love as soon as he likes." Aschenbach went off as in a dream, dazed between joy and fear, in his red neck-tie and broad straw hat with its gay striped band.

A lukewarm storm-wind had come up. It rained a little now and then, the air was heavy and turbid and smelt of decay. Aschenbach, with fevered cheeks beneath the rouge, seemed to hear rushing and flapping sounds in his ears, as though storm-spirits were abroad – unhallowed ocean harpies who follow those devoted to destruction, snatch away and defile their viands. For the heat took away his appetite and thus he was haunted with the idea that his food was infected.

One afternoon he pursued his charmer deep into the stricken city's huddled heart. The labyrinthine little streets, squares, canals, and bridges, each one so like the next, at length quite made him lose his bearings. He did not even know the points of the compass; all his care was not to lose sight of the figure after which his eyes thirsted. He slunk under walls, he lurked behind buildings or people's backs; and the sustained tension of his senses and emotions exhausted him more and more, though for a long time he was unconscious of fatigue. Tadzio walked behind the others, he let them pass ahead in the narrow alleys, and as he sauntered slowly after, he would turn his head and assure himself with a glance of his strange, twilit grey eyes that his lover was still following. He saw him – and he did not betray him. The knowledge enraptured Aschenbach. Lured by those eyes, led on the leading-string of his own passion and folly, utterly lovesick, he stole upon the footsteps of his unseemly hope – and at the end found himself cheated. The Polish family crossed a small vaulted bridge, the height of whose archway hid them from his sight, and when he climbed it himself they were nowhere to be seen. He hunted in three directions – straight ahead and on both sides of the narrow, dirty quay – in vain. Worn quite out and unnerved, he had to give over the search.

His head burned, his body was wet with clammy sweat, he was plagued by intolerable thirst. He looked about for refreshment, of whatever sort, and found a little fruit-shop where he bought some strawberries. They were overripe and soft; he ate them as he went. The street he was on opened out into a little square, one of those charmed, forsaken spots he liked; he recognized it as the very one where he had sat weeks ago and conceived his abortive plan of flight. He sank down on the steps of the well and leaned his head against its stone rim. It was quiet here. Grass grew between the stones, and rubbish lay about. Tall, weather-beaten houses bordered the square, one of them rather palatial, with vaulted windows, gaping now, and little lion balconies. In the ground floor of another was an apothecary's shop. A waft of carbolic acid was borne on a warm gust of wind.

There he sat, the master: this was he who had found a way to reconcile art and honours; who had written *The Abject*, and in a style of classic purity renounced bohemianism and all its works, all sympathy with the abyss and the troubled depths of the outcast human soul. This was he who had put knowledge underfoot to climb so high; who had outgrown the ironic pose and adjusted himself to the burdens and obligations of fame; whose renown had been officially recognized and his name ennobled, whose style was set for a model in the schools. There he sat. His eyelids were closed, there was only a swift, sidelong glint of the eyeballs now and again, something between a question and a leer; while the rouged and flabby mouth uttered single words of the sentences shaped in his disordered brain by the fantastic logic that governs our dreams.

"For mark you, Phædrus, beauty alone is both divine and visible; and so it is the senses' way, the artist's way, little Phædrus, to the spirit. But, now tell me, my dear boy, do you believe that such a man can ever attain wisdom and true manly worth, for whom the path to the spirit must lead through the senses? Or do you rather think – for I leave the point to you – that it is a path of perilous sweetness, a way of transgression, and must surely lead him who walks in it astray? For you know that we poets cannot walk the way of beauty without Eros as our companion and guide. We may be heroic after our fashion, disciplined warriors of our craft, yet are we all like women, for we exult in passion, and love is still our desire – our craving and our shame. And from this you will perceive that we poets can be neither wise nor worthy citizens. We must needs be wanton, must needs rove at large in the realm of feeling. Our magisterial style is all folly and pretence, our honourable repute a farce, the crowd's belief in us is merely laughable. And to teach youth, or the populace, by means of art is a dangerous practice and ought to be forbidden. For what good can an artist be as a teacher, when from his birth up he is headed direct for the pit? We may want to shun it and attain to honour in the world; but however we turn, it draws us still. So, then, since knowledge might destroy us, we will have none of it. For knowledge, Phædrus, does not make him who possesses it dignified or austere. Knowledge is all-knowing, understanding, forgiving; it takes up no position, sets no store by form. It has compassion with the abyss – it *is* the abyss. So we reject it, firmly, and henceforward our concern shall be with beauty only. And by beauty we mean simplicity, largeness, and renewed severity of discipline; we mean a return to detachment and to form. But detachment, Phædrus, and preoccupation with form lead to intoxication and desire, they may lead the noblest among us to frightful emotional excesses, which his own stern cult of the beautiful would make him the first to condemn. So they too, they too, lead to the bottomless pit. Yes, they lead us thither, I say, us who are poets – who by our natures are prone not to excellence but to excess. And now, Phædrus, I will go. Remain here; and only when you can no longer see me, then do you depart also."

A few days later Gustave Aschenbach left his hotel rather later than usual in the morning. He was not feeling well and had to struggle against spells of giddiness only half physical in their nature, accompanied by a swiftly mounting dread, a sense of futility and hopelessness – but whether this referred to himself or to the outer world he could not tell. In the lobby he saw a quantity of luggage lying strapped and ready; asked the porter whose it was, and received in answer the name he already knew he should hear – that of the Polish family. The expression of his ravaged features did not change; he only gave that quick lift of the head with which we sometimes receive the uninteresting answer to a casual query. But he put another: "When?" "After luncheon," the man replied. He nodded, and went down to the beach.

It was an unfriendly scene. Little crisping shivers ran all across the wide stretch of shallow water between the shore and the first sand-bank. The whole beach, once so full of colour and life, looked now autumnal, out of season; it was nearly deserted and not even very clean. A camera on a tripod stood at the edge of the water, apparently abandoned; its black cloth snapped in the freshening wind.

Tadzio was there, in front of his cabin, with the three or four playfellows still left him. Aschenbach set up his chair some half-way between the cabins and the water, spread a rug over his knees, and sat looking on. The game this time was unsupervised, the elders being probably busy with their packing, and it looked rather lawless and out-of-hand. Jaschiu, the sturdy lad in the belted suit, with the black, brilliantined hair, became angry at a handful of sand thrown in his eyes; he challenged Tadzio to a fight, which quickly ended in the downfall of the weaker. And perhaps the coarser nature saw here a chance to avenge himself at last, by one cruel act, for his long weeks of subserviency: the victor would not let the vanquished get up, but remained kneeling on Tadzio's back, pressing Tadzio's face into the sand – for so long a time that it seemed the exhausted lad might even suffocate. He made spasmodic efforts to shake the other off, lay still, and then began a feeble twitching. Just as Aschenbach was about to spring indignantly to the rescue, Jaschiu let his victim go. Tadzio, very pale, half sat up, and remained so, leaning on one arm, for several minutes, with darkening eyes and rumpled hair. Then he rose and walked slowly away. The others called him, at first gaily, then imploringly; he would not hear. Jaschiu was evidently overtaken by swift remorse; he followed his friend and tried to make his peace, but Tadzio motioned him back with a jerk of one shoulder and went down to the water's edge. He was barefoot and wore his striped linen suit with the red breast-knot.

There he stayed a little, with bent head, tracing figures in the wet sand with one toe; then stepped into the shallow water, which at its deepest did not wet his knees; waded idly through it and reached the sand-bar. Now he paused again, with his face turned seaward; and next began to move slowly leftwards along the narrow strip of sand the sea left bare. He paced there, divided by an expanse of water from the shore, from his mates by his moody pride; a remote and isolated figure, with floating locks, out there in sea and wind, against the misty inane. Once more he paused to look: with a sudden recollection, or by an impulse, he turned from the waist up, in an exquisite movement, one hand resting on his hip, and looked over his shoulder at the shore. The watcher sat just as he had sat that time in the lobby of the hotel when first the twilit grey eyes had met his own. He rested his head against the chair-back and followed the movements of the figure out there, then lifted it, as it were to Tadzio's gaze. It sank on his breast, the eyes looked out beneath their lids, while his whole face took on the relaxed and brooding expression of deep slumber. It seemed to him the pale and lovely Summoner out there smiled at him and beckoned; as though, with the hand he lifted from his hip, he pointed outward as he hovered on before into an immensity of richest expectation.

Some minutes passed before anyone hastened to the aid of the elderly man sitting there collapsed in his chair. They bore him to his room. And before nightfall a shocked and respectful world received the news of his decease.

A MAN AND HIS DOG

He Comes Round the Corner

WHEN SPRING, the fairest season of the year, does honour to its name, and when the trilling of the birds rouses me early because I have ended the day before at a seemly hour, I love to rise betimes and go for a half-hour's walk before breakfast. Strolling hatless in the broad avenue in front of my house, or through the parks beyond, I like to enjoy a few draughts of the young morning air and taste its blithe purity before I am claimed by the labours of the day. Standing on the front steps of my house, I give a whistle in two notes, tonic and lower fourth, like the beginning of the second phrase of Schubert's Unfinished Symphony; it might be considered the musical setting of a two-syllabled name. Next moment, and while I walk towards the garden gate, the faintest tinkle sounds from afar, at first scarcely audible, but growing rapidly louder and more distinct; such a sound as might be made by a metal licence-tag clicking against the trimmings of a leather collar. I face about, to see Bashan rounding the corner of the house at top speed and charging towards me as though he meant to knock me down. In the effort he is making he has dropped his lower lip, baring two white teeth that glitter in the morning sun.

He comes straight from his kennel, which stands at the back of the house, between the props of the veranda floor. Probably, until my two-toned call set him in this violent motion, he had been lying there snatching a nap after the adventures of the night. The kennel has curtains of sacking and is lined with straw; indeed, a straw or so may be clinging to Bashan's sleep-rumpled coat or even sticking between his toes – a comic sight, which reminds me of a painstakingly imagined production of Schiller's *Die Räuber* that I once saw, in which old Count Moor came out of the Hunger Tower tricot-clad, with a straw sticking pathetically between his toes. Involuntarily I assume a defensive position to meet the charge, receiving it on my flank, for Bashan shows every sign of meaning to run between my legs and trip me up. However at the last minute, when a collision is imminent, he always puts on the brakes, executing a half-wheel which speaks for both his mental and his physical self-control. And then, without a sound – for he makes sparing use of his sonorous and expressive voice – he dances wildly round me by way of greeting, with immoderate plungings and waggings which are not confined to the appendage provided by nature for the purpose but bring his whole hind quarters as far as his ribs into play. He contracts his whole body into a curve, he hurtles into the air in a flying leap, he turns round and round on his own axis – and curiously enough, whichever way I turn, he always contrives to execute these manoeuvres behind my back. But the moment I stoop down and put out my hand he jumps to my side and stands like a statue, with his shoulder against my shin, in a slantwise posture, his strong paws braced against the ground, his face turned upwards so that he looks at me upside-down. And his utter immobility, as I pat his shoulder and murmur encouragement, is as concentrated and fiercely passionate as the frenzy before it had been.

Bashan is a short-haired German pointer – speaking by and large, that is, and not too literally. For he is probably not quite orthodox, as a pure matter of points. In the first place, he is a little too small. He is, I repeat, definitely undersized for a proper pointer. And then his forelegs are not absolutely straight, they have just the suggestion of an outward curve – which also detracts from his qualifications as a blood-dog. And he has a tendency to a dewlap, those folds of hanging skin under the muzzle, which in Bashan's case are admirably becoming but again would be frowned on by your fanatic for pure breeding, as I understand that a pointer should have taut skin round the neck. Bashan's colouring is very fine. His coat is a rusty brown with black stripes and a good deal of white on chest, paws, and under side. The whole of his snub nose seems to have been dipped in black paint. Over the broad top of his head and on his cool hanging ears the black and brown combine in a lovely velvety pattern. Quite the prettiest thing about him, however, is the whorl or stud or little tuft at the centre of the convolution of white hairs on his chest, which stands out like the boss on an ancient breastplate. Very likely even his splendid coloration is a little too marked and would be objected to by those who put the laws of breeding above the value of personality, for it would appear that the classic pointer type should have a coat of one colour or at most with spots of a different one, but never stripes. Worst of all, from the point of view of classification, is a hairy growth hanging from his muzzle and the corners of his mouth; it might with some justice be called a moustache and goatee, and when you concentrate on it, close at hand or even at a distance, you cannot help thinking of an airedale or a schnauzer.

But classifications aside, what a good and good-looking animal Bashan is, as he stands there straining against my knee, gazing up at me with all his devotion in his eyes! They are particularly fine eyes, too, both gentle and wise, if just a little too prominent and glassy. The iris is the same colour as his coat, a rusty brown; it is only a narrow rim, for the pupils are dilated into pools of blackness and the outer edge merges into the white of the eye wherein it swims. His whole head is expressive of honesty and intelligence, of manly qualities corresponding to his physical structure: his arched and swelling chest where the ribs stand out under the smooth and supple skin; the narrow haunches, the veined, sinewy legs, the strong, well-shaped paws. All these bespeak virility and a stout heart; they suggest hunting blood and peasant stock – yes, certainly the hunter and game dog do after all predominate in Bashan, he is genuine pointer, no matter if he does not owe his existence to a snobbish system of inbreeding. All this, probably, is what I am really telling him as I pat his shoulder-blade and address him with a few disjointed words of encouragement.

So he stands and looks and listens, gathering from what I say and the tone of it that I distinctly approve of his existence – the very thing which I am at pains to imply. And suddenly he thrusts out his head, opening and shutting his lips very fast, and makes a snap at my face as though he meant to bite off my nose. It is a gesture of response to my remarks, and it always make me recoil with a laugh, as Bashan knows beforehand that it will. It is a kiss in the air, half caress, half teasing, a trick he has had since puppyhood, which I have never seen in any of his predecessors. And he immediately begs pardon for the liberty, crouching, wagging his tail, and behaving funnily embarrassed. So we go out through the garden gate and into the open.

We are encompassed with a roaring like that of the sea; for we live almost directly on the swift-flowing river that foams over shallow ledges at no great distance from the poplar avenue. In between lie a fenced-in grass plot planted with maples, and a raised pathway skirted with huge aspen trees, bizarre and willowlike of aspect. At the beginning of June their seed-pods strew the ground far and wide with woolly snow. Upstream, in the direction of the city, construction troops are building a pontoon bridge. Shouts of command and the thump of heavy boots on the planks sound across the river; also, from the farther bank, the noise of industrial activity, for there is a locomotive foundry a little way downstream. Its premises have been lately enlarged to meet increased demands, and light streams all night long from its lofty windows. Beautiful glittering new engines roll to and fro on trial runs; a steam whistle emits wailing head-tones from time to time; muffled thunderings of unspecified origin shatter the air, smoke pours out of the many chimneys to be caught up by the wind and borne away over the wooded country beyond the river, for it seldom or never blows over to our side. Thus in our half-suburban, half-rural seclusion the voice of nature mingles with that of man, and over all lies the bright-eyed freshness of the new day.

It might be about half past seven by official time when I set out; by sun-time, half past six. With my hands behind my back I stroll in the tender sunshine down the avenue, cross-hatched by the long shadows of the poplar trees. From where I am I cannot see the river, but I hear its broad and even flow. The trees whisper gently, song-birds fill the air with their penetrating chirps and warbles, twitters and trills; from the direction of the sunrise a plane is flying under the humid blue sky, a rigid, mechanical bird with a droning hum that rises and falls as it steers a free course above river and fields. And Bashan is delighting my eyes with the beautiful long leaps he is making across the low rail of the grass-plot on my left. Backwards and forwards he leaps – as a matter of fact he is doing it because he knows I like it; for I have often urged him on by shouting and striking the railing, praising him when he fell in with my whim. So now he comes up to me after nearly every jump to hear how intrepidly and elegantly he jumps. He even springs up into my face and slavers all over the arm I put out to protect it. But the jumping is also to be conceived as a sort of morning exercise, and morning toilet as well, for it smooths his ruffled coat and rids it of old Moor's straws.

It is good to walk like this in the early morning, with senses rejuvenated and spirit cleansed by the night's long healing draught of Lethe. You look confidently forward to the day, yet pleasantly hesitate to begin it, being master as you are of this little untroubled span of time between, which is your good reward for good behaviour. You indulge in the illusion that your life is habitually steady, simple, concentrated, and contemplative, that you belong entirely to yourself – and this illusion makes you quite happy. For a human being tends to believe that the mood of the moment, be it troubled or blithe, peaceful or stormy, is the true, native, and permanent tenor of his existence; and in particular he likes to exalt every happy chance into an inviolable rule and to regard it as the benign order of his life – whereas the truth is that he is condemned to improvisation and morally lives from hand to mouth all the time. So now, breathing the morning air, you stoutly believe that you are virtuous and free; while you ought to know – and at bottom do know – that the world is spreading its snares round your feet, and that most likely tomorrow you will be lying in your bed until nine, because you sought it at two in the morning hot and befogged with impassioned discussion. Never mind. Today you, a sober character, an early riser, you are the right master for that stout hunter who has just cleared the railings again out of sheer joy in the fact that today you apparently belong to him alone and not to the world.

We follow the avenue for about five minutes, to the point where it ceases to be an avenue and becomes a gravelly waste along the river-bank. From this we turn away to our right and strike into another covered with finer gravel, which has been laid out like the avenue and like it provided with a cycle-path, but is not yet built up. It runs between low-lying, wooded lots of land, towards the slope which is the eastern limit of our river neighbourhood and Bashan's theatre of action. On our way we cross another road, equally embryonic, running along between fields and meadows. Farther up, however, where the tram stops, it is quite built up with flats. We descend by a gravel path into a well-laid-out, parklike valley, quite deserted, as indeed the whole region is at this hour. Paths are laid out in curves and rondels, there are benches to rest on, tidy playgrounds, and wide plots of lawn with fine old trees whose boughs nearly sweep the grass, covering all but a glimpse of trunk. They are elms, beeches, limes, and silvery willows, in well-disposed groups. I enjoy to the full the well-landscaped quality of the scene, where I may walk no more disturbed than if it belonged to me alone. Nothing has been forgotten – there are even cement gutters in the gravel paths that lead down the grassy slopes. And the abundant greenery discloses here and there a charming distant vista of one of the villas that bound the spot on two sides.

Here for a while I stroll along the paths, and Bashan revels in the freedom of unlimited level space, galloping across and across the lawns like mad with his body inclined in a centrifugal plane; sometimes, barking with mingled pleasure and exasperation, he pursues a bird which flutters as though spellbound, but perhaps on purpose to tease him, along the ground just in front of his nose. But if I sit down on a bench he is at my side at once and takes up a position on one of my feet. For it is a law of his being that he only runs about when I am in motion too; that when I settle down he follows suit. There seems no obvious reason for this practice; but Bashan never fails to conform to it.

I get an odd, intimate, and amusing sensation from having him sit on my foot and warm it with the blood-heat of his body. A pervasive feeling of sympathy and good cheer fills me, as almost invariably when in his company and looking at things from his angle. He has a rather rustic slouch when he sits down; his shoulder-blades stick out and his paws turn negligently in. He looks smaller and squatter than he really is, and the little white boss on his chest is advanced with comic effect. But all these faults are atoned for by the lofty and dignified carriage of the head, so full of concentration. All is quiet, and we two sit there absolutely still in our turn. The rushing of the water comes to us faint and subdued. And the senses become alert for all the tiny, mysterious little sounds that nature makes: the lizard's quick dart, the note of a bird, the burrowing of a mole in the earth. Bashan pricks up his ears – in so far as the muscles of naturally drooping ears will allow them to be pricked. He cocks his head to hear the better; and the nostrils of his moist black nose keep twitching sensitively as he sniffs.

Then he lies down, but always in contact with my foot. I see him in profile, in that age-old, conventionalized pose of the beast-god, the sphinx: head and chest held high, forelegs close to the body, paws extended in parallel lines. He has got over-heated, so he opens his mouth, and at once all the intelligence of his face gives way to the merely animal, his eyes narrow and blink and his rosy tongue lolls out between his strong white pointed teeth.

How We Got Bashan

In the neighbourhood of Tölz there is a mountain inn, kept by a pleasingly buxom, black-eyed damsel, with the assistance of a growing daughter, equally buxom and black-eyed. This damsel it was who acted as go-between in our introduction to Bashan and our subsequent acquisition of him. Two years ago now that was; he was six months old at the time. Anastasia – for so the damsel was called – knew that we had had to have our last dog shot; Percy by name, a Scotch collie by breeding and a harmless, feeble-minded aristocrat who in his old age fell victim to a painful and disfiguring skin disease which obliged us to put him away. Since that time we had been without a guardian. She telephoned from her mountain height to say that she had taken to board a dog that was exactly what we wanted and that it might be inspected at any time. The children clamoured to see it, and our own curiosity was scarcely behind theirs; so the very next afternoon we climbed up to Anastasia's inn, and found her in her roomy kitchen full of warm and succulent steam, preparing her lodgers' supper. Her face was brick-red, her brow was wet, the sleeves were rolled back on her plump arms, and her frock was open at the throat. Her young daughter went to and fro, an industrious kitchen-maid. They were glad to see us and thoroughly approved of our having lost no time in coming. We looked about; whereupon Resi, the daughter, led us up to the kitchen table and, squatting with her hands on her knees, addressed a few encouraging words beneath it. Until then, in the flickering half-light, we had seen nothing; but now we perceived something standing there, tied by a bit of rope to the table-leg: an object that must have made any soul alive burst into half-pitying laughter.

Gaunt and knock-kneed he stood there with his tail between his hind legs, his four paws planted together, his back arched, shaking. He may have been frightened, but one had the feeling that he had not enough on his bones to keep him warm; for indeed the poor little animal was a skeleton, a mere rack of bones with a spinal column, covered with a rough fell and stuck up on four sticks. He had laid back his ears – which muscular contraction never fails to extinguish every sign of intelligence and cheer in the face of any dog. In him, who was still entirely puppy, the effect was so consummate that he stood there expressive of nothing but wretchedness, stupidity, and a mute appeal for our forbearance. And his hirsute appendages, which he has to this day, were then out of all proportion to his size and added a final touch of sour hypochondria to his appearance.

We all stooped down and began to coax and encourage this picture of misery. The children were delighted and sympathetic at once, and their shouts mingled with the voice of Anastasia as, standing by her cooking-stove, she began to furnish us with the particulars of her charge's origins and history. He was named, provisionally, Lux, she said, in her pleasant, level voice; and was the offspring of irreproachable parents. She had herself known the mother and of the father had heard nothing but good. Lux had seen the light on a farm in Hugelfing; and it was only due to a combination of circumstances that his owners were willing to part with him cheaply. They had brought him to her inn because there he might be seen by a good many people. They had come in a cart, Lux bravely running the whole twenty kilometres behind the wheels. She, Anastasia, had thought of us at once, knowing that we were on the look-out for a good dog and feeling certain that we should want him. If we so decided, it would be a good thing all around. She was sure we should have great joy of him, he in his turn would have found a good home and be no longer lonely in the world, and she, Anastasia, would know that he was well taken care of. We must not be prejudiced by the figure he cut at the moment; he was upset by his strange surroundings and uncertain of himself, but his good breeding would come out strong before long. His father and mother were of the best.

Ye-es – but perhaps not quite well matched?

On the contrary; that is, they were both of them good stock. He had excellent points – she, Anastasia, would vouch for that. He was not spoilt, either, his needs were modest – and that meant a great deal, nowadays. In fact, up to now he had had nothing to eat but potato-parings. She suggested that we take him home on trial; if we found that we did not take to him she would receive him back and refund the modest sum that was asked for him. She made free to say this, not minding at all if we took her up. Because, knowing the dog and knowing us, both parties, as it were, she was convinced that we should grow to love him, and never dream of giving him up.

All this she said and a great deal more in the same strain in her easy, comfortable, voluble way, working the while over her stove, where the flames shot up suddenly now and then as though we were in a witches' kitchen. She even came and opened Lux's jaws with both hands to show us his beautiful teeth and – for some reason or other – the pink grooves in the roof of his mouth. We asked knowingly if he had had distemper; she replied with a little impatience that she really could not say. Our next question – how large would he get – she answered more glibly: he would be about the size of our departed Percy, she said. There were more questions and answers; a good deal of warm-hearted urging from Anastasia, prayers and pleas from the children, and on our side a feeble lack of resolution. At last we begged for a little time to think things over; she agreed, and we went thoughtfully valleywards, changing impressions as we went.

But of course the children had lost their hearts to the wretched little quadruped under the table; in vain we affected to jeer at their lack of judgment and taste, feeling the pull at our own heartstrings. We saw that we should not be able to get him out of our heads; we asked ourselves what would become of him if we scorned him. Into what hands would he fall? The question called up a horrid memory, we saw again the knacker from whom we had rescued Percy with a few timely and merciful bullets and an honourable grave by the garden fence. If we wanted to abandon Lux to an uncertain and perhaps gruesome fate, then we should never have seen him at all, never cast eyes upon his infant whiskered face. We knew him now, we felt a responsibility which we could disclaim only by an arbitrary exercise of authority.

So it was that the third day found us climbing up those same gentle foothills of the Alps. Not that we had decided to buy – no, we only saw that, as things stood, the matter could hardly have any other outcome.

This time we found Frau Anastasia and her daughter drinking coffee, one at each end of the long kitchen table, while between them he sat who bore provisionally the name of Lux, in his very attitude as he sits today, slouching over with his shoulder-blades stuck out and his paws turned in. A bunch of wild flowers in his worn leather collar gave him a festive look, like a rustic bridegroom or a village lad in his Sunday best. The daughter, looking very trim herself in the tight bodice of her peasant costume, said that she had adorned him thus to celebrate his entry into his new home. Mother and daughter both told us they had never been more certain of anything in their lives than that we would come back to fetch him – they knew that we would come this very day.

So there was nothing more to say. Anastasia thanked us in her pleasant way for the purchase price – ten marks – which we handed over. It was clear that she had asked it in our interest rather than in hers or that of the dog's owners; it was by way of giving Lux a positive value, in terms of money, in our eyes. We quite understood, and paid it gladly. Lux was untied from his table-leg and the end of the rope laid in my hand; we crossed Anastasia's door-step followed by the warmest, most cordial assurances and good wishes.

But the homeward way, which it took us an hour to cover, was scarcely a triumphal procession. The bridegroom soon lost his bouquet, while everybody we met either laughed or else jeered at his appearance – and we met a good many people, for our route lay through the length of the market town at the foot of the hill. The last straw was that Lux proved to be suffering from an apparently chronic diarrhœa, which obliged us to make frequent pauses under the villagers' eyes. At such times we formed a circle round him to shield his weakness from unfriendly eyes – asking ourselves whether this was not distemper already making its appearance. Our anxiety was uncalled-for: the future was to prove that we were dealing with a sound and cleanly constitution, which has been proof against distemper and all such ailments up to this day.

Directly we got home we summoned the maids to make acquaintance with the new member of the family and express their modest judgment of his worth. They had evidently been prepared to praise; but, reading our own insecurity in our eyes, they laughed loudly, turning their backs upon the appealing object and waving him off with their hands. We doubted whether they could understand the nature of our financial transaction with the benevolent Anastasia and in our weakness declared that we had had him as a present. Then we led Lux into the veranda and regaled him with a hearty meal of scraps.

He was too frightened to eat. He sniffed at the food we urged upon him, but was evidently, in his modesty, unable to believe that these cheese-parings and chicken-bones were meant for him. But he did not reject the sack stuffed with seaweed which we had prepared for him on the floor. He lay there with his paws drawn up under him, while within we took counsel and eventually came to a conclusion about the name he was to bear in the future.

On the following day he still refused to eat; then came a period when he gulped down everything that came within reach of his muzzle; but gradually he settled down to a regular and more fastidious regimen, this result roughly corresponding with his adjustment to his new life in general, so that I will not dwell further upon it. The process of adaptation suffered an interruption one day – Bashan disappeared. The children had taken him into the garden and let him off the lead for better freedom of action. In a momentary lapse of vigilance he had escaped through the hole under the garden gate and gained the outer world. We were grieved and upset at his loss – at least the masters of the house were, for the maids seemed inclined to take light-heartedly the loss of a dog which we had received as a gift; perhaps they did not even consider it a loss. We telephoned wildly to Anastasia's inn, hoping he might find his way thither. In vain, nobody had seen him; two days passed before we heard that Anastasia had word from Hugelfing that Lux had put in an appearance at his first home some hour and a half before. Yes, he was there, his native idealism had drawn him back to the world of his early potato-parings; through wind and weather he had trotted alone the twelve or fourteen miles which he had first covered between the hind wheels of the farmer's cart. His former owners had to use it again to deliver him into Anastasia's hands once more. On the second day after that we went up to reclaim the wanderer, whom we found as before, tied to the table-leg, jaded and dishevelled, bemired from the mud of the roads. He did show signs of being glad to see us again – but then, why had he gone away?

The time came when it was plain that he had forgotten the farm – yet without having quite struck root with us; so that he was a masterless soul and like a leaf carried by the wind. When we took him walking we had to keep close watch, for he tended to snap the frail bond of sympathy which was all that as yet united us and to lose himself unobtrusively in the woods, where, being quite on his own, he would certainly have reverted to the condition of his wild forebears. Our care preserved him from this dark fate, we held him fast upon his civilized height and to his position as the comrade of man, which his race in the course of millennia has achieved. And then a decisive event, our removal to the city – or a suburb of it – made him wholly dependent upon us and definitely a member of the family.

Notes on Bashan's Character and Manner of Life

A man in the Isar valley had told me that this kind of dog can become a nuisance, by always wanting to be with his master. Thus I was forewarned against taking too personally Bashan's persistent faithfulness to myself, and it was easier for me to discourage it a little and protect myself at need. It is a deep-lying patriarchal instinct in the dog which leads him – at least in the more manly, outdoor breeds – to recognize and honour in the man of the house and head of the family his absolute master and overlord, protector of the hearth; and to find in the relation of vassalage to him the basis and value of his own existence, whereas his attitude towards the rest of the family is much more independent. Almost from the very first day Bashan behaved in this spirit towards me, following me with his trustful eyes that seemed to be begging me to order him about – which I was chary of doing, for time soon showed that obedience was not one of his strong points – and dogging my footsteps in the obvious conviction that sticking to me was the natural order of things. In the family circle he always sat at my feet, never by any chance at anyone else's. And when we were walking, if I struck off on a path by myself, he invariably followed me and not the others. He insisted on being with me when I worked; if the garden door was closed he would disconcert me by jumping suddenly in at the window, bringing much gravel in his train and flinging himself down panting beneath my desk.

But the presence of any living thing – even a dog – is something of which we are very conscious; we attend to it in a way that is disturbing when we want to be alone. Thus Bashan could become a quite tangible nuisance. He would come up to me wagging his tail, look at me with devouring gaze, and prance provocatively. On the smallest encouragement he would put his fore-paws on the arm of my chair, lean against me, and make me laugh with his kisses in the air. Then he would examine the things on my desk, obviously under the impression that they must be good to eat since he so often found me stooped above them; and so doing would smudge my freshly written page with his broad, hairy hunter's paws. I would sharply call him to order and he would lie down on the floor and go to sleep. But when he slept he dreamed, making running motions with all four paws and barking in a subterranean but perfectly audible sort of way. I quite comprehensibly found this distracting; in the first place the sound was uncannily ventriloquistic, in the second it gave me a guilty feeling. For this dream life was obviously an artificial substitute for real running, hunting, and open-air activity; it was supplied to him by his own nature because his life with me did not give him as much of it as his blood and his senses required. I felt touched; but since there was nothing for it, I was constrained in the name of my higher interests to throw off the incubus, telling myself that Bashan brought altogether too much mud into the room and also that he damaged the carpet with his claws.

So then the fiat went forth that he might not be with me or in the house when I was there – though of course there might be exceptions to the rule. He was quick to understand and submit to the unnatural prohibition, as being the inscrutable will of his lord and master. The separation from me – which in winter often lasted the greater part of the day – was in his mind only a separation, not a divorce or severance of connections. He may not be with me, because I have so ordained. But the not being with me is a kind of negative being-with-me, just in that it is carrying out my command. Hence we can hardly speak of an independent existence carried on by Bashan during the hours when he is not by my side. Through the glass door of my study I can see him on the grass-plot in front of the house, playing with the children and putting on an absurd avuncular air. He repeatedly comes to the door and sniffs at the crack – he cannot see me through the muslin curtains – to assure himself of my presence within; then he sits down and mounts guard with his back to the door. Sometimes I see him from my window prosing along on the elevated path between the aspen trees; but this is only to pass the time, the excursion is void of all pride or joy in life; in fact it is unthinkable that Bashan should devote himself to the pleasures of the chase on his own account, though there is nothing to prevent him from doing so and my presence, as will be seen, is not always an unmixed advantage.

Life for him begins when I issue from the house – though, alas, it does not always begin even then! For the question is, when I do go out, which way am I going to turn: to the right, down the avenue, the road towards the open and our hunting-ground, or towards the left and the place where the trams stop, to ride into town? Only in the first case is there any sense in accompanying me. At first he used to follow me even when I turned left; when the tram thundered up he would look at it with amazement and then, suppressing his fears, land with one blind and devoted leap among the crowd on the platform. Thence being dislodged by the popular indignation, he would gallop along on the ground behind the roaring vehicle which so little resembled the cart he once knew. He would keep up with it as long as he could, his breath getting shorter and shorter. But the city traffic bewildered his rustic brains; he got between people's legs, strange dogs fell on his flank, he was confused by a volume and variety of smells, the like of which he had never imagined, irresistibly distracted by house-corners impregnated with lingering ancient scents of old adventures. He would fall behind; sometimes he would overtake the tram again, sometimes not; sometimes he over-took the wrong one, which looked just the same, ran blindly in the wrong direction, farther and farther into a mad, strange world. Once he only came home after two days' absence, limping and starved to death, and, seeking the peace of the last house on the river-bank, found that his lord and master had been sensible enough to get there before him.

This happened two or three times. Then he gave it up and definitely declined to go with me when I turned to the left. He always knows instantly whether I have chosen the wild or the world, directly I get outside the door. He springs up from the mat in the entrance where he has been waiting for me and in that moment divines my intentions; my clothes betray me, the cane I carry, probably even my bearing: my cold and negligent glance or on the other hand the challenging eye I turn upon him. He understands. In the one case he tumbles over himself down the steps, he whirls round and round like a stone in a sling as in dumb rejoicing he runs before me to the gate. In the other he crouches, lays back his ears, the light goes out of his eyes, the fire I have kindled by my appearance dies down to ashes, and he puts on the guilty look which men and animals alike wear when they are unhappy.

Sometimes he cannot believe his eyes, even though they plainly tell him that there is no hope for the chase today. His yearning has been too strong. He refuses to see the signs, the urban walking-stick, the careful city clothes. He presses beside me through the gate, turns round like lightning, and tries to make me turn right, by running off at a gallop in that direction, twisting his head round and ignoring that fatal negative which I oppose to his efforts. When I actually turn to the left he comes back and walks with me along the hedge, with little snorts and head-tones which seem to emerge from the high tension of his interior. He takes to jumping to and fro over the park railings, although they are rather high for comfort, and he gives little moans as he leaps, being evidently afraid of hurting himself. He jumps with a sort of desperate gaiety which is bent on ignoring reality; also in the hope of beguiling me by his performance. For there is still a little – a very little – hope that I may still leave the highroad at the end of the park and turn left after all by the roundabout way past the pillarbox, as I do when I have letters to post. But I do that very seldom; so when that last hope has fled, then Bashan sits down and lets me go my way.

There he sits, in that clumsy rustic posture of his, in the middle of the road and looks after me as far as he can see me. If I turn my head he pricks up his ears, but he does not follow; even if I whistled he would not, for he knows it would be useless. When I turn out of the avenue I can still see him sitting there, a small, dark, clumsy figure in the road, and it goes to my heart, I have pangs of conscience as I mount the tram. He has waited so long – and we all know what torture waiting can be! His whole life is a waiting – waiting for the next walk in the open, a waiting that begins as soon as he is rested from the last one. Even his night consists of waiting; for his sleep is distributed throughout the whole twenty-four hours of the day, with many a little nap on the grass in the garden, the sun shining down warm on his coat, or behind the curtains of his kennel, to break up and shorten the empty spaces of the day. Thus his night sleep is broken too, not continuous, and manifold instincts urge him abroad in the darkness; he dashes to and fro all over the garden – and he waits. He waits for the night watchman to come on his rounds with his lantern and when he hears the recurrent heavy tread heralds it, against his own better knowledge, with a terrific outburst of barking. He waits for the sky to grow pale, for the cocks to crow at the nursery-gardener's close by; for the morning breeze to rise among the tree-tops – and for the kitchen door to be opened, so that he may slip in and warm himself at the stove.

Still, the night-time martyrdom must be mild compared with what Bashan has to endure in the day. And particularly when the weather is fine, either winter or summer, when the sunshine lures one abroad and all the muscles twitch with the craving for violent motion – and the master, without whom it is impossible to conceive doing anything, simply will not leave his post behind the glass door. All that agile little body, feverishly alive with pulsating life, is rested through and through, is worn out with resting; sleep is not to be thought of. He comes up on the terrace outside my door, lets himself down with a sigh that seems to come from his very heart, and rests his head on his paws, rolling his eyes up patiently to heaven. That lasts but a few seconds, he cannot stand the position any more, he sickens of it. One other thing there is to do. He can go down again and lift his leg against one of the little formal arbor-vitæ trees that flank the rose-bed – it is the one to the right that suffers from his attentions, wasting away so that it has to be replanted every year. He does go down, then, and performs this action, not because he needs to, but just to pass the time. He stands there a long time, with very little to show for it, however – so long that the hind leg in the air begins to tremble and he has to give a little hop to regain his balance. On four legs once more he is no better off than he was. He stares stupidly up into the boughs of the ash trees, where two birds are flitting and chirping; watches them dart off like arrows and turns away as though in contempt of such light-headedness. He stretches and stretches, fit to tear himself apart. The stretching is very thorough; it is done in two sections, thus: first the forelegs, lifting the hind ones into the air; second the rear quarters, by sprawling them out on the ground; both actions being accompanied by tremendous yawning. Then that is over too, cannot be spun out any longer, and if you have just finished an exhaustive stretching you cannot do it over again just at once. He stands still and looks gloomily at the ground. Then he begins to turn round on himself, slowly and consideringly, as though he wanted to lie down, yet was not quite certain of the best way to do it. Finally he decides not to; he moves off sluggishly to the middle of the grass-plot, and once there flings himself violently on his back and scrubs to and fro as though to cool off on the shaven turf. Quite a blissful sensation, this, it seems, for his paws jerk and he snaps in all directions in a delirium of release and satisfaction. He drains this joy down to its vapid dregs, aware that it is fleeting, that you cannot roll and tumble more than ten seconds at most, and that no sound and soul-contenting weariness will result from it, but only a flatness and returning boredom, such as always follows when one tries to drug oneself. He lies there on his side with his eyes rolled up, as though he were dead. Then he gets up and shakes himself, shakes as only his like can shake without fearing concussion of the brain; shakes until everything rattles, until his ears flop together under his chin and foam flies from his dazzling white teeth. And then? He stands perfectly still in his tracks, rigid, dead to the world, without the least idea what to do next. And then, driven to extremes, he climbs the steps once more, comes up to the glass door, lifts his paw and scratches – hesitantly, with his ears laid back, the complete beggar. He scratches only once, quite faintly; but this timidly lifted paw, this single, faint-hearted scratch, to which he has come because he simply cannot think of anything else, are too moving. I get up and open the door, though I know it can lead to no good. And he begins to dance and jump, challenging me to be a man and come abroad with him. He rumples the rugs, upsets the whole room and makes an end of all my peace and quiet. But now judge for yourself if, after I have seen Bashan wait like this, I can find it easy to go off in the tram and leave him, a pathetic little dot at the end of the poplar avenue!

In the long twilights of summer, things are not quite so bad: there is a good chance that I will take an evening walk in the open and thus even after long waiting he will come into his own and with good luck be able to start a hare. But in winter if I go off in the afternoon it is all over for the day, all hope must be buried for another four-and-twenty hours. For night will have fallen; if I go out again our hunting-grounds will lie in inaccessible darkness and I must bend my steps towards the traffic, the lighted streets, and city parks up the river – and this does not suit Bashan's simple soul. He came with me at first, but soon gave it up and stopped at home. Not only that space and freedom were lacking; he was afraid of the bright lights in the darkness, he shied at every bush, at every human form. A policeman's flapping cloak could make him swerve aside with a yelp or even lead him to attack the officer with a courage born of desperation; when the latter, frightened in his turn, would let loose a stream of abuse to our address. Unfortunate episodes mounted up when Bashan and I went out together in the dark and the damp. And speaking of policemen reminds me that there are three classes of human beings whom Bashan does especially abhor: policemen, monks, and chimney-sweeps. He cannot stand them, he assails them with a fury of barking wherever he sees them or when they chance to pass the house.

And winter is of course the time of year when freedom and sobriety are with most difficulty preserved against snares; when it is hardest to lead a regular, retired, and concentrated existence; when I may even seek the city a second time in the day. For the evening has its social claims, pursuing which I may come back at midnight, with the last tram, or losing that am driven to return on foot, my head in a whirl with ideas and wine and smoke, full of roseate views of the world and of course long past the point of normal fatigue. And then the embodiment of that other, truer, soberer life of mine, my own hearthstone, in person, as it were, may come to meet me; not wounded, not reproachful, but on the contrary giving me joyous welcome and bringing me back to my own. I mean, of course, Bashan. In pitchy darkness, the river roaring in my ears, I turn into the poplar avenue, and after the first few steps I am enveloped in a soundless storm of prancings and swishings; on the first occasion I did not know what was happening. "Bashan?" I inquire into the blackness. The prancings and swishings redouble – is this a dancing dervish or a berserk warrior here on my path? But not a sound; and directly I stand still, I feel those honest, wet and muddy paws on the lapels of my raincoat, and a snapping and flapping in my face, which I draw back even as I stoop down to pat the lean shoulder, equally wet with snow or rain. Yes, the good soul has come to meet the tram. Well informed as always upon my comings and goings, he has got up at what he judged to be the right time, to fetch me from the station. He may have been waiting a long while, in snow or rain, yet his joy at my final appearance knows no resentment at my faithlessness, though I have neglected him all day and brought his hopes to naught. I pat and praise him, and as we go home together I tell him what a fine fellow he is and promise him (that is to say, not so much him as myself) that tomorrow, no matter what the weather, we two will follow the chase together. And resolving thus, I feel my worldly preoccupations melt away; sobriety returns; for the image I have conjured up of our hunting-ground and the charms of its solitude is linked in my mind with the call to higher, stranger, more obscure concerns of mine.

There are still other traits of Bashan's character which I should like to set down here, so that the gentle reader may get as lively and speaking an image of him as is anyway possible. Perhaps the best way would be for me to compare him with our deceased Percy; for a better-defined contrast than that between these two never existed within the same species. First and foremost we must remember that Bashan was entirely sound in mind, whereas Percy, as I have said, and as often happens among aristocratic canines, had always been mad, through and through, a perfectly typical specimen of frantic over-breeding. I have referred to this subject before, in a somewhat wider connection; here I only want, for purposes of comparison, to speak of Bashan's infinitely simpler, more ordinary mentality, expressed for instance in the way he would greet you, or in his behaviour on our walks. His manifestations were always within the bounds of a hearty and healthy common sense; they never even bordered on the hysterical, whereas Percy's on all such occasions overstepped them in a way that was at times quite shocking.

And even that does not quite cover the contrast between these two creatures; the truth is more complex and involved still. Bashan is coarser-fibred, true, like the lower classes; but like them also he is not above complaining. His noble predecessor, on the other hand, united more delicacy and a greater capacity for suffering, with an infinitely firmer and prouder spirit; despite all his foolishness he far excelled in self-discipline the powers of Bashan's peasant soul. In saying this I am not defending any aristocratic system of values. It is simply to do honour to truth and actuality that I want to bring out the mixture of softness and hardiness, delicacy and firmness in the two natures. Bashan, for instance, is quite able to spend the coldest winter night out of doors, behind the sacking curtains of his kennel. He has a weakness of the bladder which makes it impossible for him to remain seven hours shut up in a room; we have to fasten him out, even in the most inhospitable weather, and trust to his robust constitution. Sometimes after a particularly bitter and foggy winter night he comes into the house with his moustache and whiskers like delicately frosted wires; with a little cold, even, and coughing in the odd, one-syllabled way that dogs have. But in a few hours he has got all over it and takes no harm at all. Whereas we should never have dared to expose our silken-haired Percy to such rigours. Yet Bashan is afraid of the slightest pain, behaving so abjectly that one would feel disgusted if the plebeian simplicity of his behaviour did not make one laugh instead. When he goes stalking in the underbrush, I constantly hear him yelping because he has been scratched by a thorn or a branch has struck him in the face. If he hurts his foot or skins his belly a little, jumping over a fence, he sets up a cry like an antique hero in his death-agony; comes to me hobbling on three legs, howling and lamenting in an abandonment of self-pity – the more piercingly, the more sympathy he gets – and this although in fifteen minutes he will be running and jumping again as though nothing had happened.

With Percival it was otherwise; he clenched his jaws and was still. He was afraid of the dog-whip, as Bashan is too; and tasted it, alas, more often than the latter, for in his day I was younger and quick-tempered and his witlessness often assumed a vicious aspect which cried out for chastisement and drove me on to administer it. When I was quite beside myself and took down the lash from the nail where it hung, Percy might crawl under a table or a bench. But not a sound would escape him under punishment; even at a second flailing he would give vent only to a fervent moan if it stung worse than usual – whereas the base-born Bashan will howl abjectly if I so much as raise my arm. In short, no sense of honour, no strictness with himself. And anyhow, it seldom comes to corporal punishment, for I long ago ceased to make demands upon him contrary to his nature, of a kind which would lead to conflict between us.

For example, I never ask him to learn tricks; it would be of no use. He is not talented, no circus dog, no trained clown. He is a sound, vigorous young hunter, not a professor. I believe I remarked that he is a capital jumper. No obstacle too great, if the incentive be present: if he cannot jump it he will scrabble up somehow and let himself fall on the other side – at least, he conquers it one way or another. But it must be a genuine obstacle, not to be jumped through or crawled under; otherwise he would think it folly to jump. A wall, a ditch, a fence, a thick-set hedge, are genuine obstacles; a crosswise bar, a stick held out, are not, and you cannot jump over them without going contrary to reason and looking silly. Which Bashan refuses to do. He refuses. Try to make him jump over some such unreal obstacle; in the end you will be reduced to taking him by the scruff of the neck, in your anger, and flinging him over, while he whimpers and yaps. Once on the other side he acts as though he had done just what you wanted and celebrates the event in a frenzy of barking and capering. You may coax or you may punish; you cannot break down his reasonable resistance to performing a mere trick. He is not unaccommodating, he sets store by his master's approval, he will jump over a hedge at my will or my command, and not only when he feels like it himself, and enjoys very much the praise I bestow. But over a bar or a stick he will not jump, he will crawl underneath – if he were to die for it. A hundred times he will beg for forgiveness, forbearance, consideration; he fears pain, fears it to the point of being abject. But no fear and no pain can make him capable of a performance which in itself would be child's-play for him, but for which he obviously lacks all mental equipment. When you confront him with it, the question is not whether he will jump or not; that is already settled, and the command means nothing to him but a beating. To demand of him what reason forbids him to understand and hence to do is simply in his eyes to seek a pretext for blows, strife, and disturbance of friendly relations – it is merely the first step towards all these things. Thus Bashan looks at it, so far as I can see, and I doubt whether one may properly charge him with obstinacy. Obstinacy may be broken down, in the last analysis it cries out to be broken down; but Bashan's resistance to performing a trick he would seal with his death.

Extraordinary creature! So close a friend and yet so remote; so different from us, in certain ways, that our language has not power to do justice to his canine logic. For instance, what is the meaning of that frightful circumstantiality – unnerving alike to the spectator and to the parties themselves – attendant on the meeting of dog and dog; or on their first acquaintance or even on their first sight of each other? My excursions with Bashan have made me witness to hundreds of such encounters, or, I might better say, forced me to be an embarrassed spectator at them. And every time, for the duration of the episode, my old familiar Bashan was a stranger to me, I found it impossible to enter into his feelings or behaviour or understand the tribal laws which governed them. Certainly the meeting in the open of two dogs, strangers to each other, is one of the most painful, thrilling, and pregnant of all conceivable encounters; it is surrounded by an atmosphere of the last uncanniness, presided over by a constraint for which I have no preciser name; they simply cannot pass each other, their mutual embarrassment is frightful to behold.

I am not speaking of the case where one of the parties is shut up behind a hedge or a fence. Even then it is not easy to interpret their feelings – but at least the situation is less acute. They sniff each other from far off, and Bashan suddenly seeks shelter in my neighbourhood, whining a little to give vent to a distress and oppression which simply no words can describe. At the same time the imprisoned stranger sets up a violent barking, ostensibly in his character as a good watch-dog, but passing over unconsciously into a whimpering much like Bashan's own, an unsatisfied, envious, distressful whine. We draw near. The strange dog is waiting for us, close to the hedge, grousing and bemoaning his impotence; jumping at the barrier and giving every sign – how seriously one cannot tell – of intending to tear Bashan to pieces if only he could get at him. Bashan might easily stick close to me and pass him by; but he goes up to the hedge. He has to, he would even if I forbade him; to remain away would be to transgress a code older and more inviolable than any prohibition of mine. He advances, then, and with a modest and inscrutable bearing performs that rite which he knows will soothe and appease the other – even if temporarily – so long as the stranger performs it too, though whining and complaining in the act. Then they both chase wildly along the hedge, each on his own side, as close as possible, neither making a sound. At the end of the hedge they both face about and dash back again. But in full career both suddenly halt and stand as though rooted to the spot; they stand still, facing the hedge, and put their noses together through it. For some space of time they stand thus, then resume their curious, futile race shoulder to shoulder on either side of the barrier. But in the end my dog avails himself of his freedom and moves off – a frightful moment for the prisoner! He cannot stand it, he finds it namelessly humiliating that the other should dream of simply going off like that. He raves and slavers and contorts himself in his rage; runs like one mad up and down his enclosure; threatens to jump the hedge and have the faithless Bashan by the throat; he yells insults behind the retreating back. Bashan hears it all, it distresses him, as his manner shows. But he does not turn round, he jogs along beside me, while the cursings in our rear die down into whinings and are still.

Such the procedure when one of the parties is shut up. Embarrassments multiply when both of them are free. I do not relish describing the scene: it is one of the most painful and equivocal imaginable. Bashan has been bounding lightheartedly beside me; he comes up close, he fairly forces himself upon me, with a sniffling and whimpering that seem to come from his very depths. I still do not know what moves his utterance, but I recognize it at once and gather that there is a strange dog in the offing. I look about – yes, there he comes, and even at this distance his strained and hesitating mien betrays that he has already seen Bashan. I am scarcely less upset than they; I find the meeting most undesirable. "Go away," I say to Bashan. "Why do you glue yourself to my leg? Can't you go off and do your business by yourselves?" I try to frighten him off with my cane. For if they start biting – which may easily happen, with reason or without – I shall find it most unpleasant to have them between my feet. "Go away!" I repeat, in a lower voice. But Bashan does not go away, he sticks in his distress the closer to me, making as brief a pause as he can at a tree-trunk to perform the accustomed rite; I can see the other dog doing the same. We are now within twenty paces, the suspense is frightful. The strange dog is crawling on his belly, like a cat, his head thrust out. In this posture he awaits Bashan's approach, poised to spring at the right moment for his throat. But he does not do it, nor does Bashan seem to expect that he will. Or at least he goes up to the crouching stranger, though plainly trembling and heavy-hearted; he would do this, he is obliged to do it, even though I were to act myself and leave him to face the situation alone by striking into a side path. However painful the encounter, he has no choice, avoidance is not to be thought of. He is under a spell, he is bound to the other dog, they are bound to each other with some obscure and equivocal bond which may not be denied. We are now within two paces.

Then the other gets up, without a sound, as though he had never been behaving like a tiger, and stands there just as Bashan is standing, profoundly embarrassed, wretched, at a loss. They cannot pass each other. They probably want to, they turn away their heads, rolling their eyes sideways; evidently the same sense of guilt weighs on them both. They edge cautiously up to each other with a hang-dog air; they stop flank to flank and sniff under each other's tails. At this point the growling begins, and I speak to Bashan low-voiced and warn him, for now is the decisive moment, now we shall know whether it will come to biting or whether I shall be spared that rude shock. It does come to biting, I do not know how, still less why: quite suddenly they are nothing but a raging tumult and whirling coil out of which issue the frightful guttural noises that animals make when they engage. I may have to engage too, with my cane, to forestall a worse calamity; I may try to get Bashan by the neck or the collar and hold him up at arm's length in the air, the stranger dog hanging on by his teeth. Other horrors there are, too, which I may have to face – and feel them afterwards in all my limbs during the rest of our walk. But it may be, too, that after all the preliminaries the affair will pass tamely off and no harm done. At best it is hard to part the two; even if they are not clenched by the teeth, they are held by that inward bond.

They may seem to have passed each other, they are no longer flank to flank, but in a straight line with their heads in opposite directions; they may not even turn their heads, but only be rolling their eyes backwards. There may even be a space between them – and yet the painful bond still holds. Neither knows if the right moment for release has come, they would both like to go, yet each seems to have conscientious scruples. Slowly, slowly, the bond loosens, snaps; Bashan bounds lightly away, with, as it were, a new lease on life.

I speak of these things only to show how under stress of circumstance the character of a near friend may reveal itself as strange and foreign. It is dark to me, it is mysterious; I observe it with head-shakings and can only dimly guess what it may mean. And in all other respects I understand Bashan so well, I feel such lively sympathy for all his manifestations! For example, how well I know that whining yawn of his when our walk has been disappointing, too short, or devoid of sporting interest; when I have begun the day late and only gone out for a quarter of an hour before dinner. At such times he walks beside me and yawns – an open, impudent yawn to the whole extent of his jaws, an animal, audible yawn insultingly expressive of his utter boredom. "A fine master I have!" it seems to say. "Far in the night last night I met him at the bridge and now he sits behind his glass door and I wait for him dying of boredom. And when he does go out he only does it to come back again before there is time to start any game. A fine master! Not a proper master at all – really a rotten master, if you ask me!"

Such was the meaning of his yawn, vulgarly plain beyond all misunderstanding. And I admit that he is right, that he has a just grievance, and I put out a hand to pat his shoulder consolingly or to stroke his head. But he is not, under such circumstances, grateful for caresses; he yawns again, if possible more rudely than before, and moves away from my hand, although by nature, in contrast to Percy and in harmony with his own plebeian sentimentality, he sets great store by caresses. He particularly likes having his throat scratched and has a funny way of guiding one's hand to the right place by energetic little jerks of his head. That he has no room just now for endearments is partly due to his disappointment, but also to the fact that when he is in motion – and that means that I also am – he does not care for them. His mood is too manly; but it changes directly I sit down. Then he is all for friendliness again and responds to it with clumsy enthusiasm.

When I sit reading in a corner of the garden wall, or on the lawn with my back to a favourite tree, I enjoy interrupting my intellectual preoccupations to talk and play with Bashan. And what do I say to him? Mostly his own name, the two syllables which are of the utmost personal interest because they refer to himself and have an electric effect upon his whole being. I rouse and stimulate his sense of his own ego by impressing upon him – varying my tone and emphasis – that he *is* Bashan and that Bashan is his name. By continuing this for a while I can actually produce in him a state of ecstasy, a sort of intoxication with his own identity, so that he begins to whirl round on himself and send up loud exultant barks to heaven out of the weight of dignity that lies on his chest. Or we amuse ourselves, I by tapping him on the nose, he by snapping at my hand as though it were a fly. It makes us both laugh, yes, Bashan has to laugh too; and as I laugh I marvel at the sight, to me the oddest and most touching thing in the world. It is moving to see how under my teasing his thin animal cheeks and the corners of his mouth will twitch, and over his dark animal mask will pass an expression like a human smile, or at least some ungainly, pathetic semblance of one. It gives way to a look of startled embarrassment, then transforms the face by appearing again. . . .

But I will go no further nor involve myself in more detail of the kind. Even so I am dismayed at the space I have been led on to give to this little description; for what I had in mind to do was merely to display, as briefly as I might, my hero in his element, on the scene where he is most at home, most himself, and where his gifts show to best advantage; I mean, of course, the chase. But first I must give account to my reader of the theatre of these delights, my landscape by the river and Bashan's hunting-ground. It is a strip of land intimately bound up with his personality, familiar, loved, and significant to me like himself; which fact, accordingly, without further literary justification or embellishment, must serve as the occasion for my description.

The Hunting-Ground

The spacious gardens of the suburb where we live contain many large old trees that rise above the villa roofs and form a striking contrast to the saplings set out at a later period. Unquestionably they are the earliest inhabitants, the pride and adornment of a settlement which is still not very old. They have been carefully protected and preserved, so far as was possible; when any one of them came into conflict with the boundaries of the parcels of land, some venerable silvery moss-grown trunk standing exactly on a border-line, the hedge makes a little curve round it, or an accommodating gap is left in a wall, and the ancient towers up half on public, half on private ground, with bare snow-covered boughs or adorned with its tiny, late-coming leaves.

They are a variety of ash, a tree that loves moisture more than most – and their presence here shows what kind of soil we have. It is not so long since human brains reclaimed it for human habitation; not more than a decade or so. Before that it was a marshy wilderness, a breeding-place for mosquitoes, where willows, dwarf poplars, and other stunted growths mirrored themselves in stagnant pools. The region is subject to floods. There is a stratum of impermeable soil a few yards under the surface; it has always been boggy, with standing water in the hollows. They drained it by lowering the level of the river – engineering is not my strong point, but anyhow it was some such device, by means of which the water which cannot sink into the earth now flows off laterally into the river by several subterranean channels, and the ground is left comparatively dry – but only comparatively, for Bashan and I, knowing it as we do, are acquainted with certain low, retired, and rushy spots, relics of the primeval condition of the region, whose damp coolness defies the summer heat and makes them a grateful place wherein to draw a few long breaths.

The whole district has its peculiarities, indeed, which distinguish it at a glance from the pine forests and moss-grown meadows which are the usual setting of a mountain stream. It has preserved its original characteristics even since it was acquired by the real-estate company; even outside the gardens the original vegetation preponderates over the newly planted. In the avenues and parks, of course, horse-chestnuts and quick-growing maple trees, beeches, and all sorts of ornamental shrubs have been set out; also rows of French poplars standing erect in their sterile masculinity. But the ash trees, as I said, are the aborigines; they are everywhere, and of all ages, century-old giants and tender young seedlings pushing their way by hundreds, like weeds, through the gravel. It is the ash, together with the silver poplar, the aspen, the birch, and the willow, that gives the scene its distinctive look. All these trees have small leaves, and all this small-leaved foliage is very striking by contrast with the huge trunks. But there are elms too, spreading their large, varnished, saw-edged leaves to the sun. And everywhere too are masses of creeper, winding round the young trees in the underbrush and inextricably mingling its leaves with theirs. Little thickets of slim alder trees stand in the hollows. There are few lime trees, no oaks or firs at all, in our domain, though there are some on the slope which bounds it to the east, where the soil changes and with it the character of the vegetation. There they stand out black against the sky, like sentinels guarding our little valley.

It is not more than five hundred yards from slope to river – I have paced it out. Perhaps the strip of river-bank widens a little, farther down, but not to any extent; so it is remarkable what landscape variety there is in this small area, even when one makes such moderate use of the playground it affords along the river as do Bashan and I, who rarely spend more than two hours there, counting our going and coming. There is such diversity that we need hardly take the same path twice or ever tire of the view or be conscious of any limitations of space; and this is due to the circumstance that our domain divides itself into three quite different regions or zones. We may confine ourselves to one of these or we may combine all three: they are the neighbourhood of the river and its banks, the neighbourhood of the opposite slope, and the wooded section in the middle.

The wooded zone, the parks, the osier brakes, and the riverside shrubbery take up most of the breadth. I search in vain for a word better than "wood" to describe this strange tract of land. For it is no wood in the usual sense of the word: not a pillared hall of even-sized trunks, carpeted with moss and fallen leaves. The trees in our hunting-ground are of uneven growth and size, hoary giants of willows and poplars, especially along the river, though also deeper in; others ten or fifteen years old, which are probably as large as they will grow; and lastly a legion of slender trees, young ashes, birches, and alders in a nursery garden planted by nature herself. These look larger than they are; and all, as I said, are wound round with creepers which give a look of tropical luxuriance to the scene. But I suspect them of choking the growth of their hosts, for I cannot see that the trunks have grown any thicker in all the years I have known them.

The trees are of few and closely related species. The alder belongs to the birch family, the poplar is after all not very different from a willow. And one might say that they all approach the willow type; foresters tell us that trees tend to adapt themselves to their local conditions, showing a certain conformity, as it were, to the prevailing mode. It is the distorted, fantastic, witchlike silhouette of the willow tree, dweller by still and by flowing waters, that sets the fashion here, with her branches like broom-splints and her crooked-fingered tips; and all the others visibly try to be like her. The silver poplar apes her best; but often it is hard to tell poplar from birch, so much is the latter beguiled by the spirit of the place to take on mis-shapen forms. Not that there are not also plenty of very shapely and well-grown single specimens of this lovable tree, and enchanting they look in the favouring glow of the late afternoon sun. In this region the birch appears as a slender silvery bole with a crown of little, separate leaves atop; as a lovely, lithe, and well-grown maiden; it has the prettiest of chalk-white trunks, and its foliage droops like delicate languishing locks of hair. But there are also birches colossal in size, that no man could span with his arms, the bark of which is only white high up, but near the ground has turned black and coarse and is seamed with fissures.

The soil is not like what one expects in a wood. It is loamy, gravelly, even sandy. It seems anything but fertile, and yet, within its nature, is almost luxuriantly so; for it is overgrown with tall, rank grass, often the dry, sharp-cornered kind that grows on dunes. In winter it covers the ground like trampled hay; not seldom it cannot be distinguished from reeds, but in other places it is soft and fat and juicy, and among it grow hemlock, coltsfoot, nettles, all sorts of low-growing things, mixed with tall thistles and tender young tree shoots. Pheasants and other wildfowl hide in this vegetation, which rolls up to and over the gnarled roots of the trees. And everywhere the wild grape and the hop-vine clamber out of the thicket to twine round the trunks in garlands of flapping leaves, or in winter with bare stems like the toughest sort of wire.

Now, all this is not a wood, it is not a park, it is simply an enchanted garden, no more and no less. I will stand for the word – though of course nature here is stingy and sparse and tends to the deformed; a few botanical names exhausting the catalogue of her performance. The ground is rolling, it constantly rises and falls away, so that the view is enclosed on every hand, with a lovely effect of remoteness and privacy. Indeed, if the wood stretched for miles to right and left, as far as it reaches lengthwise, instead of only a hundred and some paces on each side from the middle, one could not feel more secluded. Only by the sense of sound is one made aware of the friendly nearness of the river; you cannot see it, but it whispers gently from the west. There are gorges choked with shrubbery – elder, privet, jasmine, and wild cherry – on close June days the scent is almost overpowering. And again there are low-lying spots, regular gravel-pits, where nothing but a few willow-shoots and a little sage can grow, at the bottom or on the sides.

And all this scene never ceases to exert a strange influence upon me, though it has been my almost daily walk for some years. The fine massed foliage of the ash puts me in mind of a giant fern; these creepers and climbers, this barrenness and this damp, this combination of lush and dry, have a fantastic effect; to convey my whole meaning, it is a little as though I were transported to another geological period, or even to the bottom of the sea – and the fantasy has this much of fact about it, that water did stand here once, for instance in the square low-lying meadow basins thick with shoots of self-sown ash, which now serve as pasture for sheep. One such lies directly behind my house.

The wilderness is crossed in all directions by paths, some of them only lines of trodden grass or gravelly trails, obviously born of use and not laid out – though it would be hard to say who trod them, for only by way of unpleasant exception do Bashan and I meet anyone here. When that happens he stands stock-still and gives a little growl which very well expresses my own feelings too. Even on the fine summer Sunday afternoons which bring crowds of people to walk in these parts – for it is always a few degrees cooler here – we remain undisturbed in our fastness. They know it not; the water is the great attraction, as a rule, the river in its course; the human stream gets as close as it can, down to the very edge if there is no flood, rolls along beside it, and then back home again. At most we may come on a pair of lovers in the shrubbery; they look at us wide-eyed and startled out of their nest, or else defiantly as though to ask what objection we have to their presence or their behaviour. All which we disclaim by beating swift retreat, Bashan with the indifference he feels for everything that does not smell like game; I with a face utterly devoid of all expression, either approving or the reverse.

But these woodland paths are not the only way we have of reaching my park. There are streets as well – or rather there are traces, which once were streets, or which once were to have been streets, or which, by God's will, may yet become streets. In other words: there are signs that the pickaxe has been at work, signs of a hopeful real-estate enterprise for some distance beyond the built-up section and the villas. There has been some far-sighted planning on the part of the company which some years ago acquired the land; but their plans went beyond their capacity for carrying them out, for the villas were only a part of what they had in mind. Building-lots were laid out; an area extending for nearly a mile down the river was prepared, and doubtless still remains prepared, to receive possible purchasers and home-loving settlers. The building society conceived things on a rather large scale. They enclosed the river between dykes, they built quays and planted gardens, and, not content with that, they had embarked on clearing the woods, dumped piles of gravel, cut roads through the wilderness, one or two lengthwise and several across the width: fine, well-planned roads, or at least the first steps towards them, made of coarse gravel, with a wide foot-path and indications of a kerb-stone. But no one walks there save Bashan and myself, he on the good stout leather of his four paws, I in hobnailed boots on account of the gravel. For the stately villas projected by the company are still non-existent, despite the good example I set when I built my own house. They have been, I say, non-existent for ten, no, fifteen years; it is no wonder that a kind of blight has settled upon the enterprise and discouragement reigns in the bosom of the building society, a disinclination to go on with their project.

However, things had got so far forward that these streets, though not built up, have all been given names, just as though they were in the centre of the town or in a suburb. I should very much like to know what sort of speculator he was who named them; he seems to have been a literary chap with a fondness for the past: there is an Opitzstrasse, a Flemmingstrasse, a Bürgerstrasse, even an Adalbert-Stifterstrasse – I walk on the last-named with especial reverence in my hobnailed boots. At all the corners stakes have been driven in the ground with street signs affixed to them, as is usual in suburbs where there are no house-corners to receive them; they are the usual little blue enamel plates with white lettering. But alas, they are rather the worse for wear. They have stood here far too long, pointing out the names of vacant sites where nobody wants to live; they are monuments to the failure, the discouragement, and the arrested development of the whole enterprise. They have not been kept up or renewed, the climate has done its worst by them. The enamel has scaled off, the lettering is rusty, there are ugly broken-edged gaps which make the names sometimes almost illegible. One of them, indeed, puzzled me a good deal when I first came here and was spying about the neighbourhood. It was a long name, and the word "street" was perfectly clear, but most of the rest was eaten by rust; there remained only an *S* at the beginning, an *E* somewhere about the middle, and another *E* at the end. I could not reckon with so many unknown quantities. I studied the sign a long time with my hands behind my back, then continued along the foot-path with Bashan. I thought I was thinking about something else, but all the time my brains were privately cudgelling themselves, and suddenly it came over me. I stopped with a start, stood still, and then hastened back, took up my former position, and tested my guess. Yes, it fitted. The name of the street where I was walking was Shakespeare Street.

The streets suit the signboards and the signboards suit the streets – it is a strange and dreamlike harmony in decay. The streets run through the wood they have broken into; but the wood does not remain passive. It does not let the streets stop as they were made, through decade after decade, until at last people come and settle on them. It takes every step to close them again; for what grows here does not mind gravel, it flourishes in it. Purple thistles, blue sage, silvery shoots of willow, and green ash seedlings spring up all over the road and even on the pavement; the streets with the poetic names are going back to the wilderness, whether one likes it or not; in another ten years Opitzstrasse, Flemmingstrasse, and the rest will be closed, they will probably as good as disappear. There is at present no ground for complaint; for from the romantic and picturesque point of view there are no more beautiful streets in the world than they are now. Nothing could be more delightful than strolling through them in their unfinished, abandoned state, if one has on stout boots and does not mind the gravel. Nothing more agreeable to the eye than looking from the wild garden beneath one's feet to the humid massing of fine-leafed foliage that shuts in the view – foliage such as Claude Lorrain used to paint, three centuries ago. Such as he used to paint, did I say? But surely he painted *this*. He was here, he knew this scene, he studied it. If my building-society man had not confined himself to the literary field, one of these rusty street signs might have borne the name of Claude.

Well, that is our middle or wooded region. But the eastern slope has its own charms not to be despised, either by me or by Bashan, who has his own reasons, which will appear hereafter. I might call this region the zone of the brook; for it takes its idyllic character as landscape from the stream that flows through it, and the peaceful loveliness of its beds of forget-me-not makes it a fit companion-piece to the zone on the other side with its rushing river, whose flowing, when the west wind blows, can be faintly heard even all the way across our hunting-ground. The first of the made cross-roads through the wood runs like a causeway from the poplar avenue to the foot of the hillside, between low-lying pasture-ground on one side and wooded lots of land on the other. And from there a path descends to the left, used by the children to coast on in winter. The brook rises in the level ground at the bottom of this descent. We love to stroll beside it, Bashan and I, on the right or the left bank at will, through the varied territory of our eastern zone. On our left is an extent of wooded meadow, and a nursery-gardening establishment; we can see the backs of the buildings, and sheep cropping the clover, presided over by a rather stupid little girl in a red frock. She keeps propping her hands on her knees and screaming at her charges at the top of her lungs in a harsh, angry, and imperious voice. But she seems to be afraid of the majestic old ram, who looks enormously fat in his thick fleece and who does as he likes regardless of her bullying ways. The child's screams rise to their height when the sheep are thrown into a panic by the appearance of Bashan; and this almost always happens, quite against his will or intent, for he is profoundly indifferent to their existence, behaves as though they were not there, or even deliberately and contemptuously ignores them in an effort to forestall an attack of panic folly on their part. Their scent is strong enough to me, though not unpleasant; but it is not a scent of game, so Bashan takes no interest in harrying them. But let him make a single move, or merely appear on the scene, and the whole flock, but now grazing peacefully over the meadow and bleating in their curiously human voices, some bass, some treble, suddenly collect in a huddled mass of backs and go dashing off, while the imbecile child stoops over and screams at them until her voice cracks and her eyes pop out of her head. Bashan looks up at me as though to say: Am I to blame, did I do anything at all?

But once something quite the opposite happened, that was even more extraordinary and distressing than any panic. A sheep, a quite ordinary specimen, of medium size and the usual sheepish face, save for a narrow-lipped little mouth turned up at the corners into a smile which gave the creature an uncommonly sly and fatuous look – this sheep appeared to be smitten with Bashan's charms. It followed him; it left the flock and the pasture-ground and followed at his heels, wherever he went, smiling with extravagant stupidity. He left the path, and it followed. He ran, it galloped after. He stopped, it did the same, close behind him and smiling its inscrutable smile. Embarrassment and dismay were painted on Bashan's face, and certainly his position was highly distasteful. For good or for ill it lacked any kind of sense or reason. Nothing so consummately silly had ever happened to either of us. The sheep got farther and farther away from its base, but it seemed not to care for that; it followed the exasperated Bashan apparently resolved to part from him nevermore, but to be at his side whithersoever he went. He stuck close at my side; not so much alarmed – for the which there was no cause – as ashamed of the disgraceful situation. At last, as though he had had enough of it, he stood still, turned round, and gave a menacing growl. The sheep bleated – it was like a man's laugh, a spiteful laugh – and put poor Bashan so beside himself that he ran away with his tail between his legs, the sheep bounding absurdly behind him.

Meanwhile we had got a good way from the flock; the addle-pated little girl was screaming fit to burst, and not only bending her knees but jerking them up and down as she screamed till they touched her face, and she looked from a distance like a demented dwarf. A dairymaid in an apron came running, her attention being drawn by the shrieks or in some other way. She had a pitchfork in one hand; with the other she held her breasts, that shook up and down as she ran. She tried to drive back the sheep with the pitchfork – it had started after Bashan again – but unsuccessfully. The sheep did indeed spring away from the fork in the right direction, but then swung round again to follow Bashan's trail. It seemed no power on earth would divert it. But at last I saw what had to be done and turned round. We all marched back, Bashan beside me, behind him the sheep, behind the sheep the maid with the pitchfork, the child in the red frock bouncing and stamping at us all the while. It was not enough to go back to the flock, we had to do the job thoroughly. We went into the farmyard and to the sheep-pen, where the farm girl rolled back the big door with her strong right arm. We all went inside, all of us; and then the rest of us had to slip out again and shut the door in the face of the poor deluded sheep, so that it was taken prisoner. And then, after receiving the farm girl's thanks, Bashan and I might resume our interrupted walk, to the end of which Bashan preserved a sulky and humiliated air.

So much for the sheep. Beyond the farm buildings is an extensive colony of allotments, that looks rather like a cemetery, with its arbours and little summer-houses like chapels and each tiny garden neatly enclosed. The whole colony has a fence round it, with a latticed gate, through which only the owners of the plots have admission. Sometimes I have seen a man with his sleeves rolled up digging his few yards of vegetable-plot – he looked as though he were digging his own grave. Beyond this come open meadows full of mole-hills, reaching to the edge of the middle wooded region; besides the moles, the place abounds in field-mice – I mention them on account of Bashan and his multifarious joy of the chase.

But on the other, the right side, the brook and the hillside continue, the latter, as I said, with great variety in its contours. The first part is shadowed and gloomy and set with pines. Then comes a sand-pit which reflects the warm rays of the sun; then a gravel-pit, then a cataract of bricks, as though a house had been demolished up above and the rubble simply flung down the hill, damming the brook at the bottom. But the brook rises until its waters flow over the obstacle and go on, reddened with brick-dust and dyeing the grass along its edge, to flow all the more blithely and pellucidly farther on, with the sun making diamonds sparkle on its surface.

I am very fond of brooks, as indeed of all water, from the ocean to the smallest reedy pool. If in the mountains in the summertime my ear but catch the sound of plashing and prattling from afar, I always go to seek out the source of the liquid sounds, a long way if I must; to make the acquaintance and to look in the face of that conversable child of the hills, where he hides. Beautiful are the torrents that come tumbling with mild thunderings down between evergreens and over stony terraces; that form rocky bathing-pools and then dissolve in white foam to fall perpendicularly to the next level. But I have pleasure in the brooks of the flatland too, whether they be so shallow as hardly to cover the slippery, silver-gleaming pebbles in their bed, or as deep as small rivers between overhanging, guardian willow trees, their current flowing swift and strong in the centre, still and gently at the edge. Who would not choose to follow the sound of running waters? Its attraction for the normal man is of a natural, sympathetic sort. For man is water's child, nine-tenths of our body consists of it, and at a certain stage the fœtus possesses gills. For my part I freely admit that the sight of water in whatever form or shape is my most lively and immediate kind of natural enjoyment; yes, I would even say that only in contemplation of it do I achieve true self-forgetfulness and feel my own limited individuality merge into the universal. The sea, still-brooding or coming on in crashing billows, can put me in a state of such profound organic dreaminess, such remoteness from myself, that I am lost to time. Boredom is unknown, hours pass like minutes, in the unity of that companionship. But then, I can lean on the rail of a little bridge over a brook and contemplate its currents, its whirlpools, and its steady flow for as long as you like; with no sense or fear of that other flowing within and about me, that swift gliding away of time. Such love of water and understanding of it make me value the circumstance that the narrow strip of ground where I dwell is enclosed on both sides by water.

But my little brook here is the simplest of its kind, it has no particular or unusual characteristics, it is quite the average brook. Clear as glass, without any guile, it does not dream of seeming deep by being turbid. It is shallow and candid and makes no bones of betraying that there are old tins and the mouldering remains of a laced shoe in its bed. But it is deep enough to serve as a home for pretty, lively, silver-grey little fish, which dart away in zig-zags at our approach. In some places it broadens into a pool, and it has willows on its margin, one of which I love to look at as I pass. It stands on the hillside, a little removed from the water; but one of the boughs has bent down and reached across and actually succeeded in plunging its silvery tip into the flowing water. Thus it stands revelling in the pleasure of this contact.

It is pleasant to walk here in the warm breeze of summer. If the weather is very warm Bashan goes into the stream to cool his belly; not more than that, for he never of his own free will wets the upper parts. He stands there with his ears laid back and a look of virtue on his face and lets the water stream round and over him. Then he comes back to me to shake himself, being convinced that this can only be accomplished in my vicinity – although he does it so thoroughly that I receive a perfect shower-bath in the process. It is no good waving him off with my stick or with shoutings. Whatever seems to him natural and right and necessary, that he will do.

The brook flows on westward to a little hamlet that faces north between the wood and the hillside. At the beginning of this hamlet is an inn, and at this point the brook widens into another pool where women kneel to wash their clothes. Crossing the little foot-bridge, you strike into a road going back towards the city between wood and meadow. But on the right of the road is another through the wood, by which in a few minutes you can get back to the river.

And so here we are at the river zone, and the river itself is in front of us, green and roaring and white with foam. It is really nothing more than a mountain torrent; but its ceaseless roaring pervades the whole region round, in the distance subdued, but here a veritable tumult which – if one cannot have the ocean itself – is quite a fair substitute for its awe-inspiring swell. Numberless gulls fill the air with their cries; autumn, winter, and spring they circle screaming round the mouths of the drain-pipes which issue here, seeking their food. In summer they depart once more for the lakes higher up. Wild and half-wild duck also take refuge here in the neighbourhood of the town for the winter months. They rock on the waves, are whirled round and carried off by the current, rise into the air to escape being engulfed, and then settle again on quieter water.

And this river tract also is divided into areas of varying character. At the edge of the wood is the gravelly expanse into which the poplar avenue issues; it extends for nearly a mile downstream, as far as the ferry-house, of which I will speak presently. At this point the underbrush comes nearly down to the river-bed. And all the gravel, as I am aware, constitutes the beginnings of the first and most important of the lengthwise streets, magnificently conceived by the real-estate company as an esplanade, a carriage-road bordered by trees and flowers – where elegantly turned-out riders were to hold sweet converse with ladies leaning back in shiny landaus. Beside the ferry-house, indeed, is a sign, already rickety and rotting, from which one can gather that the site was intended for the erection of a café. Yes, there is the sign – and there it remains, but there is no trace of the little tables, the hurrying waiters and coffee-sipping guests; nobody has bought the site, and the esplanade is nothing but a desert of gravel, where sage and willow-shoots are almost as thick as in Opitz- and Flemmingstrasse.

Down close to the river is another, narrower gravel waste, as full of weeds as the bigger one. Along it are grassy mounds supporting telegraph poles. I like to use this as a path, by way of variety – also because it is cleaner, though more difficult, to walk on it than on the actual foot-path, which in bad weather is often very muddy, though it is actually the proper path, extending for miles along the river, finally going off into trails along the bank. It is planted on the river side with young maple and birch trees; on the other side the original inhabitants stand in a row – willows, aspens, and silver poplars of enormous size. The river-bank is steep and high and is ingeniously shored up with withes and concrete to prevent the flooding which threatens two or three times in the year, after heavy rains or when the snows melt in the hills. At several points there are ladderlike wooden steps leading down to the river-bed – an extent of mostly dry gravel, six or eight yards wide. For this mountain torrent behaves precisely as its like do, whether large or small: it may be, according to the conditions up above, either the merest green trickle, hardly covering the stones, where long-legged birds seem to be standing on the water; or it may be a torrent alarming in its power and extent, filling the wide bed with raging fury, whirling round tree-branches and old baskets and dead cats and threatening to commit much damage. Here, too, there is protection against floods in the shape of woven hurdles put in slanting to the stream. When dry, the bed is grown up with wiry grass and wild oats, as well as that omnipresent shrub the blue sage; there is fairly good walking, on the strip of flat stones at the extreme outer edge, and it affords me a pleasant variety, for though the stone is not of the most agreeable to walk on, the close proximity of the river atones for much, and there is even sometimes sand between the gravel and the grass; true, it is mixed with clay, it has not the exquisite cleanness of sea-sand, but after all it is sand. I am taking a walk on the beach that stretches into the distance at the edge of the wave, and there is the sound of the surge and the cry of the gulls, there is that monotony that swallows time and space and shuts one up as in a dream. The river roars eddying over the stones, and half-way to the ferry-house the sound is augmented by a waterfall that comes down by a diagonal canal and tumbles into the larger stream, arching as it falls, shining glassily like a leaping fish, and seething perpetually at its base.

Lovely to walk here when the sky is blue and the ferry-boat flies a flag, perhaps in honour of the fine weather or because it is a feast-day of some sort. There are other boats here too, but the ferry-boat is fast to a wire cable attached to another, thicker cable that is spanned across the stream and runs along it on a little pulley. The current supplies the motive power, the steering is done by hand. The ferryman lives with his wife and child in the ferry-house, which is a little higher up than the upper foot-path; the house has a kitchen-garden and a chicken-house and the man undoubtedly gets it rent-free in his office as ferryman. It is a sort of dwarf villa, rather flimsy, with funny little outcroppings of balconies and bay-windows, and seems to have two rooms below and two above. I like to sit on the little bench on the upper foot-path close to the tiny garden – with Bashan squatting on my foot and the ferryman's chickens stalking round about me, jerking their heads forward with each step. The cock usually comes and perches on the back of the bench with his green bersaglieri tail-feathers hanging down behind; he sits thus beside me and measures me with a fierce side-glance of his red eye. I watch the traffic; it is not crowded, hardly even lively; indeed, the ferry-boat runs only at considerable intervals. The more do I enjoy it when on one side or the other a man appears, or a woman with a basket, and wants to be put across; the "Boat ahoy!" is an age-old, picturesque cry, with a poetry not impaired by the fact that the business is done somewhat differently nowadays. Double flights of steps for those coming and going lead down to the river-bed and to the landings, and there is an electric push-button at the side of each. So when a man appears on the opposite bank and stands looking across the water, he does not put his hands round his mouth and call. He goes up to the push-button, puts out his hand, and pushes. The bell rings shrilly in the ferryman's villa; that is the "Boat ahoy!" even so, and it is poetic still. Then the man waits and looks about. And almost at the moment when the bell rings, the ferryman comes out of his little official dwelling, as though he had been standing behind the door or sitting on a chair waiting for the signal. He comes out, and the way he walks suggests that he has been mechanically put in motion by the ringing of the bell. It is like a shooting-booth when you shoot at the door of a little house and if you hit it a figure comes out, a sentry or a cow-girl. The ferryman crosses his garden at a measured pace, his arms swinging regularly at his sides; over the path and down the steps to the river, where he pushes off the ferry-boat and holds the steering-gear while the little pulley runs along the wire above the stream and the boat is driven across. The man springs in, and once safely on this side hands over his penny and runs briskly up the steps, going off right or left. Sometimes, when the ferryman is not well or is very busy in the house, his wife or even his little child comes out to ferry the stranger across. They can do it as well as he, and so could I, for it is an easy office, requiring no special gift or training. He can reckon himself lucky to have the job and live in the dwarf villa. Anyone, however stupid, could do what he does, and he knows this, of course, and behaves with becoming modesty. On the way back to his house he very politely says: "*Grüss Gott*" to me as I sit there on the bench between Bashan and the cock; you can see that he likes to be on good terms with everybody.

There is a tarry smell, a breeze off the water, a slapping sound against the ferry-boat. What more can one want? Sometimes these things call up a familiar memory: the water is deep, it has a smell of decay – that is the Lagoon, that is Venice. But sometimes there is a heavy storm, a deluge of rain; in my macintosh, my face streaming with wet, I take the upper path, leaning against the strong west wind, which in the poplar avenue has torn the saplings away from their supports. Now one can see why all the trees are bent in one direction and have somewhat lop-sided tops. Bashan has to stop often to shake himself, the water flies off him in every direction. The river is quite changed: swollen and dark-yellow it rolls threateningly along, rushing and dashing in a furious hurry this way and that; its muddy tide takes up the whole extra bed up to the edge of the undergrowth, pounding against the cement and the willow hurdles – until one is glad of the forethought that put them there. The strange thing about it is that the water is *quiet*; it makes almost no noise at all. And there are no rapids in its course now, the stream is too high for that. You can only see where they were by the fact that its waves are higher and deeper there than elsewhere, and that their crests break backwards instead of forwards like the surf on a beach. The waterfall is insignificant now, its volume is shrunken, no longer vaulted, and the boiling water at its base is almost obliterated by the height of the flood. Bashan's reaction to all this is simple unmitigated astonishment that things can be so changed. He cannot get over it, cannot understand how it is that the dry territory where he is wont to run about has disappeared, is covered by water. He flees up into the undergrowth to get away from the lashing of the flood; looks at me and wags his tail, then back at the water, and has a funny, puzzled way of opening his jaws crookedly, shutting them again and running his tongue round the corner of his mouth. It is not a very refined gesture, in fact rather common, but very speaking, and as human as it is animal – in fact it is just what an ordinary simple-minded man might do in face of a surprising situation, very likely scratching his neck at the same time.

Having gone into some detail in describing the river zone, I believe I have covered the whole region and done all I can to bring it before my reader's eye. I like my description pretty well, but I like the reality of nature even better. It is more vivid and various; just as Bashan himself is warmer, more living and hearty than his imaginary presentment. I am attached to this landscape, I owe it something, and am grateful; therefore, I have described it. It is my park and my solitude; my thoughts and dreams are mingled and interwoven with images from it, as the tendrils of climbing plants are with the boughs of its trees. I have seen it at all times of day and all seasons of the year: in autumn, when the chemical odour of decaying vegetation fills the air, when all the thistles have shed their down, when the great beeches in my park have spread a rust-coloured carpet of leaves on the meadow and the liquid golden afternoons merge into romantic, theatrical early evenings, with the moon's sickle swimming in the sky, when a milk-brewed mist floats above the lowlands and a crimson sunset burns through the black silhouettes of the tree-branches. In autumn, but in winter too, when the gravel is covered with snow and softly levelled off so that one can walk on it in overshoes; when the river looks black as it flows between sallow frost-bound banks, and the cries of hundreds of gulls fill the air from morning to night. But my freest and most familiar intercourse with it is in the milder months, when no extra clothing is required, to dash out quickly, between two showers, for a quarter of an hour; to bend aside in passing a bough of black alder and get a glimpse of the river as it flows. We may have had guests, and I am left somewhat worn down by conversation, between my four walls, where it seems the breath of the strangers still hovers on the air. Then it is good not to linger but to go out at once and stroll in Gellertstrasse or Stifterstrasse, to draw a long breath and get the air into one's lungs. I look up into the sky, I gaze into the tender depths of the masses of green foliage, and peace returns once more and dwells within my spirit.

And Bashan is always with me. He had not been able to prevent the influx of strange persons into our dwelling though he had lifted up his voice and objected. But it did no good, so he had withdrawn. Now he rejoices to be with me again in our hunting-ground. He runs before me on the gravel path, one ear negligently cocked, with that sidewise gait dogs have, the hind legs not just exactly behind the forelegs. And suddenly I see him gripped, as it were, body and soul, his stump of tail switching furiously, erect in the air. His head goes forward and down, his body lengthens out, he makes short dashes in several directions, and then shoots off in one of them with his nose to the ground. He has struck a scent. He is off after a hare.

The Chase

The region round is full of game, and we hunt it; that is, Bashan does and I look on. Thus we go hunting: hares, partridges, field-mice, moles, ducks, and gulls. Neither do we shrink from larger game, we stalk pheasant, even deer, if one of them, in winter, happens to stray into our preserve. It is quite a thrilling sight to see the slender long-legged creature, yellow against the snow, running away, with its white buttocks bobbing up and down, in flight from my little Bashan. He strains every nerve, I look on with the greatest sympathy and suspense. Not that anything would ever come of it, nothing ever has or will. But the lack of concrete results does not affect Bashan's passionate eagerness or mar my own interest at all. We pursue the chase for its own sake, not for the prey nor for any other material advantage. Bashan is, as I have said, the active partner. He does not expect from me anything more than my moral support, having no experience, immediate and personal, that is, of more direct co-operation. I say immediate and personal for it is more than likely that his forebears, at least on the pointer side, know what the chase should really be like. I have sometimes asked myself whether some memory might still linger in him, ready to be awakened by a chance sight or sound. At his level the life of the individual is certainly less sharply distinguished from the race than is the case with human beings, birth and death must be a less far-reaching shock; perhaps the traditions of the stock are preserved unimpaired, so that it would only be an apparent contradiction to speak of inborn experiences, unconscious memories which, when summoned up, would have the power to confuse the creature as to what were its own individual experiences or give rise to dissatisfaction with them. I indulged in this thought, but finally put it from me, as Bashan obviously put from him the rather brutal episode which gave rise to my speculations.

When we get out to follow the chase it is usually mid-day, half past eleven or twelve; sometimes, on particularly warm summer days, we go late in the afternoon, six o'clock or so – or perhaps we go then for the second time. But on the afternoon walk things are very different with me – not at all as they were on my careless morning stroll. My freshness and serenity have departed long since, I have been struggling and taking thought, I have overcome difficulties, have had to grit my teeth and tussle with a single detail while at the same time holding a more extended and complex context firmly in mind, concentrating my mental powers upon it down to its furthermost ramifications. And my head is tired. It is the chase with Bashan that relieves and distracts me, gives me new life, and puts me back into condition for the rest of the day, in which there is still something to be done.

Of course we do not select each day a certain kind of game to hunt – only hares, for instance, or only ducks. Actually we hunt everything that comes – I was going to say, within reach of our guns. So that we do not need to go far before starting something, actually the hunt can begin just outside the garden gate; for there are quantities of moles and field-mice in the meadow bottom behind the house. Of course these fur-bearing little creatures are not properly game at all. But their mysterious, burrowing little ways, and especially the slyness and dexterity of the field-mice, which are not blind by day like their brethren the moles, but scamper discreetly about on the ground, whisking into their holes at the approach of danger, so that one cannot even see their legs moving – all this works powerfully upon Bashan's instincts. Besides, they are the only wild creatures he ever catches. A field-mouse, a mole, makes a morsel not to be despised, in these lean days, when he often finds nothing more appetizing than porridge in the dish beside his kennel.

So then I and my walking-stick will scarcely have taken two or three steps up the poplar avenue, and Bashan will have scarcely opened the ball with his usual riotous plunges, when I see him capering off to my right – already he is in the grip of his passion, sees and hears nothing but the maddening invisible activities of the creatures all round him. He slinks through the grass, his whole body tense, wagging his tail and lifting his legs with great caution; stops, with one foreleg and one hind leg in the air, eyes the ground with his head on one side, muzzle pointed, ear muscles stiffly erected – so that his ear-laps fall down in front, each side of his eyes. Then with both fore-paws raised he makes a sudden forward plunge, and another; looking with a puzzled air at the place where something just now was but is not any more. Then he begins to dig. I feel a strong desire to follow him and see what he gets. But if I did we should never get farther, his whole zeal for the chase would be expended here on the spot. So I go on. I need not worry about his losing me. Even if he stops behind a long time and has not seen which way I turned, my trail will be as clear to him as though I were the game he seeks, and he will follow it, head between his paws, even if I am out of sight; already I can hear his licence-tag clinking and his stout paws thudding in my rear. He shoots past me, turns round, and wags his tail to announce that he is on the spot.

But in the woods, or out on the meadows by the brook, I do stop often and watch him digging for a mouse, even though the time allotted for my walk is nearly over. It is so fascinating to see his passionate concentration, I feel the contagion myself and cannot help a fervent wish that he may catch something and I be there to see. The spot where he has chosen to dig looks like any other – perhaps a mossy little mound among the roots at the foot of a birch tree. But he has heard and scented something at that spot, perhaps even viewed it as it whisked away; he is convinced that it is there in its burrow underground, he has only to get at it – and he digs away for dear life, oblivious of all else, not angry, but with the professional passion of the sportsman – it is a magnificent sight. His little striped body, the ribs showing and muscles playing under the smooth skin, is drawn in at the middle, his hind quarters stand up in the air, the stump of a tail vibrating in quick time; his head with his fore-paws is down in the slanting hole he has dug and he turns his face aside as he plies his iron-shod paws. Faster and faster, till earth and little stones and tufts of grass and fragments of tree-roots fly up almost into my face. Sometimes he snorts in the silence, when he has burrowed his nose well into the earth, trying to smell out the motionless, clever, frightened little beast that is besieged down there. It is a muffled snorting; he draws in the air hastily and empties his lungs again the better to scent the fine, keen, far-away, and buried effluvium. How does the creature feel when he hears the snorting? Ah, that is its own affair, or God's, who has made Bashan the enemy of field-mice. Even the emotion of fear is an enhancement of life; and who knows, if there were no Bashan the mouse might find time hang heavy on its hands. Besides, what would be the use of all its beady-eyed cleverness and mining skill, which more than balance what Bashan can do, so that the attacker's success is always more than problematical? In short, I do not feel much pity for the mouse, privately I am on Bashan's side and cannot always stick to my role of onlooker. I take my walking-stick and dig out some pebble or gnarled piece of root that is too firmly lodged for him to move. And he sends up a swift, warm glance of understanding to me as he works. With his mouth full of dirt, he chews away at the stubborn earth and the roots running through it, tears out whole chunks and throws them aside, snorts again into his hole and is encouraged by the freshened scent to renewed attack on it with his claws.

In nearly every case all this labour is vain. Bashan will give one last cursory look at the scene and then with soil sticking to his nose, and his legs black to the shoulder, he will give it up and trot off indifferently beside me. "No go, Bashan," I say when he looks up at me. "Nothing there," I repeat, shaking my head and shrugging my shoulders to make my meaning clear. But he needs no consolation, he is not in the least depressed by his failure. The chase is the thing, the quarry a minor matter. It was a good effort, he thinks, in so far as he casts his mind back at all to his recent strenuous performance – for already he is bent on a new one, and all three of our zones will furnish him plenty of opportunity.

But sometimes he actually catches the mouse. I have my emotions when that happens, for he gobbles it alive, without compunction, with the fur and the bones. Perhaps the poor little thing was not well enough advised by its instincts, and chose for its hole a place where the earth was too soft and loose and easy to dig. Perhaps its gallery was not long enough and it was too terrified to go on digging, but simply crouched there with its beady eyes popping out of its head for fright, while the horrible snorting came nearer and nearer. And so at last the iron-shod paw laid it bare and scooped it up – out into the light of day, a lost little mouse! It was justified of its fears; luckily these most likely reduced it to a semi-conscious state, so that it will hardly have noticed being converted into porridge.

Bashan holds it by the tail and dashes it against the ground, once, twice, thrice; there is the faintest squeak, the very last sound which the god-forsaken little mouse is destined to make on this earth, and now Bashan snaps it up in his jaws, between his strong white teeth. He stands with his forelegs braced apart, his neck bent, and his head stuck out while he chews, shifting the morsel in his mouth and then beginning to munch once more. He crunches the tiny bones, a shred of fur hangs from the corner of his mouth, it disappears and all is over. Bashan begins to execute a dance of joy and triumph round me as I stand leaning on my stick as I have been standing to watch the whole procedure. "You are a fine one!" I say, nodding in grim tribute to his prowess. "You are a murderer, you know, a cannibal!" He only redoubles his activity – he does everything but laugh aloud. So I walk on, feeling rather chilled by what I have seen, yet inwardly amused by the crude humours of life. The event was in the natural order of things, and a mouse lacking in the instinct of self-preservation is on the way to be turned into pulp. But I feel better if I happen not to have assisted the natural order with my stick but to have preserved throughout my attitude of onlooker.

It is startling to have a pheasant burst out of the undergrowth where it was perched asleep or else hoping to be undiscovered, until Bashan's unerring nose ferreted it out. The big, rust-coloured, long-tailed bird rises with a great clapping and flapping and a frightened, angry, cackling cry. It drops its excrement into the brush and takes flight with the absurd headlessness of a chicken to the nearest tree, where it goes on shrieking murder, while Bashan claws at the trunk and barks furiously up at it. "Get up, get up!" he is saying. "Fly away, you silly object of my sporting instincts, that I may chase you!" And the bird cannot resist his loud voice, it rises rustling from the bough and flies on heavy wing through the tree-tops, squawking and complaining, Bashan following below, with ardour, but preserving a stately silence.

This is his joy. He wants and knows no other. For what would happen if he actually caught the pheasant? Nothing at all: I have seen him with one in his claws – he may have stolen upon it while it slept so that the awkward bird could not rise – and he stood over it embarrassed by his triumph, without an idea what to do. The pheasant lay in the grass with its neck and one wing sprawled out and shrieked without stopping – it sounded as though an old woman were being murdered in the bushes, and I hastened up to prevent, if I could, something frightful happening. But I quickly convinced myself that there was no danger. Bashan's obvious helplessness, the half curious, half disgusted look he bent on his capture, with his head on one side, quite reassured me. The old-womanish screaming at his feet got on his nerves, the whole affair made him feel more bothered than triumphant. Perhaps, for his honour as a sportsman, he plucked at the bird – I think I saw him pulling out a couple of feathers with his lips, not using his teeth, and tossing them to one side with an angry shake of the head. But then he moved away and let it go. Not out of magnanimity, but because the affair seemed not to have anything to do with the joyous hunt and so was merely stupid. Never have I seen a more nonplussed bird. It had given itself up for lost, and appeared not to be able to convince itself to the contrary: awhile it lay in the grass as though it were dead. Then it staggered along the ground a little way, fluttered up on a tree, looked like falling off it, but pulled itself together and flew away heavily, with dishevelled plumes. It did not squawk, it kept its bill shut. Without a sound it flew across the park, the river, the woods on the other side, as far away as possible and certainly it never came back.

But there are plenty of its kind in our hunting-ground and Bashan hunts them in all honour and according to the rules of the game. Eating mice is the only blood-guilt he has on his head and even that is incidental and superfluous. The tracking out, the driving up, the chasing – these are ends in themselves to the sporting spirit, and are plainly so to him, as anybody would see who watched him at his brilliant performance. How beautiful he becomes, how consummate, how ideal! Like a clumsy peasant lad, who will look perfect and statuesque as a huntsman among his native rocks. All that is best in Bashan, all that is genuine and fine, comes out and reaches its flower at these times. Hence his yearning for them, his repining when they fruitlessly slip away. He is no terrier, he is true hunter and pointer, and joy in himself as such speaks in every virile, valiant, native pose he assumes. Not many other things rejoice my eye as does the sight of him going through the brush at a swinging trot, then standing stock-still, with one paw daintily raised and turned in, sagacious, serious, alert, with all his faculties beautifully concentrated. Then suddenly he whimpers. He has trod on a thorn and cries out. Ah, yes, that too is natural, it is amusing to see that he has the courage of his simplicity. It could only passingly mar his dignity, next moment his posture is as fine as ever.

I look at him and recall a time when he lost all his nobility and distinction and reverted to the low physical and moral state in which we found him in the kitchen of that mountain inn and from which he climbed painfully enough to some sort of belief in himself and the world. I do not know what ailed him; he had bleeding from the mouth or nose or throat, I do not know which to this day. Wherever he went he left traces of blood behind: on the grass in our hunting-ground, the straw in his kennel, on the floor in the house – though we could not discover any wound. Sometimes his nose looked as though it had been dipped in red paint. When he sneezed he showered blood all over, and then trod in it and left the marks of his paws about. He was carefully examined without result, and we felt more and more disturbed. Was he tubercular? Or had he some other complaint to which his species was prone? When the mysterious affliction did not pass off after some days, we decided to take him to a veterinary clinic.

Next day at about noon I kindly but firmly adjusted his muzzle, the leather mask which Bashan detests as he does few other things, always trying to get rid of it by shaking his head or rubbing it with his paws. I put him on the plaited leather lead and led him thus harnessed up the poplar avenue, through the English Gardens, and along a city street to the Academy, where we went under the arch and crossed the courtyard. We were received into a waiting-room where several people sat, each holding like me a dog on a lead. They were dogs of all sizes and kinds, gazing dejectedly at each other over their muzzles. There was a matron with her apoplectic pug, a liveried manservant with a tall, snow-white Russian greyhound, which from time to time gave a hoarse, aristocratic cough; a countryman with a dachshund which seemed to need orthopædic assistance, its legs being entirely crooked and put on all wrong. And many more. The attendant let them in one by one into the consulting-room, and after a while it became the turn of Bashan and me.

The Professor was a man in advanced years, wearing a white surgeon's coat and a gold eye-glass. His hair was curly, and he seemed so mild, expert, and kindly that I would have unhesitatingly entrusted myself and all my family to him in any emergency. During my recital he smiled benevolently at his patient, who sat there looking up at him with equal trustfulness. "He has fine eyes," said he, passing over Bashan's moustaches in silence. He said he would make an examination at once, and poor Bashan, too astounded to offer any resistance, was with the attendant's help stretched out on the table forthwith. And then it was touching to see the physician apply his black stethoscope and auscultate my little man just as I have more than once had it done to me. He listened to his quick-breathing doggish heart, listened to all his organs, in various places. Then with his stethoscope under his arm he examined Bashan's eyes and nose and the cavity of his mouth, and gave a temporary opinion. The dog was a little nervous and anæmic, he said, but otherwise in good condition. The origin of the bleeding was unclear. It might be an epistaxis or a hæmatemesis. But equally well it might be tracheal or pharyngeal hæmorrhage. Perhaps for the present one might characterize it as a case of hæmoptysis. It would be best to keep the animal under careful observation. I might leave it with them and look in at the end of a week.

Thus instructed, I expressed my thanks and took my leave, patting Bashan on the shoulder by way of good-bye. I saw the attendant take the new patient across the courtyard to some back buildings opposite the entrance, Bashan looking back at me with a frightened and bewildered face. And yet he might have felt flattered, as I could not help feeling myself, at having the Professor call him nervous and anæmic. No one could have foretold of him in his cradle that he would one day be called those things or discussed with such gravity and expert knowledge.

But after that my walks abroad were as unseasoned food to the palate; I had little relish of them. No dumb pæan of joy accompanied my going out, no glorious excitement of the chase surrounded my footsteps. The park was a desert, time hung on my hands. During the period of waiting I telephoned several times for news. Answer came through a subordinate that the patient was doing as well as possible under the circumstances – but the circumstances – for better or worse – were never described in more detail. So when the week came round again, I betook myself to the clinic.

Guided by numerous signs and arrows I arrived without difficulty before the entrance of the department where Bashan was lodged, and, warned by another sign on the door, forbore to knock and went straight in. The medium-sized room I found myself in reminded me of a carnivora-house – a similar atmosphere prevailed. Only here the menagerie odour seemed to be kept down by various sweetish-smelling medicinal fumes – a disturbing and oppressive combination. Wire cages ran round the room, most of them occupied. Loud baying greeted me from one of these, at the open door of which a man, who seemed to be the keeper, was busy with rake and shovel. He contented himself with returning my greeting whilst going on with his work, and left me to my own devices.

I had seen Bashan directly I entered the door, and went up to him. He was lying behind his bars on a pile of tan-bark or some such stuff, which contributed its own special odour to the animal and chemical smells in the room. He lay there like a leopard – but a very weary, sluggish, and disgusted leopard. I was startled by the sullen indifference with which he met me. His tail thumped the floor once or twice, weakly; only when I spoke to him did he lift his head from his paws, and even then he let it fall again at once and blinked gloomily to one side. There was an earthenware dish of water at the back of his pen. A framed chart, partly printed and partly written, was fastened to the bars, giving his name, species, sex, and age and showing his temperature curve. "Bastard pointer," it said, "named Bashan. Male. Two years old. Admitted on such and such a day of the month and the year, for observation of occult blood." Underneath followed the fever curve, drawn with a pen and showing small variations; also daily entries of his pulse. Yes, his temperature was taken, and his pulse felt, by a doctor; in his direction everything was being done. But I was distressed about his state of mind.

"Is that one yours?" asked the keeper, who had now come up, his tools in his hands. He had on a sort of gardening apron and was a squat red-faced man with a round beard and rather bloodshot brown eyes that were quite strikingly like a dog's in their humid gaze and faithful expression.

I answered in the affirmative, referred to my telephone conversations and the instructions I had had to come back today, and said I should like to hear how things stood. The man looked at the chart. Yes, the dog was suffering from occult blood, that was always a long business, especially when one did not know where it came from. But was not that always the case? No, they did not really know yet. But the dog was there to be observed, and he would be. And did he still bleed? Yes, now and then he did. And had he fever? I asked, trying to read the chart. No, no fever. His temperature and pulse were quite normal, about ninety beats a minute, he ought to have that much, and if he had not, then they would have to observe him even more carefully. Except for the bleeding, the dog was really doing all right. He had howled at first, of course; he had howled for twenty-four hours, but after that he was used to it. He didn't eat much, for a fact, but then he hadn't much exercise, and perhaps he wasn't a big eater. What did they give him? Soup, said the man. But as he had said, the dog didn't eat much at all. "He seems depressed," I remarked with an assumption of objectivity. Yes, that was true, but it didn't mean much.

After all it wasn't very much fun for a dog to lie cooped up like that under observation. They were all depressed, more or less. That is, the good-natured ones, some dogs got mean and treacherous. He could not say that of Bashan. He was a good dog, he would not get mean if he stayed there all his days. I agreed with the man, but I did so with pain and rebellion in my heart. How long then, I asked, did they reckon to keep him here? The man looked at the chart again. Another week, he said, would be needed for the observation, the Herr Professor had said. I'd better come and ask again in another week; that would be two weeks in all, then they would be able to say more about the possibility of getting rid of the hæmorrhages.

I went away, after trying once more to rouse up Bashan by renewed calls and encouragement. In vain. He cared as little for my going as for my coming. He seemed weighed down by bitter loathing and despair. He had the air of saying: "Since you were capable of having me put in this cage, I expect nothing more from you." And, actually, had he not enough ground to despair of reason and justice? What had he done that this should happen to him and that I not only let it happen but took steps to bring it about? And yet my intentions had been of the best. He had bled, and though it seemed to make no difference to him, I thought it sensible that we should call in medical advice, he being a dog in good circumstances. And then we had learned that he was anæmic and nervous – as though he were the daughter of some upper-class family. And then it had to come out like this! How could I explain to him we were treating him with great distinction, in shutting him up like a jaguar, without sun, air, or exercise, and plaguing him every day with a thermometer?

On the way home I asked myself these things; and if before then I had missed Bashan, now worry about him was added to my distress: worry over his state and reproaches to my own address. Perhaps after all I had taken him to the clinic only out of vanity and arrogance. And added to that may I not have secretly wished to get rid of him for a while? Perhaps I had a craving to see what it would be like to be free of his incessant watching of me; to be able to turn calmly to right or left as I pleased, without having to realize that I had been to another living creature the source of joy or of bitter disappointment. Certainly while Bashan was interned I felt a certain inner independence which had long been strange to me. No one exasperated me by looking through the glass door with the air of a martyr. No one put up a hesitating paw to move me to laughter and relenting and persuade me to go out sooner than I wished. Whether I sought the park or kept my room concerned no one at all. It was quiet, pleasant, and had the charm of novelty. But lacking the accustomed spur I hardly went out at all. My health suffered, gradually I approached the condition of Bashan in his cage; and the moral reflection occurred to me that the bonds of sympathy were probably more conducive to my own well-being than the selfish independence for which I had longed.

The second week went by, and on the appointed day I stood with the round-bearded keeper before Bashan's cage. Its inmate lay on his side on the tan-bark, there were bits of it on his coat. He had his head flung back as he lay and was staring with dull, glazed eyes at the bare whitewashed wall. He did not stir. I could scarcely see him breathe; but now and then his chest rose in a long sigh that made the ribs stand out, and fell again with a faint, heart-rending resonance from the vocal cords. His legs seemed to have grown too long, and his paws large out of all proportion, as a result of his extraordinary emaciation. His coat was rough and dishevelled and had, as I said, tan-bark sticking in it. He did not look at me, he seemed not to want to look at anything ever any more.

The bleeding, so the keeper said, had not altogether and entirely disappeared, it came back now and again. Where it came from was still not quite clear; in any case it was harmless. If I liked I could leave the dog here for further observation, to be quite certain, or I could take him home, because the bleeding might disappear just as well there as here. I drew the plaited lead out of my pocket – I had brought it with me – and said that I would take him with me. The keeper thought that was a sensible thing to do. He opened the grating and we summoned Bashan by name, both together and in turn, but he did not come, he kept on staring at the whitewashed wall. But he did not struggle when I put my arm into the cage and pulled him out by the collar. He gave a spring and landed with his four feet on the floor, where he stood with his tail between his legs and his ears laid back, the picture of wretchedness. I picked him up, tipped the keeper, and went to the front office to pay my debt; at the rate of seventy-five pfennigs a day plus the medical examination it came to twelve marks fifty. I led Bashan home, breathing the animal-chemical odours which still clung to his coat.

He was broken, in body and in spirit. Animals are more primitive and less inhibited in giving expression to their mental state – there is a sense in which one might say they are more human: descriptive phrases which to us have become mere metaphor still fit them literally, we get a fresh and diverting sense of their meaning when we see it embodied before our eyes. Bashan, as we say, "hung his head"; that is, he did it literally and visibly, till he looked like a worn-out cab-horse, with sores on its legs, standing at the cab-rank, its skin twitching and its poor fly-infested nose weighed down towards the pavement. It was as I have said: those two weeks at the clinic had reduced him to the state he had been in at the beginning. He was the shadow of his former self – if that does not insult the proud and joyous shadow our Bashan once cast. The hospital smell he had brought with him wore off after repeated soapy baths till you got only an occasional whiff; but it was not with him as with human beings: he got no symbolic refreshment from the physical cleansing. The very first day, I took him out to our hunting-grounds, but he followed at my heel with his tongue lolling out; even the pheasants perceived that it was the close season. For days he lay as he had lain in his cage at the clinic, staring with glazed eyes, flabby without and within. He showed no healthy impatience for the chase, did not urge me to go out – indeed it was rather I who had to go and fetch him from his kennel.

Even the reckless and indiscriminate way he wolfed his food recalled those early unworthy days. But what a joy to see him slowly finding himself again! Little by little he began to greet me in the morning in his old naïve, impetuous way, storming upon me at my first whistle instead of limping morosely up; putting his fore-paws on my chest and snapping playfully at my face. Gradually there returned to him his old out-of-doors pride and joy in his own physical prowess; once more he delighted my eyes with the bold and beautiful poses he took, the sudden bounds with his feet drawn up, after some creature stirring in the long grass.... He forgot. The ugly and to Bashan senseless episode sank into the past, unresolved indeed, unclarified by comprehension, that being of course impossible; it was covered by the lapse of time, as must happen sometimes to human beings. We went on living and what had not been expressed became by degrees forgotten.... For several weeks, at lengthening intervals, Bashan's nose showed red. Then the phenomenon disappeared, it was no more, it only had been, and so it was no matter whether it had been an epistaxis or a hæmatemesis.

Well, there! Contrary to my own intentions, I have told the story of the clinic. Perhaps my reader will forgive the lengthy digression and come back to the park and the pleasures of the chase, where we were before the interruption. Do you know that long-drawn wailing howl to which a dog gives vent when he summons up his utmost powers to give chase to a flying hare? In it rage and rapture mingle, desire and the ecstasy of despair. How often have I heard it from Bashan! It is passion itself, deliberate, fostered passion, drunkenly revelled in, shrilling through our woodland scene, and every time I hear it near or far a fearful thrill of pleasure shoots through my limbs. Rejoiced that Bashan will come into his own today, I hasten to his side, to see the chase if I can; when it roars past me I stand spellbound – though the futility of it is clear from the first – and look on with an agitated smile on my face.

And the hare, the common, frightened little hare? The air whistles through its ears, it lays back its head and runs for its life, it scrabbles and bounds with Bashan behind it yelling all he can; its yellow-white scut flies up in the air. And yet at the bottom of its soul, timid as that is and acquainted with fear, it must know that its peril cannot be grave, that it will get away, as its brothers and sisters have done before it, and itself too under like circumstances. Never in his life has Bashan caught one of them, nor will he ever; the thing is as good as impossible. Many dogs, they say, are the death of a hare, a single dog cannot achieve it, even one much speedier and more enduring than Bashan. The hare can "double" and Bashan cannot – and that is all there is to it. For the double is the unfailing natural weapon of those born to seek safety in flight; they always have it by them, to use at the decisive moment; when Bashan's hopes are highest – then they are dashed to the ground, and he is betrayed.

There they come, dashing diagonally through the brush, across the path in front of me, and on towards the river: the hare silently hugging his little trick in his heart, Bashan giving tongue in high head-tones. "Be quiet!" I think. "You are wasting your wind and your lung-power and you ought to save them if you want to catch him up." Thus I think because in my heart I am on Bashan's side, some of his fire has kindled me, I fervently hope he may catch the hare – even at the risk of seeing it torn to shreds before my eyes. How he runs! It is beautiful to see a creature expending the utmost of its powers. He runs better than the hare does, he has stronger muscles, the distance between them visibly diminishes before I lose sight of them. And I make haste too, leaving the path and cutting across the park towards the river-bank, reaching the gravelled street in time to see the chase come raging on – the hopeful, thrilling chase, with Bashan on the hare's very heels; he is still, he runs with his jaw set, scent just in front of his nose urges him to a final effort. – "One more push, Bashan!" I think, and feel like shouting: "Well run, old chap, remember the double!" But there it is; Bashan does make one more push, and the misfortune is upon us: at that moment the hare gives a quick, easy, almost malicious twitch at right angles to the course, and Bashan shoots past from his rear, howling helplessly and braking his very best so that dirt and pebbles fly into the air. Before he can stop, turn round, and get going in the other direction, yelling all the time as in great mental torment, the hare has gained so much ground that it is out of sight; for while he was braking so desperately Bashan could not watch where it went.

It is no use, I think; it is beautiful but futile; this while the chase fades away through the park. It takes a lot of dogs, five or six, a whole pack. Some of them to take it on the flank, some to cut off its way in front, some to corner it, some to catch it by the neck. And in my excited fancy I see a whole pack of bloodhounds with their tongues out rushing on the hare in their midst.

It is my passion for the chase makes me have these fancies, for what has the hare done to me that I should wish him such a horrible death? Bashan is nearer to me, of course, it is natural that I should feel with him and wish for his success. But the hare is after all a living creature too, and he did not play his trick on my huntsman out of malice, but only from the compelling desire to live yet awhile, nibble young tree-shoots, and beget his kind. It would be different, I go on in my mind, if this cane of mine – I lift it and look at it – were not a harmless stick, but a more serious weapon, effective like lightning and at a distance, with which I could come to Bashan's assistance and hold up the hare in mid career, so that it would turn a somersault and lie dead on the ground. Then we should not need another dog, and it would be Bashan's only task to rouse the game. Whereas as things stand it is Bashan who sometimes rolls over and over in his effort to brake. The hare sometimes does too, but it is nothing to it, it is used to such things, they do not make it feel miserable, whereas it is a shattering experience for Bashan, and might even quite possibly break his neck.

Often such a chase is all over in a few minutes; that is, when the hare succeeds after a short length in ducking into the bushes and hiding, or else by doubling and feinting in throwing off its pursuer, who stands still, hesitating, or makes short springs in this and that direction, while I in my bloodthirstiness shout encouragement and try to show him with my stick the direction the hare took. But often the hunt sways far and wide across the landscape and Bashan's furious baying sounds like a distant bugle-horn, now near, now remote; I go my own way, knowing that he will return. But in what a state he does return, at last! Foam drips from his lips, his ribs flutter, and his loins are lank and expended, his tongue lolls out of his jaws, which yawn so wide as to distort his features and give his drunken, swimming eyes a weird Mongolian slant. His breath goes like a trip-hammer. "Lie down and rest, Bashan," say I, "or your lungs will burst!" and I wait to give him time to recover. I am alarmed for him when it is cold, when he pumps the air by gasps into his over-heated insides and it gushes out again in a white stream; when he swallows whole mouthfuls of snow to quench his furious thirst. He lies there looking helplessly up at me, now and then licking up the slaver from his lips, and I cannot help teasing him a bit about the invariable futility of all his exertions. "Where is the hare, Bashan?" I ask. "Why don't you bring it to me?" He thumps with his tail on the ground when I speak; his sides pump in and out less feverishly, and he gives a rather embarrassed snap – for how can he know that I am mocking him because I feel guilty myself and want to conceal it? For I did not play my part in his enterprise, I was not man enough to hold the hare, as a proper master should have done. He does not know this, and so I can make fun of him and behave as though it were all his fault.

Strange things sometimes happen on these occasions. Never shall I forget the day when the hare ran into my arms. It was on the narrow clayey path above the river. Bashan was in full cry; I came from the wood into the river zone, struck across through the thistles of the gravelly waste, and jumped down the grassy slope to the path just in time to see the hare, with Bashan fifteen paces behind it, come bounding from the direction of the ferry-house towards which I was facing. It leaped right into the path and came towards me. My first impulse was that of the hunter towards his prey: to take advantage of the situation and cut off its escape, driving it back if possible into the jaws of the pursuer joyously yelping behind. I stood fixed on the spot, quite abandoned to the fury of the chase, weighing my cane in my hand as the hare came towards me. A hare's sight is poor, that I knew; hearing and smell are the senses that guide and preserve it. It might have taken me for a tree as I stood there; I hoped and foresaw it would do so and thus fall victim to a frightful error, the possible consequences of which were not very clear to me, though I meant to turn them to our advantage. Whether it did at any time make this mistake is unclear. I think it did not see me at all until the last minute, and what it did was so unexpected as to upset all my plans in a trice and cause a complete and sudden revulsion in my feelings. Was it beside itself with fright? Anyhow, it jumped straight at me, like a dog, ran up my overcoat with its fore-paws and snuggled its head into me, me whom it should most fear, the master of the chase! I stood bent back with my arms raised, I looked down at the hare and it looked up at me. It was only a second, perhaps only part of a second, that this lasted. I saw the hare with such extraordinary distinctness, its long ears, one of which stood up, the other hung down; its large, bright, short-sighted, prominent eyes, its cleft lip and the long hairs of its moustache, the white on its breast and little paws; I felt or thought I felt the throbbing of its hunted heart. And it was strange to see it so clearly and have it so close to me, the little genius of the place, the inmost beating heart of our whole region, this ever-fleeing little being which I had never seen but for brief moments in our meadows and bottoms, frantically and drolly getting out of the way – and now, in its hour of need, not knowing where to turn, it came to me, it clasped as it were my knees, a human being's knees: not the knees, so it seemed to me, of Bashan's master, but the knees of a man who felt himself master of hares and this hare's master as well as Bashan's. It was, I say, only for the smallest second. Then the hare had dropped off, taken again to its uneven legs, and bounded up the slope on my left; while in its place there was Bashan, Bashan giving tongue in all the horrid head-tones of his hue-and-cry. When he got within reach he was abruptly checked by a deliberate and well-aimed blow from the stick of the hare's master, which sent him yelping down the slope with a temporarily disabled hind quarter. He had to limp painfully back again before he could take up the trail of his by this time vanished prey.

Finally, there are the waterfowl, to our pursuit of which I must devote a few lines. We can only go after them in winter and early spring, before they leave their town quarters – where they stay for their food's sake, and return to their lakes in the mountains. They furnish, of course, much less exciting sport than can be got out of the hares; still, it has its attractions for hunter and hound – or, rather, for the hunter and his master. For me the charm lies in the scenery, the intimate bond with living water; also it is amusing and diverting to watch the creatures swimming and flying and try provisionally to exchange one's personality for theirs and enter into their mode of life.

The ducks lead a quieter, more comfortable, more bourgeois life than do the gulls. They seem to have enough to eat, on the whole, and not to be tormented by the pangs of hunger – their kind of food is regularly to be had, the table, so to speak, always laid. For everything is fish that comes to their net: worms, snails, insects – even the ooze of the river-bed. So they have plenty of time to sit on the stones in the sun, doze with their bills tucked under one wing, and preen their well-oiled plumes, off which the water rolls in drops. Sometimes they take a pleasure-ride on the waves, with their pointed rumps in the air; paddling this way and that and giving little self-satisfied shrugs.

But the nature of gulls is wilder and more strident; there is a dreary monotony about what they do, they are the eternally hungry bird of prey, swooping all day long in hordes across the waterfall, croaking about the drain-pipes that disgorge their brown streams into the river. Single gulls hover and pounce down upon a fish now and then, but this does not go far to satisfy their inordinate mass hunger; they have to fill in with most unappetizing-looking morsels from the drains, snatching them from the water in flight and carrying them off in their crooked beaks. They do not like the river-bank. But when the river is low, they huddle together on the rocks that stick out of the water – the scene is white with them, as the cliffs and islets of northern oceans are white with hosts of nesting eider-duck. I like to watch them rise all together with a great cawing and take to the air, when Bashan barks at them from the bank, across the intervening stream. They need not be frightened, certainly they are in no danger. He has a native aversion to water; but aside from that he would never trust himself to the current, and he is quite right, it is much stronger than he and would soon sweep him away and carry him God knows where. Perhaps into the Danube – but he would only arrive there after having suffered a river-change of a very drastic kind, as we know from seeing the bloated corpses of cats on their way to some distant bourne. Bashan never goes farther into the water than the point where it begins to break over the stones. Even when he seems most tense with the pleasure of the chase and looks exactly as though he meant to jump in the very next minute, one knows that under all the excitement his sense of caution is alert and that the dashings and rushings are pure theatre – empty threats, not so much dictated by passion as cold-bloodedly undertaken in order to terrify the web-footed tribe.

But the gulls are too witless and poor-spirited to make light of his performance. He cannot get to them himself, but he sends his voice thundering across the water; it reaches them, and it, too, has actuality; it is an attack which they cannot long resist. They try to at first, they sit still, but a wave of uneasiness goes through the host, they turn their heads, a few lift their wings, and suddenly they all rush up into the air, like a white cloud, whence issue the bitterest, most fatalistic screams, Bashan springing hither and thither on the rocks, to scatter their flight and keep them in motion, for it is motion that he wants, they are not to sit quiet, they must fly, fly up and down the river so that he may chase them.

He scampers along the shore far and wide, for everywhere there are ducks, sitting with their bills tucked in homely comfort under their wings; and wherever he comes they fly up before him. He is like a jolly little hurricane making a clean sweep of the beach. Then they plump down on the water again, where they rock and ride in comfort and safety, or else they fly away over his head with their necks stretched out, while below on the shore he measures the strength of his leg-muscles quite creditably against those of their wings.

He is enchanted, and really grateful to them if they will only fly and give him occasion for this glorious race up and down the beach. It may be that they know what he wants and turn the fact to their own advantage. I saw a mother duck with her brood – this was in spring, all the birds had forsaken the river and only this one was left with her fledglings, not yet able to fly. She had them in a stagnant puddle left by the last flood in the low-lying bed of the shrunken river, and there Bashan found them, while I watched the event from the upper path. He jumped into the puddle and lashed about, furiously barking, driving the family of ducklings into wild disorder. He did them no harm, of course, but he frightened them beyond measure; the ducklings flapped their stumps of wings and scattered in all directions, and the duck was overtaken by an attack of the maternal heroism which will hurl itself blind with valour upon the fiercest foe to protect her brood; more, will even by a frenzied and unnatural display of intrepidity bully the attacker into surrender. She opened her beak to a horrific extent, she ruffled up her feathers, she flew repeatedly into Bashan's face, she made onslaught after onslaught, hissing all the while. The grim seriousness of her behaviour was so convincing that Bashan actually gave ground in confusion, though without definitely retiring from the field, for each time after retreating he would bark and advance anew. Then the mother duck changed her tactics: heroics having failed, she took refuge in strategy. Probably she knew Bashan already and was aware of his foibles and the childish nature of his desires. She left her children in the lurch – or she pretended to; she took to flight, she flew up above the river, "pursued" by Bashan. At least, he thought he was pursuing her, in reality it was she who was leading him on, playing on his childish passion, leading him by the nose. She flew downstream, then upstream, she flew farther and farther away, Bashan racing equal with her along the bank; they left the pool with the ducklings far behind, and at length both dog and duck disappeared from my sight. Bashan came back to me after a while; the simpleton was quite winded and panting for dear life. But when we passed the pool again on our homeward way, it was empty of its brood.

So much for the mother duck. As for Bashan, he was quite grateful for the sport she had given him. For he hates the ducks who selfishly prefer their bourgeois comfort and refuse to play his game with him, simply gliding off into the water when he comes rushing along, and rocking there in base security before his face and eyes, heedless of his mighty barking, heedless too – unlike the nervous gulls – of all his feints and plungings. We stand there, Bashan and I, on the stones at the water's edge, and two paces away a duck floats on the wave, floats impudently up and down, her beak pressed coyly against her breast; safe and untouched and sweetly reasonable she bobs up and down out there, let Bashan rave as he will. Paddling against the current, she keeps abreast of us fairly well; yet she is being slowly carried down, closer and closer to one of those beautiful foaming eddies in the stream. In her folly she rides with her tail turned towards it – and now it is only a yard away. Bashan loudly gives tongue, standing with his forelegs braced against the stones; and in my heart I am barking with him, I am on his side and against that impudent, self-satisfied floating thing out there. I wish her ill. Pay attention to our barking, I address her mentally; do not hear the whirlpool roar – and then presently you will find yourself in an unpleasant and undignified situation and I shall be glad! But my malicious hopes are not fulfilled. For at the rapid's very edge she flutters up into the air, flies a few yards upstream, and then, oh, shameless hussy, settles down again.

I recall the feelings of baffled anger with which we looked at that duck – and I am reminded of another occasion, another and final episode in this tale of our hunting-ground. It was attended by a certain satisfaction for my companion and me, but had its painful and disturbing side as well; yes, it even gave rise to some coolness between us, and if I could have foreseen it I would have avoided the spot where it took place.

It was a long way out, beyond the ferry-house, downstream, where the wilds that border the river approach the upper road along the shore. We were going along this, I at an easy pace, Bashan in front with his easy, lop-sided lope. He had roused a hare – or, if you like, it had roused him – had stirred up four pheasants, and now was minded to give his master a little attention. A small bevy of ducks were flying above the river, in v-formation, their necks stretched out. They flew rather high and closer to the other shore, so that they were out of our reach as game, but moving in the same direction as ourselves. They paid no attention to us and we only cast casual glances at them now and then.

Then it happened that opposite to us on the other bank, which like ours was steep here, a man struck out of the bushes, and directly he appeared upon the scene he took up a position which fixed our attention, Bashan's no less than mine, upon him at once. We stopped in our tracks and faced him. He was a fine figure of a man, though rather rough-looking; with drooping moustaches, wearing puttees, a frieze hat cocked down over his forehead, wide velveteen trousers and jerkin to match, over which hung numerous leather straps, for he had a rucksack slung on his back and a gun over his shoulder. Or rather he had had it over his shoulder; for he no sooner appeared than he took it in his hand, laid his cheek along the butt, and aimed it diagonally upwards at the sky. He took a step forwards with one putteed leg, the gun-barrel rested in the hollow of his left hand, with the arm stretched out and the elbow against his side. The other elbow, with the hand on the trigger, stuck out at his side, and we could see his bold, foreshortened face quite clearly as he sighted upwards. It looked somehow very theatrical, this figure standing out above the boulders on the bank, against a background of shrubbery, river, and open sky. But we could have gazed for only a moment when the dull sound of the explosion made me start, I had waited for it with such inward tension. There was a tiny flash at the same time; it looked pale in the broad daylight; a puff of smoke followed. The man took one slumping pace forwards, like an operatic star, with his face and chest lifted towards the sky, his gun hanging from the strap in his right fist. Something was going on up there where he was looking and where we now looked too. There was a great confusion and scattering, the ducks flew in all directions wildly flapping their wings with a noise like wind in the sails, they tried to volplane down – then suddenly a body fell like a stone onto the water near the other shore.

This was only the first half of the action. But I must interrupt my narrative here to turn the vivid light of my memory upon the figure of Bashan. I can think of large words with which to describe it, phrases we use for great occasions: I could say that he was thunderstruck. But I do not like them, I do not want to use them. The large words are worn out, when the great occasion comes they do not describe it. Better use the small ones and put into them every ounce of their weight. I will simply say that when Bashan heard the explosion, saw its meaning and consequence, he started; and it was the same start which I have seen him give a thousand times when something surprises him, only raised to the *n*th degree. It was a start which flung his whole body backwards with a right-and-left motion, so sudden that it jerked his head against his chest and almost bounced it off his shoulders with the shock; a start which made his whole body seem to be crying out: What! What! What was that? Wait a minute, in the devil's name! *What was that?* He looked and listened with that sort of rage in which extreme astonishment expresses itself; listened within himself and heard things that had always been there, however novel and unheard-of the present form they took. Yes, from this start, which flung him to right and left and half-way round on his axis, I got the impression that he was trying to look at himself, trying to ask: What am I? Who am I? Is this me? At the moment when the duck's body plopped on the water he bounded forwards to the edge of the bank, as though he were going to jump down to the river-bed and plunge in. But he bethought himself of the current and checked his impulse; then, rather shame-faced, devoted himself to staring, as before.

I looked at him, somewhat disturbed. After the duck had fallen I felt that we had had enough and suggested that we go on our way. But he had sat down on his haunches, facing the other shore, his ears erected as high as they would go. When I said: "Well, Bashan, shall we go on?" he turned his head only the briefest second as though saying, with some annoyance: Please don't disturb me! And kept on looking. So I resigned myself, crossed my legs, leaned on my cane, and watched to see what would happen.

The duck – no doubt one of those that had rocked in such pert security on the water in front of our noses – went driving like a wreck on the water, you could not tell which was head and which tail. The river is quieter at this point, its rapids are not so swift as they are farther up. But even so, the body was seized by the current, whirled round, and swept away. If the man was not concerned only with sport but had a practical goal in view, then he would better act quickly. And so he did, not losing a moment – it all went very fast. Even as the duck fell he had rushed forward stumbling and almost falling down the slope, with his gun held out at arm's length. Again I was struck with the picturesqueness of the sight, as he came down the slope like a robber or smuggler in a melodrama, in the highly effective scenery of boulder and bush. He held somewhat leftwards, allowing for the current, for the duck was drifting away and he had to head it off. This he did successfully, stretching out the butt end of the gun and bending forward with his feet in the water. Carefully and painstakingly he piloted the duck towards the stones and drew it to shore.

The job was done, the man drew a long breath. He put down his weapon against the bank, took his knapsack from his shoulders, and stuffed the duck inside; buckled it on again, and thus satisfactorily laden and using his gun as a stick, he clambered over the boulders and up the slope.

"Well, he got his Sunday joint," thought I, half enviously, half approvingly. "Come, Bashan, let's go now, it's all over." Bashan got up and turned round on himself, but then he sat down again and looked after the man, even after he had left the scene and disappeared among the bushes. It did not occur to me to ask him twice. He knew where we lived, and he might sit here goggling, after it was all over, as long as he thought well. It was quite a long walk home and I meant to be stirring. So then he came.

He kept beside me on our whole painful homeward way, and did not hunt. Nor did he run diagonally a little ahead, as he does as a rule when not in a hunting mood; he kept behind me, at a jog-trot, and put on a sour face, as I could see when I happened to turn round. I could have borne with that and should not have dreamed of being drawn; I was rather inclined to laugh and shrug my shoulders. But every thirty or forty paces he *yawned* – and that I could not stand. It was that impudent gape of his, expressing the extreme of boredom, accompanied by a throaty little whine which seems to say: Fine master I've got! No master at all! Rotten master, if you ask me! – I am always sensitive to the insulting sound, and this time it was almost enough to shake our friendship to its foundations.

"Go away!" said I. "Get out with you! Go to your new friend with the blunderbuss and attach yourself to him! He does not seem to have a dog, perhaps he could use you in his business. He is only a man in velveteens, to be sure, not a gentleman, but in your eyes he may be one; perhaps he is the right master for you, and I honestly recommend you to suck up to him – now that he has put a flea in your ear to go with your others." (Yes, I actually said that!) "We'll not ask if he has a hunting-licence, or if you won't both get into fine trouble some day at your dirty game – that is your affair, and, as I tell you, my advice is perfectly sincere. You think so much of yourself as a hunter! Did you ever bring me a hare of all those I let you chase? Is it my fault that you do not know how to double, but must come down with your nose in the gravel at the moment when agility is required? Or a pheasant, which in these lean times would be equally welcome? And now you yawn! Get along, I tell you. Go to your master with the puttees and see if he knows how to scratch your neck and make you laugh. I'll wager he does not know how to laugh a decent laugh himself. Do you think he is likely to have you put under scientific observation when you decide to suffer from occult blood, or that when you are his dog you will be pronounced nervous and anæmic? If you do, then you'd better get along. But you may be overestimating the respect which that kind of master would have for you. There are certain distinctions – that kind of man with a gun is very keen on them: native advantages or disadvantages, to make my meaning clearer, troublesome questions of pedigree and breeding, if I must be plain. Not everybody passes these over on grounds of humanity and fine feeling; and if your wonderful master reproaches you with your moustaches the first time you and he have a difference of opinion, then you may remember me and what I am telling you now."

With such biting words did I address Bashan as he slunk behind me on our way home. And though I did not utter but only thought them, for I did not care to look as though I were mad, yet I am convinced that he got my meaning perfectly, at least in its main lines. In short, it was a serious quarrel, and when we got home I deliberately let the gate latch behind me so that he could not slip through and had to climb over the fence. I went into the house without even looking round, and shrugged my shoulders when I heard him yelp because he scratched his belly on the rail.

But all that is long ago, more than six months. Now, like our little clinical episode, it has dropped into the past. Time and forgetfulness have buried it, and on their alluvial deposit where all life lives, we too live on. For a few days Bashan appeared to mope. But long ago he recovered all his joy in the chase, in mice and moles and pheasant, hares and waterfowl. When we return home, at once begins his period of waiting for the next time. I stand at the house-door and turn towards him; upon that signal he bounds in two great leaps up the steps and braces his fore-paws against the door, reaching as far up as he can that I may pat him on the shoulder. "Tomorrow, Bashan," say I; "that is, if I am not obliged to pay a visit to the outer world." Then I hasten inside, to take off my hob-nailed boots, for the soup stands waiting on the table.

DISORDER AND EARLY SORROW

THE PRINCIPAL dish at dinner had been croquettes made of turnip greens. So there follows a trifle, concocted out of one of those dessert powders we use nowadays, that taste like almond soap. Xaver, the youthful manservant, in his outgrown striped jacket, white woollen gloves, and yellow sandals, hands it round, and the "big folk" take this opportunity to remind their father, tactfully, that company is coming today.

The "big folk" are two, Ingrid and Bert. Ingrid is brown-eyed, eighteen, and perfectly delightful. She is on the eve of her exams, and will probably pass them, if only because she knows how to wind masters, and even headmasters, round her finger. She does not, however, mean to use her certificate once she gets it; having leanings towards the stage, on the ground of her ingratiating smile, her equally ingratiating voice, and a marked and irresistible talent for burlesque. Bert is blond and seventeen. He intends to get done with school somehow, anyhow, and fling himself into the arms of life. He will be a dancer, or a cabaret actor, possibly even a waiter – but not a waiter anywhere else save at the Cairo, the night-club, whither he has once already taken flight, at five in the morning, and been brought back crestfallen. Bert bears a strong resemblance to the youthful manservant Xaver Kleinsgutl, of about the same age as himself; not because he looks common – in features he is strikingly like his father, Professor Cornelius – but by reason of an approximation of types, due in its turn to far-reaching compromises in matters of dress and bearing generally. Both lads wear their heavy hair very long on top, with a cursory parting in the middle, and give their heads the same characteristic toss to throw it off the forehead. When one of them leaves the house, by the garden gate, bareheaded in all weathers, in a blouse rakishly girt with a leather strap, and sheers off bent well over with his head on one side; or else mounts his push-bike – Xaver makes free with his employers', of both sexes, or even, in acutely irresponsible mood, with the Professor's own – Dr. Cornelius from his bedroom window cannot, for the life of him, tell whether he is looking at his son or his servant. Both, he thinks, look like young moujiks. And both are impassioned cigarette-smokers, though Bert has not the means to compete with Xaver, who smokes as many as thirty a day, of a brand named after a popular cinema star. The big folk call their father and mother the "old folk" – not behind their backs, but as a form of address and in all affection: "Hullo, old folks," they will say; though Cornelius is only forty-seven years old and his wife eight years younger. And the Professor's parents, who lead in his household the humble and hesitant life of the really old, are on the big folk's lips the "ancients". As for the "little folk", Ellie and Snapper, who take their meals upstairs with blue-faced Ann – so-called because of her prevailing facial hue – Ellie and Snapper follow their mother's example and address their father by his first name, Abel. Unutterably comic it sounds, in its pert, confiding familiarity; particularly on the lips, in the sweet accents, of five-year-old Eleanor, who is the image of Frau Cornelius's baby pictures and whom the Professor loves above everything else in the world.

"Darling old thing," says Ingrid affably, laying her large but shapely hand on his, as he presides in proper middle-class style over the family table, with her on his left and the mother opposite: "Parent mine, may I ever so gently jog your memory, for you have probably forgotten: this is the afternoon we were to have our little jollification, our turkey-trot with eats to match. You haven't a thing to do but just bear up and not funk it; everything will be over by nine o'clock."

"Oh – ah!" says Cornelius, his face falling. "Good!" he goes on, and nods his head to show himself in harmony with the inevitable. "I only meant – is this really the day? Thursday, yes. How time flies! Well, what time are they coming?"

"Half past four they'll be dropping in, I should say," answers Ingrid, to whom her brother leaves the major role in all dealings with the father. Upstairs, while he is resting, he will hear scarcely anything, and from seven to eight he takes his walk. He can slip out by the terrace if he likes.

"Tut!" says Cornelius deprecatingly, as who should say: "You exaggerate." But Bert puts in: "It's the one evening in the week Wanja doesn't have to play. Any other night he'd have to leave by half past six, which would be painful for all concerned."

Wanja is Ivan Herzl, the celebrated young leading man at the Stadttheater. Bert and Ingrid are on intimate terms with him, they often visit him in his dressing-room and have tea. He is an artist of the modern school, who stands on the stage in strange and, to the Professor's mind, utterly affected dancing attitudes, and shrieks lamentably. To a professor of history, all highly repugnant; but Bert has entirely succumbed to Herzl's influence, blackens the lower rim of his eyelids – despite painful but fruitless scenes with the father – and with youthful carelessness of the ancestral anguish declares that not only will he take Herzl for his model if he becomes a dancer, but in case he turns out to be a waiter at the Cairo he means to walk precisely thus.

Cornelius slightly raises his brows and makes his son a little bow – indicative of the unassumingness and self-abnegation that befits his age. You could not call it a mocking bow or suggestive in any special sense. Bert may refer it to himself or equally to his so talented friend.

"Who else is coming?" next inquires the master of the house. They mention various people, names all more or less familiar, from the city, from the suburban colony, from Ingrid's school. They still have some telephoning to do, they say. They have to phone Max. This is Max Hergesell, an engineering student; Ingrid utters his name in the nasal drawl which according to her is the traditional intonation of all the Hergesells. She goes on to parody it in the most abandonedly funny and lifelike way, and the parents laugh until they nearly choke over the wretched trifle. For even in these times when something funny happens people have to laugh.

From time to time the telephone bell rings in the Professor's study, and the big folk run across, knowing it is their affair. Many people had to give up their telephones the last time the price rose, but so far the Corneliuses have been able to keep theirs, just as they have kept their villa, which was built before the war, by dint of the salary Cornelius draws as professor of history – a million marks, and more or less adequate to the chances and changes of post-war life. The house is comfortable, even elegant, though sadly in need of repairs that cannot be made for lack of materials, and at present disfigured by iron stoves with long pipes. Even so, it is still the proper setting of the upper middle class, though they themselves look odd enough in it, with their worn and turned clothing and altered way of life. The children, of course, know nothing else; to them it is normal and regular, they belong by birth to the "villa proletariat". The problem of clothing troubles them not at all. They and their like have evolved a costume to fit the time, by poverty out of taste for innovation: in summer it consists of scarcely more than a belted linen smock and sandals. The middle-class parents find things rather more difficult.

The big folk's table-napkins hang over their chair-backs, they talk with their friends over the telephone. These friends are the invited guests who have rung up to accept or decline or arrange; and the conversation is carried on in the jargon of the clan, full of slang and high spirits, of which the old folk understand hardly a word. These consult together meantime about the hospitality to be offered to the impending guests. The Professor displays a middle-class ambitiousness: he wants to serve a sweet – or something that looks like a sweet – after the Italian salad and brown-bread sandwiches. But Frau Cornelius says that would be going too far. The guests would not expect it, she is sure – and the big folk, returning once more to their trifle, agree with her.

The mother of the family is of the same general type as Ingrid, though not so tall. She is languid; the fantastic difficulties of the housekeeping have broken and worn her. She really ought to go and take a cure, but feels incapable; the floor is always swaying under her feet, and everything seems upside-down. She speaks of what is uppermost in her mind: the eggs, they simply must be bought today. Six thousand marks apiece they are, and just so many are to be had on this one day of the week at one single shop fifteen minutes' journey away. Whatever else they do, the big folk must go and fetch them immediately after luncheon, with Danny, their neighbour's son, who will soon be calling for them; and Xaver Kleinsgutl will don civilian garb and attend his young master and mistress. For no single household is allowed more than five eggs a week; therefore the young people will enter the shop singly, one after another, under assumed names, and thus wring twenty eggs from the shopkeeper for the Cornelius family. This enterprise is the sporting event of the week for all participants, not excepting the moujik Kleinsgutl, and most of all for Ingrid and Bert, who delight in misleading and mystifying their fellow-men and would revel in the performance even if it did not achieve one single egg. They adore impersonating fictitious characters; they love to sit in a bus and carry on long lifelike conversations in a dialect which they otherwise never speak, the most commonplace dialogue about politics and people and the price of food, while the whole bus listens open-mouthed to this incredibly ordinary prattle, though with a dark suspicion all the while that something is wrong somewhere. The conversation waxes ever more shameless, it enters into revolting detail about these people who do not exist. Ingrid can make her voice sound ever so common and twittering and shrill as she impersonates a shop-girl with an illegitimate child, said child being a son with sadistic tendencies, who lately out in the country treated a cow with such unnatural cruelty that no Christian could have borne to see it. Bert nearly explodes at her twittering, but restrains himself and displays a grisly sympathy; he and the unhappy shop-girl entering into a long, stupid, depraved, and shuddery conversation over the particular morbid cruelty involved; until an old gentleman opposite, sitting with his ticket folded between his index finger and his seal ring, can bear it no more and makes public protest against the nature of the themes these young folk are discussing with such particularity. He uses the Greek plural: "themata". Whereat Ingrid pretends to be dissolving in tears, and Bert behaves as though his wrath against the old gentleman was with difficulty being held in check and would probably burst out before long. He clenches his fists, he gnashes his teeth, he shakes from head to foot; and the unhappy old gentleman, whose intentions had been of the best, hastily leaves the bus at the next stop.

Such are the diversions of the big folk. The telephone plays a prominent part in them: they ring up any and everybody – members of government, opera singers, dignitaries of the Church – in the character of shop assistants, or perhaps as Lord or Lady Doolittle. They are only with difficulty persuaded that they have the wrong number. Once they emptied their parents' card-tray and distributed its contents among the neighbours' letter-boxes, wantonly, yet not without enough impish sense of the fitness of things to make it highly upsetting, God only knowing why certain people should have called where they did.

Xaver comes in to clear away, tossing the hair out of his eyes. Now that he has taken off his gloves you can see the yellow chain-ring on his left hand. And as the Professor finishes his watery eight-thousand-mark beer and lights a cigarette, the little folk can be heard scrambling down the stairs, coming, by established custom, for their after-dinner call on Father and Mother. They storm the dining-room, after a struggle with the latch, clutched by both pairs of little hands at once; their clumsy small feet twinkle over the carpet, in red felt slippers with the socks falling down on them. With prattle and shoutings each makes for his own place: Snapper to Mother, to climb on her lap, boast of all he has eaten, and thump his fat little tum; Ellie to her Abel, so much hers because she is so very much his; because she consciously luxuriates in the deep tenderness – like all deep feeling, concealing a melancholy strain – with which he holds her small form embraced; in the love in his eyes as he kisses her little fairy hand or the sweet brow with its delicate tracery of tiny blue veins.

The little folk look like each other, with the strong undefined likeness of brother and sister. In clothing and hair-cut they are twins. Yet they are sharply distinguished after all, and quite on sex lines. It is a little Adam and a little Eve. Not only is Snapper the sturdier and more compact, he appears consciously to emphasize his four-year-old masculinity in speech, manner, and carriage, lifting his shoulders and letting the little arms hang down quite like a young American athlete, drawing down his mouth when he talks and seeking to give his voice a gruff and forthright ring. But all this masculinity is the result of effort rather than natively his. Born and brought up in these desolate, distracted times, he has been endowed by them with an unstable and hypersensitive nervous system and suffers greatly under life's disharmonies. He is prone to sudden anger and outbursts of bitter tears, stamping his feet at every trifle; for this reason he is his mother's special nursling and care. His round, round eyes are chestnut brown and already inclined to squint, so that he will need glasses in the near future. His little nose is long, the mouth small – the father's nose and mouth they are, more plainly than ever since the Professor shaved his pointed beard and goes smooth-faced. The pointed beard had become impossible – even professors must make some concession to the changing times.

But the little daughter sits on her father's knee, his Eleonorchen, his little Eve, so much more gracious a little being, so much sweeter-faced than her brother – and he holds his cigarette away from her while she fingers his glasses with her dainty wee hands. The lenses are divided for reading and distance, and each day they tease her curiosity afresh.

At bottom he suspects that his wife's partiality may have a

firmer basis than his own: that Snapper's refractory masculinity perhaps is solider stuff than his own little girl's more explicit charm and grace. But the heart will not be commanded, that he knows; and once and for all his heart belongs to the little one, as it has since the day she came, since the first time he saw her. Almost always when he holds her in his arms he remembers that first time: remembers the sunny room in the Women's Hospital, where Ellie first saw the light, twelve years after Bert was born. He remembers how he drew near, the mother smiling the while, and cautiously put aside the canopy of the diminutive bed that stood beside the large one. There lay the little miracle among the pillows: so well formed, so encompassed, as it were, with the harmony of sweet proportions, with little hands that even then, though so much tinier, were beautiful as now; with wide-open eyes blue as the sky and brighter than the sunshine – and almost in that very second he felt himself captured and held fast. This was love at first sight, love everlasting: a feeling unknown, unhoped for, unexpected – in so far as it could be a matter of conscious awareness; it took entire possession of him, and he understood, with joyous amazement, that this was for life.

But he understood more. He knows, does Dr Cornelius, that there is something not quite right about this feeling, so unaware, so undreamed of, so involuntary. He has a shrewd suspicion that it is not by accident it has so utterly mastered him and bound itself up with his existence; that he had – even subconsciously – been preparing for it, or, more precisely, been prepared for it. There is, in short, something in him which at a given moment was ready to issue in such a feeling; and this something, highly extraordinary to relate, is his essence and quality as a professor of history. Dr Cornelius, however, does not actually say this, even to himself; he merely realizes it, at odd times, and smiles a private smile. He knows that history professors do not love history because it is something that comes to pass, but only because it is something that *has* come to pass; that they hate a revolution like the present one because they feel it is lawless, incoherent, irrelevant – in a word, unhistoric; that their hearts belong to the coherent, disciplined, historic past. For the temper of timelessness, the temper of eternity – thus the scholar communes with himself when he takes his walk by the river before supper – that temper broods over the past; and it is a temper much better suited to the nervous system of a history professor than are the excesses of the present. The past is immortalized; that is to say, it is dead; and death is the root of all godliness and all abiding significance. Dr Cornelius, walking alone in the dark, has a profound insight into this truth. It is this conservative instinct of his, his sense of the eternal, that has found in his love for his little daughter a way to save itself from the wounding inflicted by the times. For father love, and a little child on its mother's breast – are not these timeless, and thus very, very holy and beautiful? Yet Cornelius, pondering there in the dark, descries something not perfectly right and good in his love. Theoretically, in the interests of science, he admits it to himself. There is something ulterior about it, in the nature of it; that something is hostility, hostility against the history of today, which is still in the making and thus not history at all, in behalf of the genuine history that has already happened – that is to say, death. Yes, passing strange though all this is, yet it is true; true in a sense, that is. His devotion to this priceless little morsel of life and new growth has something to do with death, it clings to death as against life; and that is neither right nor beautiful – in a sense. Though only the most fanatical asceticism could be capable, on no other ground than such casual scientific perception, of tearing this purest and most precious of feelings out of his heart.

He holds his darling on his lap and her slim rosy legs hang down. He raises his brows as he talks to her, tenderly, with a half-teasing note of respect, and listens enchanted to her high, sweet little voice calling him Abel. He exchanges a look with the mother, who is caressing her Snapper and reading him a gentle lecture. He must be more reasonable, he must learn self-control; today again, under the manifold exasperations of life, he has given way to rage and behaved like a howling dervish. Cornelius casts a mistrustful glance at the big folk now and then, too; he thinks it not unlikely they are not unaware of those scientific preoccupations of his evening walks. If such be the case they do not show it. They stand there leaning their arms on their chair-backs and with a benevolence not untinctured with irony look on at the parental happiness.

The children's frocks are of a heavy, brick-red stuff, embroidered in modern "arty" style. They once belonged to Ingrid and Bert and are precisely alike, save that little knickers come out beneath Snapper's smock. And both have their hair bobbed. Snapper's is a streaky blond, inclined to turn dark. It is bristly and sticky and looks for all the world like a droll, badly fitting wig. But Ellie's is chestnut brown, glossy and fine as silk, as pleasing as her whole little personality. It covers her ears – and these ears are not a pair, one of them being the right size, the other distinctly too large. Her father will sometimes uncover this little abnormality and exclaim over it as though he had never noticed it before, which both makes Ellie giggle and covers her with shame. Her eyes are now golden brown, set far apart and with sweet gleams in them – such a clear and lovely look! The brows above are blond; the nose still unformed, with thick nostrils and almost circular holes; the mouth large and expressive, with a beautifully arching and mobile upper lip. When she laughs, dimples come in her cheeks and she shows her teeth like loosely strung pearls. So far she has lost but one tooth, which her father gently twisted out with his handkerchief after it had grown very wobbling. During this small operation she had paled and trembled very much. Her cheeks have the softness proper to her years, but they are not chubby; indeed, they are rather concave, due to her facial structure, with its somewhat prominent jaw. On one, close to the soft fall of her hair, is a downy freckle.

Ellie is not too well pleased with her looks – a sign that already she troubles about such things. Sadly she thinks it is best to admit it once for all, her face is "homely"; though the rest of her, "on the other hand", is not bad at all. She loves expressions like "on the other hand"; they sound choice and grown-up to her, and she likes to string them together, one after the other: "very likely", "probably", "after all". Snapper is self-critical too, though more in the moral sphere: he suffers from remorse for his attacks of rage and considers himself a tremendous sinner. He is quite certain that heaven is not for such as he; he is sure to go to "the bad place" when he dies, and no persuasions will convince him to the contrary – as that God sees the heart and gladly makes allowances. Obstinately he shakes his head, with the comic, crooked little peruke, and vows there is no place for him in heaven. When he has a cold he is immediately quite choked with mucus; rattles and rumbles from top to toe if you even look at him; his temperature flies up at once and he simply puffs. Nursy is pessimistic on the score of his constitution: such fat-blooded children as he might get a stroke any minute. Once she even thought she saw the moment at hand: Snapper had been in one of his berserker rages, and in the ensuing fit of penitence stood himself in the corner with his back to the room. Suddenly Nursy noticed that his face had gone all blue, far bluer, even, than her own. She raised the alarm, crying out that the child's all too rich blood had at length brought him to his final hour; and Snapper, to his vast astonishment, found himself, so far from being rebuked for evil-doing, encompassed in tenderness and anxiety – until it turned out that his colour was not caused by apoplexy but by the distempering on the nursery wall, which had come off on his tear-wet face.

Nursy has come downstairs too, and stands by the door, sleek-haired, owl-eyed, with her hands folded over her white apron, and a severely dignified manner born of her limited intelligence. She is very proud of the care and training she gives her nurslings and declares that they are "enveloping wonderfully". She has had seventeen suppurated teeth lately removed from her jaws and been measured for a set of symmetrical yellow ones in dark rubber gums; these now embellish her peasant face. She is obsessed with the strange conviction that these teeth of hers are the subject of general conversation, that, as it were, the sparrows on the house-tops chatter of them. "Everybody knows I've had a false set put in," she will say; "there has been a great deal of foolish talk about them." She is much given to dark hints and veiled innuendo: speaks, for instance, of a certain Dr Bleifuss, whom every child knows and "there are even some in the house who pretend to be him". All one can do with talk like this is charitably to pass it over in silence. But she teaches the children nursery rhymes: gems like:

"Puff, puff, here comes the train!
Puff, puff, toot, toot,
Away it goes again."

Or that gastronomical jingle, so suited, in its sparseness, to the times, and yet seemingly with a blitheness of its own:

"Monday we begin the week,
Tuesday there's a bone to pick.
Wednesday we're half-way through,
Thursday what a great to-do!
Friday we eat what fish we're able,
Saturday we dance round the table.
Sunday brings us pork and greens –
Here's a feast for kings and queens!"

Also a certain four-line stanza with a romantic appeal, unutterable and unuttered:

"Open the gate, open the gate
And let the carriage drive in.
Who is it in the carriage sits?
A lordly sir with golden hair."

Or, finally that ballad about golden-haired Marianne who sat on a, sat on a, sat on a stone, and combed out her, combed out her, combed out her hair; and about bloodthirsty Rudolph, who pulled out a, pulled out a, pulled out a knife – and his ensuing direful end. Ellie enunciates all these ballads charmingly, with her mobile little lips, and sings them in her sweet little voice – much better than Snapper. She does everything better than he does, and he pays her honest admiration and homage and obeys her in all things except when visited by one of his attacks. Sometimes she teaches him, instructs him upon the birds in the picture-book and tells him their proper names: "This is a chaffinch, Buddy, this is a bullfinch, this is a cowfinch." He has to repeat them after her. She gives him medical instruction too, teaches him the names of diseases, such as inflammation of the lungs, inflammation of the blood, inflammation of the air. If he does not pay attention and cannot say the words after her, she stands him in the corner. Once she even boxed his ears, but was so ashamed that she stood herself in the corner for a long time. Yes, they are fast friends, two souls with but a single thought, and have all their adventures in common. They come home from a walk and relate as with one voice that they have seen two moollies and a teenty-weenty baby calf. They are on familiar terms with the kitchen, which consists of Xaver and the ladies Hinterhofer, two sisters once of the lower middle class who, in these evil days, are reduced to living "*au pair*" as the phrase goes and officiating as cook and housemaid for their board and keep. The little ones have a feeling that Xaver and the Hinterhofers are on much the same footing with their father and mother as they are themselves. At least sometimes, when they have been scolded, they go downstairs and announce that the master and mistress are cross. But playing with the servants lacks charm compared with the joys of playing upstairs. The kitchen could never rise to the height of the games their father can invent. For instance, there is "four gentlemen taking a walk". When they play it Abel will crook his knees until he is the same height with themselves and go walking with them, hand in hand. They never get enough of this sport; they could walk round and round the dining-room a whole day on end, five gentlemen in all, counting the diminished Abel.

Then there is the thrilling cushion game. One of the children, usually Ellie, seats herself, unbeknownst to Abel, in his seat at table. Still as a mouse she awaits his coming. He draws near with his head in the air, descanting in loud, clear tones upon the surpassing comfort of his chair; and sits down on top of Ellie. "What's this, what's this?" says he. And bounces about, deaf to the smothered giggles exploding behind him. "Why have they put a cushion in my chair? And what a queer, hard, awkward-shaped cushion it is!" he goes on. "Frightfully uncomfortable to sit on!" And keeps pushing and bouncing about more and more on the astonishing cushion and clutching behind him into the rapturous giggling and squeaking, until at last he turns round, and the game ends with a magnificent climax of discovery and recognition. They might go through all this a hundred times without diminishing by an iota its power to thrill.

Today is no time for such joys. The imminent festivity disturbs the atmosphere, and besides there is work to be done, and, above all, the eggs to be got. Ellie has just time to recite "Puff, puff", and Cornelius to discover that her ears are not mates, when they are interrupted by the arrival of Danny, come to fetch Bert and Ingrid. Xaver, meantime, has exchanged his striped livery for an ordinary coat, in which he looks rather rough-and-ready, though as brisk and attractive as ever. So then Nursy and the children ascend to the upper regions, the Professor withdraws to his study to read, as always after dinner, and his wife bends her energies upon the sandwiches and salad that must be prepared. And she has another errand as well. Before the young people arrive she has to take her shopping-basket and dash into town on her bicycle, to turn into provisions a sum of money she has in hand, which she dares not keep lest it lose all value.

Cornelius reads, leaning back in his chair, with his cigar between his middle and index fingers. First he reads Macaulay on the origin of the English public debt at the end of the seventeenth century; then an article in a French periodical on the rapid increase in the Spanish debt towards the end of the sixteenth. Both these for his lecture on the morrow. He intends to compare the astonishing prosperity which accompanied the phenomenon in England with its fatal effects a hundred years earlier in Spain, and to analyse the ethical and psychological grounds of the difference in results. For that will give him a chance to refer back from the England of William III, which is the actual subject in hand, to the time of Philip II and the Counter-Reformation, which is his own special field. He has already written a valuable work on this period; it is much cited and got him his professorship. While his cigar burns down and gets strong, he excogitates a few pensive sentences in a key of gentle melancholy, to be delivered before his class next day: about the practically hopeless struggle carried on by the belated Philip against the whole trend of history: against the new, the kingdom-disrupting power of the Germanic ideal of freedom and individual liberty. And about the persistent, futile struggle of the aristocracy, condemned by God and rejected of man, against the forces of progress and change. He savours his sentences; keeps on polishing them while he puts back the books he has been using; then goes upstairs for the usual pause in his day's work, the hour with drawn blinds and closed eyes, which he so imperatively needs. But today, he recalls, he will rest under disturbed conditions, amid the bustle of preparations for the feast. He smiles to find his heart giving a mild flutter at the thought. Disjointed phrases on the theme of black-clad Philip and his times mingle with a confused consciousness that they will soon be dancing down below. For five minutes or so he falls asleep.

As he lies and rests he can hear the sound of the garden gate and the repeated ringing at the bell. Each time a little pang goes through him, of excitement and suspense, at the thought that the young people have begun to fill the floor below. And each time he smiles at himself again – though even his smile is slightly nervous, is tinged with the pleasurable anticipations people always feel before a party. At half past four – it is already dark – he gets up and washes at the wash-stand. The basin has been out of repair for two years. It is supposed to tip, but has broken away from its socket on one side and cannot be mended because there is nobody to mend it; neither replaced because no shop can supply another. So it has to be hung up above the vent and emptied by lifting in both hands and pouring out the water. Cornelius shakes his head over this basin, as he does several times a day – whenever, in fact, he has occasion to use it. He finishes his toilet with care, standing under the ceiling light to polish his glasses till they shine. Then he goes downstairs.

On his way to the dining-room he hears the gramophone already going, and the sound of voices. He puts on a polite, society air; at his tongue's end is the phrase he means to utter: "Pray don't let me disturb you," as he passes directly into the dining-room for his tea. "Pray don't let me disturb you" – it seems to him precisely the *mot juste*; towards the guests cordial and considerate, for himself a very bulwark.

The lower floor is lighted up, all the bulbs in the chandelier are burning save one that has burned out. Cornelius pauses on a lower step and surveys the entrance hall. It looks pleasant and cosy in the bright light, with its copy of Marées over the brick chimney-piece, its wainscoted walls – wainscoted in soft wood – and red-carpeted floor, where the guests stand in groups, chatting, each with his tea-cup and slice of bread-and-butter spread with anchovy paste. There is a festal haze, faint scents of hair and clothing and human breath come to him across the room, it is all characteristic and familiar and highly evocative. The door into the dressing-room is open, guests are still arriving.

A large group of people is rather bewildering at first sight. The Professor takes in only the general scene. He does not see Ingrid, who is standing just at the foot of the steps, in a dark silk frock with a pleated collar falling softly over the shoulders, and bare arms. She smiles up at him, nodding and showing her lovely teeth.

"Rested?" she asks, for his private ear. With a quite unwarranted start he recognizes her, and she presents some of her friends.

"May I introduce Herr Zuber?" she says. "And this is Fräulein Plaichinger."

Herr Zuber is insignificant. But Fräulein Plaichinger is a

perfect Germania, blonde and voluptuous, arrayed in floating draperies. She has a snub nose, and answers the Professor's salutation in the high, shrill pipe so many stout women have.

"Delighted to meet you," he says. "How nice of you to come! A classmate of Ingrid's, I suppose?"

And Herr Zuber is a golfing partner of Ingrid's. He is in business; he works in his uncle's brewery. Cornelius makes a few jokes about the thinness of the beer and professes to believe that Herr Zuber could easily do something about the quality if he would. "But pray don't let me disturb you," he goes on, and turns towards the dining-room.

"There comes Max," says Ingrid. "Max, you sweep, what do you mean by rolling up at this time of day?" For such is the way they talk to each other, offensively to an older ear; of social forms, of hospitable warmth, there is no faintest trace. They all call each other by their first names.

A young man comes up to them out of the dressing-room and makes his bow; he has an expanse of white shirt-front and a little black string tie. He is as pretty as a picture, dark, with rosy cheeks, clean-shaven of course, but with just a sketch of side-whisker. Not a ridiculous or flashy beauty, not like a gypsy fiddler, but just charming to look at, in a winning, well-bred way, with kind dark eyes. He even wears his dinner jacket a little awkwardly.

"Please don't scold me, Cornelia," he says; "it's the idiotic lectures." And Ingrid presents him to her father as Herr Hergesell.

Well, and so this is Herr Hergesell. He knows his manners, does Herr Hergesell, and thanks the master of the house quite ingratiatingly for his invitation as they shake hands. "I certainly seem to have missed the bus," says he jocosely. "Of course I have lectures today up to four o'clock; I would have; and after that I had to go home to change." Then he talks about his pumps, with which he has just been struggling in the dressing-room.

"I brought them with me in a bag," he goes on. "Mustn't tramp all over the carpet in our brogues – it's not done. Well,

I was ass enough not to fetch along a shoe-horn, and I find I simply can't get in! What a sell! They are the tightest I've ever had, the numbers don't tell you a thing, and all the leather today is just cast iron. It's not leather at all. My poor finger" – he confidingly displays a reddened digit and once more characterizes the whole thing as a "sell", and a putrid sell into the bargain. He really does talk just as Ingrid said he did, with a peculiar nasal drawl, not affectedly in the least, but merely because that is the way of all the Hergesells.

Dr Cornelius says it is very careless of them not to keep a shoe-horn in the cloak-room and displays proper sympathy with the mangled finger. "But now you *really* must not let me disturb you any longer," he goes on. "*Auf wiedersehen!*" And he crosses the hall into the dining-room.

There are guests there too, drinking tea; the family table is pulled out. But the Professor goes at once to his own little upholstered corner with the electric light bulb above it – the nook where he usually drinks his tea. His wife is sitting there talking with Bert and two other young men, one of them Herzl, whom Cornelius knows and greets; the other a typical "Wandervogel" named Möller, a youth who obviously neither owns nor cares to own the correct evening dress of the middle classes (in fact, there is no such thing any more), nor to ape the manners of a gentleman (and, in fact, there is no such thing any more either). He has a wilderness of hair, horn spectacles, and a long neck, and wears golf stockings and a belted blouse. His regular occupation, the Professor learns, is banking, but he is by way of being an amateur folk-lorist and collects folk-songs from all localities and in all languages. He sings them, too, and at Ingrid's command has brought his guitar; it is hanging in the dressing-room in an oilcloth case. Herzl, the actor, is small and slight, but he has a strong growth of black beard, as you can tell by the thick coat of powder on his cheeks. His eyes are larger than life, with a deep and melancholy glow. He has put on rouge besides the powder – those dull carmine high-lights on the cheeks can be nothing but a cosmetic. "Queer," thinks the Professor. "You would think a man would be one thing or the other – not melancholic and use face paint at the same time. It's a psychological contradiction. How can a melancholy man rouge? But here we have a perfect illustration of the abnormality of the artist soul-form. It can make possible a contradiction like this – perhaps it even consists in the contradiction. All very interesting – and no reason whatever for not being polite to him. Politeness is a primitive convention – and legitimate. . . . Do take some lemon, Herr Hofschauspieler!"

Court actors and court theatres – there are no such things any more, really. But Herzl relishes the sound of the title, notwithstanding he is a revolutionary artist. This must be another contradiction inherent in his soul-form; so, at least, the Professor assumes, and he is probably right. The flattery he is guilty of is a sort of atonement for his previous hard thoughts about the rouge.

"Thank you so much – it's really too good of you, sir," says Herzl, quite embarrassed. He is so overcome that he almost stammers; only his perfect enunciation saves him. His whole bearing towards his hostess and the master of the house is exaggeratedly polite. It is almost as though he had a bad conscience in respect of his rouge; as though an inward compulsion had driven him to put it on, but now, seeing it through the Professor's eyes, he disapproves of it himself, and thinks, by an air of humility towards the whole of unrouged society, to mitigate its effect.

They drink their tea and chat: about Möller's folk-songs, about Basque folk-songs and Spanish folk-songs; from which they pass to the new production of *Don Carlos* at the Stadttheater, in which Herzl plays the title-role. He talks about his own rendering of the part and says he hopes his conception of the character has unity. They go on to criticize the rest of the cast, the setting, and the production as a whole; and Cornelius is struck, rather painfully, to find the conversation trending towards his own special province, back to Spain and the Counter-Reformation. He has done nothing at all to give it this turn, he is perfectly innocent, and hopes it does not look as though he had sought an occasion to play the professor. He wonders, and falls silent, feeling relieved when the little folk come up to the table. Ellie and Snapper have on their blue velvet Sunday frocks; they are permitted to partake in the festivities up to bed-time. They look shy and large-eyed as they say how-do-you-do to the strangers and, under pressure, repeat their names and ages. Herr Möller does nothing but gaze at them solemnly, but Herzl is simply ravished. He rolls his eyes up to heaven and puts his hands over his mouth; he positively blesses them. It all, no doubt, comes from his heart, but he is so addicted to theatrical methods of making an impression and getting an effect that both words and behaviour ring frightfully false. And even his enthusiasm for the little folk looks too much like part of his general craving to make up for the rouge on his cheeks.

The tea-table has meanwhile emptied of guests, and dancing is going on in the hall. The children run off, the Professor prepares to retire. "Go and enjoy yourselves," he says to Möller and Herzl, who have sprung from their chairs as he rises from his. They shake hands and he withdraws into his study, his peaceful kingdom, where he lets down the blinds, turns on the desk lamp, and sits down to his work.

It is work which can be done, if necessary, under disturbed conditions: nothing but a few letters and a few notes. Of course, Cornelius's mind wanders. Vague impressions float through it: Herr Hergesell's refractory pumps, the high pipe in that plump body of the Plaichinger female. As he writes, or leans back in his chair and stares into space, his thoughts go back to Herr Möller's collection of Basque folk-songs, to Herzl's posings and humility, to "his" Carlos and the court of Philip II. There is something strange, he thinks, about conversations. They are so ductile, they will flow of their own accord in the direction of one's dominating interest. Often and often he has seen this happen. And while he is thinking, he is listening to the sounds next door – rather subdued, he finds them. He hears only voices, no sound of footsteps. The dancers do not glide or circle round the room;

they merely walk about over the carpet, which does not hamper their movements in the least. Their way of holding each other is quite different and strange, and they move to the strains of the gramophone, to the weird music of the new world. He concentrates on the music and makes out that it is a jazz-band record, with various percussion instruments and the clack and clatter of castanets, which, however, are not even faintly suggestive of Spain, but merely jazz like the rest. No, not Spain.... His thoughts are back at their old round.

Half an hour goes by. It occurs to him it would be no more than friendly to go and contribute a box of cigarettes to the festivities next door. Too bad to ask the young people to smoke their own – though they have probably never thought of it. He goes into the empty dining-room and takes a box from his supply in the cupboard: not the best ones, nor yet the brand he himself prefers, but a certain long, thin kind he is not averse to getting rid of – after all, they are nothing but youngsters. He takes the box into the hall, holds it up with a smile, and deposits it on the mantel-shelf. After which he gives a look round and returns to his own room.

There comes a lull in dance and music. The guests stand about the room in groups or round the table at the window or are seated in a circle by the fireplace. Even the built-in stairs, with their worn velvet carpet, are crowded with young folk as in an amphitheatre: Max Hergesell is there, leaning back with one elbow on the step above and gesticulating with his free hand as he talks to the shrill, voluptuous Plaichinger. The floor of the hall is nearly empty, save just in the centre: there, directly beneath the chandelier, the two little ones in their blue velvet frocks clutch each other in an awkward embrace and twirl silently round and round, oblivious of all else. Cornelius, as he passes, strokes their hair, with a friendly word; it does not distract them from their small solemn preoccupation. But at his own door he turns to glance round and sees young Hergesell push himself off the stair by his elbow – probably because he noticed the Professor. He comes down into the arena, takes Ellie out of her brother's arms, and dances with her himself. It looks very comic, without the music, and he crouches down just as Cornelius does when he goes walking with the four gentlemen, holding the fluttered Ellie as though she were grown up and taking little "shimmying" steps. Everybody watches with huge enjoyment, the gramophone is put on again, dancing becomes general. The Professor stands and looks, with his hand on the door-knob. He nods and laughs; when he finally shuts himself into his study the mechanical smile still lingers on his lips.

Again he turns over pages by his desk lamp, takes notes, attends to a few simple matters. After a while he notices that the guests have forsaken the entrance hall for his wife's drawing-room, into which there is a door from his own study as well. He hears their voices and the sounds of a guitar being tuned. Herr Möller, it seems, is to sing – and does so. He twangs the strings of his instrument and sings in a powerful bass a ballad in a strange tongue, possibly Swedish. The Professor does not succeed in identifying it, though he listens attentively to the end, after which there is great applause. The sound is deadened by the portière that hangs over the dividing door. The young bank-clerk begins another song. Cornelius goes softly in.

It is half-dark in the drawing-room; the only light is from the shaded standard lamp, beneath which Möller sits, on the divan, with his legs crossed, picking his strings. His audience is grouped easily about; as there are not enough seats, some stand, and more, among them many young ladies, are simply sitting on the floor with their hands clasped round their knees or even with their legs stretched out before them. Hergesell sits thus, in his dinner jacket, next the piano, with Fräulein Plaichinger beside him. Frau Cornelius is holding both children on her lap as she sits in her easy-chair opposite the singer. Snapper, the Bœotian, begins to talk loud and clear in the middle of the song and has to be intimidated with hushings and finger-shakings. Never, never would Ellie allow herself to be guilty of such conduct. She sits there daintily erect and still on her mother's knee. The Professor tries to catch her eye and exchange a private signal with his little girl; but she does not see him. Neither does she seem to be looking at the singer. Her gaze is directed lower down.

Möller sings the "joli tambour":

> "*Sire, mon roi, donnez-moi votre*
> *fille* –"

They are all enchanted. "How good!" Hergesell is heard to say, in the odd, nasally condescending Hergesell tone. The next one is a beggar ballad, to a tune composed by young Möller himself; it elicits a storm of applause:

> "Gypsy lassie a-goin' to the fair,
> Huzza!
> Gypsy laddie a-goin' to be
> there –
> Huzza, diddlety umpty dido!"

Laughter and high spirits, sheer reckless hilarity, reign after this jovial ballad. "Frightfully good!" Hergesell comments again, as before. Follows another popular song, this time a Hungarian one; Möller sings it in its own outlandish tongue, and most effectively. The Professor applauds with ostentation. It warms his heart and does him good, this outcropping of artistic, historic and cultural elements all amongst the shimmying. He goes up to young Möller and congratulates him, talks about the songs and their sources, and Möller promises to lend him a certain annotated book of folk-songs. Cornelius is the more cordial because all the time, as fathers do, he has been comparing the parts and achievements of this young stranger with those of his own son, and being gnawed by envy and chagrin. This young Möller, he is thinking, is a capable bank-clerk (though about Möller's capacity he knows nothing whatever) and has this special gift besides, which must have taken talent and energy to cultivate. "And here is my poor Bert, who knows nothing and can do nothing and thinks of nothing except playing the clown, without even talent for that!" He tries to be just; he tells himself that, after all, Bert has innate refinement; that probably there is a good deal more to him than there is to the successful Möller; that perhaps he has even something of the poet in him, and his dancing and table-waiting are due to mere boyish folly and the distraught times. But paternal envy and pessimism win the upper hand; when Möller begins another song, Dr Cornelius goes back to his room.

He works as before, with divided attention, at this and that, while it gets on for seven o'clock. Then he remembers a letter he may just as well write, a short letter and not very important, but letter-writing is wonderful for the way it takes up the time, and it is almost half past when he has finished. At half past eight the Italian salad will be served; so now is the prescribed moment for the Professor to go out into the wintry darkness to post his letters and take his daily quantum of fresh air and exercise. They are dancing again, and he will have to pass through the hall to get his hat and coat; but they are used to him now, he need not stop and beg them not to be disturbed. He lays away his papers, takes up the letters he has written, and goes out. But he sees his wife sitting near the door of his room and pauses a little by her easy-chair.

She is watching the dancing. Now and then the big folk or some of their guests stop to speak to her; the party is at its height, and there are more onlookers than these two: blue-faced Ann is standing at the bottom of the stairs, in all the dignity of her limitations. She is waiting for the children, who simply cannot get their fill of these unwonted festivities, and watching over Snapper, lest his all too rich blood be churned to the danger-point by too much twirling round. And not only the nursery but the kitchen takes an interest: Xaver and the two ladies Hinterhofer are standing by the pantry door looking on with relish. Fräulein Walburga, the elder of the two sunken sisters (the culinary section – she objects to being called a cook), is a whimsical, good-natured sort, brown-eyed, wearing glasses with thick circular lenses; the nose-piece is wound with a bit of rag to keep it from pressing on her nose. Fräulein Cecilia is younger, though not so precisely young either. Her bearing is as self-assertive as usual, this being her way of sustaining her dignity as a former member of the middle class. For Fräulein Cecilia feels acutely her descent into the ranks of domestic service. She positively declines to wear a cap or other badge of servitude, and her hardest trial is on the Wednesday evening when she has to serve the dinner while Xaver has his afternoon out. She hands the dishes with averted face and elevated nose – a fallen queen; and so distressing is it to behold her degradation that one evening when the little folk happened to be at table and saw her they both with one accord burst into tears. Such anguish is unknown to young Xaver. He enjoys serving and does it with an ease born of practice as well as talent, for he was once a "piccolo". But otherwise he is a thorough-paced good-for-nothing and windbag – with quite distinct traits of character of his own, as his long-suffering employers are always ready to concede, but perfectly impossible and a bag of wind for all that. One must just take him as he is, they think, and not expect figs from thistles. He is the child and product of the disrupted times, a perfect specimen of his generation, follower of the revolution, Bolshevist sympathizer. The Professor's name for him is the "minute-man", because he is always to be counted on in any sudden crisis, if only it address his sense of humour or love of novelty, and will display therein amazing readiness and resource. But he utterly lacks a sense of duty and can as little be trained to the performance of the daily round and common task as some kinds of dog can be taught to jump over a stick. It goes so plainly against the grain that criticism is disarmed. One becomes resigned. On grounds that appealed to him as unusual and amusing he would be ready to turn out of his bed at any hour of the night. But he simply cannot get up before eight in the morning, he cannot do it, he will not jump over the stick. Yet all day long the evidence of this free and untrammelled existence, the sound of his mouth-organ, his joyous whistle, or his raucous but expressive voice lifted in song, rises to the hearing of the world above-stairs; and the smoke of his cigarettes fills the pantry. While the Hinterhofer ladies work he stands and looks on. Of a morning while the Professor is breakfasting, he tears the leaf off the study calendar – but does not lift a finger to dust the room. Dr Cornelius has often told him to leave the calendar alone, for he tends to tear off two leaves at a time and thus to add to the general confusion. But young Xaver appears to find joy in this activity, and will not be deprived of it.

Again, he is fond of children, a winning trait. He will throw himself into games with the little folk in the garden, make and mend their toys with great ingenuity, even read aloud from their books – and very droll it sounds in his thick-lipped pronunciation. With his whole soul he loves the cinema; after an evening spent there he inclines to melancholy and yearning and talking to himself. Vague hopes stir in him that some day he may make his fortune in that gay world and belong to it by rights – hopes based on his shock of hair and his physical agility and daring. He likes to climb the ash tree in the front garden, mounting branch by branch to the very top and frightening everybody to death who sees him. Once there he lights a cigarette and smokes it as he sways to and fro, keeping a look-out for a cinema director who might chance to come along and engage him.

If he changed his striped jacket for mufti, he might easily dance with the others and no one would notice the difference. For the big folk's friends are rather anomalous in their clothing: evening dress is worn by a few, but it is by no means the rule. There is quite a sprinkling of guests, both male and female, in the same general style as Möller the ballad-singer. The Professor is familiar with the circumstances of most of this young generation he is watching as he stands beside his wife's chair; he has heard them spoken of by name. They are students at the high school or at the School of Applied Art; they lead, at least the masculine portion, that precarious and scrambling existence which is purely the product of the time. There is a tall, pale, spindling youth, the son of a dentist, who lives by speculation. From all the Professor hears, he is a perfect Aladdin. He keeps a car, treats his friends to champagne suppers, and showers presents upon them on every occasion, costly little trifles in mother-of-pearl and gold. So today he has brought gifts to the young givers of the feast: for Bert a gold lead-pencil, and for Ingrid a pair of ear-rings of barbaric size, great gold circlets that fortunately do not have to go through the little ear-lobe, but are fastened over it by means of a clip. The big folk come laughing to their parents to display these trophies; and the parents shake their heads even while they admire – Aladdin bowing over and over from afar.

The young people appear to be absorbed in their dancing – if the performance they are carrying out with so much still concentration can be called dancing. They stride across the carpet, slowly, according to some unfathomable prescript, strangely embraced; in the newest attitude, tummy advanced and shoulders high, waggling the hips. They do not get tired, because nobody could. There is no such thing as heightened colour or heaving bosoms. Two girls may dance together or two young men – it is all the same. They move to the exotic strains of the gramophone, played with the loudest needles to procure the maximum of sound: shimmies, foxtrots, one-steps, double foxes, African shimmies, Java dances, and Creole polkas, the wild musky melodies follow one another, now furious, now languishing, a monotonous Negro programme in unfamiliar rhythm, to a clacking, clashing, and strumming orchestral accompaniment.

"What is that record?" Cornelius inquires of Ingrid, as she passes him by in the arms of the pale young speculator, with reference to the piece then playing, whose alternate languors and furies he finds comparatively pleasing and showing a certain resourcefulness in detail.

"*Prince of Pappenheim*: 'Console thee, dearest child,'" she answers, and smiles pleasantly back at him with her white teeth.

The cigarette smoke wreathes beneath the chandelier. The air is blue with a festal haze compact of sweet and thrilling ingredients that stir the blood with memories of green-sick pains and are particularly poignant to those whose youth – like the Professor's own – has been over-sensitive.... The little folk are still on the floor. They are allowed to stop up until eight, so great is their delight in the party. The guests have got used to their presence; in their own way, they have their place in the doings of the evening. They have separated, anyhow: Snapper revolves all alone in the middle of the carpet, in his little blue velvet smock, while Ellie is running after one of the dancing couples, trying to hold the man fast by his coat. It is Max Hergesell and Fräulein Plaichinger. They dance well, it is a pleasure to watch them. One has to admit that these mad modern dances, when the right people dance them, are not so bad after all – they have something quite taking. Young Hergesell is a capital leader, dances according to rule, yet with individuality. So it looks. With what aplomb can he walk backwards – when space permits! And he knows how to be graceful standing still in a crowd. And his partner supports him well, being unsuspectedly lithe and buoyant, as fat people often are. They look at each other, they are talking, paying no heed to Ellie, though others are smiling to see the child's persistence. Dr Cornelius tries to catch up his little sweetheart as she passes and draw her to him. But Ellie eludes him, almost peevishly; her dear Abel is nothing to her now. She braces her little arms against his chest and turns her face away with a persecuted look. Then escapes to follow her fancy once more.

The Professor feels an involuntary twinge. Uppermost in his heart is hatred for this party, with its power to intoxicate and estrange his darling child. His love for her – that not quite disinterested, not quite unexceptionable love of his – is easily wounded. He wears a mechanical smile, but his eyes have clouded, and he stares fixedly at a point in the carpet, between the dancers' feet.

"The children ought to go to bed," he tells his wife. But she pleads for another quarter of an hour; she has promised already, and they do love it so! He smiles again and shakes his head, stands so a moment and then goes across to the cloak-room, which is full of coats and hats and scarves and overshoes. He has trouble in rummaging out his own coat, and Max Hergesell comes out of the hall, wiping his brow.

"Going out, sir?" he asks, in Hergesellian accents, dutifully helping the older man on with his coat. "Silly business this, with my pumps," he says. "They pinch like hell. The brutes are simply too tight for me, quite apart from the bad leather. They press just here on the ball of my great toe" – he stands on one foot and holds the other in his hand – "it's simply unbearable. There's nothing for it but to take them off; my brogues will have to do the business.... Oh, let me help you, sir."

"Thanks," says Cornelius. "Don't trouble. Get rid of your own tormentors.... Oh, thanks very much!" For Hergesell has gone on one knee to snap the fasteners of his snow-boots.

Once more the Professor expresses his gratitude; he is pleased and touched by so much sincere respect and youthful readiness to serve. "Go and enjoy yourself," he counsels. "Change your shoes and make up for what you have been suffering. Nobody can dance in shoes that pinch. Good-bye, I must be off to get a breath of fresh air."

"I'm going to dance with Ellie now," calls Hergesell after him. "She'll be a first-rate dancer when she grows up, and that I'll swear to."

"Think so?" Cornelius answers, already half out. "Well, you are a connoisseur, I'm sure. Don't get curvature of the spine with stooping."

He nods again and goes. "Fine lad," he thinks as he shuts the door. "Student of engineering. Knows what he's bound for, got a good clear head, and so well set up and pleasant too." And again paternal envy rises as he compares his poor Bert's status with this young man's, which he puts in the rosiest light that his son's may look the darker. Thus he sets out on his evening walk.

He goes up the avenue, crosses the bridge, and walks along the bank on the other side as far as the next bridge but one. The air is wet and cold, with a little snow now and then. He turns up his coat-collar and slips the crook of his cane over the arm behind his back. Now and then he ventilates his lungs with a long deep breath of the night air. As usual when he walks, his mind reverts to his professional preoccupations, he thinks about his lectures and the things he means to say tomorrow about Philip's struggle against the Germanic revolution, things steeped in melancholy and penetratingly just. Above all just, he thinks. For in one's dealings with the young it behoves one to display the scientific spirit, to exhibit the principles of enlightenment – not only for purposes of mental discipline, but on the human and individual side, in order not to wound them or indirectly offend their political sensibilities; particularly in these days, when there is so much tinder in the air, opinions are so frightfully split up and chaotic, and you may so easily incur attacks from one party or the other, or even give rise to scandal, by taking sides on a point of history. "And taking sides is unhistoric anyhow," so he muses. "Only justice, only impartiality is historic." And could not, properly considered, be otherwise.... For justice can have nothing of youthful fire and blithe, fresh, loyal conviction. It is by nature melancholy. And, being so, has secret affinity with the lost cause and the forlorn hope rather than with the fresh and blithe and loyal – perhaps this affinity is its very essence and without it it would not exist at all!... "And is there then no such thing as justice?" the Professor asks himself, and ponders the question so deeply that he absently posts his letters in the next box and turns round to go home. This thought of his is unsettling and disturbing to the scientific mind – but is it not after all itself scientific, psychological, conscientious, and therefore to be accepted without prejudice, no matter how upsetting? In the midst of which musings Dr Cornelius finds himself back at his own door.

On the outer threshold stands Xaver, and seems to be looking for him.

"Herr Professor," says Xaver, tossing back his hair, "go upstairs to Ellie straight off. She's in a bad way."

"What's the matter?" asks Cornelius in alarm. "Is she ill?"

"No-o, not to say ill," answers Xaver. "She's just in a bad way and crying fit to bust her little heart. It's along o' that chap with the shirt-front that danced with her – Herr Hergesell. She couldn't be got to go upstairs peaceably, not at no price at all, and she's b'en crying bucketfuls."

"Nonsense," says the Professor, who has entered and is tossing off his things in the cloak-room. He says no more; opens the glass door and without a glance at the guests turns swiftly to the stairs. Takes them two at a time, crosses the upper hall and the small room leading into the nursery. Xaver follows at his heels, but stops at the nursery door.

A bright light still burns within, showing the gay frieze that runs all round the room, the large row of shelves heaped with a confusion of toys, the rocking-horse on his swaying platform, with red-varnished nostrils and raised hoofs. On the linoleum lie other toys – building blocks, railway trains, a little trumpet. The two white cribs stand not far apart, Ellie's in the window corner, Snapper's out in the room.

Snapper is asleep. He has said his prayers in loud, ringing tones, prompted by Nurse, and gone off at once into vehement, profound, and rosy slumber – from which a cannonball fired at close range could not rouse him. He lies with both fists flung back on the pillows on either side of the tousled head with its funny crooked little slumber-tossed wig.

A circle of females surrounds Ellie's bed: not only blue-faced Ann is there, but the Hinterhofer ladies too, talking to each other and to her. They make way as the Professor comes up and reveal the child sitting all pale among her pillows, sobbing and weeping more bitterly than he has ever seen her sob and weep in her life. Her lovely little hands lie on the coverlet in front of her, the night-gown with its narrow lace border has slipped down from her shoulder – such a thin, birdlike little shoulder – and the sweet head Cornelius loves so well, set on the neck like a flower on its stalk, her head is on one side, with the eyes rolled up to the corner between wall and ceiling above her head. For there she seems to envisage the anguish of her heart and even to nod to it – either on purpose or because her head wobbles as her body is shaken with the violence of her sobs. Her eyes rain down tears. The bow-shaped lips are parted, like a little *mater dolorosa*'s, and from them issue long, low wails that in nothing resemble the unnecessary and exasperating shrieks of a naughty child, but rise from the deep extremity of her heart and wake in the Professor's own a sympathy that is well-nigh intolerable. He has never seen his darling so before. His feelings find immediate vent in an attack on the ladies Hinterhofer.

"What about the supper?" he asks sharply. "There must be a great deal to do. Is my wife being left to do it alone?"

For the acute sensibilities of the former middle class this is quite enough. The ladies withdraw in righteous indignation, and Xaver Kleingutl jeers at them as they pass out. Having been born to low life instead of achieving it, he never loses a chance to mock at their fallen state.

"Childie, childie," murmurs Cornelius, and sitting down by the crib enfolds the anguished Ellie in his arms. "What is the trouble with my darling?"

She bedews his face with her tears.

"Abel... Abel..." she stammers between sobs. "Why – isn't Max – my brother? Max ought to be – my brother!"

Alas, alas! What mischance is this? Is this what the party has wrought, with its fatal atmosphere? Cornelius glances helplessly up at blue-faced Ann standing there in all the dignity of her limitations with her hands before her on her apron. She purses up her mouth and makes a long face. "It's pretty young," she says, "for the female instincts to be showing up."

"Hold your tongue," snaps Cornelius, in his agony. He has this much to be thankful for, that Ellie does not turn from him now; she does not push him away as she did downstairs, but clings to him in her need, while she reiterates her absurd, bewildered prayer that Max might be her brother, or with a fresh burst of desire demands to be taken downstairs so that he can dance with her again. But Max, of course, is dancing with Fräulein Plaichinger, that behemoth who is his rightful partner and has every claim upon him; whereas Ellie – never, thinks the Professor, his heart torn with the violence of his pity, never has she looked so tiny and birdlike as now, when she nestles to him shaken with sobs and all unaware of what is happening in her little soul. No, she does not know. She does not comprehend that her suffering is on account of Fräulein Plaichinger, fat, overgrown, and utterly within her rights in dancing with Max Hergesell, whereas Ellie may only do it once, by way of a joke, although she is incomparably the more charming of the two. Yet it would be quite mad to reproach young Hergesell with the state of affairs or to make fantastic demands upon him. No, Ellie's suffering is without help or healing and must be covered up. Yet just as it is without understanding, so it is also without restraint – and that is what makes it so horribly painful. Xaver and blue-faced Ann do not feel this pain, it does not affect them – either because of native callousness or because they accept it as the way of nature. But the Professor's fatherly heart is quite torn by it, and by a distressful horror of this passion, so hopeless and so absurd.

Of no avail to hold forth to poor Ellie on the subject of the perfectly good little brother she already has. She only casts a distraught and scornful glance over at the other crib, where Snapper lies vehemently slumbering, and with fresh tears calls again for Max. Of no avail either the promise of a long, long walk tomorrow, all five gentlemen, round and round the dining-room table; or a dramatic description of the thrilling cushion games they will play. No, she will listen to none of all this, nor to lying down and going to sleep. She will not sleep, she will sit bolt upright and suffer.... But on a sudden they stop and listen, Abel and Ellie; listen to something miraculous that is coming to pass, that is approaching by strides, two strides, to the nursery door, that now overwhelmingly appears....

It is Xaver's work, not a doubt of that. He has not remained by the door where he stood to gloat over the ejection of the Hinterhofers. No, he has bestirred himself, taken a notion; likewise steps to carry it out. Downstairs he has gone, twitched Herr Hergesell's sleeve, and made a thick-lipped request. So here they both are. Xaver, having done his part, remains by the door; but Max Hergesell comes up to Ellie's crib; in his dinner jacket, with his sketchy side-whisker and charming black eyes; obviously quite pleased with his role of swan knight and fairy prince, as one who should say: "See, here am I, now all losses are restored and sorrows end."

Cornelius is almost as much overcome as Ellie herself.

"Just look," he says feebly, "look who's here. This is uncommonly good of you, Herr Hergesell."

"Not a bit of it," says Hergesell. "Why shouldn't I come to say good-night to my fair partner?"

And he approaches the bars of the crib, behind which Ellie sits struck mute. She smiles blissfully through her tears. A funny, high little note that is half a sigh of relief comes from her lips, then she looks dumbly up at her swan knight with her golden-brown eyes – tear-swollen though they are, so much more beautiful than the fat Plaichinger's. She does not put up her arms. Her joy, like her grief, is without understanding; but she does not do that. The lovely little hands lie quiet on the coverlet, and Max Hergesell stands with his arms leaning over the rail as on a balcony.

"And now," he says smartly, "she need not 'sit the livelong night and weep upon her bed'!" He looks at the Professor to make sure he is receiving due credit for the quotation. "Ha ha!" he laughs, "she's beginning young. 'Console thee, dearest child!' Never mind, you're all right! Just as you are you'll be wonderful! You've only got to grow up.... And you'll lie down and go to sleep like a good girl, now I've come to say good-night? And not cry any more, little Lorelei?"

Ellie looks up at him, transfigured. One birdlike shoulder is bare; the Professor draws the lace-trimmed nighty over it. There comes into his mind a sentimental story he once read about a dying child who longs to see a clown he had once, with unforgettable ecstasy, beheld in a circus. And they bring the clown to the bedside marvellously arrayed, embroidered before and behind with silver butterflies; and the child dies happy. Max Hergesell is not embroidered, and Ellie, thank God, is not going to die, she has only "been in a bad way", But, after all, the effect is the same. Young Hergesell leans over the bars of the crib and rattles on, more for the father's ear than the child's, but Ellie does not know that – and the father's feelings towards him are a most singular mixture of thankfulness, embarrassment, and hatred.

"Good-night, little Lorelei," says Hergesell, and gives her his hand through the bars. Her pretty, soft, white little hand is swallowed up in the grasp of his big, strong, red one. "Sleep well," he says, "and sweet dreams! But don't dream about me – God forbid! Not at your age – ha ha!" And then the fairy clown's visit is at an end. Cornelius accompanies him to the door. "No, no, positively, no thanks called for, don't mention it," he large-heartedly protests; and Xaver goes downstairs with him, to help serve the Italian salad.

But Dr Cornelius returns to Ellie, who is now lying down, with her cheek pressed into her flat little pillow.

"Well, wasn't that lovely?" he says as he smooths the covers. She nods, with one last little sob. For a quarter of an hour he sits beside her and watches while she falls asleep in her turn, beside the little brother who found the right way so much earlier than she. Her silky brown hair takes the enchanting fall it always does when she sleeps; deep, deep lie the lashes over the eyes that late so abundantly poured forth their sorrow; the angelic mouth with its bowed upper lip is peacefully relaxed and a little open. Only now and then comes a belated catch in her slow breathing.

And her small hands, like pink and white flowers, lie so quietly, one on the coverlet, the other on the pillow by her face – Dr Cornelius, gazing, feels his heart melt with tenderness as with strong wine.

"How good," he thinks, "that she breathes in oblivion with every breath she draws! That in childhood each night is a deep, wide gulf between one day and the next. Tomorrow, beyond all doubt, young Hergesell will be a pale shadow, powerless to darken her little heart. Tomorrow, forgetful of all but present joy, she will walk with Abel and Snapper, all five gentlemen, round and round the table, will play the ever-thrilling cushion game."

Heaven be praised for that!

MARIO AND THE MAGICIAN

THE ATMOSPHERE of Torre di Venere remains unpleasant in the memory. From the first moment the air of the place made us uneasy, we felt irritable, on edge; then at the end came the shocking business of Cipolla, that dreadful being who seemed to incorporate, in so fateful and so humanly impressive a way, all the peculiar evilness of the situation as a whole. Looking back, we had the feeling that the horrible end of the affair had been preordained and lay in the nature of things; that the children had to be present at it was an added impropriety, due to the false colours in which the weird creature presented himself. Luckily for them, they did not know where the comedy left off and the tragedy began; and we let them remain in their happy belief that the whole thing had been a play up till the end.

Torre di Venere lies some fifteen kilometres from Portoclemente, one of the most popular summer resorts on the Tyrrhenian Sea. Portoclemente is urban and elegant and full to overflowing for months on end. Its gay and busy main street of shops and hotels runs down to a wide sandy beach covered with tents and pennanted sand-castles and sunburnt humanity, where at all times a lively social bustle reigns, and much noise. But this same spacious and inviting fine-sanded beach, this same border of pine grove and near, presiding mountains, continues all the way along the coast. No wonder then that the same competition of a quiet kind should have sprung up farther on. Torre di Venere – the tower that gave the town its name is gone long since, one looks for it in vain – is an offshoot of the larger resort, and for some years remained an idyll for the few, a refuge for more unworldly spirits. But the usual history of such places repeated itself: peace has had to retire farther along the coast, to Marina Petriera and dear knows where else. We all know how the world at once seeks peace and puts her to flight – rushing upon her in the fond idea that they two will wed, and where she is, there it can be at home. It will even set up its Vanity Fair in a spot and be capable of thinking that peace is still by its side. Thus Torre – though its atmosphere so far is more modest and contemplative than that of Portoclemente – has been quite taken up, by both Italians and foreigners. It is no longer the thing to go to Portoclemente – though still so much the thing that it is as noisy and crowded as ever. One goes next door, so to speak: to Torre. So much more refined, even, and cheaper to boot. And the attractiveness of these qualities persists, though the qualities themselves long ago ceased to be evident. Torre has got a Grand Hotel. Numerous pensions have sprung up, some modest, some pretentious. The people who own or rent the villas and pinetas overlooking the sea no longer have it all their own way on the beach. In July and August it looks just like the beach at Portoclemente: it swarms with a screaming, squabbling, merrymaking crowd, and the sun, blazing down like mad, peels the skin off their necks. Garish little flat-bottomed boats rock on the glittering blue, manned by children, whose mothers hover afar and fill the air with anxious cries of Nino! and Sandro! and Bice! and Maria! Pedlars step across the legs of recumbent sun-bathers, selling flowers and corals, oysters, lemonade, and *cornetti al burro*, and crying their wares in the breathy, full-throated southern voice.

Such was the scene that greeted our arrival in Torre: pleasant enough, but after all, we thought, we had come too soon. It was the middle of August, the Italian season was still at its height, scarcely the moment for strangers to learn to love the special charms of the place. What an afternoon crowd in the cafés on the front! For instance, in the Esquisito, where we sometimes sat and were served by Mario, that very Mario of whom I shall have presently to tell. It is well-nigh impossible to find a table; and the various orchestras contend together in the midst of one's conversation with bewildering effect. Of course, it is in the afternoon that people come over from Portoclemente. The excursion is a favourite one for the restless denizens of that pleasure resort, and a Fiat motor-bus plies to and fro, coating inch-thick with dust the oleander and laurel hedges along the highroad – a notable if repulsive sight.

Yes, decidedly one should go to Torre in September, when the great public has left. Or else in May, before the water is warm enough to tempt the Southerner to bathe. Even in the before and after seasons Torre is not empty, but life is less national and more subdued. English, French, and German prevail under the tent-awnings and in the pension dining-rooms; whereas in August – in the Grand Hotel, at least, where, in default of private addresses, we had engaged rooms – the stranger finds the field so occupied by Florentine and Roman society that he feels quite isolated and even temporarily *déclassé*.

We had, rather to our annoyance, this experience on the evening we arrived, when we went in to dinner and were shown to our table by the waiter in charge. As a table, it had nothing against it, save that we had already fixed our eyes upon those on the veranda beyond, built out over the water, where little red-shaded lamps glowed – and there were still some tables empty, though it was as full as the dining-room within. The children went into raptures at the festive sight, and without more ado we announced our intention to take our meals by preference in the veranda. Our words, it appeared, were prompted by ignorance; for we were informed, with somewhat embarrassed politeness, that the cosy nook outside was reserved for the clients of the hotel: *di nostri clienti*. Their clients? But we were their clients. We were not tourists or trippers, but boarders for a stay of some three or four weeks. However, we forbore to press for an explanation of the difference between the likes of us and that clientèle to whom it was vouchsafed to eat out there in the glow of the red lamps, and took our dinner by the prosaic common light of the dining-room chandelier – a thoroughly ordinary and monotonous hotel bill of fare, be it said. In

Pensione Eleonora, a few steps landward, the table, as we were to discover, was much better.

And thither it was that we moved, three or four days later, before we had had time to settle in properly at the Grand Hotel. Not on account of the veranda and the lamps. The children, straightaway on the best of terms with waiters and pages, absorbed in the joys of life on the beach, promptly forgot those colourful seductions. But now there arose, between ourselves and the veranda clientèle – or perhaps more correctly with the compliant management – one of those little unpleasantnesses which can quite spoil the pleasure of a holiday. Among the guests were some high Roman aristocracy, a Principe X and his family. These grand folk occupied rooms close to our own, and the Principessa, a great and a passionately maternal lady, was thrown into a panic by the vestiges of a whooping-cough which our little ones had lately got over, but which now and then still faintly troubled the unshatterable slumbers of our youngest-born. The nature of this illness is not clear, leaving some play for the imagination. So we took no offence at our elegant neighbour for clinging to the widely held view that whooping-cough is acoustically contagious and quite simply fearing lest her children yield to the bad example set by ours. In the fullness of her feminine self-confidence she protested to the management, which then, in the person of the proverbial frock-coated manager, hastened to represent to us, with many expressions of regret, that under the circumstances they were obliged to transfer us to the annexe. We did our best to assure him that the disease was in its very last stages, that it was actually over, and presented no danger of infection to anybody. All that we gained was permission to bring the case before the hotel physician – not one chosen by us – by whose verdict we must then abide. We agreed, convinced that thus we should at once pacify the Princess and escape the trouble of moving. The doctor appeared, and behaved like a faithful and honest servant of science. He examined the child and gave his opinion: the disease was quite over, no danger of contagion was present. We drew a long breath and considered the incident closed – until the manager announced that despite the doctor's verdict it would still be necessary for us to give up our rooms and retire to the *dépendance*. Byzantinism like this outraged us. It is not likely that the Principessa was responsible for the wilful breach of faith. Very likely the fawning management had not even dared to tell her what the physician said. Anyhow, we made it clear to his understanding that we preferred to leave the hotel altogether and at once – and packed our trunks. We could do so with a light heart, having already set up casual friendly relations with Casa Eleonora. We had noticed its pleasant exterior and formed the acquaintance of its proprietor, Signora Angiolieri, and her husband: she slender and black-haired, Tuscan in type, probably at the beginning of the thirties, with the dead ivory complexion of the southern woman, he quiet and bald and carefully dressed. They owned a larger establishment in Florence and presided only in summer and early autumn over the branch in Torre di Venere. But earlier, before her marriage, our new landlady had been companion, fellow-traveller, wardrobe mistress, yes, friend, of Eleonora Duse and manifestly regarded that period as the crown of her career. Even at our first visit she spoke of it with animation. Numerous photographs of the great actress, with affectionate inscriptions, were displayed about the drawing-room, and other souvenirs of their life together adorned the little tables and *étagères*. This cult of a so interesting past was calculated, of course, to heighten the advantages of the signora's present business. Nevertheless our pleasure and interest were quite genuine as we were conducted through the house by its owner and listened to her sonorous and staccato Tuscan voice relating anecdotes of that immortal mistress, depicting her suffering saintliness, her genius, her profound delicacy of feeling.

Thither, then, we moved our effects, to the dismay of the staff of the Grand Hotel, who, like all Italians, were very good to children. Our new quarters were retired and pleasant, we were within easy reach of the sea through the avenue of young plane-trees that ran down to the esplanade. In the clean, cool dining-room Signora Angiolieri daily served the soup with her own hands, the service was attentive and good, the table capital. We even discovered some Viennese acquaintances, and enjoyed chatting with them after luncheon, in front of the house. They, in their turn, were the means of our finding others – in short, all seemed for the best, and we were heartily glad of the change we had made. Nothing was now wanting to a holiday of the most gratifying kind.

And yet no proper gratification ensued. Perhaps the stupid occasion of our change of quarters pursued us to the new ones we had found. Personally, I admit that I do not easily forget these collisions with ordinary humanity, the naïve misuse of power, the injustice, the sycophantic corruption. I dwelt upon the incident too much, it irritated me in retrospect – quite futilely, of course, since such phenomena are only all too natural and all too much the rule. And we had not broken off relations with the Grand Hotel. The children were as friendly as ever there, the porter mended their toys, and we sometimes took tea in the garden. We even saw the Principessa. She would come out, with her firm and delicate tread, her lips emphatically corallined, to look after her children, playing under the supervision of their English governess. She did not dream that we were anywhere near, for so soon as she appeared in the offing we sternly forbade our little one even to clear his throat.

The heat – if I may bring it in evidence – was extreme. It was African. The power of the sun, directly one left the border of the indigo-blue wave, was so frightful, so relentless, that the mere thought of the few steps between the beach and luncheon was a burden, clad though one might be only in pyjamas. Do you care for that sort of thing? Weeks on end? Yes, of course, it is proper to the south, it is classic weather, the sun of Homer, the climate wherein human culture came to flower – and all the rest of it. But after a while it is too much for me, I reach a point where I begin to find it dull. The burning void of the sky, day after day, weighs one down; the high coloration, the enormous naïveté of the unrefracted light – they do, I dare say, induce light-heartedness, a carefree mood born of immunity from downpours and other meteorological caprices. But slowly, slowly, there makes itself felt a lack: the deeper, more complex needs of the northern soul remain unsatisfied. You are left barren – even, it may be, in time, a little contemptuous. True, without that stupid business of the whooping-cough I might not have been feeling these things. I was annoyed, very likely I wanted to feel them and so half-unconsciously seized upon an idea lying ready to hand to induce, or if not to induce, at least to justify and strengthen, my attitude. Up to this point, then, if you like, let us grant some ill will on our part. But the sea; and the mornings spent extended upon the fine sand in face of its eternal splendours – no, the sea could not conceivably induce such feelings. Yet it was none the less true that, despite all previous experience, we were not at home on the beach, we were not happy.

It was too soon, too soon. The beach, as I have said, was still in the hands of the middle-class native. It is a pleasing breed to look at, and among the young we saw much shapeliness and charm. Still, we were necessarily surrounded by a great deal of very average humanity – a middle-class mob, which, you will admit, is not more charming under this sun than under one's own native sky. The voices these women have! It was sometimes hard to believe that we were in the land which is the western cradle of the art of song, "*Fuggièro!*" I can still hear that cry, as for twenty mornings long I heard it close behind me, breathy, full-throated, hideously stressed, with a harsh open *e*, uttered in accents of mechanical despair. "*Fuggièro! Rispondi almeno!*" Answer when I call you! The *sp* in *rispondi* was pronounced like *shp*, as Germans pronounce it; and this, on top of what I felt already, vexed my sensitive soul. The cry was addressed to a repulsive youngster whose sunburn had made disgusting raw sores on his shoulders. He outdid anything I have ever seen for ill-breeding, refractoriness, and temper and was a great coward to boot, putting the whole beach in an uproar, one day, because of his outrageous sensitiveness to the slightest pain. A sand-crab had pinched his toe in the water, and the minute injury made him set up a cry of heroic proportions – the shout of an antique hero in his agony – that pierced one to the marrow and called up visions of some frightful tragedy. Evidently he considered himself not only wounded, but poisoned as well; he crawled out on the sand and lay in apparently intolerable anguish, groaning "*Ohi!*" and "*Ohimè!*" and threshing about with arms and legs to ward off his mother's tragic appeals and the questions of the bystanders. An audience gathered round. A doctor was fetched – the same who had pronounced objective judgment on our whooping-cough – and here again acquitted himself like a man of science. Good-naturedly he reassured the boy, telling him that he was not hurt at all, he should simply go into the water again to relieve the smart. Instead of which, Fuggièro was borne off the beach, followed by a concourse of people. But he did not fail to appear next morning, nor did he leave off spoiling our children's sand-castles. Of course, always by accident. In short, a perfect terror.

And this twelve-year-old lad was prominent among the influences that, imperceptibly at first, combined to spoil our holiday and render it unwholesome. Somehow or other, there was a stiffness, a lack of innocent enjoyment. These people stood on their dignity – just why, and in what spirit, it was not easy at first to tell. They displayed much self-respectingness; towards each other and towards the foreigner their bearing was that of a person newly conscious of a sense of honour. And wherefore? Gradually we realized the political implications and understood that we were in the presence of a national ideal. The beach, in fact, was alive with patriotic children – a phenomenon as unnatural as it was depressing. Children are a human species and a society apart, a nation of their own, so to speak. On the basis of their common form of life, they find each other out with the greatest ease, no matter how different their small vocabularies. Ours soon played with natives and foreigners alike. Yet they were plainly both puzzled and disappointed at times. There were wounded sensibilities, displays of assertiveness – or rather hardly assertiveness, for it was too self-conscious and too didactic to deserve the name. There were quarrels over flags, disputes about authority and precedence. Grown-ups joined in, not so much to pacify as to render judgment and enunciate principles. Phrases were dropped about the greatness and dignity of Italy, solemn phrases that spoilt the fun. We saw our two little ones retreat, puzzled and hurt, and were put to it to explain the situation. These people, we told them, were just passing through a certain stage, something rather like an illness, perhaps; not very pleasant, but probably unavoidable.

We had only our own carelessness to thank that we came to blows in the end with this "stage" – which, after all, we had seen and sized up long before now. Yes, it came to another "cross-purposes", so evidently the earlier ones had not been sheer accident. In a word, we became an offence to the public morals. Our small daughter – eight years old, but in physical development a good year younger and thin as a chicken – had had a good long bathe and gone playing in the warm sun in her wet costume. We told her that she might take off her bathing-suit, which was stiff with sand, rinse it in the sea, and put it on again, after which she must take care to keep it cleaner. Off goes the costume and she runs down naked to the sea, rinses her little jersey, and comes back. Ought we to have foreseen the outburst of anger and resentment which her conduct, and thus our conduct, called forth? Without delivering a homily on the subject, I may say that in the last decade our attitude towards the nude body and our feelings regarding it have undergone, all over the world, a fundamental change. There are things we "never think about" any more, and among them is the freedom we had permitted to this by no means provocative little childish body. But in these parts it was taken as a challenge. The patriotic children hooted. Fuggièro whistled on his fingers. The sudden buzz of conversation among the grown people in our neighbourhood boded no good. A gentleman in city togs, with a not very apropos bowler hat on the back of his head, was assuring his outraged womenfolk that he proposed to take punitive measures; he stepped up to us, and a philippic descended on our unworthy heads, in which all the emotionalism of the sense-loving south spoke in the service of morality and discipline. The offence against decency of which we had been guilty was, he said, the more to be condemned because it was also a gross ingratitude and an insulting breach of his country's hospitality. We had criminally injured not only the letter and spirit of the public bathing regulations, but also the honour of Italy; he, the gentleman in the city togs, knew how to defend that honour and proposed to see to it that our offence against the national dignity should not go unpunished.

We did our best, bowing respectfully, to give ear to this eloquence. To contradict the man, over-heated as he was, would probably be to fall from one error into another. On the tips of our tongues we had various answers: as, that the word "hospitality", in its strictest sense, was not quite the right one, taking all the circumstances into consideration. We were not literally the guests of Italy, but of Signora Angiolieri, who had assumed the role of dispenser of hospitality some years ago on laying down that of familiar friend to Eleonora Duse. We longed to say that surely this beautiful country had not sunk so low as to be reduced to a state of hypersensitive prudishness. But we confined ourselves to assuring the gentleman that any lack of respect, any provocation on our parts, had been the farthest from our thoughts. And as a mitigating circumstance we pointed out the tender age and physical slightness of the little culprit. In vain. Our protests were waved away, he did not believe in them; our defence would not hold water. We must be made an example of. The authorities were notified, by telephone, I believe, and their representative appeared on the beach. He said the case was "*molto grave*". We had to go with him to the Municipio up in the Piazza, where a higher official confirmed the previous verdict of "*molto grave*", launched into a stream of the usual didactic phrases – the selfsame tune and words as the man in the bowler hat – and levied a fine and ransom of fifty lire. We felt that the adventure must willy-nilly be worth to us this much of a contribution to the economy of the Italian government; paid, and left. Ought we not at this point to have left Torre as well?

If we only had! We should thus have escaped that fatal Cipolla. But circumstances combined to prevent us from making up our minds to a change. A certain poet says that it is indolence that makes us endure uncomfortable situations. The *aperçu* may serve as an explanation for our inaction. Anyhow, one dislikes voiding the field immediately upon such an event. Especially if sympathy from other quarters encourages one to defy it. And in the Villa Eleonora they pronounced as with one voice upon the injustice of our punishment. Some Italian after-dinner acquaintances found that the episode put their country in a very bad light, and proposed taking the man in the bowler hat to task, as one fellow-citizen to another. But the next day he and his party had vanished from the beach. Not on our account, of course. Though it might be that the consciousness of his impending departure had added energy to his rebuke; in any case his going was a relief. And, furthermore, we stayed because our stay had by now become remarkable in our own eyes, which is worth something in itself, quite apart from the comfort or discomfort involved. Shall we strike sail, avoid a certain experience so soon as it seems not expressly calculated to increase our enjoyment or our self-esteem? Shall we go away whenever life looks like turning in the slightest uncanny, or not quite normal, or even rather painful and mortifying? No, surely not. Rather stay and look matters in the face, brave them out; perhaps precisely in so doing lies a lesson for us to learn. We stayed on and reaped as the awful reward of our constancy the unholy and staggering experience with Cipolla.

I have not mentioned that the after season had begun, almost on the very day we were disciplined by the city authorities. The worshipful gentleman in the bowler hat, our denouncer, was not the only person to leave the resort. There was a regular exodus, on every hand you saw luggage-carts on their way to the station. The beach denationalized itself. Life in Torre, in the cafés and the pinetas, became more homelike and more European. Very likely we might even have eaten at a table in the glass veranda, but we refrained, being content at Signora Angiolieri's – as content, that is, as our evil star would let us be. But at the same time with this turn for the better came a change in the weather: almost to an hour it showed itself in harmony with the holiday calendar of the general public. The sky was overcast; not that it grew any cooler, but the unclouded heat of the entire eighteen days since our arrival, and probably long before that, gave place to a stifling sirocco air, while from time to time a little ineffectual rain sprinkled the velvety surface of the beach. Add to which, that two-thirds of our intended stay at Torre had passed. The colourless, lazy sea, with sluggish jelly-fish floating in its shallows, was at least a change. And it would have been silly to feel retrospective longings after a sun that had caused us so many sighs when it burned down in all its arrogant power.

At this juncture, then, it was that Cipolla announced himself. Cavaliere Cipolla he was called on the posters that appeared one day stuck up everywhere, even in the dining-room of Pensione Eleonora. A travelling virtuoso, an entertainer, "*forzatore, illusionista, prestidigatore*", he called himself, who proposed to wait upon the highly respectable population of Torre di Venere with a display of extraordinary phenomena of a mysterious and staggering kind. A conjuror! The bare announcement was enough to turn our children's heads. They had never seen anything of the sort, and now our present holiday was to afford them this new excitement. From that moment on they besieged us with prayers to take tickets for the performance. We had doubts, from the first, on the score of the lateness of the hour, nine o'clock; but gave way, in the idea that we might see a little of what Cipolla had to offer, probably no great matter, and then go home. Besides, of course, the children could sleep late next day. We bought four tickets of Signora Angiolieri herself, she having taken a number of the stalls on commission to sell them to her guests. She could not vouch for the man's performance, and we had no great expectations. But we were conscious of a need for diversion, and the children's violent curiosity proved catching.

The Cavaliere's performance was to take place in a hall where during the season there had been a cinema with a weekly programme. We had never been there. You reached it by following the main street under the wall of the "*palazzo*", a ruin with a "For sale" sign, that suggested a castle and had obviously been built in lordlier days. In the same street were the chemist, the hairdresser, and all the better shops; it led, so to speak, from the feudal past the bourgeois into the proletarian, for it ended off between two rows of poor fishing-huts, where old women sat mending nets before the doors. And here, among the proletariat, was the hall, not much more, actually, than a wooden shed, though a large one, with a turreted entrance, plastered on either side with layers of gay placards. Some while after dinner, then, on the appointed evening, we wended our way thither in the dark, the children dressed in their best and blissful with the sense of so much irregularity. It was sultry, as it had been for days; there was heat lightning now and then, and a little rain; we proceeded under umbrellas. It took us a quarter of an hour.

Our tickets were collected at the entrance, our places we had to find ourselves. They were in the third row left, and as we sat down we saw that, late though the hour was for the performance, it was to be interpreted with even more laxity. Only very slowly did an audience – who seemed to be relied upon to come late – begin to fill the stalls. These comprised the whole auditorium; there were no boxes. This tardiness gave us some concern. The children's cheeks were already flushed as much with fatigue as with excitement. But even when we entered, the standing-room at the back and in the side aisles was already well occupied. There stood the manhood of Torre di Venere, all and sundry, fisherfolk, rough-and-ready youths with bare forearms crossed over their striped jerseys. We were well pleased with the presence of this native assemblage, which always adds colour and animation to occasions like the present; and the children were frankly delighted.

For they had friends among these people – acquaintances picked up on afternoon strolls to the farther ends of the beach. We would be turning homeward, at the hour when the sun dropped into the sea, spent with the huge effort it had made and gilding with reddish gold the oncoming surf; and we would come upon bare-legged fisherfolk standing in rows, bracing and hauling with long-drawn cries as they drew in the nets and harvested in dripping baskets their catch, often so scanty, of *frutta di mare*. The children looked on, helped to pull, brought out their little stock of Italian words, made friends. So now they exchanged nods with the "standing-room" clientèle; there was Guiscardo, there Antonio, they knew them by name and waved and called across in half-whispers, getting answering nods and smiles that displayed rows of healthy white teeth. Look, there is even Mario, Mario from the Esquisito, who brings us the chocolate. He wants to see the conjuror, too, and he must have come early, for he is almost in front; but he does not see us, he is not paying attention; that is a way he has, even though he is a waiter. So we wave instead to the man who lets out the little boats on the beach; he is there too, standing at the back.

It had got to a quarter past nine, it got to almost half past. It was natural that we should be nervous. When would the children get to bed? It had been a mistake to bring them, for now it would be very hard to suggest breaking off their enjoyment before it had got well under way. The stalls had filled in time; all Torre, apparently, was there: the guests of the Grand Hotel, the guests of Villa Eleonora, familiar faces from the beach. We heard English and German and the sort of French that Rumanians speak with Italians. Madame Angiolieri herself sat two rows behind us, with her quiet, bald-headed spouse, who kept stroking his moustache with the two middle fingers of his right hand. Everybody had come late, but nobody too late. Cipolla made us wait for him.

He made us wait. That is probably the way to put it. He heightened the suspense by his delay in appearing. And we could see the point of this, too – only not when it was carried to extremes. Towards half past nine the audience began to clap – an amiable way of expressing justifiable impatience, evincing as it does an eagerness to applaud. For the little ones, this was a joy in itself – all children love to clap. From the popular sphere came loud cries of "*Pronti!*" "*Cominciamo!*" And lo, it seemed now as easy to begin as before it had been hard. A gong sounded, greeted by the standing rows with a many-voiced "Ah-h!" and the curtains parted. They revealed a platform furnished more like a school-room than like the theatre of a conjuring performance – largely because of the blackboard in the left foreground. There were a common yellow hat-stand, a few ordinary straw-bottomed chairs, and farther back a little round table holding a water carafe and glass, also a tray with a liqueur glass and a flask of pale-yellow liquid. We had still a few seconds of time to let these things sink in. Then, with no darkening of the house, Cavaliere Cipolla made his entry.

He came forward with a rapid step that expressed his eagerness to appear before his public and gave rise to the illusion that he had already come a long way to put himself at their service – whereas, of course, he had only been standing in the wings. His costume supported the fiction. A man of an age hard to determine, but by no means young; with a sharp, ravaged face, piercing eyes, compressed lips, small black waxed moustache, and a so-called imperial in the curve between mouth and chin. He was dressed for the street with a sort of complicated evening elegance, in a wide black pelerine with velvet collar and satin lining; which, in the hampered state of his arms, he held together in front with his white-gloved hands. He had a white scarf round his neck; a top hat with a curving brim sat far back on his head. Perhaps more than anywhere else the eighteenth century is still alive in Italy, and with it the charlatan and mountebank type so characteristic of the period. Only there, at any rate, does one still encounter really well-preserved specimens. Cipolla had in his whole appearance much of the historic type; his very clothes helped to conjure up the traditional figure with its blatantly, fantastically foppish air. His pretentious costume sat upon him, or rather hung upon him, most curiously, being in one place drawn too tight, in another a mass of awkward folds. There was something not quite in order about his figure, both front and back – that was plain later on. But I must emphasize the fact that there was not a trace of personal jocularity or clownishness in his pose, manner, or behaviour. On the contrary, there was complete seriousness, an absence of any humorous appeal; occasionally even a cross-grained pride, along with that curious, self-satisfied air so characteristic of the deformed. None of all this, however, prevented his appearance from being greeted with laughter from more than one quarter of the hall.

All the eagerness had left his manner. The swift entry had been merely an expression of energy, not of zeal. Standing at the footlights he negligently drew off his gloves, to display long yellow hands, one of them adorned with a seal ring with a lapis-lazuli in a high setting. As he stood there, his small hard eyes, with flabby pouches beneath them, roved appraisingly about the hall, not quickly, rather in a considered examination, pausing here and there upon a face with his lips clipped together, not speaking a word. Then with a display of skill as surprising as it was casual, he rolled his gloves into a ball and tossed them across a considerable distance into the glass on the table. Next from an inner pocket he drew forth a packet of cigarettes; you could see by the wrapper that they were the cheapest sort the government sells. With his finger-tips he pulled out a cigarette and lighted it, without looking, from a quick-firing benzine lighter. He drew the smoke deep into his lungs and let it out again, tapping his foot, with both lips drawn in an arrogant grimace and the grey smoke streaming out between broken and saw-edged teeth.

With a keenness equal to his own his audience eyed him. The youths at the rear scowled as they peered at this cocksure creature to search out his secret weaknesses. He betrayed none. In fetching out and putting back the cigarettes his clothes got in his way. He had to turn back his pelerine, and in so doing revealed a riding-whip with a silver claw-handle that hung by a leather thong from his left forearm and looked decidely out of place. You could see that he had on not evening clothes but a frock-coat, and under this, as he lifted it to get at his pocket, could be seen a striped sash worn about the body. Somebody behind me whispered that this sash went with his title of Cavaliere. I give the information for what it may be worth – personally, I never heard that the title carried such insignia with it. Perhaps the sash was sheer pose, like the way he stood there, without a word, casually and arrogantly puffing smoke into his audience's face.

People laughed, as I said. The merriment had become almost general when somebody in the "standing seats", in a loud, dry voice, remarked: "*Buona sera.*"

Cipolla cocked his head. "Who was that?" asked he, as though he had been dared. "Who was that just spoke? Well? First so bold and now so modest? *Paura*, eh?" He spoke with a rather high, asthmatic voice, which yet had a metallic quality. He waited.

"That was me," a youth at the rear broke into the stillness, seeing himself thus challenged. He was not far from us, a handsome fellow in a woollen shirt, with his coat hanging over one shoulder. He wore his curly, wiry hair in a high, dishevelled mop, the style affected by the youth of the awakened Fatherland; it gave him an African appearance that rather spoiled his looks. "*Bè!* That was me. It was your business to say it first, but I was trying to be friendly."

More laughter. The chap had a tongue in his head. "*Ha sciolto la scilinguàgnolo*," I heard near me. After all, the retort was deserved.

"Ah, bravo!" answered Cipolla. "I like you, *giovanotto*. Trust me, I've had my eye on you for some time. People like you are just in my line. I can use them. And you are the pick of the lot, that's plain to see. You do what you like. Or is it possible you have ever not done what you liked – or even, maybe, what you didn't like? What somebody else liked, in short? Hark ye, my friend, that might be a pleasant change for you, to divide up the willing and the doing and stop tackling both jobs at once. Division of labour, *sistema americano, sa'*! For instance, suppose you were to show your tongue to this select and honourable audience here – your whole tongue, right down to the roots?"

"No, I won't," said the youth, hostilely. "Sticking out your tongue shows a bad bringing-up."

"Nothing of the sort," retorted Cipolla. "You would only be *doing* it. With all due respect to your bringing-up, I suggest that before I count ten, you will perform a right turn and stick out your tongue at the company here farther than you knew yourself that you could stick it out."

He gazed at the youth, and his piercing eyes seemed to sink deeper into their sockets. "*Uno!*" said he. He had let his riding-whip slide down his arm and made it whistle once through the air. The boy faced about and put out his tongue, so long, so extendedly, that you could see it was the very uttermost in tongue which he had to offer. Then turned back, stony-faced, to his former position.

"That was me," mocked Cipolla, with a jerk of his head towards the youth. "*Bè!* That was me." Leaving the audience to enjoy its sensations, he turned towards the little round table, lifted the bottle, poured out a small glass of what was obviously cognac, and tipped it up with a practised hand.

The children laughed with all their hearts. They had understood practically nothing of what had been said, but it pleased them hugely that something so funny should happen, straightaway, between that queer man up there and somebody out of the audience. They had no preconception of what an "evening" would be like and were quite ready to find this a priceless beginning. As for us, we exchanged a glance and I remember that involuntarily I made with my lips the sound that Cipolla's whip had made when it cut the air. For the rest, it was plain that people did not know what to make of a preposterous beginning like this to a sleight-of-hand performance. They could not see why the *giovanotto*, who after all in a way had been their spokesman, should suddenly have turned on them to vent his incivility. They felt that he had behaved like a silly ass and withdrew their countenances from him in favour of the artist, who now came back from his refreshment table and addressed them as follows:

"Ladies and gentlemen," said he, in his wheezing, metallic voice, "you saw just now that I was rather sensitive on the score of the rebuke this hopeful young linguist saw fit to give me" – "*questo linguista di belle speranze*" was what he said, and we all laughed at the pun. "I am a man who sets some store by himself, you may take it from me. And I see no point in being wished a good-evening unless it is done courteously and in all seriousness. For anything else there is no occasion. When a man wishes me a good-evening he wishes himself one, for the audience will have one only if I do. So this lady-killer of Torre di Venere" (another thrust) "did well to testify that I have one tonight and that I can dispense with any wishes of his in the matter. I can boast of having good evenings almost without exception. One not so good does come my way now and again, but very seldom. My calling is hard and my health not of the best. I have a little physical defect which prevented me from doing my bit in the war for the greater glory of the Fatherland. It is perforce with my mental and spiritual parts that I conquer life – which after all only means conquering oneself. And I flatter myself that my achievements have aroused interest and respect among the educated public. The leading newspapers have lauded me, the *Corriere della Sera* did me the courtesy of calling me a phenomenon, and in Rome the brother of the *Duce* honoured me by his presence at one of my evenings. I should not have thought that in a relatively less important place" (laughter here, at the expense of poor little Torre) "I should have to give up the small personal habits which brilliant and elevated audiences had been ready to overlook. Nor did I think I had to stand being heckled by a person who seems to have been rather spoilt by the favours of the fair sex." All this of course at the expense of the youth whom Cipolla never tired of presenting in the guise of *donnaiuolo* and rustic Don Juan. His persistent thin-skinnedness and animosity were in striking contrast to the self-confidence and the worldly success he boasted of. One might have assumed that the *giovanotto* was merely the chosen butt of Cipolla's customary professional sallies, had not the very pointed witticisms betrayed a genuine antagonism. No one looking at the physical parts of the two men need have been at a loss for the explanation, even if the deformed man had not constantly played on the other's supposed success with the fair sex. "Well," Cipolla went on, "before beginning our entertainment this evening, perhaps you will permit me to make myself comfortable."

And he went towards the hat-stand to take off his things.

"*Parla benissimo,*" asserted somebody in our neighbourhood. So far, the man had done nothing; but what he had said was accepted as an achievement, by means of that he had made an impression. Among southern peoples speech is a constituent part of the pleasure of living, it enjoys far livelier social esteem than in the north. That national cement, the mother tongue, is paid symbolic honours down here, and there is something blithely symbolical in the pleasure people take in their respect for its forms and phonetics. They enjoy speaking, they enjoy listening; and they listen with discrimination. For the way a man speaks serves as a measure of his personal rank; carelessness and clumsiness are greeted with scorn, elegance and mastery are rewarded with social éclat. Wherefore the small man too, where it is a question of getting his effect, chooses his phrase nicely and turns it with care. On this count, then, at least, Cipolla had won his audience; though he by no means belonged to the class of men which the Italian, in a singular mixture of moral and æsthetic judgments, labels "*simpatico*".

After removing his hat, scarf, and mantle he came to the front of the stage, settling his coat, pulling down his cuffs with their large cuff-buttons, adjusting his absurd sash. He had very ugly hair; the top of his head, that is, was almost bald, while a narrow, black-varnished frizz of curls ran from front to back as though stuck on; the side hair, likewise blackened, was brushed forward to the corners of the eyes – it was, in short, the hairdressing of an old-fashioned circus-director, fantastic, but entirely suited to his outmoded personal type and worn with so much assurance as to take the edge off the public's sense of humour. The little physical defect of which he had warned us was now all too visible, though the nature of it was even now not very clear: the chest was too high, as is usual in such cases; but the corresponding malformation of the back did not sit between the shoulders, it took the form of a sort of hips or buttocks hump, which did not indeed hinder his movements but gave him a grotesque and dipping stride at every step he took. However, by mentioning his deformity beforehand he had broken the shock of it, and a delicate propriety of feeling appeared to reign throughout the hall.

"At your service," said Cipolla. "With your kind permission, we will begin the evening with some arithmetical tests."

Arithmetic? That did not sound much like sleight-of-hand. We began to have our suspicions that the man was sailing under a false flag, only we did not yet know which was the right one. I felt sorry on the children's account; but for the moment they were content simply to be there.

The numerical test which Cipolla now introduced was as simple as it was baffling. He began by fastening a piece of paper to the upper right-hand corner of the blackboard; then lifting it up, he wrote something underneath. He talked all the while, relieving the dryness of his offering by a constant flow of words, and showed himself a practised speaker, never at a loss for conversational turns of phrase. It was in keeping with the nature of his performance, and at the same time vastly entertained the children, that he went on to eliminate the gap between stage and audience, which had already been bridged over by the curious skirmish with the fisher lad: he had representatives from the audience mount the stage, and himself descended the wooden steps to seek personal contact with his public. And again, with individuals, he fell into his former taunting tone. I do not know how far that was a deliberate feature of his system; he preserved a serious, even a peevish air, but his audience, at least the more popular section, seemed convinced that that was all part of the game. So then, after he had written something and covered the writing by the paper, he desired that two persons should come up on the platform and help to perform the calculations. They would not be difficult, even for people not clever at figures. As usual, nobody volunteered, and Cipolla took care not to molest the more select portion of his audience. He kept to the populace. Turning to two sturdy young louts standing behind us, he beckoned them to the front, encouraging and scolding by turns. They should not stand there gaping, he said, unwilling to oblige the company. Actually, he got them in motion; with clumsy tread they came down the middle aisle, climbed the steps, and stood in front of the blackboard, grinning sheepishly at their comrades' shouts and applause. Cipolla joked with them for a few minutes, praised their heroic firmness of limb and the size of their hands, so well calculated to do this service for the public. Then he handed one of them the chalk and told him to write down the numbers as they were called out. But now the creature declared that he could not write! "*Non so scrivere,*" said he in his gruff voice, and his companion added that neither did he.

God knows whether they told the truth or whether they wanted to make game of Cipolla. Anyhow, the latter was far from sharing the general merriment which their confession aroused. He was insulted and disgusted. He sat there on a straw-bottomed chair in the centre of the stage with his legs crossed, smoking a fresh cigarette out of his cheap packet; obviously it tasted the better for the cognac he had indulged in while the yokels were stumping up the steps. Again he inhaled the smoke and let it stream out between curling lips. Swinging his leg, with his gaze sternly averted from the two shamelessly chuckling creatures and from the audience as well, he stared into space as one who withdraws himself and his dignity from the contemplation of an utterly despicable phenomenon.

"Scandalous," said he, in a sort of icy snarl. "Go back to your places! In Italy everybody can write – in all her greatness there is no room for ignorance and unenlightenment. To accuse her of them, in the hearing of this international company, is a cheap joke, in which you yourselves cut a very poor figure and humiliate the government and the whole country as well. If it is true that Torre di Venere is indeed the last refuge of such ignorance, then I must blush to have visited the place – being, as I already was, aware of its inferiority to Rome in more than one respect –"

Here Cipolla was interrupted by the youth with the Nubian coiffure and his jacket across his shoulder. His fighting spirit, as we now saw, had only abdicated temporarily, and he now flung himself into the breach in defence of his native heath. "That will do," said he loudly. "That's enough jokes about Torre. We all come from the place and we won't stand strangers making fun of it. These two chaps are our friends. Maybe they are no scholars, but even so they may be straighter than some folks in the room who are so free with their boasts about Rome, though they did not build it either."

That was capital. The young man had certainly cut his eye-teeth. And this sort of spectacle was good fun, even though it still further delayed the regular performance. It is always fascinating to listen to an altercation. Some people it simply amuses, they take a sort of kill-joy pleasure in not being principals. Others feel upset and uneasy, and my sympathies are with these latter, although on the present occasion I was under the impression that all this was part of the show – the analphabetic yokels no less than the *giovanotto* with the jacket. The children listened well pleased. They understood not at all, but the sound of the voices made them hold their breath. So this was a "magic evening" – at least it was the kind they have in Italy. They expressly found it "lovely".

Cipolla had stood up and with two of his scooping strides was at the footlights.

"Well, well, see who's here!" said he with grim cordiality. "An old acquaintance! A young man with his heart at the end of his tongue" (he used the word *linguaccia*, which means a coated tongue, and gave rise to much hilarity). "That will do, my friends," he turned to the yokels. "I do not need you now, I have business with this deserving young man here, *con questo torregiano de Venere*, this tower of Venus, who no doubt expects the gratitude of the fair as a reward for his prowess – "

"*Ah, non scherziamo!* We're talking earnest," cried out the youth. His eyes flashed, and he actually made as though to pull off his jacket and proceed to direct methods of settlement.

Cipolla did not take him too seriously. We had exchanged apprehensive glances; but he was dealing with a fellow-countryman and had his native soil beneath his feet. He kept quite cool and showed complete mastery of the situation. He looked at his audience, smiled, and made a sideways motion of the head towards the young cockerel as though calling the public to witness how the man's bumptiousness only served to betray the simplicity of his mind. And then, for the second time, something strange happened, which set Cipolla's calm superiority in an uncanny light, and in some mysterious and irritating way turned all the explosiveness latent in the air into matter for laughter.

Cipolla drew still nearer to the fellow, looking him in the eye with a peculiar gaze. He even came half-way down the steps that led into the auditorium on our left, so that he stood directly in front of the trouble-maker, on slightly higher ground. The riding-whip hung from his arm.

"My son, you do not feel much like joking," he said. "It is only too natural, for anyone can see that you are not feeling too well. Even your tongue, which leaves something to be desired on the score of cleanliness, indicates acute disorder of the gastric system. An evening entertainment is no place for people in your state; you yourself, I can tell, were of several minds whether you would not do better to put on a flannel bandage and go to bed. It was not good judgment to drink so much of that very sour white wine this afternoon. Now you have such a colic you would like to double up with the pain. Go ahead, don't be embarrassed. There is a distinct relief that comes from bending over, in cases of intestinal cramp."

He spoke thus, word for word, with quiet impressiveness and a kind of stern sympathy, and his eyes, plunged the while deep in the young man's, seemed to grow very tired and at the same time burning above their enlarged tear-ducts – they were the strangest eyes, you could tell that not manly pride alone was preventing the young adversary from withdrawing his gaze. And presently, indeed, all trace of its former arrogance was gone from the bronzed young face. He looked open-mouthed at the Cavaliere and the open mouth was drawn in a rueful smile.

"Double over," repeated Cipolla. "What else can you do? With a colic like that you *must* bend. Surely you will not struggle against the performance of a perfectly natural action just because somebody suggests it to you?"

Slowly the youth lifted his forearms, folded and squeezed them across his body; it turned a little sideways, then bent, lower and lower, the feet shifted, the knees turned inward, until he had become a picture of writhing pain, until he all but grovelled upon the ground. Cipolla let him stand for some seconds thus, then made a short cut through the air with his whip and went with his scooping stride back to the little table, where he poured himself out a cognac.

"*Il boit beaucoup*," asserted a lady behind us. Was that the only thing that struck her? We could not tell how far the audience grasped the situation. The fellow was standing upright again, with a sheepish grin – he looked as though he scarcely knew how it had all happened. The scene had been followed with tense interest and applauded at the end; there were shouts of "*Bravo, Cipolla!*" and "*Bravo, giovanotto!*" Apparently the issue of the duel was not looked upon as a personal defeat for the young man. Rather the audience encouraged him as one does an actor who succeeds in an unsympathetic role. Certainly his way of screwing himself up with cramp had been highly picturesque, its appeal was directly calculated to impress the gallery – in short, a fine dramatic performance. But I am not sure how far the audience were moved by that natural tactfulness in which the south excels, or how far it penetrated into the nature of what was going on.

The Cavaliere, refreshed, had lighted another cigarette. The numerical tests might now proceed. A young man was easily found in the back row who was willing to write down on the blackboard the numbers as they were dictated to him. Him too we knew; the whole entertainment had taken on an intimate character through our acquaintance with so many of the actors. This was the man who worked at the greengrocer's in the main street; he had served us several times, with neatness and dispatch. He wielded the chalk with clerkly confidence, while Cipolla descended to our level and walked with his deformed gait through the audience, collecting numbers as they were given, in two, three, and four places, and calling them out to the grocer's assistant, who wrote them down in a column. In all this, everything on both sides was calculated to amuse, with its jokes and its oratorical asides. The artist could not fail to hit on foreigners, who were not ready with their figures, and with them he was elaborately patient and chivalrous, to the great amusement of the natives, whom he reduced to confusion in their turn, by making them translate numbers that were given in English or French. Some people gave dates concerned with great events in Italian history. Cipolla took them up at once and made patriotic comments. Somebody shouted "Number one!" The Cavaliere, incensed at this as at every attempt to make game of him, retorted over his shoulder that he could not take less than two-place figures. Whereupon another joker cried out "Number two!" and was greeted with the applause and laughter which every reference to natural functions is sure to win among southerners.

When fifteen numbers stood in a long straggling row on the board, Cipolla called for a general adding-match. Ready reckoners might add in their heads, but pencil and paper were not forbidden. Cipolla, while the work went on, sat on his chair near the blackboard, smoked and grimaced, with the complacent, pompous air cripples so often have. The five-place addition was soon done. Somebody announced the answer, somebody else confirmed it, a third had arrived at a slightly different result, but the fourth agreed with the first and second. Cipolla got up, tapped some ash from his coat, and lifted the paper at the upper right-hand corner of the board to display the writing. The correct answer, a sum close on a million, stood there; he had written it down beforehand.

Astonishment, and loud applause. The children were overwhelmed. How had he done that, they wanted to know. We told them it was a trick, not easily explainable offhand. In short, the man was a conjuror. This was what a sleight-of-hand evening was like, so now they knew. First the fisherman had cramp, and then the right answer was written down beforehand – it was all simply glorious, and we saw with dismay that despite the hot eyes and the hand of the clock at almost half past ten, it would be very hard to get them away. There would be tears. And yet it was plain that this magician did not "magick" – at least not in the accepted sense, of manual dexterity – and that the entertainment was not at all suitable for children. Again, I do not know, either, what the audience really thought. Obviously there was grave doubt whether its answers had been given of "free choice"; here and there an individual might have answered of his own motion, but on the whole Cipolla certainly selected his people and thus kept the whole procedure in his own hands and directed it towards the given result. Even so, one had to admire the quickness of his calculations, however much one felt disinclined to admire anything else about the performance. Then his patriotism, his irritable sense of dignity – the Cavaliere's own countrymen might feel in their element with all that and continue in a laughing mood; but the combination certainly gave us outsiders food for thought.

Cipolla himself saw to it – though without giving them a name – that the nature of his powers should be clear beyond a doubt to even the least-instructed person. He alluded to them, of course, in his talk – and he talked without stopping – but only in vague, boastful, self-advertising phrases. He went on awhile with experiments on the same lines as the first, merely making them more complicated by introducing operations in multiplying, subtracting, and dividing; then he simplified them to the last degree in order to bring out the method. He simply had numbers "guessed" which were previously written under the paper; and the guess was nearly always right. One guesser admitted that he had had in mind to give a certain number, when Cipolla's whip went whistling through the air, and a quite different one slipped out, which proved to be the "right" one. Cipolla's shoulders shook. He pretended admiration for the powers of the people he questioned. But in all his compliments there was something fleering and derogatory; the victims could scarcely have relished them much, although they smiled, and although they might easily have set down some part of the applause to their own credit. Moreover, I had not the impression that the artist was popular with his public. A certain ill will and reluctance were in the air, but courtesy kept such feelings in check, as did Cipolla's competency and his stern self-confidence. Even the riding-whip, I think, did much to keep rebellion from becoming overt.

From tricks with numbers he passed to tricks with cards. There were two packs, which he drew out of his pockets, and so much I still remember, that the basis of the tricks he played with them was as follows: from the first pack he drew three cards and thrust them without looking at them inside his coat. Another person then drew three out of the second pack, and these turned out to be the same as the first three – not invariably all the three, for it did happen that only two were the same. But in the majority of cases Cipolla triumphed, showing his three cards with a little bow in acknowledgment of the applause with which his audience conceded his possession of strange powers – strange whether for good or evil. A young man in the front row, to our right, an Italian, with proud, finely chiselled features, rose up and said that he intended to assert his own will in his choice and consciously to resist any influence, of whatever sort. Under these circumstances, what did Cipolla think would be the result? "You will," answered the Cavaliere, "make my task somewhat more difficult thereby. As for the result, your resistance will not alter it in the least. Freedom exists, and also the will exists; but freedom of the will does not exist, for a will that aims at its own freedom aims at the unknown. You are free to draw or not to draw. But if you draw, you will draw the right cards – the more certainly, the more wilfully obstinate your behaviour."

One must admit that he could not have chosen his words better, to trouble the waters and confuse the mind. The refractory youth hesitated before drawing. Then he pulled out a card and at once demanded to see if it was among the chosen three. "But why?" queried Cipolla. "Why do things by halves?" Then, as the other defiantly insisted, "*E servito*," said the juggler, with a gesture of exaggerated servility; and held out the three cards fanwise, without looking at them himself. The left-hand card was the one drawn.

Amid general applause, the apostle of freedom sat down. How far Cipolla employed small tricks and manual dexterity to help out his natural talents, the deuce only knew. But even without them the result would have been the same: the curiosity of the entire audience was unbounded and universal, everybody both enjoyed the amazing character of the entertainment and unanimously conceded the professional skill of the performer. "*Lavora bene*," we heard, here and there in our neighbourhood; it signified the triumph of objective judgment over antipathy and repressed resentment.

After his last, incomplete, yet so much the more telling success, Cipolla had at once fortified himself with another cognac. Truly he did "drink a lot", and the fact made a bad impression. But obviously he needed the liquor and the cigarettes for the replenishment of his energy, upon which, as he himself said, heavy demands were made in all directions. Certainly in the intervals he looked very ill, exhausted and hollow-eyed. Then the little glassful would redress the balance, and the flow of lively, self-confident chatter run on, while the smoke he inhaled gushed out grey from his lungs.

I clearly recall that he passed from the card-tricks to parlour games – the kind based on certain powers which in human nature are higher or else lower than human reason: on intuition and "magnetic" transmission; in short, upon a low type of manifestation. What I do not remember is the precise order things came in. And I will not bore you with a description of these experiments; everybody knows them, everybody has at one time or another taken part in this finding of hidden articles, this blind carrying out of a series of acts, directed by a force that proceeds from organism to organism by unexplored paths. Everybody has had his little glimpse into the equivocal, impure, inexplicable nature of the occult, has been conscious of both curiosity and contempt, has shaken his head over the human tendency of those who deal in it to help themselves out with humbuggery, though, after all, the humbuggery is no disproof whatever of the genuineness of the other elements in the dubious amalgam. I can only say here that each single circumstance gains in weight and the whole greatly in impressiveness when it is a man like Cipolla who is the chief actor and guiding spirit in the sinister business. He sat smoking at the rear of the stage, his back to the audience while they conferred. The object passed from hand to hand which it was his task to find, with which he was to perform some action agreed upon beforehand. Then he would start to move zigzag through the hall, with his head thrown back and one hand outstretched, the other clasped in that of a guide who was in the secret but enjoined to keep himself perfectly passive, with his thoughts directed upon the agreed goal. Cipolla moved with the bearing typical in these experiments: now groping upon a false start, now with a quick forward thrust, now pausing as though to listen and by sudden inspiration correcting his course. The roles seemed reversed, the stream of influence was moving in the contrary direction, as the artist himself pointed out, in his ceaseless flow of discourse. The suffering, receptive, performing part was now his, the will he had before imposed on others was shut out, he acted in obedience to a voiceless common will which was in the air. But he made it perfectly clear that it all came to the same thing. The capacity for self-surrender, he said, for becoming a tool, for the most unconditional and utter self-abnegation, was but the reverse side of that other power to will and to command. Commanding and obeying formed together one single principle, one indissoluble unity; he who knew how to obey knew also how to command, and conversely; the one idea was comprehended in the other, as people and leader were comprehended in one another. But that which was *done*, the highly exacting and exhausting performance, was in every case his, the leader's and mover's, in whom the will became obedience, the obedience will, whose person was the cradle and womb of both, and who thus suffered enormous hardship. Repeatedly he emphasized the fact that his lot was a hard one – presumably to account for his need of stimulant and his frequent recourse to the little glass.

Thus he groped his way forward, like a blind seer, led and sustained by the mysterious common will. He drew a pin set with a stone out of its hiding-place in an Englishwoman's shoe, carried it, halting and pressing on by turns, to another lady – Signora Angiolieri – and handed it to her on bended knee, with the words it had been agreed he was to utter. "I present you with this in token of my respect," was the sentence. Their sense was obvious but the words themselves not easy to hit upon, for the reason that they had been agreed on in French; the language complication seemed to us a little malicious, implying as it did a conflict between the audience's natural interest in the success of the miracle, and their desire to witness the humiliation of this presumptuous man. It was a strange sight: Cipolla on his knees before the signora, wrestling, amid efforts at speech, after knowledge of the preordained words. "I must say something," he said, "and I feel clearly what it is I must say. But I also feel that if it passed my lips it would be wrong. Be careful not to help me unintentionally!" he cried out, though very likely that was precisely what he was hoping for. "*Pensez très fort,*" he cried all at once, in bad French, and then burst out with the required words – in Italian, indeed, but with the final substantive pronounced in the sister tongue, in which he was probably far from fluent: he said *vénération* instead of *venerazione*, with an impossible nasal. And this partial success, after the complete success before it, the finding of the pin, the presentation of it on his knees to the right person – was almost more impressive than if he had got the sentence exactly right, and evoked bursts of admiring applause.

Cipolla got up from his knees and wiped the perspiration from his brow. You understand that this experiment with the pin was a single case, which I describe because it sticks in my memory. But he changed his method several times and improvised a number of variations suggested by his contact with his audience; a good deal of time thus went by. He seemed to get particular inspiration from the person of our landlady; she drew him on to the most extraordinary displays of clairvoyance. "It does not escape me, madame," he said to her, "that there is something unusual about you, some special and honourable distinction. He who has eyes to see descries about your lovely brow an aureola – if I mistake not, it once was stronger than now – a slowly paling radiance . . . hush, not a word! Don't help me. Beside you sits your husband – yes?" He turned towards the silent Signor Angiolieri. "You are the husband of this lady, and your happiness is complete. But in the midst of this happiness memories rise . . . the past, signora, so it seems to me, plays an important part in your present. You knew a king . . . has not a king crossed your path in bygone days?"

"No," breathed the dispenser of our mid-day soup, her golden-brown eyes gleaming in the noble pallor of her face.

"No? No, not a king; I meant that generally, I did not mean literally a king. Not a king, not a prince, and a prince after all, a king of a loftier realm; it was a great artist, at whose side you once – you would contradict me, and yet I am not wholly wrong. Well, then! It was a woman, a great, a world-renowned woman artist, whose friendship you enjoyed in your tender years, whose sacred memory overshadows and transfigures your whole existence. Her name? Need I utter it, whose fame has long been bound up with the Fatherland's, immortal as its own? Eleonora Duse," he finished, softly and with much solemnity.

The little woman bowed her head, overcome. The applause was like a patriotic demonstration. Nearly everyone there knew about Signora Angiolieri's wonderful past; they were all able to confirm the Cavaliere's intuition – not least the present guests of Casa Eleonora. But we wondered how much of the truth he had learned as the result of professional inquiries made on his arrival. Yet I see no reason at all to cast doubt, on rational grounds, upon powers which, before our very eyes, became fatal to their possessor.

At this point there was an intermission. Our lord and master withdrew. Now I confess that almost ever since the beginning of my tale I have looked forward with dread to this moment in it. The thoughts of men are mostly not hard to read; in this case they are very easy. You are sure to ask why we did not choose this moment to go away – and I must continue to owe you an answer. I do not know why. I cannot defend myself. By this time it was certainly eleven, probably later. The children were asleep. The last series of tests had been too long, nature had had her way. They were sleeping in our laps, the little one on mine, the boy on his mother's. That was, in a way, a consolation; but at the same time it was also ground for compassion and a clear leading to take them home to bed. And I give you my word that we wanted to obey this touching admonition, we seriously wanted to. We roused the poor things and told them it was now high time to go. But they were no sooner conscious than they began to resist and implore – you know how horrified children are at the thought of leaving before the end of a thing. No cajoling has any effect, you have to use force. It was so lovely, they wailed. How did we know what was coming next? Surely we could not leave until after the intermission; they liked a little nap now and again – only not go home, only not go to bed, while the beautiful evening was still going on!

We yielded, but only for the moment, of course – so far as we knew – only for a little while, just a few minutes longer. I cannot excuse our staying, scarcely can I even understand it. Did we think, having once said A, we had to say B – having once brought the children hither we had to let them stay? No, it is not good enough. Were we ourselves so highly entertained? Yes, and no. Our feelings for Cavaliere Cipolla were of a very mixed kind, but so were the feelings of the whole audience, if I mistake not, and nobody left. Were we under the sway of a fascination which emanated from this man who took so strange a way to earn his bread; a fascination which he gave out independently of the programme and even between the tricks and which paralysed our resolve? Again, sheer curiosity may account for something. One was curious to know how such an evening turned out; Cipolla in his remarks having all along hinted that he had tricks in his bag stranger than any he had yet produced.

But all that is not it – or at least it is not all of it. More correct it would be to answer the first question with another. Why had we not left Torre di Venere itself before now? To me the two questions are one and the same, and in order to get out of the impasse I might simply say that I had answered it already. For, as things had been in Torre in general: queer, uncomfortable, troublesome, tense, oppressive, so precisely they were here in this hall tonight. Yes, more than precisely. For it seemed to be the fountain-head of all the uncanniness and all the strained feelings which had oppressed the atmosphere of our holiday. This man whose return to the stage we were awaiting was the personification of all that; and, as we had not gone away in general, so to speak, it would have been inconsistent to do it in the particular case. You may call this an explanation, you may call it inertia, as you see fit. Any argument more to the purpose I simply do not know how to adduce.

Well, there was an interval of ten minutes, which grew into

nearly twenty. The children remained awake. They were enchanted by our compliance, and filled the break to their own satisfaction by renewing relations with the popular sphere, with Antonio, Guiscardo, and the canoe man. They put their hands to their mouths and called messages across, appealing to us for the Italian words. "Hope you have a good catch tomorrow, a whole netful!" They called to Mario, Esquisito Mario: "*Mario, una cioccolata e biscotti!*" And this time he heeded and answered with a smile: "*Subito, signorini!*" Later we had reason to recall this kindly, if rather absent and pensive smile.

Thus the interval passed, the gong sounded. The audience, which had scattered in conversation, took their places again, the children sat up straight in their chairs with their hands in their laps. The curtain had not been dropped. Cipolla came forward again, with his dipping stride, and began to introduce the second half of the programme with a lecture.

Let me state once for all that this self-confident cripple was the most powerful hypnotist I have ever seen in my life. It was pretty plain now that he threw dust in the public eye and advertised himself as a prestidigitator on account of police regulations which would have prevented him from making his living by the exercise of his powers. Perhaps this eye-wash is the usual thing in Italy; it may be permitted or even connived at by the authorities. Certainly the man had from the beginning made little concealment of the actual nature of his operations; and this second half of the programme was quite frankly and exclusively devoted to one sort of experiment. While he still practised some rhetorical circumlocutions, the tests themselves were one long series of attacks upon the will-power, the loss or compulsion of volition. Comic, exciting, amazing by turns, by midnight they were still in full swing; we ran the gamut of all the phenomena this natural-unnatural field has to show, from the unimpressive at one end of the scale to the monstrous at the other. The audience laughed and applauded as they followed the grotesque details; shook their heads, clapped their knees, fell very frankly under the spell of this stern, self-assured personality. At the same time I saw signs that they were not quite complacent, not quite unconscious of the peculiar ignominy which lay, for the individual and for the general, in Cipolla's triumphs.

Two main features were constant in all the experiments: the liquor glass and the claw-handled riding-whip. The first was always invoked to add fuel to his demoniac fires; without it, apparently, they might have burned out. On this score we might even have felt pity for the man; but the whistle of his scourge, the insulting symbol of his domination, before which we all cowered, drowned out every sensation save a dazed and outbraved submission to his power. Did he then lay claim to our sympathy to boot? I was struck by a remark he made – it suggested no less. At the climax of his experiments, by stroking and breathing upon a certain young man who had offered himself as a subject and already proved himself a particularly susceptible one, he had not only put him into the condition known as deep trance and extended his insensible body by neck and feet across the backs of two chairs, but had actually sat down on the rigid form as on a bench, without making it yield. The sight of this unholy figure in a frock-coat squatted on the stiff body was horrible and incredible; the audience, convinced that the victim of this scientific diversion must be suffering, expressed its sympathy: "*Ah, poveretto!*" Poor soul, poor soul! "*Poor soul!*" Cipolla mocked them, with some bitterness. "Ladies and gentlemen, you are barking up the wrong tree. *Sono io il poveretto.* I am the person who is suffering, I am the one to be pitied." We pocketed the information. Very good. Maybe the experiment was at his expense, maybe it was he who had suffered the cramp when the *giovanotto* over there had made the faces. But appearances were all against it; and one does not feel like saying *poveretto* to a man who is suffering to bring about the humiliation of others.

I have got ahead of my story and lost sight of the sequence of events. To this day my mind is full of the Cavaliere's feats of endurance; only I do not recall them in their order – which does not matter. So much I do know: that the longer and more circumstantial tests, which got the most applause, impressed me less than some of the small ones which passed quickly over. I remember the young man whose body Cipolla converted into a board, only because of the accompanying remarks which I have quoted. An elderly lady in a cane-seated chair was lulled by Cipolla in the delusion that she was on a voyage to India and gave a voluble account of her adventures by land and sea. But I found this phenomenon less impressive than one which followed immediately after the intermission. A tall, well-built, soldierly man was unable to lift his arm, after the hunchback had told him that he could not and given a cut through the air with his whip. I can still see the face of that stately, mustachioed colonel smiling and clenching his teeth as he struggled to regain his lost freedom of action. A staggering performance! He seemed to be exerting his will, and in vain; the trouble, however, was probably simply that he could not will. There was involved here that recoil of the will upon itself which paralyses choice – as our tyrant had previously explained to the Roman gentleman.

Still less can I forget the touching scene, at once comic and horrible, with Signora Angiolieri. The Cavaliere, probably in his first bold survey of the room, had spied out her ethereal lack of resistance to his power. For actually he bewitched her, literally drew her out of her seat, out of her row, and away with him whither he willed. And in order to enhance his effect, he bade Signor Angiolieri call upon his wife by her name, to throw, as it were, all the weight of his existence and his rights in her into the scale, to rouse by the voice of her husband everything in his spouse's soul which could shield her virtue against the evil assaults of magic. And how vain it all was! Cipolla was standing at some distance from the couple, when he made a single cut with his whip through the air. It caused our landlady to shudder violently and turn her face towards him. "Sofronia!" cried Signor Angiolieri – we had not known that Signora Angiolieri's name was Sofronia. And he did well to call, everybody saw that there was no time to lose. His wife kept her face turned in the direction of the diabolical Cavaliere, who with his ten long yellow fingers was making passes at his victim, moving backwards as he did so, step by step. Then Signora Angiolieri, her pale face gleaming, rose up from her seat, turned right round, and began to glide after him. Fatal and forbidding sight! Her face as though moonstruck, stiff-armed, her lovely hands lifted a little at the wrists, the feet as it were together, she seemed to float slowly out of her row and after the tempter. "Call her, sir, keep on calling," prompted the redoubtable man. And Signor Angiolieri, in a weak voice, called: "Sofronia!" Ah, again and again he called; as his wife went farther off he even curved one hand round his lips and beckoned with the other as he called. But the poor voice of love and duty echoed unheard, in vain, behind the lost one's back; the signora swayed along, moonstruck, deaf, enslaved; she glided into the middle aisle and down it towards the fingering hunchback, towards the door. We were convinced, we were driven to the conviction, that she would have followed her master, had he so willed it, to the ends of the earth.

"*Accidente!*" cried out Signor Angiolieri, in genuine affright, springing up as the exit was reached. But at the same moment the Cavaliere put aside, as it were, the triumphal crown and broke off. "Enough, signora, I thank you," he said, and offered his arm to lead her back to her husband. "Signor," he greeted the latter, "here is your wife. Unharmed, with my compliments, I give her into your hands. Cherish with all the strength of your manhood a treasure which is so wholly yours, and let your zeal be quickened by knowing that there are powers stronger than reason or virtue, and not always so magnanimously ready to relinquish their prey!"

Poor Signor Angiolieri, so quiet, so bald! He did not look as though he would know how to defend his happiness, even against powers much less demoniac than these which were now adding mockery to frightfulness. Solemnly and pompously the Cavaliere retired to the stage, amid applause to which his eloquence gave double strength. It was this particular episode, I feel sure, that set the seal upon his ascendancy.

For now he made them dance, yes, literally; and the dancing lent a dissolute, abandoned, topsyturvy air to the scene, a drunken abdication of the critical spirit which had so long resisted the spell of this man. Yes, he had had to fight to get the upper hand – for instance against the animosity of the young Roman gentleman, whose rebellious spirit threatened to serve others as a rallying-point. But it was precisely upon the importance of example that the Cavaliere was so strong. He had the wit to make his attack at the weakest point and to choose as his first victim that feeble, ecstatic youth whom he had previously made into a board. The master had but to look at him, when this young man would fling himself back as though struck by lightning, place his hands rigidly at his sides, and fall into a state of military somnambulism, in which it was plain to any eye that he was open to the most absurd suggestion that might be made to him. He seemed quite content in his abject state, quite pleased to be relieved of the burden of voluntary choice. Again and again he offered himself as a subject and gloried in the model facility he had in losing consciousness. So now he mounted the platform, and a single cut of the whip was enough to make him dance to the Cavaliere's orders, in a kind of complacent ecstasy, eyes closed, head nodding, lank limbs flying in all directions.

It looked unmistakably like enjoyment, and other recruits were not long in coming forward: two other young men, one humbly and one well dressed, were soon jigging alongside the first. But now the gentleman from Rome bobbed up again, asking defiantly if the Cavaliere would engage to make him dance too, even against his will.

"Even against your will," answered Cipolla, in unforgettable accents. That frightful "*anche se non vuole*" still rings in my ears. The struggle began. After Cipolla had taken another little glass and lighted a fresh cigarette he stationed the Roman at a point in the middle aisle and himself took up a position some distance behind him, making his whip whistle through the air as he gave the order: "*Balla!*" His opponent did not stir. "*Balla!*" repeated the Cavaliere incisively, and snapped his whip. You saw the young man move his neck round in his collar; at the same time one hand lifted slightly at the wrist, one ankle turned outward. But that was all, for the time at least; merely a tendency to twitch, now sternly repressed, now seeming about to get the upper hand. It escaped nobody that here a heroic obstinacy, a fixed resolve to resist, must needs be conquered; we were beholding a gallant effort to strike out and save the honour of the human race. He twitched but danced not; and the struggle was so prolonged that the Cavaliere had to divide his attention between it and the stage, turning now and then to make his riding-whip whistle in the direction of the dancers, as it were to keep them in leash. At the same time he advised the audience that no fatigue was involved in such activities, however long they went on, since it was not the automatons up there who danced, but himself. Then once more his eye would bore itself into the back of the Roman's neck and lay siege to the strength of purpose which defied him.

One saw it waver, that strength of purpose, beneath the repeated summons and whip-crackings. Saw with an objective interest which yet was not quite free from traces of sympathetic emotion – from pity, even from a cruel kind of pleasure. If I understand what was going on, it was the negative character of the young man's fighting position which was his undoing. It is likely that *not* willing is not a practicable state of mind; *not* to want to do something may be in the long run a mental content impossible to subsist on. Between not willing a certain thing and not willing at all – in other words, yielding to another person's will – there may lie too small a space for the idea of freedom to squeeze into. Again, there were the Cavaliere's persuasive words, woven in among the whip-crackings and commands, as he mingled effects that were his own secret with others of a bewilderingly psychological kind. "*Balla!*" said he. "Who wants to torture himself like that? Is forcing yourself your idea of freedom? *Una ballatina!* Why, your arms and legs are aching for it. What a relief to give way to them – there, you are dancing already!

That is no struggle any more, it is a pleasure!" And so it was. The jerking and twitching of the refractory youth's limbs had at last got the upper hand; he lifted his arms, then his knees, his joints quite suddenly relaxed, he flung his legs and danced, and amid bursts of applause the Cavaliere led him to join the row of puppets on the stage. Up there we could see his face as he "enjoyed" himself; it was clothed in a broad grin and the eyes were half-shut. In a way, it was consoling to see that he was having a better time than he had had in the hour of his pride.

His "fall" was, I may say, an epoch. The ice was completely broken, Cipolla's triumph had reached its height. The Circe's wand, that whistling leather whip with the claw handle, held absolute sway. At one time – it must have been well after midnight – not only were there eight or ten persons dancing on the little stage, but in the hall below a varied animation reigned, and a long-toothed Anglo-Saxoness in a pince-nez left her seat of her own motion to perform a tarantella in the centre aisle. Cipolla was lounging in a cane-seated chair at the left of the stage, gulping down the smoke of a cigarette and breathing it impudently out through his bad teeth. He tapped his foot and shrugged his shoulders, looking down upon the abandoned scene in the hall; now and then he snapped his whip backwards at a laggard upon the stage. The children were awake at the moment. With shame I speak of them. For it was not good to be here, least of all for them; that we had not taken them away can only be explained by saying that we had caught the general devil-may-careness of the hour. By that time it was all one. Anyhow, thank goodness, they lacked understanding for the disreputable side of the entertainment, and in their innocence were perpetually charmed by the unheard-of indulgence which permitted them to be present at such a thing as a magician's "evening". Whole quarter-hours at a time they drowsed on our laps, waking refreshed and rosy-cheeked, with sleep-drunken eyes, to laugh to bursting at the leaps and jumps the magician made those people up there make. They had not thought it would be so jolly; they joined with their clumsy little hands in every round of applause. And jumped for joy upon their chairs, as was their wont, when Cipolla beckoned to their friend Mario from the Esquisito, beckoned to him just like a picture in a book, holding his hand in front of his nose and bending and straightening the forefinger by turns.

Mario obeyed. I can see him now going up the stairs to Cipolla, who continued to beckon him, in that droll, picture-book sort of way. He hesitated for a moment at first; that, too, I recall quite clearly. During the whole evening he had lounged against a wooden pillar at the side entrance, with his arms folded, or else with his hands thrust into his jacket pockets. He was on our left, near the youth with the militant hair, and had followed the performance attentively, so far as we had seen, if with no particular animation and God knows how much comprehension. He could not much relish being summoned thus, at the end of the evening. But it was only too easy to see why he obeyed. After all, obedience was his calling in life; and then, how should a simple lad like him find it within his human capacity to refuse compliance to a man so throned and crowned as Cipolla at that hour? Willy-nilly he left his column and with a word of thanks to those making way for him he mounted the steps with a doubtful smile on his full lips.

Picture a thick-set youth of twenty years, with clipped hair, a low forehead, and heavy-lidded eyes of an indefinite grey, shot with green and yellow. These things I knew from having spoken with him, as we often had. There was a saddle of freckles on the flat nose, the whole upper half of the face retreated behind the lower, and that again was dominated by thick lips that parted to show the salivated teeth. These thick lips and the veiled look of the eyes lent the whole face a primitive melancholy – it was that which had drawn us to him from the first. In it was not the faintest trace of brutality – indeed, his hands would have given the lie to such an idea, being unusually slender and delicate for a southerner. They were hands by which one liked being served.

We knew him humanly without knowing him personally, if

I may make that distinction. We saw him nearly every day, and felt a certain kindness for his dreamy ways, which might at times be actual inattentiveness, suddenly transformed into a redeeming zeal to serve. His mien was serious, only the children could bring a smile to his face. It was not sulky, but uningratiating, without intentional effort to please – or, rather, it seemed to give up being pleasant in the conviction that it could not succeed. We should have remembered Mario in any case, as one of those homely recollections of travel which often stick in the mind better than more important ones. But of his circumstances we knew no more than that his father was a petty clerk in the Municipio and his mother took in washing.

His white waiter's-coat became him better than the faded striped suit he wore, with a gay coloured scarf instead of a collar, the ends tucked into his jacket. He neared Cipolla, who however did not leave off that motion of his finger before his nose, so that Mario had to come still closer, right up to the chair-seat and the master's legs. Whereupon the latter spread out his elbows and seized the lad, turning him so that we had a view of his face. Then gazed him briskly up and down, with a careless, commanding eye.

"Well, *ragazzo mio*, how comes it we make acquaintance so late in the day? But believe me, I made yours long ago. Yes, yes, I've had you in my eye this long while and known what good stuff you were made of. How could I go and forget you again? Well, I've had a good deal to think about.... Now tell me, what is your name? The first name, that's all I want."

"My name is Mario," the young man answered, in a low voice.

"Ah, Mario. Very good. Yes, yes, there is such a name, quite a common name, a classic name too, one of those which preserve the heroic traditions of the Fatherland. *Bravo! Salve!*" And he flung up his arm slantingly above his crooked shoulder, palm outward, in the Roman salute. He may have been slightly tipsy by now, and no wonder; but he spoke as before, clearly, fluently, and with emphasis. Though about this time there had crept into his voice a gross, autocratic note, and a kind of arrogance was in his sprawl.

"Well, now, Mario *mio*," he went on, "it's a good thing you came this evening, and that's a pretty scarf you've got on; it is becoming to your style of beauty. It must stand you in good stead with the girls, the pretty pretty girls of Torre –"

From the row of youths, close by the place where Mario had been standing, sounded a laugh. It came from the youth with the militant hair. He stood there, his jacket over his shoulder, and laughed outright, rudely and scornfully.

Mario gave a start. I think it was a shrug, but he may have started and then hastened to cover the movement by shrugging his shoulders, as much as to say that the neckerchief and the fair sex were matters of equal indifference to him.

The Cavaliere gave a downward glance.

"We needn't trouble about him," he said. "He is jealous, because your scarf is so popular with the girls, maybe partly because you and I are so friendly up here. Perhaps he'd like me to put him in mind of his colic – I could do it free of charge. Tell me, Mario. You've come here this evening for a bit of fun – and in the daytime you work in an ironmonger's shop?"

"In a café," corrected the youth.

"Oh, in a café. That's where Cipolla nearly came a cropper! What you are is a cup-bearer, a Ganymede – I like that, it is another classical allusion – *Salvietta!*" Again the Cavaliere saluted, to the huge gratification of his audience.

Mario smiled too. "But before that," he interpolated, in the interest of accuracy, "I worked for a while in a shop in Portoclemente." He seemed visited by a natural desire to assist the prophecy by dredging out its essential features.

"There, didn't I say so? In an ironmonger's shop?"

"They kept combs and brushes," Mario got round it.

"Didn't I say that you were not always a Ganymede? Not always at the sign of the serviette? Even when Cipolla makes a mistake, it is a kind that makes you believe in him. Now tell me: Do you believe in me?"

An indefinite gesture.

"A half-way answer," commented the Cavaliere. "Probably it is not easy to win your confidence. Even for me, I can see, it is not so easy. I see in your features a reserve, a sadness, *un tratto di malinconia* . . . tell me" (he seized Mario's hand persuasively), "have you troubles?"

"*Nossignore*," answered Mario, promptly and decidedly.

"You *have* troubles," insisted the Cavaliere, bearing down the denial by the weight of his authority. "Can't I see? Trying to pull the wool over Cipolla's eyes, are you? Of course, about the girls – it is a girl, isn't it? You have love troubles?"

Mario gave a vigorous head-shake. And again the *giovanotto*'s brutal laugh rang out. The Cavaliere gave heed. His eyes were roving about somewhere in the air; but he cocked an ear to the sound, then swung his whip backwards, as he had once or twice before in his conversation with Mario, that none of his puppets might flag in their zeal. The gesture had nearly cost him his new prey: Mario gave a sudden start in the direction of the steps. But Cipolla had him in his clutch.

"Not so fast," said he. "That would be fine, wouldn't it? So you want to skip, do you, Ganymede, right in the middle of the fun, or, rather, when it is just beginning? Stay with me, I'll show you something nice. I'll convince you. You have no reason to worry, I promise you. This girl – you know her and others know her too – what's her name? Wait! I read the name in your eyes, it is on the tip of my tongue and yours too – "

"Silvestra!" shouted the *giovanotto* from below.

The Cavaliere's face did not change.

"Aren't there the forward people?" he asked, not looking down, more as in undisturbed converse with Mario. "Aren't there the young fighting-cocks that crow in season and out? Takes the word out of your mouth, the conceited fool, and seems to think he has some special right to it. Let him be. But Silvestra, your Silvestra – ah, what a girl that is! What a prize! Brings your heart into your mouth to see her walk or laugh or breathe, she is so lovely. And her round arms when she washes, and tosses her head back to get the hair out of her eyes! An angel from paradise!"

Mario stared at him, his head thrust forward. He seemed to have forgotten the audience, forgotten where he was. The red rings round his eyes had got larger, they looked as though they were painted on. His thick lips parted.

"And she makes you suffer, this angel," went on Cipolla, "or, rather, you make yourself suffer for her – there is a difference, my lad, a most important difference, let me tell you. There are misunderstandings in love, maybe nowhere else in the world are there so many. I know what you are thinking: what does this Cipolla, with his little physical defect, know about love? Wrong, all wrong, he knows a lot. He has a wide and powerful understanding of its workings, and it pays to listen to his advice. But let's leave Cipolla out, cut him out altogether and think only of Silvestra, your peerless Silvestra! What! Is she to give any young gamecock the preference, so that he can laugh while you cry? To prefer him to a chap like you, so full of feeling and so sympathetic? Not very likely, is it? It is impossible – we know better, Cipolla and she. If I were to put myself in her place and choose between the two of you, a tarry lout like that – a codfish, a sea-urchin – and a Mario, a knight of the serviette, who moves among gentlefolk and hands round refreshments with an air – my word, but my heart would speak in no uncertain tones – it knows to whom I gave it long ago. It is time that he should see and understand, my chosen one! It is time that you see me and recognize me, Mario, my beloved! Tell me, who am I?"

It was grisly, the way the betrayer made himself irresistible, wreathed and coquetted with his crooked shoulder, languished with the puffy eyes, and showed his splintered teeth in a sickly smile. And alas, at his beguiling words, what was come of our Mario? It is hard for me to tell, hard as it was for me to see; for here was nothing less than an utter abandonment of the inmost soul, a public exposure of timid and deluded passion and rapture. He put his hands across his mouth, his shoulders rose and fell with his pantings. He could not, it was plain, trust his eyes and ears for joy, and the one thing he forgot was precisely that he could not trust them. "Silvestra!" he breathed, from the very depths of his vanquished heart.

"Kiss me!" said the hunchback. "Trust me, I love thee. Kiss me here." And with the tip of his index finger, hand, arm, and little finger outspread, he pointed to his cheek, near the mouth. And Mario bent and kissed him.

It had grown very still in the room. That was a monstrous moment, grotesque and thrilling, the moment of Mario's bliss. In that evil span of time, crowded with a sense of the illusiveness of all joy, one sound became audible, and that not quite at once, but on the instant of the melancholy and ribald meeting between Mario's lips and the repulsive flesh which thrust itself forward for his caress. It was the sound of a laugh, from the *giovanotto* on our left. It broke into the dramatic suspense of the moment, coarse, mocking, and yet – or I must have been grossly mistaken – with an undertone of compassion for the poor bewildered, victimized creature. It had a faint ring of that "*Poveretto*" which Cipolla had declared was wasted on the wrong person, when he claimed the pity for his own.

The laugh still rang in the air when the recipient of the caress gave his whip a little swish, low down, close to his chair-leg, and Mario started up and flung himself back. He stood in that posture staring, his hands one over the other on those desecrated lips. Then he beat his temples with his clenched fists, over and over; turned and staggered down the steps, while the audience applauded, and Cipolla sat there with his hands in his lap, his shoulders shaking. Once below, and even while in full retreat, Mario hurled himself round with legs flung wide apart; one arm flew up, and two flat shattering detonations crashed through applause and laughter.

There was instant silence. Even the dancers came to a full stop and stared about, struck dumb. Cipolla bounded from his seat. He stood with his arms spread out, slanting as though to ward everybody off, as though next moment he would cry out: "Stop! Keep back! Silence! What was that?" Then, in that instant, he sank back in his seat, his head rolling on his chest; in the next he had fallen sideways to the floor, where he lay motionless, a huddled heap of clothing, with limbs awry.

The commotion was indescribable. Ladies hid their faces, shuddering, on the breasts of their escorts. There were shouts for a doctor, for the police. People flung themselves on Mario in a mob, to disarm him, to take away the weapon that hung from his fingers – that small, dull-metal, scarcely pistol-shaped tool with hardly any barrel – in how strange and unexpected a direction had fate levelled it!

And now – now finally, at last – we took the children and led them towards the exit, past the pair of *carabinieri* just entering. Was that the end, they wanted to know, that they might go in peace? Yes, we assured them, that was the end. An end of horror, a fatal end. And yet a liberation – for I could not, and I cannot, but find it so!

THE TRANSPOSED HEADS

I

THE STORY of Sita of the beautiful hips, daughter of the cattle-breeder Sumantra of the warrior caste, and of her two husbands (if one may put it like that) is so sanguinary, so amazing to the senses, that it makes the greatest demands on the hearer's strength of mind and his power to resist the gruesome guiles of Maya. It would be well for the listener to take pattern from the fortitude of the teller, for it requires, if anything, more courage to tell such a tale than to hear it. But here it is, from first to last, just as it fell out:

At the time when memory mounted in the mind of man, as the vessel of sacrifice slowly fills up from the bottom with drink or with blood; when the womb of stern patriarchal piety opened to the seed of the primeval past, nostalgia for the Mother reinvested with new shudderings the ancient images and swelled the number of pilgrims thronging in the spring to the shrines of the great World-Nurse; at such a time it was that two youths, little different in age and caste, but very unlike in body, were vowed to friendship. The younger was named Nanda, the somewhat elder Shridaman. The first was eighteen years old, the second already one-and-twenty; both, each on his proper day, had been girt with the sacred cord and received into the company of the twice-born. Their homes were in the temple village called Welfare of Cows, which had been settled in time past on a sign from the gods in its place in the land of Kosala. It was surrounded by a cactus hedge and a wooden wall; its gates, facing the four points of the compass, had been blessed by a wandering wise man and familiar of the goddess Speech – who uttered no unrighteous word, and had been given to eat in the village – with the blessing that its door-posts and lintels should drop fatness and honey.

The friendship between the two youths was based on the diversity in their I- and my-feelings, those of the one yearning towards those of the other. Incorporation, that is, makes for isolation, isolation for difference; difference makes for comparisons, comparisons give rise to uneasiness, uneasiness to wonderment, wonderment tends to admiration; and finally admiration turns to a yearning for mutual exchange and unity. *Etad vai tad*. This is that. And the doctrine applies especially in youth, when the clay of life is still soft and the I- and my-feelings not yet hardened into the conflicts of the single personality.

Young Shridaman was a merchant, and the son of a merchant; Nanda, on the other hand, both a smith and cowherd, for his father Garga not only kept cattle on the meadow and in the byre, but also plied the hammer and fanned the fire with a feather fan. As for Shridaman's sire, Bhavabhuti by name, he traced his line on the male side from a Brahman stock versed in the Vedas, which Garga and his son were far from doing. Still, they were no Sudras, and although somewhat goat-nosed, were quite distinctly members of human society. Anyhow, for Shridaman, and even for Bhavabhuti, the Brahman way of life was only a memory, for Bhavabhuti's father had deliberately abandoned it at the stage of householder, which follows that of student, and never gone on to be either forest hermit or ascetic to the end of his days. He had scorned to live only on gifts from pious respecters of his knowledge of the Vedas, perhaps he had not been content with these; for he had opened up a good business in mull, silk and calico, camphor and sandalwood. And his son in his turn, though begotten for the service of the gods, had become a vanija or merchant in the village of Welfare of Cows, and Bhavabhuti's son Shridaman followed in his father's footsteps, after having previously devoted some years to grammar and the elements of astronomy and ontology, under the supervision of a guru or spiritual preceptor.

Not so Nanda, son of Garga. His karma was otherwise; and never, either by tradition or by inheritance, had he had to do with things of the mind. No, he was just as he was, a son of the people, simple and blithe, a Krishna-manifestation, dark of skin and hair; he even had the "lucky-calf" lock on his breast. His work as a smith had made powerful his arms; that as a shepherd had been further an advantage, for he had a well-set-up body, which he loved to rub with mustard oil and drape with gold ornaments and chains of wild flowers. There was harmony between it and the pleasant beardless face, despite the rather thick lips and the suggestion of a goat-nose; even these were attractive in their way, and his black eyes almost always wore a laugh.

Shridaman very much liked all this, comparing it with himself, who was several shades lighter in both head and limbs, with a face too quite otherwise shaped. The ridge of his nose was thin as a blade; eyes he had, soft of pupil and lid, and on his cheeks a soft fan-shaped beard. Soft too were his limbs, not moulded by exercise as cowherd and smith, even rather Brahman-like, as well as clerkly, with a rather soft, narrow breast and some fat on the little belly, but otherwise flawless, with fine knee-joints and feet. It was a body proper to serve as adjunct and appendage to a noble and knowledgeable head-piece, that was of course head and front of the whole, whereas with the whole Nanda the body was, so to speak, the main thing, and the head merely a pleasing appendage. All in all the two were like Siva in his double manifestation, lying sometimes as dead, a bearded ascetic, at the feet of the goddess, but sometimes erect, a figure in the bloom of youth, stretching his young limbs as he turns towards her.

But after all they were not one like Siva, who is life and death, world and eternity in the Mother, but manifested as two entities here below; thus they were to each other like images. The my-feeling of each was tired of itself, and though each was aware that after all everything consists of what it has not got, yet on account of their very differences they intrigued each other. The fine-lipped, soft-bearded Shridaman found pleasure in the rude primeval Krishna-nature of the thick-lipped Nanda; while he, partly flattered, but partly and even more, because he felt impressed by Shridaman's light complexion, his noble head-piece and correct diction – all that, of course, being from the beginning of things inseparable from wisdom and philosophy, and one with these – on his side knew nothing more lovely than intercourse with Shridaman; thus it was they became fast friends. Certainly in the inclination of each for the other some slight humour inhered; Nanda privately made fun of Shridaman's plumpness and blondness, his thin nose and punctilious speech. Shridaman, on the other hand, smiled at Nanda's goat-nose and rustic simplicity. This sort of private criticism is a common feature of the uneasiness born of comparison; it is a tribute to the I- and my-feeling, and does no least violence to the Maya longing born of the same.

2

Well, then, it came about that in the lovely springtime, when the air was full of the song of birds, Nanda and Shridaman took a walking-tour together through the country, each on his own occasions. Nanda had from his father Garga the task of buying a certain quantity of black ore from a community of humble folk, clad only in reed aprons, who were skilful smelters and with whom Nanda knew how to talk. These folk dwelt in mud huts some days' journey from the friends' village, and nearer the town of Kurukshetra, which, in its turn, was somewhat north of the thickly populated Indraprastha, on the river Jumna. Here Shridaman's errand lay, with a business friend of the family, himself a Brahman who had not got farther than the stage of householder. With this man Shridaman was to barter to the best advantage some fine-coloured cloths woven by the village women at home, for some rice-mallets and a particularly practical kind of tinder, of which there was need at Welfare of Cows.

They had travelled a day and a half, on peopled highways and through empty woods and wastes, each bearing his fardel on his back: Nanda a box of betel-nuts, cowrie-shells, and alta-red on bast paper to redden the soles of the feet, for with these he thought to pay the humble folk for their ore; Shridaman his cloths sewed up in a doeskin. Nanda out of sheer friendliness carried the other's burden too, from time to time. They came now to a bathing-place, sacred to Kali, the All-Embracing, Mother of the worlds and of all beings, who is the dream-drunkenness of Vishnu. It lay on the stream Goldfly, which rushes, like a colt let loose, out of the mountain's womb, to moderate its flow and unite at a holy place with the river Jumna; that in its turn issuing, at a place yet more holy, into the eternal Ganges. But the Ganges flows by its many mouths into the sea. Many bathing-places of high repute, which cleanse all defilement, where one drawing up the water of life and plunging into its bosom may receive new birth – many such stand on the banks and mouths of the Ganges, and at the junction of other rivers with the terrestrial Milky Way, as at the point where Goldfly, little daughter of the snows, joins with the Jumna. Everywhere in this region, in short, such shrines and sites of purification abound, convenient to all for sacrifice and communion. They are provided with consecrated steps, so that the pious need not plump awkwardly and irreligiously through reed and lotus into the water, but may step down in dignity to drink and to lave themselves.

Now, this bathing-place the friends had hit on was not one of the larger ones, full of offerings, renowned for its miracles, and thronged by noble and simple, though at different hours. No, it was a quiet, retired little spot, not a meeting of rivers, just somewhere on the river-bank, which at that point climbed above the bed of the Goldfly. On the top of the bank stood the little temple, built simply of wood and already somewhat rickety though carved in pleasing designs. It was the temple of the Mistress of all desires and joys, with a bulbous tower above the cella. The steps leading to the spring were wooden too and rather broken, yet good enough for a dignified descent.

The youths expressed their pleasure at having hit on this spot, which gave them opportunity for worship, refreshment, and rest in the shade. It was already very hot at mid-day; the heavy summer threatened untimely, and at the sides of the little temple the growth of mangoes, teak and kadamba trees, magnolias, tamarisks, and tala palms made shelter where it would be good to rest and breakfast. The friends first performed their religious duties, as well as circumstances permitted. There was no priest from whom to purchase oil or clarified butter to anoint the stone linga images on the little terrace before the temple. They found a ladle, scooped up water from the river, and did their pious service, murmuring the appropriate words. Then they descended, cupping their hands, into the green river-bed; drank, poured the ritual water, dipped, and gave thanks. Out of pure enjoyment they stopped in the water a little longer than the spiritually requisite time; then, feeling in all their limbs the blessing of purification, returned to the resting-place they had selected under the trees.

Here like brothers they shared their bite, though one had no different from the other, and each might have eaten his own. When Nanda broke a barley cake, he handed half of it to Shridaman saying: "There, old fellow." Shridaman, dividing a piece of fruit, gave half to Nanda with the same words. Shridaman sat to eat, sideways to his food, knees and feet together, in the grass that was here still green and unsinged. Nanda squatted rustically with his knees up and feet in front of him, as one cannot long sit without being born to it. They took up these attitudes unconsciously and without thought; if they had paid heed to the manner of their sitting, Shridaman, out of sheer inclination to the primitive, would have sat with his knees up and Nanda put himself sideways in the contrary desire. He wore a little cap on his sleek black hair, still wet from the bath; a loincloth of white cotton cloth, rings on his upper arms, and round his neck a necklace of stone-pearls held together with gold bands. Through it one could see the "lucky-calf" lock on his breast. Shridaman had a white cloth wound around his head and wore his white cotton short-sleeved smock falling over his full draped apron, that hung like trousers. In the neck-opening of the smock there showed an amulet-pouch on a thin chain. Both wore the sign of their faith painted in mineral-white on their foreheads.

When they had eaten they put aside the remnants and talked. It was so delightful here that princes and kings could not have fared better. Between the tall stems of calamus and bamboo, whose foliage and clusters of blossoms made a light rustling, they could see the pool and the lower steps going down to it. Clinging water-plants made charming garlands from bough to bough. The chirping and trilling of unseen birds mingled with the humming of insects that darted to and fro returning ever and anon to the flowering grasses. The cool freshness and warm breath of all these plants perfumed the air; there was the headiness of the jasmine, the peculiar scent of the tala-fruit; sandalwood and mustard oil – Nanda had anointed himself with this last after the ritual of the bath.

"Here we seem to be beyond the six waves of hunger and thirst, age and death, suffering and blindness," said Shridaman. "It is extraordinarily peaceful. It is as though we were moved from the restless whirl of life and placed in its motionless centre where we can draw a long breath. Hark! How cosy and hushed it is here! I use the word 'hushed' because we say hush when we want to listen; and listening can only properly be done where there is a hush. It lets us listen to everything in it which is not entirely still, so that the stillness speaks as in a dream and we hear it too as though we were dreaming."

"It is verily true as thy word sayeth," responded Nanda. "In the noise of the marketplace one does not listen; that is only done where there is a hush that even so holds this and that to listen to. Quite soundless, filled with silence, is only Nirvana, and so you could never call it hushed, nor yet cosy."

"No," answered Shridaman, and could not help laughing. "It has probably not occurred to anyone to call Nirvana hushed, and certainly not cosy; yet you do it, in a sort of way, if only by negation, when you say that one cannot do it; and so you find out the funniest of all the negations – for only so can Nirvana be spoken of, of course – that could ever be uttered about it. You do say such shrewd things sometimes, if

I may use the word 'shrewd' about something which is at once absurd and perfectly correct. I like it very much, sometimes it makes my diaphragm contract suddenly, almost like a sob. Thus we see how close together are laughing and weeping; so that it is an illusion to make any distinction between pleasure and pain, and like the one and hate the other, when, after all, both can be called good and both bad. But there is a combination of laughter and tears which one can most readily assent to and call good among all things that move us in life. We have a word for it, we call it touching; it has to do with sympathy on the cheerful side, and is just what makes the contraction of my diaphragm so much like a sob. And it is that that hurts me about your shrewdness."

"But why does it hurt you?" Nanda asked.

"Because after all you are actually a child of Samsara and thus completely taken up with life," answered Shridaman; "you do not belong among the souls who feel the need to emerge above the frightful ocean of laughing and weeping as lotus flowers rise above the surface of the stream and open their cups to the sky. You are perfectly at home in the depths, where such a complex profusion and variety of shapes and forms exist. You are well off, and that is why one feels good at the sight of you. Then you suddenly get the idea in your head to meddle with Nirvana and talk about its negative condition and how it cannot be called hushed nor cosy, and all that is funny enough to make one weep, or, to use the word made on purpose, it is touching, because it makes me grieve for that well-being of yours that is so good to see."

"But listen to me," countered Nanda. "I don't understand. You might be sorry I am so taken up with Samsara and cannot go in for being a lotus. That is all right. But to be hurt because I try to take an interest in Nirvana, as well as I can – that might not be so good. You have hurt me too, let me tell you."

"And how so?" Shridaman asked.

"Because you have read the Vedas and learned about the nature of being," replied Nanda, "but even so you are more easily blinded by Samsara than people who have not. That is what really tickles me; it gives me, as you say, a feeling of sympathy on the cheerful side. It is more or less hushed in this spot where we are; so you let yourself go on about being beyond the six waves of hunger and thirst, and think you are in life's resting centre. And yet all the hush, and all the things you can listen to in it, are just a sign that there is a lot going on and your notions about peace and quiet are just notions. The birds coo because they are making love; all these bees and bugs and cockchafers are darting about in search of food; the grass is alive with sounds of life-and-death struggles we cannot hear. The very vines so tenderly embracing the trees would like to strangle them to take their sap and air to batten on. And there you have the true knowledge of life."

"I know it well," Shridaman said, "I do not blind myself to it, or at least only for the moment and because I want to. For there is not only the truth and knowledge of the understanding, but also the insight of the human heart, which sees as in an allegory and knows how to read the hand-writing of all phenomena, not only in its first and simple sense but also in its second and higher one, using it as a means whereby to look through at the pure and spiritual. How will you arrive at a perception of peace, and feel the joy of a cessation from conflict, unless you have a Maya-image to give you a hold on it – though in itself a Maya-image is by no means peace and joy! It is granted and vouchsafed to man to make actuality serve him to see the truth by; language has coined the word 'poetry' to express this boon."

"Ah, so that is what you think," laughed Nanda. "According to that, and if one listens to you, poetry would also be the stupidity that comes after the cleverness, and, suppose a man is stupid, it is in order to ask whether he is still being stupid or being stupid again. I must say, you clever ones do not make it easy for the likes of us. We think the point is to become clever; but before one reaches it, one finds out the real point is to become stupid again. You ought not to show us the new and higher stages, for fear we lose courage to climb the first ones."

"From me," said Shridaman, "you have not heard that one must be clever. Come, let us stretch out in the soft grass after our meal and look through the branches of the trees into the sky. It is such a wonderful thing to look from a station which does not actually oblige us to look up, because the eyes are already directed upwards, and to see the sky in the way that Mother Earth sees it."

"Siya, be it so," Nanda agreed.

"Siyat!" Shridaman corrected him, in the pure tongue. Nanda laughed at himself and them both.

"Siyat, Siyat!" he repeated. "Hair-splitter, leave me my lingo! When I speak Sanskrit it sounds like the snuffling of a young heifer with a rope through her nose."

At this bucolic simile Shridaman too laughed heartily; and they stretched themselves out as he had said and looked straight up through the swaying boughs and flowering bushes into the blue of Vishnu's heaven, waving broken-off branches to protect themselves from the red-and-white flies, called Children of Indra, that came to settle on their skins. Nanda had lain down, not because he cared in particular to look at the sky as Mother Earth did, merely out of good nature. He soon sat up again and assumed his Dravidian attitude, with a flower in his mouth.

"The Child of Indra is a confounded nuisance," he said, speaking of the darting host of flies as one and the same individual. "Probably he is attracted by my good mustard oil. Or it might be he has orders from his protector the elephant-rider, lord of the thunderbolt, the great god, to torment us as punishment – you know already why."

"That should not affect you," responded Shridaman; "for you voted under the tree that Indra's thanksgiving feast last autumn should be celebrated in the old or shall we rather say in the newer way, according to the ritual and the Brahmanic observance; you can wash your hands of the rest, even if we did afterwards in council decide otherwise and give Indra notice that we were turning to a newer or rather an older thanksgiving service, one which seems more natural to the religious feeling of us village folk than the patter of the Brahman service for Indra the Thunderer, who burst the strongholds of the aborigines."

"Certainly, as thy word sayeth, so is it," replied Nanda. "For my part, I still have an uncanny feeling, for even when I gave my voice under the tree for Indra, I was afraid he might not bother himself about such small matters and would just make all of us generally responsible for being done out of his feast at Welfare of Cows. Then it occurs to the people and comes into their heads, I don't know from where, that the Indra thanksgiving service is no longer the right thing, at least not for us shepherds and farmers, and we must think about pious simplification. What, said they, have we to do with the great Indra? The Brahmans, with their knowledge of the Vedas, may pay their homage with endless repetitions. As for us, we will sacrifice to the cows and mountains and forest meadows because they are our true and proper deities. And it seems to us that is what we had done before Indra came, who preceded the Coming One, and burst the strongholds of the primitive inhabitants; and even though we no longer rightly know what is to be done, yet it will come to us, and our hearts shall teach us. We will pay homage to our Bright Peak and its pastures, in our own countryside, with pious rites which are in so far new that we shall have to look for them in our hearts, remember and fetch them out again. To Bright Peak will we sacrifice the perfect of the herd, to him bring offerings of sour milk, flowers, fruit, and uncooked rice. Afterwards the herd of cows, wearing garlands of autumn flowers, shall rove over the mountain turning to him their right flanks, and the steers shall bellow to him with the thunder-voice of clouds heavy with rain. And that shall be our mountain worship, new and old. But in order that the Brahmans may have naught against it, we will feast them to the number of many hundreds; and from all the herds we will collect milk so that they can eat their fill of curds and rice-milk, and so may they be content. Thus spake some of those under the tree, and some agreed with them, but others did not. I voted from the first against the mountain rites, for I had great fear and reverence for Indra, who broke the strongholds of the blacks; and I do not hold with reviving things that nobody any longer rightly knows. But you spoke and uttered pure and right words – I mean right in respect to the language – in favour of the new form of the feast and for the renewal of the mountain rites over Indra's head, and so I was silent. For I thought: when those who have gone to school and learned something about the nature of being, speak against Indra and in favour of simplification, then we others can have nothing to say, we can only hope that the great Comer and Breaker of strongholds will have some judgment and be satisfied with the feeding of multitudes of Brahmans, so that he does not afflict us with drought or overwhelm us with rains. Perhaps, I thought, he is tired of his feast himself and thinks it would be more fun to have the mountain sacrifice and the procession of cows instead. We simple ones had great reverence for him; but perhaps he has not so much for himself these days. In the end I very much liked the revived rite and enjoyed helping to drive the garlanded cows about the mountain. Yet I will say, when you corrected my Prakrit and wanted me to say Siyat, it struck me again how strange it is that you are using your correct and cultured speech in the interest of simplification."

"You have no ground to reproach me," Shridaman answered, "for you yourself have been using the popular tongue to uphold the Brahman rites. You probably took pleasure in it. But let me tell you: there is far more pleasure in using correct and cultured words to support the claims of simplicity."

3

They were silent for a while. Shridaman still lay as he was and gazed up into the sky. Nanda held his muscular arms clasped round his knees and looked between the trees down the slope towards the bathing-place of Mother Kali.

"Sh-h! Thunder and lightning! Bolts and blazes!" he whispered all of a sudden, and laid his finger to his thick lips.

"Shridaman, brother, sit up and look very quietly. Going down to bathe, I mean. Open your eyes, it's worth the trouble! She cannot see us, but we can see her."

A young girl stood at the lonely shrine, about to perform the ritual of the bath. She had laid her sari and bodice on the steps and stood there quite nude, save only for some beads round her neck, her swaying ear-rings, and a white ribbon round her thick hair. The loveliness of her body was dazzling. Made of Maya it seemed, and of the most enchanting tint, neither too dark nor too pale, and more like a bronze with golden lights. Gloriously formed she was, after the thoughts of Brahma, with the sweetest childish shoulders, and hips deliciously curved, making a spacious pelvic cavity, with maidenly firm, budlike breasts and splendidly spreading buttocks that narrowed above to the smallest, most tender back. How supplely it curved, as she raised her slender arms and clasped her hands at the back of her neck, so that the delicate armpits showed darkly! In all this the most striking thing, the most adequately representative of Brahma's thoughts – yet without prejudice to the dazzling sweetness of the breasts, which must infallibly win over any soul to the life of sense – was the conjunction of this magnificent rear with the slimness and pliant suppleness of a back of elfin delicacy. By way of emphasis was the other contrast, between the splendid swing of the hips – this of itself worthy of a whole pæan of praise – and the dainty attenuation round the waist. Just such a shape must have had the heavenly maid Pramlocha, sent by Indra to the ascetic Kandu to wean him from his austerity lest he attain to divine power.

"Let us withdraw," Shridaman said, as he sat up, his eyes resting on the maiden's form. "It is not right that she sees us not, yet we see her."

"Why not?" answered Nanda in a whisper. "We were here first, to enjoy the peace and the hush; and whatever else may come along, we cannot help it. We will not stir; it would be cruel if we made off, crackling the bushes, and she learned she had been seen while she saw not. I look with pleasure – you do not? Your eyes are red, as when you recite texts from the Rig-Veda."

"Be quiet!" Shridaman admonished him in turn. "And be serious. This is a serious, a sacred sight; that we look on at it is only excusable if we do it with serious and pious minds."

"Yes, of course," answered Nanda. "Certainly such a thing is no joke; but say what you like, it is a pleasure. You wanted to look into the sky from the flat earth. Now you see one can sometimes see into heaven only by standing up and looking straight ahead."

They were silent awhile, moved not at all, and looked. The gold-bronze maid did as they had done a little before, laid her cupped palms together and prayed, before descending to her purification.

They saw her a little from one side, so it did not escape them that not only her body but her face as well, between the hanging ear-rings, was of the rarest sweetness: little nose, lips, brows, and especially the long slanting eyes like lotus petals. She turned her head slightly, startling the friends lest she might be aware of them; and they could see that this charming figure suffered no least detraction from an ugly face; rather that harmony ruled throughout and the loveliness of the features fully bore out the loveliness of the form.

"But I know her!" Nanda suddenly murmured, with a snap of his fingers. "This very minute do I recognize her; only up to now did she escape me. That is Sita, daughter of Sumantra from the village of the Bisons near here. She came hither from her home to do her ablutions, of course. Why should I not know her? I swung her up to the sun."

"You swung her?" asked Shridaman, low-voiced but urgently. And Nanda replied:

"Why not? With all the strength of my arms, before all the people. In her clothes I should have known her at once. But who would recognize a naked person straight off? That's Sita of Bisonbull. I was there last spring to visit my aunt, and it was at the feast of aid to the sun; but she – "

"Later, I pray you," Shridaman interrupted in an anxious

whisper. "The great good fortune that we may see her so close has also the misfortune that she might hear us. Not another word or we shall alarm her."

"Then she might run away and you would see her no more, and you have not seen your fill," Nanda said teasingly. But the other motioned him peremptorily, and once more they sat silent, watching Sita perform her ritual. She prayed first, then, with her face turned heavenwards, stepped cautiously into the pool, took up water and drank, and dipped in as far as the crown of her head, on which she laid her hand. Afterwards for a while she dipped and played and slipped in and out; after a time she stepped back on dry land, cool and dripping and most beautiful to see. Even therewith was not quite an end to the favour vouchsafed to the friends; for after the purificatory bath the maid sat down on the steps that the sun might dry her. And her native charm, released by the conviction that she was quite alone, made her fall into first one, then another most pleasing posture. Only after some little time, and then only slowly, did she don her clothes and disappear up the temple stair.

"Well, that's all there is of that," said Nanda. "Now we can at least speak and move about. In the long run it gets tiresome to act as though you were not there."

"I do not see how you can use such a word," retorted Shridaman. "Could there be a more blissful state than to lose oneself in such a sight and be present only in its presence? I should have liked to hold my breath the whole time; not out of fear of losing sight of her face, but for fear of undeceiving her belief that she was alone; for that I trembled and felt myself sacredly responsible. She is called Sita, you say? I am glad to know, it consoles me for my offence, that I may pay her honour by name to myself. And you know her from swinging her?"

"As I tell you," Nanda assured him. "She was chosen as sun-maiden last spring when I was in her village, and I swung her in aid of the sun so high in the heavens that one could hardly hear her screams. Or else they were lost in the screaming of the crowd."

"You were lucky," said Shridaman. "You are always lucky. It must have been on account of your stout arms they chose you to swing her. I can just see how she rose and flew up into the blue. My imaginary picture of her flight blends with the one we saw just now, where she stood like a statue, bowed in prayer."

"Anyhow," said Nanda, "she has ground for prayer and penance; not on account of her behaviour, for she is a very good girl, but on account of her looks. Certainly she cannot help them, yet after all, strictly speaking, she is responsible for them. A figure like that is taking. But why taking? Just because it takes us captive, makes us prisoners to the world of delights and desires. It tangles the beholder deeper in the snares of Samsara, so he simply loses consciousness just the way one loses one's breath. That is the effect she has even if it is not her intention. But her lengthening her eyes in the shape of a lotus leaf makes it look like intention. You may say the fine figure was given her, she did not deliberately take it, so she has nothing to repent on that score. But the truth is, there are cases where no real difference exists between 'given' and 'taken': she knows that herself, probably she prays for pardon just because she is so 'taking'. This figure of hers, she has taken it – not as one just accepts something that is given, she really put it on, of herself. No amount of ritual bathing can alter that: she comes out with the very same taking behind she took in."

"You should not speak so coarsely," Shridaman chided him with feeling, "of such a tender and sacred being. True, you have ventured into the field of metaphysics, but I must tell you you express yourself very rustically there; and the use you make of what knowledge you have makes it clear you were not worthy of the vision. For everything depended on the spirit in which we looked on."

Nanda received the reproach in all modesty.

"Teach me, then, Dau-ji (elder brother)," he begged, "in what spirit you looked on and how I should have done."

"Lo," said Shridaman, "all beings have two sorts of

existence: one for themselves and one for the eyes of others. They are, and also they are to be seen, soul and image; and ever is it sinful to let oneself be influenced by the image only and not to heed the soul. It is necessary to overcome the disgust inspired in us at sight of the scurvy beggar. We must not stop at the effect it has on our eyes and senses. For what affects us is impression, not reality; we must go behind it to reach the knowledge to which every phenomenon can lay claim, for it is more than appearance, and one must find the being, the soul, behind it. But not only shall we not stop at the disgust aroused in us by the sight of misery. Just as little must we dwell on the desire which the image of the beautiful inspires; this, too, being more than image, although the temptation of the senses to take it only as such is perhaps even greater than in the case of the repulsive beggar. The beautiful, that is, seems to make no claim on our conscience, no demand that we enter into its soul, whereas the image of the beggar, by its very misery, does. Yet we are equally guilty if we simply feast on the sight of beauty without inquiring into its being. And our debt to it is even greater, so it seems to me, if we see it while it does not see us. Let me tell you, Nanda, it was a real boon to me that you could name the name of her whom we watched, Sita, daughter of Sumantra; for it gave me to know something of that which is more than the image, since the name is a part of the essence and of the soul. Happier still I was to hear from you that she is a good maiden; for that was a means still more easily to go behind her image and understand her soul. And then her lengthening her eyes in the shape of a lotus leaf, and painting the lashes a little – that, you might say, is all only custom and has nothing to do with morality; she does it in all innocence, her morals being dependent upon convention. But, after all, beauty too has a duty towards its image; perhaps in fulfilling it she only seeks to increase the desire to ask after her soul. I like to imagine that she has a good father in Sumantra, and a careful mother, and has been brought up in piety; I can fancy her life and occupations as daughter of the house, how she grinds the corn on the stone, makes the porridge on the hearth, or spins the wool to a fine thread. Having been guilty of beholding her image, my heart cries out to have it become a person."

"That I can understand," responded Nanda. "But you must remember that this wish cannot be so lively with me, since she already was more of a person to me, because I swung her up to the sun."

"Only too much," replied Shridaman, whose voice had betrayed a certain quiver throughout. "Obviously only too much; for this familiarity which you were vouchsafed – whether with justice or not, I will not say, for you owed it to your strong arms and your whole sturdy body, not to your head and the thoughts of your head – this familiarity seems to have made her entirely a material being in your eyes and dulled your gaze for the higher meaning of such a manifestation. Otherwise you would not have spoken with such unpardonable coarseness of the fine shape it has taken on. Do you not know, then, that in every female shape – child, maid, mother, or grey-haired woman – *she*, the All-Mother, hides herself, the all-nourisher, Sakti, the great goddess; of whose womb all things come, into whose womb all things go; whom we honour and praise in every manifestation that bears her sign? In her most worshipful shape she has revealed herself to us here on the bank of the little stream Goldfly; shall we not then be most deeply moved by her revealing herself thus – to the extent that in fact, now that I notice it, my voice somewhat trembles – though that may in part be due to displeasure at your manner of speaking?"

"And your cheeks and forehead are red as fire," said Nanda, "and your voice, though it trembles, has a fuller ring than common. I can assure you that I too in my way was quite affected."

"Then I do not understand," answered Shridaman, "how you can talk so inadequately and reproach her for her fine figure that so confuses people that the breath of consciousness goes out of them! That is to look at things with culpable one-sidedness and to show yourself entirely empty of the true and real essence of her who revealed herself to us in so sweet an image. For she is All and not only one; life and death, madness and wisdom, enchantress and liberatress, knowest thou not that? Knowest only that she befools and bewitches the host of created beings and not also that she leads them out beyond the darkness of confusion to knowledge of the truth? Then you know very little and have not grasped a great and difficult mystery: that the very drunkenness she puts upon us is the same as the exaltation which bears us on to truth and freedom. For so it is, that what enchains us frees us, and that exaltation it is that binds together beauty of sense and beauty of spirit."

Nanda's black eyes glittered with tears, for he was easily moved and could scarcely listen to metaphysical language without weeping; especially at this moment, when Shridaman's otherwise rather thin voice had suddenly taken on a deep note that went to his heart. He drew a breath rather like a sob through his goat-nose as he said:

"How you speak today, Dau-ji, so solemnly! I think I have never heard you speak so strangely; it touches me very near. I could wish you would not go on, I feel it so much. And yet I beg you to, do please go on about the spirit and the chains and the All-Embracing one!"

"So you see," Shridaman went on in his exalted strain, "the meaning of it all, and how it is not only madness but wisdom that she confers. If what I say moves you, it is because she is mistress of the fluent word, mingled with the wisdom of Brahma. In her twofold shape we recognize her greatness; for she is the wrathful one, black and terrifying, drinking the blood of creatures out of steaming vessels; but at the same time is she the white and gracious one, source of all being, cherishing all forms of life at her nourishing breast. Vishnu's great Maya is she, she holds him embraced, he dreams in her; but we dream in him. Many waters flow into the eternal Ganges, but the Ganges flows into the sea. So we flow into Vishnu's world-dreaming godhead; but that into the sea of the Mother. Lo, we came to a place where our life-dream flowed into the sacred bathing-place, and there appeared to us the All-Mother, the All-Consumer, in whose womb we bathed, in her sweetest shape, to amaze and to exalt us – very likely as a reward, because we honoured her procreative emblem and poured water to it. Linga and Yoni – there is no greater sign and no greater hour in life than when the man is summoned with his Sakti to circle round the bridal fire, their hands are united with the flowery bond and he speaks the words: 'I have received her!' When he takes her from the hand of her parents and speaks the royal word: 'He am I, this is you; heaven I, earth you; I the music of the song, you the words; so shall we make the journey together.' When they celebrate the meeting – no longer human beings more, not he and she, one male, one female, but the great pair, he Siva, she Durga, the high and awful goddess; when their words wander and are no more *their* words, but a stammering out of the drunken deeps and they die away to the highest life in the supernal joy of their embrace. Such is the holy hour which laves us in wisdom and grants us release from the delusions of the ego in the womb of the Mother. For as sense and spirit flow together in rapture, so do life and death in love!"

Nanda was utterly ravished by these metaphysical words.

"No," said he, shaking his head, while the tears sprang from his eyes, "but the goddess of eloquence is gracious to you, endowing you with the wisdom of Brahma till I can hardly bear to listen, yet would have you go on for ever. If I could sing and say even a fifth part of all that comes out of your head-piece I would love and honour myself in all my members. That is why you are so necessary to me, my elder brother; what I have not you have, and you are my friend, so that it is almost as though I had it myself. For as your fellow I have a part in you, and so I am a little bit Shridaman; but without you I were only Nanda, and that is not enough. I tell you freely, I could not bear to survive a parting from you; I would erect the funeral pyre and burn myself. So much for that. Take this before we go!"

And he rummaged in his bundle with his dark beringed

hands and drew out a roll of betel, such as is pleasant to chew after the meal to give sweet odour to the mouth. This he handed to Shridaman, with his face averted and wet with tears, as a present-giving and a sign and seal to their friendship and their compact.

4

So they went on, and their respective errands took them for a time upon different ways. When they had reached the river Jumna with its crowding sails and saw on the horizon the outline of the city Kurukshetra, Shridaman took to the highroad full of ox-carts and entered the narrow city streets to seek the house of the man from whom he was to buy the rice-mallets and tinder. Nanda struck off on a narrow lane leading to the mud huts of the humble folk who were to give him crude iron for his father's smithy. They blessed each other and took their leave, agreeing to meet again on this same spot at a certain hour on the third day, their business being done, and then to return home as they had come.

But when the sun had risen three times, Nanda, riding a grey ass which he had got from the humble folk to transport his iron, had to wait some time at the place of parting and meeting, for Shridaman was late. At length he came along the highway with his pack; his steps were slow and dragging, his cheeks hollow in the soft fan-shaped beard, and his eyes full of gloom. He showed no joy at sight of his friend, and when Nanda hastened to take his burden and put it on the ass, Shridaman's manner did not change; he walked by Nanda's side, as drooped and depressed as before, his words were hardly more than Yea, yea, even when they ought to have been Nay, nay. He did say no, too, but precisely when he should have said yes, namely at the hour for rest and refreshment, when he declared he would not and could not eat. In answer to a question, he also said that he could not sleep.

All this looked like illness. Indeed, when on the second evening they were walking along by the light of the stars, and the anxious Nanda got him to speak a few words, he not only said that he was ill, but also added in a strangled voice that the illness was incurable, a sickness unto death. It was of such a nature, he said, that he not only must but would die, the must and the will being entirely interwoven and indistinguishable, so that they formed a single compelling desire, each issuing inevitably from the other. "If you are serious in your friendship," he said to Nanda, always in that strangled and wildly agitated voice, "then do me love's last service and build me the funeral hut that I may go into it and burn in the fire. For the incurable disease burns me within with such torments that the consuming ardour of the fire will feel by contrast like soothing oil and a healing bath in the holy stream."

Oh, ye great gods, what will become of you? thought Nanda when his ears heard this. But we must say that despite his goat-nose and his physical habit, which stood midway between the lowly folk who had sold him his iron and Shridaman, the grandchild of Brahmans, Nanda was equal to the difficult situation and did not lose his head in face of his companion's morbid state, however high-class. He made use of the advantage which the sound person has over the ailing, and, suppressing his inclination to shudder, loyally put himself at his friend's service and spoke with reason and tact.

"You may be sure," said he, "if it is true, as you say, and as I cannot doubt, that your ailment is incurable, I will not hesitate to carry out your directions and erect the pyre for you. And I will make it large enough that after I have kindled it there will be room for me beside you; for I do not think to survive the parting an hour, but will enter with you into the flames. Just for that reason, and because the thing concerns me too so nearly, you must tell me what is the matter and call your illness by name, if only so that I may gain the conviction of its incurableness and prepare to turn us both into ashes. You must admit that what I say is right and just, and if even I with my limited understanding see that, how much more must you, the wiser, agree! If I put myself in your place and try to use your head as though it sat on my shoulders, I cannot but think that my – I mean your – conviction of the incurableness of your disease needs confirmation and proof by others before we begin to carry out such far-reaching intentions. And therefore speak!"

For a long time the lank-cheeked Shridaman would not come out with it; he declared that the mortal hopelessness of his sufferings needed no evidence and no explanation. But at last after much urging he complied, with the following confession, putting as he spoke one hand over his eyes, that he need not look at his friend.

"Since," said he, "we watched that maiden, nude but virtuous, whom you once swung up to the sun, Sita, daughter of Sumantra, at the bathing-place of Devi, suffering to do with her nakedness as well as her virtue, and having its origin in both, has been planted like a seed in my soul and there flourished until it has penetrated all my limbs down to their smallest fibre; consumed my mental powers, robbed me of sleep and appetite, and now slowly but surely leads me on to destruction." He went on to say that his anguish was mortal because the cure – namely, the fulfilment of the wishes founded on the beauty and virtue of the maiden – was unthinkable, unimaginable, and of an extravagance, in short, far beyond mortal pretensions. If a man were afflicted by desire for a happiness of which no mortal but only a god might dream, and if he could not live without this happiness, then it was clear the man must die. "If," he concluded, "I may not possess her, Sita of the partridge-eyes, the glorious colour, the divine hips, then of itself my spirit will dissolve and pass away. So build me the pyre, for only in the fire is salvation from the conflict of the human and the divine. It pains me that you would enter it with me, on account of your youth and your blithe young nature and lucky-calf lock; yet there is some justice in it too. For the thought that you swung her up to the sun adds to the fire in my breast, and I should hate to leave upon earth anyone to whom this had been granted."

Nanda had no sooner heard Shridaman out than to his friend's utter amazement he burst out laughing, and continued to laugh as he danced up and down and embraced his friend by turns.

"Lovesick!" he cried. "Lovesick, lovesick! That is all there is to it. That is the mortal illness. What fun, what a joke!" And he began to sing:

> "The clever man, the clever man,
> How wisely did he reason!
> But now, alack, his wits are gone,
> His wisdom's out of season.
>
> The glances of a maiden's eye
> Have turned his head to jelly;
> A monkey tumbled from a tree
> Could not look half so silly!"

Then he went on roaring, clapping his hands on his knees, and crying out:

"Shridaman, brother, how I rejoice to know it is nothing worse, and you are only thinking of the funeral pyre because your heart is on fire like a straw thatch! The little witch stood there too long in your sight; Kama, the god with the flowery arrow, has pierced you through. What we thought was the humming of bees was the whirr of his bolt; and Rati, sister of the springtime and desire, she has done this to you. And it is all quite normal and jolly, happens every day, and is no more than proper to a man. To you it looks as though only a god could hope for such bliss; but that only shows the warmth of your desires, and proves that they do indeed come from a god, that is to say Kama, but not that they are fitting to him instead of to you. Take it not unfriendly, but only as cooling counsel to your over-heated sense, when I say that you are mistaken if you think only gods have a right to the goal of your desires. That is exaggerated; indeed, nothing is more human and natural than that you are driven to sow in this furrow." (He put it like this because the word Sita means a furrow.) "But to you," he went on, "the proverb applies: 'The owl is blind by day, by night the crow. But whom love blinds nor light nor darkness know.' I repeat this edifying saying that you may see yourself in it and bethink you that Sita of Bisonbull is no goddess, although she might so seem to you as she stood naked at the bathing-place of Durga, but a quite ordinary though extremely pretty little thing; she lives like other people, grinds the corn, cooks the porridge, and spins the wool and has parents who are like other folk, even though Sumantra, her father, can boast of a little warrior blood in his veins – too far away to amount to much! In short, they are people one can talk to; and why have you a friend like your Nanda if he should not get on his legs and arrange this whole quite regular and ordinary business for you, so you can be happy? Well? Hey? What, stupid! Instead of laying the bonfire and squatting in it beside you, I will help you build your bridal house where you can live in bliss with your bride of the beautiful hips!"

Shridaman, after a pause, answered and said: "Your words – not to mention your song – contained much that was offensive. For offensive it is to call my anguished desires quite ordinary and everyday when they are past my power to endure and are nigh to split my heart in twain. A yearning stronger than we are, too strong to sustain – we are right in calling it unfitting for man, only fit for a god to know. But I am sure you mean well by me, you want to console me, so I forgive you the vulgar and ignorant way you express yourself about my mortal illness. Indeed, not only do I forgive you; for your last words seem to hold out a possibility which has already stimulated my heart, but now resigned to death, to new and violent throbbing. It is the picture you hold up that has done this, though as yet I am incapable of belief in it. I have moments of divining that unscathed mortals, in another frame of mind than mine, may be able to judge more clearly and objectively. But I immediately mistrust any other view than my own and believe only in the way which points me to death. Consider how probable it is that the divine Sita was contracted in marriage as a child and is soon to be united with a bridegroom who grew up with her! The mere thought is such a burning torment that I can only flee from it into the coolness of the funeral pyre."

But Nanda swore by their friendship that his fear was utterly baseless; Sita was not bound by any child-marriage. Her father Sumantra had objected to such an arrangement, on the ground that it would expose her to the ignominy of widowhood in case the boy husband died untimely. In fact, she could not have been chosen as the swinging maiden if she had been betrothed. No, Sita was free, she was to be wooed; and with Shridaman's good caste, his family connections and his conversance with the Vedas, it only needed that he formally commission his friend to take the thing in hand and set in motion the negotiations between the families, to make a happy issue to the affair as good as certain.

Shridaman's cheek had twitched with pain at mention of the swinging episode. But on the whole he showed himself grateful for his friend's readiness to serve him. Slowly he let himself be turned by Nanda's sound reasoning away from his yearning for death towards a belief that the fulfilment of his desire, to enfold Sita as a bride in his arms, did not lie outside the realms of the possible and human. Even so, he stuck to it that if the wooing went wrong, Nanda would have to erect the funeral pyre with his stout arms. The son of Garga soothed him by promising this; but found it more pertinent to discuss in detail all the steps leading up to the happy consummation. Shridaman was to retire entirely and await the issue; Nanda for his part had first to open the affair to Bhavabhuti, Shridaman's father, and persuade him to undertake negotiations with the maiden's parents. Then Nanda, representing the wooer, would betake himself as suitor of the bride to Bisonbull and in his character of friend carry out the further approach between the couple.

No sooner said than done. Bhavabhuti, the *vanija* of Brahman stock, was rejoiced at the communication which his son's friend made to him. Sumantra, the cow-breeder, of warrior blood, was not displeased by the proposals, accompanied by considerable presents. Nanda in homely but convincing phrases sang the praises of his friend in the house of the wooing. Not less auspicious was the return visit of Sita's parents to Welfare of Cows, to convince themselves of the suitor's good faith. In such exchanges as these the days passed, and the maiden Sita learned from afar to see in Shridaman, the merchant's son, her destined lord and master. The marriage contract was drawn up and the signing of it celebrated with a feast and the exchange of appropriate gifts. The day of the wedding, selected by advice of those learned in the heavenly signs, drew on; and Nanda, who knew that it would do so – quite aside from the fact that Shridaman's union with Sita depended upon him, which prevented Shridaman from believing it would ever come – ran about inviting kin and friends to the nuptials. The nuptial bonfire was laid on a base of cakes of dried dung in the inner court of Sita's parents' house. Nanda's strong arms did yeoman service here too, while the priest of Brahma stood by and recited texts.

So came on the day when Sita the fine-limbed, her body anointed with sandalwood, camphor, and coconut oils, adorned with jewellery, in wedding bodice and robe, her head enveloped in a cloudy veil, for the first time set eyes on her appointed husband. He, as we are aware, had seen her before. For the first time she called him by his name. The hour had indeed been waited for, but here it was at last and took on presentness, when he spoke the words: "I have received her"; when with offerings of rice and butter he took her from her parents' hands, called himself heaven and her earth, himself the melody, her the words; and to the singing and hand-clapping of the women went with her thrice round the glowing fire. Then in solemn procession, with a team of white oxen he led her home to his village and to his mother's heart.

Here there were more good-luck ceremonies to be performed, here too they went round about the fire; he fed her with sugar-cane, let the ring fall in her lap. At the festal meal they sat again with kin and friends. But when they had eaten and drunk and been sprinkled with rose-water and water from the Ganges, they were accompanied by all the guests to the bridal chamber or "room of the happy pair", where the flower-garlanded bed had been set up. There, among kisses, jesting, and tears, everyone took leave of them. Nanda, who had been at their side throughout, was last upon the threshold.

5

Here we warn the listener, perhaps misled by the so far pleasing course of the tale, not to fall prey to a misconception of its real character. For a little space there was silence, it turned its face away; when it turns back it is no more the same, but changed to a frightful mask, a face of horror, distracting, Medusa-like, turning the beholder to stone, or maddening him to wild acts of abnegation – for so Shridaman, Nanda, and Sita saw it, on the journey which they... But everything in its turn.

Six months had passed since Shridaman's mother had taken the lovely Sita to her maternal bosom and Sita had granted to her narrow-nosed husband the full enjoyment of wedded bliss. The heavy summer had passed, and now the rainy season, covering the sky with floods of cloud, the earth with freshets of flowers, would soon be over too. Heaven's tent was spotless, the autumn lotus was in bloom, when the newly wedded pair discussed with their friend Nanda, after winning the consent of Shridaman's parents, a visit to Sita's family. Her parents had not seen her since she embraced her husband, and they wished to convince themselves that her wedded bliss became her. Although Sita had begun of late to look forward to the joys of motherhood, they ventured on the journey, which was not long and in the cool of the year not very trying.

They travelled in a cart with a top and side curtains, drawn by a zebu and a dromedary; friend Nanda being the driver. He sat in front of the wedded pair, his little cap on one ear and his legs dangling down. He seemed to be paying too much attention to his driving to turn round often to speak to his passengers. Sometimes he called out to his beasts; from time to time burst into song, very loud and clear – but after the first notes his voice would die down to a humming, ending in a vague chirrup to his team. If the burst of song was rather startling, like a relief to an overcharged breast, its dying away was no less so.

Behind him the wedded pair sat silent. They had Nanda immediately before them, their gaze if directed straight ahead would rest on the back of his neck; as the young wife's sometimes did, rising slowly from contemplation of her lap and after a short pause swiftly returning there. Shridaman avoided the sight entirely, keeping his face averted towards the canvas curtains. Gladly would he have changed places with Nanda and become the driver, in order not to have, like his wife beside him, a view of the brown back with the spinal column and the flexible shoulder-blades. But it was no matter, he thought; for any other arrangement would have been no better. And so in silence they took their way, but the breath of all three came quickly as though they had been running; their eyes were bloodshot, and that is always a bad sign. A person gifted with second sight would certainly have seen a shadow, like a black pinion, covering them as they drove.

And they drove, by preference, in the shadow of darkness; in other words, before the dawn; thus avoiding the burden of the mid-day sun – a sensible course, for which, however, they had other grounds than good sense. The confusion of their own souls was favoured by the darkness, and unconsciously they projected their inward bewilderment into outward space – with the result that they lost their way. Nanda did not guide his zebu and dromedary into the turning off the highroad that led to Sita's home. With no moon, and only the stars to guide him, he took the wrong turn, and the road they found themselves on was soon no road at all, but only a thinning among the trees, and even that only apparent, for they thickened again and became a forest wherein the thinning soon disappeared through which they might have made their way back.

It was impossible to get forward with their cart among the tree-trunks and on the soft floor of the forest. They confessed to each other that they had gone astray; but not that they had brought about a situation corresponding to confusion of their own minds. Shridaman and Sita, sitting behind Nanda as he drove, had not even been asleep; open-eyed, they allowed him to take them into the wrong road. There was nothing for it but to make a fire where they were, and await the sunrise with more security against beasts of prey. When day at length dawned, they cast about in all directions; unharnessed their team and let them go single file; then with great difficulty pushed and shoved the cart wherever the teak and sandalwood trees would let them through, and reached the edge of the jungle, where they found a stone gully. This might be possible for the cart; and Nanda declared that it would certainly lead in the direction of Sita's home.

Following the steep gully, with many jolts, they came on a temple hewn out of the rock, and recognized it as a shrine of Devi-Durga the terrible and unapproachable, Kali the dark Mother. Obeying an impulse of his heart, Shridaman expressed a wish to get out and pay honour to the goddess. "I will only look at her, say a prayer, and come back in a few minutes," he said to his companions. "Just wait here!" And he left the wagon and clambered up the rude steps leading to the temple.

It was a shrine no more important than the little mother-house by the secluded bathing-place on the river Goldfly; but its columns and ornamentation had been carved with infinite piety and care. The entrance seemed to crouch beneath the wild mountain itself, supported by columns flanked by snarling leopards. There were painted pictures to right and left, also at the sides of the inner entrance, carven out of the rock; visions of life in the flesh, all jumbled together out of skin and bones, marrow and sinews, sperm and sweat and tears and ropy rheum, filth and urine and gall; thick with passions, anger, lust, envy, and despair; lovers' partings and bonds unloved; with hunger, thirst, old age, sorrow, and death; all this for ever fed by the sweet, hot streaming blood-stream, suffering and enjoying in a thousand shapes, teeming, devouring, turning into one another. And in that all-encompassing labyrinthine flux of the animal, human, and divine, there would be an elephant's trunk that ended in a man's hand, or a boar's head seemed to take the place of a woman's. – Shridaman heeded not the pictures, he thought not to see them; yet his red-veined eyeballs skimmed them in passing, and they stirred in his soul feelings of slight giddiness and of tender pity, to prepare it for the beholding of the Mother.

Twilight reigned in the rocky cell, lighted only from above by light falling through the mountain into the audience hall, which he crossed to go into the lower vestibule adjoining it. There a door on a still lower level, to which steps led down, admitted him into the heart of the house, the womb of the great Mother.

At the foot of the steps he trembled and staggered back, his hands spread out against the two linga stones on either side. Kali's image was fearsome. Did it only seem so to his bloodshot eyes, or had he never anywhere beheld the raging one in such triumphantly horrible guise? Framed in an arch composed of skulls and hacked-off hands and feet, the idol stood out from the living rocky wall in colours that snatched up all the light to hurl it glaringly back. She was adorned with a dazzling crown; clothed and girt with bones and severed limbs, and her eighteen arms were a whirling wheel. Swords and fiery beacons the Mother brandished. Blood steamed hot in the skull she held with one hand to her lips, and blood was at her feet in a spreading pool. The frightful one stood in a bark on the flooding sea of life, it swam in a sea of blood. The very smell of blood saluted Shridaman's thin nostrils, it smelt old and sweetish in the stagnant air of this mountain cave, this subterranean charnel-house, where coagulating blood choked and made sticky the runnels in the pavement grooved to carry off the quick-flowing life-stream of the beheaded sacrifices. Four or five heads of animals, bison, swine, and goats, their eyes open and glazed, were piled in a pyramid on the altar before the image of the Unescapable, and the sword that had served to behead them, sharp-edged and shining, though spotted with dried blood, lay on the flags at one side.

Shridaman stared at the wild glaring visage, his horror mounting by the moment to fever heat. This was She, the Deathbringer-Lifegiver, Compeller of Sacrifice – her whirling arms made his own senses go round in drunken circles. He pressed his clenched fists against his mightily throbbing breast; uncanny shudderings, cold and hot, surged over his frame in successive floods. In the back of his head, in the very pit of his stomach, in the woeful excitation of his organs of sex, he felt one single urge, driving on to the extremity of a deed against his own life in the service of the eternal womb. With lips already bloodless he prayed:

"Beginningless, that wast before all created! Mother without man, whose garment none lifteth! All-embracing horror and desire, sucking back into thyself the worlds and images thou givest forth! With offerings of living creatures the people honour thee, for to thee is due the life-blood of all! How shall I not find grace to my healing, if I bring thee myself as offering? Well I know I shall not thereby escape life, even though that were desirable. But let me enter again into thee through the door of the womb that I may be free of this self; let me no more be Shridaman, to whom all desire is but bewilderment, since it is not he who gives it!"

Spoke these sinister words, seized up the sword from the floor, and severed his own head from his neck.

Quickly said; and not otherwise than quickly done. Yet the teller has here but one wish: that the hearer may not accept the fact with thoughtless indifference, as something quite common and natural, simply because it has been often told and stands in the records, that people practise cutting off their own heads. The single case is never common; the most common of all the things we think and talk about are birth and death; yet attend at a birth or a death-bed and ask yourself, ask the groaning or the parting soul, whether it is common or not. Self-beheading, however often it may be reported, is an act well-nigh impossible; to carry it through takes enormous determination, a fearful summoning up of purpose and energy. That Shridaman, the little Brahman with the mild pensive eyes and thin clerkly arms, did in fact perpetrate it, must not be taken as in the common run, but as something scarcely credible at all.

Enough, in all conscience, that he performed the gruesome sacrifice in the twinkling of an eye; here lay his noble head, with the soft beard on the cheeks, and there his body, that less important appendage, its two hands still grasping the sacrificial sword by the hilt. From the trunk the blood gushed out and ran into the channels in the floor. There was only a slight incline; so once in the channels it crept but slowly towards the pit under the altar – very like the little river Goldfly, that comes rushing, like a colt let loose, out of Himawant's gate but flows more and more quietly as it nears its mouth.

6

Returning now from the bowels of this rocky cell back to the pair waiting outside, we need not be surprised that they spent the first part of the time in silence, but after that began to question aloud. After all Shridaman had only wanted to make a brief devotion; where was he lingering so long? The lovely Sita, sitting behind Nanda in the cart, had gazed by turns at his neck and into her lap and kept as still as he, whose goat-nose and thick lips remained turned towards his team. But at length both began to wriggle in their seats, and after a while friend Nanda resolutely turned round to the young wife and asked:

"Have you any idea why he keeps us waiting and what he is doing there so long?"

"I cannot imagine, Nanda," responded she, in the sweet lilting and trilling voice he had been afraid to hear. She had quite superfluously added his name, and he had been afraid of that too – it was unnecessary, and he himself had not said: "Where is Shridaman," but simply: "Where is he?"

"I have been wondering a long time," she went on, "and if you had not turned round to me and asked me, I should very soon have asked you."

He shook his head, partly out of surprise at his friend's delay, but partly to ward off the unnecessary words she always used. "Turned round" would have been enough, the "to me", although quite correct, was unnecessary and even dangerous, spoken as it was, while they waited for Shridaman, and in that sweetly lilting, slightly affected voice.

He said nothing, afraid lest he too might speak in an unnatural voice and address her by her name, for he felt drawn to follow the example she had set. It was she who after a short pause made the suggestion:

"I will tell you what, Nanda, you must go after him and see where he is, give him a shake with those strong arms of yours, if he has forgotten himself in prayer – we cannot wait any longer, and it is very strange of him to leave us sitting here, and waste the time while the sun is getting higher. We are late anyhow by reason of losing the way, and my parents must be beginning to worry about me, for they love me beyond aught in the world. Do, pray, go fetch him, Nanda! Even though he does not want to come and protests a little, yet make him come. You are stronger than he."

"Good, I will go fetch him," Nanda replied. "Of course in all friendliness. I need only remind him of the time. It was my fault we lost the way. I had already thought of going, and only feared you might not like to wait here alone. But it is only for a few seconds."

With that he lowered himself from the driver's seat and went up into the shrine.

And we, who know what a sight awaited him there! We must accompany him through the audience hall where he walked all unconscious; and through the vestibule where still he was unaware; then finally down into the mother-cell. Now, indeed, he faltered, he staggered, a dull cry of horror on his lips, struggling to hold fast to the linga stones, just as Shridaman had done. But his horror was not, like Shridaman's, for the image, but for the awful sight on the floor. There lay his friend, the waxen face with loosened neckcloth severed from the trunk, his blood flowing by many ways towards the pit.

Poor Nanda quivered like an elephant's ear. He held his

cheeks with his dark beringed hands and from between his thick lips came chokingly over and over the name of his friend. He bent and made helpless motions towards the two parts of him on the ground, not knowing which part to embrace or to address. To the head he turned at last, that having always been so decidedly the main part; knelt down to the pallid shape and spoke, his goat-nosed face awry with bitter weeping. He laid one hand on the body and turned to it now and again as he talked.

"Shridaman," he sobbed, "dear friend, what hast thou done, and how couldst thou bring thyself to do this with thy hands and arms, a deed so hard to do! It was not anything for thee! No one urged thee to this, yet hast thou accomplished it. Always have I admired thy spirit, now must I in tears admire thy body too, because thou hast been able to do this hardest of all deeds! But what must have gone on in thy soul, to bring thee to it! How in thy breast must generosity and despair have gone hand in hand, in sacrificial dance, ere thou couldst slay thyself! Oh woe, oh woe! Severed the fine head from the fine body! Still remains the soft plumpness where it was, but reft of sense and meaning, unallied with that noble head of thine. Say, am I guilty? Am I indeed guilty of thy death by my very being, if also not by my deed? Lo, since my head still thinks, I try to think as thou wouldst, and perhaps in thy wisdom thou wouldst have called the guilt of being more essential than that of action. But what more can a man do than avoid doing? I have kept silent as much as possible in order not to speak with a cooing voice. I have said no unnecessary word, nor added her name when I addressed her. I am my own witness, there is indeed no other, that I took no advantage when she carped at you. But what good is all that, when I am guilty by my very existence in the flesh? I should have gone into the desert and as an anchorite performed strict observance! I ought to have done it, without any word from you, I confess it humbly. But in my defence I can say that had you spoken I would have done so! Why did you never speak, dear head, before you lay there sundered and still sat on your shoulders?

Aways have our heads spoken together, yours wise and mine simple; yet in the most serious and dangerous concern of all, then you were silent! Now it is too late; you have not spoken, you have acted greatly and cruelly and shown me how I too must act. Surely you did not believe I would fail you, that my strong arms would falter at a deed your slender ones have carried out! Often had I told you I did not think to survive a parting from you; when in your lovesickness you ordered me to build the funeral hut, I declared to you that if I did it at all I would do it for two and squat inside it with you. What now must happen I long have known, even though only now does it stand out clear from the confusion of my thoughts when I came in and saw you lying – by 'you' I mean body there and head here beside it – then was Nanda's resolve made on the instant. I would have burned with you, so will I also bleed with you, for nothing else remains to me. Shall I go out to her to tell her what you have done and in the cries of horror she will utter hear her secret joy? Shall I go about with tarnished name and have people say, as they certainly will: 'The villain Nanda has wronged his friend, has murdered him out of lust for his wife?' No, not that! Not ever that. I will follow you, and may the eternal womb drink my blood with yours!"

Thus saying, he turned from the head to the body, loosed the hilt of the sword from the already stiffening fingers, and with his stout arms carried out most thoroughly the sentence he himself had pronounced; so that his body, to mention it first, fell across Shridaman's, and his simple head bounced alongside that of his friend, where it lay with its eyes rolled up. But his blood too burst quick and furiously forth and then trickled slowly through the runnels to the mouth of the pit.

7

Meanwhile, Sita, the furrow, sat outside, alone in her tented cart, and the time was longer to her because she had no nape of a neck to look at any more. What – while she yielded to quite commonplace feelings of annoyance – was happening to that neck, of course she never dreamed. – Possibly, in her inmost soul – far beneath her ill-humour, which was lively, but belonged to the sphere of small possible mischances, and merely made her scuffle with her feet – the suspicion stirred of something frightful, some explanation of the delay which would make impatience and annoyance irrelevant because it belonged to an order of possibilities beyond the scope of kicking and scuffling. We must reckon with a secret receptivity of the young wife for imaginings of this order, because she had been living under certain conditions, and having certain experiences, which, to put it mildly, were themselves rather extravagant in their nature. But nothing of that sort entered into the things she was saying to herself.

"It is just unspeakable, it is almost intolerable," she thought. "Men are all alike, one must not set one above another, for there is no dependence on any. One of them leaves you sitting with the other, so that he deserves I don't know what for it; and when you send the other, then you sit here alone. And that with the sun getting high, because we had already lost so much time. I shall soon fly out of my skin with rage. There is not a single excuse, in the whole range of reasonable, sensible possibilities, for one disappearing and then the other too. The utmost I can think is that they have fallen foul of each other, because Shridaman is so set on praying that he will not stir from the spot, and Nanda is trying to force him, but out of respect for my husband's weak frame will not use his full strength; for if he wanted to, he could carry him like a child in his arms; they feel like iron when one happens to touch them. It would be humiliating for Shridaman, yet the annoyance almost makes me wish Nanda would do just that. I must say, you both deserve I should take the reins and drive on alone to my parents, and you would find me gone when you finally came out. If it were not so embarrassing to arrive alone like that, without husband or friend, because both of them went and left me, I would just do it at once. Otherwise all I can do – and it is certainly high time – is to go after them and see what in the world they are up to. No wonder I feel somewhat alarmed, being with child as I am, at their strange behaviour, for fear of what is behind it. But the worst thing I can think of, after all, is that for some reason unknown, they have quarrelled, and the quarrel is keeping them from coming back. I will just step in and straighten them both out."

With that the lovely Sita got down from the cart, her hips billowing beneath her enveloping garment, and betook herself to the shrine – and fifteen seconds later she was confronted by that most hideous of sights.

She flung up her arms, her eyes started from their sockets; bereft of her senses she sank full length on the ground. But that helped her not at all, the situation would keep, it had been keeping all the time Sita waited; and it would keep on keeping. When the unhappy Sita came to herself it was still there. She tried to faint again, but thanks to her sound constitution she could not. So she cowered on the stone pavement, her fingers in her hair, and stared at the severed heads, the bodies lying across each other, and all the crawling blood.

"Ye gods, saints, and hermits!" she whispered blue-lipped, "I am lost! Both men, both at once. All is over! My lord and husband, who went about the fire with me, my Shridaman with the estimable head and the body, which after all was warm, for he taught me lust, as far as I know it, in nights of holy wedlock – severed the honoured head from the body, lost and gone. Lost and gone – and the other, Nanda, who swung me and wooed me for Shridaman – severed and bleeding body from head – there he lies, the lucky-calf lock still on his breast – once so merry, but headless, what now? I could touch him, I could feel the strength and beauty of his arms and thighs, if I would. But I care not, blood and death have set a barrier between him and wanton desire as honour and friendship did before. They have cut off each other's heads! For a reason I no longer conceal from myself, their anger blazed up, like a fire on which one has thrown butter; their strife was such that it came to this mutual deed – I see all clearly. But only one sword is here – and Nanda holds it! How could they fight with only one? Shridaman, forgotten all wisdom and mildness, seized the sword and hewed off

Nanda's head, who then – but no! It was Nanda, for reasons at which I shudder, beheaded Shridaman, who then – oh no, oh no! Think on it no more, it avails nothing, there is nothing but blood and darkness in the darkness of this horrible place, and only one thing is clear, they behaved like savages and not for a moment thought of me. Or rather, of course they thought of me, their horrible masculine deed was on my account. Poor thing, I shudder at the thought. But only with reference to themselves did they think of me, not about me and what would become of me – that in their madness they never thought of, as little as they do now, lying there still and headless, leaving to me what I shall do next! Do? There is nothing to be done, since now I am undone. Shall I go through life a widow, shunned as a woman who cared so ill for her husband that he perished? That is a widow's common lot; but how much worse stain will attach to me when I return alone to the house of my father and my father-in-law? Only one sword – they cannot have killed each other with it in turn, one sword is not enough for two. But there is a third person left, and that is I. They will say I am an abandoned woman and murdered my husband and his foster-brother, my brother-in-law – the chain of evidence is complete. It is false, but it is conclusive and they will brand me, though innocent. Not innocent, no, there might be some sense in lying, it would be worth the trouble to lie, if everything were not at an end, but as it is there is no sense. Innocent I am not, have not been for long; and as for being abandoned there is something in it – much, much indeed, though not quite as people will think. Is there such a thing as mistaken justice? I must prevent that, I must do justice on myself. I must follow them – nothing else in the world is left me. The sword I cannot wield with my little hands, they are too small, and they tremble too much to destroy the body to which they belong, these alluring curves – that are yet naught but weakness. A pity for its loveliness – yet it must become as stiff and lifeless as these, and nevermore awake desire or suffer lust. So must it be, though the number of the sacrifice mount to four. What would it have from life, the orphaned child? Crippled by misfortune, pale and blind because I went pale with affliction when it was conceived, and shut my eyes not to see him who begot it. What I do now is what they have left me to do. Lo, then, let them see I know how to help myself!"

She pulled herself up, staggered to and fro, tottered up the step, and ran, with her gaze bent on destruction, back through the temple into the open air. A fig tree stood in front of the shrine hung with climbing vines. She seized one of these, made a noose, put it round her neck, and was just in the act to strangle herself.

8

At that moment a voice was manifest to her out of the air: no other, of course, than the voice of Devi-Durga the Unapproachable, Kali the dark, the voice of the World-Mother herself. It was a deep, harsh voice, with a maternal firmness about it.

"Will you just let that be for a minute, you silly ape!" it said. "Is it not enough to have let the blood of my sons, so that it flows in the runnels, but you will also mutilate my tree, and make your body – which is not a half-bad image of me – carrion for crows, together with the dear sweet warm little seed of life growing inside it? Perhaps you have not noticed, you goose, that you have missed your times and are in expectation from my son? If you cannot add two and two in women's matters, then hang yourself, do! But not here in my bailiwick, to make it look as though dear life should all at once perish and go out of the world, just on account of your silliness. My ears are full as it is of these quack philosophers who say that human existence is a disease, communicating itself through lust from one generation to the next – and now you, you ninny, start playing games like this with me! Take your neck out of the noose, or you'll get your ears boxed!"

"Holy goddess," answered Sita, "certainly, I obey. I hear the thunder of thy voice and interrupt of course at once my desperate enterprise as thou commandest. But I must defend myself against the idea that I did not realize my condition and not know that you had made me pause and had blessed me. I only thought it would surely be pale and blind and a child of misfortune."

"Be so good as to let me take care of that! In the first place that is a silly female superstition, and in the second, in my activities there is room for pale and blind cripples too. But justify yourself, confess why the blood of my sons has flowed to me in the pit, both of them in their way very decent youths. Not that their blood would not have been grateful to me; only I should rather have let it flow awhile yet in their veins. Speak then, but tell the truth! You realize that I know everything anyhow."

"They killed each other, holy goddess, and left me forlorn. They quarrelled on my account and with one and the same sword hewed off their – "

"Nonsense! Really, only a female can talk such sheer rubbish. They sacrificed themselves to me one after the other in manly piety, let me tell you. But why did they do it?"

The lovely Sita began to weep. She answered, sobbing:

"Ah, holy goddess, I know and confess my guilt, but how can I help it? It was such a misfortune, however inevitable; such a fatality, if you permit me to say so" (here she sobbed several times); "such a calamity, an evil and poisonous mischance, that I became a wife, being the pert and tongue-tied and ignorant girl that I was, tending in peace my father's hearth until I knew my husband and was initiated into thy matters. For the blithe child that I was, it was like eating poison berries, changing her for ever through and through, so that sin, with its irresistible sweetness, has power over her awakened senses. Not that I can wish myself back in that pert and unthinking ignorance – I cannot; it is possible to no one. I only know that in that early time I did not know man, I did not see him, he did not trouble me, and my soul was free of him and all burning curiosity about his mysteries; I tossed him jesting words and went my saucy way. Had ever I blushed at the sight of a youth's breast or felt my eyes burn when I looked at his arms and legs? No, that was all like nothing at all to me, it did not touch ever so little my coolness and poise, for I was like a closed book. A youth came, with a flat nose and black eyes, built like an image, Nanda was his name, from Welfare of Cows; he swung me up to the sun in the feast of the sun, but I felt no glow at all. I got warm – from the caressing air but from nothing else; and for thanks I gave him a tweak of the nose. Then he came back as wooer for his friend Shridaman, and our parents agreed on the marriage. Perhaps by then it was a little different; perhaps the unhappiness began in those days when he wooed me for another man who was to embrace me as his wife and who was not there. Only Nanda was there.

"He was always there; before the wedding and during the wedding feast, when we marched round the fire – and afterwards too. In the daytime, I mean, he was there, for of course he was not at night, when I slept with his friend Shridaman, my husband, and we met as the godlike pair as we had for the first time on the bed of flowers our wedding night; when he unlocked me with his manly strength and put an end to my inexperience and the pert, chaste maidenliness of my early years. That he could do, why not, he was thy son, and he knew how to impart a loftiness to our physical union, and there was nothing at all against my loving, honouring, and fearing him – ah, most high goddess, I am not so made that I should not have loved my lord and husband, and even more feared and honoured him: that head so fine and wise, the beard soft as the soft mild eyes and lids, and the body that went with them. But with all my respect, I had to ask myself whether he was really the right one to make me a wife and instruct my maidenly coldness in the sweet and awful mysteries of sense. – It always seemed to me it did not become him: it was not worthy of him, it did not go with his head, and always when his flesh rose to encounter me in those wedded nights it seemed to me like a shame, and a degradation of his refinement, a shame and debasement – and for me too when I had been aroused.

"Eternal goddess, so it was. Chide me, punish me, I thy creature confess to thee in this frightful hour without reserve just how it all was; mindful that in any case all things are open to thy wisdom. Desire did not become my noble husband Shridaman, it became neither his head nor his body, which after all, you will agree, is the important factor. His body lying there, so piteously severed from his head, did not know how to shape the rites of love so that my whole heart would hang upon them. He did indeed awake me to desire but could not still it. Have mercy, goddess! The lust of thy awakened creature was greater than its satisfaction, its craving greater than its joy.

"And by day I saw our friend Nanda with the goat-nose; and in the evening before we went to bed. I saw him and I observed him, as wedlock had now taught me to observe and judge men; and the question slipped into my head and into my dreams: what would Nanda make of the act of love and what would the godlike embrace be like with him – who is very far from talking as well as Shridaman – instead of with my husband? No different, miserable wretch, I told myself, vicious and dishonouring towards thy rightful husband! It is always the same; how could such as Nanda, who is simplicity itself in all his words and members while thy lord and husband is really a person of consequence, how could Nanda know how to make any more of it? But that was no help: the question of Nanda, the idea that his lust would become both his head and his limbs and be without shame, and he might be the man to lift my joy to the level of my desire – it stuck in my flesh and soul like a hook in a fish's mouth, and could not be pulled out because the hook was barbed.

"How could I tear it out, when he was always with us, and Shridaman and he could not live without each other because they were so different? I had to see him by day, and dream about him by night, instead of Shridaman. I would look at his breast with the lucky-calf lock, his narrow hips and very small hind-quarters, mine being so large, and Shridaman forming in this respect a mean between me and Nanda, and my self-control forsook me. When his arm touched mine the hairs on my skin rose up for very bliss. When I thought of his glorious pair of legs, with the black hair on them, saw him walk and move them and thought of their clasping me round in amorous play, a giddiness seized me and my breasts dripped with tenderness. More and more lovely he became to me day by day. I could not understand how I saw him, on the day of my swinging, and smelt the mustard oil on his skin, and remained asleep and untouched. For now he was like the prince Gandharva Citraratha in his unearthly charm, like the love-god in his sweetest guise, full of beauty and youth, ravishing to the sense, adorned with heavenly ornament, with necklaces of flowers, sweet odours, and all loveliness – Vishnu, come down to the earth in Krishna's form.

"Thus it was, when Shridaman came near me in the night, I paled for very sorrow that it was he and not the other, and closed my eyes so I might think Nanda embraced me. It came about that I forbore not, in my ardour, to murmur the name of him whom I would have wished to rouse it in me; and so Shridaman became aware that I was breaking my marriage vows in his gentle arms. And then, alas, I sometimes talk in my sleep, and I must have hurt him cruelly by uttering within his hearing the betraying substance of my dreams. I gather this from his melancholy and his withdrawal from me – for from that time he has never touched me again. Nor did Nanda touch me; not because he was not tempted, tempted he certainly was, I would vouch for it that he was sorely tempted! But in his invincible loyalty to his friend he resisted the temptation, and I too – believe me, eternal Mother, for I at least do believe it – even if his temptation had mastered him, out of honour for my lord and husband I would have showed him the door. But the issue was that I had no husband at all; and the three of us were in a state of painful renunciation.

"Under such circumstances, Mother of the world, we undertook the journey to my parents and wandering from our right ways we came on thy house. Shridaman said he would stop only a little and in passing pay you his devotions.

But in thy slaughter-cell, overcome by his plight, he did this frightful deed, robbing his limbs of their revered head, or rather his revered head of its limbs, and abandoned me to this wretched widowed state. In an agony of abnegation he did it, and with good intentions towards me, the criminal. For, gracious goddess, pardon me the truth: not to thee did he bring himself a sacrifice but to me and to his friend, that we might spend our days in full enjoyment of the joys of the flesh. Then Nanda went to seek him, and would not abide by the sacrifice but hacked his own head from his Krishna limbs, so that they are now useless. But useless, yes, and much worse than useless my life is now become; I too am as good as headless, without husband or friend. The guilt for my unhappiness I must, I suppose, ascribe to my acts in an earlier existence. But after all this, canst thou wonder that I was resolved to make an end of my present one?"

"You are an unqualified goose, and nothing else," said the goddess in her voice of thunder. "It is ridiculous, what your insatiable curiosity has made out of this Nanda, who is entirely ordinary in all his works and ways. With such arms, and on such legs, I have sons running about by the million, and you go and make a Gandharva out of him! It is pathetic, after all," added the divine voice, more mildly. "I, the Mother, find fleshly lust pathetic on the whole, and am of opinion that people are inclined to make too much of it. Anyhow, order there must be!" And the voice got suddenly harsh and blustering again. "I, indeed, am Disorder; but precisely therefore I insist on order, and I must definitely protest that the institution of marriage be kept inviolate. Everything would get into a muddle if I gave rein to my good nature. But as for you, to say I am dissatisfied is to put it mildly. You make this kettle of fish for me here and on the top of it you say all sorts of impertinent things to me. You give me to understand that my sons did not offer themselves as sacrifices, that their blood might flow to my altar – you say the first sacrificed himself to you, and then the second to the first. What kind of manners are those? How could a man hew off his head – not simply cut his throat but cut off his head according to the proper rites (and an educated man to boot, like your Shridaman, who doesn't show up so well in the business of love) – unless he got the necessary strength and wildness out of the intoxication that came to him from me? So I forbid your tone, quite aside from whether there is any truth in your words or not! For there may be truth in them, in so far that a deed has been committed with mixed motives, and is so far unclear. It was not exclusively to seek my mercy that my son Shridaman offered himself up; actually it was for affliction about you, whether he himself was clear in the matter or no. And little Nanda's sacrifice was just the inevitable consequence. I feel little inclined to receive their blood and accept the offering. Well then: if I now make good the double sacrifice and put all back as it was, may I be permitted to hope that you will behave with more decency in the future?"

"Ah, holy goddess and dear Mother!" cried Sita through her tears. "If you could do that, if you could cancel these frightful deeds and give me back husband and friend so that all were as before – how would I bless you! I would even control my dreams and the words of them so that the noble Shridaman need suffer no more. Indescribably thankful would I be to you, if you brought that about and put everything back as it was! For though it was sad enough before, and when I stood there in your Innermost before the horrible scene, I realized clear and plain that it could not have turned out otherwise, yet it would be wonderful if you had the power and could succeed in reversing the past so that next time it might have a better issue."

"What do you mean by 'if I had the power' and 'if I could succeed'?" retorted the divine voice. "I hope you do not doubt that to my power it were the merest trifle! More than once in the world it has come to pass that I showed it. But I am sorry for you, I must say, although you do not deserve it, you and the pale, blind little seedling in your womb. The two young men in there, I pity them too. So open your ears and hear what I tell you! Drop that natural noose of yours and get back with you into my shrine, before my image and the mess you have made. No fainting or whimpering, mind! You take the two heads by the hair and fit them to the poor trunks again. Then you bless the cuts with the sharp edge of the sword of sacrifice, and both times call upon my name – you may say Durga or Kali or simply Devi, it doesn't matter – and the two youths will be restored to life. Do you understand me? Do not approach the heads too quickly to the bodies, although you will feel strong attraction between head and trunk; the spilt blood must have time to run back and be sucked in again. That happens with magic quickness, but after all it takes a moment of time. I hope you have listened to me? Then run! But do the business properly, do not put the heads on wrong way round in your haste so that they have to go about with their faces backwards and make people laugh at them! Get along! If you wait till tomorrow it will be too late."

9

The lovely Sita said nothing more at all, not even "thank you"; she jumped up and ran, fast as her swathed robe would let her, back into the mother-house. She ran through the audience chamber and through the entrance hall and into the holy shrine, and there before the frightful countenance of the goddess she set to the prescribed task with flushed and feverish energy. The attraction between heads and trunks was not so strong as one might have expected from Devi's words. It was perceptible; but yet there was time for the blood to flow back up the channels, as it did with magical swiftness and a lively lapping sound. The blessing of the sword infallibly performed its office – that and the divine name which Sita, her voice breaking with joy, cried out three times in each case. Each with his head in its place, without mark or scar the youths rose before her. They looked at her and down at themselves – or rather, in so doing they looked at each other; for to look at themselves they had to look over at each other, such being the nature of their restoration.

Sita, what hast thou done? Or what has happened? Or what

in thy flurry hast thou made to happen? In a word (to put the question so that it takes proper cognizance of the fluid boundary between doing and happening), what has come to pass with you? The excitement in which you acted is understandable; but could you not have opened your eyes a little better while you did it? No, you did not put back the heads the wrong way round – this did not happen at all. But – to tell it straight out and call the amazing truth by its name – the mischance, the mistake, the mess, or whatever all three of you might feel like calling it, that confronted you was this: you have fitted on to each one and sealed fast with the sword the other's head. Nanda's to Shridaman – if we may call his trunk without the chief feature of it Shridaman at all – and Shridaman's to Nanda, if the headless Nanda was in fact still Nanda. In short, they arose before you, not husband and friend in that order, but reversed. You behold Nanda – if he is Nanda, who wears Nanda's simple head atop – in the smock and draped trousers enveloping Shridaman's plump, slender-limbed body. You behold Shridaman – if the form may be so named that is equipped with his mild and gentle head-piece – standing before you on Nanda's well-shaped legs, the lucky-calf lock framed in stone-pearls on "his" broad bronze chest!

What a state of things – all in consequence of too much haste! They lived who had been sacrifices. But they lived transformed; the body of the husband dwelt with the head of his friend, the body of the friend with the husband's head. No wonder that the rocky cave echoed and re-echoed as the three prolonged their amazed outcry! The one with the Nanda-head felt all down the limbs and the body which once had been appended, a mere detail, to the noble head of Shridaman; while that Shridaman (if we take the head as the decisive factor) stood full of embarrassment, seeking to recognize as his own the body which – when Nanda's simple head sat on its shoulders – had been the essential feature. As for the moving cause of this new order of things, she went from one to the other by turns, with cries of joy, with loud wailing and remorse; embraced first one and then the other, and at last threw herself at their feet to confess between sobs and laughter all that had happened and the late lamentable oversight.

"Forgive me, if you can!" she cried. "Forgive me, dear Shridaman" – and she turned expressly to his head, deliberately overlooking the Nanda-body it sat on – "forgive me too, Nanda" – again she spoke to the head in question as the essential thing, regarding it, despite its insignificance, as important and the Shridaman-body thereto attached as the indifferent appendage. "Oh, you ought to be able to forgive me! Think of the frightful deed to which, as you then were, you persuaded yourselves and the despair into which you flung me. Realize that I was about to strangle myself and after that had speech with the Unapproachable and heard her voice of thunder, which almost robbed me of my senses! Then you can realize that I was hardly in a frame to carry out her commands. Things swam before my eyes, I saw only unclearly whose head and limbs I had in my hands and had to trust to luck that the right would find the right. Half the chances were for it, and half against – and it has just turned out this way, and you have come out like this. How could I know whether the power of attraction between head and limbs was in the right proportion, when it was clear and strong as it was, though of course in different combination it might have been even more so? And the Unapproachable must bear some of the blame too; for she only warned me not to put your heads on wrong side before, and that I was careful about; that it could come out as it has, the high goddess never thought of that! Tell me, are you in despair over the manner of your resurrection and will you curse me for ever? If so, I will go and carry out the deed in which I was interrupted by her that was before all beginnings. Or are you inclined to forgive me, can you find it possible that under these circumstances brought about by blind chance, a new and better life could begin between us three – a better one, I mean, than would have been possible if the former situation were just restored as it was and by all human calculations must have had just the same sad issue again? Tell me, strong-limbed Shridaman! Slender Nanda, let me hear!"

The transformed youths bent over, lifted her up, the one with the other's arms, and all three stood embraced, weeping and laughing together. Two things became at once very clear: first, that Sita had been quite right in addressing the resurrected friends according to their heads; for it was definitely by these that their I- and my-feelings were conditioned. He who on narrow, light-complexioned shoulders bore the simple head of Garga's son knew himself to be Nanda. And equally the other, with the head of the grandson of Brahmans on top of a broad, bronze-coloured frame, knew and comported himself as Shridaman. But secondly, it was manifest that neither of them was angry at Sita for her mistake, but both actually found pleasure in their new guise.

"If Nanda," said Shridaman, "is not ashamed of the body that has fallen to his lot, and does not miss too much the breast-lock of Krishna, which would be painful to me, for myself I can only say that I count myself the happiest of men. I have always wished I could have a bodily form like this; when I feel the muscles of my arms, look at my shoulders and down at my magnificent legs, I am seized with unrestrained delight, and say to myself that from now on I shall hold my head high, in quite a new way; first in the consciousness of my new strength and beauty, and second because my spiritual leanings will now be in harmony with my physical build, and it will no longer be wrong or unfitting for me to speak in favour of simplification and cast my vote under the tree for the procession of cows round the mountain Bright Peak instead of for the Brahmanical rites, for it has become quite right and proper and what was strange is so no more. Of course, my dear friends, there is a certain sadness in this, that the strange is now become my own and no longer an object of desire and admiration, except that I admire myself and that I no longer serve something else in choosing the mountain feast instead of the Indra-feast, but rather that which I myself am. Yes – this kind of sadness, due to my now being that towards which

I once yearned, I feel it, I admit. But it retreats into the background at the thought of you, sweet Sita, for you come before all thought of myself, and the advantage you will reap from my new circumstances – of which I am even now so proud and glad that for my part I can only bless this whole miracle and say: Siya, be it so!"

"You might at least be correct and say Siyat," said Nanda, whose eyes at his friend's last words had sought the ground, "instead of letting your peasant limbs rule your mouth. You are welcome to them, so far as I am concerned, I have had them much too long. But neither am I angry with you, Sita. I, too, say Siyat to this miracle, for I have always wanted a slender body like this, and now, when I speak for Indra's cult of words and against simplification, it will become me better than it did before – or at least if not my face it will become my body, which has become a minor matter to you, Shridaman, but to me it is the main point. I am not at all surprised that our heads and bodies, when you put them together, Sita, displayed such strong attraction; it was the power of the friendship which bound Shridaman and me, and of which I can only hope it may suffer no breach through what has happened. But one thing I may say: my poor head cannot help thinking for the body that has fallen to its lot, and seeing where its rights lie; and therefore I am astonished and dismayed at certain of Shridaman's words and the way they took Sita's future for granted. I see nothing here that can be taken for granted. There is only a very great question, and my head answers it otherwise than yours seems to."

"How so?" cried Sita and Shridaman as with one voice.

"How so?" repeated the slender-limbed friend. "How can you even ask? To me my body is the main point, and in this I conform to the idea of marriage, for with the body are children begot and not with the head. I should like to see him who would deny that I am the father of the fruit Sita bears in her womb."

"Pull your wits together, Nanda!" cried Shridaman, with an involuntary shift of his powerful limbs, "and think what you are saying. Are you Nanda, or who are you?"

"I am Nanda," the other replied. "But as truly as I call this wedded body mine and use the word 'I' of it, just so truly is Sita of the lovely curves my wife and her fruit of my begetting."

"Indeed!" retorted Shridaman, with a quiver in his voice. "Is it really? I should not have dared to assert it, when your present body was still mine and slept at Sita's side. For it was not that body she really embraced, as I learned to my sorrow when she muttered in her sleep. Instead it was the one I now call my own. It is not in good taste, my friend, for you to touch on these painful matters and force me to speak of them. How can you insist on your head like this, or rather on your body, and behave as though you had become I, and I you? Surely it is clear that if that kind of exchange had taken place and you had become Shridaman, Sita's husband, and I Nanda, then there would be no change at all, and everything would be as it had been. The happy miracle is that only an exchange of heads and limbs has come about at Sita's hands, whereat our heads rejoice, being the decisive factor. Above all, our rejoicing is due to the happiness in store for Sita of the lovely hips. But now here you are, obstinately presuming on your present body, which is that of a married man, and assigning to me the role of friend! You display a culpable egotism, for you are thinking only of yourself and not at all of how she will profit by the change."

"She would profit, as you call it," retorted Nanda, not without bitterness, "from advantages you are now proud to call your own. You are just as egotistic as I am. And you misunderstand me besides. I do not refer to this married body I now have, but to my very own proper head, which you yourself declare to be decisive, making me Nanda even when connected with my new and finer body. You are wrong to say I am not at least as mindful of Sita as you are. When she looked at me, of late – speaking in her sweetly trilling and lilting voice, which I feared to hear lest I should answer in the same tone – she looked into my face and into my eyes, seeking to read therein with her own, calling me Nanda and dear

Nanda. At the time it seemed unnecessary, but I see it had great spiritual significance. It showed that she did not mean my body, which in and of itself does not deserve the name; you yourself have proved that, for now that you have it you still call yourself Shridaman. I did not reply to her, except for the most necessary things, and scarcely those, so as not to fall into the same trilling and thrilling key. I did not call her by name, I kept my eyes down so she could not read in them – all out of friendship for you and reverence for your wedded state. But now I have not only the head and the eyes she gazed into, so deep and questioningly, saying 'Nanda', and 'oh, dear Nanda', but the husband-body as well – and the situation is fundamentally changed in mine and Sita's favour. Hers above all! For if we are to put her happiness and satisfaction before everything else, then certainly there can be no purer and more perfect solution than the one I describe."

"No," said Shridaman, "I would not have expected this from you. I was afraid lest you might be ashamed of my body; but now my former body might blush for your head, in such contradictions do you involve yourself, arbitrarily taking now the head and now the body as the important thing in marriage! You have always been a modest youth; but now all at once you scale the heights of presumption, and declare your situation the purest and perfectest in the world to guarantee Sita's happiness, when it is obvious that it is I who have the best, that is to say at once the happiest and most reassuring possible. But there is no sense or purpose in talking further. Here stands Sita. She must say to whom she belongs and be the judge of us and her own happiness."

Sita looked bewildered from one to the other. Then she buried her face in her hands and wept.

"I cannot," she sobbed. "Do not force me to decide, I am only a poor female, it is too hard for me. At first, it seemed quite easy, and however ashamed I was of my mistake, yet I was happy about it, especially when I saw you were both happy too. But your words have bewildered my brain and cleft my heart in twain, so that one half opposes the other half as you do each other. In your words, dear Shridaman, there is much truth, and you have not ever put it beyond doubt that I can only go home with a husband who wears your features. Nanda's opinion too I sympathize with, when I remember how pathetic and insignificant his body looked without its head, I must agree with him that I probably meant his head more than his body when I said 'dear Nanda' to him. But you used the word 'reassuring', dear Shridaman; and it is difficult indeed to say whether the head or the body of my husband would reassure me more. Do not torture me! I am quite incapable of solving the riddle, I have no power to judge which of you is my husband."

"If matters stand so," said Nanda, after a helpless silence, "and Sita cannot decide and judge between us, then judgment must come from a third or rather from a fourth party. When Sita just now said that she can only go home with a man who wears Shridaman's features, then I thought in my own mind that she and I would not go home but live somewhere in retirement, in case she should find a reassuring life with me as her husband. The thought of retirement and solitude has long been attractive to me, for when Sita's voice made me doubt the loyalty of my friendship, I would think that perhaps I might become a hermit. And I made acquaintance with such a man, practised in self-mortification, Kamadamana by name, that he might give me instruction in that kind of life. I visited him in the Dankaka forest where he lives, and where there are very many other holy men all about. His family name is just Guha; but he took the name of Kamadamana, by which he desires, as anchorite, to be called – so far as anybody has a chance to call him anything. For many years he has lived in the Dankaka forest with strict vows concerning bathing and speaking. I should say he cannot be far from his transfiguration. Let us go to this wise man, who knows and has vanquished life. Let us tell him our story and put him as judge over Sita's happiness. Let him decide, if you are agreed, which of us two is her husband, and may his words prevail."

"Yes, yes," cried Sita with relief, "Nanda is right, let us get up and go to the holy man."

"I see," said Shridaman, "that what we have here is an objective problem not to be solved from within but only by outward wisdom; I agree to the suggestion and am ready to submit to the judgment of the wise man."

Being now so far agreed, they left the mother-house together and returned to their conveyance standing down in the gully. Here the question arose which of the friends should drive, that being a matter of the body and the head both. Nanda, of course, knew the way to the Dankaka forest, which was two days' journey away. He had it all in his head; while Shridaman was now better adapted to hold the reins, just as Nanda had been before. He gave up the office to Shridaman and sat down behind him with Sita; but prompted his friend on the way he should take.

10

On the third day they reached the Dankaka forest, which was green with the rains and thickly populated with holy men, though large enough to afford each one sufficient seclusion and his own little holding of desolation void of human kind. It was not easy for the pilgrims to question their way through from solitude to solitude and find Kamadamana, the vanquisher of desires. All the hermits were one in wishing to know nothing of each other and each protested his conviction that he was alone in the wood, surrounded by unpeopled space. Holy men of various degrees were here: some of them had passed the stage of householder, and now, sometimes accompanied by their wives, were devoting the remainder of their lives to a mild form of contemplativeness. Others were yogi of the thick and thin kind, so to speak: they had as good as completely bridled the steeds of sense, by mortification and abstention fought their flesh to the knife, and managed to carry through the most awful vows. They fasted to the point of death; slept naked in the rain on the ground, and in the cold season wore their clothing wet. In the summer heat they lay between four firebrands to consume their earthly flesh – in part it dripped from them, in part it was consumed in the parching heat. To this they added further discipline by rolling days at a time on the ground, or stood continuously on the tips of their toes, or kept in constant motion by standing up and sitting down in quick succession. If by such practices they injured their health and the approach of their apotheosis was indicated, then they set forth on their final pilgrimage north and east, taking neither herbs nor roots to their nourishment but only water and air, until their bodies gave way and their souls were united with Brahma.

The seekers after decision encountered these various kinds as they wandered through the holdings of successive solitaries, having first left their conveyance at the edge of the woods with a hermit family they found leading a relatively light-minded life there, in touch, to some extent, with the outer world. The path to the particular unpeopled void where Kamadamana dwelt, was, as we said, hard to find. True, Nanda had once already found the way thither through the trackless waste. But he had done so in another body, and this hampered his intuition and sense of locality. The denizens of the caves and hollow trees were either ignorant or pretended to be so. It was only with the help of the wives of some former householders who behind the backs of their lords good-heartedly pointed out the way, and after another whole day and night spent in the wilderness, that they arrived in the preserve of their particular saint, and saw his whitewashed head with its sausage of braided hair, and his arms like dried branches reared up heavenwards, rising out of a swampy pool where he had been standing, God knows how long, up to his neck in water, his spirit gathered to a fine point. They refrained from calling to him out of reverence for so much burning zeal, and waited patiently for him to intermit his discipline. However he did not do so for a long time; either because he had not seen them or else just because he had. They had to wait for as much as an hour, keeping a modest distance from the pool, before he came out, quite naked, his beard and his body hair dripping with mud. His body was as good as fleshless, consisting merely of skin and bones; so there was, in a manner of speaking, nothing at all to his nakedness. As he approached the waiting group he swept the ground before his feet with a broom which he had taken from the bank. This, they knew, was in order not to crush any living creature that might be there. But he was not nearly so gentle to his unbidden guests: for as he came on he threatened them with uplifted broom, heedless that something irretrievable might happen to the creeping and crawling things where he trod, and that theirs would be the blame.

"Away," he shouted, "ye idlers and gapers! What seek ye in my unpeopled void?"

"O Kamadamana, vanquisher of desire," answered Nanda with due modesty, "forgive us that in our need we have so boldly approached you! The fame of your self-conquest has tempted us hither, driven by the urges of this fleshly life. Deign then, O most lion-hearted among wise men, to give us advice and useful counsel. Pray be so good as to remember me! Once already have I confided in you, to partake of your wisdom on the subject of the solitary life."

"It is possible that I may recognize you," said the recluse, looking at Nanda out of the deep caverns of his eyes, from under their threatening thatch of brow. "At least I might recognize your face; but your form seems in the meantime to have gone through a certain refining process which I suppose I may ascribe to your former visit."

"It did me a great deal of good," Nanda answered evasively. "But the change you perceive has a different cause and belongs to a story full of strangeness and stress, which is precisely the story of us three who petition you. It has set us face to face with a question we cannot solve by ourselves; we must obtain your advice and judgment. We have hope that your self-conquest may be so great that you can bring yourself to hearken to us."

"It shall be," answered Kamadamana. "No one shall say that it would not. Of course it was my first impulse to chase you out of my preserve; but that too was an impulse which I reject and a temptation I am minded to resist. For if it is self-denial to avoid men, it is still greater self-denial to put up with them. Trust me, your nearness and the fumes of life you give out lie heavy on my chest and bring an unpleasant flush to my cheeks, as you could see were it not for their seemly coating of ashes. But I am ready to bear with you and your vapours, particularly since I have observed from the first that among the three of you is a woman grown, whom the senses find glorious; slender as a vine, with soft thighs and full breasts, oh yea, oh fie! Her navel is beauteous, her face lovely with partridge-eyes, and her breasts, I repeat, are full and upstanding. Good-day, O woman! When men look upon you, do not the hairs of their bodies rise up for lust? And the troubles of the three of you, are they not due to your snares and allurements? Hail! I should most likely have sent these young men to the devil, but since you are with them, my dear, pray stay, stop as long as you like! I rejoice to invite you to my hollow tree, when I will regale you with the jujube berries I have gathered there in leaves, not to eat but to renounce, and with them in my sight gnaw roots instead, since this earthly frame must from time to time be fed. And I will listen to your tale, though the fumes of life it exhales will come nigh to choke me. Word for word will I listen to it, for no one shall ever tax Kamadamana with lack of courage. True, it is hard to distinguish between courage and curiosity. It might be that I listen to you because I have got hungry here in my retreat, and lustful to have the fumes of real life in my nostrils. But the idea must be rejected, and no less the further suggestion that curiosity here too acts to prompt the rejection and nip it in the bud, so that actually it is the curiosity that ought to be nipped. But if so, then what about my courage? It is the same as it is with the jujube berries. The thought probably tempts me that I keep them beside me not so much to renounce them as to enjoy the sight of them. To which I make bold to reply that the pleasure of looking at them constitutes the temptation to eat them. Thus I should make life too easy for myself if I did not keep them beside me. And so the suspicion is done away with, that I have thought of this answer just for the sake of being able to share the alluring sight – since, even if I do not eat the berries myself but give them to you to eat, I can enjoy seeing you put them down. And that, in view of the illusory character of the divers manifestations on this earth, and of any distinction between the I and the you, is almost the same as though I ate them myself. In short, asceticism is a bottomless pit; unfathomable because the temptations of the spirit are mingled therein with the temptations of the flesh, until the whole thing is like the snake that grows two heads as soon as you cut off one. But it is all quite right, and after all the main thing is to have courage. So come with me, you life-reeking mortals of both sexes, come with me to my hollow tree and tell me of all life's manifold uncleanliness; tell me as much as you like, and I will listen, for my correction and to get rid of the idea that I am doing it for my own entertainment – the more one gets rid of, the better!"

With these words the holy man led the way for some distance through the jungle, always carefully sweeping before him with his broom. And they arrived at his own place, a huge, very old kadamba tree, still green though it was only a gaping hollow inside. Kamadamana had chosen this mossy, earthy home not for protection against the weather, for he constantly exposed his frame to the storm, wore wet clothing in cold weather, and sat between firebrands in the time of greatest heat. No, it was only that he might know where he belonged, and have a place to store his supply of roots, tubers, and fruits to eat, and firewood, flowers, and grasses for offerings.

Here he bade his guests sit down, which they hastened to do, in all modesty, well knowing that they were here only for his asceticism, so to speak, to sharpen its teeth on. He gave them the jujube berries as he had promised and they were no little refreshed. He himself meanwhile assumed an ascetic attitude, which is called the Kajotsarga position: with motionless limbs, arms directed stiffly downwards, and rigid knee-joints. He contrived to keep separate, somehow or other, not only his fingers but his toes as well; and thus remained, his spirit summoned to its height, in all his nakedness, which signified so very little because of the lack of flesh. To Shridaman, because of his head-piece, the office of narrator had fallen; so he stood in all the magnificence of his present form beside the other, and spoke of the events which had brought them hither and the vexed question which could only be solved by a fourth party, as some saint or king.

He told it truthfully, as we have told it, in part in the same words. To make clear the disputed point, it would have been enough to tell only the final stage. But he reported it from the beginning just as it happened in order to give the holy man something to think about in his solitude. He began with an account of Nanda's life and his own, the friendship between them, and the way they broke their journey at the river Goldfly. He described his lovesickness, his wooing and marriage, weaving in such earlier information as Nanda's acquaintance with Sita, at the feast of the swinging. Other points, such as the bitter experience of his married life, he touched on with delicacy or only by inference, not to spare himself, since his were now the strong arms that had swung Sita up to the sun, and his the living body of which she had dreamed in his former arms. No, it was out of regard for Sita herself, for whom none of this could be very pleasant and who throughout the narrative kept her little head shrouded in her embroidered scarf.

The powerful Shridaman, thanks to his head-piece, proved a good and skilful narrator. Even Sita and Nanda, who knew the whole thing, of course, heard their own story, horrible as it was, with pleasure from his lips, and Kamadamana, although he maintained his Kajotsarga position unchanged, presumably found it arresting too. Shridaman recounted his own and Nanda's grisly deed, the relenting of the goddess to Sita, and Sita's pardonable error at the work of restoration. At last he got to the end, and put the question.

"Thus and thus was it," said he. "The husband's head was bestowed on the body of his friend, the friend's on the body of the husband. Be so gracious, then, as to pronounce in your wisdom upon our bewildered state, holy Kamadamana! As thou decreest, so will we be bound and act according, for we ourselves cannot decide. To whom now belongs this all-round fine-limbed woman, and who is truly her husband?"

"Yes, tell us, tell us, O vanquisher of desire!" cried Nanda loudly and with confidence. Sita only hastily pulled her veil from her head to direct her lotus-eyes expectantly upon Kamadamana.

The latter drew his fingers and toes together and sighed deeply. Then he took his broom, swept himself a spot on the ground free from vulnerable insects, and sat down with his guests.

"Faugh!" said he. "You three are certainly the right people for me! I was prepared of course for a tale full of life's headiest fumes. But this of yours, you could fairly cut it with a knife. It is easier for me to hold out between my four firebrands in the hottest summer heat than to breathe in the stream you are giving out. If I had not rouged my face with ashes you could see the flush on my decently lank cheeks or rather on the ascetic bones of them. Ah children, children! Like to the ox that with his eyes bound up turns the oil-mill round and round, so you are turned upon the wheel of life, anguished with appetite, pricked and twitched in your flesh by the six miller's men of the passions. Could you not leave off? Must you still go on, with your ogling, licking, slavering, your knees giving way with desire when the object of your delusion heaves in sight? Yes, yes, I know, I know it all: the body of love, with bitter lust bedewed – limb-play 'neath satin skin, unguent-imbrued – the noble vault the shoulder makes – the sniffing nose, loose mouth that seeks – sweet breasts adorned with tender stars – the armpits' hollow with sweat-drenched hairs – oh, pasturage for hands to rove, fair hips, fine loins, back supple, belly breathing love – the bliss-embrace of arms, the bloomy thighs, cool twin delight of hillocks that behind them lies – till all agog with lust at pitch they work at coupling play in hot and reeking dark, each urging other on more bliss to capture, they flute each other to a heaven of rapture – and this and that and here and there – I know it all, of all I am aware!"

"But so are we – we know all that ourselves and of ourselves, great Kamadamana," said Nanda with suppressed impatience in his voice. "Will you not be so good as to come to the point and instruct us, who is Sita's husband, that we many finally know and act according?"

"The judgment," replied the holy man, "is as good as given. It is clear that I am surprised you are not far enough along in knowledge of the right things that you need a judge in so clear and self-evident a matter. The little tidbit there, of course, is the wife of him who has his friend's head on his shoulders. For in the marriage one reaches the right hand to the bride; but the hand belongs to the body; and the body is the friend's."

With an exultant cry Nanda leaped to his finely shaped feet. Sita and Shridaman sat still with bowed heads.

"But that is only the premise," Kamadamana went on in a louder voice. "The conclusion follows to surmount and outsound it, and crown it with truth. Please wait a moment."

With that he stood up and went inside his hollow, fetched a rude garment, a sort of apron made out of thin bark, and clothed his nakedness with it. Then he spoke:

"Husband is, who wears the husband's head.
Here lies no doubt at all, must it be said,
As woman is the highest bliss and bourne of songs,
So among limbs to head the highest rank belongs."

It was Sita's and Shridaman's turn to lift their heads and look joyfully at each other. Nanda, who had but now been so glad, remarked in a crestfallen voice:

"But you said something quite different before!"

"What I said last," replied Kamadamana, "is decisive."

So now they had their verdict. Nanda, in his refined state, could least of all murmur against it, since he himself had proposed to take the holy man for their judge. Nor could he object to the irreproachable gallantry on which Kamadamana had based his decree.

They all bowed low before Kamadamana and departed hence. Together they went, not speaking, for some distance through the Dankaka forest, green with the rains. Then Nanda stopped in his tracks and took leave of them.

"All the best to you," said he. "I will now go my ways. I will find me an unpeopled void and become a hermit, as I previously intended. Anyway, in my present incorporation I feel myself a little too good for the world."

Neither of them could blame him for his decision. They agreed with him, though it made them feel slightly depressed; and bade him farewell with the friendliness one shows towards a man who has drawn the shorter straw. Shridaman clapped him encouragingly on the shoulder that once was his own, and advised him, with a concern such as one seldom feels for anybody else, not to plague his body with extravagant discipline, and not to eat too many tubers, for he knew that a monotonous diet did not suit him.

"Let that be my affair," said Nanda ungraciously. And when Sita tried to utter words of consolation he only shook his goat-nosed head, in bitter melancholy.

"Don't take it too much to heart," said she. "Don't forget that you nearly triumphed, and that you might be now about to share with me the legal joys of wedlock. Be sure I shall always feel the sweetest tenderness from head to foot for all that once was yours, and with hand and lips show gratitude for my joy, in ways so choice that only the eternal Mother can teach them to me!"

"Of all that I shall have nothing," he replied obstinately. She even whispered to him: "Sometimes I will dream of thy head too"; but his mien did not change, he only said sadly and stubbornly: "Of that I shall have nothing."

So they parted, the one and the two. But Sita turned back when Nanda was already a little distant, and flung her arms about him.

"Farewell," said she. "After all, you were my first husband, you first awakened me and taught me love so far as I know it; and whatever that dried-up holy man may think and sing about wives and heads, the fruit beneath my heart comes from you after all!"

With that she ran back to Shridaman the strong.

II

Once back at Welfare of Cows, Sita and Shridaman spent their days and nights in full enjoyment of the pleasures of sense; nor did any shadow trouble at first the cloudless heaven of their bliss. The little words "at first", a faint premonitory troubling of their unclouded sky, are an addition by one narrating the story from outside; whereas they who lived in it, whose story it is, knew of no "at first", but were only aware of their joy, which both sides considered no common thing.

It was, indeed, a happiness such as belongs to paradise and seldom to this earth. The common earthly joys, the gratifications falling to the lot of mortals in all the conditions of the moral order and social pressure under which we live, are circumscribed indeed. Makeshifts, renunciations, and resignation are the common lot. Our desires are boundless, their fulfilment sharply restricted; "If I only could" is met on all sides by the stern "It won't do". Life soberly bids us put up with what we can get. A few things are granted, but more denied; that they will one day be granted is and remains a dream. A paradisial dream, of course; for in paradise, surely, that which is forbidden and that which is granted, so diverse here below, must there become one. The lovely forbidden must be crowned with legality, while the legal attains to all the charms of the forbidden. For in what other guise can paradise appear to the hankering man?

Well, it was just this unearthly kind of happiness that a capricious fate had dealt out to the wedded lovers on their return to Welfare of Cows. They drank it down in thirsty gulps – at first. For Sita, the awakened lover and friend had been two different people; but now, oh joy, they were one, and – by inevitable destiny – the best of each. What had been most individual in each had joined to form a new individuality surpassing all desire. Nightly on her lawful couch she nestled in the strong arms of Shridaman's friend and experienced his raptures as once on her husband's tender bosom she had closed her eyes and dreamed of them. Yet it was the head-piece of the descendant of Brahmans that she kissed in gratitude – the most highly favoured woman in all the world, for she possessed a husband who, so to speak, consisted of nothing but principal features.

And Shridaman, the transformed husband – how proud and glad was he not in his turn! We need not be concerned lest the change in him made an unpleasant impression on Bhavabhuti his father or on his mother (whose name does not occur in the story because she plays so modest a role) or on any other member of the Brahman merchant's family or the other inhabitants of the temple village. The idea that there was anything wrong or unnatural about Shridaman's physical improvement (as though the natural things were the only right ones!) might easily have arisen, if the metamorphosed Nanda had been there too. But he was far away, leading the hermit life, to which he had previously sometimes shown a leaning. The change in him, which might have been striking when viewed together with his friend's, was known to nobody; there was only Shridaman, whose bronzed and beauteous limbs might be credited (so far as they were noticed at all) to the beneficial effect of married life on his masculine development. Sita's lord and husband, of course, did not go about in Nanda's loincloth, arm-bands, and stone-pearl necklace. Conformably to his head-piece, he wore as before the draped trousers and cotton smock which had always been his garb. And in all this we must see undeniable proof of the contention that the head is the all-important factor in establishing the human being's identity. Try to imagine your son or your brother or some acquaintance entering the room with his perfectly well-known head on his shoulders; whatever might be out of order with the rest of his appearance, would you entertain the smallest doubt that this was actually the brother, son, or acquaintance in question?

The description of Sita's bliss has been given precedence over Shridaman's in this narrative just as he himself, directly after his transformation, placed it, as we saw, before his own. But his happiness was in fact equal to hers and wore the same paradisial face. Indeed, I cannot sufficiently adjure the listener to put himself in Shridaman's place. Here was a lover who had shrunk in profound dejection from the beloved object, being driven to realize that she longed for the embraces of another. And now he was in the incomparable position of offering her everything she had so mortally craved. One feels tempted to rank his good fortune above that of the charming Sita. That love for Sumantra's golden child that had seized upon Shridaman when he saw her at her ritual bath – a love so deep and ardent that he had thought he must die of it, to the great amusement of Nanda's vulgar mind; that violent, anguished attack of tenderness, kindled by a lovely image on which he at once hastened to confer a human dignity; that rapture, in short, born, of course, of spirit and sense combined, and of his whole personality – had been above all and in essentials a matter of his Brahman head, gifted by the goddess of speech with fervour of thought and power of imagination. That head's mild appendage, Shridaman's body, was no equal partner to it, and must in the marriage relation have betrayed the fact. Can we now realize the joy, the satisfaction of such a being, when to such a gifted, ardent, subtle head was added a good, gay, ordinary body, a body simple and strong, accurately corresponding to the spiritual passions conceived in the head? It is idle to imagine the blisses of paradise – in other words, life in the pleasure-grove called "Joy" – otherwise than in the image of this perfection.

Even the depressing "at first" does not come into the above description; and indeed is not pertinent there since it is not in the consciousness of those concerned, but belongs solely to the controlling sphere of the narrator's mind and thus casts only an objective, impersonal shadow. But now, indeed, it must be told that very soon, very early, it began to glide into the personal sphere; yes, probably from the beginning it played its earthly role to limit and condition in a way surely unknown in paradise. We must admit that Sita of the lovely hips had made a mistake when she carried out in the way she did the goddess's gracious command: a mistake not only in so far as she carried it out in blind haste, but also in so far as she carried it out not quite and altogether in blind haste. This sentence has been well considered and must be well understood.

Nowhere does the magic of Maya the preserver, life's fundamental law of illusion, deception, imagination, which holds all creatures in thrall – nowhere does it more show its deluding power than in love, in that tender craving of one single creature for another, which is so precisely the pattern and prime content of all the attachment, all the involvement and entanglement, all the delusions on which life feeds and by which it is lured to perpetuate itself. Not for nothing is lust called the love-god's most cunning mate; not in vain is that goddess called "gifted with Maya"; for she it is which makes any phenomenon charming and worthy of desire, or rather makes it seem so; the sense-element is already apparent in the word itself, linking it with ideas of brilliance and beauty. Lust it was, the goddess and deceiver, made Sita's form so dazzling fair, so worship-ripe, to the youths at Durga's bathing-place, especially to the suggestible Shridaman. But note how glad and grateful the friends had been when the bather turned her head and they saw her face, that it too was lovely, the little nose and lips, and brows and eyes; so that the sweet form had not been deprived of value and meaning by ugly features. We need only recall that to realize how much obsessed a man is, not only with the desired one but with desire itself; how he is not seeking sanity but intoxication and yearning, and fears nothing more than to be undeceived, that is to say relieved of his delusion.

And now see how this concern, that the little face the friends were spying on might be pretty too, proves dependence of the body, by its Maya-meaning and value, upon the head to which it belongs! Rightly had Kamadamana, vanquisher of desire, declared the head to be the highest of the limbs and on that statement based his judgment. Indeed, the head decides the value of the body for love, and the impression it makes. It is not enough to say that if it wore another head it would not be the same. Let one single feature, one expressive line be changed, and the whole is altered. Herein lay the error which Sita in error committed. She counted herself happy to have made it, because it seemed to her paradisial – and perhaps in the beginning had appeared so – to possess the friend's body in the sign of the husband's head. But she had not foreseen – nor in her happiness would at first admit it – that the Nanda-body, when combined with the narrow-nosed Shridaman-head, the thoughtful, mild eyes and cheeks covered with soft fan-shaped beard, was no longer Nanda's lively body but another altogether.

Another it was, at once and from the first minute after his Maya. But not only of this do I speak. For in time – the time that Sita and Shridaman spent "at first" in perfect relish of their sensual joys, in the incomparable delights of love – the body of the friend, so hotly coveted and won at last (if one may still so designate the body of Nanda in the sign of Shridaman's head, when in actual fact the far-away husband-body had become the friend-body); in time, then, and indeed in no long time, the Nanda-body, crowned with the honoured husband-head, became of itself, and aside from any Maya, quite a different one. Under the influence of the head and the laws of the head, it gradually became like a husband-body.

That is the common lot, the regular effect of married life. Sita's melancholy experience differed on this point not greatly from that of another woman who presently no longer recognizes in her easy-going spouse the slender lusty youth who wooed her. Yet here the common lot had a special bearing and cause.

The Shridaman-head had shown its influence when Sita's wedded lord continued to dress his new body as he had the old and not as Nanda did. Again, he did not follow Nanda's practice of anointing his skin with mustard oil. His head could not tolerate this odour on his own person; he stopped using the oil and that was rather disappointing to Sita. Another slight disappointment was the fact that when Shridaman sat on the ground his posture – as need hardly be said – was conditioned not by his body but by his head. He had contempt for the rustic position beloved of Nanda, and sat sidewise as he always had. But all these were trifles and belonged to early days.

Shridaman, the Brahman's grandson, continued, even with Nanda's body, to be what he had been and to live as he had lived. He was no smith nor herd, but a vanija and son of a vanija, who helped his father carry on a respectable trade; as the father declined in strength the son took over the business. No heavy hammer did he wield, nor pastured the kine on the mountain Bright Peak; but bought and sold mull and camphor, silk and calico, likewise rice-mallets and fire-lighters to supply the needs of the folk at Welfare of Cows. Between times he read in the Vedas. It was no miracle then, however miraculous the tale may otherwise sound, that Nanda's arms soon began to lose their strength and grow thinner; his chest to narrow and relax and some slight fat to gather on his little belly – in short that he fell more and more into the husband pattern. Even the lucky-calf lock failed him; not altogether, it merely grew thinner, so that it was scarcely recognizable as Krishna's sign – Sita his wife observed with pain. It is undeniable that a certain refinement, in part Brahman, in part clerkly, an ennoblement, if you like, was – aside from any Maya – bound up with the change, and extended even to his complexion, which turned some shades lighter; his hands and feet grew smaller and finer, more delicate the bones and knee-joints. And in short the joyous friend-body, in its former life the chief of the whole, turned into a tame appendage to a head, into whose noble impulses it soon neither could nor would enter with any paradisial completeness, and even bore them company with a certain reluctance.

Such was Sita's and Shridaman's wedded experience, once the truly incomparable joys of the honeymoon were past.

Things did not get so far that the Nanda-body changed back completely into the Shridaman-body – when indeed everything would have been as before. Our narrative will not exaggerate, rather it emphasizes the factors limiting the bodily change, and its restriction to unmistakable signs, in order to gain understanding for the fact that the effect was reciprocal between head and limbs; since the Shridaman-head, conditioning his I- and my-feeling, underwent adaptation in its turn. This might be explained on natural grounds by secretions common to head and body; but on philosophical ones by loftier considerations.

There is an intellectual beauty and one that speaks to the senses. Some people will have it that the beautiful belongs solely to the field of sense; they separate the intellectual entirely from it, so that our world presents a picture of cleavage between the two. This is the basis of the Vedic teaching; "Bliss experienced in all the universe is of two kinds only: the joys received through the body and those through the redeeming peace of the spirit." Yet it follows directly from the doctrine that the spirit does not stand in the same relation to the beautiful that the ugly does and is not inevitably one and the same. The things of the spirit and mind are not synonymous with the ugly, nor need they be; for they take on beauty through knowledge of the beautiful and love of it, and express that love as spiritual beauty. So their love is by no means an irrelevant and hopeless thing; for by the law of attraction of opposites the beautiful yearns in its turn towards the spiritual, admires it and welcomes its wooing. This world is not so made that spirit is fated to love only spirit, and beauty only beauty. Indeed the very contrast between the two points out, with a clarity at once intellectual and beautiful, that the world's goal is union between spirit and beauty, a bliss no longer divided but whole and consummate. This tale of ours is but an illustration of the failures and false starts attending the effort to reach the goal.

Shridaman, son of Bhavabhuti, had by mistake been given a beautiful, sturdy body to accompany his noble head, where love of the beautiful reigned. And his mind straightaway found something sad in the fact that the strange had now become his and was no longer an object of admiration – in other words, that he was not himself that after which he had yearned. This "sadness" unfortunately persisted throughout the changes which his head suffered in combination with the new body; for these changes were such as go on in a head that through possession of the beautiful more or less loses the love of it and therewith its own spiritual beauty.

The question remains open whether this process would not have taken place anyhow, without the bodily change, simply because Shridaman now possessed the lovely Sita. We have already said that the case in general was like the common run of cases, though exaggerated by special circumstances. To the objective listener, it is merely an interesting fact, but to the lovely Sita it must have been a distressing and sobering sight, that her husband's fine thin lips got fuller and thicker in his soft beard until they finally curled over in a roll of flesh; that his nose, once thin as a knife blade, took on fleshiness too, and showed an undeniable inclination to droop and decline into the goat-like. His eyes in time wore an expression of rather heavy joviality. The final product was a Shridaman with a finer Nanda-body and a coarser Shridaman-head; there was no longer anything right about him at all. And here the narrator would particularly invoke the sympathy of his hearers for Sita's feelings as she watched the changes and drew inevitable conclusions about corresponding changes which might have taken place in the distant friend.

She thought about her husband's body, which she had embraced in not precisely blissful but sanctified and provocative bridal nights, and which she no longer possessed – or which, if you like, as it was now the friend-body, she still did not possess – and she doubted not where the lucky-calf lock was to be found. Moreover she definitely suspected that a refining process must have taken place in the loyal friend-head which now sat atop the husband-body, in the same way that the friend-body was now crowned by the husband-head. It was this speculation, even more than the other, that moved her. Soon she had no more rest by day or night, not even in her husband's moderated arms. The lonely and doubtless beautified husband-body hovered before her, wearing a pathetically refined Nanda-head, and suffering spiritually from the separation. Longing and pity for him so far away were born and grew in her, so that she closed her eyes in Shridaman's wedded embraces and in lust waxed pale for very woe.

12

When her time was come, Sita bore to Shridaman the fruit of her womb, a little boy, to whom they gave the name of Samadhi, which means "collection". They waved a cow's tail above the new-born to ward off evil, and put cow-dung on his head to the same end – as was right and proper. The joy of the parents (if that is the right word) was very great, for the boy was neither pale nor blind. True, he was very light-skinned; but that might come from his mother's Kshatriya or warrior blood. He turned out later to be very near-sighted. Thus do prophecies and folk-lore get themselves fulfilled, somewhat darkly and imperfectly. You may say they have "come true", or that they have not, as you like.

After a while Samadhi got the nick-name of Andhaka (little blind one) on account of his near-sightedness, and the name gradually ousted the first one. But the weakness lent his gazelle-like eyes a soft appealing gloss and made them even lovelier than Sita's, which they resembled. All together, he took far more after her than after either of his two fathers. She was obviously the clearest and most unequivocal element in his composition, and it was natural that his form should shape itself to hers. He was pretty as a picture; and once he had got past the stage of soiled and crippling swaddlings he proved to be a model of symmetry and strength. Shridaman loved him as his own flesh and blood; and his soul began to register certain feelings of abdication, a desire to hand over the business of living to his son.

But the years in which Samadhi-Andhaka developed into loveliness at his mother's breast and in his hammock cradle were just the ones during which the changes slowly took place in Shridaman's head and limbs, turning his whole person so decisively into the husband-form that Sita could endure it no longer. She felt an overmastering sympathy with the far-off friend in whom she envisaged the begetter of her little son. The longing to see him again, to see what he in his turn might have become by operation of the law of assimilation; to show him his delightful offspring, that he too might have his joy in him, that longing filled her soul to overflowing, yet she dared not communicate it to her husband-head. So when Samadhi was four years old, and was called Andhaka more often than by his name; when he could run, but more often fell down, it happened that Shridaman went away on business, and Sita made up her mind, whatever the cost, to seek out Nanda the hermit to console him.

One morning in spring, by starlight and before the dawn, she put on her pilgrim shoes, took staff to hand and with the other clasped that of her little son, dressed in his shirt of cotton from Kalikat. With a sack of provisions on her back she stole away unseen, and by great good luck was soon off with him out of house and village.

Her courage in face of the hardships and perils of her pilgrimage is evidence of the great urgency of her desire. Her warrior blood, watered down though it might be, may have come to her aid; certainly her beauty did so, as well as that of her son; for everybody rejoiced to help the lovely pilgrim and her shining-eyed companion on their way with word and deed. She told people that she was journeying in search of her husband, father of her child, who had felt irresistible craving to contemplate the nature of things and so had become a forest hermit. She wished, she said, to conduct her son hither, that his father might bless and instruct him; and this too made folk's hearts soft, reverent, and gracious to her. In the villages and resting-places she got milk for her little one, almost always she procured a night's lodging for herself and him in hay-barns and on the earthen banks of furnaces. Often the jute and rice farmers took her long distances in their carts, and when there was no such conveyance, she paced onwards with her staff undaunted, in the dust of the highroads. She held Andhaka's hand and he took two steps to one of hers and with his shining eyes saw only a little space of the road before him. But she saw far ahead into the distance to be travelled, the goal of her pity and yearning fixed before her eyes.

Thus in her wanderings she reached the Dankaka forest, having guessed that her friend had sought himself out a solitude in that place. But she learned from the holy men she asked that he was not there. Many could or would say nothing more; but some good-hearted hermit-wives who had fed and petted little Samadhi told her kindly where Nanda was. For the world of the hermit is very like other worlds: when you belong to it you know your way about there, and all the gossip and jealousy and rivalry and back-biting that go on. One hermit of course knows where another hermit lives and what he is doing. So these good women could betray to Sita that Nanda the hermit had set up his rest near the river Gomati (the Cow River), seven days' journey distant by south and west. It was, they said, a spot to gladden the heart, with all kinds of trees, flowers, and clinging vines, full of bird-song and herds of animals; the river-bank had roots, tubers and fruits in plenty. All in all Nanda had chosen his retreat in almost too pleasant a spot, and the more austere among the saints did not take his asceticism very seriously, particularly as he observed no vows save bathing and silence, and ate the fruits of the forest as they came to hand, with wild rice in the rainy season and even now and then a roast bird. In short, he was merely contemplative after the fashion of any disappointed and dejected man. As for the way thither, it was without special difficulties or hardships, except for the robbers' pass, the gorge of tigers, and the vale of serpents, where certainly one needed to have a care and to take one's courage in both hands.

Thus instructed, Sita took leave of the friendly women of the Dankaka and with fresh hopes continued her journey as before. She surmounted the difficulties each day as they came, and haply Kama the god of love, in bond with Shri-Lakshme, mistress of good fortune, guided her steps aright. Unassailed she put behind her the robbers' pass; the gorge of tigers she went round, by instruction from some friendly shepherds, and in the vale of serpents, which lay directly on her route, she carried little Samadhi-Andhaka the whole way in her arms.

But when she came to the Cow River she set him down and led him by the hand, with the other planting her staff. It was a morning shimmering with dew. A while she paced onwards along the flowery banks; then as she had been instructed turned landwards across the plain to a strip of woods behind which the sun was just rising. The blossoms of the red ashoka and the kinshuka tree made the woodland glow like fire. Her eyes were dazed by the bright sun; but when she shaded them with her hand she distinguished a hut at the edge of the clearing, thatched with straw and bark, and behind it a youth in bast garments girdled with grasses, working at the structure with an axe. As she drew yet nearer she saw that his arms were strong like those that had swung her up to the sun; but his nose came down towards the only moderately thick lips in a way that could not be called goat-like but only refined.

"Nanda!" she cried, her heart on fire with joy. He seemed to her like Krishna, who is overflowing with the juices of great tenderness. "Nanda, look, it is Sita coming to you."

He let fall his axe and ran towards her and on his breast he had the lucky-calf lock. With a hundred welcomes and by a hundred pet names he spoke to her, for he had yearned sorely for her in her entirety, with body and soul. "Art thou come at last," he cried, "thou mild moon, thou partridge-eyed, thou altogether lovely-limbed, fair-hued thou, Sita, my wife, with the glorious hips! How many nights have I dreamed that you came so to the outcast and solitary across the wastes, and now it is really you, and you have conquered the robbers' pass, the tigers' gorge, and the serpents' vale, that I wilfully put between us out of anger at the judgment of fate! Ah, what a splendid woman! And who is this you bring with you?"

"It is the fruit," she said, "that you gave me in the first holy wedded night, when you were not yet Nanda."

"That will not have been much," said he. "What is he called?"

"He is named Samadhi," she replied, "but more and more he is called Andhaka."

"Why so?" he asked.

"Do not think he is blind," she responded. "He is no more blind than he is pale, despite his fair complexion. But he is truly very short-sighted, so that he can only see three paces before him."

"That has its good side," Nanda said. They set the boy a little distance from the hut, in the fresh green grass, and gave him flowers and nuts to play with. Thus he was busy; and what they played – fanned about with the fragrance of the mango flowers spring sends to heighten desire, and to the music of the kokils' trilling in the sunlit tree-tops – that lay outside the range of his vision.

13

The story goes on to tell that the wedded bliss of these lovers lasted but a day and a night. The sun had not risen for the second time above the fiery blossoms of the wood beside Nanda's hut when Shridaman came on the scene. He had known as soon as he got back to his empty house whither it was his wife had gone. His family at Welfare of Cows had tremblingly announced the disappearance of Sita, and had surely expected that his anger would blaze up like a fire into which butter is cast. But that did not happen; he had only nodded slowly like a man who had known it all before. Nor had he set out after his wife in wrath and lust for revenge; he went indeed without rest but also without haste, direct to Nanda's retreat, having long known the precise spot and kept the knowledge from Sita in order not to hasten fate.

Mildly, with drooping head, he came riding on a yak; dismounted under the morning star before the hut, and did not even disturb the embraces of the pair within, but sat and waited for day to break them off. For his jealousy was of no ordinary kind such as is commonly suffered with furious sighs by dissevered lovers. It was lightened by the knowledge that this was his former body with which Sita was now renewing her marriage vows – an act that might as well be called faithfulness as the reverse. Shridaman's knowledge of the nature of things taught him that it was in principle unimportant with whom Sita slept, with him or with his friend, since even though one of them had nothing from it, she always did it with both of them.

Hence his lack of haste on the journey and his patience and composure as he sat in front of the hut and awaited the dawning of day. But we shall see that notwithstanding he was not minded to let matters take their course. The story says that at the first ray of dawn, while little Andhaka still slept, Sita and Nanda came out of the hut with towels round their necks, to bathe in the near-by stream; thus they perceived the friend and husband, who sat with his back to them and did not turn round as they appeared. They came before him, greeted him with humility, and in the end wholly united their wills to his, recognizing as inevitable what he had excogitated on the way about their problem and its solution.

"Shridaman, my lord and honoured husband-head," said Sita as she bowed low before him, "greetings and hail – and believe not that your coming is unwelcome and awful to us. For where two of us are, the third will always be lacking; forgive me then, that I could not hold out longer with you but overcome by pity sought out the lonely friend-head."

"And the husband-body," answered Shridaman. "I forgive you. I forgive you too, Nanda, as on your side you may forgive me for acting on the judgment of the holy man and taking Sita for myself, only considering my own I- and my-feeling and not troubling about yours. You would have done just the same if the holy man's judgment had been in your favour. For in the madness and divisions of this life it is the lot of human beings to stand in one another's light, and in vain do the better-constituted long for an existence in which the laughter of one would not be the weeping of another. All too much have I insisted on my head, which rejoiced in your body. For with these somewhat diminished arms you swung Sita up to the sun and in our new distribution I flattered myself I had everything to offer for which she yearned. But love has to do with the whole. So I had to suffer that our Sita abode by your head and went out of my house. If I could now believe she would find her lasting joy and satisfaction in you, my friend, I would go away and make my own retreat in the house of my fathers. But I do not believe it. Possessing the husband-head on the friend-body, she yearned for the friend-head on the husband-body. And just as certainly would she feel pity and sympathy for the husband-head on the friend-body, nor would she find any peace and satisfaction, the distant husband would ever be the friend whom she loves, to him would she bring our son Andhaka, because she sees the father in him. But with both of us she cannot live, since polyandry is not permitted among superior beings. Am I right, Sita, in what I say?"

"As thy word sayeth, so, alas, is it, my lord and friend," answered she. "My regret, however, which I sum up in the word 'alas', refers only to part of your words, and has no reference to the abomination of polyandry, for I cannot regret that it does not come into consideration for a woman like me. Rather I am proud. From my father Sumantra's side some warrior blood still flows in my veins, and against anything so base as polyandry everything in me rises up. In all the weakness and bewilderment of the flesh one has yet one's pride and honour as a superior being."

"I had not expected otherwise," answered Shridaman. "You may be sure that I have from the beginning taken into consideration this attitude, as distinct from your female feebleness. Since you cannot live with both of us, I am certain that this youth here, Nanda, my friend, with whom

I exchanged heads, or bodies as you like, Nanda will agree with me that neither of us can live, and nothing remains but to put off the division we have exchanged and unite our essences once more with the All. For where the single essence has fallen into such conflict as in our case, it were best it melt in the flame of life as an offering of butter in the sacrificial fire."

"Most rightly, Shridaman, my brother," said Nanda, "do you count on my agreement with your words. It is unconditional. I should not know what we could still have to seek in the flesh, since both of us have gratified our desires and slept at Sita's side. My body could rejoice in her in the consciousness of your head and yours in the consciousness of mine, as she rejoiced in me in the sign of your head and in you in the sign of mine. But our honour may count as saved, for I have only betrayed your head with your body, and that is quitted, in a way, by the fact that Sita the lovely-hipped betrayed my head with your body. Brahma has preserved us from the worst; that I who once shared the betel-roll with you in sign of loyalty should have betrayed you with her as Nanda in head and body both! But even so we cannot honourably go on like this, since we are too enlightened for polyandry and promiscuity; certainly Sita is, and so are you, even when you have my body; and I myself too, now that I have yours. Therefore I unreservedly agree with everything you say about mingling our essence. Here are these arms, they have been strengthened in the wilderness, I offer them to build the funeral pyre. You know I have already offered before. You know too that I was always resolved not to outlive you, and I followed you without hesitation into death when you sacrificed yourself to the goddess. I only betrayed you when my husband-body gave me a certain right and Sita brought me the little Samadhi, whose bodily father I must consider myself, though I willingly and respectfully concede your parenthood according to the head."

"Where is Andhaka?" asked Shridaman.

"He is lying in the hut," answered Sita, "collecting in sleep strength and beauty for his older days. It is time we spoke of him; for his future ought to be more important to us than the question of how we shall come with honour out of all these perplexities. But his case and ours are closely related, and we shall be acting for his honour in acting for ours. Were I to stay behind with him, as I might, I suppose, when you withdraw into the All, then he would pass through life as a wretched orphan child forsaken of honour and joy. Only if I follow the example of those noble Satis who united themselves to the bodies of their dead husbands, and mounted with them into the fire, and monuments, a stone tablet, and obelisks were erected to their memory on the place of their burning – only if I leave him will his life be honourable and the favour of men fall upon him. Therefore I, the daughter of Sumantra, demand that Nanda build the funeral pyre for three. As I have shared the couch of life with you both, so shall also death's fiery bed unite us three. For after all, on the other we were always three."

"Never," said Shridaman, "would I expect anything else from you; for from the first I have known your high spirit and your pride, and that they dwell in you along with the weakness of the flesh. In the name of our son I thank you for your resolve. But we must consider well how to rescue our honour and human pride out of the desolation into which the flesh has brought us. We must take great care for the form that rescue takes; and in this particular my thoughts and plans as I have developed them on the way hither differ somewhat from yours. The high-hearted widow turns herself to ashes beside her dead husband. But you are not a widow as long as one of us is alive; and it is a question whether you would become a widow by sitting living with us in the fire and dying as we died. To make you a widow Nanda and I must kill ourselves, I mean we must each kill the other; in our case either is right and both come to the same thing. We must fight like bucks for the doe; I have provided two swords, they hang on the girth of my yak. But it may not be that one shall win and survive and carry off the fine-hipped Sita for himself. That would do no good, for ever would the dead man be the friend after whom she would consume herself with longing, till she faded away in the arms of her husband. No, we must both fall, each struck to the heart by the other's sword – for only the sword is the 'other's', not the heart. That will be better than if each of us turned the sword against his own present division; for it seems to me our heads have no right to decree death to the body attached to each, any more than our bodies would have the right to wedded bliss wearing heads that do not belong to them. Indeed the battle will be sore; for the head and body of each of us must take care not to fight for itself and the possession of Sita, but to remember the double duty of giving and receiving the mortal blow. Still, each of us brought himself to cut off his own head – and this mutual suicide cannot be harder than that."

"Bring on the swords," cried Nanda. "I am ready for the fray, and find it is a just solution to our rivalry. It is just, because in the process of adaptation of our bodies to our heads, our arms have come to be of almost equal strength – yours stronger on my body, mine weaker on yours. Gladly will I offer my heart to your weapon. But yours I will pierce through that Sita may not pale for love of me in your arms, but doubly widowed join us in the flames."

Sita professed herself satisfied with these arrangements, she said they appealed to her warrior blood. Wherefore she would not withdraw from the combat but look on unflinching. So then this mortal meeting took place forthwith in front of the hut where Andhaka lay asleep, and on the flowery mead between the Cow River and the red-blossoming woodland; and both young men sank down into the flowers, each pierced through the other's heart. Their funeral, because of the religious ceremonial of suttee combined with it, became a great festival. Thousands gathered on the place of burning to watch the little Samadhi, called Andhaka. As next of kin male he brought his near-sighted gaze to bear and laid the torch to the pyre built of mango and sweet-smelling knots of sandalwood, the interstices filled with dry straw soaked in melted butter that it might catch quickly. Within the pyre Sita of Bisonbull had found her place between her husband and her friend. The pile blazed heavenwards to a most unusual height; and if the lovely Sita shrieked awhile – because fire when one is not already dead is frightfully painful – her voice was drowned out by the yelling of conches and rolling of drums so that it was just as though she had not shrieked. But the story says, and we would believe it, that the heat was cool to her in the joy of being united with her twain beloved.

An obelisk was set up on the spot in memory of her sacrifice, and what was not entirely burnt of the bones of the three was collected, drenched with milk and honey, and buried in an earthen pot which was thrown into the holy Ganges.

But the little fruit of her womb, Samadhi, who was soon called nothing but Andhaka, he prospered upon earth. He enjoyed fame and favour as the son of a monument-widow, and to that was added a love called forth by his increasing beauty. Even at twelve years old he was like an incarnation of a Gandharva for charm and supple strength; and on his breast the lucky-calf lock began to show. His poor eyesight, far from being a handicap, kept him from living too much in the body's concerns and directed his head towards the things of the mind. A wise and learned Brahman took charge of the seven-year-old lad; and taught him right and cultured speech, grammar, astronomy, and the art of thought. At the youthful age of twenty he was already reader to the King of Benares. On a splendid palace terrace he sat, in fine garments, under a white silk umbrella, and read aloud to that prince in a pleasing voice, from the sacred and profane writings, holding his book close in front of his shining eyes.

THE TABLES OF THE LAW

I

HIS BIRTH was disorderly. Therefore he passionately loved order, the immutable, the bidden, and the forbidden.

Early he killed in frenzy; therefore he knew better than the inexperienced that, though killing is delectable, *having* killed is detestable; he knew you should not kill.

He was sensual, therefore he longed for the spiritual, the pure, and the holy – in a word, the *invisible* – for this alone seemed to him spiritual, holy, and pure.

Among the Midianites, a nimble tribe of shepherds and merchants strewn across the desert, to whom he had to flee from Egypt, the land of his birth, because he had killed, he made the acquaintance of a god whom one could not see but who saw you. This god was a mountain-dweller who at the same time sat invisible on a transportable chest in a tent and there dispensed oracles by the drawing of lots. To the children of Midian this numen, called Jahwe, was one god among many; they did not bother very much about serving him. What service they undertook they did to be on the safe side, just in case. For it had occurred to them that among the gods there could possibly be a bodiless one whom one did not see, and they sacrificed to him so as not to miss anything, not to offend anybody, to forestall any unpleasantness from any quarter.

But Moses, because of his desire for the pure and the holy, was deeply impressed by the invisibility of Jahwe; he believed that no visible god could compete in holiness with an invisible one, and he marvelled that the children of Midian attached so little importance to a characteristic which seemed to him full of immeasurable implications. While he minded the sheep belonging to the brother of his Midianite wife, he plunged himself into long, deep, and violent cogitations. He was moved by inspirations and visions which in one case even left his inner consciousness and returned to his soul as a flaming vision from without, as a precisely-worded pronouncement, and as an unshrinkable command. Thus he reached the conviction that Jahwe was none other than El'eljon, the Only-Highest, El ro'i, the God who sees me, He who had always been known as El Schaddai, "the God of the Mountain", El 'olām, the God of the World and the Eternities – in short, the God of Abraham, Isaac, and Jacob, the God of the Father. And that meant the God of the poor, dumb, in their worship completely confused, uprooted, and enslaved tribes at home in Egypt, whose blood, from his father's side, flowed in the veins of Moses.

Full of this discovery, his soul heavy with command but trembling also with the wish to fulfil the mission, Moses ended his stay of many years with the children of Midian. He placed his wife Zipporah (a sufficiently noble woman because she was a daughter of Reuel, the priest-king of Midian, and the sister of his herd-owning son, Jethro) on a mule. He took along also his two sons, Gershom and Eliezer, and returned, travelling westward in seven day-journeys through many deserts, to the land of Egypt. That is to the lower land, the fallow country where the Nile branches out into the district called Kos, and variously known as Goschem, Gosem, and Goshen. It was here that the tribes of his fathers lived and drudged.

Here he immediately began to communicate his great experience to his kinsfolk; he talked to them whenever he went and stood, in their huts, their grazing grounds, and their workplaces. When he spoke he had a certain way of letting his arms hang limp at his sides, while his fists shook and trembled. He informed them that the God of their Fathers was found again, that He had made himself known to him, Moscheh ben 'Amram, on the mountain Hor in the desert Sin from a bush which burned but never burned out. This God was called

Jahwe, which name is to be understood as "I am that I am, from eternity to eternity", but also as flowing air and as mighty sound. This God was inclined towards their tribe and was ready under certain conditions to enter into a covenant with them, choosing them above all other peoples. The conditions were that they would devote themselves in full exclusiveness to him, and that they would form a sworn brotherhood to serve him alone in worship of the invisible, a worship without images.

Moses stormed at them and the fists on his broad wrists trembled. Yet he was not completely honest with them, and kept under cover much, indeed the essential thought, he had in mind. Fearing he might scare them off, he said nothing of the implications of invisibility, that is, its spirituality, its purity, its holiness. He preferred not to point out that as sworn servants of the invisible they would have to be a separated people, a people of the spirit, of purity and of holiness. Afraid to frighten them he kept silent. They were so miserable, so oppressed, and in their worship so confused, this kin of his father. He mistrusted them though he loved them. Yes, when he announced to them that Jahwe the Invisible was inclined towards them, he really ascribed to the God and interpreted for the God what possibly was true of the God but what certainly was true of him: for he himself was inclined to his father's kin, as the sculptor is inclined towards the shapeless lump from which he hopes to carve a high and fine figure, the work of his hands. Hence his trembling desire, hence too the great heaviness of soul which filled him directly after his departure from Midian.

He also kept back the second half of the secret; for it was a double secret. It included not only the message to his tribe of the rediscovery of their father's God and the God's inclination towards them; it included also his own belief that he was destined to guide them out of Egypt's house of bondage, out into the open, and through many deserts into the land of promise, the land of their fathers. That destiny was part of the mission, inseparably linked with it. God – and liberation for the return home; the Invisible – and release from foreign yoke: to him these were one and the same thought, but to the people he as yet said nothing of this second part of the mission, because he knew that one would inevitably follow from the other; also because he hoped that he himself could negotiate the release with Pharaoh, King of Egypt, with whom he had not-too-remote connection.

Was it, however, that his speech displeased the people – for he spoke badly and haltingly and often could not find the right word – or did they divine, while he shook his trembling fists, the implications of invisibility as well as those of the covenant? Did they perceive that they were being lured towards strenuous and dangerous matters? Whatever the reason they remained mistrustful, stiff-necked, and fearful of his storming. They ogled their Egyptian whip-masters and mumbled between their teeth:

"Why do you spout words? And what kind of words are these you spout? Likely somebody set you up as chief or as judge over us? Well, we want to know who."

That was nothing new to him. He had heard it from them once before he had fled to Midian.

2

His father was not his father, nor was his mother his mother. So disorderly was his birth.

One day the second daughter of the Pharaoh, Ramessu, was amusing herself – under the watchful eye of the armed guard and in company of her serving maidens – in the royal garden on the Nile. There she espied a Hebrew labourer who was carrying water. She became enamoured of him. He had sad eyes, he had a young beard encircling his chin, and he had strong arms, as one could clearly see when he drew the water. He worked by the sweat of his brow and had his troubles, but to Pharaoh's daughter he was the image of beauty and desire. She commanded that he should be admitted to her pavilion. There she plunged her precious little hands through his sweat-drenched hair, she kissed the muscles of his arms and charmed his manhood to wakefulness, so that he took possession of her;

he, the foreign slave, took possession of the child of a king. When she had had enough, she let him go. But he did not go far; after thirty paces he was slain and quickly buried, so that nothing remained of the pleasure of the Sun-Daughter.

"The poor man," said she when she heard about it. "You are always such busybodies. He would have kept quiet. He loved me." After that she became pregnant, and after nine months she gave birth in all secrecy to a boy. Her serving woman placed the boy in a box fashioned of tarred reeds, and they hid the box in the bulrushes on the edge of the water. There in due time they found it and exclaimed, "O magic! A foundling, a boy from the bulrushes, an abandoned child! It is like the old tales, exactly as it happened with Sargon, whom Akki the Water Carrier found in the rushes and reared in the goodness of his heart. Such things happen all the time. What shall we do now with our find? It would be wisest if we gave it to a nursing mother, a woman of simple station who has milk to spare, so that the boy may grow up as her son and the son of her lawful husband." And they handed the child to a Hebrew woman who carried it down into the region of Goshen and there gave it to Jochebed, the wife of Amram, who belonged to the tribe of the Tolerated Ones, to the descendants of Levi. She was nursing her son Aaron and had milk to spare. Therefore, and also because once in a while and quite secretly substantial gifts arrived at her hut from sources higher up, did she rear the unclassified child in the goodness of her heart. Before the world Amram and Jochebed became his parents and Aaron became his brother. Amram possessed cattle and fields, Jochebed was the daughter of a stonemason. She did not know how she should name the questionable child. Therefore she gave him a half-Egyptian name, that is to say, the half of an Egyptian name. For the sons of the land were often called Ptach-Moses, Amen-Moses, or Ra-Moses. They were named as sons with the names of the gods. Amram and Jochebed preferred to omit the name of the god, and called the child simply Moses. Thus he was called plain "Son". The only question was, whose son?

3

He grew up as one of the Tolerated Ones, and expressed himself in their dialect. The ancestors of this tribe had come into the land long ago at the time of the Drought. They whom Pharaoh's historians described as the "hungry Bedouins from Edom" had come with the due permission of the frontier officials. They had received pasture privileges in the district of Goshen in the lower land. Anybody who believes that they received these privileges for nothing does not know their hosts, the children of Egypt. Not only did they have to pay taxes out of their cattle, and that so heavily that it hurt, but also all who had strength were forced to do manual services at the several building operations which in a country like Egypt are always under way. Especially since Ramessu, the second of his name, had become Pharaoh in Thebes, excessive building was going on, for building was his pleasure and his royal delight. He built prodigal temples all over the land. And down in the Delta region he not only renewed and greatly improved the long-neglected canal which connected the eastern arm of the Nile with the Bitter Lakes and thus the great ocean with the corner of the Red Sea, but he also constructed two arsenal cities on the banks of the canal, called Pithom and Rameses. It was for this work that the children of the Tolerated Ones were drafted. They baked bricks and carried them and drudged in the sweat of their bodies under Egypt's cudgel.

This cudgel was hardly more than a symbol of the authority vested in Pharaoh's overseers. The workers were not unnecessarily beaten with it. They also had good food with their drudgery: much fish from the Nile, bread, beer, and beef, quite as plentiful as they needed. Nevertheless, they did not take to or care for this work, for they were nomads, full of the tradition of a free, roaming life. Labour by the hour, labour which made them sweat, was foreign and insulting to their nature. The tribes, however, were far too tenuously connected and insufficiently conscious of themselves to be able to signal their dissatisfaction to each other, or to become of one firm mind about it. Because several of their generations had lived in a transitional land, pitching their tents between the home of their fathers and the real Egypt, they were now unanchored souls, wavering in spirit and without a secure doctrine. They had forgotten much; they had half assimilated some new thoughts; and because they lacked real orientation, they did not trust their own feelings. They did not trust even the bitterness that they felt towards their bondage, because fish and beer and beef made them uncertain.

Moses, also, as the supposed son of Amram, was destined to form bricks for Pharaoh as soon as he had outgrown his boyhood. But this did not come to pass; the youth was taken away from his parents and was brought to Upper Egypt into a school, a very elegant academy where the sons of the Syrian town kings and the scions of the native nobility were educated. There was he taken, because his real mother, Pharaoh's child, who had delivered him into the bulrushes, was, though somewhat lascivious, not devoid of sentiment. She had remembered him for the sake of his buried father, the water carrier with the beard and the sad eyes. She didn't want Moses to remain with the savages, but wished him to be educated as an Egyptian and to achieve a court position. His half descent from the gods was thus to be half recognized in silence. Clothed in white linen and with a wig on his head, Moses acquired the knowledge of stars and of countries, the art of writing and of law. Yet he was not happy among the snobs of the elegant academy, but lonely was he among them, filled with aversion towards all of Egypt's refined culture. The blood of the buried one who had been sacrificed to this culture was stronger in him than was his Egyptian portion. In his soul he sided with the poor uncertain ones at home in Goshen, who did not even have the courage of their bitterness. He sided with them against the lecherous arrogance of his mother's kin.

"What was your name again?" his comrades at the school asked him.

"I am called Moses," he answered.

"Ach-Moses or Ptach-Moses?" they asked.

"No, simply Moses," he responded.

"That's inadequate and paltry," said the snobs. And he became enraged, so that he almost wanted to kill and bury them. For he understood that with these questions they simply wished to pry into his uncertain history, which in nebulous outlines was known to everybody. He himself could hardly have known that he was the discreet result of Egyptian pleasure, if it had not been common though somewhat inexact knowledge. Pharaoh himself was as well aware of the trifling escapade of his child as was Moses of the fact that Ramessu, the master builder, was his illegitimate grandfather, and that his paternity was the result of iniquitous, lecherous, and murderous pleasure. Yes, Moses knew this, and he also knew that Pharaoh knew it. And when he thought about it he inclined his head menacingly, inclined it in the direction of Pharaoh's throne.

4

When he had lived two years among the whelps of the school in Thebes, he could stand it no longer, fled by night over the wall, and wandered home to Goshen to his father's tribe. With severe countenance he roamed among them, and one day he saw at the canal near the new buildings in Rameses how an Egyptian overseer beat with his cudgel one of the workers, who probably had been lazy or obdurate. Moses paled. With flaming eyes he challenged the Egyptian, who in short response smashed his nose so that Moses all his life had a nose with a broken flattened bridge. Moses seized the cudgel from the overseer, swung it mightily, and demolished the man's skull so that he lay dead on the spot. Not even once did Moses glance about to find out if anybody had observed him. Fortunately it was a lonely place and not a soul was near. Alone he buried the murdered man; for he whom Moses had defended had instantly taken to his heels. After it was over, he felt that killing and burying were what he had always desired in his soul.

His flaming deed remained hidden at least from the Egyptians, who never did find out what had become of their man. A year and a day passed over the deed. Moses continued to roam among his people and to probe into their frays with a peculiar air of authority. So it happened that once he saw two slaves quarrelling with each other. They were at the point of violence. "Wherefore do you quarrel and seek to strike each other?" he said to them. "Are you not miserable enough and neglected? Would it not be better for kin to side with kin, instead of baring your teeth to each other? This one is in the wrong: I saw it. Let him give in and be content; nor let the other triumph."

But as usually happens, suddenly both of them were united against him, and they said, "What business is it of yours?" Especially he who was in the wrong was extremely snappy and shouted quite loudly, "Well, this caps everything! Who are you that you stick your ugly nose into things that don't concern you? Ahah! You are Moscheh, son of Amram, but that means very little. Nobody really knows who you are, not even you yourself. Curious are we to learn who has appointed you master and judge over us. Perhaps you want to choke me too, as you choked the Egyptian and buried him?"

"Be quiet," whispered Moses, alarmed. And he thought, "How did this get out?" But that very day he understood that it would be no longer possible for him to remain in the country, and he fled across the frontier where the frontier had a loophole, near the muddy shallows of the Bitter Lakes. Through many deserts of the land of Sinai he wandered, and came to Midian, to the Midianites, and to their priest-king, Reuel.

5

When he returned to Egypt, fraught with his discovery and his mission, he was a man at the height of his powers, sturdy, with a sunk-in nose and prominent cheek-bones, with a divided beard, eyes set far apart, and wrists that were unusually broad. He had a habit when he meditated of covering his mouth and beard with his right hand, and it was then that those broad wrists were especially noticeable. He went from hut to hut and from workplace to workplace, he shook his fists at the sides of his body and discoursed on the Invisible One, the God of the Fathers, who was ready for the covenant. Actually Moses did not speak well. His nature was halting and pent-up, and when he became excited he was apt to stammer. Nor was he master of any one language, but floundered in three. The Aramaic-Syro-Chaldee, which was the language of his father's kin and which he had learned from his parents, had been glossed over by the Egyptian which he had had to learn at school. And to this was added the Midianitic-Arabic which he had spoken so long in the desert. All of these he jumbled together.

Very helpful to him was his brother Aaron, a tall man with a black beard and with black curls at the nape of his neck. Aaron was gentle and held his large and curved eyelids piously lowered. Moses had initiated Aaron into all his beliefs and had won him over completely to the cause of the Invisible and all its implications. Because he knew how to speak from under his beard fluently and unctuously, he accompanied Moses on his preaching tours and did the talking for him. Admittedly, he spoke in a somewhat oily fashion, and not nearly transportingly enough to suit Moses, so that Moses, accompanying the speech with his shaking fists, sought to put more fire into his brother's words, and sometimes would blurt helter-skelter into the oration with his own Aramaic-Egyptian-Arabic.

Aaron's wife was named Elisheba, daughter of Amminadab. She too partook of the oath and the propaganda, and so did a younger sister of Moses and Aaron called Miriam, an inspired woman who knew how to sing and play the timbrel. Moses was especially fond of yet another disciple, a youth who devoted himself body and soul to his plans, and who never left his side. His real name was Hosea, son of Nun (that means "fish"), of the kin of Ephraim. Moses, however, had given him the Jahwe name, Jehoschua – Joshua for short. Joshua was erect and sinewy and curly-headed, had a prominent Adam's-apple and a clearly defined wrinkle between his brows. He carried his new name with pride, though he had his own views of the whole affair, views which were not so much religious as military. For him Jahwe, God of the Fathers, was first of all God of the fighting forces. The idea connected with the God, that is, the idea of flight from the house of bondage, was to him identical with the idea of the conquest of a new grazing ground which would belong solely to the Hebraic tribes. This was logical enough, for they had to live somewhere and nobody was going to hand them any land, promise or not, as a gift.

Joshua, young as he was, carried all the salient facts in his clear-eyed, curly head, and discussed them unceasingly with Moses, his older friend and master. Without having the means of carrying out an exact census, Joshua was able to calculate that the strength of the tribes tenting in Goshen or living in the slave cities, Pithom and Rameses, and including also the slaves who were farflung over the country, was about twelve or thirteen thousand people. This meant that there were possibly three thousand men capable of bearing arms. Later on these figures were immeasurably exaggerated, but Joshua knew them fairly correctly, and was little satisfied with them. Three thousand men – that was no terror-inspiring fighting force, even if you count on the fact that once on the way several kindred tribes roaming the desert would join them for the sake of winning new land. With such a force one could not dream of any major expeditions; with such a force it was impractical to hew one's way into the promised land. Joshua well understood that. His plan, therefore, was to seek first of all a spot in the open, a marking time and resting place, where the tribes could settle and devote themselves to the business of natural multiplication under more or less favourable circumstances. This natural growth amounted to – as Joshua knew his people – two and a half per cent. per year. The youth was constantly on the lookout for such a hedged-in hatching place where they could grow further fighting forces. In his frequent consultations with Moses it appeared that Joshua saw with surprising clarity where one place in the world lay in relation to another place. He carried in his head a kind of map of all the interesting districts; he knew their dimensions measured in daytime marches, their watering places, and especially the fighting strength of their inhabitants.

Moses knew what a treasure he possessed in Joshua, knew also that he would have need of him, and loved his ardour, though he was little concerned with the immediate objectives of that ardour. Covering mouth and beard with his right hand, he listened to the strategic theories of the youth, thinking all the while of something else. For him also Jahwe meant an exodus, but not an exodus for a war of land seizure; an exodus rather for seclusion. Out in the open Moses would have his father's kin to himself, those swaying souls confused in their beliefs, the procreating men, the nursing women, the awakening youths, the dirty-nosed children. There in the open he would be able to imbue them with the holy, invisible God, the pure and spiritual God; there he could give them this God as the centre which would unite and form them, form them to his image, form them into a people different from all other peoples; a people belonging to God, denoted by the holy and the spiritual, and distinguished from all others through awe, restraint, and fear of God. That is to say that his people would hold in awe a restraining, pure, spiritual code, a code which, since the Invisible One was in truth the God of the entire world, would in the future bind and unite all peoples, but would at first be given to them alone and be their stern privilege among the heathen.

Thus was Moses's inclination towards his father's blood; it was the sculptor's inclination, and he identified it with the God's choice and the God's desire for the covenant. Because Moses believed that the education towards God must precede all other enterprises, such enterprises as the young Joshua carried in his head, and because he knew that such education would take time – free time out in the open – he did not mind that there was so far many a hitch to Joshua's plans, that these plans were thwarted by an insufficient number of fighters.

Joshua needed time so that his people could multiply in a natural way; he also needed time so that he himself could become older, old enough to set himself up as commander in chief. Moses needed time for the work of education, which for the God's sake he desired. So they both agreed, if for different reasons.

6

In the meantime he, God's delegate, and his immediate followers, the eloquent Aaron, Elisheba, Miriam, Joshua, and a certain Caleb, who was Joshua's bosom friend, of the same age, and also a strong, simple, courageous youth – in the meantime, they were not idle, not a single day. They were busy spreading Jahwe's message and his flattering offer of alliance among their people. They continued to stoke the people's bitterness against slavery under the Egyptian cudgel, and they planted ever deeper the thought that the yoke must be thrown off through migration. Each of them did it in his own way: Moses himself through halting words and shaking fists; Aaron in unctuously flowing speech, Elisheba with persuasive chatter; Joshua and Caleb in the form of military command, in short and terse slogans; and Miriam, who was soon known as "the Prophetess", in elevated tone to the accompaniment of the timbrel. Their preaching did not fall on barren ground. The thought of allying themselves with Moses's agreeable god to become the chosen people of the Invisible One and under his and his proclaimer's banner to depart for the open – this thought took root among the tribes and began to be their uniting centre. This especially because Moses promised, or at least put it forth as a hopeful possibility, that he would be able to obtain the permission for their departure from Egypt through negotiations in the highest place, so that this departure would not have to take the form of a daring uprising, but of an amicable agreement. The tribes knew, if inexactly, Moses's half-Egyptian birth in the bulrushes. They knew, too, of his elegant education and of his ambiguous connections with the court. What used to be a cause of distrust and aversion, namely the fact that he was half foreign, and stood with one foot in Egypt, now became a source of confidence and lent him authority. Surely, if anybody, he was the man to stand before Pharaoh and plead their cause. And so they commissioned him to attempt to obtain their release from Ramessu, the master builder and master. They commissioned both him and his foster brother, Aaron. Moses planned to take Aaron along first because he himself could not speak fluently while Aaron could; but also because Aaron had at his disposal certain tricks with which he hoped to make an impression at court in Jahwe's honour. He could take a hooded snake and by pressing its neck make it rigid as a rod. Yet as soon as he cast this rod to the ground, it would curl up and "it became a serpent". Neither Moses nor Aaron took into account the fact that these miracles were quite well known to Pharaoh's magicians, and that they therefore could hardly serve as frightening proof of Jahwe's power.

Altogether, they did not have much luck – it may as well be mentioned beforehand – craftily as they had planned their campaign in counsel with the youths Joshua and Caleb. In this council it had been decided to ask the king for permission only that the Hebrew people might assemble and voyage three days across the frontier into the desert so that they could there hold a feast of offering to the god who had called them. Then they would return to work. They did not expect, of course, that Pharaoh would swallow such a subterfuge and really believe that they would return. It was simply a mild and polite form in which to submit their petition for emancipation. Yet the king did not thank them for it.

However, it must be counted to the credit of the brothers that at least they succeeded in getting into the Great House and before Pharaoh's throne. And that not once but again and again for tenaciously prolonged conferences. In this Moses had not promised too much to his people, for he counted on the fact that Ramessu was his secret and illegitimate grandfather, and that they both knew that each knew it. Moses had a trump card in his hand which, if it was not sufficient to achieve from the king permission for the exodus, was at least potent enough to grant him audience again and again with the mighty one. For he feared Moses. To be sure, a king's fear is dangerous, and Moses was playing a dangerous game. He was courageous – how very courageous and what impression he was able to make through this courage on his people, we shall soon see. It would have been easy for Ramessu to have had Moses quietly strangled and buried, so that at last really nothing would remain of his child's escapade. But the princess cherished a sentimental memory of that hour, and very obviously did not want harm to befall her bulrush boy. He stood under her protection, ungrateful as he had been for her solicitude and for all her plans of education and advancement.

Thus Moses and Aaron were able to stand before Pharaoh, even if he refused categorically the festival-vacation out into the open to which their god had supposedly summoned them. It availed nothing that Aaron spoke with unctuous logic, while Moses shook his fists passionately. It availed nothing that Aaron changed his rod into a snake, for Pharaoh's magicians without further ado did the same thing, proving thereby that the Invisible One in whose name both of them were talking could claim no superior powers, and that Pharaoh need not listen to the voice of such a lord.

"But pestilence or the sword shall visit our people if we do not voyage three days and prepare a feast for our God," said the brothers.

The king responded, "That is not my affair. You are numerous enough, more than twelve thousand strong, and you will be able to stand some diminution, whether it be by pestilence or sword or hard work. What you, Moses and Aaron, really want is to permit slothfulness to your people, and to allow them to idle in their lawful labours. But that I cannot suffer nor permit. I have several unprecedented temples in work; furthermore I want to build a third arsenal city in addition to Pithom and Rameses. For that I need the arms of your people. I am obliged to you for your fluent recital, and you, Moses, I dismiss more or less with particular favour. But not a word more of desert festivals."

The audience was terminated, and not only did it result in nothing good but it afterwards had decidedly bad consequences. For Pharaoh, his zeal for building affronted, and annoyed because he could not very well strangle Moses to death – for otherwise his daughter would have made a scene – issued the order that the people of Goshen were to be more pressed with labour than before, and that the cudgel was not to be spared should they be dilatory; on the contrary, they should be made to slave until they fell exhausted, so that all idle thoughts of a desert festival would be driven out of them. Thus it happened. The drudgery became harder from one day to the next for the very reason that Moses and Aaron had talked to Pharaoh. For example, the straw which they needed for the glazing of bricks was no longer furnished to them. They themselves had to go into the fields to gather the stubbles, nor was the number of bricks to be delivered diminished. That number had to be reached or the cudgel danced upon their poor backs. In vain did the Hebrew foremen protest to the authorities because of the exorbitant demands. The answer was, "You are lazy, lazy are you. Therefore you cry and say, 'We want to migrate and make offerings.' The order remains: Gather the straw yourselves – and make the same number of bricks."

7

For Moses and Aaron this was no small embarrassment. The foremen said to them, "There you have it. And this is all the good the pact with your god has done us. Nothing have you accomplished except that you have made our savour worse before Pharaoh and his servants, and that you have given the sword into their hands for them to slaughter us."

It was difficult to answer, and Moses had heavy hours alone with the god of the thorn bush. He confronted the god with the fact that from the very beginning he was against this mission, and from the beginning he had implored that whomsoever the god wanted to send, he should not in any case send him, for he could not speak properly. But the god answered him that Aaron was eloquent. True enough, Aaron had done the speaking, but in much too oily a fashion, and it appeared how absurd it was to undertake such a cause if one had a heavy tongue and was forced to have others plead as deputy. But the god consoled Moses and meted punishment to him from his own soul. He answered Moses from his own soul that he should be ashamed of his half-heartedness. His excuses were pure affectation, for at bottom he himself had longed for the mission, because he himself was as much inclined towards his people and the forming of them as the god. Yes, it was impossible to distinguish his own inclination from the inclination of the god; it was one and the same. This inclination had driven him to the work, and he should be ashamed to be despondent at the first misadventure.

Moses let himself be persuaded, the more so as in counsel with Joshua, Caleb, Aaron, and the inspired women they reached the conclusion that the greater oppression, though it did cause bad blood, was, rightly understood, not such a bad beginning. For the bad blood would form itself not only against Moses but also and especially against the Egyptians. It would make the people all the more receptive to the call of the saving God and to the idea of the exodus. Thus did it happen. Among the workers the discontent caused by straw and bricks was fomented, and the accusation that Moses had made their savour worse before Pharaoh and had only harmed them took second place to the wish that Amram's son should once again exploit his connections and once again go for them to Pharaoh.

This he did, but not with Aaron. Alone he went, not caring how haltingly he spoke. He shook his fists before the throne and demanded in stammering and plunging words permission for the exodus for the sake of the festival in the desert. Not once did he do so but a dozen times, for Pharaoh simply could not deny him admission to his throne, so excellent were his connections. It came to a combat between Moses and the king, a tenacious and protracted combat, the result of which was not that the king agreed to the petition and permitted the departure, but rather that one day he drove and chased the people of Goshen from his land, very glad to get rid of them. There has been much talk about this combat and the various threatening measures which were employed against the stubbornly resisting king. This talk is not entirely without basis, though it has been subjected to much ornamentation. Tradition speaks of ten plagues, one after the other, with which Jahwe smote Egypt, in order to wear down Pharaoh, while at the same time he purposely hardened Pharaoh's heart against Moses's demands, for the sake of proving his might with ever-new plagues. Blood, frogs, vermin, wild beasts, boils, pestilence, hail, locusts, darkness, and death of the first-born, these were the names of the ten plagues. And any or all of them could have happened. The question is only whether any of them, excepting the last, which has an opaque and never fully elucidated explanation, did contribute materially to the final result. Under certain circumstances the Nile takes on a blood-red colouring. Temporarily its waters become undrinkable and the fish die. That is as likely to happen as that the frogs of the marshes multiply unnaturally or that the propagation of the constantly present lice grows to the proportion of a general affliction. There were plenty of lions left in Egypt prowling along the edge of the desert and lurking in the dried-up stream beds of the jungle. And if the number of their rapacious attacks on man and beast suddenly increased, one could very well designate that as a plague. How usual are sores and blains in the land of Egypt, and how easily uncleanliness causes cankers which fester among the people like a pestilence! The heavens there are usually blue, and therefore the rare and heavy thunderstorm makes all the deeper an impression, when the descending fire of the clouds mixes with the sharp gravel of the hail, which flails the harvest and rends the trees asunder – all this without any definite purpose. The locust is an all-too-familiar guest; against their mass advance man has invented many a repellent and barricade. Yet again and again these yield to greed, so that whole regions remain gaping in bare baldness. And he who has experienced the dismal darkling mood which a shadowed sun produces on the earth can well understand that a people spoiled by the luxury of light would give to such an eclipse the name of a plague.

With this all the reported evils are accounted for. For the tenth evil, the death of the first-born, does not properly belong among them. It represents a dubious by-product of the exodus itself, one into which it is uncomfortable to probe. Some of the others, or even all of them, if spread over a sufficient period of time, could have occurred. One need consider them as merely more or less decorative circumlocutions of the only actual pressure which Moses could use against Ramessu, namely and quite simply the fact that Pharaoh was his illegitimate grandfather and that Moses had the means to bruit this scandal abroad. The king was more than once at the point of yielding to this pressure; at least he made considerable concessions. He consented that the men depart for the feast of offering if their wives, children, and cattle remained behind. Moses did not accept this; with young and old, with sons and daughters, with sheep and cows, would they have to depart, to do justice to the feast of the Lord. So Pharaoh conceded wives and brood and excepted only the cattle, which were to remain as forfeit. But Moses asked where they were expected to find offerings to be burned and slaughtered if they lacked their cattle. Not one single hoof, he demanded, might remain behind, whereby, of course, it became apparent that it was not a question of a holiday but of a departure.

This resulted in a last stormy scene between His Egyptian Majesty and Jahwe's delegate. During all the negotiations Moses had shown great patience, though there was fist-shaking rage in his soul. It got to the point that Pharaoh staked all and literally showed him the door. "Out," he screamed, "and beware lest you come again into my sight. If you do, so shall you die."

Then Moses, who had just been fiercely agitated, became

completely calm, and answered only, "You have spoken. I shall go and never again come into your sight." What he contemplated when he thus took leave in terrible calm was not according to his desire. But Joshua and Caleb, the youths, they liked it well.

8

This is a dark chapter, one to be voiced only in half-whispered and muffled words. A day came, or more precisely a night, a wicked vesper, when Jahwe or his destroying angel went about and smote the children of Egypt with the tenth and last plague. That is, he smote a part of them, the Egyptian element among the inhabitants of Goshen and those of the towns of Pithom and Rameses. Those huts and houses whose posts were painted with the sign of blood he omitted, passed by, and spared.

What did he do? He caused death to come, the death of the Egyptian first-born, and in doing so he may well have met half-way many a secret wish and helped many a second-born to the right which would otherwise have been denied him. One has to note the difference between Jahwe and his destroying angel. It was not Jahwe himself who went about, but his destroying angel, or more properly, a whole band of such, carefully chosen. And if one wishes to search among the many for one single apparition, there is much to point to a certain straight, youthful figure with a curly head, a prominent Adam's-apple, and a determined, wrinkled brow. He becomes the traditional type of the destroying angel, who at all times is glad when unprofitable negotiations are ended and deeds begin.

During Moses's tenacious audiences with Pharaoh, the preparations for decisive deeds had not been neglected. Moses's part in them was limited: he merely sent his wife and sons secretly to Midian to his brother-in-law, Jethro. Expecting serious trouble, he did not wish to be burdened with their care. Joshua, however, whose relationship to Moses was recognizably similar to the relationship of the destroying angel to Jahwe, had acted according to his nature; though he did not possess the means or as yet the prestige to get three thousand arm-bearing comrades ready for war under his command, he at least had selected a group, had armed them, exercised them, and reared them in discipline. For a beginning, a good deal could be accomplished with them.

What then occurred is shrouded in darkness – the very darkness of that certain vesper night which was supposed to be a holiday night for the slave tribes. The Egyptians assumed that these tribes wanted to have some compensation for the festival in the desert which had been denied to them, and thus had planned to hold a celebration enhanced by feasting and illumination. For they had even borrowed gold and silver vessels from their Egyptian neighbours. Instead of this there occurred that appearance of the destroying angel, that death of the first-born, in all those dwellings unmarked with blood by the bundle of hyssop. It was a visitation which caused so great a confusion, and so sudden a revolution of legal claims and property rights, that in the next hour the way out of the land not only stood open to the people of Moses, but they were actually forced on the way. Their departure could not be quick enough for the people of Egypt. Indeed, it seems as if the second-born were less zealous to avenge the death of those to whose place they succeeded than to hasten the disappearance of those who had caused their advancement.

The word of history has it that the tenth plague at last broke Pharaoh's pride so that he dismissed Moses's people from bondage. Soon enough, however, he sent after the departed ones a pursuing armed division which miraculously came to grief.

Be that as it may, it is certain that the exodus took the form of expulsion. The haste with which it happened is indicated by the fact that nobody had time to leaven his bread for the journey. The people were provided only with unleavened emergency cakes. Later Moses formed of this occurrence a memorial feast for all time. But in other respects everybody, great and small, was quite prepared for the departure. While the destroying angel went about, they sat with girded loins near their fully packed carts, their shoes already on their feet, their staffs in their hands. The gold and silver vessels which they had borrowed from the children of the land they took with them.

My friends, at the departure from Egypt there was killing and there was theft. It was Moses's determined will that this should happen for the last time. How can people free themselves from uncleanliness without offering to that uncleanliness a last tribute, without soiling themselves thoroughly for the last time? Now Moses had the unformed mass, his father's kin, out in the open. He, with his sculptor's desire, believed that out in the open, out in freedom, the work of cleansing could begin.

9

The migrants, though their number was much smaller than the legend narrates, were yet numerous enough to be difficult to manage, to guide, and to provision. They were a heavy enough burden for him who had the responsibility for their fate and for their survival out in the open. The tribes chose the route which chose itself, for with good reason they wanted to avoid the Egyptian frontier fortifications, which began north of the Bitter Lakes. The way they took led through the Salt Lake district, a district into which projects the larger, more westerly of the two arms of the Red Sea. These arms frame the Sinai peninsula. Moses knew this district because on his flight to Midian and on his return from there he had passed and repassed it. Its characteristics were better known to him than to young Joshua, who knew it only as a map he had learned by heart. Moses had seen these strange reedy shallows, which sometimes formed an open connection between the Bitter Lakes and the sea, and which at other times and under certain peculiar conditions could be traversed as dry land. If there was a strong east wind and if the sea was at low tide, the shallows permitted free passage. The fugitives found them in this condition, thanks to Jahwe's favourable disposition.

Joshua and Caleb were the ones who spread the news among the multitude that Moses, calling to God, had held his rod over the waters, had caused the waters to divide and make way for the people. Very probably Moses actually did this, and thus assisted the east wind with solemn gesture and in Jahwe's name. In any case, the faith of the people in their leader could at this moment well do with confirmation, because right here it was subjected to the first heavy trial. For it was here that Pharaoh's mighty battalion, the mounted men in those grim, scythe-studded chariots all too familiar to the people, caught up with the fugitives and were within a hair's breadth of putting a bloody end to the whole pilgrimage to God.

The news of their coming, announced by Joshua's rear guard, caused extreme terror and wild despair among the people. Regret at having followed "that man Moses" immediately flared up, and the mass murmuring arose which was to occur, to his grief and bitterness, at every succeeding difficulty. The women whined, the men cursed and shook their fists at the sides of their bodies as Moses himself was wont to do when he was excited.

"Were there no graves in Egypt," thus was the speech, "which we could have entered peacefully at our appointed hour if we had stayed at home?" Suddenly Egypt was "home", that very Egypt which used to be the foreign land of slavery. "For it had been better for us to serve the Egyptians than that we should die in the wilderness."

This Moses had to hear from a thousand throats. The cries even galled his joy in the deliverance, which when it came was overwhelming. He was "the man Moses who has led us out of Egypt" – which phrase was a pæan of praise as long as everything went well. When things went badly the phrase immediately changed colour and became a menacingly murmured reproach, a reproach never far removed from the thought of stoning.

Well, then, after a short fright everything went miraculously and shamefully well. Through God's miracle Moses stood before his people in all his greatness and was "the man who has led us out of Egypt", once again with a different connotation. The people pushed through the dry shallows, after them the might of the Egyptian chariots. Suddenly the wind dies down, the flood returns, and man and horse perish gurgling in the engulfing waters.

The triumph was unprecedented. Miriam the prophetess, Aaron's sister, played the timbrel and led the round dance of the women. She sang: "Praise the Lord – a wondrous deed – steed and man – he has flung them into the ocean." She had written this herself. One has to imagine it to the accompaniment of the timbrel.

The people were deeply moved. The words "mighty, holy, terrifying, praiseworthy, and miracle-dispensing" fell incessantly from their lips, and it was not clear whether these words were meant for the divinity or for Moses, delegate of the god. For they now believed that it was Moses's rod which had drawn the drowning flood over the might of Egypt. This substitution was ever present. At those times when the people were not murmuring against him, he always had his troubles trying to prevent them from looking on him as God instead of as God's proclaimer.

10

At the bottom this was not so ridiculous. For what Moses began to exact of those wretched people went far beyond the humanly customary, and could hardly have sprung from the brain of a mortal. They stood agape at hearing it. He immediately forbade Miriam's dance of triumph and all further jubilation over the destruction of the Egyptians. He proclaimed: Jahwe's heavenly hosts were at the point of joining in the song of victory, but the holy one had rebuked them. "How so! My creatures sink into the sea, and you want to sing?" This short and surprising pronouncement Moses spread among the people. And he added, "Thou shalt not rejoice over the fall of thine enemy, nor shall thy heart be glad over his misfortune." This was the first time he addressed the entire mob, some twelve thousand people with three thousand capable of bearing arms, with "Thou". It was a form of speech which embraced them in their entirety and at the same time designated each individual, man and woman, the aged and the child, pointing a finger against each one's breast.

"Thou shalt not utter a cry of joy over the fall of thine enemy." That was to the highest degree unnatural! But obviously this unnaturalness had some relation to the invisibility of Moses's god, who desired also to be their god. The more thinking ones among the dark-skinned mob began dimly to perceive what it meant to have allied themselves with an invisible god, and what uncomfortable and exigent matters they could expect.

The people were now in the land of Sinai, in the desert of Shur, an unlovely region which once left behind would only lead to yet another lamentable district, the desert of Paran. Why these deserts had different names is inexplicable. Barrenly they joined one another, and were both quite the same, that is, stony, waterless, and fruitless – accursed plains, dotted with dead hills, stretching for three days or four or five. It was lucky for Moses that he had fortified his reputation by impressing them with the supernatural occurrences at the shallows. For soon enough was he again "that man Moses who has led us out of Egypt", which meant "into misfortune". Loud murmurings rose to his ears. After three days the water which they had taken along gave out. Thousands thirsted, the inexorable sun above their heads, and under their feet bare disconsolateness, whether it was the desert Shur or by this time the desert Paran.

"What shall we drink?" they called loudly, without consideration for the leader, who suffered because he was responsible. Gladly would he have wished that he alone had nothing to drink, that he alone would never drink again, if only he did not have to hear continually, "Why did you carry us forth out of Egypt?" To suffer alone is little torment compared to the trial of having to be responsible for such a multitude. Moses was a much tried man, and remained so all his life, tried more than all the other people on earth.

Very soon there was nothing more to eat, for how long could the flat cakes which they had taken with them last? "What shall we eat?" Now this cry arose, tearful and abusing, and Moses had heavy hours alone with God. He complained how unfair it was that God had placed all the burden of all the people on one servant alone, on Moses.

"Did I conceive all these people and give them birth," he asked, "so that you have the right to say to me, 'Carry them in your arms'? Where can I find the nourishment to give to all? They cry before me and speak, 'Give us meat that we may eat!' Alone I cannot bear the weight of so many people; it is too heavy for me. And if you demand this of me, it would be better that you strangle me to death so that I need not see their misfortune and mine."

Jahwe did not entirely leave him in the lurch. On the fifth day they espied on a high plateau a spring surrounded by trees, which incidentally was marked as the "spring Marah" on the map which Joshua carried in his head. Unfortunately, the water tasted vile, because of certain unsalutary additions. This caused bitter disappointment and far-rumbling murmurs. However, Moses, made inventive by necessity, inserted a kind of filter apparatus which held back the foul additions, if not entirely, at least largely. Thus he performed the miracle of the spring, which changed the plaints into pæans and did much to cement his reputation. The phrase, "He who has led us out of Egypt", immediately took on again a rosy glow.

A miracle occurred also with the nourishment, a miracle which at first caused exultant astonishment. It appeared that great stretches of the desert Paran were covered with a lichen which was edible. This "manna-lichen" was a sugary tomentum, round and small, looked like coriander seed and like bdellium, and was highly perishable. If one did not eat it at once, it began to smell evil. But otherwise it made quite tolerable emergency food, mashed and powdered and prepared like an ash cake. Some thought that it tasted almost like rolls with honey; others it reminded of oil cakes.

This was the first favourable judgment, which did not last. Soon, after a few days, the people became wearied of this manna and tired of staying their hunger with it. Because it was their only nourishment, they sickened of it; it made them nauseated and they complained, "We remember the fish which we got in Egypt for nothing, the squash, the cucumbers, the leeks, the onions, and the garlic. But now our souls are weary, for our eyes see nothing but manna." This, in addition of course to the question, "Why did you carry us forth out of Egypt?" Moses had to hear in pain. What he asked God was, "What shall I do with the people? They no longer want their manna. You will see, soon they shall stone me."

II

However, from such a fate he was tolerably well protected by Jehoschua, his youth, and by the able guards whom he already had called on in Goshen and who surrounded the liberator as soon as the menacing murmurs rose among the crowd. For the time being this armed guard was small and consisted only of young men, with Caleb as lieutenant. Joshua was waiting for the right occasion to set himself up as commander in chief and leader of the battle, and to bind into a regular military force under his command *all* those capable of bearing arms, all the three thousand. He knew that such an occasion was coming.

Moses owed much to the youth whom he had baptized in the name of God. Without him he would have been lost many a time. He himself was a spiritual man and his virility, though it was strong and sturdy, though it had wrists as broad as a stonemason's, was a spiritual virility, a virility turned inward, nourished and fired by God, unconscious of outer happenings, concerned only with the holy. With a kind of foolhardiness, which stood in peculiar contrast to his reflective musings when he covered mouth and beard with his hand, all his thoughts and endeavours dealt only with his desire to have his father's kin alone for himself in seclusion, so that he might educate them, and sculpt into God's image the amorphous mass which he loved. He was little or not at all concerned with the dangers of freedom, the difficulties of the desert, and with the question how one could safely steer such a crowd out of the desert. He did not even know precisely to what spot he must guide the people. In short, he had hardly prepared himself for practical leadership. Therefore he could be doubly glad to have Joshua at his side, who in turn admired the spiritual virility in his master and placed his own direct, realistic, and useful virility unconditionally at his disposal.

It was thanks to him that they made planned progress through the wilderness and did not stray or perish. He determined the direction of the marches according to the stars, calculated the distances of the marches, and arranged it so that they arrived at watering places at bearable if sometimes even just bearable intervals. He it was who had found out that the round lichen was edible. In short, he looked after the reputation of the leader and master. He saw to it that when the phrase, "He who has led us out of Egypt", became a murmur, it would soon again take on a laudatory meaning. He kept the goal clearly in his head, and there he steered with the help of the stars and in accord with Moses, on the shortest route. Both of them were agreed that a first provisional goal was needed. Even if this was a temporary shelter, it would be an abode where one could live and where one could gain time. Much time had to be gained, partly (in Joshua's view) that the people might multiply and furnish him as he grew older a stronger number of warriors; partly (in Moses's view) that he might lead the mass towards God and hew them into a shape that would be holy, decent, and clean. For this his soul and his wrists longed.

The goal was the oasis Kadesh. Just as the desert Shur touches the desert Paran, so does the desert Sin adjoin Paran in the south. But not on all sides and not closely. Somewhere in between lay the oasis of Kadesh. This oasis was like a precious meadow, a green refreshment amid waterless waste, with three strong springs and quite a number of smaller springs, a day's march long and half a day's march broad, covered with fresh pasture and arable ground, and enticing landscape rich in animals and in fruits and large enough to quarter and nourish a multitude like theirs.

Joshua knew of this attractive spot: it was scrupulously marked out on the map which he carried in his head. Moses too had heard something about it. But it was really Joshua who had contrived to select Kadesh as their destination. His opportunity – it lay there. It goes without saying that such a pearl as Kadesh was not without its owner. The oasis was in firm possession. Well, perhaps not too firm, Joshua hoped. To acquire it, one had to fight those who possessed it, and that was Amalek.

A part of the tribe of Amalek held Kadesh occupied and would most certainly defend it. Joshua made it clear to Moses that this meant war, that a battle between Jahwe and Amalek was inevitable, even if it resulted in eternal enmity from generation to generation. The oasis they would have to have; it was their predestined place for growth and consecration.

Moses had his reservations. In his view one of the implications of the invisible god was that one should not covet the house of one's neighbour. He said as much to the youth, but Joshua responded: Kadesh is not, strictly speaking, Amalek's house. He knew his way about not only in space but in historic pasts, and he knew that long ago – though he could not precisely say just when – Kadesh had been inhabited by Hebrew people, and that they had been dispossessed by the people of Amalek. Kadesh was property through robbery – and one may rob a robber.

Moses doubted that, but he had his own reasons for believing that Kadesh truly was the property of Jahwe and should belong to those who were allied to him. The place bore the name of Kadesh, which means "sanctuary", not only because of its natural charm but also because it was in a certain sense a sanctuary of the Midianitic Jahwe, whom Moses had recognized as the God of the Fathers. Not far from it, towards the east and towards Edom, lay the mountain Horeb, which

Moses had visited from Midian and on whose slope the god had appeared to him in the burning bush. Horeb the mountain was the dwelling-place of Jahwe – at least it was one of them. His original dwelling was Mount Sinai in that range which lay towards mid-day. Thus between Sinai and Horeb there was a close connection – that is, that they both were Jahwe's dwelling-places. You could perhaps name one after the other, you could call Horeb Sinai. And you could call Kadesh what it was actually called because, speaking somewhat loosely, it lay at the foot of the sanctified mountain.

Therefore Moses consented to Joshua's scheme and permitted him to make his preparations for the combat with Amalek.

12

The battle took place – that is an historic fact. It was a bloody, fluctuating battle. But Israel emerged the victor. Moses had given this name Israel, which means "God makes war", to his people before the battle, to strengthen them. He had explained that it was a very old name which had slipped into oblivion. Jacob, the original father, had first won it, and had thus called his kin. Now indeed it benefited Moses's people. The tribe which previously had only loosely held to each other, now that they were all called Israel, fought united under this armoured name. They fought grouped in battle ranks and led by Joshua, the war-worthy youth, and Caleb, his lieutenant.

The people of Amalek had no illusions as to the meaning of the approach of the wanderers. At all times such approaches have only one meaning. Without waiting for the attack on the oasis, they burst in bulging bands into the desert, greater in number than Israel, and better armed. Amid swirling dust, amid tumult and martial cries, the battle began. It was an uneven battle, uneven also because Joshua's people were troubled by thirst and had eaten nothing but manna for many days. On the other hand, they had Joshua, the clear-seeing youth, who led their movements, and they had Moses, the man of God.

At the beginning of the engagement Moses, together with Aaron, his half-brother, and Miriam, the prophetess, retired to a hill from which he could view the field of combat. Virile though he was, his duty was not to do battle. His was a priest's duty, and everyone agreed without hesitancy that that could be his only duty. With raised arms he called to the god, and voiced enflaming words, as "Arise, Jahwe, appear to the myriads, to the thousands of Israelites, so that your enemies shall scatter and those who hate you flee before your sight."

They did not flee nor did they scatter. Or if they did, they did so only in a few places and temporarily. For though Israel was made fierce by thirst and by satiety with manna, Amalek disposed of more "myriads". And, after a brief discouragement, they again and again pressed forward, at times dangerously close to the commanding hill. It clearly appeared that Israel conquered as long as Moses held up his arms in prayer to heaven. But if he let his arms sink, then Amalek was victorious. Because he could not continuously hold up his arms with his own strength, Aaron and Miriam supported him under the armpits, and even held his arms so that they might remain raised. What that means one can measure by the fact that the battle lasted from morn to evening, and in all this time Moses had to retain his painful position. Judge from that how difficult is the duty assigned to spiritual virility, up there on the hill of prayer – in truth more difficult than the duty of those who hack away below in the turmoil.

Nor was he able to perform this duty all day long. Intermittently, and for a moment only, his helpers had to let down the arms of the master. And immediately this caused much blood and affliction among Jahwe's warriors. Then the arms were again hoisted, and those below took fresh courage. What also helped to veer the battle in their favour was the strategic gift of Joshua. He was a most ingenious apprentice of war, a youth with ideas and vision. He invented manoeuvres which were utterly novel and quite unprecedented, at least in the desert. He was also a commander stoical enough to be able to view with calmness the temporary loss of territory. He assembled his prize warriors, the carefully chosen destroying angels, on the right flank of the enemy, pushed against this flank determinedly, deflected it, and harried it sufficiently to be victorious in that one spot. It mattered not that the main force of Amalek had the advantage against the ranks of the Hebrews, and storming ahead gained considerable territory from them. Because of the break-through at the flank, Joshua penetrated to the rear of Amalek's force so that now they had to turn around towards him, without being able to cease fighting against the main might of Israel. And they who a moment ago had almost been vanquished now took new courage. With this the Amalekites lost their head and despaired. "Treason," they cried, "all is lost. Do not hope any longer to be victorious! Jahwe is above us, a god of unbounded malice." And with this password of despair, the warriors of Amalek let their swords sink and were overcome.

Only a few succeeded in fleeing north towards their people, where they found refuge with the main tribe. Israel occupied the oasis Kadesh, which proved to be traversed by a broad, rushing stream, rich with nut bushes and fruit trees and filled with bees, song-birds, quails, and rabbits. The children of Amalek who had been left behind in the village tents augmented the number of their own progeny; the wives of Amalek became Israel's wives and servants.

13

Moses, though his arms hurt him long afterwards, was a happy man. That he remained a much tried man, tried more than all the people on earth, we shall soon see. For the time being he could well be pleased with the state of affairs. The exodus had been successful, Pharaoh's avenging might had drowned in the sea of reeds, the desert voyage was mercifully completed, and the battle for Kadesh had been won with Jahwe's help. Now he stood in all his greatness before his father's kin, in the esteem which springs from success, as "the man Moses who has led us out of Egypt". He needed this esteem to be able to begin his work, the work of cleansing and shaping in the sign of the Invisible One, the work of hewing, chiselling, and forming of the flesh and blood, the work for which he longed. He was happy to have this flesh and blood at last all to himself out in the open, in the oasis which bore the name "sanctuary". Here was his workplace.

He showed his people a certain mountain which lay towards the east of Kadesh behind the desert. This was Horeb, which one could also call Sinai. Two-thirds of it was overgrown with bushes, but at the summit it was bare, and there was the seat of Jahwe. This was plausible, for it was a peculiar mountain, distinguished among its neighbours by a cloud which never vanished and which lay like a roof on its peak. During the day this cloud looked grey, but at night it glowed. There, he told the people, on the bushy slope beneath the rocky top, Jahwe had talked to him from the burning thorn bush, and had charged him to lead them out of Egypt. They listened to the tale with fear and trembling. They could not as yet feel reverence or devotion. All of them, even the bearded men, shook at their knees like cowards when he pointed to the mountain with the lasting cloud, and when he taught them that this was the dwelling of the god who was inclined towards them and was to be their sole god. Moses, shaking his fists, scolded them because of their uncouth behaviour, and endeavoured to make them feel more courageous towards Jahwe, and more intimate with him, by erecting right in their midst, in Kadesh itself, a shrine in his honour.

For Jahwe had a mobile presence. This was another attribute of his invisibility. He dwelt on Sinai, he dwelt on Horeb. And hardly had the people begun to make themselves at home in the camp of the Amalekites when Moses gave him a dwelling even there. It was a tent right next to one's own tent. He called it the meeting or assembly tent, and also the tabernacle. There he housed holy objects which would serve as aids in the service of the Invisible. Most of these objects traced back to the cult of the Midianitic Jahwe as he remembered it. First, a kind of chest carried on poles, on which, according to Moses's explanation (and he was the man to know such things), the invisible divinity was enthroned. This chest they could take along into the field and carry before them in battle, should Amalek approach and endeavour to seek revenge. Next to this chest he kept a brass rod with a serpent's head, also called the "Brass Serpent". This rod commemorated Aaron's well-meant trick before Pharaoh, but with the additional import that it be also the rod which Moses had held over the sea of reeds to part the waters. He also kept in the tent a satchel called an ephod, from which the oracle lots were drawn. These were the yes and no, the right and wrong, the good and bad, the "Urim and Thummim" judgments which were Jahwe's direct decisions in those difficult disputes which man alone could not solve.

For the most part Moses himself did the judging in Jahwe's stead, in all kinds of controversies and contentions which arose among the people. As a matter of fact, the first thing he did in Kadesh was to erect a tribunal where, on designated days, he passed judgment and settled differences. There, where the strongest spring bubbled, the spring which was already called Me-Meribah, meaning "water of the law", there he pronounced his verdicts and let the holy judgment flow even as the water flowed from the earth. If one considers that there were twelve thousand five hundred souls who looked up to him alone for justice, then one can well imagine how sorely tried was he.

For more and more of them sought their rights and pressed towards his seat near the spring, as the idea of right was something utterly new to these forsaken and lost souls. Up to now they had hardly known that there was such a thing. Now they learned first that right was directly connected with the invisibility and holiness of God and stood under his protection, and second that the conception of right also included the conception of wrong. The mob could not understand this for a long time. They thought that there, where right was dispensed, everybody had to be in the right. At first they could not and did not want to believe that a person might obtain his right through the very fact that he was judged in the wrong and had to slink away with a long face.

Such a man regretted that he had not decided the matter with his adversary as he used to decide in former times, that is, with stone in fist, even if the affair might then have had a different outcome. With difficulty did this man learn from Moses that such an action was offensive to the invisibility of God, and that no one should slink away with a long face if right had declared him wrong. For right was equally beautiful and equally dignified in its holy invisibility whether it said yea or nay to a man.

Thus Moses not only had to pass judgment but to teach judgment. And greatly was he tried. He had studied law in the academy in Thebes, and knew the Egyptian law scrolls and the Code of Hammurabi, king of the Euphrates. This knowledge helped him to a decision in many a case. For example: if an ox had gored a man or a woman to death, then the ox had to be stoned and his meat could not be eaten. But the owner of the ox was innocent unless he knew that that ox previously was wont to push with his horns and had not kept him in. Then his life was forfeit, except that he could ransom it with thirty shekels of silver. Or if somebody dug a pit and did not cover it properly, so that an ox or an ass fell into it, then the owner of that pit should make restitution in money to the other man for his loss, but the carcass should belong to the first man. Or whatever else occurred in matters of violence, mistreatment of slaves, theft and burglary, destruction of crops, arson, or abuse of confidence – in all these and a hundred other cases Moses passed judgment, leaning on the Code of Hammurabi, and decided what was right and what wrong. But there were too many cases for one judge, and his seat near the spring was overrun. If the master probed the various cases only half-way-conscientiously, he was never finished and had to postpone much. Ever-new problems arose, and he was tried above all people.

14

Therefore, it was a stroke of great good fortune that his brother-in-law, Jethro, came from Midian to visit him in Kadesh and give him good counsel, counsel in such as the over-conscientious Moses could never have found for himself. Soon after the arrival in the oasis, Moses had sent to Midian to his brother-in-law for the return of his wife Zipporah and his two sons, who had been entrusted to the safety of Jethro's tent during the Egyptian tribulations. Accommodatingly, Jethro came in person to deliver wife and sons, to embrace Moses, to look around, and to hear from him how everything had gone off.

Jethro was a corpulent sheik with a pleasant mien, with even and deft gestures, a man of the world, a paladin of a civilized, mundane, and experienced people. Received with much splendour, he put up at Moses's hut. There, not without astonishment, he learned how one of his own gods – peculiarly enough, the imageless one – had done so extraordinarily well for Moses and his people, and had, as he already knew, delivered them from Egypt's power.

"Well, who would have thought it?" he said. "Obviously this god is greater than we suspected, and what you tell me now makes me fear that we have cultivated him too negligently. I shall see to it that we shall accord him more honour in future."

The next day public sacrifices were ordered. Moses arranged these seldom, as he had little use for a custom common to all the people in the world. Sacrifice was not essential, said he, to the Invisible One. "Not offerings do I want," spoke Jahwe, "but that ye shall listen to my voice, and that is the voice of my servant, Moses. Then shall I be your God and ye my people." Nevertheless, this once they did arrange slaughter and burnt offerings in Jahwe's honour as well as to celebrate Jethro's arrival. And again the next day, early in the morning, Moses took his brother-in-law along to the Spring of the Law so that he could attend a court session and observe how Moses sat and judged the people. And the people stood round him from morn to evening, and there was no end to it, no question of being finished.

"Now, let me ask you one thing, my honoured brother-in-law," said the guest when, after the session, he walked home with Moses. "Why do you plague yourself like that? There you sit all alone and all the people stand around you from morn until evening. Why do you do it?"

"I have to," answered Moses. "The people come to me that I may judge one and all and show them the right of God and his laws."

"But, my good friend, how can you be so inefficient?" said Jethro. "Is that the way to govern, and is it right that the ruler should have to work himself to the bone because he does everything himself? It is a shame that you drive yourself so that you can hardly hold your head up. What is more, you lose your voice with all that judging. Nor are the people any less tired. That is no way to begin. As time passes you will not be able to transact all business yourself. Nor is this necessary – listen to my voice. If you act as the delegate of your people before God, and personally bring before him only the most important cases, those cases which concern everybody, that is all you can possibly be expected to do. As for the other cases – well, look around you," said he with easy gestures, "look around among the mob and search for respectable men, men of some standing, and place them as judges above the people. Let one of these men rule a group of a thousand, another a hundred, still another fifty and even ten, and let them all rule according to the law and tenets which you have set up. Only if it is a great matter should you be called. The lesser questions they can settle themselves; you do not even need to know about it. That is how we do it, and so shall it be easier for you. I would not today have been able to get away to visit you, if I took it into my head that I had to know about everything that is going on and if I burdened myself as you do."

"But the judges will accept gifts," answered Moses with a heavy heart, "and will declare the godless ones in the right. For gifts blind those who see and turn awry the cause of the just."

"I know that," answered Jethro, "I know it quite well. But one has to close one's eyes to that, just a little. Wherever order reigns, wherever law is spoken, wherever judgments are made, they become a little involved through gifts. Does that matter so much? Look, those who accept presents, they are ordinary folk. But the people themselves are ordinary folk; therefore they understand the ordinary and the ordinary is comfortable to the community. Moreover, if a man has been wronged because the judge of the ten has accepted gifts from his godless adversary, then let that man pursue an ordinary process of law. Let him appeal to the judge who rules over the fifty, then to the one who rules over the hundred; and finally, to the one who rules over the thousand: that one gets the most gifts and has therefore the clearest vision. Our man will find his rights with this last judge, that is, if in the meantime the fellow has not wearied of the whole affair."

Thus did Jethro discourse with even gestures, gestures which made life easier if one but saw them. Thus did he show that he was indeed the priest-king of a civilized desert people. With a heavy heart did Moses listen and nod. His was the pliable soul of the lonely spiritual man, the man who nods his head thoughtfully at the cleverness of the world and understands that the world may well be in the right. He followed the counsel of his deft brother-in-law – it was absolutely necessary. He appointed lay judges who, according to his tenets, let judgment flow next to the great spring and next to the smaller one. They judged the everyday cases (such as if an ass fell into the pit); only the capital cases came to Moses, the priest of God. And the greatest matters were decided by the holy oracles.

Moses no longer had his hands tied with everyday affairs; his hands were free for the larger work, the work of sculpting for which Joshua, the strategic youth, had won the work-place, Kadesh the oasis. Undoubtedly, the doctrine of right and wrong was one important example of the implications inherent in the invisible God. Yet it was only one example. Much work remained to be done. Mighty and long labour lay ahead, labour which would have to be achieved through anger and patience before the uncouth hordes could be formed into a people who would be more than the usual community to whom the ordinary was comfortable, but would be an extraordinary, a separated people and a unique monument erected to the Invisible One and dedicated to him.

15

The people soon learned what it meant to have fallen into the hands of an angrily patient workman who held himself accountable to an invisible god. They began to realize that that unnatural suggestion to omit the shout of triumph over the drowning of the enemy was but a beginning, though a portentous beginning, which already lay well within the domain of holiness and purity. It was a beginning which presupposed a certain understanding; the people would have to acquire that understanding before they could view Moses's command as anything less than unnatural.

What the mob was really like, to what degree it was the rawest of raw material and flesh and blood, lacking the most elementary conception of purity and holiness, how Moses had to begin at the beginning and teach them beginnings, that is to be deduced from the simple precepts with which he started to work and chisel and blast. Not to their comfort, certainly, for the stone does not take sides with the master but against him; to the stone the first stroke struck to form it appears as a most unnatural action.

Moses, with his wide-set eyes and his flattened nose, was always in their midst, here, there, in this and that encampment. Shaking his broad-wristed fists, he jogged, censured, chided, and churned their existence; he reproved, chastised, and cleansed, using as his touchstone the invisibility of the God Jahwe who had led them out of Egypt in order to choose them as his people and make them into a holy people, even as holy as himself. For the time being they were nothing more than rabble, a fact which they proved by emptying their bodies simply wherever they lay. That was a disgrace and a pestilence. Ye must have a place outside the camp where ye shall go when ye need to. Do ye understand me? And take along a little scoop and dig a pit before ye sit down, and after ye have sat then shall ye cover it. For the Lord your God walks in your camp, therefore your camp must be holy. And that means clean, so that the Lord need not hold his nose and turn away from you. For holiness begins with cleanliness, which is purity in the rough, the rough beginning of all purity. Dost thou comprehend this, Ahiman, and thou, wife Naemi? The next time I want to see everybody with that scoop, or ye shall have to reckon with the destroying angel.

Thou must be clean and wash thyself often with live water for the sake of thy health. For without water there is no cleanliness or holiness, and disease is unclean. But if thou thinkest that vulgarity is healthier than clean custom, then thou art an imbecile and thou shalt be visited by jaundice, fig warts, and the boils of Egypt. If ye do not practise cleanliness, then evil black blains shall grow up in you and the seeds of pestilence shall travel from blood to blood. Learn to distinguish cleanliness from uncleanliness, or else ye shall fail before the Invisible One and ye are nothing but rabble. Therefore if a man or a woman have a cankerous sore or an evil fistule, if he suffer with rash or ulcers, then he or she shall be declared unclean and not permitted in the encampment, but shall be put outside, separated in uncleanliness even as the Lord has separated you that ye may become clean. And whatever such a one has touched, on whatever he has lain, the saddle on which he has sat, that shall be burned. But if he has become clean again in separation, then he shall count seven days to make sure that he be truly clean, then he shall bathe thoroughly in water and then may he return.

Distinguish, I say unto you, and be holy before God. For how else can ye be holy as I want you to be? Ye eat everything together without choice or daintiness, and to me who have to watch you that is an abomination. There are certain things that ye may eat and others that ye may not, for ye shall have your pride and your disgust. Those animals which have cloven hoofs and chew their cud, those ye may eat. But those which chew their cud and divide not the hoof, like the camel, those shall be unclean to you and ye shall not eat them. Notice well:

the good camel is not unclean as a living creature of God; it is merely unfit for food, as little fit as the pig, which, though it has cloven hoofs, does not chew its cud. Therefore distinguish! What creatures in the water have fins and scales, those ye may eat, but those which slither in the element without fins or scales, the entire breed of salamanders, they, though they also are from God, ye shall shun as nourishment. Among the birds disdain ye the eagle, the hawk, the osprey, the vulture, and their ilk. Furthermore, all ravens, the ostrich, the night owl, the cuckoo, the screech owl, the swan, the horned owl, the bat, the bittern, the stork, the heron, and the jay, as well as the swallow. Who would eat the weasel, the mouse, the toad, or the hedgehog? Who shall be so gross as to eat the lizard, the mole, and the blindworm – in fact, anything which creeps on the earth and crawls on its belly? But ye do it, and turn your souls into loathsomeness. The one whom I shall next see eating a blindworm I shall deal with so that he will never do it again. For though one does not die from eating it, though it is not harmful, yet it is reprehensible, and much shall be reprehensible to you. Therefore ye also shall eat no carcass, for that is even harmful.

Thus did he give them precepts of nourishment and circumscribe them in matters of food, though not alone in those. He did likewise in matters of lust and love, for there too were they disorderly in rabble fashion. Ye shall not commit adultery, he told them, for marriage is a holy barrier. But do ye really know what that means: ye shall not commit adultery? It means a hundred curbs out of regard for the holiness of God. It does not mean only that thou shalt not covet the wife of your neighbour: that is the least. For though ye are living in the flesh, ye are allied in oath to Invisibility. And marriage is the essence of all purity of flesh before God's visage. Therefore thou shalt not take unto thyself a wife and her mother, to name only one example; that is not seemly. And thou shalt never and under no conditions lie with thy sister so that thou shalt see her shame and she yours. For that is incest. Not even with thine aunt shalt thou lie. That is not worthy of her nor of thyself: thou shalt keep clear from it. If a woman have a sickness, then thou shalt shun her and not approach the fountain of her blood. And if something shameful should happen to a man in his sleep, then shall he be unclean until the next evening, and he shall bathe carefully in water.

I hear that thou causest thy daughter to be a whore and that thou takest whore money from her? Do this no longer, for if thou perseverest, then shall I let thee be stoned. What art thou thinking of, to sleep with a boy as well as with a woman? That is iniquity and rabble depravity. Both of you shall be put to death. But if somebody consort with an animal, be it man or woman, they shall be completely exterminated, and they and the animal choked to death.

Imagine their bewilderment over all these curbs! At first they felt life would hardly be worth living if they should observe them all. Moses struck at them with the sculptor's chisel so that the chips flew. Deadly serious was he about meting out the chastisements which he had placed on the worse transgressions. And behind his ordinances stood the young Joshua and his destroying angels.

"I am the Lord thy God," said he, risking the danger that they might in truth take him for God, "who have led thee out of Egypt and separated thee from all the peoples. Therefore shall ye separate, the clean from the unclean, and not follow in whoredom the other tribes but be holy to me. For I, thy Lord, am holy, and have separated you so that ye shall become mine. Of all the unclean actions the one most unclean is to care for any other god. For I am a jealous god. The most unclean action is to make yourself an image, be it the likeness of a man or a woman, of an ox or a hawk, a fish or a worm. In doing that ye shall become faithless to me, even if the image shall be in my likeness, and thou mightest as well sleep with thy sister or with an animal. Such an action is not far removed and soon follows quite by itself. Take care! I am among you and I see everything. Whosoever shall whore after the animal-and-death gods of Egypt, him shall I drown. I shall drive him into the desert and banish him like an outcast. And the same shall I do with him who sacrifices to the Moloch, whom I know ye still carry in your memory. If ye consume your force in its honour, I shall deem it evil, and heavily shall I deal with you. Nor shalt thou let thy son nor thy daughter walk through fire according to the stupid old custom, nor shalt thou pay attention to the flight of the birds and their cry, nor whisper with fortune-tellers, destiny predictors, or augurs, nor shall ye question the dead nor practise magic in my name. If one among you is a scoundrel and takes my name in false testimony, he shall not profit by such tale-bearing, for I shall devour him. It is even magic and abomination to print marks on one's body, to shave one's eyebrows and make cuttings on one's face as a sign of sorrow for the dead – I shall not suffer it."

How great was their bewilderment! They were not even allowed to cut their faces in mourning, not even allowed to tattoo themselves a little bit. They realized now what is meant by the invisibility of God. It meant great privation, this business of being in league with Jahwe. But because behind Moses's prohibition stood the destroying angels, and because nobody wanted to be driven into the desert, that which he prohibited soon appeared to them to be worthy of fear. At first it was fearworthy only in relation to the punishment, but by and by the action itself took on the stamp of evil, and if they committed it they became ill at ease without even thinking of the punishment.

Bridle your hearts, he said to them, and do not cast your eyes on somebody else's possessions. If ye desire them, it soon follows that ye take them, be it through stealthy purloining, which is cowardice, or by killing the other, which is brutality. Jahwe and I do not want you either cowardly or brutal, but ye shall be in the middle between these two; that means decent. Have ye understood that much? To steal is slinking wretchedness, but to murder, be it from rage or from greed, or from greedy rage or from raging greed, that is flaming wrong, and against him who shall commit such a wrong shall I set my countenance so that he will not know where to hide himself.

For he has shed blood and blood is holy awe and a deep secret offering for my altar and atonement. Ye shall not eat blood nor any meat in the blood, for blood is mine. And he who is smeared with the blood of human beings, his heart shall sicken in cold terror and I shall drive him that he run away from himself unto the ends of the world. Say ye Amen to that.

And they said Amen, still hoping that with the ban on murder killing alone was meant. For few of them had the desire to kill, and those who did had it only occasionally. But it turned out that Jahwe gave that word as wide a meaning as he had given the word adultery and that he meant by it all sorts of things, so that "murder" and "killing" began with almost any transgression of the code. Almost every wound which one man inflicted upon another, whether through deceit or through fraud (and almost all of the people hankered a little after deceit and fraud), Jahwe considered bloodshed. They should not deal falsely with one another nor bear false witness against their neighbours, and they should use just weights, and just measures. It was to the highest degree unnatural, and for the time being it was only the natural fear of punishment which gave an aspect of naturalness to all this bidding and forbidding.

That one should honour one's father and mother as Moses demanded, that also had a wider meaning, wider than one suspected at first blush. Whosoever raised his hand against his progenitor and cursed him, well, yes, he should be done away with. But that respect should also be extended to those who merely could be your progenitors. Ye shall arise before a grey head. Ye shall cross your arms and incline your stupid head. Do ye understand me? Thus demands the decency of God. The only consolation was that since your neighbour was not permitted to kill you, you had a reasonable prospect of becoming yourself old and grey, so that the others would have to arise before you.

Finally, it appeared that old age was a symbol of what was old in general, everything which did not happen from today to tomorrow but which came from long ago: the piously traditional, the custom of the fathers. To that one had to pay the tribute of honour and awe in God. Ye shall keep my sabbaths, the day on which I led you out of Egypt, the day of the unleavened bread, and the day when I rested from the labours of my creation. Ye shall not defile my day with the sweat of your brow: I forbid it. For I have led thee out of the Egyptian house of bondage with mighty hand and with outstretched arm, where thou wert a slave and a work animal. And my day shall be the day of thy freedom, which thou shalt keep holy. Six days shalt thou be a tiller or a plough-maker or a potter or a coppersmith or a joiner. But on my day shalt thou put on clean garments and thou shalt be nothing, nothing but a human being who raises his eyes to the Invisible.

Thou wert an oppressed servant in the land of Egypt. Think of that in your behaviour towards those who are strangers amongst you: for example, the children of Amalek, whom God gave into your hands. Do not oppress them. Look on them as ye look on yourself and give them equal rights, or I shall crash down upon you. For they too stand under the protection of Jahwe. In short, do not make such a stupid, arrogant distinction between thyself and the others, so that thou thinkest that thou alone art real and thou alone countest while the others are only a semblance. Ye both have life in common, and it is only an accident that thou art not he. Therefore do not love thyself alone but love him in the same way, and do unto him as thou desirest that he do unto you. Be gracious with one another and kiss the tips of your fingers when ye pass each other and bow with civility and speak the greeting, "Be hale and healthy." For it is quite as important that he be healthy as that thou be healthy. And even if it is only formal civility that ye do thus and kiss your finger-tips, the gesture does leave something in your heart of that which should be there of your neighbour. To that say ye Amen!

And they all said Amen.

16

Actually, that Amen did not mean very much. They only said it because Moses was the man who had led them successfully out of Egypt, who had drowned Pharaoh's chariots, and had won the battle of Kadesh. It took a long time before what he had taught them, what he enjoined upon them – all those barriers, laws, and prohibitions – sank into their flesh and blood. It was a mighty piece of work which he had undertaken, the work of changing the rabble into a people dedicated to the Lord, and to a clean image which could pass muster before the Invisible. In the sweat of his brow he worked in his workplace, Kadesh. He kept his wide-set eyes on all. He chiselled, blasted, formed, and smoothed the unwilling stone with tenacious patience, with repeated forbearance and frequent forgiving, and also with flaming anger and chastising sternness. Yet often did he almost despair when once again the flesh relapsed into stubbornness and forgetfulness, when once again the people failed to use the scoop, when they ate blindworms, slept with their sisters or their animals, painted marks upon themselves, crouched with fortune-tellers, slunk towards theft, and killed each other. "O rabble," said he to them, "ye shall see. The Lord shall appear above you and devour you." But to the Lord himself he said, "What shall I do with this flesh and why have you withdrawn your graces from me, that you burden me with a thing I cannot bear? I would rather clean a stable untouched for years by water or spade, I would rather clear a thicket with my bare hands, and turn it into a garden, than try to form for you a clean image out of them. Wherefore must I carry these people in my arms as if I had given them birth? I am but half related to them from my father's side; therefore I pray you let me enjoy my life and free me from this task. Or else strangle me rather!"

But God answered Moses out of his inner consciousness with so clear a voice that he could hear it with his ears and he fell upon his face:

"Just because you are only half related to them from the side of the buried one are you the man to form them for me and to raise them to a holy people. For if you were wholly and only one of them, then you could not see them as they are nor work upon them. Anyway, that you complain to me and wish to excuse yourself from your work is pure affectation. For you know quite well that your work is beginning to take effect. You know that you have already given them a conscience so that they are ill at ease when they do ill. Therefore do not pretend to me that you do not desire your travail. It is my desire, God's desire, which you have, and lacking it you would sicken of life as our people sickened of manna after a few days. Of course, if I decided to strangle you, then yes, then would you be rid of that desire."

The much-troubled Moses understood this, nodded his head at Jahwe's words as he lay there, and stood up once again to his travail. But now he had problems, not only in his capacity as a sculptor of the people; trouble and grief began to creep into his family life. Anger, envy, and bickering arose around him and there was no peace in his hut. Perhaps it was his own fault, the fault of his senses. For his senses, stirred up by overwork, hung on a Negro girl, the well-known Negro girl.

One knows that at this time he lived with an Ethiopian girl as well as with his wife Zipporah, the mother of his sons. She was a wench from the land of Kush who as a child had arrived in Egypt, had lived among the Hebrew tribes in Goshen, and had joined the exodus. Undoubtedly she had known many a man, yet Moses now chose her as the companion of his bed. She was a magnificent specimen of her type, with erect breasts, with rolling eyes, thick deep lips, to sink into which may well have been an adventure, and a skin redolent of spice. Moses doted on her mightily; she was his recreation, and he would not let go of her, though he drew upon himself the enmity of his whole house. Not only his Midianite wife and her sons looked askance at the affair, but also and especially his half-sister Miriam and his half-brother Aaron. Zipporah, who possessed much of the even worldliness of her brother Jethro, got along tolerably well with her rival, particularly since the Ethiopian girl knew how to hide her feminine triumph and conducted herself most subserviently towards her. Zipporah treated the Ethiopian girl more with mockery than hate, and adopted towards Moses a light tone of irony which hid the jealousy she felt. His sons, Gershom and Eliezer, members of Joshua's dashing troop, possessed too much sense of discipline to revolt openly against their father; yet they let it be known unmistakably that they were angry and that they were ashamed of him.

Matters stood yet differently with Miriam the prophetess and Aaron the unctuous. Their hatred towards the Ethiopian mistress was more venomous than that of the others, because that hatred was the expression of a deeper and more general grudge which united them against Moses. For a long time now had they envied Moses his intimate relation with God and his spiritual master. That he felt himself to be God's elect worker they thought was largely conceit; they deemed themselves just as good as he, perhaps better. To each other they said, "Does the Lord talk only through Moses? Does he not also talk through us? Who is this man Moses? that he has exalted himself above us?" That then was the real cause of the indignation which they manifested towards this affair with the Ethiopian. And every time they noisily reproached their unfortunate brother with the passion of his nights, they soon departed into more general complaints. Soon they would be harping on the injustice which was their fate because of Moses's elevation.

Once as the day was drawing towards an end, they were in his hut, and harassed him in a way I said they were wont to harass him: the Ethiopian here and the Ethiopian there, and that he was thinking of nothing but her black breasts, and what a scandal it was, what a disgrace to his wife Zipporah, and what exposure for himself who claimed to be a prince of God and Jahwe's sole mouthpiece on earth. . . .

"Claimed?" said he. "What God has commanded me to be

I am. How ugly of you, how very ugly, that you envy my pleasure and my relaxation on the breasts of the Ethiopian. For it is no sin before God, and there is no prohibition among all the prohibitions which he gave to me which says that one may not lie with an Ethiopian. Not that I know of."

But they answered that he chose his own prohibitions according to his own tastes, and quite possibly he would soon preach that it was compulsory to lie with Ethiopians. For did he not consider himself Jahwe's sole mouthpiece? The truth was that they, Miriam and Aaron, were the proper children of Amram and the grandchildren of Levi, while he, when all was said and done, was only a foundling from the bulrushes; he might learn a little humility and not insist quite so much on his Ethiopian nor ignore their displeasure quite so offhandedly. Such behaviour was proof of his pride and his conceit.

"Who can help it that he is called?" answered he. "Can any man help it if he comes upon the burning thorn bush? Miriam, I have always thought highly of your prophetic gifts and never denied your accomplishments on the timbrel. . . ."

"Then why did you disallow my hymn 'Steed and Man' and why did you prohibit me from leading the round dance of the women? You pretended that God forbade his flock to triumph over the downfall of the Egyptians. That was abominable of you."

"And you, Aaron," continued the hard-pressed Moses, "you I have employed as the high priest in the tabernacle, and I have entrusted the Chest, the Ephod, and the Brass Serpent unto your care. Thus do I value you."

"That was the least that you could have done," answered Aaron. "For without my eloquence could you never have persuaded the people to the cause of Jahwe, nor won them for the exodus. Consider how awkward is your mouth! But now you call yourself the man who has led us out of Egypt! If you really valued us, if you really did not exalt yourself so arrogantly over your blood relatives, then why do you not pay heed to our words? Why do you remain deaf to our admonition that you imperil our whole tribe with your black paramour? To Zipporah, your Midianite wife, she is a draught as bitter as gall, and you offend all of Midian with your action, so that Jethro your brother-in-law might soon declare war on us – all for the sake of your coloured caprice."

"Jethro," said Moses with restraint, "is an even man of the world who well understands that Zipporah – praised be her name! – no longer can offer the necessary recreation to a highly overworked and heavily burdened man. But the skin of my Ethiopian is like cinnamon and perfumed of carnation in my nostrils; all my senses long for her, and therefore I beg of you, my good friends, grant her to me."

But that they did not want to do. They screeched and demanded not only that he should part from the Ethiopian and forbid her his bed, but also that he drive her into the desert without water.

Thereupon veins of anger rose on his forehead and terribly did his fists begin to tremble. But before he could open his mouth to respond, a very different trembling began – Jahwe interposed and set his visage against the hard-hearted brother and sister, and came to his servant's aid in a way they never forgot. Something frightful, something never before seen, now happened.

17

The foundations trembled. The earth shook, shivered, and swayed under their feet so that they could not stand upright but tottered to and fro in the hut, whose posts seemed to be shaken by giant fists. What had been firm began to waver, not only in one direction but in crooked and dizzying gyrations. It was horrible. At the same time there occurred a subterranean growling and rumbling and a sound from above and from outside like the blare of a great trumpet, followed by a droning, a thundering, and a rustling. It is very strange and peculiarly embarrassing if you are on the point of breaking out into a rage and the Lord takes the words out of your mouth and himself breaks out much more mightily than you yourself could have done it, and shakes the world where you could only have shaken your fists.

Moses was the least pale with fright, for at all times he was prepared for God. With Aaron and Miriam, who were deathly pale, he rushed out of the house. Then they saw that the earth had opened its jaws and that a great gap yawned right next to their hut. Obviously this rent had been destined for Miriam and Aaron, and had missed them only by a few yards. And they looked towards the mountain in the east behind the desert, Horeb and Sinai – but what was happening on Horeb, what was taking place on Sinai? It stood there enveloped from foot to summit in smoke and flames, and threw glowing crumbs towards heaven, with a far-off sound of fearful crackling. Streams of fire ran down its sides. Its vapour, crossed by lightning, obscured the stars above the desert, and slowly a rain of ashes began to descend upon the oasis Kadesh.

Aaron and Miriam fell upon their foreheads; the cleft destined for them had filled them with terror. This revelation of Jahwe showed them that they had gone too far and had spoken foolishly. Aaron exclaimed:

"O my master, this woman my sister has jabbered ugly words. Accept my prayer and let not the sin remain upon her, the sin with which she sinned against the man anointed by the Lord."

Miriam also screamed to Moses and spoke: "Master, it is impossible to speak more foolishly than spoke my brother Aaron. Forgive him and let not the sin remain upon him, so that God may not devour him just because he has twitted you a little about the Ethiopian."

Moses was not quite certain if Jahwe's revelation was really meant for his brother and sister and their lack of love, or if it was the call meant for him, the call for which he had waited hourly, the call that summoned him to commune with God about his people and the work of their education. But he let them suppose what they supposed and answered:

"There, you see. But take courage, children of Amram.

I shall put forth a good word for you up there with God on the mountain, whither he calls me. For now you shall see, and all the people shall see, whether your brother has become unmanned by his black infatuation or if the courage of God still dwells in his heart stronger than in other hearts. To the fiery mountain shall I go, quite alone, upward to God, to hear his thoughts and to deal without fear with the fearful one, on familiar terms, far from the people, but in their cause. For a long time have I known that he wishes to write down all that I have taught you for your salvation into binding words, into an eternal condensation, that I might carry it back to you from his mountain, and that the people may possess it in the tabernacle together with the Chest, the Ephod, and the Brass Serpent. Farewell. I may perish in God's tumult, in the fire of the mountain; I have to reckon with that. But should I return, then shall I bring out of his thunder the eternal word, God's law."

Such was his firm resolve; whether for life or death, that had he decided. For in order to root the obdurate, always backsliding rabble in God's morality, in order to make them fear his laws, nothing was more effective than that he, bare and alone, should dare to climb up to Jahwe's terror, up the spewing mountain, and thence carry down the dictates. Then, thought he, would they observe the laws.

When the people came running from all sides to his hut, trembling at the knees, frightened by the signs and by the terrible undulations of the earth, which occurred once and twice again, though weaker, Moses forbade them their commonplace quaking and admonished them to decent composure. God called him, said he, for their sake, and he was to climb up to Jahwe, up to the summit of the mountain, and bring something back for them, with God's will. They, however, should return to their homes and should prepare for a pilgrimage. They should hold themselves clean and wash their garments and abstain from their wives, and tomorrow they should wander out from Kadesh into the desert near the mountain. There should they encamp and wait for him until he returned from the fearful interview, perhaps bringing something back for them.

And thus it happened, or at least almost thus. Moses in his fashion had only remembered to tell them to wash their garments and to abstain from their wives. Joshua, the strategic youth, had remembered what else was necessary for such an excursion; with his troop he provided the proper quantities of water and nourishment needful to the thousands in the desert. And he also established a line of communication between Kadesh and the encampment near the mountain. He left Caleb his lieutenant in Kadesh with a police detail to supervise those who could not or would not come along. When the third day had dawned and all preparations had been made, all the others set out with their carts and their slaughter animals. They journeyed towards the mountain, a journey of a day and still a half. There, at a respectable distance from Jahwe's fuming dwelling, Joshua erected an enclosure. He enjoined the people most strictly, and in Moses's name, not to think of climbing that mountain nor even to set foot upon it. The master alone was privileged to approach so near to God. Moreover, it was highly dangerous, and whoever touched the mountain should be stoned or pierced with the arrow. They took this command in their stride, for rabble has no desire whatever to come all too near to God. To the common man the mountain did not in the least look inviting, neither by day, when Jahwe stood upon it in a thick cloud crossed by lightning, nor certainly by night, when the cloud and the entire summit glowed.

Joshua was extremely proud of the courage of his master, who the very first day and before all the people set out on his way to the mountain, alone and on foot with his pilgrim's staff, provided only with an earthen flask, a few crusts, and some tools, an axe, a chisel, a spade and a stylus. Very proud was the youth, and pleased at the impression which such holy intrepidity would surely make on the multitude. But anxious was he too about the man he worshipped, and he implored him not to approach too near to Jahwe and to be careful of the hot molten streams which ran down the sides of the mountain. Also, said he, he would visit Moses once or twice and look after him, so that the master would not in God's wilderness lack the simplest necessities.

18

Moses, leaning on his staff, traversed the desert, his wide-set eyes fixed on God's mountain, which was smoking like an oven and spewed forth many times. The mountain was of peculiar shape: it had fissures and veins which seemed to divide it into terraces and which looked like upward-leading paths, though they were not paths, but simply gradations of yellow walls. On the third day, after climbing several foothills, God's delegate arrived at the bare foot of the mountain. Then he began to ascend, his fist grasping the pilgrim's staff which he set before him. He climbed without path or track many an hour, step by step, higher, always higher, towards God's nearness. He climbed as far as a human being could, for by and by the sulphurous fumes which smelled of hot metals and which filled the air choked him, and he began to cough. He arrived at the top-most fissure and terrace right underneath the summit, where he could have a wide view of the bald and wild mountain ranges on both sides, and out over the desert as far as Kadesh. Closer by he could see the people in their enclosure, far below and small.

Here the coughing Moses found a cave in the mountain wall, a cave with a projecting roof of rock which could protect him from the falling stones and the flowing broth. There he took up his abode and arranged himself to start, after a short breathing spell, the work which God had ordered from him. Under the difficult circumstances – for the metal vapours lay heavily on his breast and made even the water taste of sulphur – this work held him fast up there not less than forty days and forty nights.

But why so long? Idle question! The eternal had to be recorded, the binding word had to be briefed, God's terse moral law had to be captured and graved into the stone of the mountain, so that Moses might bring it down to the vacillating mob, to the blood of his buried father, down into the encampment where they were waiting. There it was to stand from generation to generation, unbreakable, graved also into their minds and into their flesh and blood, the quintessence of human decency.

From his inner consciousness God directed him to hew two tablets from the rock and to write upon them his dictate, five words on the one and five words on the other, together ten words. It was no easy task to build the two tablets, to smooth them and to shape them into fit receptacles of eternal brevity. For a lone man, even if he had drunk the milk of a mason's daughter, even if he had broad wrists, it was a piece of work subject to many a mishap. Of the forty days it took a quarter. But the actual writing down was a problem the solution of which could well have prolonged the number of Moses's mountain days far over forty.

For in what manner should he write? In the academy of Thebes he had learned the decorative picture writing of Egypt with all its current amendments. He had also learned the stiffly formal arrow script of Euphrates, in which the kings of the world were wont to exchange their thoughts on fragments of clay. In Midian he had become acquainted with still a third magic method of capturing meaning. This one consisted of eyes, crosses, insets, circles, and variously formed serpentine lines. It was a method used in Sinai which had been copied with desert awkwardness from the Egyptians. Its marks, however, did not represent whole words or word pictures, but only their parts. They denoted syllables which were to be read together.

None of these three methods of fastening thought satisfied him, for the simple reason that each of them was linked to a particular language and was indigenous to that language. Moses realized perfectly well that it would never under any conditions be possible for him to set upon the stone the dictate of ten words either in Babylonian or in Egyptian language, nor yet in the jargon of the Sinai Bedouins. The words on the stone could be only in the language of his father's blood, the very dialect which they spoke and which he himself employed in his teachings. It did not matter whether they would be able to read it or not. In fact, how could they be expected to read a language which no one could as yet write? There was no magic symbol at hand to represent and hold fast their speech.

With all his soul Moses wished that there existed such a symbol, one which they could learn to read quickly, very quickly; one which children, such as they were, could learn in a few days. It followed, then, that somebody could think up and invent such a symbol in a few days, with the help of God's nearness. Yes, because it did not exist, somebody had to think up and invent this new method of writing.

What a pressing and precious task! He had not considered it in advance, had simply thought of "writing" and had not taken into account that one could not write just like that! Fired by his fervent search for symbols his people could understand, his head glowed and smoked like an oven and like the summit of the mountain. It seemed to him as if rays emerged from his head, as if horns sprang from his forehead, so great was his wishing exertion. And then a simple, illuminating idea came to him. True, he could not invent signs for all the words used by his kin, nor for the syllables from which they formed their words. Even if the vocabulary of those down in the enclosure was paltry, yet would it have required too many marks for him to build in the span of his mountain days and also for the others to learn to read quickly. Therefore he thought of something else, and horns stood upon his forehead out of pride over the flash of God's inspiration. He gathered the sounds of the language, those formed by the lips, by the tongue, by the palate, and by the throat; he put to one side the few open sounds which occurred every so often within the words, which in fact were framed by the others into words. He found that there were not too many of these framing sonant sounds – hardly twenty. If one ascribed definite signs to them, signs which everybody could alike aspirate and respirate, mumble and rumble, gabble and babble, then one could combine these signs into words and word pictures, leaving out the open sounds which followed by themselves. Thus one could form any word one liked, any word which existed, not only in the language of his father's kin, but in all languages – yes, with these signs one could even write Egyptian or Babylonian.

A flash from God. An idea with horns. An idea such as could be expected from the Invisible and the spiritual one, him to whom the world belonged, him who, though he had chosen those down below as his people, was yet the Lord of all the earth. It was an idea also which was eminently fitting to the next and most pressing purpose for which and out of which it was created: the text of the tablets, the binding briefed text. This text was to be coined first and specifically for the tribe which Moses had led out of Egypt because God and he were inclined towards them. But just as with a handful of these signs all the words of all the languages of all the people could, if need be, be written, just as Jahwe was the God of all the world, so was what Moses meant to brief and write of such a nature that it could serve as fundamental precept, as the rock of human decency, to all the peoples of the earth.

Moses with his fiery head now experimented with signs loosely related to the marks of the Sinai people as he remembered them. On the wall of the mountain he graved with his stylus the lisping, popping, and smacking, the hissing, and swishing, the humming and murmuring sounds. And when he had all the signs together and could distinguish them with a certain amount of assurance, lo! with them one could write the whole world, all that which occupied space and all that which occupied no space, all that was fashioned and all that was thought. In short, all.

He wrote. That is to say, he jabbed, chiselled, and hacked at the brittle stone of the tablets, those tablets which he had hewn laboriously and whose creation went hand in hand with the creation of the letters. No wonder that it took him forty days!

Joshua, his youth, came to see him several times. He

brought him water and crusts, without precisely telling the people of his visits. The people thought that Moses lived up there in God's proximity and communed with him quite alone. And Joshua deemed it best to let them believe this. Therefore his visits were short and made by night.

From the dawn of the light of day above Edom to its extinction, Moses sat behind the desert and worked. One has to imagine him as he sat up there with bare shoulders, his breast covered with hair, with his powerful arms which he may have inherited from his ill-used father, with his eyes set far apart, with his flattened nose, with the divided now greying beard – chewing his crust, now and then coughing from the metal vapours of the mountain, hammering, scraping, and polishing his tablets in the sweat of his brow. He crouched before the tablets propped against the rocky wall, and painstakingly carved the crow's-feet, then traced them with his stylus, and finally graved the omnipotent runes deep into the flatness of the stone.

On one tablet he wrote:

> I, Jahwe, am thy God; thou shalt have
> no other gods before me.
> Thou shalt not make unto thee any
> image.
> Thou shalt not take my name in vain.
> Remember my day, to keep it holy.
> Honour thy father and thy mother.

And on the other tablet he wrote:

> Thou shalt not murder.
> Thou shalt not commit adultery.
> Thou shalt not steal.
> Thou shalt not harm thy neighbour by
> false witness.
> Thou shalt not cast a covetous eye on
> the possessions of thy neighbour.

That is what he wrote, omitting the open sounds which formed themselves. And always it seemed to him as if rays like two horns stood out from the locks of his forehead.

When Joshua came for the last time to the mountain, he remained a little longer, two whole days. For Moses was not finished with his work and they wanted to descend together. The youth admired wholeheartedly what his master had accomplished. He comforted him because a few letters were cracked and unrecognizable in spite of all the love and care which Moses had expended. Joshua assured him that this did no harm to the total impression.

The last thing that Moses did while Joshua looked on was to paint the sunken letters with his blood so that they would stand out better. No other pigment was at hand. Therefore he cut his strong arm with his stylus and smeared the trickling blood into the letters so that they glowed rosily in the stone. When the writing had dried, Moses took one tablet under each arm, gave his pilgrim's staff, with which he had ascended, to the youth, and thus they wandered down from the seat of God towards the encampment of the people near the mountain in the desert.

19

When they had arrived at a certain distance from the encampment, just within hearing distance, a noise penetrated to them, a hollow screeching. They could not account for it. It was Moses who heard it first and Joshua who mentioned it first.

"Do you hear this peculiar clatter," he asked, "this tumult, this uproar? There is something doing, I think, a brawl, a bout, or I am much mistaken. And it must be violent and general, that we hear it as far as this. If it is what I think it is, then it is good that we come."

"That we come," answered Moses, "is good in any case. But as far as I can make out, this is no scuffle and no tussle, but something like a feasting or a dance of triumph. Do you not hear the high-pitched jubilation and clash of timbrels? Joshua, how is it that they celebrate without my permission? Joshua, what has got into them? Let us hurry."

He grasped his two tablets higher under his arms and strode faster with the puzzled Joshua.

"A dance of triumph . . . a dance of triumph," he repeated uneasily and finally in open terror. For it appeared all too clearly that this was not an ordinary brawl in which one person lay on top and the other below; this was a general united carousal. And now it was only a question of what kind of unity it was in which they thus revelled.

Even that question answered itself too soon, if indeed it need ever have been asked. The mess was horrible. As Moses and Joshua passed the high posts of the encampment they saw it in shameless unequivocalness. The people had broken loose. They had thrown off everything that Moses had laid upon them in holiness, all the morality of God. They wallowed in relapse.

Directly behind the portals was a free space which was the assembly place. There things were happening, there they were carrying on, there they wallowed, there they celebrated their miserable liberty. Before the dance they had all stuffed themselves full. One could see that at first glance. Everywhere the place showed the traces of slaughtering and gluttony. And in whose honour had they sacrificed, slaughtered, and stuffed themselves? There it stood. In the midst of barrenness, set on a stone, set on an altar pedestal, an image, a thing made by their hands, an idolatrous mischief, a golden calf.

It was no calf, it was a bull, the real, ordinary stud bull of all the peoples of the world. A calf it is called only because it was no more than medium size, in fact rather less, and also misshapen and ludicrously fashioned; an awkward abomination, yet all too recognizable as a bull.

Around this thing a multitudinous round dance was in progress, a dozen circles of men and women, hand in hand, accompanied by timbrels and by cymbals. Heads were thrown far back, rolling eyes were upturned, knees jerked towards chins; they screeched and they roared and made crass obeisance. In different directions did the dance turn, one shameful circle turning towards the right, another towards the left. In the very centre of the whirlpool, near the calf, Aaron could be seen hopping around in his long-sleeved garment which he used to wear as the guardian of the tabernacle, and which he had gathered high so that he could jig with his long, hairy legs. And Miriam led the women with her timbrel.

But this was only the round dance near the calf. Farther on what was to be expected was taking place. It is difficult to confess how far the people debased themselves. Some ate blindworms, others lay with their sisters and that publicly, in the calf's honour. Others simply squatted and emptied themselves, forgetting the scoop. Men offered their force to the calf. Somewhere someone was cuffing his own mother.

At these gruesome sights, the veins of anger swelled to bursting on Moses's forehead. His face flaming red, he cut his way through the circles of the dancers – straight to the calf, the seed, the fountain, the womb of the crime. Recognizing the master, they gaped with embarrassed grins. High up he lifted one of the tablets of the law with mighty arms, and smashed it down on the ridiculous beast, so that its legs crumbled. Once again did he strike, and with such rage that though the tablet broke into pieces, nothing but a formless mass remained of the thing. Then he swung the second tablet and gave the abomination a final blow, grinding it completely to dust. And because the second tablet remained still intact, he shattered it with a blow on the pedestal. Then he stood still with trembling fists, and deeply from his breast he groaned: "Ye rabble, ye Godforsaken! There lies what I have carried down from God, what he has written for you with his finger as your talisman against the misery of ignorance. There it lies in ruins near the fragments of your idol. And what shall I now tell my Lord so that he will not devour you?"

He saw Aaron the jumper standing near with downcast eyes, and with oily locks at the nape of his neck; he stood silent and stupid. Moses seized him by his garment, shook him, and spoke: "Where did the golden Belial come from, this excrescence, and what did the people do to you that you push them to their destruction while I am up on the mountain? Why do you yourself bray before them in their dance of debauchery?"

And Aaron answered, "O my master, let not your anger be heaped on me and on my sister. We had to give in. You know that the people are evil. They forced us. You were away so long, you remained an eternity on the mountain, so that we all thought that you would never return. Then the people gathered against me and screamed, 'Nobody knows what has become of that man Moses, who has led us out of Egypt. He shall not return. Probably the spewing mouth of the mountain has swallowed him. Arise, make us gods which shall go before us when Amalek comes. We are a people like other peoples, and want to carouse before gods which are like the gods of other peoples!' Thus they spoke, master, for if you pardon me, they thought they were rid of you. But now tell me what I could have done when they banded together against me. I asked them to break off the golden ear-rings from their ears. These I melted in the fire and made a form, and cast the calf as their god."

"It is not even a good likeness of a calf," interposed Moses contemptuously.

"They were in such a hurry," answered Aaron. "The very next day, that is, today, they wanted to hold their revels in honour of the sympathetic gods. Therefore I handed over to them the image as it was, a piece of work to which you ought not deny a certain amount of verisimilitude. And they rejoiced and spoke, 'These are your gods, Israel, which have led you out of Egypt.' And we built an altar and they offered burnt sacrifices and thank offerings and ate, and after that they played and danced a little."

Moses let him stand there and made his way back to the portal through the scattered circles of dancers. There with Joshua he placed himself beneath the birchen crossbeam and called with all his might:

"Who is on the Lord's side, let him come unto me."

Many came, those who were of sound heart and had not

willingly joined the revels. Joshua's armed troop assembled around him.

"Ye unfortunate people," said Moses, "what have ye done, and how shall I now atone for you before Jahwe, that he shall not blot you out as an incorrigibly stiff-necked people and shall not devour you? As soon as I turn my back, ye make yourselves a golden Belial. Shame on you and on me! Do ye see these ruins – I do not mean those of the calf, let the pest take them! – I mean the others? That is the gift which I had promised you and which I have brought down to you, the eternal condensation, the rock of decency, the ten words which I, in God's nearness, wrote down in your language and wrote with my blood, with the blood of my father; with your blood did I write them. Now lies the gift in fragments."

Then many who heard this wept and there was a great crying in the encampment.

"Perhaps it will be possible to replace them," said Moses. "For the Lord is patient and of infinite mercy, and forgives missteps and trespasses. But" – he thundered of a sudden, while his blood rose to his head and his veins swelled to bursting – "he lets no one go unpunished. For, says the Lord, I visit the iniquity of the fathers upon the children unto the third and fourth generation as the jealous God that I am. We shall hold court here," exclaimed Moses, "and shall order a bloody cleansing. It shall be determined who were the ringleaders who first screamed for golden gods and insolently asserted that the calf has led you out of Egypt, where I alone have done it, says the Lord. They shall all have to deal with the destroying angels, regardless of their rank or person. To death shall they be stoned and shot by the arrow, even if there are three hundred of them. And the others shall strip off their ornaments and mourn until I return – for I shall again ascend the mountain of God, and shall see what in any case I can do for you, ye stiff-necked people."

20

Moses did not attend the executions which the golden calf had made necessary. That was the business of the dashing Joshua. Moses himself was once again up on the mountain in his cave underneath the rumbling summit. While the people mourned he again remained forty days and forty nights alone among the vapours. But why so long? The answer is thus: not only because Jahwe directed him to form the tablets anew and to write down the dictate afresh – that task went more quickly because he had acquired practice and knew how to write – but also because he had to fight a long fight with the Lord before he would permit the renewal. It was a wrestling in which anger and mercy, fatigue over the work and love for the undertaking, were in turn victorious. Moses had to use much power of persuasion and many clever appeals to prevent God from declaring the covenant broken. For almost did God cast himself loose from the stiff-necked rabble, almost did he smash them as Moses in flaming anger had smashed the first tablets of the law.

"I shall not go before them," said God, "to lead them into the land of their fathers. Do not ask this of me – I cannot depend upon my patience. I am a jealous God and I flame up, and you shall see one day I shall forget myself and I shall devour them altogether."

And he proposed to Moses that he would annihilate these people, who were as miscast as the golden calf and as incorrigible. It would be impossible, said he, to raise them into a holy people, and there was nothing left but to consume Israel and root it out. But of him, Moses, he would make a great nation and live with him in covenant. But this Moses did not want, and he said to him, "No, Lord," said he, "forgive them their sins; if not, then blot me out of the book also, for I do not wish to survive them. For my part, I wish for no other holy people but them."

And he appealed to the Lord's sense of honour and spoke: "Imagine, holy one, what is going to happen. If you kill these people as one man, then the heathen who shall hear their screams will say, 'Bah! The Lord was not able to bring the people into the land which he had promised them. He was not powerful enough. Therefore did he slaughter them in the wilderness.' Do you want that said of you by all the peoples of the world? Therefore let the power of the Lord appear great, and be lenient with the missteps of your children according to your mercy."

It was this last argument which won God and decided him towards forgiveness. With the restriction, however, that of this generation none except Joshua and Caleb should ever see the promised land. "Your children," decided the Lord, "I shall lead there. But all those who are above twenty in their age, they shall never see the land. Their bodies shall fall in the desert."

"It is well, Lord, all shall be well," answered Moses. "We shall leave it at that." For because this decision agreed with his and Joshua's purposes, he argued against it no longer. "Now let me renew the tablets," said he, "that I may take your brevity down to the human beings. After all, perhaps it was just as well that I smashed the first in my anger. There were a few misshaped letters in them. I shall now confess to you that I fleetingly thought of this when I dashed the tablets to pieces."

And again he sat, secretly nourished and succoured by Joshua, and he jabbed and he chiselled, he scraped and he smoothed. Wiping his brow from time to time with the back of his hand, he wrote, hacking and graving the letters into the tablets. They came out a good deal better than the first time. Then again he painted the letters with his blood and descended, the law under his arms.

It was announced to Israel that the mourning had come to an end, and that they again might put on their ornaments, except of course the ear-rings: these had been used up to bad purpose. And all the people came before Moses that he might hand them what he had brought down, the message of Jahwe from the mountain, the tablets with the ten words.

"Take them, blood of our fathers," said he, "and hold them

sacred in the tent of God. But what they tell ye, that hold sacred in your actions. For here is briefed what shall bind you; here is the divine condensation; here is the alpha and omega of human behaviour; here is the rock of decency, which God has inscribed in lapidary writing, using my stylus. In your language did he write, but in symbols in which if need be all the languages of all peoples could be written. For he is the Lord of all, and therefore is the Lord of ABC, and his speech, addressed to you, Israel, is at the same time a speech for all.

"Into the stone of the mountain did I grave the ABC of human behaviour, but it must be graved also into your flesh and blood, Israel. So that he who breaks but one word of the ten commandments shall tremble before his own self and before God and an icy finger shall be laid on his heart, because he has stepped out of God's confines. I know well and God knows in advance that his commandments will not be obeyed, and they will be transgressed at all times and everywhere. But at least the heart of everyone who breaks them shall turn icy, for the words are written in every man's flesh and blood and deep within himself he knows that the words are all-valid.

"But woe to the man who shall arise and speak: 'They are no longer valid.' Woe to him who teaches you: 'Arise and get rid of them! Lie, murder, rob, whore, rape, and deliver your father and mother to the knife. For this is the natural behaviour of human beings and you shall praise my name because I proclaim natural licence.' Woe to him who erects a calf and speaks: 'This is your god. In his honour do all of this, and whirl around the image I have fashioned in a round dance of debauchery.' He shall be mighty and powerful, he shall sit upon a golden throne, and he shall be looked up to as the wisest of all. For he knows that the inclination of the human heart is evil, even in youth. But that is about all that he will know, and he who knows only that is as stupid as the night and it would be better for him never to have been born. For he knows nothing of the covenant between God and man, a covenant that none may break, neither man nor God, for it is unbreakable. Blood shall flow in torrents because of his black stupidity, so much blood that the redness shall vanish from the cheeks of mankind. But then the people shall hew down the monster – inevitably; for they can do naught else. And the Lord says, I shall raise my foot and shall trample him into the mire, to the bottom of the earth shall I cast the blasphemer, one hundred and twelve fathoms deep. And man and beast shall describe an arc around the spot into which I have cast him; and the birds of the heavens, high in their flight, shall shun the place so that they need not fly over it. And he who shall speak his name, he shall spit towards the four corners of the earth and shall wipe his mouth and say, 'Forfend!' That the earth may again be the earth, a vale of want, yes, but not a sty of depravity. To that say ye Amen!"

And all the people said Amen.

THE BLACK SWAN

IN THE twenties of our century a certain Frau Rosalie von Tümmler, a widow for over a decade, was living in Düsseldorf on the Rhine, with her daughter Anna and her son Eduard, in comfortable if not luxurious circumstances. Her husband, Lieutenant-Colonel von Tümmler, had lost his life at the very beginning of the war, not in battle, but in a perfectly senseless automobile accident, yet still, one could say, "on the field of honour" – a hard blow, borne with patriotic resignation by his wife, who, then just turned forty, was deprived not only of a father for her children, but, for herself, of a cheerful husband, whose rather frequent strayings from the strict code of conjugal fidelity had been only the symptom of a superabundant vitality.

A Rhinelander by ancestry and in dialect, Rosalie had spent the twenty years of her marriage in the busy industrial city of Duisburg, where von Tümmler was stationed; but after the loss of her husband she had moved, with her eighteen-year-old daughter and her little son, who was some twelve years younger than his sister, to Düsseldorf, partly for the sake of the beautiful parks that are such a feature of the city (for Frau von Tümmler was a great lover of Nature), partly because Anna, a serious girl, had a bent for painting and wanted to attend the celebrated Academy of Art. For the past ten years, then, the little family had lived in a quiet linden-bordered street of villas, named after Peter von Cornelius, where they occupied the modest house which, surrounded by a garden and equipped with rather outmoded but comfortable furniture dating from the time of Rosalie's marriage, was often hospitably opened to a small circle of relatives and friends – among them professors from the Academies of Art and Medicine, together with a married couple or two from the world of industry – for evening gatherings which, though always decorous in their merriment, tended, as the Rhineland custom is, to be a little bibulous.

Frau von Tümmler was sociable by nature. She loved to go out and, within the limits possible to her, to keep open house. Her simplicity and cheerfulness, her warm heart, of which her love for Nature was an expression, made her generally liked. Small in stature, but with a well-preserved figure, with hair which, though now decidedly grey, was abundant and wavy, with delicate if somewhat ageing hands, the backs of which the passage of years had discoloured with freckle-like spots that were far too many and far too large (a symptom to counteract which no medication has yet been discovered), she produced an impression of youth by virtue of a pair of fine, animated brown eyes, precisely the colour of husked chestnuts, which shone out of a womanly and winning face composed of the most pleasant features. Her nose had a slight tendency to redden, especially in company, when she grew animated; but this she tried to correct by a touch of powder – unnecessarily, for the general opinion held that it became her charmingly.

Born in the spring, a child of May, Rosalie had celebrated her fiftieth birthday, with her children and ten or twelve friends of the house, both ladies and gentlemen, at a flower-strewn table in an inn garden, under the parti-coloured light of Chinese lanterns and to the chime of glasses raised in fervent or playful toasts, and had been gay with the general gaiety – not quite without effort: for some time now, and notably on that evening, her health had been affected by certain critical organic phenomena of her time of life, the extinction of her physical womanhood, to whose spasmodic progress she responded with repeated psychological resistance. It induced states of anxiety, emotional unrest, headaches, days of depression, and an irritability which, even on that festive evening, had made some of the humorous discourses that the gentlemen had delivered in her honour seem insufferably stupid. She had exchanged glances tinged with desperation with her daughter, who, as she knew, required no predisposition beyond her habitual intolerance to find this sort of punch-inspired humour imbecilic.

She was on extremely affectionate and confidential terms with this daughter, who, so much older than her son, had become a friend with whom she maintained no taciturn reserve even in regard to the symptoms of her state of transition. Anna, now twenty-nine and soon to be thirty, had remained unmarried, a situation which was not unwelcome to Rosalie, for, on purely selfish grounds, she preferred keeping her daughter as her household companion and the partner of her life to resigning her to a husband. Taller than her mother, Fräulein von Tümmler had the same chestnut-coloured eyes – and yet not the same, for they lacked the naïve animation of her mother's, their expression being more thoughtful and cool. Anna had been born with a club-foot, which, after an operation in her childhood that produced no permanent improvement, had always excluded her from dancing and sports and indeed from all participation in the activities and life of the young. An unusual intelligence, a native endowment fortified by her deformity, had to compensate for what she was obliged to forgo. With only two or three hours of private tutoring a day, she had easily got through school and passed her final examinations, but had then ceased to pursue any branch of academic learning, turning instead to the fine arts, first to sculpture, then to painting, in which, even as a student, she had struck out on a course of the most extreme intellectualism, which, disdaining mere imitation of nature, transfigured sensory content into the strictly cerebral, the abstractly symbolical, often into the cubistically mathematical. It was with dismayed respect that Frau von Tümmler looked at her daughter's paintings, in which the highly civilized joined with the primitive, the decorative with profound intellection, an extremely subtle feeling for colour combinations with a sparse asceticism of style.

"Significant, undoubtedly significant, my dear child," she

said. "Professor Zumsteg will think highly of it. He has confirmed you in this style of painting and he has the eye and the understanding for it. One has to have the eye and the understanding for it. What do you call it?"

"Trees in Evening Wind."

"Ah, that gives a hint of what you were intending. Are those cones and circles against the greyish-yellow background meant to represent trees – and that peculiar spiralling line the wind? Interesting, Anna, interesting. But, heavens above, child, adorable Nature – what you do to her! If only you would let your art offer something to the emotions just once – paint something for the heart, a beautiful floral still life, a fresh spray of lilac, so true to life that one would think one smelt its ravishing perfume, and a pair of delicate Meissen porcelain figures beside the vase, a gentleman blowing kisses to a lady, and with everything reflected in the gleaming, polished table-top. . . ."

"Stop, stop, Mama! You certainly have an extravagant imagination. But no one can paint like that any more!"

"Anna, you don't mean to tell me that, with your talent, you can't paint something like that, something to refresh the heart!"

"You misunderstand me, Mama! It's not a question of whether I can. Nobody can. The state of the times and of art no longer permits it."

"So much the more regrettable for the times and art! No, forgive me, child, I did not mean to say quite that. If it is life and progress that make it impossible, there is no room for regret. On the contrary, it would be regrettable to fall behind. I understand that perfectly. And I understand too that it takes genius to conceive such an expressive line as this one of yours. It doesn't express anything to me, but I can see beyond doubt that it is extremely expressive."

Anna kissed her mother, holding her palette and wet brush well away from her. And Rosalie kissed her too, glad in her heart that her daughter found in her work – which, if abstract and, as it seemed to her, deadening, was still an active handicraft – found in her artist's smock comfort and compensation for much that she was forced to renounce.

How greatly a limping gait curtails any sensual appreciation, on the part of the opposite sex, for a girl as such, Fräulein von Tümmler had learned early, and had armed herself against the fact with a pride which (in turn, as these things go), in cases where a young man was prepared despite her deformity to harbour an inclination towards her, discouraged it through coldly aloof disbelief and nipped it in the bud. Once, just after their change of residence, she had loved – and had been grievously ashamed of her passion, for its object had been the physical beauty of the young man, a chemist by training, who, considering it wise to turn science into money as rapidly as possible, had, soon after attaining his doctorate, manoeuvred himself into an important and lucrative position in a Düsseldorf chemical factory. His swarthy, masculine handsomeness, together with an openness of nature which appealed to men too, and the proficiency and application which he had demonstrated, aroused the enthusiasm of all the girls and matrons in Düsseldorf society, the young and the old being equally in raptures over him; and it had been Anna's contemptible fate to languish where all languished, to find herself condemned by her senses to a universal feeling, confronted with whose depth she struggled in vain to keep her self-respect.

Dr Brünner (such was the paragon's name), precisely because he knew himself to be practical and ambitious, entertained a certain corrective inclination towards higher and more recondite things; and for a time openly sought out Fräulein von Tümmler, talked with her, when they met in society, of literature and art, tuned his insinuating voice to a whisper to make mockingly derogatory remarks to her concerning one or another of his adorers, and seemed to want to conclude an alliance with her against the mediocrities, who, refined by no deformity, importuned him with improper advances. What her own state was, and what an agonizing happiness he aroused in her by his mockery of other women – of that he seemed to have no inkling, but only to be seeking and finding protection, in her intelligent companionship, from the hardships of the amorous persecution whose victim he was, and to be courting her esteem just because he valued it. The temptation to accord it to him had been strong and profound for Anna, though she knew that, if she did, it would only be in an attempt to extenuate her weakness for his masculine attraction. To her sweet terror, his assiduity had begun to resemble a real wooing, a choice, and a proposal; and even now Anna could not but admit that she would helplessly have married him if he had ever come to the point of speaking out. But the decisive word was never uttered. His ambition for higher things had not sufficed to make him disregard her physical defect nor yet her modest dowry. He had soon detached himself from her and married the wealthy daughter of a manufacturer, to whose native city of Bochum, and to a position in her father's chemical enterprise there, he had then betaken himself, to the sorrow of the female society of Düsseldorf and to Anna's relief.

Rosalie knew of her daughter's painful experience, and would have known of it even if the latter, at the time, in a moment of uncontrollable effusion, had not wept bitter tears on her mother's bosom over what she called her shame. Frau von Tümmler, though not particularly clever in other respects, had an unusually acute perception, not malicious but purely a matter of sympathy, in respect to everything that makes up the existence of a woman, psychologically and physiologically, to all that Nature has inflicted upon woman; so that in her circle hardly an event or circumstance in this category escaped her. From a supposedly unnoticed and private smile, a blush, or a brightening of the eyes, she knew what girl was captivated by what young man, and she confided her discoveries to her daughter, who was quite unaware of such things and had very little wish to be made aware of them. Instinctively, now to her pleasure, now to her regret, Rosalie knew whether a woman found satisfaction in her marriage or failed to find it. She infallibly diagnosed a pregnancy in its very earliest stage, and on these occasions, doubtless because she was concerned with something so joyously natural, she would drop into dialect – "*Da is wat am kommen*," she would say, meaning "something's on the way". It pleased her to see that Anna ungrudgingly helped her younger brother, who was well along in secondary school, with his homework; for, by virtue of a psychological shrewdness as naïve as it was keen, she divined the satisfaction that the superiority implied by this service to the male sex brought to the jilted girl.

It cannot be said that Rosalie took any particular interest in her son, a tall, lanky red-headed boy, who looked like his dead father and who, furthermore, seemed to have little talent for humanistic studies, but instead dreamed of building bridges and highways and wanted to be an engineer. A cool friendliness, expressed only perfunctorily, and principally for form's sake, was all that she offered him. But she clung to her daughter, her only real friend. In view of Anna's reserve, the relation of confidence between them might have been described as one-sided, were it not that the mother simply knew everything about her repressed child's emotional life, had known the proud and bitter resignation her soul harboured, and from that knowledge had derived the right and the duty to communicate herself with equal openness.

In so doing, she accepted, with imperturbable good humour, many a fondly indulgent or sadly ironical or even somewhat pained smile from her daughter and confidante, and, herself kindly, was glad when she was kindly treated, ready to laugh at her own simple-heartedness, convinced that it was happy and right – so that, if she laughed at herself, she laughed too at Anna's wry expression. It happened quite often – especially when she gave full rein to her fervour for Nature, to which she was for ever trying to win over the intellectual girl. Words cannot express how she loved the spring, *her* season, in which she had been born, and which, she insisted, had always brought her, in a quite personal way, mysterious currents of health, of joy in life. When birds called in the new mild air, her face became radiant. In the garden, the first crocus and daffodil, the hyacinths and tulips sprouting and flaunting in the beds around the house, rejoiced the good soul to tears. The darling violets along country roads, the gold of flowering broom and forsythia, the red and the white may trees – above all, the lilac, and the way the chestnuts lighted their candles, white and red – her daughter had to admire it all with her and share her ecstasy. Rosalie fetched her from the north room that had been made into a studio for her, dragged her from her abstract handicraft; and with a willing smile Anna took off her smock and accompanied her mother for hours together; for she was a surprisingly good walker and if in company she concealed her limp by the utmost possible economy of movement, when she was free and could stump along as she pleased, her endurance was remarkable.

The season of flowering trees, when the roads became poetic, when the dear familiar landscape of their walks clothed itself in charming, white and rosy promise of fruit – what a bewitching time! From the flower catkins of the tall white poplars bordering the watercourse along which they often strolled, pollen sifted down on them like snow, drove with the breeze, covered the ground; and Rosalie, in raptures again, knew enough botany to tell her daughter that poplars are "diœcious", each plant bearing only flowers of one sex, some male, others female. She discoursed happily on wind pollination – or, rather, on Zephyrus' loving service to the children of Flora, his obliging conveyance of pollen to the chastely awaiting female stigma – a method of fertilization which she considered particularly charming.

The rose season was utter bliss to her. She raised the Queen of Flowers on standards in her garden, solicitously protected it, by the indicated means, from devouring insects; and always, as long as the glory endured, bunches of duly refreshed roses stood on the whatnots and little tables in her boudoir – budding, half-blown, full-blown – especially red roses (she did not favour the white), of her own raising or attentive gifts from visitors of her own sex who were aware of her passion. She could bury her face, eyes closed, in such a bunch of roses and, when after a long time she raised it again, she would swear that it was the perfume of the gods; when Psyche bent, lamp in hand, over sleeping Cupid, surely his breath, his curls and cheeks, had filled her sweet little nose with this scent; it was the aroma of heaven, and she had no doubt that, as blessed spirits there above, we should breathe the odour of roses for all eternity. Then we shall very soon, was Anna's sceptical comment, grow so used to it that we simply shan't smell it any more. But Frau von Tümmler reprimanded her for assuming a wisdom beyond her years: if one was bent on scoffing, such an argument could apply to the whole state of beatitude, but joy was none the less joy for being unconscious. This was one of the occasions on which Anna gave her mother a kiss of tender indulgence and reconciliation, and then they laughed together.

Rosalie never used manufactured scents or perfumes, with the single exception of a touch of Eau de Cologne from C. M. Farina in the Jülichsplatz. But whatever Nature offers to gratify our sense of smell – sweetness, aromatic bitterness, even heady and oppressive scents – she loved beyond measure, and absorbed it deeply, thankfully, with the most sensual fervour. On one of their walks there was a declivity, a long depression in the ground, a shallow gorge, the bottom of which was thickly overgrown with jasmine and alder bushes, from which, on warm, humid days in June with a threat of thunder showers, fuming clouds of heated odour welled up almost stupefyingly. Anna, though it was likely to give her a headache, had to accompany her mother there time and again. Rosalie breathed in the heavy, surging vapour with delighted relish, stopped, walked on, lingered again, bent over the slope, and sighed: "Child, child, how wonderful! It is the breath of nature – it is! – her sweet, living breath, sun-warmed and drenched with moisture, deliciously wafted to us from her breast. Let us enjoy it with reverence, for we too are her children."

"At least you are, Mama," said Anna, taking the enthusiast's arm and drawing her along at her limping pace. "She's not so fond of me, and she gives me this pressure in my temples with her concoction of odours."

"Yes, because you are against her," answered Rosalie, "and pay no homage to her with your talent, but want to set yourself above her through it, turn her into a mere theme for the intellect, as you pride yourself on doing, and transpose your sense perceptions into heaven knows what – into frigidity. I respect it, Anna; but if I were in Mother Nature's place. I should be as offended with all of you young painters for it as she is." And she seriously proposed to her that if she was set upon transposition and absolutely must be abstract, she should try, at least once, to express odours in colour.

This idea came to her late in June, when the lindens were in flower – again for her the one lovely time of year, when for a week or two the avenues of trees outside filled the whole house, through the open windows, with the indescribably pure and mild, enchanting odour of their late bloom, and the smile of rapture never faded from Rosalie's lips. It was then that she said: "That is what you painters should paint, try your artistry on that! You don't want to banish Nature from art entirely; actually, you always start from her in your abstractions, and you need something sensory in order to intellectualize it. Now, odour, if I may say so, is sensory and abstract at the same time, we don't see it, it speaks to us ethereally. And it ought to fascinate you to convey an invisible felicity to the sense of sight, on which, after all, the art of painting rests. Try it! What do you painters have palettes for? Mix bliss on them and put it on canvas as chromatic joy, and then label it 'Odour of Lindens', so that people who look at it will know what you were trying to do."

"Dearest Mama, you are astonishing!" Fräulein von Tümmler answered. "You think up problems that no painting teacher would ever dream of! But don't you realize that you are an incorrigible romanticist with your synæsthetic mixture of the senses and your mystical transformation of odours into colours?"

"I know – I deserve your erudite mockery."

"No, you don't – not any kind of mockery," said Anna fervently.

Yet on a walk they took one afternoon in mid-August, on a very hot day, something strange befell them, something that had a suggestion of mockery. Strolling along between fields and the edge of a wood, they suddenly noticed an odour of musk, at first almost imperceptibly faint, then stronger. It was Rosalie who first sniffed it and expressed her awareness by an "Oh! Where does that come from?" but her daughter soon had to concur: Yes, there was some sort of odour, and, yes, it did seem to be definable as musky – there was no doubt about it. Two steps sufficed to bring them within sight of its source, which was repellent. It was there by the roadside, seething in the sun, with blowflies covering it and flying all around it – a little mound of excrement, which they preferred not to investigate more closely. The small area represented a meeting-ground of animal, or perhaps human, fæces with some sort of putrid vegetation, and the greatly decomposed body of some small woodland creature seemed to be present too. In short, nothing could be nastier than the teeming little mound; but its evil effluvium, which drew the blowflies by hundreds, was, in its ambivalence, no longer to be called a stench but must undoubtedly be pronounced the odour of musk.

"Let us go," the ladies said simultaneously, and Anna, dragging her foot along all the more vigorously as they started off, clung to her mother's arm. For a time they were silent, as if each had to digest the strange impression for herself. Then Rosalie said:

"That explains it – I never did like musk, and I don't understand how anyone can use it as a perfume. Civet, I think, is in the same category. Flowers never smell like that, but in natural-history class we were taught that many animals secrete it from certain glands – rats, cats, the civet-cat, the musk-deer. In Schiller's *Kabale und Liebe* – I'm sure you must remember it – there's a little fellow, some sort of a toady, an absolute fool, and the stage direction says that he comes on screeching and spreads an odour of musk through the whole parterre. How that passage always made me laugh!"

And they brightened up. Rosalie was still capable of the old warm laughter that came bubbling from her heart – even at this period when the difficult organic adjustments of her time of life, the spasmodic withering and disintegration of her womanhood, were troubling her physically and psychologically. Nature had given her a friend in those days, quite close to home, in a corner of the Palace Garden ("Paintbox" Street was the way there). It was an old, solitary oak tree, gnarled and stunted, with its roots partly exposed, and a squat trunk, divided at a moderate height into thick knotty branches, which themselves ramified into knotty offshoots. The trunk was hollow here and there and had been filled with cement – the Park Department did something for the gallant centenarian; but many of the branches had died and, no longer producing leaves, clawed, crooked and bare, into the sky; others, only a scattered few but on up to the crown, still broke into verdure each spring with the jaggedly lobed leaves, which have always been considered sacred and from which the victor's crown is twined. Rosalie was only too pleased to see it – about the time of her birthday she followed the budding, sprouting, and unfolding of the oak's foliage on those of its branches and twigs to which life still forced its way, her sympathetic interest continuing from day to day. Quite close to the tree, on the edge of the lawn in which it stood, there was a bench; Rosalie sat down on it with Anna, and said:

"Good old fellow! Can you look at him without being touched, Anna – the way he stands there and keeps it up? Look at those roots, woody, and thick as your arm, how broadly they clasp the earth and anchor themselves in the nourishing soil. He has weathered many a storm and will survive many more. No danger of his falling down! Hollow, cemented, no longer able to produce a full crown of leaves – but when his time comes, the sap still rises in him – not everywhere, but he manages to display a little green, and people respect it and indulge him for his courage. Do you see that thin little shoot up there with its leaf-buds nodding in the wind? All around it things haven't gone as they should, but the little twig saves the day."

"Indeed, Mama, it gives cause for respect, as you say," answered Anna. "But if you don't mind, I'd rather go home now. I am having pains."

"Pains? Is it your – but of course, dear child, how could I have forgotten! I reproach myself for having brought you with me. Here I am staring at the old tree and not worrying about your sitting there bent over. Forgive me. Take my arm and we will go."

From the first, Fräulein von Tümmler had suffered severe abdominal pains in advance of her periods – it was nothing in itself, it was merely, as even the doctors had put it, a constitutional infliction that had to be accepted. Hence, on the short walk home, her mother could talk about it to the suffering girl soothingly and comfortingly, with well-intentioned cheerfulness, and indeed – and particularly – with envy.

"Do you remember," she said, "it was like this the very first time, when you were still just a young thing and it happened to you and you were so frightened, but I explained to you that it was only natural and necessary and something to be glad over and that it was really a sort of day of glory because it showed that you had finally ripened into a woman? You have pains beforehand – it's a trial, I know, and not strictly necessary, I never had any; but it happens; aside from you, I know of two or three cases where there are pains, and I think to myself: Pains, *à la bonne heure*! – for us women, pains are something different from what they are elsewhere in Nature and for men; they don't have any, except when they're sick, and then they carry on terribly; even Tümmler did that, your father, as soon as he had a pain anywhere, even though he was an officer and died the death of a hero. Our sex behaves differently about it; it takes pain more patiently, we are the long-suffering, born for pain, so to speak. Because, above all, we know the natural and healthy pain, the God-ordained and sacred pain of childbirth, which is something absolutely peculiar to woman, something men are spared, or denied. Men – the fools! – are horrified, to be sure, by our half-unconscious screaming, and reproach themselves and clasp their heads in their hands; and, for all that we scream, we are really laughing at them. When I brought you into the world, Anna, it was very bad. From the first pain it lasted thirty-six hours, and Tümmler ran around the apartment the whole time with his head in his hands, but despite everything it was a great festival of life, and I wasn't screaming myself, *it* was screaming, it was a sacred ecstasy of pain. With Eduard, later, it wasn't half so bad, but it would still have been more than enough for a man – our lords and masters would certainly want no part in it. Pains, you see, are usually the danger-signals by which Nature, always benignant, warns that a disease is developing in the body – look sharp there, it means, something's wrong, do something about it quick, not so much against the pain as against what the pain indicates. With us it can be like that too, and have that meaning, of course. But, as you know yourself, your abdominal pain before your periods doesn't have that meaning, it doesn't warn you of anything. It's a sport among the species of women's pains and as such it is honourable, that is how you must take it, as a vital function in the life of a woman. Always, so long as we are that – a woman, no longer a child and not yet an incapacitated old crone – always, over and over, there is an intensified welling up of the blood of life in our organ of motherhood, by which precious Nature prepares it to receive the fertilized egg, and if one is present, as, after all, even in my long life, was the case only twice and with a long interval between, then our monthly doesn't come, and we are pregnant. Heavens, what a joyous surprise when it stopped the first time for me, thirty years ago! It was you, my dear child, with whom I was blessed, and I still remember how I confided it to Tümmler and, blushing, laid my face against his and said, very softly: 'Robert, it's happened, all the signs point that way, and it's my turn now, *da is wat am kommen. . . .*'"

"Dearest Mama, please just do me the favour of not using dialect, it irritates me at the moment."

"Oh, forgive me, darling – to irritate you now is the last thing I meant to do. It's only that, in my blissful confusion, I really did say that to Tümmler. And then – we are talking about natural things, aren't we? – and, to my mind, Nature and dialect go together somehow, as Nature and the people go together – if I'm talking nonsense, correct me, you are so much cleverer than I am. Yes, you are clever, and, as an artist, you are not on the best of terms with Nature but insist on transposing her into concepts, into cubes and spirals, and, since we're speaking of things going together, I rather wonder if they don't go together too, your proud, intellectual attitude towards Nature, and the way she singles you out and sends you pains at your periods."

"But, Mama," said Anna, and could not help laughing, "you scold me for being intellectual, and then propound absolutely unwarrantable intellectual theories yourself!"

"If I can divert you a little with it, child, the most naïve theory is good enough for me. But what I was saying about women's natural pains I mean perfectly seriously, it should comfort you. Simply be happy and proud that, at thirty, you are in the full power of your blood. Believe me, I would gladly put up with any kind of abdominal pains if it were still with me as it is with you. But unfortunately that is over for me, it has been growing more and more scanty and irregular, and for the last two months it hasn't happened at all. Ah, it has ceased to be with me after the manner of women, as the Bible says, in reference to Sarah, I think – yes, it was Sarah, and then a miracle of fruitfulness was worked in her, but that's only one of those edifying stories, I suppose – that sort of thing doesn't happen any more today. When it has ceased to be with us after the manner of women, we are no longer women at all, but only the dried-up husk of a woman, worn out, useless, cast out of nature. My dear child, it is very bitter. With men, I believe, it usually doesn't stop as long as they are alive. I know some who at eighty still can't let a woman alone, and

Tümmler, your father, was like that too – how I had to pretend not to see things even when he was a lieutenant-colonel! What is fifty for a man? Provided he has a little temperament, fifty comes nowhere near stopping him from playing the lover, and many a man with greying temples still makes conquests even among young girls. But we, take it all in all, are given just thirty-five years to be women in our life and our blood, to be complete human beings, and when we are fifty, we are superannuated, our capacity to breed expires, and, in Nature's eyes, we are nothing but old rubbish!"

To these bitter words of acquiescence in the ways of Nature, Anna did not answer as many women would doubtless, and justifiably, have answered. She said:

"How you talk, Mama, and how you revile and seem to want to reject the dignity that falls to the elderly woman when she has fulfilled her life, and Nature, which you love after all, translates her to a new, mellow condition, an honourable and more lovable condition, in which she still can give and be so much, both to her family and to those less close to her. You say you envy men because their sex life is less strictly limited than a woman's. But I doubt if that is really anything to be respected, if it is a reason for envying them; and in any case all civilized peoples have always rendered the most exquisite honours to the matron, have even regarded her as sacred – and we mean to regard you as sacred in the dignity of your dear and charming old age."

"Darling" – and Rosalie drew her daughter close as they walked along – "you speak so beautifully and intelligently and well, despite your pains, for which I was trying to comfort you, and now you are comforting your foolish mother in her unworthy tribulations. But the dignity, and the resignation, are very hard, my dear child, it is very hard even for the body to find itself in its new situation, that alone is torment enough. And when there are heart and mind besides, which would still rather not hear too much of dignity and the honourable estate of a matron, and rebel against the drying up of the body – that is when it really begins to be hard. The soul's adjustment to the new constitution of the body is the hardest thing of all."

"Of course, Mama, I understand that very well. But consider: body and soul are one; the psychological is no less a part of Nature than the physical; Nature takes in the psychological too, and you needn't be afraid that your psyche can long remain out of harmony with the natural change in your body. You must regard the psychological as only an emanation of the physical; and if the poor soul thinks that she is saddled with the all too difficult task of adjusting herself to the body's changed life, she will soon see that she really has nothing to do but let the body have its way and do its work on herself too. For it is the body that moulds the soul, in accordance with its own condition."

Fräulein von Tümmler had her reasons for saying this, because, about the time that her mother made the above confidence to her, a new face, an additional face, was very often to be seen at home, and the potentially embarrassing developments which were under way had not escaped Anna's silent, apprehensive observation.

The new face – which Anna found distressingly commonplace, anything but distinguished by intelligence – belonged to a young man named Ken Keaton, an American of about twenty-four whom the war had brought over and who had been staying in the city for some time, giving English lessons in one household or another or simply commandeered for English conversation (in exchange for a suitable fee) by the wives of rich industrialists. Eduard had heard of these activities towards Easter of his last year in school and had earnestly begged his mother to have Mr Keaton teach him the rudiments of English a few afternoons a week. For though his school offered him a quantity of Greek and Latin, and fortunately a sufficiency of mathematics as well, it offered no English, which, after all, seemed highly important for his future goal. As soon as, one way or another, he had got through all those boring humanities, he wanted to attend the Polytechnic Institute and after that, so he planned, go to

England for further study or perhaps straight to the El Dorado of technology, the United States. So he was happy and grateful when, respecting his clarity and firmness of purpose, his mother readily acceded to his wish; and his work with Keaton, Mondays, Wednesdays and Saturdays, gave him great satisfaction – because it served his purpose, of course, but then too because it was fun to learn a new language right from the rudiments, like an abecedarian, beginning with a little primer: words, their often outlandish orthography, their most extraordinary pronunciation, which Ken, forming his *l*'s even deeper down in his throat than the Rhinelanders and letting his *r*'s sound from his gums unrolled, would illustrate with such drawn-out exaggeration that he seemed to be trying to make fun of his own mother tongue. "Scrr-ew the top on!" he said. "I sllept like a top." "Alfred is a tennis play-err. His shoulders are thirty inches brr-oaoadd." Eduard could laugh, through the whole hour and a half of the lesson, at Alfred, the broad-shouldered tennis player, in whose praise so much was said with the greatest possible use of "though" and "thought" and "taught" and "tough", but he made very good progress, just because Ken, not being a learned pedagogue, used a free and easy method – in other words, improvised on whatever the moment brought and, hammering away regardless, through patter, slang, and nonsense, initiated his willing pupil into his own easy-going, humorous, efficient vernacular.

Frau von Tümmler, attracted by the jollity that pervaded Eduard's room, sometimes looked in on the young people and took some part in their profitable fun, laughed heartily with them over "Alfred, the tennis play-err", and found a certain resemblance between him and her son's young tutor, particularly in the matter of his shoulders, for Ken's too were splendidly broad. He had, moreover, thick blond hair, a not particularly handsome though not unpleasant, guilelessly friendly boyish face, to which in these surroundings, however, a slight Anglo-Saxon cast of features lent a touch of the unusual; that he was remarkably well built was apparent despite his loose, rather full clothes; with his long legs and narrow hips, he produced an impression of youthful strength. He had very nice hands, too, with a not too elaborate ring on the left. His simple, perfectly unconstrained yet not rude manner, his comical German, which became as undeniably English-sounding in his mouth as the scraps of French and Italian that he knew (for he had visited several European countries) – all this Rosalie found very pleasant; his great naturalness in particular prepossessed her in his favour; and now and again, and finally almost regularly, she invited him to stay for dinner after Eduard's lesson, whether she had been present at it or not. In part her interest in him was due to her having heard that he was very successful with women. With this in mind, she studied him and found the rumour not incomprehensible, though it was not quite to her taste when, having to eructate a little at table, he would put his hand over his mouth and say "Pardon me!" – which was meant for good manners, but which, after all, drew attention to the occurrence quite unnecessarily.

Ken, as he told them over dinner, had been born in a small town in one of the Eastern states, where his father had followed various occupations – broker, manager of a gas station – from time to time too he had made some money in the real-estate business. Ken had attended high school, where, if he was to be believed, one learned nothing at all – "by European standards", as he respectfully added – after which, without giving the matter much thought, but merely with the idea of learning something more, he had entered a college in Detroit, Michigan, where he had earned his tuition by the work of his hands, as dishwasher, cook, waiter, campus gardener. Frau von Tümmler asked him how, through all that, he had managed to keep such white, one might say aristocratic, hands, and he answered that, when doing rough work, he had always worn gloves – only a short-sleeved polo shirt, or nothing at all from the waist up, but always gloves. Most workmen, or at least many of them – construction workers, for example – did that back home, to avoid getting horny proletarian hands, and they had hands like a lawyer's clerk, with a ring.

Rosalie praised the custom, but Keaton differed. Custom? The word was too good for it, you couldn't call it a "custom", in the sense of the old European folk customs (he habitually said "Continental" for "European"). Such an old German folk custom, for example, as the "rod of life" – village lads gathering fresh birch and willow rods at Christmas or Easter and striking ("peppering" or "slashing", they called it) the girls, and sometimes cattle and trees, with them to bring health and fertility – that was a "custom", an age-old one, and it delighted him. When the peppering or slashing took place in spring, it was called "Smack Easter".

The Tümmlers had never heard of Smack Easter and were surprised at Ken's knowledge of folk-lore. Eduard laughed at the "rod of life", Anna made a face, and only Rosalie, in perfect agreement with their guest, showed herself delighted. Anyhow, he said, it was something very different from wearing gloves at work, and you could look a long time before you found anything of the sort in America, if only because there were no villages there and the farmers were not farmers at all but entrepreneurs like everyone else and had no "customs". In general, despite being so unmistakably American in his entire manner and attitude, he displayed very little attachment to his great country. He "didn't care for America"; indeed, with its pursuit of the dollar and insensate church-going, its worship of success and its colossal mediocrity, but, above all, its lack of historical atmosphere, he found it really appalling. Of course, it had a history, but that wasn't "history", it was simply a short, boring "success story". Certainly, aside from its enormous deserts, it had beautiful and magnificent landscapes, but there was "nothing behind them", while in Europe there was so much behind everything, particularly behind the cities, with their deep historical perspectives. American cities – he "didn't care for them". They were put up yesterday and might just as well be taken away tomorrow. The small ones were stupid holes, one looking exactly like another, and the big ones were horrible, inflated monstrosities, with museums full of bought-up European cultural treasures. Bought, of course, was better than stolen, but not *much* better, for, in certain places things dating from A.D. 1400 and 1200 were as good as stolen.

Ken's irreverent chatter aroused laughter; they took him to task for it too, but he answered that what made him speak as he did was precisely reverence, specifically a respect for perspective and atmosphere. Very early dates, A.D. 1100, 700, were his passion and his hobby, and at college he had always been best at history – at history and at athletics. He had long been drawn to Europe, where early dates were at home, and certainly, even without the war, he would have worked his way across, as a sailor or dishwasher, simply to breathe historical air. But the war had come at just the right moment for him; in 1917 he had immediately enlisted in the army, and all through his training he had been afraid that the war might end before it brought him across to Europe. But he had made it – almost at the last minute he had sailed to France, jammed into a troop transport, and had even got into some real fighting, near Compiègne, from which he had carried away a wound, and not a light one, so that he had had to lie in hospital for weeks. It had been a kidney wound, and only one of his kidneys really worked now, but that was quite enough. However, he said, smiling, he was, in a manner of speaking, disabled, and he drew a small disability pension, which was worth more to him than the lost kidney.

There was certainly nothing of the disabled veteran about him, Frau von Tümmler observed, and he answered: "No, thank heaven, only a little cash!"

On his release from the hospital, he had left the service, had been "honourably discharged" with a medal for bravery, and had stayed on for an indefinite time in Europe, which he found "wonderful" and where he revelled in early dates. The French cathedrals, the Italian campaniles, *palazzi*, and galleries, the Swiss villages, a place like Stein am Rhein – all that was "most delightful indeed". And the wine everywhere, the *bistros* in France, the *trattorie* in Italy, the cosy *Wirtshäuser* in Switzerland and Germany, "at the sign of the Ox", "of the

Moor", "of the Star" – where was there anything like that in America? There was no wine there – just "drinks", whisky and rum, and no cool pints of Elsässer or Tiroler or Johannisberger at an oak table in a historical taproom or a honeysuckle arbour. Good heavens! People in America simply didn't know how to live.

Germany! That was the country he loved, though he really had explored it very little and in fact knew only the places on the Bodensee, and of course – but that he knew really well – the Rhineland. The Rhineland, with its charming, gay people, so amiable, especially when they were a bit "high"; with its venerable cities, full of atmosphere. Trier, Aachen, Coblenz, "Holy" Cologne – just try calling an American city "holy" – "Holy Kansas City", ha-ha! The golden treasure, guarded by the nixies of the Missouri River – ha-ha-ha – "Pardon me!" Of Düsseldorf and its long history from Merovingian days, he knew more than Rosalie and her children put together, and he spoke of Pepin the Short, of Barbarossa, who built the Imperial Palace at Rindhusen, and of the Salian Church at Kaiserswerth, where Henry IV was crowned King as a child, of Albert of Berg and John William of the Palatinate, and of many other things and people, like a professor.

Rosalie said that he could teach history too, just as well as English. There was too little demand, he replied. Oh, not at all, she protested. She herself, for instance, whom he had made keenly aware of how little she knew, would begin taking lessons from him at once. He would be "a little shy" about it, he confessed; in answer she expressed something that she had feelingly observed: It was strange and to a certain degree painful that in life shyness was the rule between youth and age. Youth was reserved in the presence of age because it expected no understanding of its green time of life from age's dignity, and age feared youth because, though admiring it wholeheartedly, simply as youth, age considered it due to its dignity to conceal its admiration under mockery and assumed condescension.

Ken laughed, pleased and approving. Eduard remarked that

Mama really talked like a book, and Anna looked searchingly at her mother. She was decidedly vivacious in Mr Keaton's presence, unfortunately even a little affected at times; she invited him frequently, and looked at him, even when he said "Pardon me" behind his hand, with an expression of motherly compassion which to Anna – who, despite the young man's enthusiasm for Europe, his passion for dates like 700, and his knowledge of all the time-honoured pot-houses in Düsseldorf, found him totally uninteresting – appeared somewhat questionable in point of motherliness and made her not a little uncomfortable. Too often, when Mr Keaton was to be present, her mother asked, with nervous apprehension, if her nose was flushed. It was, though Anna soothingly denied it. And if it wasn't before he arrived, it flushed with unwonted violence when she was in the young man's company. But then her mother seemed to have forgotten all about it.

Anna saw rightly: Rosalie had begun to lose her heart to her son's young tutor, without offering any resistance to the rapid budding of her feeling, perhaps without being really aware of it, and in any case without making any particular effort to keep it a secret. Symptoms that in another woman could not have escaped her feminine observation (a cooing and exaggeratedly delighted laughter at Ken's chatter, a soulful look followed by a curtaining of the brightened eyes), she seemed to consider imperceptible in herself – if she was not boasting of her feeling, she was not too proud of it to conceal it.

The situation became perfectly clear to the suffering Anna one very summery, warm September evening, when Ken had stayed for dinner and Eduard, after the soup, had asked permission, on account of the heat, to take off his jacket. The young men, was the answer, must feel no constraint; and so Ken followed his pupil's example. He was not in the least concerned that, whereas Eduard was wearing a coloured shirt with long sleeves, he had merely put on his jacket over his sleeveless white jersey and hence now displayed his bare arms – very handsome, round, strong, white young arms, which made it perfectly comprehensible that he had been as good at athletics in college as at history. The agitation which the sight of them caused in the lady of the house, he was certainly far from noticing, nor did Eduard have any eyes for it. But Anna observed it with pain and pity. Rosalie, talking and laughing feverishly, looked alternately as if she had been drenched with blood and frighteningly pale, and after every escape her fleeing eyes returned, under an irresistible attraction, to the young man's arms and then, for rapt seconds, lingered on them with an expression of deep and sensual sadness.

Anna, bitterly resentful of Ken's primitive guilelessness, which, however, she did not entirely trust, drew attention, as soon as she found even a shred of an excuse, to the evening coolness, which was just beginning to penetrate through the open French window, and suggested, with a warning against catching cold, that the jackets be put on again. But Frau von Tümmler terminated her evening almost immediately after dinner. Pretending a headache, she took a hurried leave of her guest and retired to her bedroom. There she lay stretched on her couch, with her face hidden in her hands and buried in the pillow, and, overwhelmed with shame, terror, and bliss, confessed her passion to herself.

"Good God, I love him, yes, love him, as I have never loved, is it possible? Here I am, retired from active service, translated by Nature to the calm, dignified estate of matronhood. Is it not grotesque that I should still give myself up to lust, as I do in my frightened, blissful thoughts at the sight of him, at the sight of his godlike arms, by which I insanely long to be embraced, at the sight of his magnificent chest, which, in wretchedness and rapture, I saw outlined under his jersey? Am I a shameless old woman? No, not shameless, for I am ashamed in his presence, in the presence of his youth, and I do not know how I ought to meet him and look him in the eyes, the ingenuous, friendly boy's eyes, which expect no burning emotion from me. But it is I who have been struck by the rod of life, he himself, all unknowing, has slashed me and peppered me with it, he has given me my Smack Easter!

Why did he have to tell us of it, in his youthful enthusiasm for old folk customs? Now the thought of the awakening stroke of his rod leaves my inmost being drenched, inundated with shameful sweetness. I desire him – have I ever desired before? Tümmler desired me, when I was young, and I consented, acquiesced in his wooing, took him in marriage in his commanding manhood, and we gave ourselves up to lust when he desired. This time it is I who desire, of my own will and motion, and I have cast my eyes on him as a man casts his eyes on the young woman of his choice – this is what the years do, it is my age that does it and his youth. Youth is feminine, and age's relationship to it is masculine, but age is not happy and confident in its desire, it is full of shame and fear before youth and before all Nature, because of its unfitness. Oh, there is much sorrow in prospect for me, for how can I hope that he will be pleased by my desire, and, if pleased, that he will consent to my wooing, as I did to Tümmler's. He is no girl, with his firm arms, not he – far from it, he is a young man, who wants to desire for himself and who, they say, is very successful in that way with women. He has as many women as he wants, right here in town. My soul writhes and screams with jealousy at the thought. He gives lessons in English conversation to Louise Pfingsten in Pempelforter Strasse and to Amélie Lützenkirchen, whose husband, the pottery-manufacturer, is fat, short-winded, and lazy. Louise is too tall and has a bad hairline, but she is only just thirty-eight and knows how to give melting looks. Amélie is only a little older, and pretty, unfortunately she is pretty, and that fat husband of hers gives her every liberty. Is it possible that they lie in his arms, or at least one of them does, probably Amélie, but it might be that stick of a Louise at the same time – in those arms for whose embrace I long with a fervour that their stupid souls could never muster? That they enjoy his hot breath, his lips, his hands that caress their bodies? My teeth, still so good, and which have needed so little attention – my teeth gnash, I gnash them, when I think of it. My figure too is better than theirs, worthier than theirs to be caressed by his hands, and what tenderness I should offer him, what inexpressible devotion! But they are flowing springs, and I am dried up, not worth being jealous of any more. Jealousy, torturing, tearing, crushing jealousy! That garden party at the Rollwagens' – the machine-factory Rollwagen and his wife – where he was invited too – wasn't it there that with my own eyes, which see everything, I saw him and Amélie exchange a look and a smile that almost certainly pointed to some secret between them? Even then my heart contracted with choking pain, but I did not understand it, I did not think it was jealousy because I no longer supposed myself capable of jealousy. But I am, I understand that now, and I do not try to deny it, no, I rejoice in my torments – there they are, in marvellous disaccord with the physical change in me. The psychological only an emanation of the physical, says Anna, and the body moulds the soul after its own condition? Anna knows a lot, Anna knows nothing. No, I will not say that she knows nothing. She has suffered, loved senselessly and suffered shamefully, and so she knows a great deal. But that soul and body are translated together to the mild, honourable estate of matronhood – there she is all wrong, for she does not believe in miracles, does not know that Nature can make the soul flower miraculously, when it is late, even too late – flower in love, desire, and jealousy, as I am experiencing in blissful torment. Sarah, the old grey crone, heard from behind the tent door what was still appointed for her, and she laughed. And God was angry with her and said: Wherefore did Sarah laugh? I – I will not have laughed. I will believe in the miracle of my soul and my senses, I will revere the miracle Nature has wrought in me, this agonizing shy spring in my soul, and I will be shamefaced only before the blessing of this late visitation. . . ."

Thus Rosalie, communing with herself, on that evening. After a night of violent restlessness and a few hours of deep morning sleep, her first thought on waking was of the passion that had smitten her, blessed her, and to deny which, to reject it on moral grounds, simply did not enter her head. The poor woman was enraptured with the survival in her soul of the ability to bloom in sweet pain. She was not particularly pious, and she left the Lord God out of the picture. Her piety was for Nature, and it made her admire and prize what Nature, as it were against herself, had worked in her. Yes, it was contrary to natural seemliness, this flowering of her soul and senses; though it made her happy, it did not encourage her, it was something to be concealed, kept secret from all the world, even from her trusted daughter, but especially from him, her beloved, who suspected nothing and must suspect nothing – for how dared she boldly raise her eyes to his youth?

Thus into her relationship to Keaton there entered a certain submissiveness and humility which were completely absurd socially, yet which Rosalie, despite her pride in her feeling, was unable to banish from it, and which, on any clear-sighted observer – and so on Anna – produced a more painful effect than all the vivacity and excessive gaiety of her behaviour in the beginning. Finally even Eduard noticed it, and there were moments when brother and sister, bowed over their plates, bit their lips, while Ken, uncomprehendingly aware of the embarrassed silence, looked questioningly from one to another. Seeking counsel and enlightenment, Eduard took an opportunity to question his sister.

"What's happening to Mama?" he asked. "Doesn't she like Keaton any more?" And as Anna said nothing, the young man, making a wry face, added: "Or does she like him too much?"

"What are you thinking of?" was the reproving answer. "Such things are no concern of yours, at your age. Mind your manners, and do not permit yourself to make unsuitable observations!" But she went on: he might reverently remind himself that his mother, as all women eventually must, was having to go through a period of difficulties prejudicial to her health and well-being.

"Very new and instructive for me!" said the senior in school ironically; but the explanation was too general to suit him. Their mother was suffering from something more specific, and even she, his highly respected sister, was visibly suffering –

to say nothing of his young and stupid self. But perhaps, young and stupid as he was, he could make himself useful by proposing the dismissal of his too attractive tutor. He had, he could tell his mother, got enough out of Keaton; it was time for him to be "honourably discharged" again.

"Do so, dear Eduard," said Anna, and he did.

"Mama," he said, "I think we might stop my English lessons, and the constant expense I have put you to for them. Thanks to your generosity, I have laid a good foundation, with Mr Keaton's help; and by doing some reading by myself I can see to it that it will not be lost. Anyway, no one ever really learns a foreign language at home, outside of the country where everybody speaks it and where one is entirely dependent on it. Once I am in England or America, after the start you have generously given me, the rest will come easily. As you know, my final examinations are approaching, and there is none in English. Instead I must see to it that I don't flunk the classical languages, and that requires concentration. So the time has come – don't you think? – to thank Keaton cordially for his trouble and in the most friendly way possible to dispense with his services."

"But Eduard," Frau von Tümmler answered at once, and indeed at first with a certain haste, "what you say surprises me, and I cannot say that I approve of it. Certainly, it shows great delicacy of feeling in you to wish to spare me further expenditure for this purpose. But the purpose is a good one, it is important for your future, as you now see it, and our situation is not such that we cannot meet the expenses of language lessons for you, quite as well as we were able to meet those of Anna's studies at the Academy. I do not understand why you want to stop half-way in your project to gain a mastery of the English language. It could be said, dear boy – please don't take it in bad part – that you would be making me an ill return for the willingness with which I met your proposal. Your final examinations – to be sure, they are a serious matter, and I understand that you will have to buckle down to your classical languages, which come hard to you. But your English lessons, a few times a week – you don't mean to tell me that they wouldn't be more of a recreation, a healthy distraction for you, than an additional strain. Besides – and now let me pass to the personal and human side of the matter – the relationship between Ken, as he is called, or rather Mr Keaton, and our family has long since ceased to be such that we could say to him: 'You're no longer needed,' and simply give him his marching orders. Simply announce: 'Sirrah, you may withdraw.' He has become a friend, almost a member of the family, and he would quite rightly be offended at such a dismissal. We should all feel his absence – Anna especially, I think, would be upset if he no longer came and enlivened our table with his intimate knowledge of the history of Düsseldorf, stopped telling us all about the quarrel over right of succession between the duchies of Jülich and Cleves, and about Elector John William on his pedestal in the marketplace. You would miss him too, and so, in fact, should I. In short, Eduard, your proposal is well meant, but it is neither necessary nor, indeed, really possible. We had better leave things as they are."

"Whatever you think best, Mama," said Eduard, and reported his ill success to his sister, who answered:

"I expected as much, my boy. After all, Mama has described the situation quite correctly, and I saw much the same objections to your plan when you announced it to me. In any case, she is perfectly right in saying that Keaton is pleasant company and that we should all regret his absence. So just go on with him."

As she spoke, Eduard looked her in the face, which remained impassive; he shrugged his shoulders and left. Ken was waiting for him in his room, read a few pages of Emerson or Macaulay with him, then an American mystery story, which gave them something to talk about for the last half hour, and stayed for dinner, to which he had long since ceased to be expressly invited. His staying on after lessons had become a standing arrangement; and Rosalie, on the recurring days of her untoward and timorous, shame-clouded joy, consulted with Babette, the housekeeper, over the menu, ordered a choice repast, provided a full-bodied Pfälzer or Rüdesheimer, over which they would linger in the living-room for an hour after dinner, and to which she applied herself beyond her wont, so that she could look with better courage at the object of her unreasonable love. But often too the wine made her tired and desperate; and then whether she should stay and suffer in his sight or retire and weep over him in solitude became a battle which she fought with varying results.

October having brought the beginning of the social season, she also saw Keaton elsewhere than at her own house – at the Pfingstens' in Pempelforter Strasse, at the Lützenkirchens', at big receptions at Chief Engineer Rollwagen's. On these occasions she sought and shunned him, fled the group he had joined, waited in another, talking mechanically, for him to come and bestow some notice on her, knew at any moment where he was, listened for his voice amid the buzz of voices, and suffered horribly when she thought she saw signs of a secret understanding between him and Louise Pfingsten or Amélie Lützenkirchen. Although the young man had nothing in particular to offer except his fine physique, his complete naturalness and friendly simplicity, he was liked and sought out in this circle, contentedly profited by the German weakness for everything foreign, and knew very well that his pronunciation of German, the childish turns of phrase he used in speaking it, made a great hit. Then, too, people were glad to speak English with him. He could dress as he pleased. He had no evening clothes; social usages, however, had for many years been less strict, a dinner-jacket was no longer absolutely obligatory in a box at the theatre or at an evening party, and even on occasions where the majority of the gentlemen present wore evening dress, Keaton was welcome in ordinary street clothes, his loose, comfortable apparel, the belted brown trousers, brown shoes, and grey woollen jacket.

Thus unceremoniously he moved through drawing-rooms, made himself agreeable to the ladies to whom he gave English lessons, as well as to those by whom he would gladly have been prevailed upon to do the same – at table first cut a piece of his meat, then laid his knife diagonally across the rim of his plate, let his left arm hang, and, managing his fork with the right, ate what he had made ready. He adhered to this custom because he saw that the ladies on either side of him and the gentleman opposite observed it with such great interest.

He was always glad to chat with Rosalie, whether in company or *tête-à-tête* – not only because she was one of his sources of income but from a genuine attraction. For whereas her daughter's cool intelligence and intellectual pretensions inspired fear in him, the mother's true-hearted womanliness impressed him sympathetically, and, without correctly reading her feelings (it did not occur to him to do that), he allowed himself to bask in the warmth that radiated from her to him, took pleasure in it, and felt little concern over certain concomitant signs of tension, oppression, and confusion, which he interpreted as expressions of European nervousness and therefore held in high regard. In addition, for all her suffering, her appearance at this time acquired a conspicuous new bloom, a rejuvenescence, upon which she received many compliments. Her figure had always preserved its youthfulness, but what was so striking now was the light in her beautiful brown eyes – a light which, if there was something feverish about it, nevertheless added to her charm – was her heightened colouring, quick to return after occasional moments of pallor, the mobility of feature that characterized her face (it had become a little fuller) in conversations that inclined to gaiety and hence always enabled her to correct any involuntary expression by a laugh. A good deal of loud laughter was the rule at these convivial gatherings, for all partook liberally of the wine and punch, and what might have seemed eccentric in Rosalie's manner was submerged in the general atmosphere of relaxation, in which nothing caused much surprise. But how happy she was when it happened that one of the women said to her, in Ken's presence: "Darling, you are astonishing! How ravishing you look this evening! You eclipse the girls of twenty. Do tell me, what fountain of youth have you discovered?" And even more when her beloved corroborated: "Right you are! Frau von Tümmler is perfectly delightful tonight." She laughed, and her deep blush could be attributed to her pleasure in the flattery. She looked away from him, but she thought of his arms, and again she felt the same prodigious sweetness drenching, inundating her inmost being – it had been a frequent sensation these days, and other women, she thought, when they found her young, when they found her charming, must surely be aware of it.

It was on one of these evenings, after the gathering had broken up, that she failed in her resolve to keep the secret of her heart, the illicit and painful but fascinating psychological miracle that had befallen her, wholly to herself and not to reveal it even to Anna's friendship. An irresistible need for communication forced her to break the promise she had made to herself and to confide in her brilliant daughter, not only because she yearned for understanding sympathy but also from a wish that what Nature was bringing to pass in her should be understood and honoured as the remarkable human phenomenon that it was.

A wet snow was falling; the two ladies had driven home through it in a taxicab about midnight. Rosalie was shivering. "Allow me, dear child," she said, "to sit up another half hour with you in your cosy bedroom. I am freezing, but my head is on fire, and sleep, I fear, is out of the question for some time. If you would make tea for us, to end the evening, it wouldn't be a bad idea. That punch of the Rollwagens' is hard on one. Rollwagen mixes it himself, but he hasn't the happiest knack of it, pours a questionable orange cordial into the Moselle and then adds domestic champagne. Tomorrow we shall have terrible headaches again, a bad 'hangover'. Not you, that is. You are sensible and don't drink much. But I forget myself, chattering away, and don't notice that they keep filling my glass and think it is still the first. Yes, make tea for us, it's just the thing. Tea stimulates, but it soothes at the same time, and a cup of hot tea, taken at the right moment, wards off a cold.

The rooms were far too hot at the Rollwagens' – at least, I thought so – and then the foul weather outdoors. Does it mean spring already? At noon today in the park I thought I really sniffed spring. But your silly mother always does that as soon as the shortest day has passed and the light increases again. A good idea, turning on the electric heater; there's not much heat left here at this hour. My dear child, you know how to make us comfortable and create just the right intimate atmosphere for a little *tête-à-tête* before we go to bed. You see, Anna, I have long wanted to have a talk with you, and – you are quite right – you have never denied me the opportunity. But there are things, child, to express which, to discuss which, requires a particularly intimate atmosphere, a favourable hour, which loosens one's tongue . . ."

"What sort of things, Mama? I haven't any cream to offer you. Will you take a little lemon?"

"Things of the heart, child, things of Nature, wonderful, mysterious, omnipotent Nature, who sometimes does such strange, contradictory, indeed incomprehensible things to us. You know it too. Recently, my dear Anna, I have found myself thinking a great deal about your old – forgive me for referring to it – your *affaire de cœur* with Brünner, about what you went through then, the suffering of which you complained to me in an hour not unlike this, and which, in bitter self-reproach, you even called a shame, because, that is, of the shameful conflict in which your reason, your judgment, was engaged with your heart, or, if you prefer, with your senses."

"You are quite right to change the word, Mama. 'Heart' is sentimental nonsense. It is inadmissible to say 'heart' for something that is entirely different. Our heart speaks truly only with the consent of our judgment and reason."

"You may well say so. For you have always been on the side of unity and insisted that Nature, simply of herself, creates harmony between soul and body. But that you were in a state of disharmony then – that is, between your wishes and your judgment – you cannot deny. You were very young at the time, and your desire had no reason to be ashamed in Nature's eyes, only in the eyes of your judgment, which called it debasing. It did not pass the test of your judgment, and that was your shame and your suffering. For you are proud, Anna, very proud; and that there might be a pride in feeling alone, a pride of feeling which denies that it has to pass the test of anything and be responsible to anything – judgment and reason and even Nature herself – that you will not admit, and in that we differ. For to me the heart is supreme, and if Nature inspires feelings in it which no longer become it, and seems to create a contradiction between the heart and herself – certainly it is painful and shameful, but the shame is only for one's unworthiness and, at bottom, is sweet amazement, is reverence, before Nature and before the life that it pleases her to create in one whose life is done."

"My dear Mama," replied Anna, "let me first of all decline the honour that you accord to my pride and my reason. At the time, they would have miserably succumbed to what you poetically call my heart if a merciful fate had not intervened; and when I think where my heart would have led me, I cannot but thank God that I did not follow its desires. I am the last who would dare to cast a stone. However, we are not talking of me, but of you, and I will not decline the honour you accord me in wishing to confide in me. For that is what you wish to do, is it not? What you say indicates it, only you have spoken in such generalities that everything remains dark. Show me, please, how I am to refer them to you and how I am to understand them!"

"What should you say, Anna, if your mother, in her old age, were seized by an ardent feeling such as rightfully belongs only to potent youth, to maturity, and not to a withered womanhood?"

"Why the conditional, Mama? It is quite obvious that you are in the state you describe. You're in love?"

"The way you say that, my sweet child! How freely and bravely and openly you speak the words which would not easily come to my lips, and which I have locked up in me so long, together with all the shameful joy and grief that they imply – have kept secret from everyone, even from you, so closely that you really used to be startled out of your dream, the dream of your belief in your mother's matronly dignity! Yes, I'm in love, I love with ardour and desire and bliss and torment, as you once loved in your youth. My feeling can as little stand the test of reason as yours could, and if I am even proud of the spring with which Nature has made my soul flower, which she has miraculously bestowed upon me, I yet suffer, as you once suffered, and I have been irresistibly driven to tell you all."

"My dear, darling Mama! Then do tell me! When it is so hard to speak, questions help. Who is it?"

"It cannot but be a shattering surprise to you, my child. The young friend of the house. Your brother's tutor."

"Ken Keaton?"

"Yes."

"Ken Keaton. So that is it. You needn't fear, Mother, that I shall begin exclaiming 'Incomprehensible!' – though most people would. It is so easy and so stupid to call a feeling incomprehensible if one cannot imagine oneself having it. And yet – much as I want to avoid hurting you – forgive my anxious sympathy for asking a question. You speak of an emotion inappropriate to your years, complain of entertaining feelings of which you are no longer worthy. Have you ever asked yourself if he, this young man, is worthy of your feelings?"

"He – worthy? I hardly understand what you mean. I love, Anna. Of all the young men I have ever seen, Ken is the most magnificent."

"And that is why you love him. Shall we try reversing the positions of cause and effect and perhaps get them in their proper places by doing so? May it not be that he only seems so magnificent to you because you are . . . because you love him?"

"Oh, my child, you separate what is inseparable. Here in my heart my love and his magnificence are one."

"But you are suffering, dearest, best Mama, and I should be so infinitely glad if I could help you. Could you not try, for a moment – just a moment of trying it might do you good – not to see him in the transfiguring light of your love, but by plain daylight, in his reality, as the nice, attractive – that I will grant you! – attractive lad he is, but who, such as he is, in and for himself, has so little to inspire passion and suffering on his account?"

"You mean well, Anna, I know. You would like to help me, I am sure of it. But it cannot be accomplished at his expense, by your doing him an injustice. And you do him injustice with your 'daylight', which is such a false, misleading light. You say that he is nice, even attractive, and you mean by it that he is an average human being with nothing unusual about him. But I tell you he is an absolutely exceptional human being, with a life that touches one's heart. Think of his simple background – how, with iron strength of will, he worked his way through college, and excelled all his fellow-students in history and athletics, and how he then hastened to his country's call and behaved so well as a soldier that he was finally 'honourably discharged' . . ."

"Excuse me, Mama, but that is the routine procedure for everyone who doesn't actually do something dishonourable."

"Everyone. You keep harping on his averageness, and, in doing so, by calling him, if not directly, then by implication, a simple-minded ingenuous youngster, you mean to talk me out of him. But you forget that ingenuousness can be something noble and victorious, and that the background of his ingenuousness is the great democratic spirit of his immense country. . . ."

"He doesn't like his country in the least."

"And for that very reason he is a true son of it; and if he loves Europe for its historical perspectives and its old folk customs, that does him honour too, and sets him apart from the majority. And he gave his blood for his country. Every soldier, you say, is 'honourably discharged'. But is every soldier given a medal for bravery, a Purple Heart, to show that the heroism with which he flung himself on the enemy cost him a wound, perhaps a serious one?"

"My dear Mama, in war, I think, one man catches it and another doesn't, one falls and another escapes, without its having much to do with whether he is brave or not. If somebody has a leg blown off or a kidney shot to pieces, a medal is a sop, a small compensation for his misfortune, but in general it is no indication of any particular bravery."

"In any case, he sacrificed one of his kidneys on the altar of his fatherland!"

"Yes, he had that misfortune. And, thank heaven, one can at a pinch make do with only one kidney. But only at a pinch, and it *is* a lack, a defect, the thought of it does rather detract from the magnificence of his youth, and in the common light of day, by which he ought to be seen, does show him up, despite his good – or let us say normal – appearance, as not really complete, as disabled, as a man no longer perfectly whole."

"Good God – Ken no longer complete, Ken not a whole man! My poor child, he is complete to the point of magnificence and can laugh at the lack of a kidney – not only in his own opinion, but in everyone's – that is, in the opinion of all the women who are after him, and in whose company he seems to find his pleasure! My dear, good, clever Anna, don't you know why, above all other reasons, I have confided in you, why I began this conversation? Because I wished to ask you – and I want your honest opinion – if, from your observation, you believe that he is having an affair with Louise Pfingsten, or with Amélie Lützenkirchen, or perhaps with both of them – for which, I assure you, he is quite complete enough! That is what keeps me suspended in the most agonizing doubt, and I hope very much that I shall get the truth from you, for you can look at things more calmly, by daylight, so to speak. . . ."

"Poor, darling Mama, how you torture yourself, how you suffer! It makes me so unhappy. But, to answer you: I don't think so – of course, I know very little about his life and have not felt called upon to investigate it – but I don't think so, and I have never heard anyone say that he has the sort of relationship you suspect, either with Frau Pfingsten or Frau Lützenkirchen. So please be reassured, I beg of you!"

"God grant, dear child, that you are not simply saying it to comfort me and pour balm on my wound, out of pity! But pity, don't you see, even though perhaps I am seeking it from you, is not in place at all, for I am happy in my torment and shame and filled with pride in the flowering spring of pain in my soul – remember that, child, even if I seem to be begging for pity!"

"I don't feel that you are begging. But in such a case the happiness and pride are so closely allied with the suffering that, indeed, they are identical with it, and even if you looked for no pity, it would be your due from those who love you and who wish for you that you would take pity on yourself and try to free yourself from this absurd enchantment. . . . Forgive my words; they are the wrong ones, of course, but I cannot be concerned over words. It is you, darling, for whom I am concerned and not only since today, not only since your confession, for which I am grateful to you. You have kept your secret locked within you with great self-control; but that there has been some secret, that, for months now, you have been in some peculiar and crucial situation, could not escape those who love you, and they have seen it with mixed feelings."

"To whom do you refer by your 'they'?"

"I am speaking of myself. You have changed strikingly in these last weeks, Mama – I mean, not changed, I'm not putting it right, you are still the same, and if I say 'changed', I mean that a sort of rejuvenescence has come over you – but that too isn't the right word, for naturally it can't be a matter of any actual, demonstrable rejuvenescence in your charming person. But to my eyes, at moments, and in a certain phantasmagoric fashion, it has been as if suddenly, out of your dear matronly self, stepped the Mama of twenty years ago, as I knew her when I was a girl – and even that was not all, I suddenly thought I saw you as I had never seen you, as you must have looked, that is, when you were a girl yourself. And this hallucination – if it was a mere hallucination, but there was something real about it too – should have delighted me, should have made my heart leap with pleasure, should it not? But it didn't, it only made my heart heavy, and at those very moments when you grew young before my eyes, I pitied you terribly. For at the same time I saw that you were suffering, and that the phantasmagoria to which I refer not only had to do with your suffering but was actually the expression of it, its manifestation, a 'flowering spring of pain', as you just expressed it. Dear Mama, how did you happen to use such an expression? It is not natural to you. You are a simple being, worthy of all love; you have sound, clear eyes, you let them look into Nature and the world, not into books – you have never read much. Never before have you used expressions such as poets create, such lugubrious, sickly expressions, and if you do it now, it has a tinge of – "

"Of what, Anna? If poets use such expressions it is because they *need* them, because emotion and experience force them out of them, and so it is, surely, with me, though you think them unbecoming in me. You are wrong. They are becoming to whoever needs them, and he has no fear of them, because they are forced out of him. But your hallucination, or phantasmagoria – whatever it was that you thought you saw in me – I can and will explain to you. It was the work of *his* youth. It was my soul's struggle to match his youth, so that it need not perish before him in shame and disgrace."

Anna wept. They put their arms around each other, and their tears mingled.

"That too," said the lame girl with an effort, "what you have just said, dear heart, that too is of a piece with the strange expression you used, and, like that, coming from your lips, it has a ring of destruction. This accursed seizure is destroying you, I see it with my eyes, I hear it in your speech. We must check it, put a stop to it, save you from it, at any cost. One forgets, Mama, what is out of one's sight. All that is needed is a decision, a saving decision. The young man must not come here any longer, we must dismiss him. That is not enough. You see him elsewhere when you go out. Very well, we must prevail upon him to leave the city. I will take it upon myself to persuade him. I will talk to him in a friendly way, point out to him that he is wasting his time and himself here, that he has long since exhausted Düsseldorf and should not hang around here for ever, that Düsseldorf is not Germany, of which he must see more, get to know it better, that Munich, Hamburg, Berlin are there for him to sample, that he must not let himself be tied down, must live in one place for a time, then in another, until, as is his natural duty, he returns to his own country and takes up a regular profession, instead of playing the invalid language-teacher here in Europe. I'll soon impress it upon him. And if he declines and insists on sticking to Düsseldorf, where, after all, he has connections, we will go away ourselves. We will give up our house here and move to Cologne or Frankfurt or to some lovely place in the Taunus, and you will leave here behind you what has been torturing you and trying to destroy you, and with the help of 'out of sight', you will forget. Out of sight – it is all that is needed, it is an infallible remedy, for there is no such thing as not being able to forget. You may say it is a disgrace to forget, but people do forget, depend upon it. And in the Taunus you will enjoy your beloved Nature and you will be our old darling Mama again."

Thus Anna, with great earnestness, but how unavailingly!

"Stop, stop, Anna, no more of this, I cannot listen to what you are saying! You weep with me, and your concern is affectionate indeed, but what you say, your proposals, are impossible and shocking to me. Drive him away? Leave here ourselves? How far your solicitude has led you astray! You speak of Nature, but you strike her in the face with your demands, you want me to strike her in the face, by stifling the spring of pain with which she has miraculously blessed my soul! What a sin that would be, what ingratitude, what disloyalty to her, to Nature, and what a denial of my faith in her beneficent omnipotence! You remember how Sarah sinned? She laughed to herself behind the door and said: 'After I am waxed old shall I have pleasure, my lord being old also?' But the Lord God was angry and said: 'Wherefore did Sarah laugh?' In my opinion, she laughed less on account of her own withered old age than because her lord, Abraham, was likewise so old and stricken in years, already ninety-nine. And what woman could not but laugh at the thought of indulging in lust with a ninety-nine-year-old man, for all that a man's love life is less strictly limited than a woman's. But my lord is young, is youth itself, and how much more easily and temptingly must the thought come to me – Oh, Anna, my loyal child, I indulge in lust, shameful and grievous lust, in my blood, in my wishes, and I cannot give it up, cannot flee to the Taunus, and if you persuade Ken to go – I believe I should hate you to my dying day!"

Great was the sorrow with which Anna listened to these unrestrained, frenzied words.

"Dearest Mama," said she in a strained voice, "you are greatly excited. What you need now is rest and sleep. Take twenty drops of valerian in water, or even twenty-five. It is a harmless remedy and often very helpful. And rest assured that, for my part, I will undertake nothing that is opposed to your feeling. May this assurance help to bring you the peace of mind which, above all things, I desire for you! If I spoke slightingly of Keaton, whom I respect as the object of your affection, though I cannot but curse him as the cause of your suffering, you will understand that I was only trying to see if it would not restore your peace of mind. I am infinitely grateful for your confidence, and I hope, indeed I am sure, that by talking to me you have somewhat lightened your heart. Perhaps this conversation was the prerequisite for your recovery – I mean, for your restored peace of mind. Your sweet, happy heart, so dear to us all, will find itself again. It loves in pain. Do you not think that – let us say, in time – it could learn to love without pain and in accordance with reason? Love, don't you see? – " (Anna said this as she solicitously led her mother to her bedroom, so that she could herself drop the valerian into her glass) "love – how many things it is, what a variety of feelings are included in the word, and yet how strangely it is always love!

A mother's love for her son, for instance – I know that Eduard is not particularly close to you – but that love can be very heartfelt, very passionate, it can be subtly yet clearly distinguished from her love for a child of her own sex, and yet not for an instant pass the bounds of mother love. How would it be if you were to take advantage of the fact that Ken could be your son, to make the tenderness you feel for him maternal, let it find a permanent place, to your own benefit as mother love?"

Rosalie smiled through her tears.

"And thus establish the proper understanding between body and soul, I take it?" she jested sadly. "My dear child, the demands that I make on your intelligence! How I exhaust it and misuse it! It is wrong of me, for I trouble you to no purpose. Mother love – it is something like the Taunus all over again. . . . Perhaps I'm not expressing myself quite clearly now? I *am* dead tired, you are right about that. Thank you, darling, for your patience, your sympathy! Thank you too for respecting Ken for the sake of what you call my affection. And don't hate him at the same time, as I should have to hate you if you drove him away! He is Nature's means of working her miracle in my soul."

Anna left her. A week passed, during which Ken Keaton twice dined at the Tümmlers'. The first time, an elderly couple from Duisburg were present, relatives of Rosalie's; the woman was a cousin of hers. Anna, who well knew that certain relationships and emotional tensions inevitably emanate an aura that is obvious, particularly to those who are in no way involved, observed the guests keenly. Once or twice she saw Rosalie's cousin look wonderingly first at Keaton, then at the hostess; once she even detected a smile under the husband's moustache. That evening she also observed a difference in Ken's behaviour towards her mother, a quizzical change and readjustment in his reactions, observed too that he would not let it pass when, laboriously enough, she pretended not to be taking any particular notice of him, but forced her to direct her attention to him. On the second occasion no one else was present. Frau von Tümmler indulged in a scurrilous performance, directed at her daughter and inspired by her recent conversation with her, in which she mocked at certain of Anna's counsels and at the same time turned the travesty to her own advantage. It had come out that Ken had been very much on the town the previous night – with a few of his cronies, an art-school student and two sons of manufacturers, he had gone on a pub-crawl that had lasted until morning, and, as might have been expected, had arrived at the Tümmlers' with a "first-class hangover" as Eduard, who was the one to let out the story, expressed it. At the end of the evening, when the good-nights were being said, Rosalie gave her daughter a look that was at once excited and crafty – indeed, kept her eyes fixed on her for a moment as she held the young man by the lobe of his ear and said:

"And you, son, take a serious word of reproof from Mama Rosalie and understand hereafter that her house is open only to people of decent behaviour and not to night-owls and disabled beer-swillers who are hardly up to speaking German or even to keeping their eyes open! Did you hear me, you good-for-nothing? Mend your ways! If bad boys tempt you, don't listen to them, and from now on stop playing so fast and loose with your health! Will you mend your ways, will you?" As she spoke, she kept tugging at his ear, and Ken yielded to the slight pull in an exaggerated way, pretended that the punishment was extraordinarily painful, and writhed under her hand with a most pitiable grimace, which showed his fine white teeth. His face was near to hers, and speaking directly into it, in all its nearness, she went on:

"Because if you do it again and don't mend your ways, you naughty boy, I'll banish you from the city – do you know that? I'll send you to some quiet place in the Taunus where, though Nature is very beautiful, there are no temptations and you can teach the farmers' children English. This time, go and sleep it off, you scamp!" And she let go of his ear, took leave of the nearness of his face, gave Anna one more pale, crafty look, and left.

A week later something extraordinary happened, which astonished, touched, and perplexed Anna von Tümmler in the highest degree – perplexed her because, though she rejoiced in it for her mother's sake, she did not know whether to regard it as fortunate or unfortunate. About ten o'clock in the morning the chambermaid brought a message asking her to see the mistress in her bedroom. Since the little family breakfasted separately – Eduard first, then Anna, the lady of the house last – she had not yet seen her mother that day. Rosalie was lying on the chaise-longue in her bedroom, covered with a light cashmere shawl, a little pale, but with her nose flushed. With a smile of rather studied languor, she nodded to her daughter as she came stumping in, but said nothing, so that Anna was forced to ask:

"What is it, Mama? You aren't ill, are you?"

"Oh no, my child, don't be alarmed, I'm not ill at all. I was very much tempted, instead of sending for you, to go to you myself and greet you. But I am a little in need of coddling, rest seems to be indicated, as it sometimes is for us women."

"Mama! What do you mean?"

Then Rosalie sat up, flung her arms around her daughter's neck, drew her down beside her onto the edge of the chaise-longue, and, cheek to cheek with her, whispered in her ear, quickly, blissfully, all in a breath:

"Victory, Anna, victory, it has come back to me, come back to me after such a long interruption, absolutely naturally and just as it should be for a mature, vigorous woman! Dear child, what a miracle! What a miracle great, beneficent Nature has wrought in me, how she has blessed my faith! For I believed, Anna, and did not laugh, and so now kind Nature rewards me and takes back what she seemed to have done to my body, she proves that it was a mistake and re-establishes harmony between soul and body, but not in the way that you wished it to happen. Not with the soul obediently letting the body act upon it and translate it to the dignified estate of matronhood, but the other way around, the other way around, dear child, with the soul proving herself mistress over the body.

Congratulate me, darling, there is reason for it! I am a woman again, a whole human being again, a functioning female, I can feel worthy of the youthful manhood that has bewitched me, and no longer need lower my eyes before it with a feeling of impotence. The rod of life with which it struck me has reached not my soul alone but my body too and has made it a flowing fountain again. Kiss me, my darling child, call me blessed, as blessed I am, and, with me, praise the miraculous power of great, beneficent Nature!"

She sank back, closed her eyes, and smiled contentedly, her nose very red.

"Dear, sweet Mama," said Anna, willing enough to rejoice with her, yet sick at heart, "this is truly a great, a moving event, it testifies to the richness of your nature, which was already evident in the freshness of your feeling and now gives that feeling such power over your bodily functions. As you see, I am entirely of your opinion – that what has happened to you physically is psychological in origin, is the product of your youthfully strong feeling. Whatever I may at times have said about such things, you must not think me such a Philistine that I deny the psychological any power over the physical and hold that the latter has the last word in the relationship between them. Each is dependent upon the other – that much even I know about Nature and its unity. However much the soul may be subject to the body's circumstances – what the soul, for its part, can do to the body often verges on the miraculous, and your case is one of the most splendid examples of it. Yet, permit me to say that this beautiful, animating event, of which you are so proud – and rightly, you may certainly be proud of it – on me, constituted as I am, it does not make the same sort of impression that it makes on you. In my opinion, it does not change things much, my best of mothers, and it does not appreciably increase my admiration for your nature – or for Nature in general. Clubfooted, ageing spinster that I am, I have every reason not to attach much importance to the physical. Your freshness of feeling, precisely in contrast to your physical age, seemed to me splendid enough, enough of a triumph – it almost seemed to me a purer victory of the soul than what has happened now, than this transformation of the indestructible youth of your heart into an organic phenomenon."

"Say no more, my poor child! What you call my freshness of feeling, and now insist that you enjoyed, you represented to me, more or less bluntly, as sheer folly, through which I was making myself ridiculous, and you advised me to retreat into a motherly dowagerhood, to make my feeling maternal. Well, it would have been a little too early for that, don't you think so now, my pet? Nature has made her voice heard against it. She has made my feeling her concern and has unmistakably shown me that it need not be ashamed before her nor before the blooming young manhood which is its object. And do you really mean to say that does not change things much?"

"What I mean, my dear, wonderful Mama, is certainly not that I did not respect Nature's voice. Nor, above all things, do I wish to spoil your joy in her decree. You cannot think that of me. When I said that what had happened did not change things much, I was referring to outward realities, to the practical aspects of the situation, so to speak. When I advised you – when I fondly wished that you might conquer yourself, that it might not even be hard for you to confine your feeling for the young man – forgive me for speaking of him so coolly – for our friend Keaton, rather, to maternal love, my hope was based on the fact that he could be your son. That fact, you will agree, has not changed, and it cannot but determine the relationship between you on either side, on your side and on his too."

"And on his too. You speak of two sides, but you mean only his. You do not believe that he could love me except, at best, as a son?"

"I will not say that, dearest and best Mama."

"And how could you say it, Anna, my true-hearted child! Remember, you have no right to, you have not the necessary authority to judge in matters of love. You have little perception in that realm, because you gave up early, dear heart, and turned your eyes away from such things. Intellect offered you a substitute for Nature – good for you, that is all very fine! But how can you undertake to judge and to condemn me to hopelessness? You have no power of observation and do not see what I see, do not perceive the signs which indicate to me that his feeling is ready to respond to mine. Do you mean to say that at such moments he is only trifling with me? Would you rather consider him insolent and heartless than to grant me the hope that his feeling may correspond to mine? What would be so extraordinary in that? For all your aloofness from love, you cannot be unaware that a young man very often prefers a mature woman to an inexperienced girl, to a silly little goose. Naturally, a nostalgia for his mother may enter in – as, on the other hand, maternal feelings may play a part in an elder woman's passion for a young man. But why say this to you? I have a distinct impression that you recently said something very like it to me."

"Really? In any case, you are right, Mama, I agree with you completely in what you say."

"Then you must not call me past hope, especially today, when Nature has recognized my feeling, You must not, despite my grey hair, at which, so it seems to me, you are looking. Yes, unfortunately I am quite grey. It was a mistake that I didn't begin dyeing my hair long ago. I can't suddenly start now, though Nature has to a certain extent authorized me to. But I can do something for my face, not only by massage, but also by using a little rouge. I don't suppose you children would be shocked?"

"Of course not, Mama! Eduard will never notice, if you go about it a little discreetly. And I . . . though I think that artificiality will not go too well with your deep feeling for Nature, why, it is certainly no sin against Nature to help her out a little in such an accepted fashion."

"So you agree with me? After all, the thing is to prevent a fondness for being mothered from playing too large a part, from predominating, in Ken's feeling. That would be contrary to my hopes. Yes, dear, loyal child, this heart – I know that you do not like talking and hearing about the 'heart' – but my heart is swollen with pride and joy, with the thought of how very differently I shall meet his youth, with what a different self-confidence. Your mother's heart is swollen with happiness and life!"

"How beautiful, dearest Mama! And how charming of you to let me share in your great happiness! I share it, share it from my heart, you cannot doubt it, even if I say that a certain concern intrudes even as I rejoice with you – that is very like me, isn't it? – certain scruples – *practical* scruples, to use the word which, for want of a better, I used before. You speak of your hope, and of all that justifies you in entertaining it – in my opinion, what justifies it above all is simply your own lovable self. But you fail to define your hope more precisely, to tell me what its goal is, what expression it expects to find in the reality of life. Is it your intention to marry again? To make Ken Keaton our stepfather? To stand before the altar with him? It may be cowardly of me, but as the difference in your ages is equivalent to that between a mother and her son, I am a little afraid of the astonishment which such a step would arouse."

Frau von Tümmler stared at her daughter.

"No," she answered, "the idea is new to me, and if it will calm your apprehensions, I can assure you that I do not entertain it. No. Anna, you silly thing, I have no intention of giving you and Eduard a twenty-four-year-old stepfather. How odd of you to speak so stiffly and piously of 'standing before the altar'!"

Anna remained silent; her eyelids lowered a little, she gazed past her mother into space.

"Hope – " said her mother, "who can define it, as you want me to? Hope is hope – how can you expect that it will inquire into practical goals, as you put it? What Nature has granted me is so beautiful that I can only expect something beautiful from it, but I cannot tell you how I think that it will come, how it will be realized, and where it will lead. That is what hope is like. It simply doesn't think – least of all about 'standing before the altar'."

Anna's lips were slightly twisted. Between them she spoke softly, as if involuntarily and despite herself:

"That would be a comparatively reasonable idea."

Frau von Tümmler stared in bewilderment at her crippled daughter – who did not look at her – and tried to read her expression.

"Anna!" she cried softly. "What are you thinking, what does this behaviour mean? Allow me to say that I simply don't recognize you! Which of us, I ask you, is the artist – I or you? I should never have thought that you could be so far behind your mother in broad-mindedness – and not only behind her, but behind the times and its freer manners! In your art you are so advanced and profess the very latest thing, so that a simple person like myself can scarcely follow you. But morally you seem to be living God knows when, in the old days, before the war. After all, we have the republic now, we have freedom, and ideas have changed very much, towards informality, towards laxity, it is apparent everywhere, even in the smallest things. For example, nowadays young men consider it good form to let their handkerchiefs, of which you used to see only a little corner protruding from the breast pocket, hang far out – why, they let them hang out like flags, half the handkerchief; it is clearly a sign, even a conscious declaration, of a republican relaxation of manners. Eduard lets his handkerchief hang out too, in the way that is the fashion, and I see it with a certain satisfaction."

"Your observation is very fine, Mama. But I think that, in Eduard's case, your handkerchief symbol is not to be taken too personally. You yourself often say that the young man – for such by this time he has really become – is a good deal like our father, the lieutenant-colonel. Perhaps it is not quite tactful of me to bring Papa into our conversation and our thoughts at the moment. And yet – "

"Anna, your father was an excellent officer and he fell on the field of honour, but he was a rake and a Don Juan to the very end, the most striking example of the elastic limits of a man's sexual life, and I constantly had to shut both eyes on his account. So I cannot consider it particularly tactless that you should refer to him."

"All the better, Mama – if I may say so. But Papa was a gentleman and an officer, and he lived, despite all that you call his rakishness, according to certain concepts of honour, which mean very little to me, but many of which Eduard, I believe, has inherited. He not only resembles his father outwardly, in figure and features. In certain circumstances, he will involuntarily react in his father's fashion."

"Which means – in what circumstances?"

"Dear Mama, let me be perfectly frank, as we have always been with each other! It is certainly conceivable that a relationship such as you vaguely anticipate between Ken Keaton and yourself could remain completely concealed and unknown to society. However, what with your delightful impulsiveness and your charming inability to dissimulate and bury the secrets of your heart, I have my doubts as to how well it could be carried off. Let some young whippersnapper make mocking allusions to our Eduard, give him to understand that it is known that his mother is – how do people put it? – leading a loose life, and he would strike him, he would box the fellow's ears, and who knows what dangerous kind of official nonsense might result from his chivalry?"

"For heaven's sake, Anna! What things you imagine! You are excruciating. I know you are doing it out of solicitude, but it is cruel, your solicitude, as cruel as small children condemning their mother. . . ."

Rosalie cried a little. Anna helped her to dry her tears, affectionately guiding the hand in which she held her handkerchief.

"Dearest, best Mama, forgive me! How reluctant I am to hurt you! But you – don't talk of children condemning! Do you think I would not look – no, not tolerantly, that sounds too supercilious – but reverently, and with the tenderest concern, on what you are determined to consider your happiness? And Eduard – I hardly know how I happened to speak of him – it was just because of his republican handkerchief. It is not a question of us, nor only of people in general. It is a question of you, Mama. Now, you said that you were broad-minded. But are you, really? We were speaking of Papa and of certain traditional concepts by which he lived, and which, as he saw them, were not infringed by the infidelities to upset you with. That you forgave him for them again and again was because, fundamentally, as you must realize, you were of the same opinion – you were, in other words, conscious that they had nothing to do with real debauchery. He was not born for that, he was no libertine at heart. No more are you. I, at most, as an artist, have deviated from type in that respect, but then again, in another way, I am unfitted to make use of my emancipation, of my being morally *déclassée*."

"My poor child," Frau von Tümmler interrupted her, "don't speak of yourself so gloomily!"

"As if I were speaking of myself at all!" answered Anna. "I am speaking of you, of you, it is for you that I am so deeply concerned. Because, for you, it would really be debauchery to do what, for Papa, the man about town, was simply dissipation, doing violence neither to himself nor to the judgment of society. Harmony between body and soul is certainly a good and necessary thing, and you are proud and happy because Nature, your beloved Nature, has granted it to you in a way that is almost miraculous. But harmony between one's life and one's innate moral convictions is, in the end, even more necessary, and where it is disrupted the only result can be emotional disruption, and that means unhappiness. Don't you feel that this is true? That you would be living in opposition to yourself if you made a reality out of what you now dream? Fundamentally, you are just as much bound as Papa was to certain concepts, and the destruction of that allegiance would be no less than the destruction of your own self. . . . I say it as I feel it – with anxiety. Why does that word come to my lips again – 'destruction'? I know that I have used it once before, in anguish, and I have had the sensation more than once. Why must I keep feeling as if this whole visitation, whose happy victim you are, had something to do with destruction? I will confess something to you. Recently, just a few weeks ago, after our talk when we drank tea late that night in my room and you were so excited, I was tempted to go to Dr Oberloskamp, who took care of Eduard when he had jaundice, and of me once, when I had laryngitis and couldn't swallow – you never need a doctor; I was tempted, I say, to talk to him about you and about what you had confided to me, simply for the sake of setting my mind at rest on your account. But I rejected the idea, I rejected it almost at once, out of pride, Mama, out of pride in you and for you, and because it seemed to me degrading to turn your experience over to a medical man who, with the help of God, is competent for jaundice and laryngitis, but not for deep human ills. In my opinion, there are sicknesses that are too good for the doctor."

"I am grateful to you for both, my dear child," said Rosalie, "for the concern which impelled you to talk with Oberloskamp about me, and for your having repressed the impulse. But then what can induce you to make the slightest connection between what you call my visitation – this Easter of my womanhood, what the soul has done to my body – and the concept of sickness? Is happiness – sickness? Certainly, it is not light-mindedness either, it is living, living in joy and sorrow, and to live is to hope – the hope for which I can give no explanation to your reason."

"I do not ask for any explanation from you, dearest Mama."

"Then go now, child. Let me rest. As you know, a little quiet seclusion is indicated for us women on such crowning days."

Anna kissed her mother and stumped out of the bedroom. Once separated, the two women reflected on the conversation they had just held. Anna had neither said, nor been able to say, all that was on her mind. How long, she wondered, would what her mother called "the Easter of her womanhood", this touching revivification, endure in her? And Ken, if, as was perfectly plausible, he succumbed to her – how long would *that* last? How constantly her mother, in her late love, would be cast into trepidation by every younger woman, would have to tremble, from the very first day, for his faithfulness, even his respect! At least it was to the good that she did not conceive of happiness simply as pleasure and joy but as life with its suffering. For Anna uneasily foresaw much suffering in what her mother dreamed.

For her part, Frau Rosalie was more deeply impressed by her daughter's remonstrances than she had allowed to appear. It was not so much the thought that, under certain circumstances, Eduard might have to risk his young life for her honour – the romantic idea, though she had wept over it, really made her heart beat with pride. But Anna's doubts of her "broad-mindedness", what she had said about debauchery and the necessary harmony between one's life and one's moral convictions, preoccupied the good soul all through her day of rest and she could not but admit that her daughter's doubts were justified, that her views contained a good part of truth. Neither, to be sure, could she suppress her most heartfelt joy at the thought of meeting her young beloved again under such new circumstances. But what her shrewd daughter had said about "living in contradiction to herself", she remembered and pondered over, and she strove in her soul to associate the idea of renunciation with the idea of happiness. Yes, could not renunciation itself be happiness, if it were not a miserable necessity but were practised in freedom and in conscious equality? Rosalie reached the conclusion that it could be.

Ken presented himself at the Tümmlers' three days after Rosalie's great physiological reassurance, read and spoke English with Eduard, and stayed for dinner. Her happiness at the sight of his pleasant, boyish face, his fine teeth, his broad shoulders and narrow hips, shone from her sweet eyes, and their sparkling animation justified, one might say, the touch of artificial red which heightened her cheeks and without which, indeed, the pallor of her face would have been in contradiction to that joyous fire. This time, and thereafter every time Ken came, she had a way, each week, of taking his hand when she greeted him and drawing his body close to hers, at the same time looking earnestly, luminously, and significantly into his eyes, so that Anna had the impression that she very much wished, and indeed was going, to tell the young man of the experience her nature had undergone. Absurd apprehension! Of course nothing of the sort occurred, and all through the rest of the evening the attitude of the lady of the house towards her young guest was a serene and settled kindliness from which both the affected motherliness with which she had once teased her daughter, as well as any bashfulness and nervousness, any painful humility, were gratifyingly absent.

Keaton, who to his satisfaction had long been aware that, even such as he was, he had made a conquest of this grey-haired but charming European woman, hardly knew what to make of the change in her behaviour. His respect for her had, quite understandably, diminished when he became aware of her weakness; the latter, on the other hand, had in turn attracted and excited his masculinity; his simple nature felt sympathetically drawn to hers, and he considered that such beautiful eyes, with their youthful, penetrating gaze, quite made up for fifty years and ageing hands. The idea of entering into an affair with her, such as he had been carrying on for some time – not, as it happened, with Amélie Lützenkirchen or Louise Pfingsten, but with another woman of the same set, whom Rosalie had never thought of – was by no means new to him, and, as Anna observed, he had begun, at least now and again, to change his manner towards his pupil's mother, to speak to her in a tone that was provocatively flirtatious.

This, the good fellow soon found, no longer seemed quite to come off. Despite the handclasp by which, at the beginning of each meeting, she drew him close to her, so that their bodies almost touched, and despite her intimate, searching gaze into his eyes, his experiments in this direction encountered a friendly but firm dignity which put him in his place, forbade any establishment of what he wished to establish, and, instantly dispelling his pretensions, reduced his attitude to one of submission. The meaning of the repeated experience escaped him. "Is she in love with me or not?" he asked himself, and blamed her repulses and her reprobation on the presence of her children, the lame girl and the schoolboy. But his experience was no different when it happened that he was alone with her for a time in a drawing-room corner – and no different when he changed the character of his little advances, abandoning all quizzicalness and giving them a seriously tender, a pressing, almost passionate tone. Once, using the unrolled palatal "*r*" which so delighted everyone, he tried calling her "Rosalie" in a warm voice – which, simply as a form of address, was, in his American view, not even a particular liberty. But, though for an instant she had blushed hotly, she had almost immediately risen and left him, and had given him neither a word nor a look during the rest of that evening.

The winter, which had proved to be mild, bringing hardly any cold weather and snow, but all the more rain instead, also ended early that year. Even in February there were warm, sunny days redolent of spring. Tiny leaf buds ventured out on branches here and there. Rosalie, who had lovingly greeted the snowdrops in her garden, could rejoice far earlier than usual, almost prematurely, in the daffodils – and, very soon after, in the short-stemmed crocuses too, which sprouted everywhere in the front gardens of villas and in the Palace Garden, and before which passers-by halted to point them out to one another and to feast on their particoloured profusion.

"Isn't it remarkable," said Frau von Tümmler to her daughter, "how much they resemble the autumn colchicum? It's practically the same flower! End and beginning – one could mistake them for each other, they are so alike – one could think one was back in autumn in the presence of a crocus, and believe in spring when one saw the last flower of the year."

"Yes, a slight confusion," answered Anna. "Your old friend Mother Nature has a charming propensity for the equivocal and for mystification in general."

"You are always quick to speak against her, you naughty child, and where I succumb to wonder, you mock. Let well enough alone; you cannot laugh me out of my tender feeling for her, for my beloved Nature, least of all now, when she is just bringing in my season – I call it mine because the season in which we were born is peculiarly akin to us, and we to it. You are an Advent child, and you can truly say that you arrived under a good sign – almost under the dear sign of Christmas. You must feel a pleasant affinity between yourself and that season, which, even though cold, makes us think of joy and warmth. For really, in my experience, there is a sympathetic relation between ourselves and the season that produced us. Its return brings something that confirms and strengthens, that renews our lives, just as spring has always done for me – not because it is spring, or the prime of the year, as the poets call it, a season everyone loves, but because I personally belong to it, and I feel that it smiles at me quite personally."

"It does indeed, dearest Mama," answered the child of winter. "And rest assured that I shan't speak a single word against it!"

But it must be said that the buoyancy of life which Rosalie was accustomed – or believed she was accustomed – to receive from the approach and unfolding of "her" season was not, even as she spoke of it, manifesting itself quite as usual. It was almost as if the moral resolutions which her conversation with her daughter had inspired in her, and to which she so steadfastly adhered, went against her nature, as if, despite them, or indeed because of them, she were "living in contradiction to herself". This was precisely the impression that Anna received, and the limping girl reproached herself for having persuaded her mother to a continence which her own liberal view of life in no sense demanded but which had seemed requisite to her only for the dear woman's peace of mind. What was more, she suspected herself of unacknowledged evil motives. She asked herself if she, who had once grievously longed for sensual pleasure, but had never experienced it, had not secretly begrudged it to her mother and hence had exhorted her to chastity by all sorts of trumped-up arguments. No, she could not believe it of herself, and yet what she saw troubled and burdened her conscience.

She saw that Rosalie, setting out on one of the walks she so loved, quickly grew tired, and that it was she who, inventing some household task that must be done, insisted on turning home after only half an hour or even sooner. She rested a great deal, yet despite this limitation of her physical activity, she lost weight, and Anna noticed with concern the thinness of her forearms when she happened to see them exposed. People no longer asked her at what fountain of youth she had been drinking. There was an ominous, tired-looking blueness under her eyes, and the rouge which, in honour of the young man and of her recovery of full womanhood, she put on her cheeks created no very effective illusion against the yellowish pallor of her complexion. But as she dismissed any inquiries as to how she felt with a cheerful, "I feel quite well – why should you think otherwise?" Fräulein von Tümmler gave up the idea of asking Dr Oberloskamp to investigate her mother's failing health. It was not only a feeling of guilt which led her to this decision; piety too played a part – the same piety that she had expressed when she said that there were sicknesses which were too good to be taken to a doctor.

So Anna was all the more delighted by the enterprise and confidence in her strength which Rosalie exhibited in connection with a little plan that was agreed on between herself, her children, and Ken Keaton, who happened to be present, one evening as they lingered over their wine. A month had not yet passed since the morning Anna had been called to her mother's bedroom to hear the wonderful news. Rosalie was as charming and gay as in the old days that evening, and she could have been considered the prime mover of the excursion on which they had agreed – unless Ken Keaton was to be given the credit, for it was his historical chatter that had led to the idea. He had talked about various castles and strongholds he had visited in the Duchy of Berg – of the Castle on the

Wupper, of Bensberg, Ehreshoven, Gimhorn, Homburg, and Krottorf; and from these he went on to the Elector Carl Theodore, who, in the eighteenth century, had moved his court from Düsseldorf, first to Schwetzingen and then to Munich – but that had not prevented his Statthalter, a certain Count Grottstein, from embarking on all sorts of important architectural and horticultural projects here: it was under him that the Electoral Academy of Art was conceived, the Palace Garden was first laid out, and Jägerhof Castle was built – and, Eduard added, in the same year, so far as he knew, Holterhof Castle too, a little to the south of the city, near the village of the same name. Of course, Holterhof too, Keaton confirmed, and then, to his own amazement, was obliged to admit that he had never laid eyes on that creation of the late Rococo nor even visited its park, celebrated as it was, which extended all the way to the Rhine. Frau von Tümmler and Anna had, of course, taken the air there once or twice, but they had never succeeded in viewing the interior of the charmingly situated castle, nor had Eduard.

"*Wat et nit all jibt!*" said the lady of the house, using, in jocular disapproval, the local equivalent of "Will wonders never cease!" It was always an indication of good spirits when she dropped into dialect. "Fine Düsseldorfers you are," she added, "the lot of you!" One had never been there at all, and the others had not seen the interior of the jewel of a castle which every tourist made it a point to be shown through! "Children," she cried, "this has gone on too long, we must not allow it. An excursion to Holterhof – for the four of us! And we will make it within the next few days! It is so beautiful now, the season is so enchanting and the barometer is steady. The buds will be opening in the park, it may well be pleasanter in its spring array than in the heat of summer, when Anna and I went walking there. Suddenly I feel a positive nostalgia for the black swans which – you remember, Anna – glided over the moats in such melancholy pride with their red bills and oar-feet. How they disguised their appetite in condescension when we fed them! We must take along some bread for them.... Let's see, today is Friday – we will go Sunday, is that settled? Only Sunday would do for Eduard, and for Mr Keaton too, I imagine. Of course there will be a crowd out on Sunday, but that means nothing to me, I like mixing with people in their Sunday best, I share in their enjoyment, I like being where there's 'something doing' – at the outdoor carnivals at Oberkassel, when it smells of fried food and the children are licking away at red sugar-sticks and, in front of the circus tent, such fantastically vulgar people are tinkling and tootling and shouting. I find it marvellous. Anna thinks otherwise. She finds it sad. Yes, you do, Anna – and you prefer the aristocratic sadness of the pair of black swans in the moat.... I have an inspiration, children – we'll go by water! The trip by land on the street railway is simply boring. Not a scrap of woods and hardly an open field. It's much more amusing by water, Father Rhine shall convey us. Eduard, will you see to getting the steamer timetable? Or, just a moment, if we want to be really luxurious, we'll indulge ourselves and hire a private motor-boat for the trip up the Rhine. Then we'll be quite by ourselves, like the black swans.... All that remains to be settled is whether we want to set sail in the morning or the afternoon."

The consensus was in favour of the morning. Eduard thought that, in any case, he had heard that the castle was open to visitors only into the early hours of the afternoon. It should be Sunday morning, then. Under Rosalie's energetic urging, the arrangements were soon made and agreed on. It was Keaton who was designated to charter the motor-boat. They would meet again at the point of departure, the Rathaus quay, by the Water-gauge Clock, the day after tomorrow at nine.

And so they did. It was a sunny and rather windy morning. The quay was jammed with a crowd of pushing people who, with their children and their bicycles, were waiting to go aboard one of the white steamers of the Cologne-Düsseldorf Navigation Company. The chartered motor-boat lay ready for the Tümmlers and their companion. Its master, a man with rings in his ear-lobes, clean-shaven upper lip, and a reddish mariner's beard under his chin, helped the ladies aboard. The party had hardly seated themselves on the curved bench under the awning, which was supported by stanchions, before he got under way. The boat made good time against the current of the broad river, whose banks, incidentally, were utterly prosaic. The old castle tower, the crooked tower of the Lambertuskirche, the harbour installations, were left behind. More of the same sort of thing appeared beyond the next bend in the river – warehouses, factory buildings. Little by little, behind the stone jetties which extended from the shore into the river, the country became more rural. Hamlets, old fishing villages – whose names Eduard, and Keaton too, knew – lay, protected by dykes, before a flat landscape of meadows, fields, willow-bushes, and pools. So it would be, however many windings the river made, for a good hour and a half, until they reached their destination. But how right they had been, Rosalie exclaimed, to decide on the boat instead of covering the distance in a fraction of the time by the horrible route through the suburbs! She seemed to be heartily enjoying the elemental charm of the journey by water. Her eyes closed, she sang a snatch of some happy tune into the wind, which at moments was almost stormy: "O water-wind, I love thee; lovest thou me, O water-wind?" Her face, which had grown thinner, looked very appealing under the little felt hat with the feather, and the grey-and-red-checked coat she had on – of light woollen material with a turn-down collar – was very becoming to her. Anna and Eduard had also worn coats for the voyage, and only Keaton, who sat between mother and daughter, contented himself with a grey sweater under his tweed jacket. His handkerchief hung out, and, suddenly opening her eyes and turning, Rosalie stuffed it deep into his breast pocket.

"Propriety, propriety, young man!" she said, shaking her head in decorous reproof.

He smiled: "Thank you," and then wanted to know what song it was she had just been singing.

"Song?" she asked. "Was I singing? That was only singsong,

not a song." And she closed her eyes again and hummed, her lips scarcely moving: "How I love thee, O water-wind!"

Then she began chattering through the noise of the motor, and – often having to hold on to her hat, which the wind was trying to tear from her still abundant, wavy grey hair – expatiated on how it would be possible to extend the Rhine trip beyond Holterhof, to Leverkusen and Cologne, and from there on past Bonn to Godesberg and Bad Honnef at the foot of the Siebengebirge. It was beautiful there, the trim watering-place on the Rhine, amid vineyards and orchards, and it had an alkaline mineral spring that was very good for rheumatism. Anna looked at her; she knew that her mother now suffered intermittently from lumbago, and had once or twice considered going to Godesberg or Honnef with her in the early summer, to take the waters. There was something almost involuntary in the way she chattered on about the beneficial spring, catching her breath as she spoke into the wind; it made Anna think that her mother was even now not free from the shooting pains that characterize the disease.

After an hour they breakfasted on a few ham sandwiches and washed them down with port from little travelling-cups. It was half past eleven when the boat made fast to a flimsy landing-stage, inadequate for larger vessels, which was built out into the river near the castle and the park. Rosalie paid off the boatman, as they had decided that it would after all be easier to make the return journey by land, on the street railway. The park did not extend quite to the river. They had to follow a rather damp footpath across a meadow, before a venerable, seignorial landscape, well cared for and well clipped, received them. From an elevated circular terrace, with benches in yew arbours, avenues of magnificent trees, most of them already in bud, though many shoots were still hidden under their shiny brown covers, led in various directions – finely gravelled promenades, often arched over by meeting branches, between rows, and sometimes double rows, of beeches, yews, lindens, horse chestnuts, tall elms. Rare and curious trees, brought from distant countries, were also to be seen, planted singly on stretches of lawn – strange conifers, fern-leafed beeches, and Keaton recognized the Californian sequoia and the swamp cypress with its supplementary breathing-roots.

Rosalie took no interest in these curiosities. Nature, she considered, must be familiar, or it did not speak to the heart. But the beauty of the park did not seem to hold much charm for her. Scarcely glancing up now and again at the proud tree-trunks, she walked silently on, with Eduard at her side, behind his young tutor and the bobbling Anna – who, however, soon hit on a manoeuvre to change the arrangement. She stopped and summoned her brother to tell her the names of the avenue they were following and of the winding footpath that crossed it just there. For all these paths and avenues had old, traditional names, such as "Fan Avenue", "Trumpet Avenue", and so on. Then, as they moved on, Anna kept Eduard beside her and left Ken behind with Rosalie. He carried her coat, which she had taken off, for not a breath of wind stirred in the park and it was much warmer than it had been on the water. The spring sun shone gently through the high branches, dappled the roads, and played on the faces of the four, making them blink. In her finely tailored brown suit, which closely sheathed her slight, youthful figure, Frau von Tümmler walked at Ken's side, now and again casting a veiled, smiling look at her coat as it hung over his arm. "There they are!" she cried, and pointed to the pair of black swans; for they were now walking along the poplar-bordered moat, and the birds, aware of the approaching visitors, were gliding nearer, at a stately pace, across the slightly scummy water. "How beautiful they are! Anna, do you recognize them? How majestically they carry their necks! Where is the bread for them?" Keaton pulled it out of his pocket, wrapped in newspaper, and handed it to her. It was warm from his body, and she took some of the bread and began to eat it.

"But it's stale and hard," he cried, with a gesture that came too late to stop her.

"I have good teeth," she answered.

One of the swans, however, pushing close against the bank, spread its dark wings and beat the air with them, stretching out its neck and hissing angrily up at her. They laughed at its jealousy, but at the same time felt a little afraid. Then the birds received their rightful due. Rosalie threw them the stale bread, piece after piece, and, swimming slowly back and forth, they accepted it with imperturbable dignity.

"Yet I fear," said Anna as they walked on, "that the old devil won't soon forget your robbing him of his food. He displayed a well-bred pique the whole time."

"Not at all," answered Rosalie. "He was only afraid for a moment that I would eat it all and leave none for him. After that, he must have relished it all the more, since I relished it."

They came to the castle, to the smooth circular pond which mirrored it and in which, to one side, lay a miniature island bearing a solitary poplar. On the expanse of gravel before the flight of steps leading to the gracefully winged structure, whose considerable dimensions its extreme daintiness seemed to efface, and whose pink façade was crumbling a little, stood a number of people who, as they waited for the eleven-o'clock conducted tour, were passing the time by examining the armorial pediment with its figures, the clock, heedless of time and supported by an angel, which surmounted it, the stone wreaths above the tall white portals, and comparing them with the descriptions in their guide-books. Our friends joined them, and, like them, looked at the charmingly decorated feudal architecture, up to the *œils-de-bœuf* in the slate-coloured garret storey. Figures clad with mythological scantiness, Pan and his nymphs, stood on pedestals beside the long windows, flaking away like the four sandstone lions which, with sullen expressions, their paws crossed, flanked the steps and the ramp.

Keaton was enthusiastic over so much history. He found everything "splendid" and "excitingly continental". Oh dear, to think of his own prosaic country across the Atlantic! There was none of this sort of crumbling aristocratic grace over there, for there had been no Electors and Landgraves, able, in absolute sovereignty, to indulge their passion for magnificence, to their own honour and to the honour of culture. However, his attitude towards the culture which, in its dignity, had not moved on with time, was not so reverent but that, to the amusement of the waiting crowd, he impudently seated himself astride the back of one of the sentinel lions, though it was equipped with a sharp spike, like certain toy horses whose rider can be removed. He clasped the spike in front of him with both hands, pretended, with cries of "Hi!" and "Giddap!", that he was giving the beast the spurs, and really could not have presented a more attractive picture of youthful high spirits. Anna and Eduard avoided looking at their mother.

Then bolts creaked, and Keaton hastened to dismount from his steed, for the caretaker, a man wearing military breeches and with his left sleeve empty and rolled up – to all appearances a retired non-commissioned officer whose service injury had been compensated by this quiet post – swung open the central portal and admitted the visitors. He stationed himself in the lofty doorway and, letting them file past him, not only distributed entrance tickets from a small pad, but managed too, with his one hand, to tear them half across. Meanwhile, he had already begun to talk; speaking out of his crooked mouth in a hoarse, gravelly voice, he rattled off the information which he had learned by rote and repeated a thousand times: that the sculptured decoration on the façade was by an artist whom the Elector had summoned for the purpose from Rome; that the castle and the park were the work of a French architect; and that the structure was the most important example of Rococo on the Rhine, though it exhibited traces of the transition to the Louis Seize style; that the castle contained fifty-five rooms and had cost eight hundred thousand taler – and so on.

The vestibule exhaled a musty chill. Here, standing ready in rows, were large boat-shaped felt slippers, into which, amid much snickering from the ladies, the party were obliged to step for the protection of the precious parquets, which were, indeed, almost the chief objects of interest in the apartments dedicated to pleasure, through which, awkwardly shuffling and sliding, the party followed their droning one-armed guide. Of different patterns in the various rooms, the central intarsias represented all sorts of star shapes and floral fantasies. Their gleaming surfaces received the reflections of the visitors, of the cambered state furniture, while tall mirrors, set between gilded pillars wreathed in garlands and tapestry fields of flowered silk framed in gilded listels, repeatedly interchanged the images of the crystal chandeliers, the amorous ceiling paintings, the medallions and emblems of the hunt and music over the doors, and, despite a great many blind-spots, still succeeded in evoking the illusion of rooms opening into one another as far as the eye could see. Unbridled luxuriousness, unqualified insistence on gratification, were to be read in the cascades of elegant ornamentation, of gilded scrollwork, restricted only by the inviolable style and taste of the period that had produced them. In the round banquet room, around which, in niches, stood Apollo and the Muses, the inlaid woodwork of the floor gave place to marble, like that which sheathed the walls. Rosy *putti* drew back a painted drapery from the pierced cupola, through which the daylight fell, and from the galleries, as the caretaker said, music had once floated down to the banqueters below.

Ken Keaton was walking beside Frau von Tümmler, with his hand under her elbow. Every American takes his lady across the street in this fashion. Separated from Anna and Eduard, among strangers, they followed close behind the caretaker, who hoarsely, in stilted text-book phrases, unreeled his text and told the party what they were seeing. They were not, he informed them, seeing everything that was to be seen. Of the castle's fifty-five rooms, he went on – and, following his routine, dropped for a moment into vapid insinuation, though his face, with its crooked mouth, remained wholly aloof from the playfulness of his words – not all were simply open without further ado. The gentry of those days had a great taste for jokes and secrets and mysteries, for hiding-places in the background, retreats that, offering opportunities, were accessible through mechanical tricks – such as this one here, for example. And he stopped beside a pier glass, which, in response to his pressing upon a spring, slid aside, surprising the sightseers by a view of a narrow circular staircase with delicately latticed banisters. Immediately to the left, on a pedestal at its foot, stood an armless three-quarters torso of a man with a wreath of berries in his hair and kirtled with a spurious festoon of leaves; leaning back a little, he smiled down into space over his goat's beard, priapic and welcoming. There were ah's and oh's. "And so on," said the guide, as he said each time, and returned the trick mirror to its place. "And so too," he said, walking on; and made a tapestry panel, which had nothing to distinguish it from the others, open as a secret door and disclose a passageway leading into darkness and exhaling an odour of mould. "That's the sort of thing they liked," said the one-armed caretaker. "Other times, other manners," he added, with sententious stupidity, and continued the tour.

The felt boats were not easy to keep on one's feet. Frau von Tümmler lost one of hers; it slid some distance away over the smooth floor, and while Keaton laughingly retrieved it and, kneeling, put it on her foot again, they were overtaken by the party of sightseers. Again he put his hand under her elbow, but, with a dreamy smile, she remained standing where she was, looking after the party as it disappeared into further rooms; then, still supported by his hand, she turned and hurriedly ran her fingers over the tapestry, where it had opened.

"You aren't doing it right," he whispered, "Let me. It was here." He found the spring, the door responded, and the mouldy air of the secret passageway enveloped them as they advanced a few steps. It was dark around them. With a sigh drawn from the uttermost depths of her being. Rosalie flung her arms around the young man's neck; and he too happily embraced her trembling form. "Ken, Ken," she stammered, her face against his throat, "I love you, I love you, and you know it, I haven't been able to hide it from you completely, and you, and you, do you love me too, a little, only a little, tell me, can you love me with your youth, as Nature has bestowed it on me to love you in my grey age? Yes? Yes? Your mouth then, oh, at last, your young mouth, for which I have hungered, your dear lips, like this, like this – Can I kiss? Tell me, can I, my sweet awakener? I can do everything, as you can. Ken, love is strong, a miracle, so it comes and works great miracles Kiss me, darling! I have hungered for your lips, oh how much, for I must tell you that my poor head slipped into all sorts of sophistries, like thinking that broad-mindedness and libertinism were not for me, and that the contradiction between my way of life and my innate convictions threatened to destroy me. Oh, Ken, it was the sophistries that almost destroyed me, and my hunger for you. . . . It is you, it is you at last, this is your hair, this is your mouth, this breath comes from your nostrils, the arms that I know are around me, this is your body's warmth, that I relished and the swan was angry. . . ."

A little more, and she would have sunk to the ground before him. But he held her, and drew her along the passage, which grew a little lighter. Steps descended to the open round arch of a door, behind which murky light fell from above on an alcove whose tapestries were worked with billing pairs of doves. In the alcove stood a sort of causeuse beside which a carved Cupid with blindfolded eyes held a thing like a torch. There, in the musty dampness, they sat down.

"Ugh, it smells of death," Rosalie shuddered against his shoulder. "How sad, Ken my darling, that we have to be here amid this decay. It was in kind Nature's lap, fanned by her airs, in the sweet breath of jasmines and alders, that I dreamed it should be, it was there that I should have kissed you for the first time, and not in this grave! Go away, stop it, you devil, I will be yours, but not in this mould. I will come to you tomorrow, in your room, tomorrow morning, perhaps even tonight. I'll arrange it, I'll play a trick on my would-be-wise Anna. . . ." He made her promise. And indeed they felt too that they must rejoin the others, either by going on or by retracing their steps. Keaton decided in favour of going on. They left the dead pleasure chamber by another door, again there was a dark passageway, it turned, mounted, and they came to a rusty gate, which, in response to Ken's strenuous pushing and tugging, shakily gave way and which was so overgrown outside with leathery vines and creepers that they could hardly force their way through. The open air received them. There was a plash of waters; cascades flowed down behind broad beds set with flowers of the early year, yellow narcissuses. It was the back garden of the castle. The group of visitors was just approaching from the right; the caretaker had left them; Anna and her brother were bringing up the rear. The pair mingled with the foremost, who were beginning to scatter towards the fountains and in the direction of the wooded park. It was natural to stand there, look around, and go to meet the brother and sister. "Where in the world have you been?" And: "That's just what we want to ask *you*!" And: "How could we possibly lose sight of one another so?" Anna and Eduard had even, they said, turned back to look for the lost couple, but in vain. "After all, you couldn't have vanished from the face of the earth," said Anna. "No more than you," Rosalie answered. None of them looked at the others.

Walking between rhododendrons, they circled the wing of the castle and arrived at the pond in front of it, which was quite close to the street-railway stop. If the boat trip upstream, following the windings of the Rhine, had been long, the return journey on the tram, speeding noisily through industrial districts and past colonies of workmen's houses, was correspondingly swift. The brother and sister now and again exchanged a word with each other or with their mother, whose hand Anna held for a while because she had seen her trembling. The party broke up in the city, near the Königsallee.

* * *

Frau von Tümmler did not go to Ken Keaton. That night, towards morning, a severe indisposition attacked her and alarmed the household. What, on its first return, had made her so proud, so happy, what she had extolled as a miracle of Nature and the sublime work of feeling, reappeared calamitously. She had had the strength to ring, but when her daughter and the maid came hurrying in, they found her lying in a faint in her blood.

The physician, Dr Oberloskamp, was soon on the spot. Reviving under his ministrations, she appeared astonished at his presence.

"What, Doctor, you here?" she said. "I suppose Anna must have troubled you to come? But it is only 'after the manner of women' with me."

"At times, my dear Frau von Tümmler, these functions require a certain supervision," the grey-haired doctor answered. To her daughter he declared categorically that the patient must be brought, preferably by ambulance, to the gynæcological hospital. The case demanded the most thorough examination – which, he added, might show that it was not dangerous. Certainly, the metrorrhagias – the first one, of which he had only now heard, and this alarming recurrence – might well be caused by a myoma, which could easily be removed by an operation. In the hands of the director and chief surgeon of the hospital, Professor Muthesius, her dear mother would receive the most trustworthy care.

His recommendations were followed – without resistance on Frau von Tümmler's part, to Anna's silent amazement. Through it all, her mother only stared into the distance with her eyes very wide open.

The bimanual examination, performed by Muthesius, revealed a uterus far too large for the patient's age, abnormally thickened tissue in the tube, and, instead of an ovary already greatly reduced in size, a huge tumour. The curettage showed carcinoma cells, some of them characteristically ovarian; but others left no doubt that cancer cells were entering into full development in the uterus itself. All the malignancy showed signs of rapid growth.

The professor, a man with a double chin, a very red complexion, and water-blue eyes into which tears came easily – their presence having nothing whatever to do with the state of his emotions – raised his head from the microscope.

"Condition extensive, if you ask me," he said to his assistant, whose name was Dr Knepperges. "However, we will operate, Knepperges. Total extirpation, down to the last connective tissue in the true pelvis and to all lymphatic tissue, can in any case prolong life."

But the picture that the opening of the abdominal cavity revealed, in the white light of the arc-lamps, to the doctors and nurses, was too terrible to permit any hope even of a temporary improvement. The time for that was long since past. Not only were all the pelvic organs already involved; the peritoneum too showed, to the naked eye alone, the murderous cell groups, all the glands of the lymphatic system were carcinomatously thickened, and there was no doubt that there were also foci of cancer cells in the liver.

"Just take a look at this mess, Knepperges," said Muthesius. "Presumably it exceeds your expectations." That it also exceeded his own, he gave no sign. "Ours is a noble art," he added, his eyes filling with tears that meant nothing, "but this is expecting a little too much of it. We can't cut all that away. If you think that you observe metastasis in both ureters, you observe correctly. Uremia cannot but soon set in. Mind you, I don't deny that the uterus itself is producing the voracious brood. Yet I advise you to adopt my opinion, which is that the whole story started from the ovary – that is, from immature ovarian cells which often remain there from birth and which, after the menopause, through heaven knows what process of stimulation, begin to develop malignantly. And then the organism, *post festum*, if you like, is shot through, drenched, inundated, with estrogen hormones, which leads to hormonal hyperplasia of the uteral mucous membrane, with concomitant hæmorrhages."

Knepperges, a thin, ambitiously conceited man, made a brief, covertly ironical bow of thanks for the lecture.

"Well, let's get on with it, *ut aliquid fieri videatur*," said the professor. "We must leave her what is essential for life, however steeped in melancholy the word is in this instance."

Anna was waiting upstairs in the hospital room when her mother, who had been brought up by the elevator, returned on her stretcher and was put to bed by the nurses. During the process she awoke from her post-narcotic sleep and said indistinctly:

"Anna, my child, he hissed at me."

"Who, dearest Mama?"

"The black swan."

She was already asleep again. But she often remembered the swan during the next few weeks, his blood-red bill, the black beating of his wings. Her suffering was brief. Uremic coma soon plunged her into profound unconsciousness, and, double pneumonia developing, her exhausted heart could only hold out for a matter of days.

Just before the end, when it was but a few hours away, her mind cleared again. She raised her eyes to her daughter, who sat at her bedside, holding her hand.

"Anna," she said, and was able to push the upper part of her body a little towards the edge of the bed, closer to her confidante, "do you hear me?"

"Certainly I hear you, dear, dear Mama."

"Anna, never say that Nature deceived me, that she is sardonic and cruel. Do not rail at her, as I do not. I am loth to go away – from you all, from life with its spring. But how should there be spring without death? Indeed, death is a great instrument of life, and if for me it borrowed the guise of resurrection, of the joy of love, that was not a lie, but goodness and mercy."

Another little push, closer to her daughter, and a failing whisper:

"Nature – I have always loved her, and she – has been loving to her child."

Rosalie died a gentle death, regretted by all who knew her.

This book is set in BEMBO which was cut
by the punch-cutter Francesco Griffo
for the Venetian printer-publisher
Aldus Manutius in early 1495
and first used in a pamphlet
by a young scholar
named Pietro
Bembo.